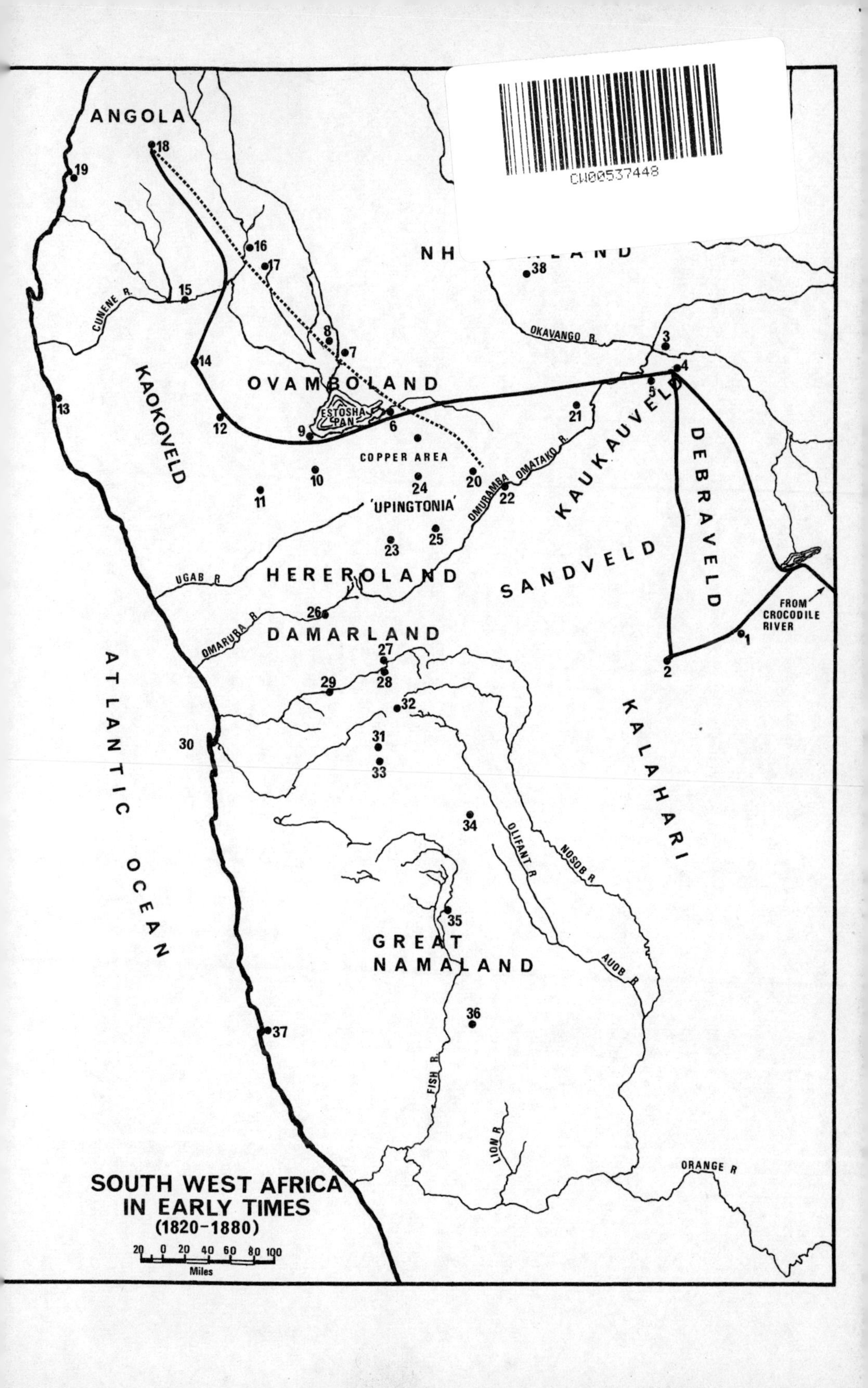

ANGOLA
CUNENE R.
KAOKOVELD
OVAMBOLAND
ESTOSHA PAN
COPPER AREA
'UPINGTONIA'
OKAVANGO R.
OMURAMBA OMATAKO R.
KAUKAUVELD
DEBRAVELD
SANDVELD
FROM CROCODILE RIVER
UGAB R
HEREROLAND
OMARURA R
DAMARLAND
KALAHARI
ATLANTIC OCEAN
OLIFANT R
NOSOB R
GREAT NAMALAND
AUOB R
FISH R
LION R
ORANGE R
SOUTH WEST AFRICA IN EARLY TIMES (1820-1880)
20 0 20 40 60 80 100
Miles

The Thirstland

An historical novel in the first person presupposes a kind of heavenly recorder which finds an equivalent in the 'ghost writer' of our times. It has for example become established practice in some countries that a public figure does not write his own biography, but pays for the services of some professional journalist. W. W. Jordan's account of the happenings in Damaraland and elsewhere from November 1879 to July 1886 should be seen in this light.

It is relevant here to remember what Marguerite Yourcenar said about this in her excellent *Memoires d'Hadrien* (1951). 'The reconstruction of an historical figure and the world of his time', Mme Yourcenar said, 'drafted in the first person, borders on the fictitious, but also on the poetic.' That is why a work of this nature can dispense with the formal references to sources relating to the historical facts. Because it has been the main purpose of the present writer to reconstruct an inner reality of which the particular facts were a unique expression, he has tried to stay as close to them as possible. What fiction there is in this chronicle consists mainly of the play of the imagination in dialogue. Only a few of the lesser figures are not historical. As Mme Yourcenar says: a faithfulness to historical facts in this kind of writing can only serve to enhance its human value.

The Thirstland

W. A. DE KLERK

REX COLLINGS LONDON 1977

First published in English by Rex Collings Ltd
69 Marylebone High Street, London W1

ISBN 0 860 36045 8

Distributed in Southern Africa by
Aloe Book Agency

Typesetting by Malvern Typesetting Services
Printed in Great Britain by
The Pitman Press, Bath

CONTENTS

For Laurens van der Post
lover of Southern Africa

PRELUDE

On a night in June 1886 a wagon stood among a group of makalani palms on the great plain south-west of Ondangua in Ovamboland. It was a starlit night and wonderfully clear, as it nearly always is in South West Africa—Namibia—during winter. A disintegrating moon hung low in the western sky; the constellation Scorpio, which at midnight had been some way above the eastern horizon, had now passed the zenith.

The quietness was that of clear winter nights on the Southern African highveld: nights when the frost seemed to grow out of the silence, and the silence itself was only at times disturbed by the far-off roar of a lion, or the howling of a jackal.

The wagon stood between two palms. From a distance it was the sort of scene which would have caught the attention of a recorder of the times like the artist, Thomas Baines, from the Cape. There were the slender makalanis with their feathery tops. There was the wagon with its recumbant draught-pole. There were the ruminating oxen tied to yokes, as a precaution against the lions.

The camp-fire had left a silver smudge of ash where leadwood logs had burnt themselves out. Two servants, Izak, a yellow Ai-Bushman, and Kairob, a black Bergdamara, each lay in a shallow trench in the sand in which they had buried live coals from the fire. They were covered with skins in which they had rolled themselves. A mare with drooping head stood tied to a wheel of the wagon.

Under the canopy a man lay on a bed of rough mahogany, fitted with a mat of eland thongs. Only his head and one shoulder were visible. The night was cold, and he had drawn the blankets up high. His name was Will Worthington Jordan.

Earlier that night the Bushman had arisen from his hollow in *the sand to put fresh wood on the fire. Jordan had heard him. He had lifted a corner of the wagon canvas and enquired:* 'Bambuse!* *Is there coffee*?'

In his own language he muttered affirmatively: 'Dira ma!', *meaning 'I go!'. Then he walked back to the fire, lifted the kettle off the warm ash and poured a bowl of coffee.*

Now Jordan lay in the back of the wagon nursing the warm bowl between his hands, and reclining against a pillow of soft skin, staring through the front of the canopy at a segment of the night sky. Sleep was difficult, he thought, for a man facing what was likely to be the most momentous day of his life.

The next twelve hours would be of critical importance, not only for him personally, but also for those in his charge. Here he was now on his way to see Kambonde Kampingana, king of the Ondonga tribe in southern Ovamboland. In all likelihood the chief had received word of his coming: news always preceded one's travelling in this country. At least all the fluid uncertainty of things would now be at an end. A man had the right to know where he stood, and what was expected of him.

Sometimes Jordan remembered a great, clear-running river, rising in the far north, coming down into the Thirstland. This was a river that gradually lost its life in the sand marshes of the Kalahari. It never reached the sea. Associated with the river there was also a memory, heavy with decay and the smell of death.

One might fight one's enemies in the flesh; but what about those that remained unseen? How long could one continue the struggle? When did one give up? On the other hand, without courage there was no hope . . .

There was a time when he had stood on a desert shore, lost in his own thinking, conscious of the emptiness of his life up to that stage. Night was falling. A ceiling of high cloud covered the heavens. Far out to sea the day still gleamed in a ribbon of light. Then at last it faded and died.

Time was always dying . . . It was dying now under this frosty sky . . . If sleep were impossible and things seemed to be winding up, it was better to remember all that had happened, all that had led to this point in time . . .

*In effect: 'Batman!'

THE MARSH

November 1878–1879

1

It was November of 1878 and a dry year. I was on my way to Andara on the Okavango to keep an appointment with Charles Thomas, when we came across the Zulu, Kleinveld Labuschagne, in the veld. My *bambuse*, Izak, had first noticed the man. His clothes had been torn by the dry mucharra and the black hookthorn. For a moment I thought that I could hear his bones rattling as he came towards us, grey with dust and with shredded lips, a tattered hat pressed close to his chest. Only his eyes were gleaming above the prominent cheekbones. Kairob, my wagon-driver, offered him a calabash of water. He drank this so greedily that the water spilled over his chest and emerged from the bottoms of his trousers.

Later I discovered that he was a Zulu with a Boer name. I had known that he could be no Ovambo or 'Galagadi from the Kalahari Thirstland. Nor was he a wandering Omuherero or Bergdamara. In fact, he spoke Dutch like Roets and Holtzhausen, like Alberts and Van der Merwe. 'I am Kleinveld Labuschagne, Master,' he said at last, 'I am the wagon-driver of *Bass* Hans Lombard, who is dead now. I have been walking for four days from where our people are in the *vleis*.* Little Master is also dead, some time already of the fever. Only Old Miss Ella keeps upright; and *Oumie* who is called Dina . . . And little Miss Lisa, who also has the sickness . . . Now I come to hear, Master: is there perhaps someone to help us? Our oxen are all dead of the fly.'

He stood in front of me with his tattered hat between his bony fingers. It suddenly seemed as if he were drifting on the burning sand. We walked to the shady side of the wagon.

There were the people, he said, who had kept to the waters,

*Shallow lakes.

when the others had crossed the Thirstland to Rietfontein. They belonged to *Baas* Kreling. But Kreling (whose real name was Greyling) and his followers had gone off on their own. These River Trekkers, he said, had remained in the outveld for some time because of the fever, and the fly. Thirst had driven them back again. Once more they had gone down to the waters. There all had fallen ill. He himself had buried more people than he could remember. Food was scarce and the survivors had little strength left.

That very morning I set off in the direction of the great inland delta of the Okavango in the north-western Kalahari. I struck a course just south of east. According to the Zulu, the trek had come to a standstill not far from the most northern reaches of the marshes. I had calculated that I would strike the river where it still flowed strongly and freely in an open channel. The Toahke was the western arm of the great delta. I would keep to the Toahke, leaving a spoor for the wagon to follow southwards.

The land had been full of rumours. There had been a Boer Trek from the Transvaal, coming west. There had been talk of a new Boer republic somewhere here in Damaraland.

At Gobabis the Orlam Chief, Andreas Lamberts, had already given an advance group of the Trekkers permission to stay at Rietfontein on the edge of the Thirstland. Kamaherero, paramount chief of the Ovaherero, had been deeply perturbed by the news. Rietfontein, he said, was Herero property. All the Namas, including the Orlams, were his underlings.

This was only a threat. But Kamaherero's attitude could well be understood. There was talk everywhere: at Walwich Bay, at Otjimbingue, Omaruru and Rehoboth . . . All the Transvaal Boers, so it was said, had decided to get out before the Imperial British.

Here in the far west the Boers would try to win a new land. This had already taken place in Natal, in the Transvaal, and in the Orange Free State.

At that time I was still at Rehoboth, in partnership with Gunning. I was curious to find out what exactly was taking place. As a young man at the Cape I had been intrigued by the northern treks of the pioneer Boers. Among my friends the Boers had never been popular. But I admired them.

In March 1877 I was in Windhoek when Gert Alberts, Gert van der Merwe, and a few others arrived on horseback from

Rietfontein, to ask Jan Jonker Afrikaander, paramount chief of the Afrikaander-Namas, for more grazing and for water for their flocks. Other treks were on their way from the Transvaal.

The story went that they were from the Transvaal and were coming through the Kalahari Thirstland. Yes, the visitors from Rietfontein confirmed, a number of Boers, mostly from the western areas of the Transvaal, had decided to trek. The Rev Thomas Burgers, the new president, was too free-thinking. Some also believed that the British at the Cape and in Natal would soon reassert their authority over the inland republics. Whatever the causes, there was a general feeling among the Trekboers to get out before the changes came; to seek, perhaps, 'some fine land to the north-west where we may live unhindered and in peace'.

What did that mean, I enquired. What if the 'fine land' was not to be had by treaty or by peaceful occupation? Alberts and his fellow Boers looked at me in some surprise. I was merely enquiring, I said. There was a general feeling among the aboriginal peoples of the Transgariep that conquest was intended.

No, Gert Alberts solemnly assured me, there was no desire at all to take anybody else's land. All the Trekboers wanted was an 'own country to live in, where with God's help and all possible co-operation on the part of the "nations", they might be themselves.' 'No man can deny his own past,' he added, 'without suffering the punishment of the Lord.'

That first trek of the Albertses and the Van der Merwes had been successful. Without undue trouble they had journeyed from the Crocodile River, to the Botletle, Lake Ngami and Ghanzi. From there they had progressed to Rietfontein, which was a meeting point between Damaraland and Namaland. Effective leadership had ensured the safe crossing of hundreds of miles of thirstland and fever marsh.

Alberts and his party must have been back at Rietfontein for some time, when the news began to reach us: the treks still in the Thirstland were in great difficulties. Many people had already died. All along the spoor to the east empty wagons could be found. Goods of all sorts had been abandoned . . .

The reports were disturbing. At Otjimbingue John Caine had told me that he had had positive information that the Trekboers were on their way. Dr Theo Hahn of Rehoboth confirmed this. He added that a message from Rietfontein had said that Alberts had heard from the treks still at the Botletle: nearly all their animals including their trek-oxen had died. The parties under one Kreling (Greyling) and Du Plessis were badly straitened.

Theo Hahn had always had a certain sympathy for the Boers. He had even incurred the anger of Hermanus van Wyk and his Basters, by asking Hendrik van Zyl of Ghanzi to invite the Boers to Rehoboth as settlers. Unfortunately the letter had fallen into the hands of Kamaherero at Okahandja. Kamaherero had since never ceased ranting about the 'threat of the Boers'.

It was only towards the end of 1877, while on a trading expedition to Gobabis, that I could hear the facts for myself. My information again came from a party from Rietfontein.

Machiel Roets and Dolf Holtzhausen came to my wagon with some ivory to sell. Yes, he and Holtzhausen said, it was true: the various treks which had left the Crocodile River in April of that year had been badly stricken. From the very start the leaders had quarrelled. The result was that the whole trek had fallen into disunity. Many lives had been lost, and much property had been thrown away. The way back to the Transvaal had been marked by the graves of their children. Those who survived had at last managed to reach the Botletle and Lake Ngami. Here an even later trek, that of J. F. Botha, the Robbertzes and others, eventually had caught up with them. Botha and Co were a small company and had avoided the hazards of the treks.

What about the men from Rietfontein, who had taken the trek-oxen to those at the Botletle? Had they arrived there?

Yes, Machiel Roets and Dolf Holtzhausen affirmed, they had got to the Botletle and had delivered the trek-oxen; but the groups there were still too exhausted to resume their journey. Terrible things had happened; and the people had suffered. 'Jan Kreling was forever arguing with Moreem, who is the king of the Lake people,' Roets said. 'Moreem refused to allow us to trek back through his country to Rietfontein. It was only after Field-Cornet van der Merwe spoke to Moreem that he gave us permission. Kreling was still very angry and he trekked away, following the Okavango. Only fourteen families came back with us. With all this coming and going it was four months before we got back to Rietfontein. The River Trekkers? We heard that they were suffering great hardships. There was so much fever among them.'

From Gobabis I went back to Rehoboth, to Otjimbingue, and the Bay. Then I trekked northwards to Ovamboland again, crossing the Cunene at Humbe; crossing the High Serras, and going down to Moçamedes. From there I duly returned to the Bay. At the end of 1879 I went via the Waterberg, Otavi Spring and the Omuramba Omatako* to eastern Ovamboland. This was the area south of the middle-reaches of the Okavango. All the time I was conscious of the strange wanderings of a people now taking place in these largely unpopulated areas of Southern Africa. According to reports, the main parties of the Trek were somewhere in the country north-west of Lake Ngami and the marshes. As far as I could make out, most of them were near the left bank of the Toahke. Why hadn't they gone back to the Transvaal when things had become so difficult? What positive destination did they have which justified all this suffering? Eighteen months had passed since I had first heard of the treks.

I remembered what Pieter Maritz-Botha had once told me at the Bay. Sir Bartle Frere, governor of the Cape Colony, had heard of the emigration from the western Transvaal and had shown great interest in it, he said. Axel Eriksson, who had also been present on that occasion, had lauded the Bay as a harbour and trading centre. Hendrik van Zyl, who lived at Ghanzi like a sultan, organizing great hunting expeditions in the Debra from his castle on the veld, had supported Eriksson. The Transgariep was an excellent pastoral country, Botha had said. With all this in view, the Trekboers would be the right material to help develop the country. Sir Bartle had considered it all. Sir Bartle had suggested that the Kaoko, which was mainly uninhabited, might serve this purpose. The Kaoko was a wild, inhospitable country.

On trek one would meet fellow hunter-traders, or just hunters, who would exchange their latest bit of news for what you yourself had to tell. Some said that they had heard that not a single Trekboer was still living: all had died in the marshes. Only a few had escaped this fate by returning to the Transvaal. Kamaherero had warned the Trekboers, some said, that he would not allow them to enter Damaraland. Violence would be met with violence.

It was usually Kairob, my wagon-driver, and Izak, my *bambuse,* who provided me with the most dependable information. Africa had its own ways of spreading the news. The Trekboers had left Rietfontein, my servants said. The people who had been there were now moving northwards to the river. Others were still somewhere in the Sandveld, in the delta of the

* Omuramba—a shallow, tree-rich watercourse. Omatako is the greatest.

Okavango.

On a November afternoon in '78 I finally heard the true facts. I had known that the Erikssons and some of the other Swedes were up at the Okavango. I had met Pieter Maritz-Botha and Barend Bouwer a week or so before at Andara. Both had just completed a spell of service with Hendrik van Zyl. They had hunted elephants for him from Ghanzi. Now they had had enough of the old chap, and had come to join the Erikssons.

Hunter-traders in the Transgariep had their own lives to see to. At times, however, we would meet, set up a laager, and sit around the fire, exchanging news. For some time now the main subject for discussion had been the westward emigration of the Boers through the Thirstland. Everywhere little groups were still wandering about, it now appeared. Some were in the Debra west of Lake Ngami. Others, in spite of everything, were staying close to the marshes. Some had trekked down to Rietfontein. But from Rietfontein itself portions of the Trek had moved northwards again. To what end? Nobody could say.

I had offered Botha a partnership, and he had been eager to accept, his connections with the Erikssons being tenuous. What attracted me to Botha in those days was his zest for life. He could handle a gun, and spin a yarn, and charm the ladies. What I later discerned in him was a certain element of ruthlessness.

On occasion we were around a laager fire down there where the Omuramba Omatako enters the river. 'Mester,' Barend Bouwer said—he always called me Mester—'we have hunted all there is in the Debra while with old Hendrik. Now there is not so much left. The elephants have got rather wise to us, after the great battle we had at the pan!'

He was referring to what had happened at Olifants Pan near Andara on a Sunday afternoon, about a year previously. Botha, Bouwer, and other hunters in the employ of Hendrik van Zyl, had shot one hundred and three elephants here in one terrible slaughter. The animals had fled into the pan and had got stuck in the deep mud of the bowl.

'We have heard that Alberts and his people are on their way to Olifants Pan,' Bouwer said. 'So, if there are no more elephants for us to hunt, let us join the Trek and see what lies in other places.'

'If the Trek is on its way to Olifants Pan, Brother Barend,' Botha said, 'then we must go down and see the tree with our names on it.'

This was a baobab near the pan on which the hunters of the previous years had cut their names. One stack of names was under a heading: *Van Zyl Battle, October 1878.*

Strange, intriguing people these, I sometimes thought. They were solidly cast in the puritan mould. I, on the contrary, had hardly been conservative in my opinions. How would we get through to each other?

I played with the thought. I was a physician, they said. I was 'the best doctor in the country'. That was like Cyclops being king of the blind. Yet, I had learnt some things when helping at Cape hospitals. Sometimes I even believed that I was qualified. I picked up things so easily, not only languages . . .

Quinine was better than marula bark or gunpowder-and-vinegar. With some ipecac, calomel, arnica, tincture of opium and phenol, I could get along. Sterile bandages could be made from old linen sheets. With a scalpel, a needle-and-horsehair, and a few other surgical instruments, I could do minor operations. Add to this a clinical thermometer, and a medical home-counsellor. Nobody paid for my services.

Axel Eriksson once looked closely at me. Things I had mentioned in conversation soon put him wise. 'We must go down to Olifants Pan and see what you can do for the Trekboers,' he said.

We sat under wild-figs around the laager fire, drinking Cape brandy and strong, black coffee. We talked about hunting, trading, and the seemingly endemic wars of the nations in the Transgariep. We also discussed the Trek. What was at the root of it all? Nobody knew . . .

Barend Bouwer now told of how the Trek had got to Ghanzi where Hendrik van Zyl had built his castle. The Trek had wanted to water its animals there, but Old Hendrik had said the thirsty animals would damage his wells. The old man was tough and difficult. He had one good eye; and when he looked at you it was like Old Nick himself. In the end he relented and the animals were watered, but only with the greatest difficulty. Axel Wedburg, a countryman of Eriksson, had once told about Hendrik van Zyl executing thirty-three Bushmen for murdering a boy from the Trek.

Was it true, I now asked. Bouwer and Botha remained silent. Thereupon Eriksson said: it might well be true. Van Zyl was Lord of Ghanzi, and dispensed justice as he knew it. 'Yes, it happened,' Botha suddenly said. 'We were all there. But it was necessary. The Bushmen were murderers.' He was reluctant to tell the whole story. It was best forgotten, he explained. Remember, old Hendrik is a friend of the governor of the Cape.

'We have heard at Andara,' Eriksson said, tugging at his red beard, 'that there is a whole collection of wagons at Olifants Pan. The people are hungry, they say, and sick! Chief Andara sent some corn for them. Everywhere in the Debra wagons still stand about. Down at the waters too. Ugh, for what? Perhaps we still go out to look for some. But we must first go to the Pan.' His thick, strong arms were arched over his knees.

'You are right, Karevapu,' I said.

'There is great sorrow at the Pan,' Eriksson continued. 'So we go, Will. Tomorrow, eh?'

'I have an appointment with Charles Thomas at Andara,' I said. 'Fine, I go to Andara; and from Andara to the Pan; the day after tomorrow. Meanwhile you go ahead, Axel. Take all the quinine we have. I hear Robert Lewis is up at the river. Is that true?'

Lewis, true to form, had told Coates Palgrave all sorts of stories about where the boundaries of Damaraland were. It was fictitious, but plausible. Poor Coates had been impressed . . .

We filled our glasses. Barend Bouwer, however, had fallen asleep. Now he was snoring pleasantly.

2

It was on the way to Andara that I had met Ella Lombard's wagon-driver in the dry, sun-smitten veld. That same day I changed my plans and rode in a south-easterly direction, towards the marshes of the Okavango.

I kept going that whole day, and a good part of the night. The next morning when the early shadows had already disappeared, I once again saw the blue streak of the river in the distance. Straight ahead, against a blue-white sky, I could see vultures wheeling. This was the left bank of the Okavango. In time it became the Toahke.

By midday all had been flattened to a featureless, motionless landscape. It was a naked sun in a naked sky. Even the game—a few herds of blue wildebeest; Chapman's zebra; at odd intervals a giraffe—seemed tardy in their movements. On a dead leadwood between thin acacias a row of vultures sat. A few marabous had got lost in the haze. Between the trees I could now see the carrion, or what remained of it. The birds had all eaten their fill. Now shaggy hyaenas were skulking in the bush. In places the remains of dead long-horned cattle lay shrivelling in the sun.

The veld was full of wagon-spoors, seemingly leading to nowhere. Tensely I now discerned the wagons themselves, gaunt and empty: ten of them, each standing forlornly on its own little *werf.** The wind had blown the ashes of old fires in between the trees. Heaps of freshly dug soil, covered with branches of hookthorn, showed where they who had until recently still lived here, lay buried. A vulture on the draught-pole of a wagon clumsily launched itself into flight, a black shadow moving swiftly, silently over the bare earth. Approaching the wagon, I raised myself in the stirrups and peered in under the canopy. A man, a woman, and two children lay close to each other on the *katel*:† the man with a Bible clutched between lifeless fingers.

Turning my horse, I was suddenly conscious of my own heartbeat. I stopped at other wagons, some being empty, others, too, containing their dead. Under rough shelters next to black, three-legged pots, greasy with old fat, the remains of those who had been servants lay. Some were lying out in the open and the vultures and hyaenas had got at them. Others lay under branches of hookthorn they had drawn over them. I sensed that the hyaenas were watching me. Warily I looked around me. Had nobody survived?

In the putrid air I suddenly felt sick. What had possessed these people? Why had they invited death in this way? One single night in these depressions where the river broadened into lagoons, slowly moving between the reeds, could be fatal. If one had a mosquito net and enough quinine, one might survive. I had heard that the Trekboers made smoke-screens by burning green branches over an open fire. This is what the Bushmen did. But white people were not Bushmen: the smoke afforded them but little protection. Out of the stagnant pools, where the river reached into the flatland, the mosquitoes arose in dense clouds

*The area around a farmhouse, wagon laager, etc, where the main activity takes place.
†Wagon bed.

shortly after sunset. There was also fly lower down in the mosheshe bush, west of the Toahke. Herdsmen walked behind cattle with branches in their hands, waving them about, scaring off the tsetse. Nevertheless, sooner or later the animals were stung, became ill, and died.

The Zulu servant had said that some of his 'people' had gone to the outveld, away from the marshes. Thirst had driven them back again; to the waters. In a normal year they might have stayed in the outveld. But the year had been wrong. The land had been blighted by lung-sickness, and everywhere cattle were dying.

There were also the rumours about an impending new war between the Orlam Namas and the Ovaherero. They had been fighting each other for forty years. War, disease, poverty, drought had numbed the country. Now there were these others who had come from the west and had got lost in a hard land . . .

I stood there on a bare patch of earth between straggly trees, trodden to dust by animals and men. The mare next to me drooped her head, as if she were mourning my sudden helplessness. What had I come here for? To bury the dead? There seemed to be nothing else to do. I was shivering slightly.

I looked up and suddenly noticed the movement between the trees. Was it some animal? Then I realized that it was two women. They were kneeling at the carcase of an ox, carving out pieces of meat.

'Hallo there!' My voice sounded far-off, and faint. I saw them start up and stand staring at me. I led the mare and walked slowly towards them.

'Hallo!' I shouted. 'I've come to look for you!'

The mare plodded on behind me. It was a homely sound and it seemed to ease the tension. I saw a black woman let a piece of meat fall into a bucket she was carrying. A white woman was slowly coming towards me, the pale smudge of her face framed in her bonnet.

'I met your servant in the veld and he told me about you!' I said, when we finally met. 'I have come to bring you to Olifants Pan!' We shook hands. Her fingers were hot and sticky from cutting the meat. The hand itself was limp, as if the body to which it belonged had lost all its strength. Beads of perspiration and deeply incised lines showed on her face.

'Are you then alone, *Meneer*?'

'The others are on their way.' I indicated the north-west with a movement of the head. 'We heard that there were still people at the river. So I came ahead to see!'

She was now drying her tears with a corner of her apron. 'Are you a hunter?' she asked.

'I am a hunter too,' I replied. 'But I am more of a trader!'

The black woman, too, had now reached us, wailing aloud: 'Old Miss, Old Miss! This is what we have been praying should happen . . . Mister, I greet you! This is Dina who is here before you now. And this is my Old Miss. My little Missie lies there in the wagon, very ill. It is only Old Miss and *Ai** Dina who are still living of all who were here; and Little Miss. It is Kleinveld who went out to look for someone to help us. The Lord is good to us, Old Miss. Not so? Eh?'

'Old Dina, Dina . . .!' The white woman, stoically calm up till now, was suddenly overcome by emotion. '*Meneer*,' she said, looking up, making a vague gesture to indicate the desolation about us. 'All is just as you see it here.' The tears were now coursing down her cheeks. It seemed as if all the feeling that had been suppressed by hunger, thirst, shock, had suddenly been loosed in her.

'Here, *Meneer*, there was nothing else except death and sorrow. But when we laid our troubles before Him who is our Lord, He heard us. The Lord's will be done.'

I slowly undid my saddle bags. There was sufficient food and medicine here to last until the wagon arrived. 'Are you the only survivors?' I asked.

The white woman nodded. '*Meneer*, there are no others,'

'There is only Little Miss, who is ill in the wagon,' the black woman said. 'But how does Mister come so quietly? We did not hear a sound!'

'It is because we have been so busy at this one place, Dina,' her mistress answered. 'When one is in need one only sees the ground in front of you.' Turning to me again, she added: '*Meneer*, we are still alive, because we were mostly in the outveld; until there was no more food and no more water. So we had to come here. Come now, *oumeid*,† we must help this *Meneer*!'

She took the things from me, as I unpacked them from the saddle bags. There were flour, sugar, coffee and dried beans.

*Meaning 'old woman'; a term of affection.

†Old servant.

I sat on a three-legged stool in the wagon. A young girl of about twelve or thirteen lay on the *katel* in a blaze of dry fever. She was very ill. Yet her eyes showed a certain resistance to me. I was there with the bottle of quinine in one hand and a spoon in the other. The old woman sat at the foot of the bed. Dina—Dina Lombard, as I later heard, because she had always 'belonged to the Lombards'—sat on the *voorkist** at the front of the canopy. Her black forehead was drawn tightly into a frown, as she watched me pour the quinine. 'It is bitter-tasting,' I said to the girl, 'but you must take it. It will make you well again.' The girl moved a corner of her mouth and seemed to withdraw into herself. 'Come!' I said. Now her eyes moved, quickly and anxiously.

'Oh, my child,' her mother said, 'you must do as this *Meneer* says. Soon *Meneer's* wagon will be here; and then we can all go to where all our friends are. Open your mouth, Little Heart. Come now!'

There was always the possibility that things had already gone too far, I thought. This was a lovely child. I would not like to see her die.

'Come now!' her mother said again, and helped to raise her head. 'It will only do you good!'

'Bitter things are always good things,' the black woman cried, 'except when they are poison!'

Quinine was a fine remedy, I thought. It had brought relief to thousands. It was not a complete cure. When the bitterness had become diluted in your blood, the parasites came back. It might happen in a few minutes. You would think the weather was uncommonly hot; but the next moment you would feel a chill striking your bones. You would make your way back to your wagon. Blindly you would grope for your blankets, then flop down on your *katel*. There you would lie like a sick dog under a bush, your teeth chattering until you feared that they might break. Soon there were those sweeping chills, then the dry fever, drawing you down relentlessly into a pit. You might imagine you were a palla head the Bushmen had baked in a hole in the ground. Everything seemed to have been caught up in a luminous, brittle glow . . .

I looked at my patient. This, it seemed to me, was the condition she was in now. If that were the case, the quinine could still do

*Chest in front part of wagon.

something for her.

'My dear child,' I wanted to say to her, 'you may drink this without fear. I have taken it so many times, I have lost count. It is bad-tasting, but it keeps one going. There were times when I could not see the silhouette of a camelthorn at fifty yards. My ears felt as if they had been stopped with beeswax. On my face and hands and chest there were brackish spots. But this medicine kept me going; and I could always live again. Come now, little one, drink this, please!'

It suddenly seemed as if my thoughts had penetrated her consciousness. She pushed herself up, rested on an elbow, and pointed to the spoon.

'Oh, my child, my child,' her mother said.

'It is good for Little Miss,' the black woman sang. 'This *Mister*, he is *mos* a doctor! Oh, but the Lord has helped us, eh?'

Lisa was back on her pillows, and her mother was wiping her forehead with a wet rag. She would be all right, I said to myself.

Outside again, I looked about me. The whole abominable scene seemed to be overwhelmed by the sun.

Ella Lombard came towards me. Her eyes were smiling, and there was a new erectness in her bearing. She had put on her Sabbath dress. Even her bonnet was fresh. Her hands were rough from much work, but the nails had been tended. There was a gold wedding-ring on her finger. Dina Lombard, too, had put on a clean apron.

We sat on the shady side of the wagon, engulfed in the midday heat. Around us was a vibrant landscape. This was an old flood area of the river. There were many like it, strips of higher-lying land densely overgrown with mosheshe and magonomo, with forests of camelthorn, intersected by old *malappos*. You could walk due east and after a few miles you would reach the first stagnant water.

It would not be easy to determine the main channel. There was a tangle of waterways in most of which it was impossible to distinguish the flow of the river. If you went further, following the water, you might presently decide that it was, after all, a lagoon: stagnant water, choked with reeds, spawning mosquitoes. At places were islets crowned by makalani palms. It was a brooding, depressing, introverted world, populated by smaller game, and a great variety of birds. Those who had laagered nearby had probably thought that they were far enough from the waters. But the contagion reached up into the low-lying bush, bordering on the marshes.

I listened, my arms dangling over my knees. The old woman's voice was monotonously toned, as if she were speaking in her sleep, cracking at times like glass against the incandescence of the day.

'This was the way of our people,' she said in her strange archaic Dutch. 'We always wished to be on our own. Hans Lombard, who was my husband and lies beneath the tree . . .' The peak of the *kappie** indicated the spot. 'Hans Lombard always said so. Said, too, that we would keep on trekking; keep on to where we would find our *own* land; troubling none; being troubled by none. *Meneer*, you are an Englishman?'

I caught her glance, and smiled. Yes, I was an Englishman.

'Yet I do not think so. Because, *Meneer*, you speak our language. So we trekked, and while trekking suffered all that took place. From here, to the Letter Tree; and the Lake; to the wells and the *vleis*, across the Great Thirst; to the Crocodile River, where we all had gathered.'

I was making a few notes for the Cape newspapers. 'The trek of Alberts, Van der Merwe, Holtzhausen and others started in '74?' I presently enquired: I had heard of this at Gobabis from Roets and Holtzhausen. 'That was four and a half years ago.'

'The Alberts people were at Crocodile River for a whole year before they entered the Thirst, *Meneer*.'

She was like other Boer women. They were not illiterate, as many thought. It was rather the old Calvinist pattern: a world built around the Old Testament. This was the mould for all their spiritual and intellectual life.

Others judged these people on the surface. From my colleagues in the Bay or at Otjimbingue I had often heard sharp words. Hunter-traders like Rule, Stevens, even John Caine, had little time for the Boers. Robert Lewis set the pace. He had said the most trenchant things. This was quite logical in view of the fact that he was Kamaherero's man, since the Palgrave mission had come to grief. And if Kamaherero had decided that the Boers were his real enemies, not the Namas, Lewis would play up to him.

*Poke-bonnet.

'*Oom* Gert and his people were but a few,' the woman said. 'So they came well through the Thirst. And they could come to rest at Rietfontein. Some time back they left Rietfontein and came to the Debra. There they found the Krelings; with others who had trekked away with them. No, *Meneer*, as I hear it from you, they are all at Olifants Pan.'

'When did you leave the Crocodile River?'

'In May of seventy-five,' she said. 'We were two treks, because the people could not agree. Because of the argument between our leaders, Jan Kreling and Louw du Plessis, the Trek was in disorder. So when we arrived at the wells all were falling over each other to get in first.'

'Who started the argument?'

'Kreling went to King Kgama to ask for a way through his country. But Kgama was not satisfied. Kreling then came back from the kraal and some wished to know what had happened. Kreling said there was no need to tell. Then the people chose Louw du Plessis in his place as commandant. Kreling was angry. "Tonight," he said, "we shall trek into the Thirst! Every man shall stand on the soles of his own feet!"—So they trekked; and we, who were with Louw du Plessis, followed the next day. *Meneer*!' She hesitated. 'By the third day we found all that they had left behind: pieces of furniture; sacks of meal; coffee; many other things. There were ploughs and harrows, too; and where the dunes rise, there were empty wagons. By this time our children, too, were crying for water. So it came about that when our distress was at its highest, the Lord looked down upon us. The people had followed a 'Galagadi who had brought water to the laager in ostrich-egg shells. They had spied on him and had seen how he sucked the water up from a little hidden well among the dunes. He emptied it into the shells from his mouth. There we dug and found the water.'

'. . . We were in the desert, *Meneer*, for the Lord's account. So we were punished for all our sins and disunity. We, too, left wagons and things behind. We struggled on through the sand, to where there might be water. But remember, the other trek was ahead; and on arriving at a water-hole we would find only dead cattle in the mud; and no water. So we took the mud, and pressed it in a cloth till at last there were a few drops. The oxen were running about, bellowing. Sometimes they would come to the wagons and lick the iron bands of the wheels, imagining it to be water. Others were drinking the blood of animals they had slaughtered; or the stomach sap. Then the Lord heard our prayers, *Meneer.* An Englishman with a wagon-load of water came our way from Lake Ngami. His name was Hepburn and he was a minister to the nations there. He helped us when there was no hope and many were already lying down to die. After many days we arrived at Tlakaan, and Lake River.'

This was the Botletle, a strange river which sometimes reversed its flow. Some called it the Zouga; a river like an appendix, coming out of the north-eastern extremity of Lake Ngami, ending in a shallow depression, sometimes referred to as Lake Kawaetu, little more than a sponge, receiving the surplus water from Lake Ngami in times of flood.

'So you were there at the Botletle,' I enquired, 'when the message asking for assistance was sent to Rietfontein?'

'Kreling and Du Plessis met each other again. Peace was made, *Meneer.* But Kreling was still in the wrong. There was soon fresh trouble. Kreling insisted on following his own head.'

'As far as I know only a few people left for Rietfontein from Ngami. The others remained at the waters. The Botletle is all right in winter. But it is bad in summer; unless you have quinine. There is the fly down there as well!'

She was wiping her eyes. 'We had all been scared by the Thirst,' she said, 'everywhere in the sand people had been buried. As you have said, because it was winter, we had no trouble with fever. But other things happened. I had four sons, and one daughter: Lisa who lies here in the wagon. I had four sons, and all are dead. Some died in the wars of our people: since the days when we came out of the Old Colony, and trekked to Natal; and from Natal to the highveld and Mooidorp, which is also called Potchefstroom.' She was looking distantly at the grave beneath the tree. 'When Burgers became president my husband said we must carry the *Vierkleur** to some land where it could fly safely, for all to see. Our trek consisted of my husband and I; Willem, who was the only son we had left; and Lisa, who arrived when I thought that I had passed my years. But Willem was killed by a lion, when we were still at the river. He was out hunting, and got lost. And afterwards he had to walk, because his horse had taken fright, and had run off. The next day my husband found him there beside the

*The old flag of the South African Republic (Transvaal).

lion. The lion had charged and had been struck by a bullet. But Willem, too, was dead.'

The *kappie* moved towards me. 'Kreling had many supporters,' she said, sensing what I wished to know. 'We had to vote; and so he was chosen.'

'How long were you at the Botletle: at Lake River?'

'A long time,' she answered. 'But then we left for the Lake itself, where Moreem was the king. You know, he enquired whether we had a young girl for him to be his wife. It was because of trouble with Moreem that some of us refused to take the trek route to Rietfontein, as the others had done. So we stayed at the waters. Kreling wished to trek northwards. And so he did, because he is the kind of man, who, once on his way, even the sea couldn't stop. Later the Trek reached the Letter Tree . . .'

It was a great camelthorn between the nineteenth and twentieth latitude, I remembered, where hunters and traders on trek in the country above Lake Ngami had always left messages, and mail. Axel Eriksson and I had laagered there once.

'But we were not yet there when Louw du Plessis decided he would go off on his own to Rietfontein, taking all his people.'

'But you remained at the river?'

'Hans said we must stay near the waters. In time the *vleis* would be fewer. We had heard that it was fine there: one might even sow corn, and reap enough for all to eat. We had our own plans to make.

'Were there any who returned?'

'A few, yes; but not many. They could follow our trekspoor in the sand; look for the graves we had made. Well, before long there was trouble again: some wished to go this way, others that way. Kreling and his party went to the outveld. Some remained at the Letter Tree. Some others, led by Jurie Snyman, followed the river, which comes down into the marshes . . .

'At the waters people were falling ill. In the outveld, however, there was the Thirst again. And dust . . . In the dry season, before the rains come, it is hard to see oxen-at-six from the *voorkist.* The dust got into one's throat and into one's eyes. In the end one always fled down to the waters again.'

'Where did the Snyman's go?'

'To Rietfontein to take the trekspoor back as we had come. We just went on. Afterwards we heard that Kreling and his people were in the outveld. But some left them and also came down to the waters. We were then still with the Prinsloos: old Diederick and the others. Old Died was landdrost and Orphan Master. He has three sons: Jan, Machiel, and Willem: leaders in the laager. Some days we would see curtains of rain falling in the distance; then we would trek again to the outveld, to see if we could reach a small pan with some water in it. There we would remain until the pan was dry. Then we would trek down to the *vleis* again. With all these doings the Prinsloos got lost. Then we heard that they were down here at the waters. Our own animals were suffering badly by this time. There was no other way for us. We, too, had to leave the outveld again and go in search of the others. So, *Meneer*, we managed to get here after some time, with but half a team of oxen left; and Hans now very ill.'

'How many had died?'

'Quite a few, *Meneer*. There was no hope of continuing our trek: the oxen were too weak.'

'Who lies buried here? Whose bodies are still in the wagons?'

Between the straggly branches of the trees gleamed the off-white of canopies. Her eyes seemed to rest on a heap of soil covered with hookthorn nearby. Hans Lombard lay there.

A jackal stared at me through a tunnel in the bush. The sun was beating down on the rusty red of his fur. On the dead branches of the leadwood the vultures had gathered. A marabou beat its wings. Billowy thunderheads were pushing up beyond the north-eastern horizon.

' . . . Van Voors* we were; and Coppenhagens; and Groblers; and Bothmas . . .'

The black woman was approaching with a coffee kettle.

'Old Miss Ella now thinks of other times,' she said. 'The Bothma people were there at the Tree!'

'The Letter Tree . . . Yes, I am confused by all that happened. We buried them as best we could.'

'Mister, he who is Kleinveld found the spoor of the Prinsloos in the outveld. They had trekked past.'

'Where to?'

'We did not know. Kleinveld was out looking for veld foods. And then he found the spoor. Now, he said, this must certainly be Old Master Prens* and his people. And so they did not even know

*Van Vuuren.

*Prinsloo.

of us down here.'

My clothes were sticking to my body. On the seat of the stool a wet patch had formed.

'Ma!' It was a choking sound from the wagon. Ella Lombard peered into the gloom under the canopy.

'Ma!' The voice from inside choked again, 'I am not going to die, Ma!'

I wished that I could put the girl out here under a shade-tree. A wagon-tent was close on a day like this. I would give her as much quinine as she could take. By the morning one should know what her chances were.

I walked around the wagon. Now I could see her. She had raised herself on the *katel* and was sitting up, her hands behind her back.

' . . . Is this *Meneer* a doctor?'

'Not in the ordinary sense of the word, young Missie,' I answered. 'But you just keep kicking. One of these days you will be running around again. Come on, swallow the bitter stuff. It will make you well. That fever of yours has broken. You'd better keep down.'

Her face was shiny wet against the dirty white of the canvas. Tears suddenly broke from her eyes and slipped over her gleaming cheeks. '*Meneer*,' she stuttered, 'I *do* feel better!'

'You get some sleep now,' I answered. 'You're not altogether well yet.'

'Can I have some water, Ma?'

Her sudden liveliness was to be wondered at. I had not expected the fever to break so soon. I unhooked my water-bottle from the broken limb of a tree, and handed it to Dina Lombard. 'Give it to Little Miss.'

Ella Lombard was now sitting on the *voorkist*. 'Oh, my child,' she sighed, 'Death had already taken down our names. But the dangers have now passed. See how wet you are. Here is a *lappie*!'*

When the white-hot sun had already begun cooling off to redness by the late afternoon, I followed a *malappo* in the direction of the main stream, or where I calculated it to be. The first *vleis* and lagoons were close by. Perhaps I would find some duck, muscovy, or a spurwing goose. I well knew that it might demand more skill and judgement than I could muster. The white-

*Literally: a little rag.

backed duck and the muscovy were clever birds. They kept low when danger threatened. Then they suddenly reappeared and swept away over the water, beating the surface with their wings. Then they were in the air. The trouble was: even if you got one with the Winchester, it had to be fetched. I did not relish the idea of wading into the lagoons.

I found a single marula on a hillock which would probably be an island in times of flood. There, a hundred yards away, was the first lagoon. A great many birds were to be seen. Dotted lines were moving over the shining surface. There was the smack of wings upon the water.

To the south and to the east the marshes extended to the horizon. To the north there were indications of a narrowing down. About a day's journey from here the Okavango still ran deeply in its ancient channel. Here the river had already fanned out. The eastern stream was now the Toahke, and would be about a mile away. It lay there between islets, *vleis*, and old lagoons.

John Gunning and I had once got so far. Even the main arms of the delta often failed to indicate the flow. Strange, I thought, while precariously balanced in the cleft of a tree, that such a fine river should lose its life in the sand . . .

Like the Trek, I suddenly thought. The start had been vigorous, hopeful, even heady. But what had it all come to? One could never know . . . If these people had not yet turned back after all that had happened, they would continue their journey. To where?

At least, one had to recognize the strength of their feeling. They lived on their emotions, but yet were inhibited. Only at rare intervals would they cry out to their God, beseeching his intervention. . . .

I wandered back the way I had come. If only the rains would come, I thought. It could change everything.

A bustard went scurrying up a sand dune. On the crest it paused, silhouetted against the darkening sky. I held my breath and supported the gun on the wreck of an old acacia. When the bullet struck, the great bird climbed into the air, but the next moment it fell steeply and hit the sand.

It was already dark when I finally returned with my booty to the wagon, where a fire was burning.

That night it did rain. I lay there under the camelthorn. When I awoke the heavens were illuminated and the rain was coming down. It was cool and wonderful. I lay there without moving, quietly happy. Even the mosquitoes, which earlier that evening had appeared in black clouds, had been taken by surprise.

Perhaps I imagined that the storm would soon pass. But after an hour the rain was still coming down and I was getting wet. I was also beginning to feel the cold, so I removed myself to under Ella Lombard's wagon. Up above they must have heard me, for presently the old woman enquired whether it was *Meneer.* Yes, I answered, it was *Meneer.*

There was a moment of silence. Then I heard her say: 'Oh, my child, but you must be wet. Nor have you any coffee!' It took a moment to realize that she was addressing me, not her daughter.

I chuckled. I made myself comfortable against a wagon-wheel and lit a cigar. 'Never mind, *Tante,*' I answered, 'fresh water is as pleasant to the taste!' I heard her laugh: a short dry laugh, but not without humour.

And leaning against the wheel, with the driest of my blankets drawn up around me, sucking at my cigar, I thought: 'I am happy . . .'

Late the following afternoon, while expended rain-clouds were slowly drifting southwards, my wagon arrived. The servants greeted me with shouts of joy. Their master was still alive. Almost certainly they had feared the worst.

'Greetings, Bushman. Greetings, Dama!' I, too, was relieved.

They stood there before me grinning: Izak the Ai-Bushman, and Kairob the Bergdamara. They had long been members of my firm. Kleinveld Labuschagne, thin as a reed, but tough, came to kneel before his Old Miss, hands clasped together, thankful, too, for finding her alive. His true joy, however, was the sight of his Little Miss. She had dressed herself and was now walking about the *werf*, pale and slight.

'Because of all the bitter stuff this Mister has given our child,' Dina Lombard explained.

Kleinveld nodded: 'I hear you, *Oumie.* I, too, have learnt to know this Mister.'

We should be off now, I said. We should get away from here as soon as possible. This place still smelt of death.

The sun was behind low cloud in the west when at last we were ready. My Damara oxen, with the few reserves which always accompanied us, would suffice for the two wagons. The rain had hardened the sand and the going would be good.

Ella Lombard took a last, lonely look at the grave covered with hookthorn among the trees. Those who had died here would lie here in the bush, with their graves untended. How would one ever return to this place? I watched her as she walked back to her wagon. The girl suddenly ran up and embraced her mother.

We trekked, following a north-westerly course, and spent the night out in the open veld under a clear sky. The next day we regularly struck small pans filled with fresh water. Late on the second afternoon we sighted the thin blue smoke of laager fires.

3

Olifants Pan is situated twenty-five miles south of the river where it flows due east. Here I met most of these with whom I would still undertake strange things in this strange land.

There were the Prinsloos, with Old Diederick at the head of the clan: well in the seventies, but still straight as a rifle barrel. Like Saul, from the shoulders upwards, Ella Lombard explained, he stood out among the crowd.

There were the Du Plessis (Louw and Jan), Gallic in appearance, Gallic in temperament. There was good, sober-minded David Black. There were the Holtzhausens, presided over by the inimitable Dolf. There were the Oppermans, the Labuschagnes: both sizable clans. There were many others, including those I had judged fit to confer with: the Albertses led by the dauntless Gert; the Van der Merwes, solid in physique, solid in attitude. There were the Bothas: the J.F.'s who had been the leaders of the successful Third Trek from the Crocodile. Some time later at Leeu Pan, some distance to the south-west, J.F. would become commandant of the Trek. There were also those who had been grievously tried by all that had happened. They had now lost heart, thinking of little else but the long road back: following the sandspoor, for more than a thousand miles . . .

The leader here was Jan Kreling, a closed-up man; a bitter man. Kreling flatly refused to recognize my presence and ignored my greetings. Often one would hear his voice climbing out above the others. Enough of all this wandering about, he would shout. It was now time to go home. And indeed, two days after our arrival, he trekked out of the laager in a huff, heading south for Rietfontein. The little line of wagons crept away into the sunlight. I watched them go. The bush swallowed them up . . .

Nearly all thc missing people had now been accounted for. Ella Lombard and her little circle had been the last to arrive. There was also great interest in the 'Englishman' who had brought them in. Women, led by Jet du Plessis, Jan's wife, ran out into the sun. Around me there was much embracing, blowing of noses, and wiping of cheeks. Jan Labuschagne, hunter *par excellence*, six foot six, with shoulders like an ox-yoke, came marching into the laager with little Lisa perched on his neck. The Oppermans fired a welcoming salvo and a smell of powder hung in the air. People were cheering.

But even before being informed of the situation by my friends, Axel Eriksson and Pieter Maritz-Botha, I knew the worst. People in the laager were very ill. Many had died. Many had been buried among the trees fringing the pan. Our stock of quinine had run low.

Charles Thomas, with whom I had had an appointment in Andara, however, turned up with quinine to spare. It was good to see him. Charles, an American, was a hunter-trader in the best tradition. He brought a wagon full of much needed provisions, and sold it to the Trekkers at reasonable prices. At Andara, said Charles, the chief had provided some of the River Trekkers with corn. They were the Prinsloos. Doubtless more could be had. He would trade in the vicinity for a while, and also spy out the land.

We sat around the laager fire and talked of old times. Back to America? I asked. Not in a hurry, said Charles. This was a man's country and he loved it.

This was a man's country; and we all loved it. We loved its vastness, its wildness, its beauty. In a way we even loved its terrible hardness.

Look at the Boers, I said. They were almost destitute. They were suffering badly from fever. Many were grief-stricken by the loss of their loved ones, but here they were, and here they would remain. No, they would not return, in spite of Kreling and his ilk. Note how they had kept their dignity. This was beyond disease, and beyond poverty.

'Come again Charles!' I said. He left in the early morning, and I held his hand.

At dawn, and after sunset, the laager would assemble for devotions. It happened four times on a Sunday. There was the long prayer, with the prayer-leader calling for divine intervention on behalf of all who were afflicted. There was the heavy solemnity of the psalms, with the older women keening in nasal tones, the men droning along with them. Then they would stand in the sun with bared heads. Nowhere was there sufficient shade for the whole assembly. Sweat crept down their bearded cheeks and their eyes were tightly shut.

Each little *werf* was well ordered and neat. Black retainers bent over smoking *erds.** Sundays everybody would dress. The men wore short jackets and trousers of corduroy or nankeen. The women exchanged their work-a-day dresses for better ones of print or cambric.

It was a day for visiting, especially the ill. The leaders—Gert Alberts, Louw du Plessis, Diederick Prinsloo—would pray powerfully, movingly. But the burials continued.

One would see the little groups down there by the marulas or acacias, or sometimes at a baobab. Of the women one would see only the *kappies.* These were directed to the ground.

The breeze would stir, bringing with it a snatch of song, or of prayer. At times one would also hear the dull thud of soil on wood. Rough planks had been sawn, and Dolf Holtzhausen was the carpenter. Dolf would work deep into the night. Sometimes even Dolf and his sons could not cope. People were buried in their clothes.

Meanwhile the news had spread that I was a 'doctor'. From all sides I was summoned. I did what was in my power, but our supply of quinine was exhausted. Now I had to look to the Trek's own medicine chests.

My *bambuse* also fell ill. Nights I watched over him, thinking that he would die: Izak, the little yellow man who had led my oxen teams so many miles through this vast land. I had always thought Bushmen to be immune from fever. Apparently they were not. Izak suddenly folded up and lay there in his *scherm,*† panting like a dog. 'Dama,' I said to Kairob, 'the medicine is *opu.*‡ You'll have to find some more!'

*The hearth of the wagon *werf.*

†A rough shelter of grass and poles.

‡A Herero corruption of the Dutch *op*: finished.

He took me seriously. He disappeared that night and only returned the next afternoon with another Bushman. Who was he precisely? I never discovered.

The newcomer, festooned with bones and bits of skin, carried his charms in a leather bag. I let him have his way. I looked up strangely when he suddenly began an incantation over Izak's prostrate body. It rose to a climax. Then he grabbed the patient fast and sucked violently at his chest. With a sudden scream he let go again. Then he stood there waving something aloft. This he quickly buried under a flat stone: I recognized it as a veld cacoon.

By evening when our visitor had left I was surprised to see Izak struggle up from his bed. '*Ara!*' he clicked, and shook his head. For a while he still seemed to move about unsteadily. By nightfall, however, he was again going about his duties.

There he sat, stirring the hunter's pot, batting his eyes against the smoke, serene.

But the Trekkers themselves had their own way of doing things.

A child in the laager was suffering from croup. Many remedies had already been tried. There had been dried hyaena-dung ground to a powder and blown into the child's throat. There had been an extraction of acacia bark. There had been the juice of a finely crushed tortoise . . .

Kappies nodded around a wagon while I was told all this. Meanwhile there were the raspings of tight breath, coming from under the canopy, with a worried mother begging me to do something. Ella Lombard and old Dina luckily arrived, and I asked them to bring me a tub with warm water and some mustard. This they did, and I put the patient in the tub. I mixed the mustard with a pint of water and proceeded to pour it down the child's throat. Soon the child was contorting in a most violent manner. Around me women were wailing, while some were denouncing me. I held on grimly, praying to God that I would succeed. The next moment the child started retching. The constricted throat had burst open. A few minutes later he fell asleep . . .

4

We shared a laager site: Eriksson, Botha, and I. Evenings we would talk. Around us, following the contour of the pan, were winking fires. Two other hunter-traders of the territory turned up unexpectedly: McNab, who had just come to the country, and Gerald McKierman, who was in the service of his fellow American, Charles Thomas. Both had heard of the assembly of destitute Boers. McKierman could supply us with some quinine. He and McNab lent a hand at digging graves.

Axel Eriksson led us all and there was no sparing of himself. This was Karevapu Katiti, I thought, the boy from Vänersborg who now stood at the summit of his career. He was thirty-three and acknowledged by all to be the Trader King of Damaraland. His headquarters were at Omaruru, but his contacts were everywhere in the territory. There were no less than twenty white hunter-traders in his employ. The latest recruits were Piet Botha and Barend Bouwer.

Axel also had much influence at the Cape. People had always respected his views. He would walk through the laager here at the pan, the friend of all, listening to the many tales of hardship, encouraging the weak. Material assistance would bc given, he assured them, as soon as he could get to the Cape.

Botha had also by this time established himself, largely because of the legend spun around his name after the great battle with the elephants. But with his easy approach, his style, especially as far as the fair sex was concerned, he was much in demand. He would wear a bowler hat, bought at the Cape, sport a cane with a silver head and always listen attentively to the many tales of privation; of death in the Thirst, and in the marshes. Often he would laugh with abandon, regaling audiences with stories of his heroics in the Debra.

Here in the pan were the sun-bleached bones of one hundred and three African elephants, half hidden in the mud. Botha would walk about, using his silver-headed cane, pointing out all.—This was a herd in flight, he said; mostly cows and young bulls, with relatively little ivory . . . This lot here *he* had shot. Those were Barend Bouwer's . . .

At the big baobab in the south-eastern bend of the pan he would point out the names carved into the bronze bark, then read them out aloud: *Bouwer, Botha, McDonald, Van Zyl, Van Zyl, Van Zyl* . . . The latter three were sons of old Hendrik.

The young men would stretch their necks. The older hunters would shake their heads, chew their tobacco, spit upon the ground. Jan Labuschagne, who himself had shot his way through the bush and plains of Africa, would roar: 'That needs doing,

Cousin Piet, eh!'

'A fortnight had not yet passed,' Piet would relate, 'when we had already notched up fifty elephants. Sixty-nine had already been accounted for. In all, we brought down one hundred and seventy-eight. This gave us two whole tons of ivory. Of course, it all belonged to old Hendrik: we were in his employ, and entitled only to our share.'

Now he was with Eriksson. This was to tide him over. Tentatively we had discussed a joint venture. John Gunning and I had ceased doing business together at Rehoboth. I needed a new partner. There was already in me the dim outline of an ideal. It was growing perceptibly.

I was thirty and had spent eight years in the country. What exactly were my ambitions? I had heard it said that I was gifted. The question nevertheless remained: what could outlast my time? One could not just spend one's days trading, hunting, wandering. I was a bachelor and I had no plans for marriage. The land itself had claimed me. I was bound to its vastness, its poetry. I had grown in it, and it had grown in me . . .

'It is not so easy to decide,' I said while making coffee, 'whether all who were in the Trek have been accounted for. The Snyman group, as you know, returned to the Transvaal via Rietfontein. Kreling and Co were brought in by the Albertses. And now the Krelings too have elected to go back the way they came. What about the River Trekkers? The Prinsloos got up as far as Andara, and are now here. We have picked up a few odd stragglers here and there, like my Lombard woman, and her child. But who can say whether there are not people still in the marshes?'

'Who could survive it?' Botha asked. 'You know what it is like down there.'

I agreed, but added: 'These people have a knack of surviving. The marvel is that only two hundred were claimed by the marshes and the Thirstland.'

'Ugh, Will,' Eriksson said, pushing his fingers through his thinning red hair. 'My friend: with all that is so sadly lacking in the laager, here we should remain. Must I give an account? So then, I agree. All who are still alive and have not gone back are now here. The question remains: where must we put these people? Before God and man I must admit I do not know their destination, and what it should be. There are so many here sick unto death. And so many are poor!'

'They need their own country,' Botha said. 'Well, that is why they trekked, isn't it?'

'Damaraland can be ruled out,' I said at length. 'With Kamaherero and his *Missionare* in their present mood, it would be dangerous. As for Robert Lewis at Otjimbingue? As for his partners in the trading business? Coates Palgrave has already decided on the Kaoko, which is no pleasant prospect.'

'Lewis is up at the river,' Botha reminded. 'We must get him here. To talk.'

'He talks too much,' I said. 'Lewis has told the Ovaherero that the Trekboers are out to take Damaraland.'

Lewis could hardly sign his name. Yet he was, in the eyes of Kamaherero, his 'legal adviser'. Maybe this was because he had once been a partner of Spence, Pass and Co, of the Bay. So, too, was Palgrave, the Cape commissioner, 'enquiring into the resources of the country'. Theo Hahn was right: *Missionar* Diehl at Okahandja would wake up one day and discover that Robert Lewis had become the owner of all the mineral rights of Damaraland.

'Lewis!' Eriksson snorted. 'He must come down to see what "evil people" the Trekboers are!'

'He's an old hand,' I said. 'He has had his share in the pioneering of this country. The hard fact is that our friends at the Pan cannot stay here. They know all about Palgrave. He wrote to Alberts and Co at Rietfontein and suggested the Kaoko. But some have been talking about Angola.'

Axel struck his knees with his big hands. 'Do they know where Angola lies?'

'Our people are land-tamers, Karevapu,' Botha said. 'They follow the sun; and they get where they want to be. They know of Angola. That is enough.'

I looked at Piet. I was doubtful of this. I did not agree that the Trekboers knew where they were heading. I doubted whether they had much idea of the map of Africa.

'Follow the sun, eh?' Eriksson asked. 'Now what if the sun goes down into the big ocean?'

'My grandfather,' Botha said, sucking at his pipe, 'was Harbour Master of Port Natal. That was in the days when our people trekked up from the Old Colony across the Drakensberg and down into Natal. He knew the sea! And except him, there were only a few that knew the sea. Among those here in the laager it is only Ignatius Labuschagne, as far as I know. As a young man he worked for my grandfather.'

'Angola!' I played with the thought. Eriksson looked at me. We had been down to Moçamedes together on more than one occasion. Eriksson knew what I was thinking. The whole vast hinterland of Portuguese West Africa was still undeveloped country. For more than three centuries the Portuguese had been glued to the coast. Those that went into the interior traded *aguardente*, kept black concubines, and took slaves down to Luanda or Lobito. These worked in the cocoa plantations of Sao Thome. *Minha terra* was big and empty. The Serras could well do with the Boers. But could the Boers well do with the Portuguese?

'Down at the Cape they will know all about the Trekboers,' Botha said.

'Not about present conditions,' I said. 'When you get down there, Karevapu, as you shortly will, you can inform the newspapers.'

Premier Molteno had once talked freely of extending the Colonial rule from the mouth of the Orange to Cape Frio on the Kaoko coast. Coates Palgrave had been specially briefed to consider the Trekboers as possible colonists. I nursed the idea and suddenly found it attractive. The Transgariep had great need of a civilized, stable element. Hugo Hahn, who was the founder of the Rhenish Mission in the country and the greatest of the *Missionare*, had once stressed this very point. We were traders and hunters, he had said. But we were also educated, civilized people. Anarchy could not be suffered. And anarchy was prevalent.

No one lived here for more than a day ahead. Palgrave had come here with the finest of ideals. He, too, had soon discovered that as far as the Transgariep was concerned *Pax Britannica* was little more than a pious sentiment.

'What Palgrave probably forgot, or never knew,' I said, 'was that the Ovaherero left the Kaoko more than a century ago, because of famine.'

'Palgrave talks like the wind blows,' Eriksson said. 'Now here, now there. And he dreams!'

That was putting it gently. There was no part of the sub-continent more inhospitable, more demanding than the Kaoko. The mountainous country directly south of the Cunene was an impenetrable wilderness. It was only good for primitive Ovahimba, Ovatjimba and elephants.

'Palgrave must think it suitable for our people,' Botha continued, 'because he believes we are nothing but hunters. He hoisted a Union Jack at Okahandja and thought it was British.'

The well-meant, tireless efforts of the special commissioner had culminated in a series of conferences. During September '76 they had gathered at Okahandja: the entire Herero hierarchy, and two hundred others. Robert Lewis duly informed us of the unanimous desire on the part of the Ovaherero that somebody should be sent by the Cape Government 'to rule us and be the head of our country'. My way of answering was to put the difficult question whether 'our country' indeed included the whole vast area from the mouth of the Cunene to Rietfontein in the east. This was exactly what Lewis thought fit to tell. What nonsense! Since when, and in what manner, had all this land been Damara pasture? During the previous October Palgrave duly returned from the Cape, bringing with him a Union Jack and a flag-pole.

'Theo Hahn informed me,' I said, 'that when the flag was at last hoisted, old man Diehl looked up at it and remarked: *"Glück zu!"* Then he just shook his head.'

'I have heard them tell at Omaruru,' Eriksson added, 'that the king himself—Kamaherero—said the flag was very pretty.'

The problem, I thought, was not so much whether protection would come to anything or not. The whole thing was more a comic performance than serious statecraft. What was indeed worthy of more positive action was the increasing anarchy. Had the land itself invited it? Here it lay, spread out over twelve latitudes on both sides of Capricorn. To whom did it belong in ages past? And to whom did it belong today? A cynic might answer: to those who excelled best in the art of murder. At present it was the Ovaherero. And the underdogs were Nama, Saan, Bergdamara and Bushmen . . .

At the beginning of the century Herero herdsmen had driven their cattle through Great Namaland. They claimed the water and the grazing for themselves. Where Namas tried to stop them, they were struck down. Then Jonker Afrikaander arrived from distant Waveren in the Cape. He swore to restore the Nama honour. The vengeance he exacted, in time, was frightful. He and his soldiers rode into the heart of Damaraland. Every black body was shot down without quarter. Andersson reported in his journal that the Ovaherero had by the end of the fifties almost ceased to exist.

Jonker ruled from Windhoek and at his 'court', in humiliating circumstances, was Tjamuaha (Copper Foot), once king of the Ovaherero. There was also Maherero, his son, the very man who was now dispensing 'justice' from Okahandja.

In '57 Jonker and Copper Foot had died within a month of each other on opposite sides of the Swakop. They had barely departed when the successors grabbed at each other's throats: Jan Jonker Afrikaander, and Kamaherero, as he now was called. Followed a decade of inglorious warfare. Eight years previously, when *Missionar* Hahn could stand it no longer, he had forced the warring parties to sign a peace. But he soon lost faith in the sincerity of the agreement, so after five years he packed up and left for the Cape.

Peace, they said, but there was no peace. Coates Palgrave had done his best, but his best was little more than a posture. He and Manning, who gloried in the official title of Resident Magistrate at Okahandja, tried hard to promote the idea of British justice. The Ovaherero still preferred their own 'legality', implemented by human massacre.

A story did the rounds that Kamaherero had come to Palgrave with a cravat around his neck. 'I thought,' he complained, 'that you were going to make me an even greater chief than what I am. Now I see that you merely wish to blind me.'

'It seems to me Palgrave is sick of all these doings,' Eriksson observed. 'The chief's son, Wilhelm, who has been a student at Hahn's Augustineum, talks as a Christian.'

'I respect Wilhelm Maherero,' I said. 'But he is a voice crying in the wilderness. Hugo Hahn's idea to establish a White Colony on the banks of the Swakop at Otjimbingue was excellent. However, with all respect to men like Haelbich, Redecker, and the others, the chances for success, using colonists from the Old World, were slight. What Africa demands is people from Africa itself. Theo Hahn was right when he said that Boers should go to Rehoboth. True, Okahandja did not like the thought. But the idea was sound. We can keep this in mind. Meanwhile what needs our attention is the matter of provisions for the laager.'

'Food, clothing, medicine,' Botha said. 'Karevapu, this is your task. You'll be at the Cape in the New Year!'

'Write to the press,' I suggested. I had great faith in the Cape newspapers.

'That I could well do, Will,' Erikkson answered. 'But then I would look to you so that you may help me. My learning stopped too soon, you know.'

'Your learning, Karevapu,' I reflected, 'is a model for all of us. A long and useful life.'

'Am I then so old, my friend?' His eyes shone as he grinned.

'Not old, Karevapu, just very much alive, and very human. What we need is a schooner, to bring whatever provisions can be obtained to some place on the Kaoko coast where they may be landed.'

'So you, too, will have them in the Kaoko?' Eriksson looked at me. Izak was filling our tin cups with coffee.

'Yes,' I answered, 'it seems that till such time as we are able to settle them elsewhere, the Kaoko may well be a temporary resting place.'

Charles Thomas turned up unexpectedly the next day. With him was Robert Lewis. The latter, I forthwith decided, had come to Olifants Pan because he was curious. His manner, however, was friendly enough. He would walk around, distributing greetings and questions at the wagons. At times he would even offer cigars and bon-bons. Far more important was the small supply of quinine he could provide us with. For the rest he was having a field-day exercising his Dutch. The bon-bons had made him popular with the children.

My own subtle discomfort at his presence, however, was in a way relieved when he directly addressed me on the question of the Trekboers. 'Well, Jordan,' he enquired, 'what exactly do you envisage for these people?'

'That is surely not for me to say.' I answered: 'nevertheless, *pro tempore* it seems to be the Kaoko.'

5

I was indebted to Charles Thomas. He had brought some post from the Bay. It included a letter from my mother. I went and sat under a tree and read it, and for a while I was back at the Cape.

At times, my mother wrote, they wondered if I was still alive. Damaraland was so far away. When a letter arrived from me after months of silence, it was a real event. She and my sisters would then read and re-read it. Georgina, who was the eldest, believed I would be home for Christmas.

'Please look after yourself,' my mother wrote. 'There are so many dangers in that wild country. So, will you please make your fortune soon and then return, this time for good.'

In the Cape they were having the sort of summer I liked: dry and brilliant, with lots of south-easter. They had been down to Muizenberg and Hout Bay. My mother often thought of me and my playmates catching rock-lobster at Hout Bay in the icy Atlantic. 'Look after yourself,' she said in conclusion.

That same afternoon I sat down at my little X-table and wrote back. I told my mother of the latest trek up here to the Okavango. I gave an account of my journey to the marshes, and of the sufferings of the Trekboers. I felt singularly attached to these people, I said. One could not see their plight from close quarters and remain unmoved. I would record what I had heard and what I had seen. A dependable, factual record of the wanderings of the Trekboers was necessary. The mere physical performance of the Trek itself was without parallel. What about the future? No one could say. There were a number of possibilities . . .

A touch of nostalgia took hold of me as I sealed the letter. Lewis was going down to Otjimbingue that week. He could take the letter along with him. From Otjimbingue it would catch a wagon going down to the Bay. With luck, my mother could have the letter by the end of January.

Late that afternoon Charles Thomas came to my laager. 'Come along with us, Will,' he said, 'to across the river, and beyond!'

Charles had always wanted to go beyond the Okavango into what we knew as Nhembaland. Nobody could tell us much about it. We shared the view that between the upper reaches of the Zambezi and the Okavango was perhaps the greatest virgin country in Africa.

'Charles,' I said after a moment's thought, 'in any other circumstances I would not have hesitated.'

'What we want now, Will,' he explained, 'is merely some form of reconnaissance with a view to the future.'

Maybe this linked up with some talk in the laager of crossing the river and continuing the Trek in a northerly direction. One Van Staden had done that. Accompanied by his brother, wife and child, he had gone off on his own, out into the blue.

'See what you can find, Charles,' I said musingly. 'One day we'll set off together; you, Karevapu, Piet Botha, myself; and whoever else would join us.'

He left the following morning. That was the last I ever saw of him.

Almost forty people had already been buried at the Pan.

Daily I had to employ myself in more respects than I had ever bargained for. Main reason for this was my search for the material to complete this chapter of my journal. Axel had said that he would be with us for another week. Then he had to get back to Omaruru. My provisional chronicle of the Trekboers and their wanderings would go with him.

There I was, suddenly cast into a part I had no experience of, nor had striven for. I was the mentor, I was the general source of information regarding the country and its future. I was the comforter of the sick . . .

Take a man like Eloff who came to me with a septic finger, the result of his carving out hippo sjamboks during a hunt up at the river.

'Cut it off, Sir!' he demanded, holding the poisoned finger up for me to see.

I looked quickly at him. When I was satisfied, however, that his condition was serious, I obliged. I amputated the finger on a bread-board, then disinfected the wound with tincture of iodine and phenol, stitching it with horsehair. All the while my patient stood firm. Only his moustache showed a nervous twitch at times, and around his nostrils beads of sweat had formed. His wife and children watched silently from a distance.

Then there was the weary Trekker who came to me complaining that the Thirst had destroyed his wife's reason. I went with him and found the woman walking aimlessly between the trees, haggard, unkempt, obviously disorientated. I could do nothing for her.

In the meanwhile there was much talk of the boy who had got lost in the Debra and had been murdered by the Bushmen. Everywhere questions were being whispered. Was it true that old Van Zyl, who had refused water for the Trekboers at Ghanzi, had caught the murderers? Was it true that he had passed sentence of death on them?

Pieter Maritz-Botha was the likely one to tell. But Botha, in his easy way, laughed it off. 'That's old Hendrik's doing,' he said. 'Ask him!'

So many things were now coming my way. It was difficult to

know just what to record. Every wagon, every family, had its own saga. Every story had its variants. I imagined that in lost, heroic ages people had gathered around their fires in just this fashion. I imagined they had sat there telling each other stories like these we were now hearing.

6

I listened to Ella Lombard: 'That time when the old 'Galagadi came to us while we were in the Thirst,' she said, 'he carried the water in a calabash and two ostrich-egg shells. Machiel Prinsloo paid one blanket, five bags of powder, one bar of lead, and one tin of percussion caps. Everything had to be spread out in front of him in the sand. But of course, the water was not enough. So we said we would pay for more. We gave him a cask and he crept away into the bush. After some time the men-folk started following his spoor. Then they came to a sand-dune and spied on him while he was busy sucking up water through a reed from a little covered well, then spitting it into the cask. So, *Meneer*, can you realize how we felt, knowing that we had already used such water. The old *schelm.** He got such a fright, when the men surprised him, that at once he began talking Dutch! Here was the little reed still sticking into the ground. At the end was a knot of grass with which the eye of the fountain had been stopped. Everyone now set to work digging. The deeper it went, the wetter it became. Suddenly there was the water itself: spurting out, forming a little pool. Everybody just lay down and drank. The cask was filled with the new water, then taken back to those of us who were still at the wagons. Everybody hurried to come and see with their own eyes what miracle this was: some with a beaker in the hand, others with a bowl or a cup. During all the days of our suffering *so* much water had never been seen. There was now a large hole full, and still more came from the spring. Ah, and the poor oxen! Some had been blinded by thirst.

'We had to mind the animals rushing down to get to the water. So we made troughs of hide, and filled them with water. The blinded oxen were brought up and watered, one by one. After a while they began to see again! In this way we saved a great many

*Rascal.

people, and a great many oxen.'

'What caused all the dissension?' I enquired from Louw du Plessis, for it was he who had first questioned Kreling's leadership. Instinctively I trusted this man.

'We gathered at Pienaar's River,' Du Plessis said with his thoughts afar. 'That was the first meeting-place. Erasmus and his people with thirty-four wagons turned up. Kreling was there with fourteen. We had seven. Kreling stopped an hour's ride on horseback from us. Still, I invited him to come along and join our laager. No, he would not come. But he and his people nevertheless did show up after some time. From Erasmus he demanded to know where the meeting-place was, becoming so angry that people had to intervene. Still, we decided there had to be firm trek regulations to ensure law and order. The clauses were drawn up and accepted by general vote. Provision was also made for a commandant, field-cornets, and a triumvirate, to whom the commandant had to make a regular report. Well, in spite of what had happened, Kreling was then elected commandant by vote. Thereupon he left for Kgama's country, to ask for trekking rights through the king's territory. This was refused. On his return he summoned the triumvirate, but insisted on acting as his own chairman. When it was explained to him that he could not be chairman and *also* report on his journey, he said: then no report! The triumvirate now decided on a point of order to resign. So enmity grew between us. Meanwhile I had been chosen to be landdrost, to sanctify marriages. Kreling, however, was still commandant; and Gert Meyer was his field-cornet. Soon Meyer, too, resigned, and I had to take his place.

'*Meneer*, regarding the question of Kreling's bad behaviour, in the final run he was found guilty and dismissed from office. In his place I was appointed. Yet, Kreling still had his own following. It was now December of '76.

'Well, we had to wait for another trek which was on its way. It was April of '77 when it eventually arrived. Meanwhile quite a number of people had fallen ill. Because King Kgama had now denied us a way through his land, we were compelled as in former times to take the long way around. At the Magalepsies a letter from Kgama arrived, informing us that we had five days to get out of his country: all this while the people were ever more being struck down by fever, some dying. Water, too, was getting scarce. So we trekked again; and after some days we stood on the very edge of the Thirst, on the way to the Lake. Here I thought it best to come to an agreement with Kreling, to get us through the Thirst. But that was the day he shouted out to all who were present: Every man must now stand on the soles of his own feet! Well, I said, if Jan Kreling has oxen for his followers, so have I! One hundred and thirty wagons there were, all ready to enter the Thirst together, which was hazardous. A second great mistake was that six thousand oxen had been sent on ahead of us. Well, on the 9th of May '77, we then entered the Thirst. How it all turned out, you already know.'

There was an ever-present interest in the 'Englishman' who had taken it upon himself to record the events of the Trek. My *passe-partout*, however, was my fluency in Dutch. Add to this the important fact that I was the 'doctor'. Maybe I exploited all this: as recorder, yes; but perhaps with the feeling that momentous things were afoot. The first glimmerings of an ideal now began to appear in me. Truth was that the relatively peaceful pattern of my existence had suddenly been upset. The sudden contact with these people seemed to have broken through some shell. The sun, the dust, the ever recurring bouts of fever, had dimmed the life in me. Now I was strangely conscious of myself again: questioning things, questioning myself; walking around with sharpened powers of observation and deduction.

It was like coming to the end of a hard day's trek. Your wagons had at long last reached great sycamores grouped around a silver spring. You were pale with dust, dog-tired, and almost dehydrated. You stripped the clothes from your body and stood there in the moonlight, scrubbing yourself. You dived into the shining pool, feeling the wetness and the coolness fold around you like love itself. You stood there in your nakedness under a starry sky. You became a man again . . .

' . . . At one of our outspans I went to look for a little wild buck. Some way from the outspan I found a kudu spoor.' From within the circle of firelight, but distant as a dream, the voice impinged on my consciousness. 'I followed the spoor, to where the spoor of five eland crossed it. So I left the kudu and went after the eland. These I found under a thorn tree in a dip in the veld. I shot the bull and covered him with hookthorn. To find the place again, I dragged a stump of wood behind me for some distance. What then? After some time I crossed my own spoor, and then saw that I was lost. That night I slept in the open; and the next day

I started searching for the wagons, but all in vain. The bush lay flat and thick around me. I could be no wiser. I ate veld-food: berries and roots, wherever it could be found. There was no water. This had long since been used up. Eventually I was so thirsty, I drank my own water. The third day everything turned grey in front of me. I could only see for a short distance. Later I could only see a hole in the ground, when I had already landed in it. My own people had been searching round about for me. On the eighth day they decided to trek on. They thought me dead. Happily, on my wife's begging them to do so, they remained till the next day. Nearby the outspan was a little pan. And there, just by accident, I arrived on the ninth day. Now I was so weak that I could not walk any more. When I saw the water in the pan, however, I gathered all my remaining strength to get there. Around the pan was a little ridge about half a foot high. It was but a few feet from the water. When I trod this down, I collapsed. I was so spent now, I could only creep towards the water . . .'

And yet another told of the Thirst itself.

'The sand, *Meneer*? The sand is good and soft. One does not get shaken so much as when trekking over the hardveld. But the sand, too, is difficult. The sand sometimes covers the rims of the wheels: it is so loose. Twelve to fourteen oxen then struggle to drag the wagon with but half a load. The sand is hot, too, during the day when the sun bakes upon it. Barefoot one cannot walk on it. And when it creeps into your *veldschoens*, it burns your feet. At night that same sand is as cold as iron. If you do not cover yourself well with a karross,* if you do not bury live coals in a trench you have dug (as Bushmen do), at daybreak you are stiff as a plank. Yet, one accustoms oneself to everything, *Meneer*. You must still trek to where you want to be!'

'A good day to you, *Oom* Roets!' I greeted the man to whom I had spoken with Holtzhausen that time at Gobabis. 'And a good day to you, *Tante*!' I greeted his wife. She was wearing a black dress and a *kappie*. This was something each woman in the laager always kept in readiness. Roets himself had a black crepe band around his arm.

'It grieves me to hear of the death of your child,' I said. It was a son, and they had buried him the previous day. I had sent as much quinine as I could spare, but it was too late. The fever was in a

*A skin blanket.

virulent form.

Tante Roets wiped her eyes: '*Meneer*,' she said, 'should there be one who would seek the road by which we have come, let him but look for the graves of our children in the sand.'

Machiel Roets, whose gentle ways gave little indication of his skill as a hunter, nodded slowly. 'To trek back, *Meneer*?' he said. '*That* we shall never do. We shall each but try to do his duty. We must keep on trekking, *Meneer*: until we reach that land where there is no more Thirst. The Lord will provide!'

The Lord will provide . . .

Others, many others, confirmed this.

'There was the time in the outveld,' one said, 'when we had to leave the waters, because of the fever. The pans were all dry. The eyes of our oxen were already deep-set with thirst. The people, too, were suffering. What was there to do? We could but return to the waters, where so many had died. We had but two days left. Then we would just have to lie down in the sand and die. What else to do but to call on the God of our fathers. There we stood, lost in the terrible Thirstland: and now only the Lord could pity us . . . And he heard our prayers . . . It was late afternoon; the sun was already setting. A cloud as big as a man's hand now appeared in the sky. We all stood looking at it, when there was a sudden clap of thunder and the sky became overcast. Suddenly it was raining, yes, it was raining straight down on us! As quick as possible we spread out canvases and caught all the water we could, in every hollow thing we could find: buckets, calabashes, casks, kettles . . . In the canvases there was still enough for the oxen, too. So we were saved, and we praised God for it.

In my journal, that night, I noted: '*No pen can describe the horrors and painful scenes that took place during the Trek. At one wagon you would see a family who had by chance caught a stray sheep or buck which they had slaughtered, eagerly drinking the warm blood, while others were fighting for possession of the paunch for the sake of the water contained therein. The noises made by the various animals in their agony of thirst had a most unearthly sound. The memories of which will never be forgotten by those who have heard them. The unfortunate men could do nothing to relieve their fearful sufferings; but through the whole of these trying scenes the courage of the Afrikaner never failed them; they still persevered and were determined to overcome all obstacles.*'

So I sat there under a baobab, considering the uncertain future of my newfound friends.

What would be the end to it all? What would happen now to the Albertses, the Van der Merwes, Prinsloos, Du Plessis, Holtzhausens and all the others? Here they were, strong in their resolve to build a future in a new and yet undiscovered land, but with no idea as yet of their final destination.

'Karevapu!' I looked up to where Eriksson was sitting in the shade. 'What I have been noting down has been for the purpose of giving a correct and factual record of the Trek. The question yet remains, and we have indeed put it to one another at times: was all this sacrifice worth so much? And if it was, for what reason?'

'Does the human being not dream of things which lie far away?' Eriksson asked. 'And neither does he rest till he has found this happiness.'

'Our people have been trekking for so long now,' Botha remarked, 'that it is in their blood.'

This, indeed, accorded with what Gert Alberts, the leader of the first trek had said: 'Freedom!—We must trek, *meneer*, until we have found that which is our own and will remain our own.' The small tough man had looked shrewdly at Botha, and had said: 'And your name is Maritz-Botha. And you should know it all well enough!'

It was a Sunday afternoon and groups of people were gathered under the trees, drinking their shepherd's-tree coffee. J. F. Botha, who would shortly be elected as the new commandant of the reunited trek, then added his own admonishment: 'Cousin, our wish is that you should join the Trek. We have need of you. Keep with us, to where we shall discover our Land of Rest.'

But it was Diederick Prinsloo who spoke the conclusive word: 'It is the Voice of the Blood which one hears and cannot deny.' Turning to me he added, 'This is as it should be; and he who denies it, will pay for it. Dost thou understand me, *Meneer*?'

He always addressed me in his own particular brand of High Dutch. Tall and erect in his frockcoat, with the late sun slanting over his gaunt features, he waited for my full attention.

'In our hearts the spirit of trek had come, *Meneer.* Of this the cause and the reason was not to be divined. Complaints against the authorities in our country we had none. Nor did we feel the burden of taxation. Nor was our form of worship threatened. Our homes, there where we had lived, were quiet and good. Our cattle and crops were always sufficient. But, *Meneer*! This thou shalt know: in our hearts there was always this driving force of *trek*. Of this we could not determine the moving cause. We knew, as we know now, this was the way we should go: northwards, in order to seek for us a peaceful land, in which we all could settle, and be happy.'

7

One day Botha and I went down to the pan and came to the Tree. This was the baobab on which the names of the hunters of the previous year had been cut out. We saw someone watching us from behind the elephantine bole. It seemed as if he had been there for some time, awaiting our arrival. He suddenly appeared, a boy with gun-blue eyes and fair hair. There was something odd about him. I could detect a suggestion of defiance.

'What are you up to, eh?' Botha asked. He laughed and put a hand on the boy's shoulder. The air of resistance vanished and we suddenly had before us a youngster with an open admiration for the man with whom he was talking. Here was Pieter Maritz-Botha: a great hunter. And this was the very tree on which his great battle with the elephants had been recorded . . .

'What is your name?' Botha asked.

'Venter, *Oom*!' He looked one squarely in the eyes.

'From which Venters would that be?'

'My father was Willem Venter, *Oom*; but he is dead. Ma is also dead. There by the Letter Tree, *Oom*, where our wagons once stood.'

Botha nodded. 'And now,' he asked, 'who remains?'

'I, and Eldest Brother Hans; and Brother Jan, *Oom*!'

'Hans Venter!' Piet said. 'Were your brothers with *Oom* Barend Bouwer and the others when they went up to the river to hunt hippo?'

'Yes, *Oom*, they have just returned!'

'So! Old Barend too, eh?'

'Brother Jan said that *Oom* Barend and his people would now go with us in the Trek, *Oom*.'

The boy's attitude had now become more confident.

Botha seemed to be surprised. He pursed his lips, and dipped his imperial. 'Well! My friend Barend too!'

'Yes, *Oom*. I have heard it said that *Oom* is also joining us. Is this true?' He was speaking, as the custom was, in the third person.

'You hear what is being said about me?' Botha looked at me.

'I hear,' I said, smiling to myself.

Well, why not, I thought. Our partnership, as was customary in this part of the world, was on an easy basis.

'My boy, you now tell me strange things,' Botha declared. 'But I believe that you are only being light-hearted, eh?'

'No, *Oom*, I have heard them talking this way!'

Botha was enjoying this. 'What is your first name?'

'Adriaan, *Oom.*'

'Adriaan, boy, when a hunter notices all that is taking place around him, so it should be. But things might trick him!'

The boy now seemed embarrassed. His ears had reddened. 'I ask your pardon, *Oom.*' But Botha laughed.

'How old was *Oom* when *Oom* shot *Oom's* first elephant?'

'About seventeen. How old are you?'

'I am fourteen, *Oom*!'

He was rather small for his age, as Boer boys went. I recognized in him another type; slight, but extremely self-reliant. Gert Alberts was like that.

'Who, do you now reckon, excepting your own brothers, are the best hunters in the laager?'

He thought for a moment. 'It is *Oom* Jan Labuschagne, *Oom*,' he said at once. 'And *Oom* Jan Robbertze. And *Oom* Louw du Plessis. We were with *Oom* Louw in the Trek, *Oom.* There is also *Oom* Machiel Roets, *Oom* Piet du Prés, and many others. Now there is also *Oom* Barend Bouwer, who is with us now. And perhaps he is *still* the best!'

'What have you shot?'

'Buck, *Oom*! Many. And one lion!'

Piet nodded by way of approval. 'So! And how did you shoot the lion?'

'It was at the Lake. The lion charged me, *Oom.* Eldest Brother Hans's gun failed him. I shot the lion through the right shoulder, *Oom.* Then through the head, while it lay there.'

'So! I see you know exactly where to shoot, eh? What gun did you use?'

'A Star Barrel Six-pounder, *Oom.* That is what my father left me when he died.' I noticed that he was eyeing my gun. '*Oom*

Machiel had such a one,' he said.

'This is a Winchester Repeater.' I unhooked it from my shoulder. His face lighted up as he took it.

'*Oom*!' he said after a while. 'One would have to sell a lot of ivory before one could buy a gun like this. I know *Oom* Machiel had one.'

'It costs a little, son,' I said. 'But not really so much.'

'See what you can get together,' Botha remarked. 'If you are clever, you will have enough some day. Quick, tell me, where would you aim when a great bull elephant comes at you with his trunk in front of him, waving like a flag?'

'Between the eyes, *Oom*,' the answer came. 'Or a heart-shot, above and next to the left-front thigh. That is, from where *I* would be looking at him!'

'Very nice!' Botha said. 'I see that you have been taught correctly. Say, what did Eldest Brother Hans and the others get? Where have they been to?'

'As I now understand it, they were in the Ombongo bush, *Oom*. They brought quite a lot of ivory back: about a wagon-load full. They say more is yet to come.'

Botha was interested now. 'In Ombongo one can still find elephants,' he said. 'But round about here, and down in the Debra, where we hunted in other times? With all the hunting from old Van Zyl's place at Ghanzi, the elephants have all fled.'

'Where to, *Oom*?'

'Well, in Ombongo, as you have heard, there are still some to be had. But the great herds have all taken another course.

'Down this way,' he said, pointing his imperial to the south-west, 'one eventually strikes the great maramba* of Damaraland. The elephants always trekked through there on their way to the White Pan, where there is so much other game.

'Up that way . . .' The beard now pointed to the north-west, ' . . . one comes, in time, to the Shimborro. You must ask Mister Jordan here more about that. He knows the country up there better than I do. To the west is the Cunene river, where the hippo are in such great numbers. On the underside lies the Kaoko. Well, what do you think, Will, are there still elephants there?'

'I have not been there for a long while,' I said. 'But I imagine there would still be a great many. That country, as you know, is empty of people. To hunt between all these wild hills would not be easy.'

*The Trekkers' abbreviation of omuramba.

'I have heard it said,' Botha declared, 'that the Trek intends going that way. Now, Adriaan boy, you must remember that it might still take place. Keep your powder dry!'

'Eldest Brother Hans said that we would certainly trek to where the sun sets, *Oom*.'

'Yes, keep towards sundown,' I affirmed, 'and you will come to the Kaoko.'

A sudden movement in the tree above us drew our attention. I saw the boy's eyes widen.

'It's a girl, *Oom*!' he blurted out.

It seemed as if he had long been itching to tell us this. His face was scarlet.

Botha opened his mouth in surprise. 'Would you imagine it!' he breathed.

There she sat in an alcove of the baobab. She had pressed herself against the bronze bark so closely that she seemed almost to be part of the tree.

'How on earth . . . !' I said.

'She herself climbed into the tree, *Oom*! Then she could not get out again.'

'Good for you,' Botha said. 'And so you had to come to her assistance, eh?'

The boy's cheeks were still burning. I chuckled. He had either had to tell the truth or keep up his acting.

He looked at me. '*Meneer* . . .' he said, but seemed to lose his words.

'Never mind, hunter,' I comforted him. 'This is no sin. Come along, let's help her down.'

Clearly the girl could only have got into the tree with some assistance. And without jumping down the twelve feet of baobab she could not reach the ground on her own again.

'Pooh!' There was a measure of contempt in the way she said it.

I recognized her. It was Lisa Lombard—my child of the marshes. For a moment it seemed as if she were going to cry. Then, suddenly her eyes were laughing.

'Well!' I said. 'Is this you? Come along, Missie, let's give you a hand!'

Now she was keeping her tears back. '*Oom*!' she said, throwing a quick glance at the boy who was standing behind us. 'It is *he* who said I must climb up here!'

Botha and I laughed. Lisa looked away from us, blushing. Her shoulders were trembling. I could not believe that this was because of tears.

I was the tallest. 'Come,' I said again. 'Let me help you down!'

She hesitated, then with sudden impulsiveness took my outstretched hands. I was standing on an elevation formed by one of the great roots of the baobab. Botha was supporting me from behind. This was not necessary, for Lisa suddenly seemed to take flight. The next moment she had reached the ground next to us. With one quick, indignant look at the boy, she jumped away. The wind caught her *kappie* and it fell to the ground. She snatched it up quickly, and started down the edge of the pan, running like a filly.

The water in the hollow of the pan had become brackish and low. J. F. Botha, the Albertses, the Prinsloos, had investigated Leeu Pan, some fifteen miles to the south-west.

Forty-three people already lay buried here at Olifants Pan. But the previous week there had been no deaths. The special work I had taken upon me regarding the Trekboers was as far as it could be brought, at this stage, at least.

Some addenda to my report had still to be seen to. There were copies of letters which had been sent to the Trek leaders by native chiefs. There was a letter from Moreem of Ngami, and a letter from Kido Witbooi of Gibeon, in far away Great Namaland. There were letters from Andries Lambert and Saul Sheppard of Barmen in Damaraland. There was also an answer to Moreem by Gert Alberts. This was from the laager at Rietfontein. Louw du Plessis, Gert Alberts, and J. F. Botha had also handed me the Trek Regulations. This served as a civil and criminal code.

I carefully copied all these documents. This was certainly no band of desert nomads. This was an ordered, civilized community, which set a great price on its own traditional values. I had spoken with many of the young people here. None of them were illiterate. The Bible had been the firm basis of their education. Diederick Prinsloo, landdrost and Orphan Master of the Trek, was reputed to know all 150 Psalms by heart. He also knew great pieces of Scripture, and the whole Reformed Catechism.

All this had now struck me anew, because I myself had never attached any particular value to formal religion. I might well have mentioned these things in a special note. Yet I preferred to be careful.

Meanwhile I was watching my friend Botha exercising his charms. Once more he was the centre of groups of young people, with the girls listening ardently and the young men, like Adriaan Venter, regarding him as a giant.

'At the moment,' I once facetiously remarked, 'you are easily the most eligible bachelor in all the Transgariep!'

There was that special care he now exhibited towards his person: the fancy waistcoat he had once bought at the Cape; the way in which he combed his hair, and carefully tended his beard . . .

In the old Colonial homes of the Cape he had been a popular guest. When a man like Pieter Maritz-Botha, after two years of isolation in the wilds of Ghanzi, suddenly turned up among a group of attractive ladies, results were to be expected. Before the comfort of married life and a tendency to put on weight spoilt them, Boer girls were rather charming. The question was now: who would it be?

Amusing myself with such thoughts, I looked up and saw a rider coming in from a northerly direction. I watched him closely. This was Robert Lewis. He was alone, and this was rather strange. Lewis got off his horse and threw the reins to Kairob. I went up to meet him.

'Charles Thomas has been murdered,' he said. He spoke loudly, but tersely. 'He was killed while fording the river. He was shot from cover. Then set upon and stabbed to death!'

I stood there in my tracks. Such news I had heard before. News of death had in these past weeks been plentiful enough. But this was different. Charles Thomas was my friend and fellow hunter-trader. We had been discussing the trip to Nhembaland. And now he was dead . . . I was shocked to silence.

'*Bambuse*, bring us some coffee!' It was Lewis ordering the Bushman, where he was sitting at the *erd*.

We sat down at my table. I was still slightly dazed.

'What should be done about it?' I asked quietly when the coffee came. 'Charles Thomas was a fine man, and a fine friend.' Something pushed up inside of me. 'God damn his murderers!' I added with anger.

'Some of your friends of the laager were in the vicinity,' Lewis said. 'No doubt they will be back one of these days to give their own version of what happened. For my part, Jordan, I opine that a commando should be formed to cross the river and punish the offenders.'

'Of course,' I decided. 'At the earliest opportunity.'

A few days later, with the Trek at Leeu Pan, a commando under J. F. Botha left for the river. The murderers would be punished. Botha said the Lord was with the just.

There was no lack of volunteers. Barend Bouwer, who with his whole family was now part of the Trek, the Prinsloos, the Albertses, the Holtzhausens, the Oppermans and Du Plessis were all there. Lewis, Pieter Maritz-Botha, and I would also take part. At the river we were joined by another American, in the person of Gerald McKiernan.

The enemy took flight and all that we could find was empty kraals. These we burnt to the ground after the contents of a number of grain baskets had been seized. Wagons were brought up and the Trek was suddenly a few hundred bushel of corn the richer. It was a rather bitter thought: the death of a man like Charles Thomas had provided us with this much-needed food.

For some days I still felt sick at heart. Charles Thomas had been among the best of us who were hunter-traders in the Transgariep. He had been a friend of all the native people of the country. Now his blood had mingled with the waters of the river and it had been carried away to its distant marshes.

8

Botha and I trekked with four wagons loaded with about half a ton of ivory we had bought from the Ombongo hunters in the Trek. I was glad to have this because I needed a worthwhile load before I could undertake the long journey to the Bay. I was also glad for the sake of the Trekker community. A little ready cash had been brought into circulation again.

The hard fact was that the Trek itself had fallen into penury. True, the outward appearance of dignity had always been maintained. But one could see beneath the surface. I was thankful that Axel Eriksson would now get to the Cape and could make a public appeal for assistance.

Meanwhile the Trek had left Leeu Pan and had followed a course almost due west in the direction of the White Pan. At

Namutoni on the south-eastern corner of this great, shimmering expanse, on the old trek-route to Ovamboland, was a magnificent fountain. The surroundings were congenial. There was good pasture, the danger of fever was not so acute here, and there was an abundance of game. The Trekker community could well be able to provide for itself here, until such time as a decision had been reached about the future.

We followed the trek-road down to the Bay from the Okavango. This was the old route of the pioneers: westwards to Shonango on the lower Omuramba Omatako; then the Omuramba itself to Kora Kobis, Buchuvlei and Otjituuo; from here south-west to Otjozandjupa at the Waterberg, where there had once been a mission station; then the road to Okalimba and Omaruru. The north bank of the Swakop could now be reached in easy stages. Across the Swakop lay the Kuiseb. The dry bed of this ancient river led eventually to the Bay.

This was the old road of Andersson. It was also the road of Sir Francis Galton, Fred Greene, the Chapmans, and the Erikssons. There it lay in the sand and in the limestone, wandering incalculably through the bush.

Andersson had discovered the Okavango in 1857. It was a river that never reached the sea. He saw it one morning shining in the distance and thought ecstatically: at last the Cunene he had sought for so long! When he eventually reached the waters, however, he discovered that they were flowing eastwards, not westwards. The river, he heard later, was the Okavango.

Andersson's friend, Francis Galton, had swum 'bottomless' Lake Otjikoto, with the Bushmen watching in horror from the rocky walls. Andersson had once led a Herero army with Fred Greene against Jan Jonker Afrikaander. Tom Baines had sat there painting the grand, military march past the Holy Fire. Chapman had crossed the whole breadth of the sub-continent from Port Natal to Walwich Bay. There were many others discovering this country of whom the world would never know . . .

The spring had been dry. But now, during January of 1879, good rains had fallen. The veld was growing with an almost sensual licence. The Omuramba was a shallow broad river-bed with pools of water here and there, covered in places with stately acacia. In the outveld, where the Bushmen had brought fire in the late autumn, the new grass was pushing up its shiny green. Great herds of palla were grazing there: also kudu, eland and hartebeest.

In the early mornings the veld rang with the cry of francolin.

Journey hopefully, and see that you arrive, my father had always said. At such times I could sit for hours on my horse, taking in the landscape. I loved watching Kairob handle the tall driving whip, making it crack like gun-fire. He could flick a fly off the nose of the left fore-ox.

'*Vaaat*!' he would shout to set the team straining at their yokes. '*Vaaat*!' Then he would make great play with the names of the oxen.

The incantation was in Dutch, larded with snatches of Otjiherero, Nama, Ai. At the head of the procession pranced Izak, the team-leader.

Where the veld was full of wild fruit trees, we would stop. The omuandis bore wagon-loads of fruit. The marulas lay upon the ground, quietly fermenting. The elephants were addicted to them. In a week or two one would find their drunken spoors, listen to their uproarious, brassy carousal.

At times Kairob would lay mupels at our feet like a sacrifice. For this he had earned a tot. The trees—leadwood, marula, tamboti, teak, mahogany, mulemba—stood with their boles in pools of deep shadow. We drank Cape brandy, ate roasted palla and warm pot-bread. It was a lovely life . . .

'What is the truth about Old Hendrik and the thirty-three Bushmen?' I again asked Botha one day. 'You were there?'

'I was there,' he answered. 'But one should not talk of these things. You know what a story is.'

After a while, however, he opened up.

'It was at the time when the Trek was on its way from the Debra to the river,' he said. 'Alberts and his people had already left Rietfontein. Many of our people, however, were still wandering around in the veld near the marshes. The Prinsloos were at New Year's Pan, but wished to get out of the Thirst. At the same time they wished to get away from the places where the fever had been so bad. We were hunting on the flats above the Lake and we found the wagon-spoor of the Alberts people.

'The Prinsloos were now trekking about in all directions. While all this was happening, the boy disappeared one day. By nightfall he had not yet been found. After three days, they discovered his remains in the bush. You have heard it said, Will, that Old Hendrik was partial to the English, and did not like his own people. True, he refused water to the Trek when it arrived at

Ghanzi. Nevertheless, in the end the old man did allow the people to water their cattle. And he was very angry when the news of the murder reached him. Some of our own Bushmen trackers came to tell us all about it. Then Old Hendrik said: "Take the servants and send them into the veld with messengers. Let it be known that here in the laager is any amount of tobacco and brandy: for the fetching!"

'About three or four days later little groups of Bushmen began to arrive. Old Hendrik was now playing host to them in a big way. Everywhere there was smoking and drinking. Eventually enough Bushmen had gathered to the old man's liking. The Bushmen were all inside a kraal he had specially constructed. While they were all sitting there, waiting for more of the good things to come, the old chap had the men caught and bound. Then he took them to the edge of the very pan where the Prinsloo boy had been murdered. There all the Bushmen then sat, bound hands and feet, the women and children to one side, crying and lamenting. But *Oom* Hendrik simply said: "Go ahead now!" Some of us tried to persuade him to let the captives go, but he would have none of it. We then decided that we would have no hand in the shooting. So Old Hendrik gave the guns to our own Bushmen and said: "Shoot, and get over with it!"

'Well, the air soon became thick with gun-smoke. When the last shot rang out, old Hendrik walked nearer, smoking his pipe, quietly counting the bodies. He looked at them with his one good eye: the old chap had a squint, as you know. There the dead Bushmen lay in the sand and the vultures were already landing on the trees around the pan. Afterwards we all helped to pile thornwood over the bodies. When at last there was enough, we set fire to it. Then we rode back to our laager south of the pan. For a long while the dark smoke hung in the air behind us. *Oom* Hendrik did not say very much. That evening after we had had supper, however, he said we should hold devotions. He read a chapter out of the Bible and prayed: "The Lord would look down with approval on a just man who demanded eye for eye, tooth for tooth, and hand for hand." '

Such things happened often enough, I thought. The fact that Hendrik van Zyl could execute thirty-three Bushmen by way of cold-blooded reprisal would not necessarily count as unusual in the Transgariep. Van Zyl could at least lay claim to a virtue of sorts: he had wished to avenge the cruel death of a boy who had got lost in the veld. Nevertheless, Botha's story had disturbed me.

Still, I had no illusions. It was a thirst for adventure that had brought me to this country, and had kept me here. There was the feeling that I was treading in the footsteps of the great. They were the men whose records of their travels had once carried me away . . .

A teacher had once given me Andersson's books to read. They were the records on his journeys to Lake Ngami and the Okavango. I lay there reading by candlelight and at three in the morning my mother looked into my little room, so that I had to adjust my eyes to see her properly. I should blow out the candle, she said, and brought me a cup of milk. In the dark I still lay there thinking, dreaming of what I had read.

A new country and far, new horizons . . . The whole vast area of the Transgariep was there to explore. It extended eastwards to Matabeleland; northwards to Ovamboland; and far beyond. It reached into the Portuguese territories of West Africa.

When I had made my fortune I should return home to a safer, more restful existence, my mother had said. Perhaps she saw me at the head of the family, living in some quiet Cape suburb. Maybe at times I saw myself like that. Feathers were selling at £45 a pound, and ivory at 7/-. The chances were good that I could in fact raise a fortune within a few years. Were that to happen, I thought, I would like to visit Europe. I might even resume my studies again, perhaps qualify as a doctor . . .

But this land around Capricorn . . . It cared but little for those who dealt in dreams. It was a beautiful, jealous land. It seized you and demanded you for itself. You always returned in the end. It took you far into its own turbulent interior. You got lost in its great, amorphous life.

The contours were too hard, too defined here. The light was too brittle, the climate too cruel, the distances too vast . . . Human beings were few and the landscape dwarfed them all. Only if you were ever on your guard could you survive.

A sudden harsh turn of events often brought you back to reality. You paused a while and asked yourself: 'Were I to come to some bad end here, what would remain?'

What was there beyond this incessant wandering about in a land where every man, like old Hendrik van Zyl, concocted his own brand of justice? I had carefully read the Trek Regulations drafted by Alberts, Du Plessis and Botha. I had met these people when their poverty and confusion had brought them almost to a standstill. If there had ever been an opportunity for general decay, the Trek had afforded it. But what was the evidence? It was all to the contrary. Law and order prevailed. There was an almost too conspicuous attention to God . . .

All this cogitation would soon turn to introspection. What was the true compass of my knowledge, I asked myself. I had heard it said that I was the best medical man in the country. What a distinction! My mother fondly believed that I was doing good business among the native tribes. Indeed, I had dispatched sizable loads of ivory, skins, feathers and trophies to Krynauw at the Cape. But what of it?

I had now been in the Transgariep for eight years. At forty a man here should consider retirement. But what I had collected did not amount to much. There were my wagons, some cattle, my guns. There was a *kist* with botanical and geological specimens, gathered on my many journeys. There were my clothes, and a few dozen books. There were my writing materials, my journals. Nearest to me perhaps was the old *katel*: a rough frame-bed with a mat of eland thongs, a thin coir mattress, and a pillow of soft skin . . .

What had I written? Very little. Months sometimes passed without my making entries in my journal. There were many odd scraps of paper with jottings on them. These gathered in the tin box under the *katel.*

What had I effected to help matters reach some condition of order in this country? It was a country torn by warfare, intrigue, and general violence. But I loved it . . .

At Rehoboth I had seen how Kamaherero had come down from the north, his armies driving great herds of cattle before them. These, Kamaherero had declared, would be freely watered at the wells dug by Nama hands. Whoever ventured to offer resistance would be struck down. Within a few months one hundred and eighteen Namas had been killed. There was daily talk of all this at our trading store in Rehoboth. The theme was consistent: the Ovaherero would not rest until they had washed the blood off their spears in the waters of the Orange. The position of the Namas was that of slaves. At times I had expressed myself forcibly regarding this *Pax Herero.*

What had I accomplished? Not even as much as a man like Robert Lewis. Lewis's motives were suspect; yet, he had brought about some stability in the rickety framework of Okahandja.

What about my eminence as a hunter? Dear Lord . . . I was a fair shot, and an indifferent tracker . . .

'*Oom* Hendrik,' Piet recounted, lying on his back, 'I knew as a child at Potchefstroom. In '77 I was somewhere near Rustenburg, where I had a store. Man, it was the time of the great war against Chief Secucuni. There was no price to be had for any farm produce anywhere in Pretoria. I talked to my uncle, Cornelis Maritz, my mother's brother. He was the son of my grandfather, Gert Maritz, leader of the Great Trek of '36. *Oom* Cornelis had already heard of people who wished to trek on to seek a new land. The talk was that they feared the return of the Union Jack to the *Raadzaal* in Pretoria.

'Up there round and about Lake Ngami, *Oom* Cornelis said, was a fine land for hunting. We should stick together. We should buy trading goods and set off. I would be a working partner. A third of the profits would be mine . . .

'You see, with Old Hendrik everything was done on strict business lines. He would bear all the costs. We had to give him half of the ivory we brought in. The sons of Old Hendrik, Marthinus and Andrew, also McDonald and Barend Bouwer, were all in the team. But I had a personal arrangement with the old chap. That enabled me to make a fair profit. I doubt whether in all the history of Africa there have been greater hunts than in those days . . . !'

At the back of my mind there was the constant thought that my own experience had not included such things. These weeks trekking down to the Bay had been for me a time of reassessment. What, in fact, did I want of life? What had been dormant for many years was now newly alive in me. My previous slumber had been induced by the dust, the sun, the many weary miles of this vast country . . .

One considered these things on hot, sticky afternoons, when the spotted turtle called and the cicadas droned. Then one would lie in the shade of great acacias, reduced to a pleasant stupor.

All this had changed now. There was this growing restlessness in me. Dimly I already knew where my new field of endeavour lay. What I did not know yet was the shape of the encounter.

Before sleep led me finally away, there was the subtle, comforting reminder that Andersson, too, had known his times of doubt. There had been occasions of inward searching, of threatening disillusionment. During visits to his widow, Sarah Jane, down at the Cape, I had discerned this.

On 1 January 1867, not long before he died, Andersson had written: 'In a few months I shall have passed my fortieth year. Forty years! An ordinary lifetime; and what have I done? A bankrupt in purse and in health; and as to what I have performed, it is apparently very little; and yet I have worked desperately hard, setting danger, fatigue, pain and troubles at nought. God help me, poor fellow . . .'

The very next thought comforted me again: after all, the name of Andersson was still alive. As far as I could see, it would yet live on. Considering this, I could whisper to myself: 'Something should remain . . . God help me.'

It was a tattered little prayer. Yet it had some meaning.

9

When our trek remained at Otjituuo for a day or two to replenish our larder, we had unexpected visitors. These were Jan Labuschagne and the fair-haired boy, Adriaan Venter.

The main party was hunting in the fine game country south of the White Pan. But Labuschagne himself had heard from the Bushmen that we were down here and had decided to come and look us up. He brought encouraging news. The Trek had progressed well and was now at Namutoni at the south-east corner of the great White Pan. Here they were resting. The health of the people was improving and there was an abundance of game.

Namutoni was ten days' trek from here on the old road to Ovamboland. The laager, according to Labuschagne, had all its members, except the Van Stadens, who had disappeared into the unknown bush country west of the Zambezi. It was the very country I myself had been wanting to investigate.

At Namutoni the Trekkers intended remaining until such time as the 'temporary resting-place' could be found, perhaps further to the north-west. The idea still was to find a suitable area in the Kaoko. With this in view a commission under Gert Alberts had been sent out to investigate the land westwards. Reports had already been brought in that good water had been found.

This I could confirm. Ninety miles south of the Cunene was the great fountain of Kaoko Otavi. Forty miles further south were other springs. Should the commission reach them, they would probably find them suitable for their purpose. When did the people in the laager expect the commission to return? I myself provided the answer. It was a long journey over difficult terrain. From Namutoni to Kaoko Otavi was more than three hundred miles. Even if the Alberts party had no intention of examining other parts of the Kaoko, they could not be expected to return within a month. If the Trek itself had then to move on to the new area, the laagers there could be established before the autumn.

This would give us the opportunity to conduct our business in the Bay and at other places. Then we could trek northwards again in search of our friends. By that time, I silently hoped, I would be in a position to present the Trekkers with certain positive proposals.

Jan Labuschagne was telling the boy tall stories, causing his eyes to widen. A team of oxen, Jan said, even when fatigued after a hard day's trek, could pull a fully loaded wagon through the toughest mire or the deepest sands, as long as the wagon-driver had seen to it that the lash of the longwhip had been stroked with lion-fat. Jan's sense of humour was as broad as his shoulders. When he laughed around the laager fire, the jackals fell silent.

'An ox is a wonderful animal,' he declared. 'Keep him on the right course, as you should, and in no time you will return to from where you set out. The world is round, man! Ask Mister Jordan if you don't believe me.'

Yes, I remarked, it was perfectly true. If one were to keep on trekking in the same direction, some time or other you would strike your own spoor again. The trouble was, the land ended where the sea began . . .

'Have you not yet seen oxen *swim* with a loaded wagon?' Labuschagne asked.

'Yes,' I conceded, 'that I have seen.'

A good team could easily swim with its full load through a river in flood. I myself had done this on many occasions when returning from Angola and crossing the Cunene. The difficulty was, where the waters were too vast, where would one find an outspan? Such things were scarce, especially in the ocean . . .

The boy was mystified. But when Botha completed the banter with the remark that lion-fat on the *voorslag* could possibly cause the team to swim so powerfully that no outspan would be necessary, laughter from all sides rose above the crackling of the fire.

'So, young man,' I said at last, 'you see that one should not swallow all one hears!'

'Yes, *Meneer*!'

His seriousness was comic. But he was learning fast.

'How is *Tante* Lombard, and Lisa?'

His cheeks were alight. 'It goes well with them, *Meneer*. They are in good health.'

'It pleases me to hear it,' I said.

'What are you hunting up here?'

'Birds, Mister,' Labuschagne answered. 'Birds' were ostriches. 'I have a mind to buy myself a new Schneider. So I am collecting feathers. Mister, I expect that you will come to where the Trek is going?'

'That is my intention.'

'I am looking for a good horse,' Botha said.

'Cousin Piet,' Labuschagne declared, 'if you are looking for a horse, then you must talk to Machiel Prinsloo.'

'I have an eye on that part-bred Arab of his. Fine horse that! Do you know it?'

'Yes, I know it,' Labuschagne said. 'That is a salted horse. Machiel is very proud of it.'

'What have you shot?' I asked the boy. 'How is the Star Barrel behaving? You should also collect feathers, son. See if you can get a Schneider for yourself.'

'Well, he has already done that,' Labuschagne said.

I saw the boy's pride rise in him.

'I was but as high as this stool you are sitting on,' Labuschagne said to Adriaan, 'well, a little higher!—I and my elder brother were already shooting with a gun that had been in the Trek of '36. We had to light the powder in the pan with a burning ember. But we kept on shooting: down there at Elands River in the Rustenburg country. Afraid of nothing; and what we shot we skinned and ate out there in the veld.'

Adriaan was listening intently: but needing no encouragement, I thought. He, too, was cut out of the hardwood of the veld . . .

10

The gold watch I had inherited from my father showed it to be two o'clock in the morning. I had slept, but was now wide awake. Now I lay there with my senses alerted. A strange tension had hold of me. Old thoughts kept trembling through my mind.

With my school days over, I had spent four relatively useless years in Cape Town. Still, I undertook a few journeys overland with my father to the north-west of the colony. Once we even ventured over the Orange into Great Namaland. We touched at Steinkopf, where my mother had come from. I enjoyed these journeys. Strangely enough, I had never seen myself at that time as a hunter-trader. My father had discouraged it. His idea was that I should carry on with my studies. But how? There was never enough money for study in a foreign country. I was not the only child.

The treks with my father had developed in me a taste for the outdoor life. I did attempt once or twice to accommodate myself to clerical work. Soon, however, I knew this would not do.

For some time I acted as a kind of orderly to a well-known Cape doctor. I accompanied him on his rounds. I helped him dress wounds. I even learned to draw teeth. Week-ends I sometimes worked in the hospitals. I looked for a better opportunity, but it never came.

And yet it did. My true opportunity, ironically, was the sudden death of my father. Within a few hours after the news had reached us, I had decided on my future.

QUEST
(March 1879 - December 1882)

1

February of that year had almost spent itself when we eventually reached Omaruru.

At the trading station Albert Eriksson informed us that his brother Axel had had a good voyage to the Cape. Surprisingly soon news was received—due to a fortunate availability of ships—that Axel had already written to the Cape newspapers. He had given details of the Trekboers and their circumstances, as we had found them in the Okavango country.

There was great interest in the sudden reappearance of people whom many had regarded as lost. In his letter to his brother, Axel Eriksson had mentioned that the chances of a special relief fund were good. Mr Hofmeyr, an honoured leader of the Dutch-speaking colonists at the Cape, had taken a personal interest in the matter.

In my journal I had noted down the strange history of the Trek up to the point of the various parties reaching Olifants Pan. But this was by no means the whole story. From Labuschagne we had heard how the Trek had journeyed to Namutoni. The intention was now to find a 'temporary resting-place', somewhere in the Kaoko. To complete my chronicle I would have to join the laager again. Meanwhile Axel Eriksson and others could inform the Cape of the hardships the emigrants had already suffered.

A harsher note was sounded, however, when Albert Eriksson warned me that the local *Missionar*, Gustav Viehe, whose spiritual charges were the Hereros under Manasse Tjisiseta, was not sympathetic. He had never been a friend of the Trekboers. This had notably been the case when Gert Alberts and his party had been staying at Rietfontein.

Meeting Viehe in the trading store one morning, he said to me in German:

'I am the adviser and the secretary here to the Damara* people. I deem it necessary to know exactly what the intentions of your friends are. We have heard it said that they intend settling somewhere in Damaraland. That, of course, would not be acceptable!'

I considered my words. 'As far as I know,' I said, 'the Trek has no firm idea at all where it could come to a stop.'

'You will of course admit that they *do* intend settling somewhere?'

'Quite probably,' I answered. 'When we last heard of them they were at Namutoni. According to the reports they were on their way to the Kaoko.'

He nodded. 'It is to be the Kaoko then,' he said. 'And what will they do when they get there? The land there is a wilderness. The Ovaherero left the Kaoko a century ago.'

'I have already said,' I answered, 'that they will only be there for a while.'

'And after that?'

'There are a number of possibilities,' I said. 'The land is vast.'

'But it is also necessary, *Herr* Jordan, that the Trekboers should know to whom the land *belongs*.' He was stressing his words. '*Wir ängstigen uns um Sie!*'

'That is hardly necessary,' I assured him. 'If it will put your mind at rest, I can tell you that the Trekboers are an orderly and civilized group. They have no intention of attacking any people; or of driving any of them out of their ancestral lands. Where the Trekboers eventually will be settled? Wherever it might be, you may rest assured that it will only take place as a result of proper consultation of all the peoples affected. That, by the way, is rather more than can be said for any other nation in this country.'

'What the Ovaherero have been fighting for,' he replied sharply, 'is to have and to hold what is theirs.'

'Maybe,' I conceded. 'But don't think that I have forgotten that Kamaherero once came to see Andersson at Otjimbingue, complaining that he had been treated like a dog by Jan Jonker Afrikaander. It is, however, also a fact that he was trembling for fear of his own skin. Fine, the Ovaherero broke out in revolt, and threw off the yoke. Against that one could have no objection. The prime difficulty, however, is that the roles have now been

*Damara and Herero are interchangeable terms here.

reversed. The Ovaherero are the lords and masters, the Namas being their serfs. In what way, do you think, has the general situation improved since the rise of the Ovaherero?'

He looked at me, then turned away and said loudly, so that people in the store could hear: 'The Hottentots are a bad and lazy lot! Andersson himself said as much, seeing that you have mentioned his name!'

'As far as I know,' I said, 'Andersson was not an enemy of any single people in this country. He was against tyranny and crime, yes. With the Ovaherero in a dominant position at the moment, this is precisely what is taking place. You, as a *Missionar* in a fine tradition, ought to take note of this. Have you not heard that the Namas were attacked by Kamaherero's people at Taniep some time ago? This was at the dead of night, and a number of them were slaughtered. Maybe you are also aware of what happened at Windhoek, when women from the tribe of Jan Jonker had their hands and feet cut off!'

'That is exactly what the Afrikaanders led by Jan Jonker's father did to the Damara women in 1853,' he rejoined.

'You have missed the point,' I answered. 'It surely does not suit a Christian minister to try to condone such cruelty, wherever it might have taken place.'

'That I am not doing, Sir!' He was angry now. '*Blödsinn!*'

'Nama hunters have been killed at Omatako,' I persisted.

'What were Nama hunters doing in Damara territory?' he asked.

'They were there with the permission of the paramount chief.'

'Regarding what happened at Taniep,' he persisted, 'I simply do not believe that the Damaras were the guilty ones. If that were the case, my own Christian Damaras would surely have told me of it!'

The argument was becoming embarrassing. Bystanders in the store, mostly Hereros of the tribe of Tjisiseta, had by this time grasped enough to realize what it all meant. Obviously they were not on my side. Neither could I have expected it to be otherwise.

The position as such had to be accepted. I had long had the intention of writing to the Cape press, setting out the true facts of conditions here. Viehe might well read this, in time.

Regarding the Trekboers and their future plans, I now had no further illusions. I knew the general attitude. To meet this situation would not be easy. Even my friends showed antipathy.

A week later at Otjimbingue—headquarters of the 'British' trade in the Transgariep, with the headquarters of the Rhenish Mission also situated there—I was to experience this.

John Caine and I had on a number of occasions expressed different views on the matter. Nevertheless I liked Caine, and regarded him as my friend. The feeling, I believe, was reciprocal. Usually when passing through Otjimbingue, I would visit Caine and we would discuss the latest news from the Cape. On this occasion I told him of my argument with Viehe. He poured us some brandy, and said: 'Well, you should know better than to get involved in such an argument. Let's hear all about it. First tell me about these Trekboers. Where are they off to?'

At the moment this was not so important, I assured him. What was important was the necessity of a proper appreciation of the intentions of the emigrants. Robert Lewis had told Caine about his meeting with them. According to Lewis, conditions were chaotic.

'These people just seem to be wandering,' Caine said. 'That is, according to Robbie Lewis.'

'That is not so,' I countered. 'They are fundamentalists, yes; Calvinist puritans. But for that very reason it would be foreign to their tradition to go wandering about aimlessly.'

'You must admit,' Caine said, 'that in view of the fact that even you who have become their confidant and friend have no idea what their destination might be, in view of all the evidence it does not seem unreasonable to ask: *cui bono?* Or must it all be a miasma? Granted, your friends have all shown great courage in crossing the Thirstland. They have also no doubt borne their sufferings with great courage. Still, to what end? Indeed, great ends may in time be accomplished by small means; but the opposite also holds true. The hardships of these people seem to be out of all proportion to the causes of their wandering. I have generally heard good reports of the pioneer Boers. But it does seem strange that they should so take fright of the British that they should leave homes, farms, established enterprises, and just set off—to where?'

I could admit that the Trekboers were isolated from the modern world, I said. I could also admit that they were limited by their own attitudes. Their many virtues, however, were also apparent.

To what extent the Trek had really been justified in the first instance was indeed a debatable question. Personally I was not prepared to admit that what had been undertaken at such an inordinate cost, was entirely without meaning. The Boers had always had a deep urge for freedom. Even if they had fared better by remaining in the land of their birth, here they were now, looking for some land where they might set up on their own. They were patently sincere.

'You have now touched on an important point,' Caine said after a moment. 'I imagine we all love independence dearly. That, by the way, may account for our own presence as hunter-traders here. But now, don't you see that precisely *this* might also be the cause of Viehe feeling a little riled?'

The decision regarding the ultimate destination of the Trek was a matter for the Trek itself, I answered. I was quite convinced that there could only be two possible destinations. The one was Angola, which was a Portuguese colony, therefore a Catholic country. Unless the immigrants could acquire some area for themselves where they would be autonomous, it was difficult to see how they could find any permanence there. The other possibility was an area somewhere between the Orange and the Cunene. The previous year my thoughts had turned increasingly towards Rehoboth. Strictly speaking, Rehoboth, which included some of the best pasture lands in the Transgariep, was *terra derelicta.* Legally it belonged to the Swartbooi-Namas; but we all knew what had happened there. In 1864 Charles John Andersson and Fred Greene had led an Herero army from Okahandja to Rehoboth as a punitive measure. Jan Jonker Afrikaander, who had been freely asserting Nama hegemony by general murder and freebooting, was to be taught a lesson.

The Afrikaanders had taken up position in the mountains to the south. The Hereros, assisted by the Swartboois, had emerged as victors. Andersson himself had been badly wounded in the leg, otherwise the battle might have been decisive. As matters developed, however, the Afrikaanders maintained sufficient strength to return to the fight. Now they were supported by Hendrik Ses and his *Veldschoendragers.**

The combined fury of these Orlam Hottentots was then directed towards the Swartboois. This was because of the treason they had allegedly committed when fighting with the Ovaherero against their fellow Namas. Under the care of their *Missionar,* the Rev

*Literally: the wearers of *veldschoens.*

Kleinschmidt, they then fled to the north, seeking refuge with their friends beyond the Swakop.

The whole population trekked over the Khomas *Hochland*, ostensibly because they were trying to avoid the lung-sickness of the plains. Soon they discovered they were being pursued by Hendrik Ses. Eventually they were forced to form a laager of their wagons. Thereupon Ses set fire to the veld. A strong wind carried the flames to the Swartbooi laager, and a great many perished. Others were shot down in the ensuing panic. The Rev Kleinschmidt and his family had to flee for days through the veld under a cruel sun with only a loaf of bread amongst them to eat. The Rev Hugo Hahn sent a wagon to fetch them when they were still some distance from Otjimbingue. It was too late, however. Kleinschmidt died a few days later in the arms of his friend.

To whom did Rehoboth belong? John Gunning and I had set up a trading centre there. Presumably we were in a position to know. A handful of newly-arrived Basters under Hermanus van Wyk had come to live there. They, however, had no ground for claiming Rehoboth. The Swartboois were still the rightful owners. True enough, since the sixties the Swartboois had been living at Otjitambi in the north. There they had been given land by Kamaherero. Chief Petrus Swartbooi and his council had declared themselves willing to sell the whole of Rehoboth. Who could rightfully object? The Basters could remain at Rehoboth. There was no reason why they could not share the area peacefully with the Trekboers.

Caine listened to me carefully, nodding approval at times. We sat there before the window in the front room of the very house in which Andersson had lived. Here he had lain for nine months, nursing his wounded leg. From here he had eventually departed for the Cape to get proper treatment. There he rejoined his wife and child.

The dry bed of the Swakop curved away in the midday haze. One might dig a few feet into the sand and find water. Since the earliest days people had established gardens there. In times of flood everything was destroyed. But for the greater part of the year the gardens were a delight.

There it lay before us on that tranquil February afternoon. Dominating all was the Church with its steep roof thatched with veld-grass, and its white-washed walls. To one side were the flat-roofed houses of *Frau* Kleinschmidt, *Missionar* Brincker, and others. Scattered about were the huts of the Hereros, made of fire-bent poles, supporting a covering of hides and mud. Here and there stood a covered trek-wagon, with its draught-pole on the ground. Cattle grazed on the high banks of the river. The dense green bush on the opposite side swept up to the blue crests of the Khomas *Hochland.* Herero tribesmen with filed teeth, iron snuff-spoons in their hair, and aprons of soft skin, came padding by, raising little puffs of dust. A female convert, wearing a narrow-bodiced dress topped by a colourful cloth, walked slowly by, balancing on her head a pot of water. A dog was barking.

How peaceful . . . Yet nowhere in all the land had more blood been spilt than at this very place. Caine should have known all this. Perhaps he did know it, but refused to remember it. He would have to be reminded.

'The most violent wars in Southern Africa,' I said, 'have swept over the Swakop here. For what reason? Mostly according to the whims and fancies of whoever happened to be in power. Remember 1863, and 1865, John! The Swakop carried more blood than water those years. *Frau* Kleinschmidt remembers it all. Agreed, the Hereros were much abused in the days of Nama dominance. But today it is the Namas who have been forced into serfdom. How much longer do you think is this 'peace' going to last, my friend? Every two-legged creature is free to murder and rob as it pleases him. The land is utterly devoid of laws. There is no administration of justice. There is no central authority. Such efforts as have been made, like those of Coates Palgrave, have been a waste of time. Great Britain has seen fit to establish but a semblance of British rule over a fragment of the country: Walwich Bay. For the rest? It might go to hell, for all they care. Is it not time that we who have become part of this land take matters into our own hands? Consider what it might mean to the country as a whole, if but *one* stable society were to be established here. This is what Hugo Hahn tried to do, but with the wrong material. We have to start afresh!'

'There is some truth in what you say,' he said, staring out of the window. 'Indeed, things here leave much to be desired. However, having the same affection for you I have always had, Will, I feel the need to warn you: don't let your eagerness to assist the Trekboers outrun your discretion.'

'There is more to it than that,' I said.

'Of course there is. Yet on the whole you are precipitate. This is because you have met the remnants of the Trek.'

I suddenly realized the futility of words. What could I say to Caine that he would not discount? He had his own ideas.

My own I would pursue to their logical end. I had given myself to this cause. It had grown in me, and there was no discarding it now. It still had to be developed, but in time it would mature.

'On the whole the native chiefs of this country are well disposed towards us,' Caine added. 'It would be rash to do anything which would antagonize them. Better to leave well alone, my boy, believing that progress must inevitably come, if each one does his duty.'

That is exactly what it is, I thought to myself—a matter of discovering one's duty. Of primary importance was that those things at least should be enforced without which no society could function. Law, like politics, was a compromise. Lawlessness in this land was like lung-sickness among cattle, or fever among human beings: it was endemic. Quinine was no perfect remedy, but it made things livable.

I was preparing to leave. My host, however, had not yet had his say. There was something else which I should take into account. Ka-Robbie—Robert Lewis—he said, should be consulted before any steps were taken regarding Rehoboth. Lewis had the confidence of Kamaherero. One should not forget that when Dr Theo Hahn had presented the Boers with an invitation via Hendrik van Zyl to settle at Rehoboth, Kamaherero had strongly protested. He saw in the coming of the Boers an attempt to take possession of Damara territory. He, Caine, accepted that Hahn's intentions were honourable. The fact was, however, that Kamaherero saw the letter in an ominous light. Robert Lewis's co-operation should therefore be obtained. This should not prove so difficult. After all, Ka-Robbie had accompanied the Boers on a successful punitive expedition to the other side of the river. This had certainly been necessary. The Ovambos, Lewis maintained, were a fickle and murderous nation. One could not trust them beyond sight. It was high time somebody taught them a lesson. All Caine now wished to say was conditional on the possibility of my ideal being practical politics.

I resisted in silence. In the first place I would hesitate to ask any favours of Lewis, even if he had had a part in the Okavango expedition; even if it were true that he were the power behind the Damara throne. Like Viehe he closed his eyes too easily to injustice. Far was it from me to pretend that the Ovambos had never perpetrated barbarisms. They, too, were a primitive people. But this at least could be said for them: conditions there were never as bad as they were here in Damaraland or in Great Namaland. Hugo Hahn, Francis Galton, and others, had often told of the terrible night of 23 August 1850, when Jan Jonker Afrikaander, with an army consisting of his own Nama-Afrikaanders, Bergdamaras and subservient Hereros under Tjamuaha, Kamaherero's own father, had attacked the Herero villages on the Swakop, near Grosz Barmen and Okahandja. Almost the whole black population, except a few, had been killed.

In pitiless thoroughness Jonker Afrikaander had completed his task. Then, celebrating his triumph by freely drinking all the brandy he could lay his hands on, he walked about the field of 'honour', acclaiming his victory. His drunken bragging could be heard for hours, mingling with the cries of the dying.

The part Tjamuaha had played in all this was despicable. In his slavish way he had looked on while the massacre of his own people was taking place, feeling perfectly secure, as far as his own skin was concerned. All that had happened he could justify on the grounds of his personal feud with the old chief Kahitjene, who had fled to Barmen, seeking asylum with Hugo Hahn. In Ovamboland, at least, there had never been this massive spilling of blood, There had never been this general murder and horror, which had changed a shining landscape into a field of death. Other massacres had followed. With the booty guns and brandy were bought from unscrupulous traders, all with a view to taking 'further steps'.

The story was told that at the beginning of the sixties there had lived at Windhoek—Jonker's old capital—a mad Bushman prophet, who used to run about at night shouting: 'Woe to you Afrikaanders! Your day will yet come!' The wife of Jan Aries, a sister of Jan Jonker and a daughter of Jonker himself, could stand it no longer. She had had the Bushman bound, so that she could burn holes in his flesh with live embers. Nevertheless, the old man still went around at night, shouting his mad talk for all to hear, dragging his festered body over the ground, mouthing his curses, crying out to the heavens that the sins of the Namas would yet be avenged. In Ovamboland things like this had never happened . . .

There was also Hugo Hahn and Brincker, who had been near

Omakuru on their way to Okahandja, some ten years before. Kamaherero was then on the ascendant against Jan Jonker, after a bloody fight here at Otjimbingue, five years earlier. This was the famous Battle of the Dappled Ox. Kamaherero now avenged himself with measureless fury. Apparently he had forgotten all about his own subservience to the Namas. Hahn and Brincker had also told how the Hereros had cut down the tribe of Jacobus Booi to a man. The two missionaries had walked around the veld, collecting the bones so as to put them into a common grave. This grave had become a seed-bed for the growing hegemony of the Ovaherero. In that hole in the ground, they informed the world, lay the last of their enemies.

I thought about all this while sitting there in the old house of Andersson, on that shimmering February afternoon. I remembered too that Caine himself had been present when Robert Lewis had described the boundaries of Damaraland to Coates Palgrave. The boundaries, Lewis declared, ran from the mouth of the Cunene to Rietfontein in the east. If my information were correct, that had also been the occasion on which Kamaherero, in the presence of all sorts, had declared that the Trekboers were his true and lasting enemies.

The cause I had taken up was a worthy one, I quietly decided. What had started as a rather loose thought was now a burning reality.

2

Our trek-route followed the old road via Tsaobis on the south bank of the Swakop. Here we turned away in a south-westerly direction, the road taking us to the north bank of the Kuiseb. From here it led us down to the bed of the river; and so to the Bay. It was still partly the road Jonker Afrikaander had made: one of the few things of positive worth he had done.

The days were hot. Mirages trembled against a succession of horizons. Cumulo-nimbus clouds came drifting silently down from the north. Vultures and marabou storks wheeled at great heights. Martial eagles took advantage of the wind from the sea, gliding lazily, gracefully, against a blue-white sky. Large herds of oryx with wonderful markings on their supple, shiny bodies came galloping through the dry grass. Sometimes they would pause against a dune, their V-shaped horns black against the brilliance of the day. Where the savannah highlands became sparse and hard, breaking down dramatically to the coastal desert, it suddenly seemed as if one had wandered to the moon. One could stand and stare again, as on so many previous occasions, wondering at nature.

We were in good spirits. Botha would amuse me by discussing in detail the various attributes of the Trekker-girls. What he wanted, he declared, was someone who would go where he went; and that could be far! She had to be a good cook, but also sharp-witted, daring, efficient, and pleasing to the eye. Virtue lasted longer than beauty, so the old people said. Nevertheless, virtue could be acquired, and beauty not . . .

Pieter Maritz-Botha would enjoy these speculations. 'Of course,' I would solemnly declare, 'you might still end up with some prim little housewife: one who would duly wear the breeches.'

'No point in my pretending to be so superior,' Botha would then rejoin. 'After all, wasn't I a man? Even Robert Lewis had a wife!'

We discussed my Rehoboth scheme, for the idea had now taken hold of me. 'When Gunning and I had the store there,' I said, 'we had to pay £25 a year to Hermanus van Wyk and his Baster Council. That was merely for the right to stay there; and never doubt it. When the Basters began blasting open the springs some time ago, they sent the Swartboois an offer to purchase Rehoboth. Petrus Swartbooi and his Council would hear nothing of it. It was quite true that the Basters eventually offered a substantial sum for the Swartboois to reconsider: 120 horses and five new wagons. I have it on good authority that Hermanus van Wyk and Abraham Swartbooi agreed that Rehoboth would be sold to the Basters, should the Swartboois decide to relinquish ownership. Van Wyk asserted himself in turn and told Theo Hahn and his partner Steyn that not a sod of land would be turned, nor one stone laid upon another without the authority of the Council. By the way, the reason for this "command" was Hahn's invitation to the "hundred Boers" to come and settle at Rehoboth. Hahn appealed to the Swartboois to intervene; and the Basters went to ask the Nama chiefs for assistance. The rub of it all was that everybody—Kamaherero, the primitive Bergdamaras down along the Kuiseb, or Jan Jonker Afrikaander at Windhoek—were busy helping themselves to whatever Baster property they could lay hold of. This fragment of a nation has been fighting the flames on all sides. Jan Jonker did his worst to make life as difficult for them as he could. Kamaherero himself has said on a number of occasions that there is no question of anything like Baster rights. His cattle are watered freely at the wells of Rehoboth. When they return, Baster cattle are brought back as part of the bargain. When the Basters are so rash as to go out searching for their lost cattle, they are threatened by armed guards. Namas and Bergdamaras, admittedly, also have no qualms when it comes to helping themselves to whatever is at hand. The Basters are powerless, and have little hope of ever being able to defend themselves. With a strong Trekboer community, however, conditions would improve overnight. This sham peace has lasted now for almost ten years. I have a feeling that an explosion is near. One develops a nose for it!'

Botha looked at me with but the suggestion of doubt. Concerning the facts of the situation, he said, there could be no dispute. However, it should be a matter for the Trekboers themselves to decide on. Whenever we should reach the laager again, the people would in all probability have decided on their future. As far as he was concerned, he always believed: *haast uw langzaam—festina lente.*

'Let's first get some fresh air,' he concluded jovially. 'We all need to cool off here at the coast, after all those months in the sun. Then we can set out to find the Trek!'

I quietly considered this. My friend, I decided, was still getting the feel of the land. Of course, there was no particular reason why he should devote time and attention to things beyond his immediate interest. After all, he was young, attractive, adventuresome. It seemed as if the afflictions affecting others in this country—fever, dysentery, enmity—has almost wholly passed him by. Secretly I envied him the ability to take things in his stride. Temperamentally, I supposed, I was different. There was an abiding restlessness in me. Things inordinate upset me. I was constantly putting questions to myself. At night I often lay awake, thinking and planning . . .

3

Trekking up from the mouth of the Kuiseb, between the high Namib dunes and the Atlantic we were met by a cold west wind blowing from the sea. Mornings the mist would creep up the sides of the dunes with thin white fingers, feeling its way over the tawny sand. Gradually it would spread over the smooth slopes, then gather in the hollows between the dunes, finally lying there like cotton wool. It was uncomfortably cold. I wrapped myself in a skin jacket, but still shuddered when the wind moaned through the wagon-rigging.

A great tiredness had crept over me, and my thoughts had became sluggish. I knew what lay ahead; I was already resigned to my fate. As usual I had brought it upon myself. If I took my quinine regularly, I could keep in reasonable health. But often, in the daily business of getting everything done, I would forget about it. Then I would try and make up for the lapse with double doses. This was looking for trouble.

Late one afternoon, we suddenly spied the Union Jack rising behind a wind-sculptured dune. Our journey had come to an end, but by now I was a sick man. My body seemed to have been gripped by some unseen force. My teeth were chattering.

I drank what quinine I had left and crept into bed at the Erikssons' storehouse, moaning like a sick dog looking for a sheltered corner. For the next thirty-six hours I had no proper knowledge of my whereabouts. Neither did I care whence I had come, and where I was going. Finally when the fever broke, the sheet around my body was limp and wet, clinging to my legs.

Sounds of revelry were dimly coming from a distance. Drinking and card-playing, I supposed. This was the usual routine when traders gathered at the Bay. There was a whole concourse this time: the 'British' traders Lewis, Rule, Lyon, Todd, and others; the Swedes in the service of the Erikssons; the few British officials, looking after trading rights, and customs. Well, I decided, the party might well now be celebrating my return to the living . . .

My urine had become like weak black coffee. I looked at it with faint disgust, wondering whether I had got over the worst. Who could say? From somewhere I discerned Pieter Maritz-Botha roaring with laughter.

I had been vaguely conscious of his coming to my bed. He had stood there, smoking a cigar, smiling down at me. At least, he had shown some sympathy . . . Not that I needed it. By this time I had surely learnt to know what this sort of life demanded. Now I thought of my mother, my sisters, and was suddenly moved. So it always happened—after the fever had got hold of me again. But I would be up in a day or two. I would be up and able to join my noisy colleagues next door. I would be able to join in a game of cards, talk, take my brandy. Yes, I would do all that. But there were always more important things. I was in a hurry to get away now, to go looking for the Trek . . .

I poured my coffee-like urine from its calabash out of the window. Then I sank back exhausted on my bed. There I lay, thinking faintly. Life, after all, even the meanest sort of life, or life with all its risks, anxieties, disappointments, was desirable. I *wanted* to live. I had not yet even properly *begun* to live. What a lot there was still to do . . . Suddenly I remembered Axel Eriksson, now far away at the Cape. Karevapu . . . good old Karevapu. I wished he were back . . . There was no one here to comfort a man in distress like Karevapu . . .

In the old days there was almost nothing else at the Bay but the sea, the desert, the unending sky. Then gradually a few shacks had been erected alongside the lagoon for the benefit of those who came trading, hunting or exploring. Life here was never more than the bare bones of existence. When trade with the interior started expanding, especially with the coming of the Erikssons, the Bay took on a kindlier aspect.

A few more buildings of wood and iron had been erected. Some were substantial enough to house the goods brought by schooner from the Cape, or to be loaded here. The traffic of wagons itself had increased. There were new faces now: on each return to the Bay. There were wagons, oxen, men. And always there was the sea, and the mist, and the burning, far-off mountains . . . The sea was to the west and was blue-green and icy. The mountains were to the east and were magenta and blue. As they grew larger on approaching them, they became unreal, seemingly floating there on beds of iridescent opal. The land started with the dunes, billowing up against a steely sky. Beyond the dunes were the gravelly flats . . .

During March of the previous year *HMS Industry* had been here. The flag was hoisted ceremoniously. The Bay and its immediate surroundings were declared British territory, to the accompaniment of gun-fire.

Some more buildings had been erected. A few officials were left on the desert coast. They had to watch over the interests of Her Britannic Majesty. Coates Palgrave was the first magistrate; and Musgrave succeeded him . . .

Musgrave . . . The great land lying there beyond the dunes, in the end, had proved too much for him. Poor man, he had lost his nerve, and had fled to the Cape . . .

But the general pattern of life here had never changed so much. Almost daily the trek-wagons still arrived from the interior. They left wagon-spoors like furrows in the sand. Sometimes they got stuck and had to be hauled out by double teams of oxen. They brought ivory, skins, feathers, trophies; and returning, they took with them guns, ammunition, brandy, and the general necessities of life.

Those who arrived here were Germans, Colonials, Swedes, Boers, British . . . A tough breed of men who regarded the Bay as their headquarters . . . They could drink, tell earthy stories, and gamble. Those who could not get a white woman to share the wilderness, took what came to hand. The wind blew daily from the west, heavy with salt, dense with cold. Constantly one sought sunny spots behind walls or pieces of canvas. Sometimes the wind blew from the east and brought the Namib with it. The sand scoured the life out of you. Everything seemed to dry up and shrink.

Water had to be fetched from wells in the dry bed of the Kuiseb. The cattle were posted at Rooibank, some way up the river, where there was sufficient grazing. There your servants had remained, squatting around their little fires, waiting for the day when you would send for them; or you yourself would arrive. Everywhere were wagon spoors. Izak the Bushman always approached them warily. He would jump over them. This was the custom of his people.

Three, four months of letters and newspapers usually collected here. One would spend days reading and studying it all. One would marvel that so much was taking place in the world. This time there was news that in the Cape Mr Hofmeyr had extended his influence. In the Boer Republics, lying to the north, his slogan had taken on a new meaning: *Africa for the Afrikaner.*

This was the white Afrikaner, the Boer, not the Nama Afrikaander of the Transgariep. Adapting Terence I might well have remarked: *Africanus sum, nihil Africani a me alienum puto.* Perhaps it applied now to both these groups . . .

In Egypt Britain was preparing to drive out the Turks. Germany was arrogantly triumphant after her defeat of France . . . There was much talk of the 'larger role' she was still destined to play: also in Africa merchants from the Hansa cities had already established themselves in the Cameroons.

Leopold II of Belgium was opening mid-western Africa for colonization, with the Congo as main artery. In this venture he was partnered by the American, Henry Morton Stanley. In the Transvaal the British imperium had returned . . .

It was doubtful whether the petition against annexation, taken to No 10 Downing Street by Kruger and Joubert, had any chance of success. Certainly there were also adventurous souls in France, Italy—even in Spain and Portugal—bent on finally dividing up the Dark Continent. With rueful satisfaction, I said to myself: all that; and none of the Great Powers has any interest at all in this western land around Capricorn . . .

Strange, on the one hand I knew that matters could not go on in the same old way. On the other hand I had sufficient reason to be wary of European colonization.

The ideal nevertheless was a civilized order. This could serve as a general norm, to be looked up to by all the nations lying within its compass. In a sense it would also serve as a necessary authority. What this country needed more than anything else was authority . . .

With whom was I to discuss all this? Was it to be my friend, Pieter Maritz-Botha? At the moment he was far too popular to break his head about politics. Everybody at the Bay thought him a fine fellow. He was drinking brandy, but with discretion. He never tired of telling of his many adventures in the elephant country with Van Zyl and Co. Merriment was invariably caused by his descriptions of *Oom* Hendrik, who was so incurably squint-eyed that his guns were fitted with double sights. Who could outshoot Old Hendrik?

Concerning the situation in the Transvaal and after studying the newspapers, he would say: 'You see that our people up there in the Kaoko were not quite so wrong as you might have imagined. Well. Look, man, England is already on the highveld. And the Transvaal will just have to see to it. I tell you, we have not yet trekked far enough!'

I found it difficult to reconcile such words with his general attitude. Was the true destination of the Trek after all Angola? Such isolationism was contradictory in a man like Botha. Hail fellow, have a drink, he was everybody's friend. Robert Lewis, often in his company, spoke with appreciation of 'this unusual young Boer' . . .

Ah, well, I eventually decided, the trouble was probably to be traced to Will Jordan himself. Pieter Maritz-Botha was addicted to the sunny side of life. Jordan had the burden of an analytic mind.

I walked down the coast one afternoon, following the curve of the lagoon. Flocks of pink-winged flamingoes were rising from the shallows. Beyond the lagoon lay the cold, blue-green Atlantic, magnificent in its loneliness.

There was the continuous roar of the surf in my ears and the damp salt-laden wind on my cheeks. Extending to the horizon was a firm bank of cloud. A great cosmic silence seemed to lie over the world, above the beating surf, above the cry of the gulls.

I stood at the water's edge and felt myself caught in some sombre world-flood, beyond my understanding. Soon I was lost in it. Only a thin ribbon of the day still glowed in the extreme west. There it stretched above a sea as wine-dark as Homer pictured it.

I climbed a dune and saw the night spreading over the land, the sea, the sky itself. This was one human being trying to understand what he was doing here; whence he had come, whither he was heading. But this could so easily become sickly . . . And in the final run one had to get back to life . . .

I strode over to the damp sand of the lagoon shore. In the curve of the Bay the lights of the *Swallow* flickered. The night sky was afire.

In the building erected by Spence, De Pass and Co there was a party going. Robert Lewis and others were initiating Piet Botha into the secrets of American poker.

'Hi, Will!' It was a general welcome and it warmed me. I was susceptible to attention. Someone presented me with a cigar. Another poured me a drink. Readily I entered into the spirit of the company.

Towards ten o'clock, however, while the others were still going strongly, I had had enough of it all. I retired to my room in the Erikssons' store.

There I sat on my bed, taking in the things around me: a bed . . . A table . . . A chair . . . A piece of tattered canvas in front of the window . . . There were my wagon *kists,* some choice skins and feathers; some trophies I intended for friends at the Cape . . .

The table was covered with books, letters, newspapers, documents of various kinds. Most had arrived with the *Swallow.* My mother had written that Chris Leen and my sister Georgina were to be married in the New Year. My mother had not yet heard from me; but Dr Palgrave, she said, was at the Cape. Krynauw, my agent, had informed her that he had heard that I had been up to the north-eastern parts of the territory, looking for the Trekboers . . .

The company here at the Bay had told me that Palgrave had left in the middle of January for the Cape. With him he had taken the two sons of Kamaherero, Wilhelm and Samuel. Wilhelm was his father's successor. He had been trained by the Rhenish missionaries. What did Palgrave want with him? Lyon, Behan, Todd, all good fellows, with a great deal of interest in the Trekboers, thought that Palgrave was doing his best to see Wilhelm on the throne at Okahandja. Fine, I commented, if that were the case. Unfortunately we had already learnt that Palgrave rarely regarded the facts. Kamaherero, Lyon said, was too shrewd to hand over power while still alive. What did Robert Lewis say? Would Kamaherero accept this? Lyon smiled a little wryly. He would just have to accept it, he said: Lewis was leading him by the nose.

I had reasonable expectations that with Wilhelm Maherero ruling the Ovaherero things would improve. His wife, Magdalena, had been trained as a teacher at Stellenbosch. With these two in charge, my own schemes for the Trekboers would stand a far better chance of being accepted in Okahandja.

Todd had brought news from the interior that the situation in the central parts of the country was getting worse. Another string of murders had taken place. These things would have to be brought to the public attention at the Cape and elsewhere. Wilhelm Maherero might well read all about it in the local press. As a Christian he would admit the truth.

I finished my personal correspondence. I then wrote to *The Cape Times.* I told about my objection to what *Missionar* Vollmer had said to me about atrocities in Damaraland. I had at that time referred him to specific crimes committed by the Ovaherero. To this, according to Todd's information, and also that of others, there were others to be added. There were, for example, the fifty Swartbooi-Namas who had been arbitrarily killed in the Kaokoveld. There was a Bergdamara family at Pallafontein who had suffered a similar fate.

Other murders of Ovambos at Omaruru had been committed. The body of a Nama woman, showing distinct signs of having been used for ritual purposes, was discovered in the same area. I had told the Swedes here at the Bay—Axel Wedburg, Emil Trettow and others—about all this. The Swedes, surely, had the soundest reasons of us all to side with the Ovaherero. That, after all, was the assurance of their continued trading-rights in Damaraland. Nevertheless, they admitted the facts collected by Lyon, Todd and others. Wedburg said that many other things had happened of which the world would never know. It was necessary to bring such facts into the open. The public itself should judge.

From Axel Eriksson only a short letter had arrived, drafted in his inimitable mixture of English, Swedish and Dutch. It confirmed all that I had already heard from his brothers at Omaruru. At the Cape Mr Hofmeyr had taken the first positive steps to start the relief fund. Money would be collected to purchase foodstuffs and clothing. This would be sent up the coast by schooner. To what harbour? If the news were correct that the Trek was now somewhere in the Kaoko, an attempt would be made to land the goods in some sheltered spot. This would be somewhere between Walwich Bay and the mouth of the Cunene. Could I suggest a likely place? Admittedly the coast there seemed to follow a fairly undented line. But perhaps there was some haven which had as yet been overlooked. The alternative, I had already decided, was to land the goods at the Bay. The Kaoko coast was one of the most inhospitable in the world.

Such were my thoughts as I sat there in a box of a room, in a box of a storehouse, in an embryonic seaport, on a desert coast . . . The night mist crept up silently from the Atlantic; and the jackals howled in the dunes.

Even in a great, empty land, the demands of existence, in the more sophisticated sense, could often be extreme.

4

During the following three months Pieter Maritz-Botha and I, in pursuance of our partnership, undertook a journey to the hinterland. We first went to Rehoboth, and from Rehoboth to the borders of Great Namaland. From here we returned to Windhoek, where Jan Jonker Afrikaander and his people were still living. The final stages of the journey were, as always: Otjimbingue, the Lower Kuiseb, and finally the Bay.

I undertook this journey mainly for financial reasons. I also undertook it because I wished to see for myself what was taking place in the country.

At Rehoboth I found some confirmation for what John Caine had said at Otjimbingue. The Basters under Hermanus van Wyk were having a difficult time. Kamaherero was behaving in a high-handed way. He had already moved his cattle posts further southwards to some twenty miles north of the Rehoboth settlement. It was Piet who summed matters up and said: 'Trouble is brewing. When one people's cattle are watered at another people's wells, and destroy its grazing, war will most surely come.'

The little group of Basters sat under their camelthorns: smoking, talking, solemnly discussing the highness and mightiness of the black intruders. What the Hereros were doing was grossly unfair, they said. What could we propose? I could only remind them that they could hardly expect anything from the Namas under Jan Jonker Afrikaander. After all, he was stealing Baster cattle himself whenever it seemed to please him. He also aided and abetted the Bergdamaras. These then fled with their booty into the wilderness of the Lower Kuiseb. I added that this lawlessness would certainly continue until such time as proper authority, backed with sufficient armed strength, could be established in the country.

Hermanus van Wyk and his men blew great clouds of tobacco smoke into the quiet air. They looked at me askance. Yes, they understood what I was saying to them. But they would make no concessions. Van Wyk himself wished to know whether 'Mister' had any great plans in mind. Employing what diplomacy I could muster, I answered that time would bring wisdom. I would return to have further talks. One thing had to be remembered: they alone were by no means strong enough to prevent raids on their property.

At Hoachanas, where twenty years earlier, in all solemnity, Jonker Afrikaander himself had presided over the drafting of the 'Twelve Peace Articles', we stayed for a while. This had been the scene of the *Pax Nama,* which in the end had meant nothing.

Jonker himself had taken the lead. He had been here with twenty-seven wagons, one hundred mounted guards, and a great retinue of advisors and subsidiary chiefs. All the proceedings were conducted in Dutch. From the rest of Great Namaland representatives of the tribes arrived.

The Twelve Articles had indicated clearly that Jonker had known what the country still lacked. A general peace had to be established. The Ovaherero would be included. Anybody caught stealing cattle from either the Namas or the Hereros, or anybody else for that matter, would be severely punished. To this end a police force would be established. The pity was that no one had any idea what a police force was.

Had Jonker lived, he himself would probably have come to the conclusion that assistance from outside, from groups with a stronger tradition in the maintenance of civilized authority, was necessary. Only on this basis could order be established.

The apple, as they say in Dutch, had fallen far from the tree. Hoa-Arab (Cat Ribs), as Jan Jonker had been nicknamed, had long since forgotten that there had ever been anything like a peace conference at Hoachanas. True, the immediate danger in the country was Herero hegemony. Nevertheless, when it came to the propensities of the Afrikaanders under Jan Jonker to cause havoc, I had no illusions.

We found an opportunity to sound Jan Jonker out on the way back from Gobabis. He received us in some style. From the start, however, he would not stop talking about the many injustices his people were suffering. He spoke feelingly about the great 'war' (army) he was intending to take through Damaraland to Okahandja. The peace which *Missionar* Hahn had established nine years previously meant nothing at all. Kamaherero had grown too rich. There were also far too many evil people advising him. By way of answering this, I advised circumspection, pointing out that any sort of war would cause nameless misery for all concerned. His only enemies were the Ovaherero, Jonker assured us. *They* had to be punished, and punished severely . . .

There he stood before me, a typical Nama: small and wiry, with a reddish-yellow skin, and prominent cheekbones.

Windhoek itself with its dreary collection of reed huts, the two-room brick house of Jan Jonker himself, the veld which had been badly over-grazed, the powerful springs, had deteriorated since the great days when this man's father had ruled here. The decadence was symptomatic of the general decay of the Afrikaander tribe. But Jan Jonker's thin lips and pale eyes reminded me that the Namas had great powers of endurance. They were also shrewd masters of their own particular strategies. If indeed a new struggle were to develop, it would by no means be an easy matter for the Ovaherero.

I shuddered to think what might happen to the country as a whole. At the same time I knew that bringing my own plans to fruition would serve the general good. From all the overwrought talk by Jan Jonker I could deduce something else. He was not only watching the north with hatred in his heart. His eyes also looked enviously at his own blood-relations in Great Namaland.

Had I perhaps heard of any 'works' being undertaken by the Witbooi-Namas? he asked. Old Moses Witbooi, the Chief, had according to reports said that his son Hendrik had tried to usurp the Gibeon throne. Beware of Hendrik, Jonker advised with singular passion. He (Jonker) had heard that *Missionar* Olpp had 'salved' Hendrik with his own hands. This was possible because Hendrik was an elder in Olpp's church. The talk was that Hendrik carried a picture of the *Missionar* in his Bible, on which some words had been written in German. That was proof of the salving; exactly as Samuel had done to Saul. What he, Jan Jonker, now wished to know, was whether 'Mister' knew anything about Hendrik's plans.

About Hendrik Witbooi's movements or motives I knew nothing. My father had sometimes travelled to Gibeon, but my own wagon spoors were almost exclusively to be found in the north. Well, Jonker persisted, should things come to a pass, would 'Mister' provide *skietgoed*—things for shooting? Once again I was called upon to act the diplomat. No, I said, why meet trouble half-way? What we all had to strive for was a consolidation of the peace.

Jan Jonker's eyes became little black slits. Flies crawled around their corners. He smiled slowly, and grunted. The atmosphere by this time had become tense and I was not enjoying it. Gladly I would have told this shape of arrogance to clear off and leave me in peace. At the same time I reminded myself that whatever the faults of the Namas, at present it was the sins of the Ovaherero which were most destructive. Jonker sensed my apathy, then turned to Botha. Would the Boers in the coming struggle give 'us Red people a piece of meat', he asked. At that moment Botha himself was busy enjoying a lamb cutlet, with the fat streaming down his chin.

'Meat, Captain,' Botha eventually answered and wiped his mouth, 'there is surely enough of it in the land. All that you need to do is to shoot well!'

Jan Jonker thought deeply about this. Then he nodded solemnly, weighing it all in his mind. Botha closed his pocket-knife with a snap, stretched himself, and ambled away to a shady camelthorn. Soon he was lying stretched out on his back, hat over his eyes, belt loosened, snoring.

By the middle of June that year we began to prepare for our trek to the north. The news reaching the Bay indicated that the Trek had already left the waters at Namutoni and was heading for the Kaoko. Charles Lyon, just back from Ovamboland, told us that the Finnish Mission at Ondangua already knew about the Trekboers. According to them Gert Alberts and his fellow riders had already returned from their long reconnaissance to the west. The Trek itself was moving slowly in a north-westerly direction. Ovambo hunters of Kambonde Kampingana, king of the Ondonga tribe, had informed him that the mounted commission had reached the waters at Kaoko Otavi and Otjitundua. Presumably the Trek was now on its way to these springs.

I knew these waters. They were situated in the hard dolomite of the wild country south of the Cunene. Kaoko Otavi was the great eye of the Kaoko. Otjitundua lay some two days' trek to the south. There, too, were fine waters, fresh and shiny. There was also sufficient arable land nearby for the Trek to raise crops. Game was plentiful in the high valleys and plains to the east of the mountains. The Cunene, less than a hundred miles north of Kaoko Otavi, had an abundance of hippo. A successful hunt on these animals would provide the Trek with a variety of necessities, including food. This would suffice until the goods from the Cape could reach the laager.

Albert Eriksson confirmed what Charles Lyon had said. The Boers were at the Kaoko waters, which they had reached without trouble in sixteen stages. I could now conclude my report and send it by the first available schooner to the Cape. With luck it might be there before the end of December and be in the *Cape Review* in the new year.

Axel Eriksson's letters to the press had already stimulated public interest. Coates Palgrave would no doubt support him, be it for purely humanitarian reasons. How soon could things start moving? Time was necessary for the buying of provisions; for the chartering of the ship or ships; for the voyage up the desert coast.

I was constantly re-examining old charts, hoping that my own conclusions would soon be corrected; that there was in fact some place due west of the Kaoko springs where a ship might lie. From the inland waters to the coast was about one hundred and fifty miles. Accepting that wagons could cross the mountains of the western Kaoko, a long trek of some eight hundred miles down to the Bay and back would be obviated.

All this I discussed with Piet Botha, Charles Lyon and others. 'If they off-load on the Kaoko coast,' Botha said, 'we'll go down to the sea. We are used to finding our way through hard country. If they off-load at the Bay, we'll come down to the Bay.'

Our larders were carefully replenished. Special attention was given to the medicine chests, with Lyon assisting. The probability was that fever had by this time set in anew among members of the Trek.

'Well, Charles,' I said, 'when we have finally established the New Republic, we shall send for you to act as secretary of state!' He took this seriously. 'Who knows?' he said. 'Should you need me, my dear Will, please let me know!'

I had once treated him for dysentery up at Andara, and he had never stopped being grateful.

Charles creased his face into a smile and added: 'I shall consider whatever you have to propose. Please keep me informed.'

A day after our departure Robert Lewis and John Caine arrived from Otjimbingue. Caine had heard of what I had written to *The Cape Times* regarding the increasing number of murders in Damaraland.

'What do you hope to effect?' he asked. 'Circumstanced as we are, it is, according to my lights, advisable to tread softly. These things happening in the country are disheartening indeed. But at this stage it is better to leave well alone.' In a fatherly way he reminded me that sufficient unto the day was the evil thereof. Most certainly, I said, but that did not mean indifference to whatever happened. I nevertheless maintained a light-hearted air, assuring Caine that he had no need to worry. He referred again to my Rehoboth scheme. To this I rejoined that all was tentative. It was a matter for the Trekboers themselves. *They* would finally decide. Was this my new-found diplomacy at work? I was beginning to feel at home in it.

We sat there in the house which Sarah Jane Andersson, after the death of her husband, had used as a shop and as living-quarters. It was cold outside. The wind from the sea brought with it a smell of sulphur, due to some kind of submarine disturbance.

We drank brandy, played poker, and talked. Robert Lewis joined us, wearing a Norfolk jacket and knee-breeches. He also wore a ring, the seal of which was that of an antelope within a circle: the sign of his 'office'. Generally he was now regarded as being Kamaherero's personal adviser: 'prime minister', Charles Lyon had said in jest.

'Well, Jordan,' Lewis said, 'so you're off to your friends in the Kaoko!'

I looked at my cards. 'So I am,' I said.

'Intending to establish them in some part of your own choosing?'

It could have been that he was now referring to Rehoboth. I scraped the ash off my cigar. 'Intending nothing,' I said drily.

'Of course, there is great concern in Damaraland regarding the secret intentions of the Trekboers.'

'Why do you call it secret?'

He smiled weakly. 'I and others would like to know what they—your friends—have in mind,' he said. 'But granted, the Boer mind is not easily penetrated. They believe, so I surmise, that they have been called into the Thirstland by the Most High, like ancient Israel. You will understand why we who have the interest of the country at heart, are on the *qui vive*!'

He added something in Otjiherero which he spoke fluently. From this I could deduce that he preferred the god of the Ovaherero, Karunga, and the Holy Fire, to the God of Hosts, on trek in a wagon.

'What keeps me guessing,' John Caine interposed, 'is the why and wherefore of the whole affair. The Boers did surely not expect to find a land there in the far west free for the picking! How did they imagine they could escape the British and set up on their own, somewhere where the land does not belong to them? The numbers of the Trekboers hardly warrant anything of size. Has all this death and misery, have all these tears, been justified?'

One should hesitate to draw conclusions, I said. Few of those here at the Bay had any first-hand knowledge of the Trekboers and their motives. In any event, the prime fact was their presence in the country. However they might have erred and wandered, they were a civilized group of men, women and children with a strict code of conduct. Whatever their intentions might have been, they might still serve an excellent purpose.

I must ever remember, Lewis said, that any Boer settlement in or near Damaraland without the authority of the king himself would be viewed in a serious light.

I might have reacted sharply to this, but Botha suddenly opened the outside door. A blast of icy wind swept into the room as he noisily saluted us. With the cold and the smell of sulphur descending upon the company like death itself, the intruder was by no means popular.

'Shut the door!' voices barked out in unison. Botha, looking innocent, surveyed the scene. He kicked the door shut. Broadly seating himself, and quaffing a tot of brandy presented to him, he had much to tell concerning himself. He had been taking leave of friends setting off on new journeys to the hinterland. He was sporting a new waistcoat.

Botha was at home in this company, motley as it was. Perhaps his free-and-easy adaptability was a legacy of his paternal grandfather, Captain Botha, who had been the first Harbour Master of Port Natal.

Through the window, so clouded by the thick sea air that one could hardly see through it, I could dimly discern the form of our wagons. They were already loaded for the next day's trek. The figure of Izak appeared through the murk. He was finding shelter in the lee of the house. Soon his face appeared around an inner door, grinning at me. Should he prepare something to eat? 'Fry some fish, *Bambuse*,' I said. Botha poured him a drink. The Bushman looked at what he had received. *'Ara!'* He smacked his lips.

From the gloom of the kitchen, which was merely a lean-to behind the building, I would see Kairob's eyes shining white in the blackness of his face.

We drank brandy, ate fish, and played poker. Afterwards Charles Lyon, Albert Eriksson, Todd and some others joined the company. It was almost homelike.

5

It was the open road again.

All that had been so fluid now took shape. Days had come when I had feared that what had been so urgent in me had lost its momentum, trapped in the morass of dailiness. This had happened often enough in the past. Now Pieter Maritz-Botha and I had come to the implementation of our plans. We were setting out to find the Trek. It was an exciting thought. We had heard where the laagers might be, but nothing was certain. We would find the Trek and discuss the future.

A year before I was trekking alone, finding old spoors, laagering at old outspans. A year before I was still feeling angry, sad, lonely, brave, and not getting anywhere. Now all this had changed. My new self-consciousness was driving me forward. To where? It did not matter. I was moving.

We stuck to the south bank of the Swakop until we got to Otjimbingue. From there we followed the route northwards to Omaruru. The Erongo range lay to our left. In the east we could see the great twin peaks of Omatako. For days it was the focal point of the eastern horizon. Mornings the sun would rise like a ripe Cape apricot. Oryx would stare at us through white masks, displaying the sheen of supple skin, rapier-like horns, luminous black eyes . . .

We trekked west of the rock-pyramid of Okonjenje, where Charles John Andersson, during an early search for the Cunene, had been compelled to turn back. The route lay through dense mopani to Otjitambi, where the Swartbooi Namas had been given land by Kamaherero. This was for services rendered in the wars against Jan Jonker.

The Swartboois were still the rightful owners of Rehoboth. They had been banished here to the far north. We met Petrus Swartbooi, who looked like a Redskin, but was all Nama. He was glad to see 'Mister'. He was also thankful for the 'thought': the little cask of Cape brandy we had presented him with. Oh, yes, he knew all about the Trekboers. They had passed to the north, keeping to the lower fringe of the White Pan. They had touched at Okaukueyo, where there were powerful springs. Some of his people at Zesfontein, in the heart of the Kaoko, had informed him that Trekboer laagers had been established at the Kaoko waters to the north.

The chief confirmed his tribe's claim to Rehoboth. No, he said, they had never abandoned it. They had merely been driven out. He had heard that 'Mister' was interested in buying Rehoboth for the Trekboers. Somehow I avoided the answer.

'I have no wrong ideas about this lot,' I said when we finally resumed our journey. 'They are like the rest. They'll take what they can get.'

Botha, riding a fine gelding he had bought at Omaruru, adjusted his hat to a rakish angle. 'Yes,' he said, 'they'll take what they can get. When one is not strong, one must be clever!'

'Let's find the laagers first,' I said. 'I cannot wait to meet our friends again. It's like returning to my own people at the Cape!'

Our friends, I had said. I had consciously used the plural. Botha and I were partners in more than just the business sense. He was an excellent link between the Trekboers and Will Jordan. His maternal grandfather had been Gert Maritz, the leader of the Great Trek of the late thirties.

Things seemed to be falling into place. I was by no means religious, yet I was becoming conscious of something in all this beyond my comprehension. I was awed by nature. I was awed by its vastness, its mystery. Nights I would lie awake, staring at the brilliance of the night sky. This and the 'moral law within' proved to me that God lived. Emmanuel Kant had said that. I liked to read the Authorized Version. I liked to read Shakespeare . . .

Did Botha care for these things? Hardly. He liked to give the impression of being light-hearted, superficial. But there was a harder, more serious side to the man. He could even be pedantic. And he was a staunch Calvinist.

The Boer people had always had it in their blood to stand on their own feet, however difficult, however dangerous, he said. They preferred places where the grazing was good. They always wanted good hunting and good waters. 'So,' he concluded, 'we must also take a look at the land beyond the river!'

The 'river' now was the Cunene. The river divided the Kaoko from Angola. I had often told people of the attractions of Angola. It was still a big, empty country, with fine highlands, great rivers and magnificent forests. The hunting, too, was good.

'We must go and look at it,' Botha said, 'even if the Portuguese are as they are. They tell me they are a weak nation who sleep with the blacks.'

'The Portuguese have been there for centuries,' I said. 'They have their own customs.'

'If they are weak, we can go there. A country like that needs men. Our people are used to taming the wilderness.'

6

One afternoon, at long last, it was the laager itself. It was the group that had gathered around the more southerly waters of Otjitundua. The others were at Kaoko Otavi, six hours on horseback in a northerly direction, towards the Cunene.

Smoke was visible for many miles before we could identify it. To the east an extensive bush plain, blue-green and lush, filled the horizon. To the far west successive ranges of mountain were rising, seemingly floating in the haze. In the middle-distance were broken island hills of black dolomite, densely overgrown with grass and trees.

At about three o'clock that afternoon, against one of these, we distinguished the white dots of wagon-hoods. Half an hour later the first welcoming shots rang out. Two riders were coming out through the dry grass of an omuramba to meet us. They were Barend Bouwer and Louw du Plessis.

'Mester Will! Cousin Piet!' It was Stentor in the shape of Barend. Behind him was Louw du Plessis, holding up his hat by way of a salute.

From all sides people were now appearing. Men were coming to meet us, on foot and on horseback. Women rose from their stools around their smoking *erds,* gazing steadily at us through *kappies.* Children alongside the wagon were laughing, skipping, screaming with delight.

Izak, prancing for their benefit, was the cause of much of this. Kairob, manipulating the longwhip with more than his usual dexterity, shone with pride. Another long trek had come to an end.

The general welcome became a triumphal procession. Other volleys sounded from wagons lying further afield. Our horses, tired after being pushed over the last twenty miles, had suddenly livened up again. More riders came to join us. Together we proceeded to an open slope where a clear spring ran. Close to the water stood a solitary shepherd's tree, crowned with a head of fresh green leaves. In front of a house built of rough limestone, I spied Old Diederick, landdrost and Orphan Master, in a frock-coat and a high white collar. A gnarled hand rested on an olive-wood stick.

A little figure in a white *kappie* and clutching a wild orange in her right hand waved to us, calling out. I waved back. It was my child of the marshes. It was she who had once stood in the niche of the baobab at Olifants Pan; who had petulantly denied all knowledge of the attention of a young Adriaan Venter. There, behind her, was her mother, Ella Lombard. Next to her was the Roets couple. Behind them was the Lombard wagon with a Transvaal *Vierkleur* held aloft by Dina Lombard. There, too, was Kleinveld Labuschagne, pressing his hat to his chest, watching us with eyes deep-set above sunken cheeks.

There, too, was Dolf Holtzhausen and his clan appearing from all sides and corners of their wagons. There, too, were the Van Voors gathered around their own patriarchal head, who was resting on a stool. There, too, was David Black and his people, quietly smiling; and Machiel Prinsloo, riding his Arab, coming up to meet us, shaking hands and assuring us that we were very welcome. There, too, were the Oppermans, the Louwrenses, the Du Plessis, of whom Louw was the head . . .

The water—fresh, shiny and euphonious—coursed down the limestone slope, following the contour, to where the fields had already been cleared for sowing. In some the young corn was already showing. Patches of bright green stood out against the blue- and olive-green of the bush, the bleached yellow of the grass. Four or five limestone houses, thatched with veld-grass, had been built here on the slope.

Barend Bouwer, his face aglow with pleasure, laid a heavy but friendly hand upon my shoulder: 'Mester Will,' he said, 'for many days now we have thought never to see you again. And yet, here you are. Cousin Piet, you would know about the hunting here. Man, here is more than what we can deal with.'

And Louw du Plessis looked at me and said: 'So, Brother Jordan, our people have come a long way, as you can see. But I think that they have now reached a place where they may rest for a while. It is fine here!'

To this Botha remarked: 'Cousin Louw, for us it is a great

pleasure to see you all in good health. And we, having arrived here safely, are thankful too!'

'In good health, yes, Cousin Piet,' Louw answered. 'And thankful! So we all are for blessings received. We are poor because we have trekked many a year now. What we had has all been used up. Now we are greatly heartened that you have come. The people here all wish us to go on a hippo-hunt up at the river. And should Brother Jordan have knowledge of the country up there, it would be of great assistance to us. Cousin Piet, if you, too, could go along with us, the hunt will be successful.'

What was the news, I was constantly being asked. This I could only answer to the best of my ability. We ourselves had been on trek from the Bay for more than a month now. Yes, I confirmed, I had heard from the Cape that a Relief Committee had been established. It was collecting funds. It would send ships with food and clothing and medicine up the coast. It might well be that all this could come about before the end of the year. Axel Eriksson had taken the matter upon himself. He had written letters to the newspapers. These had been read by many people. Dr Palgrave, too, had promised support.

'God has blessed us,' Diederick Prinsloo intoned. 'This has happened, because it is God's people who are on trek!'

That evening, at the time of devotions, Old Diederick addressed those gathered under the trees: 'The Lord is my strength and song, and He is become my salvation: He is my God, and I will prepare Him an habitation; My father's God, and I will exalt Him . . .'

The psalm drew itself out through the tranquil air:

'Nor will God's truth as token,
Nor will His covenant e'er be broken . . .'

Everywhere against the slopes and under the trees the fires were now winking. The heavens had become frostily clear.

Ella Lombard brought me a bowl of coffee. 'This is from a handful of real beans that I have saved,' she said. 'Oh, my child, the coffee made from the roots of the shepherd's tree sometimes has strange workings on one's stomach!'

A week later we had reached the rest of the Trek at Kaoko Otavi. Here was the laager of Commandant J. F. Botha. Here, too, were the Albertses, the Van der Merwes, the Labuschagnes, Venters, Louwrenses . . .

The expedition of Gert Alberts and his fellow riders to

investigate the land to the west, looking for the 'temporary resting place', had been entirely successful. Shortly after his return, however, his wife had died. Now she lay there in the limestone on the south edge of the White Pan, a day's trek west of Namutoni.

The Trek itself had got to Kaoko Otavi, the finest water of the region, without undue trouble. Members of the laager had left for the Cunene shortly after arriving here to get the feel of the land. They had now returned with the news that the other side of the river looked promising. In the river itself there were a great many hippos.

Plans for a great hunt were well advanced. Meanwhile there was much shooting in the vicinity. Elephants were abundant. Jan Robbertze believed that good profits could be made by hunting the animals for their ivory by means of big, organized expeditions. In Jan Labuschagne Robbertze found an enthusiastic supporter. Jan had many stories to tell about the great elephant orgy in the marula season.

Young Adriaan Venter turned up at the wagon, informing us that shortly after meeting us at Otjitundua he had shot his first elephant. 'With the Star Barrel, *Meneer.*' He looked at me with level eyes.

Well, I said, and now it was time for him to get a modern gun. He immediately wished to know how much ivory would be necessary to buy a gun like mine. I handed him the Winchester, and he held it gently, lovingly.

'This is what the old people called a "thigh-loader",' Barend Bouwer said. 'Look, man!' He took the gun from the boy. 'You load it like this!' He demonstrated the loading. 'On the side here, see? On the thigh! Listen, young fellow, this gun is good for the usual kind of shooting. There is nothing better. But for an elephant? Don't try it, *boetie**. It is far too light!'

'There are new guns coming,' I said.

'Schneiders, *Meneer*?'

'There are others too, even better than the Schneider. There are guns good enough for anything one needs to shoot; but lighter than your Star Barrel.'

'That is what we need, *Meneer.*'

There was the suggestion of a dream in his words.

*Literally: little brother.

7

So many other things were also needed. In spite of considerable improvement in general conditions in the laager—compared with Olifants Pan—it was yet apparent that the people were weary.

By now they had wandered for many years. What did the future hold? I did not easily touch upon the matter. With a general air of contentment in the laager, it was, as yet, uncalled for. Here at Kaoko Otavi and Otjitundua was the 'temporary resting-place'. In time this might well lead to the 'Land of Rest'. The idea had, for so many years, served this community. Thinking of it in these terms caused me to remind myself: rather a Land of the Living than a Land of Rest.

Main task now was to get the Trekboers properly settled; to win their confidence and their friendship.

As far as Rehoboth was concerned, the idea should mature. The leaders themselves would in time see the advantages of a settlement somewhere in the Transgariep. Then I would discuss the intended purchase.

'Rehoboth,' I said casually to a group of Trek leaders one day, 'has much of the best grazing in the whole of the land between the Orange and the Cunene. Here in the Kaoko it is fine, but the land is too remote. For a modern state there should be some contact with the world.'

The company was silent. It was Gert Alberts who then answered: 'The Lord had an object with this Trek, *Meneer*. It is our *own* land that we must find.'

They kept on putting questions to me concerning opportunities in Angola.

'The interior of Angola is still wild country,' I said. 'No doubt the Portuguese will develop it some day. They are enterprising enough in their way, and tough. They hang on to what they have. To keep a country as large as that for centuries takes some doing. Nevertheless, I have good reason to believe that the authorities in Moçamedes and other places would welcome a Boer settlement somewhere in the interior. There are fine, healthy highlands in the Huila Province, with an abundance of water. There are also fine lands and forests.'

My audience silently considered this. 'We have heard of this province,' Commandant J. F. Botha said at last. 'We have also heard that there is a chance for us Boers to obtain land there where it is high and there is no fever. We wish to obtain a country where no one will trouble us, and where we can be on our own. We have feelings of great thankfulness towards Mister Jordan that there may also be a new Boer Republic in the South where the Basters live . . .'

'An own, free republic,' Gert Alberts emphasized.

To this Louw du Plessis added: 'With all the nations here living in strife with each other, Brother Jordan, will they suffer us Boers to go and live down there?'

'I believe that the Boers have it in them to demonstrate to the other people of the Transgariep how a civilized community should live,' I said.

'But are we then there on our *own*?' Gert Alberts asked.

'If we should be there, Brother Jordan,' the Commandant added, 'with another nation, how will the old Boer way of life be preserved? Yes, you say that the Basters are but a handful. Still, they are not white!'

Pieter Maritz-Botha finalized the matter: '*Oom* Jacobus,' he said, 'what Brother Jordan has just said is that we must never forget that Angola is a Portuguese country. They have kept it that way for a long time. They are also a jealous nation who hold on to what they have. So we, too, would be if we had possessed that land. Another thing: it is a Romish country; and we are of the Reformed Faith. Our forefathers died for it. Still, I am not saying that we should not consider it. Jordan can yet take us there. He speaks the language; and he knows the country. He is also a good friend of the people in Moçamedes.'

He looked at me. 'If we have to stay for some time under the Portuguese,' he said, 'and even if the Portuguese are a jealous nation, we may yet buy land which appeals to us!'

It had to be faced: all these years of wandering had left my friends with an insufficient knowledge of the modern world. Their own world was still very much the laager. It was a world which they had brought along with them in their wagons to this distant corner of the continent. Here the laager had been finally isolated. Here the members declared themselves well satisfied with life as they knew it.

Their heroic qualities had always appealed to me. In the pieces I had sent for publication to the *Cape Review* I had underlined this. The firm religious values of the Boers had always impressed me too. They were not always my values, yet one had to respect them.

One had to respect, too, the way in which they were kept alive. They had done this in the face of the Thirstland, the fever marshes, the threats of enemies. These trials had brought them to penury. They were living here with a minimum of the accepted necessities which made life bearable. In ordinary circumstances conditions might have given rise to moral decay. This had not happened. Their strict moral code was as strong as ever.

As pioneers the Trekboers were outstanding. But one thing was becoming increasingly clear: there was no future at all in a continuing isolation. It was now necessary for these people to return to the world, and to find their true place in it.

Already I had admitted to myself the validity of the question put to me by John Caine at Otjimbingue: 'To what end? Great ends may at times be accomplished by small means; but the opposite also holds true . . .'

The suffering of my friends could only become meaningful if it could be directed to reality. There was only one possibility: they had to find some place to settle in South West Africa. There they should establish themselves as an ordered community. Angola? True, it was a land of possibilities. Success there would only come, however, if the Boers were prepared to accept not only Portuguese living but also the Portuguese themselves. This meant Roman Catholicism . . .

Looking at it in all honesty it would indeed have been better for them to have found the long way back.

But this was impracticable. The latest news was that the Union Jack had been hoisted in Pretoria. There it would remain, as far as I could see.

Was I now becoming conscious of some personal loss should the Trek abandon its search for a new land? Their quest had strangely become part of my own life. I liked to think of myself as the small means by which the great end might yet be accomplished.

These people here were a community in more than just the physical sense. There was some mystique which held them together. It had grown through generations. It was tempered by the heat, the cold, the fire of Africa. It had been formed by its hard contours, the sharpness of its light. It had taken over the unremitting nature of its bush, plains, deserts, mountains . . .

One could divine this best at nights around the laager fires. The heavens were silent; but far down on the plains the lions would roar. Here the circle seemed to close. Little ones lay asleep in their mothers' arms. The old people would re-tell the old stories. The young ones would listen. The circle had closed. These were moments of renewed dedication. The great deeds of the past were once more recalled. These were the things which had made these people.

Hendrikus van Voor, Diederick Prinsloo, Gert Alberts, Ella Lombard . . .

'*Tante*?' Tina du Plessis, Louw's eldest daughter, would ask: '*Tante*, I have heard it said that *Tante* was at the massacre of Blaauwkrantz in Natal. That was more than forty years ago!'

'Yes, my child,' Ella Lombard would presently answer, as she had often answered, 'it is a long time since all that happened. But no one outgrows such things. Neither should they.'

Once I had come to her wagon unexpectedly while she had been kneading bread. I had noticed the scars on the inside of her arms: where the assegais had struck. She showed no embarrassment, but bared her arms to above the elbows.

'We were attacked by the Amazulu,' she said. 'I was still a young girl, not yet married.'

More she would not say. Neither did I enquire. Blaauwkrantz was part of the Great Trek of the thirties. It was the Trek from the Old Colony to Natal. It had ended in the Battle of Blood River, where the Zulu power had finally been broken.

Around the Kaoko fires she would re-tell the stories she had so often told.

'With us all there at Blaauwkrantz there was still another called Betta de Beer. That night the Amazulu attacked us. Betta fled from her wagon with her child of but nine months in her arms. She crept under the hind-axle of another wagon and lay there in the dark. But the evil-doers saw her and struck at her with their assegais between the spokes of the wheels. So they managed to kill her child while it still lay there in her arms. She too was wounded. The wagon stood on a high bank, next to a sluit. When the chance came, Betta jumped from the bank into the sluit with her dead child in her arms. Down there in the darkness at the bottom of the sluit she laid her child down. Then she crept away to a tree and climbed into it, wounded as she was. She reached a fork of the tree and hung there exhausted. Two Zulus came past and saw her there. First they struck at her with their assegais. She was far too high for them to reach. Then one climbed up and grabbed Betta by the hair. She had hair which reached down to her hips. The Zulus grabbed her by the hair and tried to drag her from the tree. She wedged herself fast into the fork, however, and would not let go. So there they hung: the Zulu to her long hair, and Betta to the tree. All the while she was shouting. Some people heard her and presently shots rang out. Then the evil-doers took flight. So tightly was she drawn into the fork of the tree that four men had to pull her out again . . .'

And leathery Gert Alberts, who had led the riders over the high mountains of the Kaoko to the distant west, looking for the waters . . .

'So we then left the White Pan, eight of us, on horseback,' he recounted. 'Our course was to follow the sun. So we rode; and came the same way as the Trek itself, later. After ten days we got to these waters and saw that they were good. But we wished to go further for we had not yet seen what happens to the sun when it disappears behind the mountains. So we left the waters and rode down the 'maramba as you see it here, going towards the mountains. One day we got to a good water and lay down to drink. But suddenly we noticed many dead birds lying about. Others which were drinking were presently falling down and dying. Then we knew that the water was poisoned. We then rode on through the mountains to where a great *poort** opened. We followed the dry stony bed of a steep river, going down, down all the way. Eventually we emerged where the mountains ended in dunes. The dunes were like hills, and we rode over them. The sun was still in the west and we had not yet seen it disappear where the earth was flat again. So we rode on for three more days. The dunes were now as high as mountains. We followed the sun, and that afternoon we heard a strange roaring noise like thunder from the west. It did not stop, but kept on. But the skies were clear, and nowhere was there a cloud. Then we thought it might be game storming over a stony ridge. We looked for dust, but there was none. Then one said it might be the earth itself, roaring from its inside. But then it would shake; and all was still quiet. Then Naas Labuschagne came up and said: "*Oom* Gert, listen! This roaring sound is the sea of which you have heard but have not yet seen!" "Naas," I asked, "how do you know that?" "*Oom* Gert," he said, "but you know that I have been down to Port Natal and

*Opening through a mountain range.

have seen the sea. I know the great sound it makes when the surf is strong, because the wind blows from far away towards the land.'' So we went further to see for ourselves what Ignatius—old Naas!—had told us. Then after another hour we crossed another high dune; and suddenly there was the sea! It was as beautiful and wide as the grass plains of Transvaal in a year of good rains. A great thundering came from the waters which yet looked so peaceful. We rode down to the white strand and let the horses play in the water. Cold it was; and saltier than the saltiest water of the White Pan. But where the river came through the dunes we dug in the sand and found fresh water to drink. We rode south then, following the strand. When after four days we got to the mouth of the big dry river, we turned inland to the mountains. The mountains now lay to the west with the sun rising behind the peaks. Through the mountains we went to the waters of Zesfontein. So we named it because there are six big springs there. Good waters these, and fine soil! But there are far too many mountains there. It closes one in and oppresses one. There was not much game, so we rode further to the west. After many days we saw the White Pan again. Like the sea, it was shining white and vast there in the distance. So we had got back to the laager after many weeks; and we thanked the Lord that we had been spared to see our loved ones again.'

Gert Alberts and his fellow-riders had ridden nearly a thousand miles through a wild country, I thought. They had gone to beyond the mountains, to see where the sun disappeared. They had then returned, and then their leader's wife had died . . .

One who listened to this story, in the audience around the laager fire, was Nellie la Grange, then a girl of seventeen. I would remember this later, when we were up at the river, shooting hippo.

8

Those evenings around the laager fires . . . Those Sundays when little family groups visited each other between the many religious services . . .

The visitors would be given folding stools made of tamboti to sit on. They would drink their shepherd's tree coffee out of bowls or decorated cups. They would eat doughnuts made from corn flour with veld-honey as a special treat.

At times I would grow critical, impatient. Had these good people any idea of where they were heading to, what they were looking for? Had anything of any real significance regarding this country and its peoples ever penetrated their consciousness? Inevitably my natural sympathy would restore the balance, would cause me to say: 'In time all will find its true place and meaning. Patience! After all, these people are poor, lonely, lost in the world. They are no different to what people have ever been. Of main importance to them is the old way of life . . .'

Little children would run about in moleskin trousers or print dresses and in *veldschoens.* They would play under the shade of trees with clay oxen or knucklebones, inspanned to miniature wagons. Evenings at devotions they would sit there sweetly, fingers on their mouths, watching their elders, never daring to utter a word. The children in their early teens were growing up awkwardly, noticing each other. There were those like Adriaan Venter who at fifteen were already men. There were young girls like Lets Labuschagne, Tina du Plessis, Hannie Venter, Lisa Lombard, who were reaching out eagerly for life. What did it matter if there was a great outside world beyond their knowing? What did it matter if much had happened which was not part of their own intimate history? Here in the laagers of Otjitundua and Kaoko Otavi was still all the world they needed. Behind them they had a study of the *Steps of Youth,* the *Thunderbolt of the Godless.* That was enough. They wrote carefully and precisely. They read slowly but correctly. They knew a great many psalms and a great many pieces of Scripture. Solemnly they sang:

> '*Those who on the oceans wander*
> *In ships so richly loaded,*
> *Look at the mighty waves and ponder*
> *God's mightiness and wrath.*'

Of all the original Trekkers it was only Ignatius Labuschagne who had ever seen the sea. Of all the Boers in the laager it was only Pieter Maritz-Botha who had an inkling of how big the world was, or how many people lived in it. Of all together here, it was only Will Jordan who wondered. This was he who put questions to himself on the how and the why of things, who lay thinking at night . . .

The tightly closed life of the laager . . .

Each one had his appointed place. Dolf Holtzhausen and his

sons were the carpenters. They made coffins, rifle-butts, wheel-spokes, wheel-rims, wheel-hubs, yoke-skeys, and yokes. Sometimes they would also make a fine bench, a folding stool with a leather seat, or a *kist*. They would use the teak of this northern region. It had been given the name *Dolfzijnhout*—Dolf's wood.

There were the gunsmiths who could fix anything from six or twelve pound muzzle-loader, to the Schneiders and Wesley-Richards of the modern day. They were Jan du Plessis—brother of Louw—Albert and Johannes Opperman, and Hermanus Grobler. There were the land surveyors, who were also the agriculturists. They carefully constructed water furrows, saw to the levelling of fields: the Van der Merwes, the Du Prés, Van Voors. There were the hunters who constantly saw to it that the larders of all were sufficiently stocked: Barend Bouwer, the Robbertzes, the Labuschagnes, the Venters and Pieter Maritz-Botha. There were the ironsmiths, who could repair a trek-chain, and could shoe a horse: the Prinsloos, Bothmas, De Klerks. There were the leather-workers who made *veldschoens,* longwhips, sjamboks, bridles, saddles, and thong-mats for the *katels*: the Van Deventers, Snymans, De Beers, De Klerks. There were the wagon-smiths who could shoe a wheel with either a new shoe or by shortening the old one: the Du Toits, Van den Bergs, Prinsloos . . .

The smiths of the Trek were masters of their craft. The iron had first to be turned, measured, welded, then fitted to the wood. The work proceeded with the assistance of hammers, fire-tongs, anvils. Combretum—the leadwood of this country—burning slowly but fiercely to a silver-white ash, was used for heating. The fitting had to be deftly, swiftly done. Water was poured over the glowing iron. Black figures loomed up through clouds of steam. When the fit was true, the shoe would be rivetted to the wood with pins. Now the wheel would be ready again. The Trek could continue.

There were the women who made the clothes of the Trek: a frock-coat of broadcloth; a polonaise of cambric or print. Nearly all of them could do this, with but a few sewing machines between them. Among the women there, too, were those who had a wide knowledge of veld fruits and tubers. Ella Lombard and her Dina produced candles of mopani-wax or wildebeest-fat. They also made a variety of sweet-meats.

There were the *tantes*: Louwrens, Du Plessis, Prinsloo, and many others. They could cut up a hippo into strips of fat to dry in the sun. This was food for harder days. There were the midwives who performed their tasks in the wagon tents. There were the remedy-givers who would sometimes ask the 'doctor' what he thought of their medicines. There was the teacher of the young whose approach was gentle but whose cane was ready: Andries Alberts, son of Gert; at times also David Black. There were the musicians who could sound festive notes when required, playing the violin, whistle, and at times the harmonica: the Louwrens brothers. There were the story-tellers who were experts in transporting their listeners to regions finer, better, more heroic even than what they knew: old Hendrikus van Voor; Gert Alberts, Ella Lombard; last but not least—Pieter Maritz-Botha.

There was the landdrost and Orphan Master of the Trek: Old Diederick Prinsloo, perhaps the worthiest of them all. There was the Field-Cornet, who had to be constantly alert to all that was going on: Louw du Plessis. There was at the head of the *Bestuur*—the Council—Commandant J. F. Botha, solidly capable of gracing an authority in a more sophisticated environment. He, with Diederick Prinsloo, was the *voorlezer*—the reader—at devotions: always reminding those present that they were the Lord's own people.

'*Nor will His covenant e'er be broken* . . .'

Such was this tightly organized, closed community of the Trek. Such was this strange company into which I, Will Worthington Jordan, had so precipitately entered: I who was not only of another language and cultural background, but also of another race . . .

9

The Cunene hippo-hunt would be undertaken without further delay. For people such as these, isolated here in one of the most inaccessible parts of Africa, a hippo-carcase was a rare prize.

At the beginning of August that year we trekked in a convoy of twenty wagons through the dense bush country north of Kaoko Otavi, due south of the final one hundred mile reach of the Cunene on its way to the sea. For long distances we had to hack our way through primeval forest. Mopani here was sixty to eighty feet high. On the Ehombo heights, above the river, there were giant anas, baobab, mulemba, omuandi and omumborombonga. Far to the north-west lay a range of mountains showing remarkable vertical layers of black dolomite, sandwiched in between blue shale.

'The Zebra Mountains,' Gert Alberts said. The name had been given by those who had already got to the river.

Wary but inquisitive Ovahimba—first cousins of the Ovaherero—appeared from out of the bush, and watched the Trek go by. The men laughed at us with filed teeth. The women shook their *ekori* headpieces and clapped their hands, shaking bracelets of heavy red copper.

From the top of the Ehombo we descended into the humid valley, at a point where the river ran blue-green and deep between high banks overgrown with the greatest anas in all Africa. *Oorkant*—the other side—was now visible through the dense haze. There it was, a tremendous expanse of bush with a range of great mountains showing up faintly in the far distance.

'Angola,' I said as I stood on my wagon. Others had scrambled into trees or climbed rocks to see better. It was the first time I had seen that country from afar. It gripped us all.

'Some two days' trek from down below here lies the great waterfall,' I said. 'Above that is Humbe. If I judge well, the trek road to Moçamedes lies over the far mountains. They are the Serra da Chela. There are excellent highlands there!'

We completed the last stages of the journey down to the river itself. The calm, Rhine-like flow of the water was suddenly changed into the flood of the Tjimahaka rapids. Here the laager would be sited. Up river was the hippo-water, extending some forty miles to the great waterfall.

Full, exciting days down there at the river . . .

Days of gunsmoke, hippo fat, and endless talk around endless fires . . .

Mornings with the sun rising, the hunters would go up river to the open waters. The hippos would come up from blue-green depths, blowing and snorting, watching us warily over bulging eye-ridges. When the sun grew hotter, they would take shelter in the dense reeds of the river banks. At night they would graze among the waterberry trees and the lush grass of marshy banks. Like little drifting islands they would float in the water.

Shots would ring out, echoing back from black dolomite hills.

The green-blue water would turn red. On the sandbanks crocodiles would crash into the stream. After a while, if one were lucky, the carcase of the shot hippo woud rise to the surface. Then one would go out in a dug-out canoe. The carcase would be secured with ropes. Slowly it would be pulled towards the south bank. With the aid of Himbas drawn to the river by the sound of shooting, and teams of oxen, the carcases would then be dragged up the bank to level ground under giant anas.

The prospects were that the great fat-hunger of the Trek would eventually be appeased. Under the trees, at roughly constructed tables, the womenfolk stood cutting up hunks of fat into strips, trimming it, washing it all to a shiny whiteness. The young girls carried the strips on wooden trays to sunny flats, setting them out on the grass. There it lay, like snow on the Cape mountains. The Himbas, hacking at the carcases, fought noisily with each other for choice titbits. The hunters, tired after a hard day's work, sat under the anas. Clouds of tobacco smoke hung in the lifeless air. There they sat, drinking coffee, cleaning their guns, talking, and ever talking.

The sunlight lay pleasantly on the waters of the river. Only the fish-eagles cried from the heavens; their strange, lonely cry . . .

At nights the elephants came down to the river. When they discovered our presence, they trumpeted and thundered away into the bush, crashing tremendously through the trees.

'Brother Jordan,' Gert Alberts said one day, 'I have investigated the chances of getting through the river here. One can do it at Tjimahaka. The water there is not too deep. We would like to go to *oorkant*.'

And Barend Bouwer said: '*Oom* Gert, I have heard that the nations are particularly fierce over there. Mester Will? You must tell us, because our people are eager to find out for themselves. Maybe there are good hunting grounds!'

'The hippo-water here has been emptied!' Botha said. He lay there, stretched out on his back, smoking, watching the sky through the foliage above him. 'Will? We must form a commando. *Oom* Gert, we must do it!'

Stout womenfolk gathered around the tables, talking, laughing, slashing with their knives. They were dressed in print dresses, workaday *kappies*, flat *veldschoens* and aprons. Mountains of fat were heaped up by the Himbas on their tables.

I listened to their lively talk and divined something I had long suspected: this sweet-faced girl who had listened so intently to Gert Alberts telling about the long ride to the sea . . .

The *tantes* winked at each other. Did Nellie la Grange perhaps know what *Oom* Gert had said on such and such a day, at such and such a time? When, for instance, would the dried fat be enough for them to load on the wagons and take back to the laagers? Nellie blushed. The *tantes* slapped their strips of fat on the tables, bayed with laughter until Nellie herself could suffer it no longer, and fled . . .

Dina Lombard brought me gifts of dried hippo fat and well-filled honey-comb. 'This is now for Mister,' she said, as if in confidence, 'who came to fetch us there where we once stood at the poisonous waters.'

'Mister,' Kleinveld Labuschagne explained, 'this honey is as white as hippo fat, as Mister may see. This is because it is from the flowers of the baobab, which are as big as saucers.'

'*Meneer*,' Lisa Lombard said, gazing at me with level eyes, 'will *Meneer* also go to to *oorkant*?'

'Why do you ask, dear child?'

'So everybody says, *Meneer*!'

'Who knows, Lisa.' Her face was turned up towards me. There was the freshness of the morning on it. 'We shall have to see. Would you also like to go to *oorkant*?'

'I wish to be there where the water is strong, *Meneer*. I wish to see water which will never come to a standstill; and which is good and pure to drink!'

She had grown out of the fever, she had shaken it off completely, but some memory remained. Yet, her youth had triumphed.

'This *Oom* Gert,' *Tante* Louwrens said, coming up from behind, 'is like an old goat among the young ewes.'

The *tantes*, slapping down their hippo-fat on the tables, laughed again. 'Yet a good man, cousin Lenie,' Ella Lombard said, 'is a rare treasure. Nell*ieee*? Where are you, my child? All heaven above, she is so shy. But go now, Lisa child, and tell Nellie to come back from where she is hiding. We must make coffee.' Turning towards me again, she added: '*Meneer*, you must know: it is not easy for a woman to be alone when once she has had a man. One has deep thoughts. So, too, it is with a man.'

10

Then came the day when the commando left for *oorkant.*

One morning we were shocked by the news that Pieter Maritz-Botha had been killed during a brush with the Ombalantu Ovambos on the north bank of the river above the great waterfall.

The commando, having safely crossed at Tjimahaka, had visited a number of Angolan villages, looking for corn which might be purchased. At the same time they had wished to find out whether there were any Portuguese in the vicinity.

I had intended accompanying the group, but a bout of fever had kept me to my wagon. 'You will have to hack your way through much of the bush on the other side,' I had said by way of farewell. 'It is even denser than that of Ehombo. On the heights above the big waterfall there is an Ombalantu kraal. You will meet some Portuguese officials at Humbe, busy looking after the slave trade, the sale of *aguardente,* and their black concubines. In Ukuanyama, in the country of King Nambadi, you may come across two Catholic priests, Fathers Delpech and Rothan, who will offer you excellent coffee. The road from Ondangua to Humbe runs through Ukuanyama. Ride warily, my friends; and look after yourselves!'

The commando, led by Gert Alberts and Louw du Plessis, included Pieter Maritz-Botha; Andries Alberts, son of Gert; two brothers of Louw du Plessis, Jan and Phillip; Johannes Grobler; Gert and Freek van der Merwe, and others.

'To Humbe and back you can trek in fourteen days,' I said to the leaders. 'If the bush is not too difficult. Above the great waterfall you may find a wagon-drift. Please investigate it; and see if it is negotiable.'

'Our intention, *Meneer,*' Gert Alberts answered, 'is to investigate all we find. The land *oorkant* looks good and healthy to us. Our people back at the laagers would like to know all about it.'

For days I lay in my wagon, fretting about the safety of the commando. Sometimes I would ask myself: 'Am I really where I am; or is it just some strange fantasy of a fever-stricken body?' At such times resistance would painfully assert itself. No sense, I would decide, in nursing such thoughts. Patience was still the watchword: patience and the clear will to create something orderly out of all this chaos. This at least was certain: whatever happened, we would not turn back.

Then, at last there was the morning the commando returned . . . I heard the splashing of the horses as they came through the drift at Tjimahaka, rising above the dull thunder of the rapids. Perhaps it was the calling of the women, telling me that the commando was approaching, which suddenly sharpened my senses. Peering out of my wagon I saw the riders come up one by one, haggard and tattered . . .

Now they all stood before me with wet, shivering, bare-backed horses. I climbed out of the wagon, greeting them as they dismounted. What on earth had happened, I enquired.

A lot had happened. Could I not see? They had barely escaped with their lives. A nice ending for a commando expedition!

Now the womenfolk were coming up from all sides, to embrace their men. Then they stood silently listening as the story was told. But even before that they heard the news: one of the party had not returned: Pieter Maritz-Botha. Loud wailing immediately rose on all sides. Soon mothers were comforting their daughters, and the daughters themselves were sobbing. Jan Labuschagne, with head hanging and with arms resting on his knees, glowered and said: 'Is it a true heart-sore you feel? No, that man was a favourite amongst you! And now he is dead!'

At that there was more wailing, then a sharp reprimand from *Tante* Louwrens. What now? Did they not know how to behave at the news of death? What sort of weakness was this?

Perched on my wagon *kist* I remained unmoved. Perhaps I knew my friend too well. Pieter Maritz-Botha was just not the sort to end his life in a tragic way.

'*Meneer*,' Gert Alberts explained, 'we rode as you told us, keeping towards sunrise. The bush was so thick, often we could not find a way through it, and had to hack a lot to clear a way. This had to be done for many miles. After two days we came to the 'Vambo kraal you spoke of. There the chief told us to wait some time, because he first wished to consult king Nambadi, who was above him. He gave us two guides, however, to show us where we could off-saddle and stay overnight. *Meneer*, it was above the great waterfall where a branch comes into the Cunene from the south. The guides showed us where we could stay: where the Cunene makes a sharp bend, just above the place where the drift is of which you spoke; where one may cross with the horses without even wetting your feet. I thought to myself, this place we have been shown here is dangerous. "Men, be on your guard!" I said. "As sure as the sun will rise, the nations will come! They will come and kill us here!" However, there we slept. The men were tired, and it was already getting dark. Two stood guard all night. But nothing happened. By morning we were feeling safer, but too soon. The whole bush there is full of mupel trees, and there was a good crop of fruit on them. So we gathered the mupels, because we were hungry. The sun had not yet risen. Suddenly we heard a great noise coming from the bush. It was where the river straightens out again. Suddenly it was if hell itself had opened and all its devils were pouring out. There they came, blowing their battle horns and screaming terribly. Gert van der Merwe climbed into a tree, from where he could see an army of 'Vambos coming through the bush. But all our things were still there where we had laagered. So we ran back and looked for our horses, which had not been saddled. These we caught as best we could. *Meneer*, have you ever tried to saddle a horse when the enemy attacks from all sides: blowing its battle horns, screaming to high heaven, and shooting arrows? On three sides we had the river, and only one small *poort* through which we could escape. We jumped on the horses, just as they were. Everywhere one looked there were nothing but 'Vambos. So we had to shoot while galloping bare-backed through the trees. *Meneer*, that is no easy thing to do. Yet, by the grace of God we could flee to safety. And here we are now, all except Pieter Botha.'

Around us sobbing and wailing set in anew. Dina Lombard clicked her tongue and looked about her. I, still there on my *kist,* sat wondering.

'Pieter Botha was the last of us to mount his horse,' said Louw du Plessis. 'When Piet got hold of him at last, there was only one thing to do: take to the river. The last we saw of Pieter Botha, he was in mid-stream, still on the horse, his gun-bearer clinging to the horse's tail.'

Above the keening of the women, somebody asked: 'But what about the crocodiles?'

There was all that sudden clamour from the river. Strange, I seemed to realize at once what it was. 'Someone is in trouble,' I said, looking up sharply.

We had all got up from where we were sitting. The next moment we were running down to the water's edge. We were running to a quiet little bay where some women and girls had been bathing in seclusion. We were running through the trees, and the shouting had increased.

In after years I would tell: 'I was there at the river that day when Hester Bouwer dragged Nellie la Grange from the jaws of death. You might think this is hyperbole, but this is exactly what took place. The crocodile had taken Nellie, and Hester went into the river and grabbed her by her long black hair. There was a terrible tug of war, and Hester pulled Nellie from the river, crocodile and all. I saw it happen.'

And I remembered the shouting, the shooting, the curses, the tears. I remembered the cheers too, when the reptile splashed back into the river. Its jaws were bloody.

I remembered Gert Alberts falling over the white river stones to get to Nellie. I remembered him kneeling next to her with a tortured face, trying in vain to stop the blood flowing from a lacerated thigh. Sweat was streaming down his face. From the high bank of the river men were shooting at the water.

I remembered Hester Bouwer, still standing in the water, beating wildly around her, challenging the river. She came wading back, her dress clinging to her thighs, like some legendary figure. Her eyes blazed and her lungs heaved. She was covered with blood. She had only her dress on, but she showed no shame.

'We had someone watching,' she said, choking in her words, 'but it came so swiftly and silently.'

'Yes, my child,' Ella Lombard said. 'But this is Satan in the flesh. And his ways are secret.' She removed her apron and gave it to Hester, who covered herself with it, restfully but deliberately.

'The next thing I saw,' said Hester, 'was Nellie disappearing.' She looked at the girl, lying on her back, moaning softly, holding on to her lacerated leg, with the blood seeping through her fingers. Barend Bouwer and two others were still patrolling the river bank, shooting at all that moved in the water. Meanwhile I had fashioned a tourniquet from a piece of linen, and now applied it to the injured thigh. Someone had gone to my wagon to fetch my medicine chest.

'Luckily,' I said, examining the wounds, 'the crocodile seems to have been a relatively young one.'

'Yet it was heavy,' said Hester.

'That I can well believe.' I was filled with admiration for what this woman had done.

Quite a crowd had now gathered. From various quarters sympathy and a great deal of advice was being offered. *Oom* Gert himself was now on his knees next to Nellie, holding her hand and comforting her with endearing words. 'Just lie still, Little One,' he kept on saying. 'All will be well!' He looked up at me and I sensed what he wanted to say.

'Just please stand back,' I said to the crowd. 'Please don't excite her unnecessarily.' The onlookers drew back, watching us in silence now from a short distance. Dina Lombard brought my medicine chest and Kleinveld Labuschagne brought a can of hot water. I cleansed the wounds, disinfecting them with phenol. No arteries had been injured, as far as I could judge.

While the stitching was being done, Nellie bit her lip and sometimes twitched as the needle penetrated her tender flesh. Both *Oom* Gert's horny hands were clasped around hers. 'It will soon be over, Little One,' he kept assuring her. 'It will soon be over!'

When at last it was all done *Oom* Gert kept kneeling at her side. Now she was smiling through her tears. A *katel* was brought, and on this she was carried to *Oom* Gert's wagon. Next to me Dina Lombard was clapping her hands for joy, muttering: 'My doctor, oh yes, my doctor!'

Re-packing my medicine chest, I thought to myself: So they survived . . . They had lived through two and a half centuries of Africa, ever treading the tight thin line between tragedy and comedy . . . Africa had done its best to get them down . . . There had been the Xhosa of the Eastern Border, the Ndebele of Great Marico, the Zulu of Natal . . . There had been the soaring heights of Quatlamba, the endless plains of the Highveld . . . There had been the Kalahari Thirstland, the marshes of the Okavango . . . There had been the myriad snapping, roaring, trumpeting animals of grasslands, bush and rivers . . . All had been met . . . A great many had fallen by the wayside . . . Hardly anyone had not had his or her share of suffering . . . They were hardened men like *Oom* Gert, Louw du Plessis, Barend Bouwer . . . They were big-hearted *tantes* like Chrissie Louwrens, Mina Botha or Sannie Robbertze . . . They were slim girl-women like Tina du Plessis, or Nellie la Grange . . .

The talk around us now was about the seven-year-old child of Andries Alberts who threw sand into the crocodile's eyes when Hester Bouwer pulled it out of the water, hanging on to

Nellie's leg. Only then would it let go . . .

I marvelled at it all. I felt the keen pleasure of knowing that my judgement of my friends had not been altogether wrong. They were simple, complicated souls. They were not easily to be dismissed.

This was further confirmed when the missing and prematurely mourned-for Pieter Maritz-Botha himself turned up one afternoon just as the sun was setting.

There he was, none the worse for his adventures. He came galloping up between the trees of the south bank, waving his hat. Although his horse was foam-flecked, he still rode in a spirited way. The mucharra and hookthorn had torn his fine skin-jacket to shreds. Still, there was no mistaking the old self-assurance. It was that of a man who believed that life was on his side.

'Hallo, hallo!' he greeted all who came tumbling out of their wagons. And when handshakes, kisses, hugs and embraces had run their course, he sat there in the midst of a throng. He sat there drinking coffee, eating doughnuts, and accepted from me a tot of good Cape brandy.

'The story, my friend,' I said cosily, 'the *full* story is what we need.' For his sense of the dramatic had made him give it in instalments; and more people had now gathered.

And the full story was eventually told.

There he had been, he said, trying to catch his horse, with a blood-thirsty enemy storming at them from all sides, blowing their battlehorns, sending down swarms of arrows. By the time he had his horse bridled and saddled—no bare-back flight for Pieter Maritz-Botha!—there was no escape except by way of the river. The current was strong; the river, as everyone knew, was swarming with crocodiles. The gun-bearer had hold of the horse's tail. For some while all went well. They could use the current. Alas, within a few yards of the south bank, the gun-bearer suddenly yelled and disappeared.

'I turned back,' Botha said in conclusion. 'I looked for the poor sinner. But he was gone; as gone as gone can be! Now I had to get to the bank, or be taken myself!'

Darkness caught him at last and he lost his way in the dense forest. For many hours he had to ride detours through the Kaoko hills to avoid being torn to pieces by the mucharra and the hookthorn.

11

Early in November, with the heat lying in a motionless haze over everything, we got back to the laagers with our wagons loaded to the tent-ribbings with dried hippo fat, dried meat, sjamboks made of hippo hide, honey, and a little ivory. At Kaoko Otavi and Otjitundua there was great joy at our return, and even greater joy at the produce of the hunt.

A Bushman had brought a letter for me in a cleft stick from Namutoni. It was from Harry Hart, who worked for the Erikssons. Even in a wild and inaccessible country news travelled in its own, secret way. Hart had heard that I was with the Trekboers. Now he and his colleagues needed me. Axel Eriksson had not yet returned from the Cape and his brothers were at Ghanzi, Ngami, and in the Okavango country.

The letter was disturbing. Hunters left by Hart at Namutoni had been visited by a band of Ovambos from Ondangua. They were perfectly friendly and only wished to exchange some corn for tobacco and knives. On the morning of 15 July, however, the three white men were surprised while enjoying their early morning coffee, and taken prisoner. The Ovambos claimed their guns and horses.

'. . . Thereupon they were taken to the kraal of Chief Kambonde,' the letter said. 'Headman Himene stated that the prisoners were Boers who had been captured. Whereupon the chief ordered the prisoners to be killed, which sentence was duly carried out. It seems that there is a great fear of the Boers amongst the Chief's people. Please come to assist us in the investigations, also to reassure Kambonde . . .'

Piet Botha, the Labuschagnes, Jan Robbertze, the Venters (with young Adriaan) had left on an elephant-hunt near the Zebra Mountains. Barend Bouwer, Louw du Plessis and a group of others had gone south to the Otjikuvare flats. It would have been inadvisable to take more of the menfolk out of the laager. There was no alternative: I had to go to Namutoni.

It was managed in twelve stages, thanks to the faithful assistance of my two servants. I met Hart at Namutoni and he was relieved to see me. With him were Bjorklund and Skoglund, who were also in Eriksson's employ. The same day we left Namutoni, travelling northwards, following the old trek-route on the east rim of the White Pan. A week later we reached Olukonda and

Ondangua. Olukonda was the Finnish mission-station on the outskirts of Kambonde's kraal.

Rautanen and Reignonen, who had founded the mission a few years earlier, led the way to the kraal. Kambonde, who had just recently acceded to the throne of Ovamboland, was locked in a struggle with his brother Nehale. Nehale, although younger, had claimed the throne.

Kambonde, in his early twenties, appeared to me to be intelligent, arrogant, and on the defensive. Yet, Rautanen had assured me that what had happened to Eriksson's men was unlike the Ovambos. I was inclined to agree. Still, I found little comfort in knowing the reason for the excesses. It had all happened, they said, because of fear of the Boers.

I talked to Kambonde in Otjiherero in his holy of holies. This was the heart of the intricate maze of pallisaded compartments and passageways which constitutes an Ovambo kraal.

'The Boers the king has been hearing about are the most peaceful people I have yet met in this country,' I said. 'The king need not fear any attack on his land by them. Whatever land they seek will be purchased in a lawful manner.' Rautanen supported me; and Kambonde, with sweatbeads gleaming on his forehead, seemed to be comforted.

Who would sell the Boers land? he asked. It was far too early to tell, I answered. At the moment it seemed as if the Trek might continue into Portuguese territory. But nothing, as yet, had been decided. This seemed to pacify the king. For the truth of what Jordan had stated, he could vouch, Rautanen said in Oshindango. The Trekboers were a peace-loving people. It was a great pity that the hunters had been mistaken for Boers . . .

Interjections by members of Kambonde's council now convinced me that news of the Ombalantu skirmish had reached Ondangua. Yes, I said, there had been this brush between the exploring party and the people of the kraal. They were Ombalantus. They had unnecessarily attacked the Boer horsemen. Did I know of the people who had been shot by the Boers? No, I answered. In any event, if it had taken place, I could assure the king (mindful of my own future safety when travelling through his country) that the Boers had acted in self-defence.

Kambonde and his council considered my words. Yes, I heard them say, this man Jordan was known to them. They trusted him . . .

I was greatly relieved. Still, neither Kambonde nor any of his headmen would commit themselves. Rautanen and I were allowed to go, and there were no more questions.

Back at Olukonda that afternoon, where the Finns had created a part of their northern homeland for themselves in buildings of compacted earth and steep, grass-thatched roofs, Rautanen said: 'We all regret the things that have happened. That is what men come to when they are moved by fear. We have been hearing of this panic about the Trekboers for some time now.'

Rautanen fell silent. Then he said quietly: 'We have but one thing to do as missionaries: to continue to preach the Word of God, to the best of our ability.'

His words returned to me as I trekked back in easy stages to the laagers in the Kaoko. I went via Ogandjera and Ombombo-Ovambo, due west of Ondangua. This was a more direct route than the way I had come. Heavy rain, however, delayed our progress. At least a dozen times we got bogged down in the mud. Days came when Izak would lead the team of oxen for hours with the waters swirling about his hips. So, it took us more than a fortnight to reach the western limestone—the hardveld. Here for the first time we could give our sorely tried animals some decent rest.

The slowness of the trek back to the Kaoko afforded me much opportunity for thought. One fact I had ignored in the past had now to be recognized: the Boers were not popular. That, and the fact that they had inspired general anxiety, had to be faced, deplorable as it was. Now I was again reminded of what John Caine had said.

Gert Alberts had written to Coates Palgrave from Rietfontein, asking whether there would be room for the Boers in Damaraland. That was just about the time Robert Lewis had caused Palgrave to believe that Damaraland extended from the mouth of the Cunene to Rietfontein. At Okahandja Palgrave had said: 'The hatred of the Damaras for the Trekboers continues unabated. Every proposal I have made for locating them has been unfavourably received.'

This was Caine's evidence and what had now happened in Ovamboland seemed to confirm it. The fact was, the native peoples feared and hated the immigrants. Yet, knowing the Trekboers as intimately as I did, I could find no grounds for it. Indeed, uncompromising toughness had expressed itself in individual characters like Hendrik van Zyl of Ghanzi. But Van Zyl regarded himself as a 'Colonial Englishman'. His massacre of the Bushmen had also shocked the ordinary God-fearing Trekboer.

A clue was afforded by what had happened in Natal nearly forty years earlier. The greatest of all indigenous African armies had been defeated. The Boers had purchased part of Natal from Dingane, king of the Amazulu. Dingane had lured a party of sixty under Pieter Retief into his kraal, and had killed them all. The Zulu had then sought a general massacre of all the Boer immigrants in Natal. It had ended in the Battle of Blood River, where the Zulu had been broken by a handful of Trekkers. Had the history of Blood River now penetrated so far to the west? Was that the cause of all this hatred? Was it indeed a matter of dread, as Rautanen had stated?

The laager was a tightly closed institution. No one from outside could penetrate its fastness. For such it remained an unknown quantity. But one thing was abundantly clear: the Trekboers were concerned with finding their own land, their own distinctive future. 'Freedom!' Gert Alberts had said in his staccato manner. 'To where we have our own!'

And Diederick Prinsloo, gripping his shiny olive-wood stick, had added: 'To continue northwards, to where we may find a Land of Rest; through the way of the wilderness . . . Thou shalt bring them in, and plant them in the mountain of thine inheritance!'

The heart of the matter, I decided, was that no one here in the far west could see this as a legitimate passion. Yet it was the will of a people to find its own future. It was strictly confined, but it was not inhuman.

Jolting onwards on my wagon, I finally concluded: there was always still Rehoboth. It was a question of attitude. I still had hopes of convincing my friends, for common sense supported me.

12

At the beginning of February I was back at the laagers.

A surprise awaited me. The Cape Relief Committee, which had only seriously begun its work the previous September, had acted swiftly. The two schooners *Swallow* and *Christina* had been chartered, loaded and sent up to Fort Rock on the Kaoko coast. This information was contained in a letter from one Haybittel, awaiting me at Kaoko Otavi. The Relief Committee, Haybittel wrote, had hoped to land the goods at Fort Rock with the assistance of small boats. He himself would then lead an expedition inland to search for the Trek.

Alas, the schooners, on completing their voyage of some 1,500 miles, had discovered Fort Rock to be little more than a name. There was nothing to afford shelter. So the ships had returned to Walwich Bay, and Haybittel had come to the Kaoko to seek out the Trekboers. The goods would have to be fetched at the Bay. Commandant Botha had told him that for the forty wagons necessary to convey the goods there were not enough trek-oxen. He would therefore return to the Bay at once and make arrangements for oxen to be sent.

On board the *Swallow* were also Dr Palgrave, Axel Eriksson and the Reverend Lion Cachet, who had also undertaken the voyage. The Reformed Church was anxious to regain contact with those of its members who had now been lost for years.

Matters in the two laagers had, however, in some ways deteriorated. The heavy rains had brought the fever back, and a great many people were confined to their wagons and some had died. There was also a great shortage of clothing.

With Haybittel's oxen only arriving at the end of the month, the second week in March was already approaching before the convoy of wagons could begin the long journey down to the Bay and back. In his letter Haybittel had also given the assurance that the Herero chiefs had promised a safe passage for the Trek through their territory. That, at least, was comforting.

Since my return from Ovamboland I had been hearing more and more talk of Angola as the true destination of the Trek. Especially those who had skirmished with the Ombalantus on the far side of the Cunene thought this way. According to Botha, he had even been in contact with some Portuguese officials. These had promised the Trekboers a golden future in Angola. I offered no comment.

During March, trekking down to the Bay in that long line of wagons, one could sense the growing tension in the country. It was in the very dust one breathed. Then, during the short stop-over at Omaruru there were the first visible signs of something brewing.

Where was Axel Eriksson? He would have pinpointed it all. He would have given me the exact information. But Eriksson had left for the Okavango country a few days before our arrival. So I was left with a sense of loss at having missed my friend. His months at the Cape had probably, as in the case of his mentor, Andersson, given rise in him to a great longing for the open veld. It happened to us all.

It was *Missionar* Viehe who at last supplied the information. Things were getting troubled in Damaraland, he said. To this he quickly added: 'Your letter in the Cape newspaper, *Herr* Jordan, was of no assistance.'

I looked up in surprise. It was the letter I had written to *The Cape Times* from the Bay. In it I had deplored the increasing lawlessness. This, I had pointed out, was taking place with the Union Jack flying from a pole in Okahandja. Surely, I said to Viehe, I had merely done my simple duty. Or did he wish to condone atrocities?

I had no right, Viehe said, to make such an allegation. The sooner I realized, too, that Kamaherero took a serious view of my press-writing, the better.

I had had enough of it all. 'The facts stated in the letter can easily be checked,' I said abruptly. 'If they can seriously be disputed, then you may well do so. I am sure the press will accommodate you.'

'That is not the point,' Viehe answered emotionally. 'There is a time for everything. *Herr* Jordan, you go about things in a way which can profit no one. One should take a realistic view of things.'

'Agreed,' I answered, checking my temper. 'But the essence of realism here is to acknowledge the lawlessness which exists and the need for security. If things are allowed to go their own rotten way, we shall have new explosions before many months have passed.'

Thereupon he started a long discourse on his knowledge of the territory and what was taking place. This, he said, was true of all the missionaries devoting their lives to the native peoples of the country. What they were doing, they were doing to serve God and their fellow man. Agreed, I said. Who could dispute that? However, it would be better to make allowances for each other's mistakes as well as for each other's sincerity.

I made little impression on Viehe. I would have liked to have discussed the matter with Manasse Tjisiseta, but the meeting could not be arranged.

There was a feeling of growing enmity in the air. My *bambuse* came and told me that he, in fact, had been threatened with death. He had also heard that 'Mister' could be 'seen to' at the first possible opportunity. 'Mister' was no friend of the Ovaherero. I shrugged my shoulders at this information, saying: 'Well, let them do what they will. They will soon find out that we won't take things lying down. Meanwhile, you, Izak, and you, Kairob, stick around where we can see you!'

Everywhere people were carrying guns: mainly cap-locks and muzzle-loaders, lethal enough in the hands of those who knew how to use them. Signs of nervousness had now also become apparent among the Namas living there in their reed-huts along the Swakop. Was the ten years of 'peace' for which Hugo Hahn had once laid the foundation now nearing its end? If so, what about all my fine plans for a civilized order? Perhaps Viehe had been right. Perhaps it was time to face the facts in the light of my own, heart-felt ideals.

At Otjimbingue a week or so later I saw John Caine, just about to leave for Okahandja, where Robert Lewis had been 'very busy' and from where he had asked for Caine's assistance. Busy with what? Assisting in what? Caine like everybody else was on his guard, referring darkly to my writing in the Cape press, indicating that it had caused considerable reaction at Okahandja. The suggestion was that he did not like it either. To this I answered that I had never imagined the truth to be popular. Caine once more admonished me in his old way, saying that there were better means to effect what one wished to do without being blunt. Bluntness, I answered, was the right medicine for blunt people.

We parted company and I felt that our friendship had suffered. 'By the way,' I remarked, as a sort of parting shot, 'you know of course that Coates Palgrave is here? I think you will find that he agrees with us!'

Palgrave and I ran into each other in front of *Hälbichs Anwesen*, a few days later.

'Coates!' I exclaimed.

'Will!'

We shook hands heartily. I was genuinely glad to see him. He had just arrived from Otjimbingue.

So, where was he off to, I asked. To Okahandja, he replied.

Musgrave was still there. Poor Musgrave, I thought, still there looking after the Union Jack on its tall flag-pole . . . Things were rather uncertain, Palgrave assured me. He seemed to want to avoid the subject and switched it to the Trek. So, the Trek had got settled, he asked. And we were on our way to pick up the goods? Glad to have been of assistance! Was it true that the Trekboers had decided on Angola? Perhaps that would be best in the circumstances . . .

The day was hot, and I was weary. I wanted to get back to my wagon: to take a rest before setting off on the final stages of our 800-mile journey to the Bay. One would have to wait and see whether the peace could be maintained, I said. Things seemed to be deteriorating. There was all this tension in the air. It was like dust in August before the rains came.

Poor Palgrave. He looked tired and disappointed, standing there in front of me under a straggly camelthorn, seeming to be fishing around in his own mind for the right things to say. This was a frustrated man, I decided. The chances of British Protection had receded and the Transgariep was a forgotten country. Nobody wanted it. General murder and anarchy seemed to be the only definite promise for the future.

'What have you seen, Coates?' I asked presently. 'Do you agree that things here are getting worse?'

'You are right, Will,' he conceded. 'The situation is bad. The first shot fired will plunge this country into war again.' His eyes found mine. 'You know, of course, that I took Wilhelm Maherero with me to Cape Town. He is the one stable element in the Herero order. Wilhelm might yet have a good influence on his father. You agree, surely?'

'Wilhelm seems to be the only pebble on the beach at the moment,' I said. 'A very lonely pebble.'

'One can only do one's duty,' he said after a while. 'I have given much of my life for the cause of better government in this country . . .' Now he shrugged his shoulders. 'To what effect? I have not given up all hope yet. By the way, did you hear what happened to Old Hendrik van Zyl?'

Now I looked at him in surprise, anticipating what he was going to tell me.

'The old man had it coming to him for a long time, I suppose. It was that arch scoundrel Paul Visser that got him in the end.'

Visser, I quickly reminded myself, was an Orlam chief with

headquarters at Gobabis. He was given to freebooting and brigandage.

'Paul Visser and his gang went to Ghanzi and took Old Hendrik prisoner. They had some sort of a mock trial, it seems, with Visser himself acting as judge and prosecutor. The end of the matter was that Old Hendrik was sentenced to death!'

Now I was shocked.

'. . . Presumably because Van Zyl himself had sentenced others to death. You know about that.'

'I can't see Visser as an avenging angel,' I said. 'What happened?'

'Van Zyl managed to escape, while Visser and his lot were helping themselves to his brandy. Well, he's at Okahandja now, from what I hear. Of course, all that he possessed at Ghanzi has been stolen. The old man has been reduced to poverty.'

'Well,' I said, with a touch of bitterness, 'this all goes to show just how far we have got. You will now understand why I have given so much thought and time to the idea of settling the Trekboers at Rehoboth. No doubt you have heard about it.'

He nodded, looking glum. 'At the moment Rehoboth seems to be the main trouble centre. You realize that, of course!'

'The Basters are getting it from all sides. Jan Jonker utters threats from Windhoek; Kamaherero does it from Okahandja. To this they add almost daily robbery. The Bergdamaras come down from the mountains and do likewise. You can see now what an ordered, civilized community, acting as a buffer between Namaland and Hereroland, might well have meant.'

He looked vaguely at me. 'But are you sure now that the Trekboers would fall in with such a scheme? As far as I can see, they are not interested in any settled occupation like agriculture. If they come to settle at Rehoboth, their hunting fervour would soon bring them into conflict with the Hereros and the Namas. You may find, instead of a buffer, a strange new alliance being formed to defeat a common enemy.'

There was a certain harsh truth in what he was saying. However, he was over-simplifying things.

'I must be off,' I said, shaking his hand. 'When are you leaving?'

'In the early morning.'

'Good luck!'

I smiled and slapped him lightly on the shoulder. I was

dogweary tired. The heat was oppressive. Why the shoulder-slapping gesture, I asked myself as I walked off. Palgrave was a defeated man. He knew it, and I knew it. Perhaps I had clumsily tried to comfort him; and perhaps comfort myself. This great, lovely, cruel land of South West Africa had defeated him, as it had defeated so many.

13

The question of the Trek's final destination was decided by events beyond our control a month or so after reaching the Bay.

While loading the goods from the *Swallow* and *Christina* onto forty wagons, there was ample opportunity to sound the Trek leaders who had come along on the future of their people. In the light of the growing unrest in the country Rehoboth was not mentioned any more. Instead the conversation seemed to drift easily to the subject of Angola.

Those highlands I had spoken of: where exactly were they situated? What was the climate like? How was the soil? How were the waters? Was there good hunting? Could the Cunene be reached in a week of easy trekking?

Yes, I would answer, perhaps a little diffidently. The Serras were more than six thousand feet high. There was fine water and an excellent climate. There were also good forests and good land for agriculture. The Cunene was an easy five days' trek from the central highlands. All this was meant as preface to what I usually wound up with: 'Gentlemen,' I would say again, 'you must not forget that Angola is a Portuguese country. Your ideal of an independent Boer state will have to be suspended, if not abandoned, if you decide to go there. Consider this well: the Portuguese are not going to give away anything, however much they might need you at the moment.'

For some reason or other my words never seemed to be taken seriously. Gert Alberts would always return to the idea that in such a 'big empty land' there would surely be some place which could, in time, become entirely their own. This was the prevalent belief.

My friends seemed to have boundless faith that, once settled in Angola, they could 'manage things'.

This was vague. Sometimes it smacked of danger. I got the

impression that some of the wilder ones like Jan Labuschagne even envisaged establishing themselves in Angola, then telling the Portuguese that they claimed the land by effective occupation.

Gert Alberts, however, would fly into a temper whenever there was even a remote suggestion of this. Would I be prepared to act as mediator, Alberts asked. Would I take a commission of riders over the river, over the mountains and down to Moçamedes? Would I negotiate with the Portuguese on their behalf? Of course, I assured him. Why not? I had said so in the Kaoko, and I had meant it. But the matter should only be finalized on the return of the convoy to the Kaoko. I would try to be there in the spring. Then, I supposed, things would be clearer.

The wagons, fully loaded, left the Bay at the end of July. Three weeks later, on the night of 23 August 1886, while I was busy attending to my accumulated mail, the turn of events decided for us.

I should have known just how near the explosion was. After all, hadn't two of my wagons which I had sent to Rehoboth been diverted by Kamaherero's people? Had they not been 'off-loaded' to the value of hundreds of pounds? This, I had duly been informed, was by way of reprisal for my 'enmity' towards the Herero nation.

It was a serious blow. For days I felt depressed. Sometimes I would even give vent to my feelings and damn the name of Kamaherero. At the same time I knew full well how futile this was. I had chosen to make my bed in a particular way. Now I had to lie on it.

The worst was that there was no longer any particular reason why I should expect better things from the Namas. Jan Jonker Afrikaander had sent me a message to the effect that he badly needed *skietgoed.** Mister Jordan had to 'make a plan', he said. The Red People were having a hard time of it.

I was still considering all this when the news from Okahandja reached the Bay. The night of 23 August had been a night of blood.

The trouble apparently had started some weeks before at Gurumanas, near Rehoboth village. The Ovaherero had illegally been using this place as a cattle post. A cow had disappeared from the Herero herds there. Immediately on discovering the loss, the

*Literally: shooting things i.e. ammunition.

local Herero headman, one Karuvingo, had attacked a neighbouring Nama village. Karuvingo had been killed in the ensuing fight, but so had the Nama headman, one Nu-Namab. The next day at dawn the Namas were again attacked, but the Hereros had been driven off. Thirty of the attackers were killed, but only a few Namas. Within a day or two the news of all this reached Okahandja: at precisely the same time as a group of prominent Namas, including Jan Aries, brother of Jan Jonker, had been attending a court case there. Musgrave, the 'British magistrate,' was at least maintaining a semblance of justice.

That very night Kamaherero, enraged at the news from Gurumanas, ordered his soldiers to kill each and every Nama in and around Okahandja. By a strange coincidence it was thirty years to the day after Jonker Afrikaander had slaughtered the Hereros here in similar fashion. This had happened on the 23 August 1850. This was vengeance as complete as could be wished for. Before the sun rose the next morning, every Nama within reach of the Hereros had been summarily killed. Nobody escaped.

At the Bay, with each new arrival of a wagon, or even people on horseback or on foot, the news was added to. In the whole country lying above and below the Middle Swakop, not a single Nama had been left alive. The slain, some declared, had been dragged to a deep hole at the foot of a mountain just outside of Okahandja. This hole, which some said was 'bottomless', had now been filled with dead.

Whatever hyperbole was attached to all this, one thing was clear: this was war and the end of the ten years of peace. It was no different to war anywhere. In many ways it was a lot worse. Knowing this country as I did, I knew that there would be no quick end to it. This would drag on for years. It would be mass attrition. It would continue until the struggling nations had finally worn each other down.

I wanted to get away from it all. I was sick unto death of all the violence, deceit, intrigue, robbery around me. I had done my best to bring the facts of the situation before the civilized world. But my voice was a small one. Now I just wanted to get away from it all, back to my friends of the laager.

Better things might well return. For the moment, however, it all looked pretty hopeless. Bouts of fever had been plaguing me. Maybe my reaction to the news from the interior was the flight of someone whose blood was running low. Maybe I had been too much of an individualist. Maybe I was, in fact, just another Palgrave . . .

I wanted to get to my friends. I had recorded the history of their wanderings and my pieces had appeared in the *Review*. I had not said anything about their future. Now I knew: I would lead a commission of riders to Moçamedes and act as the Trek's mediator with the Portuguese. Whether Portuguese West Africa could in fact give the Trek what it had so long been looking for was hardly an issue any more. War had broken out. The Trek had no alternative.

It would have to be Angola. On the High Serras this puritan community might well find sufficient to enable itself to lead the 'old Boer way of life'. Whether this could be meaningful, only the future would tell. For my part I would just be thankful to see them settled.

So, I would lead the commission; and all things going well, I would return with them to the laagers. After that I would come down to the Bay. Here I would wait for a schooner to take me to the Cape. I had not been home for years.

I could swim again in the cold, clear water of Hout Bay . . . wander on a misty morning along the eastern slopes of Table Mountain . . . go looking for mushrooms in the woods . . .

My mother's face would light up at my unexpected arrival at the little house under the oaks of Wynberg. She would shed tears at my safe return. She would look at me, hardly believing that it was I who had returned from the far country . . .

Yes, there was even the possibility that Axel Eriksson and I might undertake that long discussed journey to Nhembaland. We might do this together. We might do this even before my taking ship on the *Isabella*.

Good old Karevapu . . . I found him at Omaruru and his welcome was as heart-warming as ever. Concerning the things that had taken place at Okahandja, he could now give more details. Nobody could say how many people had been killed. There had been a lull in the fighting. But what had taken place was only the start. Everywhere one went there were preparations for war.

'Is Palgrave still at Okahandja?' I asked.

'The news has come here that he is at Gobabis!'

'Anyway, Karevapu, he is near enough to see the end of

Protection.'

'They tell of Kamaherero that when the killing started, he looked at the flag on its pole and said: "It blew this way, it blew that way. It blew us with it—this way, that way!" ' I stood wondering at all this. I looked up and saw Eriksson grinning at me.

'Maybe he is sharper than I imagined,' I said.

'We may still see that all is not so bad as it seems, eh?' He shrugged his powerful shoulders. 'There are yet the Erikssons of Omaruru, providing all the necessities for Damaraland. When the war comes in a bad way? Not so good for trade, Will. Not so good for anything; but my trust is in God.'

'My trust is in God,' I quietly repeated. 'Thank you, Karevapu.'

We took leave of each other. There were still sixteen days ahead of me on my way to the Kaoko. How I would have liked to have had Axel Eriksson with me . . .

'Axel,' I said before finally saying goodbye, 'if all goes well, you will have me here in the new year. Then if things have not got too bad, we'll set off together. To Nhembaland.'

His face lighted up with pleasure. He stroked his thick red beard. He rubbed his pate and confirmed: 'To Nhembaland, then!'

14

Before mid-September of that year I led the mounted commission of Trekboers to Moçamedes, as I had promised. The party included the laager commandant, J. F. Botha, Gert and Paul van der Merwe, Gert Alberts and his son Andries and Louw du Plessis. In spite of ever-present dangers, all went well. Andries Alberts, who kept the journal, wrote in firelight of the 'proud and arrogant nations we met'. Between Humbe and Huila, north-west of the Cunene, six men stood guard at night, guns at the ready. I was taking no chances. It was the old situation: a general dread of the Boers was preceding us.

Fifteen days out from Kaoko Otavi we passed over the Serra da Chela. The landscape was impressive. Grass slopes were like corn fields and forests with excellent workable timber were everywhere. There was also an abundance of lively streams. This was paradise after the brooding heat of the plains.

We descended from the six thousand foot escarpment of the Serras down to the coastal desert. We went via Capengombe and Pedra Grande, where granite monoliths reared themselves massively out of the desert floor, as at Ameib in the Namib.

An afternoon came when the glowing desert heat seemed to become milder. Then one could suddenly smell it—the sea.

It was a Friday afternoon. As we rounded a dune, the little white port of Moçamedes came into view. Soon gulls were riding the wind above us, squawking a welcome.

The Portuguese received us with great hospitality.

The war had shown no signs of abating. I had already forgotten about the dream of Rehoboth. My friends of the Trek were on the move again: a final trek from the waters of the Kaoko to the Highlands of the Serras. Matters had been settled easily, quickly and effectively with the Portuguese. Yes, they would be only too pleased to have settlers of the calibre of the Boers on their empty inland highlands. All the details could be worked out in time. The Trek had meanwhile to come and get settled at Humpata.

One should enjoy what one could, while there was still life to do so, I quietly decided. Life was short. Andersson had died at forty: in a lonely place, in the far northern bush of Ovamboland . . . It would need a search to find his grave.

The year 1880 had almost come to a close when I returned to Omaruru from the Kaoko. The Trek was at this time probably fording the Cunene above the great waterfall. Here I was at last; and here again was Axel Eriksson. And the war was around us.

'Has trade suffered?' I enquired as we sat drinking beer under the camelthorns.

He indicated a fleet of empty wagons standing about under the trees. 'It is as you see it, Will.'

'It's damnable, but it is also fine, Karevapu. Because now you can forget your worries, as I shall forget mine; and we set off on our trek!'

He rubbed his hands together and grinned. 'Nhembaland might even compensate one for some of the losses suffered,' he said. 'I believe we shall find the greatest virgin hunting country in all Africa up there: between the Cunene and the Zambesi. Can't wait to investigate it. But first, Will, you rest here at Omaruru, eh? We arrange our trek in plenty of time! Did I tell you of Palgrave?'

I looked up in surprise. 'Don't tell me he also got caught by Paul Visser and his gang!'

'Palgrave got away though, and lucky for him. All his great ideas—phewt!' He blew between his fingers. 'So we have justice, eh?'

'Justice is a prerogative of the powerful,' I said. 'And when every puny chieftain thinks himself to be God Almighty, there simply *is* no justice.'

Palgrave had indeed arrived at Okahandja. This was the tenor of a letter reaching Omaruru within the next few days. 'This accursed place', Palgrave had called Gobabis. Back at Okahandja, he had apparently discovered that Wilhelm Maherero, on whom all his hopes had been pinned, was no longer on speaking terms with his father. This was because of Kamaherero's attack on the unsuspecting Namas. Nevertheless, he and Palgrave did make an attempt to convince Wilhelm's father that a cease-fire was necessary. Kamaherero, sulking and proud, would have nothing to do with it. Not even Palgrave's warning that his name would yet stink in history had any effect on him.

After all, I now pointed out to Eriksson, why should Kamaherero not carry on with a successful war? It was all going his way at present. At Witvlei, according to reports, he had almost exterminated the Namas. Apparently about the only Nama to escape was Hendrik Witbooi, of whom Jan Jonker had once complained that he had been 'salved' by *Missionar* Ollp. Now all sorts of rumours were doing the rounds. While fleeing for his life through the Auas Mountains near Windhoek, Witbooi had heard a Heavenly Voice which had told him to stand firm, and take on him a 'hard task'. He should conquer the whole country for the Nama people . . .

Kamaherero obviously wished the war to continue. After all, why should he not consolidate his already impressive gains? At the same time it seemed as if the Namas themselves were finding a new unity. Jacobus Izak had sent a letter through Great Namaland summoning all Namas to the struggle.

'The stories fly like vultures,' Eriksson declared. 'They come from nowhere. What must we believe?'

What one could believe were the visible signs of continuing warfare. There was a never-ending line of black warriors coming to Omaruru. They bought what they needed, then disappeared again. Meanwhile their trade was of little use. They simply said that Kamaherero would pay for everything—later. Eriksson and

Co were expected to help finance the war.

A day or two later news reached us that the Basters, after some hesitation, had now finally decided to throw in their lot with the Namas. This was confirmed by Charles Lyon who arrived at Omaruru from the Okavango country. Lyon also told us that McNab, who had once accompanied us on the punitive expedition across the Okavango when the Trek was at Olifants Pan, had been hunting in the Waterberg, with a group of Basters. A band of Hereros had attacked them one night while they lay sleeping. All had been killed.

Irle, the Rhenish *Missionar* at Okahandja, had arrived a few days earlier and was staying with Viehe. I would have liked to have spoken to Irle, but had no desire to see Viehe again. So again it was Eriksson who kept me informed. Concerning the murder of McNab and his fellow-hunters, both Viehe and Irle had declared that it had all been a mistake. The attackers had taken the hunters for Namas belonging to Moses Witbooi, acting on instructions from Jan Jonker Afrikaander.

The very next day, however, I did get to see Viehe again. We were having coffee at the Erikssons when he walked in. Viehe greeted Axel and his wife—who was an Englishwoman—but ignored me. Had we heard the latest reports, he asked. Without more ado, he proceeded to give a dramatic account of an attack by the Namas under Jan Jonker on the Hereros under Aponda. This had happened at Barmen on 10 December, he said.

Studiously denying my very presence, Viehe then proceeded to give the details, obliquely directing them at me. I felt it was an easy victory for Jan Jonker. As one could expect from the Namas, however, they fell victims to their own arrogance. So busy were they celebrating their victory, gorging themselves on roast meat and getting drunk on gallons of rough brandy, that no watch was set out. The next morning, while they were still sleeping off their stupor, they were attacked by Wilhelm Maherero and eight hundred men. Fleeing in complete disorder, the Namas were shot to pieces, leaving all their wagons behind them. Alas, though, the news was also bad, for Wilhelm Maherero himself had been mortally wounded.

After having been taken to the mission house, he had died there. His wife, Magdalena, and Bam, the storekeeper at Okahandja, had come to fetch the body. Wilhelm had now been buried next to the church at Okahandja.

'Irle says that Kamaherero himself has now sworn never to put a foot inside his church again,' Viehe concluded.

It was suddenly quiet in the room. Mrs Eriksson wiped a tear from her eyes. Axel stroked his beard and said: 'This is a bad thing!' And I, at a loss to communicate my feelings, stood at a window and stared at the sunlight on the dusty road; at the silent green bush, and the deep pools of shadow under the trees.

'I'm sorry to hear it,' I said after a while. 'Wilhelm might yet have effected something. He was one of a few who still kept his head.' I was conscious of Viehe looking sharply at me.

Later that evening when Axel Eriksson and I were sitting at my laager fire, I said: 'Well, Karevapu, I take it that we are going on our journey. But first you take your wife and children down to the Bay. They need a change—some sea air, and a rest!'

He rubbed his pate, grinned. 'Yes, when all has been settled here, we go!' he said.

15

Towards the end of the first half of 1881 a measure of peace had returned to the country. Jan Jonker, according to reports, had gathered the remnants of his 'war' and was now reassembling them in the fastnesses of Gamsberg. This was a seven thousand foot mountain on the escarpment between Rehoboth and the Bay. There it stood like a Crusaders' castle, crowned with a layer of shimmering quartzite.

Meanwhile stories had reached me that Jan Jonker had been down to the Bay, enquiring after 'Mister Jordan', who would surely supply him with the 'necessary', so as to enable him to return to the fight.

But I was not in the Bay. Even if I had been, it would have made little difference. Apart from the fact that I had little desire to be embroiled in the new power struggle in any way, my business as a trader had suffered. This, at least, I could say for Jan Jonker and his Afrikaanders: they would not admit defeat. In a way, this showed character.

Character, in fact, was everywhere in evidence on the subcontinent. Bundles of newspapers reaching us in the Bay during March and April of that year brought us the first detailed news of the Boer rebellion in the Transvaal. Great Britain, it appeared, had had but a few thousand regular soldiers in the whole vast area south of the Limpopo. Even these had not yet fully recovered from the mauling which they had received at Isandhlwana in the Anglo-Zulu war. Bill Clay, arriving with the newspapers in the schooner, drily added to this that the whole Cape Colony was full of British soldiers who had deserted. No wonder the Transvaal Boers had been able to cut up a British force at Bronkhorstspruit near Pretoria. The Boers, Clay said, had been armed with Wesley Richards and could shoot straight. What about the Imperial troops? For some time their shooting was the theme for funny stories. But when the *Isabella* returned a month later, it brought the news that the war in the Transvaal had abruptly ended. The Boers, so the reports said, had attacked a strong Imperial force under General Pomeroy Colley on the lofty crest of Majuba Mountain in northern Natal. In spite of their meagre numbers, and the advantage for the British situated at the top of the mountain, the Republicans had triumphed.

This was not pleasant news at all for men like John Caine, Robert Lewis, Rule, Stevens, all staunch Empire loyalists. Robert Lewis had once remarked cuttingly that although I liked to refer to myself as an Englishman, in fact I was worse than the Boers. I shrugged this off. Being human, I said, was more important than being an Englishman.

At the Bay there was a general feeling that we had to get moving again. The weeks of forced leisure had been depressing. If, as hunter-traders, we could not trade, I suggested, then at least we could hunt. What about our virgin country to the far north, up between the two great rivers. Axel Eriksson grinned approvingly. 'Yes, of course,' he said, 'but why not. Let's see what we can get together.'

The group seemed to constitute itself. There were Charles Lyon, Todd, Behan and Llewellyn Andersson. He was a son of Charles John Andersson and had once worked for Hendrik van Zyl in the company of Pieter Maritz-Botha and Barend Bouwer. On his enquiring, I told him the story of Botha's narrow escape at the Cunene. 'At present he is somewhere in Angola,' I said. 'Elephant hunting. At the same time probably keeping his eyes skinned for the right wife. We may yet see him on our journey!'

The party finally consisted of thirteen hunters, fifty-eight servants, thirteen wagons and fifty-eight horses. We left Omaruru on a June morning, happy as schoolboys at the end of term. Women and children had all now been safely posted in the Bay for the duration. A message had also been received that the Colonial government would send a gunboat to lie in the lagoon and protect the harbour against attack. Was there any likelihood of this? We did not think so. Both parties in the struggle knew on which side their bread was buttered. The Bay was British territory.

So we then left for Nhembaland, and it became a great and happy experience. I loved it all. I loved the lordly trees; and sometimes even lordlier animals; I loved the landscape which never, even in its hardness, seemed to lose its poetry. I could abandon myself to the pleasant tension of venturing into the unknown. This, I reminded myself, must have been the way of the early pioneers: men like Sir James Alexander; Sir Francis Galton; Charles John Andersson, Fred Greene; the Chapmans . . .

What did it matter if the hunting was less successful? In the course of six months we could do no better than six elephants. We also shot fifty or sixty ostriches, a dozen or so lions, a fair collection of hippos, buffaloes, giraffes, and as many antelopes as we required. The bag could surely have been more profitable, but it became a secondary consideration. We were enjoying the land itself.

Axel Eriksson had turned ornithologist again, and was collecting birds as we trekked along: new species in a new country. In doing so, he was adding to his already magnificent collection. This would all go to the museum in Vänersborg, Sweden, where he had been born.

Even when the trek took us high up into the land of the Evares under King Nambinga, we enjoyed good health, only Axel Eriksson suffering from an attack of dysentery.

The company was lively, amusing, stimulating. Evenings would be spent around the laager fire, relaxing after a hard day's work, cutting a road for the wagons through dense bush. Charles Lyon solemnly proposed that Mr Gladstone of No 10 Downing Street be asked to accompany us on our next trek. The Prime Minister, according to the newspapers, had taken to tree-felling—for exercise . . .

All the old tales of our many wanderings were aired again. At times it would give rise to so much laughter that the animals in the bush for miles around must have started. At other times the talk would cause us to remember those who had accompanied us on our many treks and whose graves were now in lost and lonely places.

Some of the party even trekked to Humbe to take in provisions. The Catholic fathers there—Delpech and Rothan—told our men that the Trekboers at Humpata had become well-established. They had reached a working agreement with the Portuguese. 'Excellent', I said.

Maybe I could get to the highlands myself some day, I decided: see what was shaping there. In my innermost thoughts I still had doubts about my bedrock Calvinist friends. There they were now—in a Catholic country.

I suddenly found myself longing to see them all again: the Du Plessis, the Albertses, the Prinsloos, the Barend Bouwers . . . I thought of Hester Bouwer and the way she had stood there in the river that day. Before I had taken leave of the Trek in the Kaoko, she had come to my wagon to fetch some medicine.

'It was a brave thing you did,' I said to her again. 'I won't forget it.'

She was a handsome woman. She looked at me and said: 'But anybody else would have done the same.'

'Not everybody,' I answered. 'You got Nellie out alive, you know, crocodile and all. That took some doing.'

She smiled wanly, then thanked me for the medicine, and walked back to her wagon. Towards evening a servant brought me a little jar of veld-fruit preserves: 'for the medicine'.

I missed my friends. I missed Pieter Maritz-Botha: his very *panache*. I even missed the long-limbed, loud-mouthed Jan Labuschagne, ever ready to recount his weird experiences. Most of all I missed my little family of the marshes—old Ella Lombard and her child; *Ai* Dina and Kleinveld . . .

Charles Lyon, arriving back later than the others from Humbe, brought the choicest bit of gossip: Pieter Maritz-Botha had got married. To whom? To the demurest of the bunch . . . to Johanna Meyer, of all people. Botha himself had come down to the Cunene on a hippo-hunt, and had brought the news.

Well, I thought, timid little Johanna . . . What had happened to all the attractive, vivacious, impertinently pretty lasses of the Trek? I couldn't even remember Botha ever mentioning Johanna. What I did recall, however, was Johanna sitting there very primly at his feet, while he was telling of his epic adventures, her pale, serious little face turned up towards him. Quite clearly, there was more in that primness than was apparent to the eye.

Botha had arrived at Humbe on a lively Arab, Lyon said: hat cocked and wearing a fancy waistcoat . . .

'The Arab,' I commented, 'must be his purchase from Machiel Prinsloo. Piet always had an eye on it.'

Another bit of news concerned the fifteen-year-old daughter of Commandant Botha, who had married Arthur de Paiva, the Portuguese commander at Humpata. This was indeed another surprise. I could never have imagined a Trek girl marrying outside her own, intimate circle. Yet it had happened.

In turn, while at Humbe, our own people could tell of the battle of Majuba Hill, where the Boers had gained a great and decisive victory. In this way the news had at last reached Humpata.

All these things had been but an interlude. The journey to Nhembaland now seemed to take us further and further away from all that had previously weighed upon us. Strivings, hopes, disappointments seemed to lose their importance. Even the fact that we lost seventeen horses on the trek hardly worried us. *Carpe diem* was our motto. We were enjoying a new freedom.

16

On 18 December of that year we again reached Omaruru, travel-weary but in high spirits.

The whole settlement was humming with the talk of what *Missionar* Viehe was proudly referring to as 'the greatest battle that ever took place in the Transgariep'.

It appeared that Moses Witbooi and Jan Jonker Afrikaander, having regained their strength, had marched on Okahandja. At Osona, a few miles outside the town, Kamaherero and his army had awaited them. On 22 and 23 November the battle had raged. Once again the Namas were defeated, suffering severe losses. The story was that the road from Okahandja to Windhoek was strewn with the bodies of hundreds of dead Namas. Moses Witbooi fled back to the far south. And Jan Jonker returned to his impregnable Gamsberg.

We had forgotten about all this. Returning to Omaruru and being suddenly faced by it all again, I was sickened. Dear God, I had had enough of it. After all those wonderful, carefree days in an untroubled land, all this now fell upon me like a stench.

This latest exhibition of primitive savagery was just too much. Within even a few miles of Omaruru it was impossible to ride through the veld without being nauseated. Rotting bodies were lying everywhere. There had always been an element of risk journeying through the country. Now it had become well-nigh impossible.

Of all the hunter-traders in the territory, it was now apparent that the Erikssons of Omaruru had been most affected. The turnover of the once so flourishing business had dropped by two-thirds. Goods were daily being 'bought' by people who had no intention of ever paying for them. Wagons could no longer follow the old trek-routes. The long overland route through Great Namaland to the Cape was impossible. In spite of everything, my friend, Axel, still remained his old, large-hearted self.

'So, we see whether we can go east with cattle through the Thirstland,' he said. I looked at him and saw that he was serious. 'Friend Will! And if it does not work?' He gestured with his hands. 'I buy a good farm for me where your Trekboers are. That would do me fine. I retire, eh?'

'Do you mean it, Karevapu?'

'How should I not mean it?'

'Fine, Karevapu, I'll remember it. I'll let you know—in time.'

He laughed, and put his arm around me. 'First, you go back home,' he said.

'I'll go to the Cape. But I'll come back, my friend. You know it!'

He poured us some brandy. We lifted our glasses and drank to each other's health.

Two months after our return from the distant north, the Reverend Hugo Hahn arrived at the Bay. The Colonial government had sent him to try and act as a mediator in the war. The character of the struggle had clearly become too much for even the lethargic Colonials. Nama and Herero were mutually destroying each other. Who was better fitted for the task of mediator than Hugo Hahn? It was he who had laid the foundations of the Rhenish Mission in the Transgariep as far back as 1842. As such he had proved his mettle. He had told Jonker Afrikaander—Nkuru, God of the World!—in the clearest of terms that he would suffer nobody trying to deter him from preaching the Gospel. He did more than just preach. He worked for the cause of an ordered community.

In a way, I reflected, Hugo Hahn and I had tried to do the same thing. In the early sixties Hahn had played with the idea of establishing at Otjimbingue a centre of civilized authority. This was to act as a stabilizing element in a country torn by anarchy. I had thought of something similar at Rehoboth.

Hahn had been given money by Princess Augusta von Lippe. With this he had built the Augustineum, a training centre for the native peoples. In 1869, he curbed Kamaherero who had named himself 'the Great, the Rich, the Almighty', then irrigated the sub-chiefs of Damaraland with holy water from his mouth. It was the Herero custom. Kamaherero, said Hahn, was to make peace with Jan Jonker, and would allow them to live in Windhoek.

Hahn's work as a philologist had already earned him a D Phil, *honoris causa.* This distinction was conferred on him by a great European university. He set the pace and the example for men like Rath, Kleinschmidt and others. But Rath, who had founded Otjimbingue, had given up after seventeen years of hard, self-sacrificing work, and had settled at Sarepta in the Cape. I myself read what he had written there: '*Solange das Volk in solcher Versunkenheit sitzt wie gegenwärtig, ist an kein Christentum zu denken.*' And even the tireless Hahn, after a quarter of a century of courageous service, wrote: '*War nicht alles umsonst?*' It was indeed an excruciating question for a man like Hahn. Eight years earlier he had shaken the dust of the country from his feet. He had gone to the Cape, and had become the spiritual head of the Lutheran community. To him, too, Diehl's words at Okahandja could be applied: '*Glück zu!*'

In spite of everything, I would have liked to have seen Hahn's new mission have some success. The Swartbooi tribes of Otjitambi had now, rather strangely, become the allies of their fellow Namas against the Ovaherero. Hahn saw in them the weakest link. After all, they had always fought with the Ovaherero against their fellow Namas. The Swartboois, Hahn decided, could be prevailed upon to make a separate peace. Kamaherero had given them Franzfontein and Zesfontein, where they were now living. Hermanus van Wyk, chief of the Basters, could also be moved to make peace with Okahandja. The real enemy was still Jan Jonker.

If you went south from the Bay, following the coastline, eventually you would come to Sandfish Harbour. That was where some of Jan Jonker's arms and ammunition were being landed. From near Sandfish Harbour one could see, on a clear day, the great quartzite citadel of Gamsberg in the distance.

Hahn had brought some of his Rhenish colleagues from Stellenbosch to help him. They were working at Jan Jonker's place at Gamsberg. Hahn himself would approach Kamaherero, although the Stellenbosch men had had but little success. Charles Lyon, returning from Otjimbingue, told that these two gentlemen—Krönlein and Hegner—had been scurvily received by Jan Jonker. Moses Witbooi was also there. With much posturing the Namas declared that there would be only one sort of peace: that which the Namas themselves would enforce. They would do it at Okahandja.

17

The *Christina* lay in the lagoon, her slender masts and fine lines reflected in the water.

The time had come for me to leave. I could hardly believe it. Was I really going to say goodbye to this land which had claimed so much of my life? I would rather not think of it that way, in spite of all. Nevertheless, I kept an open mind.

I took leave of my two faithful servants. They had been my companions on so many journeys. They had served me so well.

They had walked beside me and been my companions for many miles: Izak, the Ai-Bushman; and Kairob, the Bergdamara. Now they would trek back to Omaruru with the wagons and the cattle. They would serve with the Erikssons. At Omaruru they would wait for me to return. It might be in six months' time. It might be never.

This was the simple truth. My part in the story of this country had never matured. I had spent eleven years here. What had I to show for it? The most promising days had undoubtedly been those which started one hot November day in the marshes of the Okavango. Something might have grown out of this. But fortune had not been my friend.

Now the land was disappearing behind the surf. All that I could still see were the red dunes of the Namib, catching the last light of day. Faintly visible, too, was the group of buildings thrown together there beside the quiet waters of the lagoon.

I could imagine Izak and Kairob still standing there on the wet sand, watching the *Christina* grow fainter as it rounded Pelican Point, heading for the open sea. Izak had knelt and folded his hands together in an attitude of prayer as the dinghy had taken me out to the schooner.

I had never thought of leaving this country in this fashion. My wagon spoors were still in many places: in the sand; in the limestone; in the bush; in the mountains. They were there over the endless sun-smitten plains of this country. As far as I was concerned, they would always be there. Sometimes I had seen my own spoors in the sand of the Omaheke on my way to Ngami. This was after eight years. But even if great rains came and wiped them out, they would still be there.

They said one always returned . . . Look at Andersson, Hahn, Palgrave and even Van Zyl. Van Zyl had built a castle for himself in the wilds of Ghanzi. Why had he not rather built his castle at the Cape? Now he had been reduced to poverty; and he had been threatened with death.

Many came back but some did not. To whom did I belong?

I stood there, clinging to the deck-rail, feeling the salt swish of the wind, the stinging coolness of the spray. There was a dull weariness inside me.

The summer was passing. Autumn had tinged the sea. It was now a deeper, colder green. Soon the fog would creep up out of the sea into the Namib, lie among the dunes like the ghost of a dead land. The sleek oryx would loom up out of the mist, and to the west the dull thunder of the surf would sound.

A deck hand brought me a message. The captain would like me to join him in his cabin. I nodded, and wiped the salt spray from my face. This was a kindly gesture towards a man who had almost lost his way.

The old Cape records said that the first mate in founder Van Riebeeck's ship *Dromedaris* had promised a handful of Spanish ducats to the one who, after months at sea, first sighted the great, flat crest of Table Mountain, rising out of the southern ocean. After one's own seventeen days at sea, one could appreciate this.

A Malay with a *toering** on his head took me by hansom from the harbour. We went through the city to my parental home. The hansom was drawn by a dappled horse with bells on its harness.

*A conical straw hat.

Great south-easter clouds were pouring over the precipitous ridge of Table Mountain. So they had done through the ages.

We drove cheerfully through the cobbled streets of the city. Little Cape boys were selling the morning paper. I read it, and it was strange to hear of international affairs but a few days old.

Much of what we had heard bit by bit in the Transgariep these past months was now confirmed. In the Transvaal, after the Convention of Pretoria, there had been a gradual withdrawal of British interest. So, Majuba *had* been decisive. What remained of British power in the Transvaal was some vague 'suzerainty'. Of greater import was the news that British troops marched down from Laingsnek into Natal. The correspondence columns of the newspapers showed that there were still many who were by no means happy about British prestige. In the Colony feelings were running high.

I sat in the cab, jogging along with the newspaper spread open on my knees. Dimly I wondered whether my friends up there on a lost highland in Portuguese West Africa had any inkling of what was taking place. In Nhembaland I had asked myself whether the successful outcome of the War in the Transvaal could possibly cause them to change their minds. Maybe this would finally bring them to the realization that there was little future for them as Calvinist puritans in a Catholic country. If there had been a substantive motive for the Trek in the first instance, it was the fear of a new British intervention. There was, however, more to it than this. So I had long decided. The true reasons for this strange *Völkerwanderung* lay deeper.—How deep? And where precisely? I did not know.

The jolly *rare-rare* of a fish-bugle sounded in my ears. I listened to it with particular pleasure. This was the ancient way of Cape fishermen. In this way they announced their wares.

Going past the Grand Parade in the centre city, I watched the usual Saturday morning crowd going about their traditional activities. At the one end of the square a horse-sale was in progress. The auctioneer wore a frock-coat and topper—looking for all the world like Robert Lewis in his robes of 'office'. He was offering two fine cart-horses for sale. A young farmer from the wine districts, wearing riding boots, spurs, and on his head a flat felt hat adorned with a white scarf, was examining the pair. A group of riding-horses which might have pleased the heart of Pieter Maritz-Botha was secured to a line of posts. There were

Arabs, English thoroughbreds, and some fine locally bred Hantams. A Malay in a fez stroked the glossy hindquarters of one of the Arabs. Sailors and soldiers gathered around fruit-sellers sitting under sunshades with Malay sandals on their feet, offering apples, sweet melons, grapes. An auctioneer of second-hand goods, sporting a bowler, was directing his clerk to strike a copper gong, announcing the start of the proceedings.

Nearing Rondebosch, I saw the sun flooding over the wooded eastern slopes of Table Mountain. By eleven o'clock we got to Wynberg. There, suddenly, under great oaks, was my parental home. Humble as it was, it was my own.

Georgina, my eldest sister, was busy cutting autumn roses in the garden. She looked up, recognized me, and turned pale. Her hand started to her mouth. Then she dropped her flowers, and came running towards me.

We embraced. She was crying, and shouting to those inside the house: 'Mama! Mama! It is Will who has come!'

Those were happy days. It rained as I had forgotten it could rain. On the great mountain ranges to the east the first snow of winter fell.

The sunny days reappeared. Everything was green and fresh, and the fever in my blood was nourished by such conditions. I had to keep to my bed for days. My mother seemed to welcome this in a way: it gave her the opportunity of nursing me. There she would sit for hours with me, listening to all I had to tell, captivated by my stories of the Trekboers and how I had taken them to Angola.

Friends and relations came in a steady stream. Time and time again I had to tell about my life in 'Damaraland'. Was it really true, they asked? Had I been chosen to be leader of the Trekboers? I had simply given them advice, I said. I was their friend and counsellor. Nothing more. The whole story had appeared in the *Cape Quarterly Review.*

Lying in bed, I worked at an account of our journey to Nhembaland. The editor of the *Review* read and accepted it. 'Please let us have more like it,' he wrote.

A frequent visitor those days was Chris (C. L.) Leen, married to Georgina. Chris had long played with the idea of joining me in the Transgariep. He should have no illusions, I said. It was a hard life in a hard country. There were adventures, and new worlds to discover, yes, but that was the romantic side of it. It was firstly a job, and not an easy job . . .

He considered it all, then reaffirmed: he would yet like to be there. It was a new country. It seemed as if there were opportunities. When would I return? Time would tell, I said. I had come back to the Cape more or less resigned to the final dissolution of any plans I might have had. South West Africa would have to look after itself. The Trekboers were perfectly happy where they were. Rehoboth? It was sometimes difficult to remember with what devotion to the idea I had once been filled. My friends were at Humpata on the High Serras. The indications were that they would remain there.

Chris Leen was the serious, rangy type one usually consulted when a sober account of things was required. He was also the kind my mother could well depend on when things around the house needed seeing to. He did a good deal of business with the Cape farming community, and was well-disposed towards them. On the whole he had all the qualities necessary for a successful hunter-trader. What would Georgina say? I doubted very much if she would accompany Chris. She would not easily leave my mother and the younger sisters to look after themselves. Krynauw, my agent, and the agent of most of the hunter-traders—a shrewd judge of character with a wide knowledge of Africa—kept saying:

'Take Chris along with you when you go back.'

We would talk to him, hear all the latest news the schooners had brought from the Bay. At times we would meet old friends and acquaintances, share remembrances, anecdotes, some strange longing of the heart, some laughter. Krynauw himself complained rather bitterly that the Herero-Nama war had cut his imports to almost nothing. There was news that a peace treaty between Kamaherero, the Swartboois, and the Basters had already been signed. According to the reports Jan Jonker and Moses Witbooi, however, thought it all a joke. They were still threatening the Basters. There was no sign of order yet.

We stood talking at Krynauw's one afternoon when the post arrived. There was a letter from Axel Eriksson. Trade had almost come to a standstill, he wrote. Jan Jonker's threats against Rehoboth had not been empty. The new 'peace treaty' had hardly been old enough to allow Krönlein to get back to Stellenbosch, when the Afrikaanders left their Gamsberg citadel, and descended upon Rehoboth. Hermanus van Wyk had sent an urgent appeal to Okahandja for assistance. Even before the message could get there, however, Rehoboth town had been burnt to the ground.

The most piquant element in all this news, however, was to the effect that Jan Jonker's attack had been strongly supported by the Swartboois. They were the very people who had just signed the peace treaty with Okahandja. It was patently absurd. 'That, my dear Chris, is the country and its people,' I said. 'Yet? You still see how attached I am to it, in spite of everything. Let there be *wet en regel* . . . Law and order, and positive results can be expected.'

Chris said: 'Some time or other you will return.'

'Some time or other,' I answered vaguely. 'Meanwhile . . . ?'

Meanwhile I was still at home, and enjoying the way my mother pampered me. She would bring me early morning coffee. She would sit there next to my bed, talking to me. I would look at her and think that she had the kind of face I would like to draw. There was character in that delicate nose, those fine lines around the eyes, that expression of humour but also sadness around the mouth.

'So you still have your dreams of fortune, Will,' she would say and look tenderly at me.

I would smile and stir my coffee. 'We shall have to see,' I would say. 'All is very real at present. And I am thankful for it.'

Margaret Jordan, my mother, sometimes reminded me of Ella Lombard.

'I hear that you have been to see Mrs Andersson?' she enquired one evening.

'So I have!'

This was Sarah Jane, the widow of Charles John.

'I had the regards of the Erikssons to convey to her. Llewellyn was there too. Fine boy that. He was with us on the journey to Nhembaland.'

Georgina appeared in the door of my little room. She stood leaning there against the jamb, smiling strangely at me.

'Will,' she said, 'I have spoken to Chris. Or rather, Chris has spoken to me. He wants to go along with you, whenever that may be.'

I looked up in surprise. 'He seems to accept it that I have plans to leave for the north again?'

'I have said to him, if that is what he wants to do, he must do it. One day I shall join him there.'

'The land is still at war!'

'The war will come to an end.'

This is what Sarah Jane had said. Llewellyn had a good appointment in the post office. Sarah Jane's brother was Postmaster-General of the Colony. But Llewellyn would also like to return to Damaraland when the war came to an end. 'He has followed the trails his father cut,' Sarah Jane said. 'I advised him to settle down now. Charles went back when he was a sick man, you know.'

Judging by the way Sarah Jane looked at me I could tell that she was eager to know of my plans. Instead of telling her, I asked: 'Would you like to visit Damaraland again?'

She smiled, and I remembered how Andersson himself had referred to her in his journal as a 'strong little blue-eyed woman'. This she was.

'Yes,' she answered presently, 'I would like to return; be it just for a while. And journey to the river.'

The river was the Okavango. Charles John Andersson had been the first white man to see it. Not even Livingstone had reached it. But there was another river which had got a hold on Andersson. It was the Cunene. He had searched for it for years, and soon after he had found it, he had died: far out there in the wilderness.

Weeks passed and even the newspapers were bringing the facts of the continent back to me. It was now the *Scramble for Africa.* Livingstone and Stanley had opened the great central part. The Brussels Conference had shown how it was to be exploited. Even *Fürst* von Bismarck at the Congress of Berlin had alleviated some of the French humiliation at the hands of the Prussians by declaring that Africa was waiting—for the French, too. France did not need much encouragement. She had already established herself in Tunisia and equatorial Africa. Leopold of Belgium was active in the Congo. Italy had moved in Eritrea. The *Fürst* himself had referred rather carelessly to South West Africa; but the Hansa-inspired *Koloniale Gesellschaft* had been making demands that Germany had by no means found her own rightful place in Africa.

At the beginning of November I read with some surprise that a merchant of Bremen, one Alfred Lüderitz, had purchased land from the Namas at Angra Pequena, on the southern desert coast.

I lay awake that night, thinking hard about it. With the British removing the last remnants of Protection from Okahandja, with the Ovaherero and the Namas wearing each other down, the country was wide open. How far would the Germans go?

I had nothing against their presence. I only had a formless urge to be there where it was all taking place. If German colonization could establish a civilized order, well and good. There were, however, still other possibilities, should peace return. My thoughts had often moved to the distant hinterland of the Marutze-Mapunda empire, beyond the Zambesi. If a railway could be built from the Bay through the unclaimed land lying between Damaraland and Ovamboland, it could lead to a tremendous development of Southern Africa.

The thought was exciting. I sat propped up in my bed against the cushions, making notes. Just before dawn my mother appeared with my early morning coffee. She brought it to me in a little pewter pot to which I had become attached. Coffee tasted better out of it.

'Take it along with you when you go back,' my mother said. She filled my cup. The lamplight was soft over the smooth brown of her skin, over the black hair intertwined with grey, drawn severely over her head and gathered in a bun.

Maybe it was a premonition, I do not know. I arranged with my bank for the withdrawal of bigger sums of money than usual.

It was farewell again: *avsked* as Axel Eriksson would say. We did the rounds and said goodbye to friends and relations. This time I was not alone. Chris Leen was with me looking the part with a new, wide-brimmed hat, Norfolk jacket of corduroy, and knickerbockers.

On 10 November 1881, the *Louis Alfred* lay in Table Bay Harbour. A fresh southerly wind was blowing. It had drawn a cloth of white cloud over the table of the mountain, and promised a good start to the voyage up the west coast.

It was the old approach. I had learnt it when I had been little more than a boy. You took the matter as lightly as you could. You kept talking about it all as if it were just an excursion.

This time, however, it proved to be more difficult. My mother and Georgina remained standing there on the quay long after we had slowly drifted out of the harbour. Georgina, who had been very workmanlike in her preparations for her husband's leaving, had suddenly shown signs of emotion. It affected us all, and handkerchiefs appeared. I laughed it off, and said: 'We'll be back to come and fetch you all one of these days.' My mother smiled, and I kissed her. Her cheeks were moist.

The sails of the *Louis Alfred* slowly unfurled. On the distant head of concrete two small figures were still visible. We rounded the breakwater. The wind filled the sails and the ship began cleaving through the blue water of the bay. I watched the sails, and saw the rigging grow tense.

The ship was moving fast now, heading for its far destination. In a sense this was always the unknown. Blow wind, I said to myself, fill ye sails, draw tight ye ropes . . .

In a fortnight, if we were lucky, we could be on the trek-road again.

What did the future hold? It was unimportant to know the answer. What was important was that we were journeying again.

FEVER
(November 1884 - September 1885)

1

Sunday, 14 December 1884, at Humbe on the Cunene . . . In my journal I noted the date.

I had then spent some two and a half years with the Trekboers at Humpata. I had operated as a hunter-trader. I had farmed. I had been their friend and adviser. At the end of a year in Angola I had already known that in spite of the enthusiastic letters I had written to Cape newspapers, asking for more people from the country districts of the Cape to come and settle in this Land of Plenty, there was no future here for them—as themselves.

On that Sunday I sat there next to the river under a giant mulemba. I sat there writing at my little X-table, the same one which had accompanied me on so many journeys through Southern Africa.

The heat lay over the river valley, quietly, oppressively. Where the sun was reflected back on the blue waters of the river, one had to close one's eyes against it. The air was vibrant with the screech of the cicadas.

What should I record? So many days had passed without my making any entries. But now it had to be done: by day when sitting under the shade of the mulemba; by night when sitting by lamplight under a mosquito net in the wagon.

Those faintly droning, those deeply incubating, Sunday afternoons at Humbe on the river . . .

Paper work, Gert Alberts insisted on calling it, as he saw me writing . . . Paper work it was. Gert Alberts referred to it as many Boers did: with a certain disdain. Yet he knew how necessary it was. There was, for instance, the matter of completing the draft constitution for the new Republic.

Rehoboth had finally crumbled to pieces as a scheme. Times had come when the old idea would suddenly live again. But gradually I had seen the possibilities of the other areas: the 'unclaimed' land lying between Damaraland and Ovamboland, south-east of the White Pan, west of the Omuramba Omatako. 'Unclaimed' it was, only because the Ovambos whose rights were beyond dispute had never occupied it effectively. The only people who had really lived there were the few nomadic Bushmen. They dug copper ore for Kambonde Kampingana, as tribute.

When had I first thought of this land of promise? How had it happened that I had always disregarded it until it finally presented itself? There was a time when I trekked back to the Bay from the Okavango, down the Omuramba Omatako. Piet Botha was with me. He was then still my partner, my friend.

Rehoboth had dominated my thoughts, until German *Schutz* finally disposed of it. During March of this year I had written to Dr Nachtigall of the German Foreign Office. What right did the Reich have, I had asked him, to disregard the solemn contract of sale entered into between Petrus Swartbooi and myself. The tribe was still the legal owner of Rehoboth. The sale of the territory to me was for the sum of £1,500. In the letter to Nachtigall I stressed that there were increasing difficulties for the Trekboers at Humpata. Belck, who was a German geologist, had turned up at Otjitambi and brought the news of the development. The Reich was taking *Schutzherrschaft* seriously, he assured me. It had started with Lüderitz at Angra Pequena. Now it was at Rehoboth. More was to come . . . What, I asked, the whole country? Belck was non-committal. Who could say, he said.

Well, I decided, I had my own task. True, the news about Rehoboth had left me with some bitterness. My interests, and the interests of my charges, had been completely disregarded. Still, there were other possibilities. Perhaps I had, unconsciously, kept it in reserve all these years. There was the fine area around Otavi Spring, west of the Omuramba Omatako. On the heights of Otjovanda Tjongue was one of the strongest waters in the country. In good years this was paradise. To whom did it belong? If anybody, the Ovambos. Strange that nobody had settled there, except a few wandering Bushmen. Why? I could not say.

Dolf Holtzhausen, who was the carpenter of the Trek, would sometimes bring his string of sons along to watch me at my labours. The steady movement of my pen over the paper would amuse them. They themselves wrote slowly, carefully. They would sit around on stools, which Dolf himself had made. They would laugh uproariously at some remark I would innocently make concerning them.

Meester—which means teacher—Dolf called me. Barend Bouwer called me *Mester*. Hester, his wife, like many others, called me *Meneer*. To quite a few I had permanently become *Doctor*.

'*Meester*,' Dolf said one Sunday, addressing me on behalf of himself and all his sons. 'Thou knowest what has been written in the Scriptures: "six days shalt thou labour and do all thy work . . ." '

I kept up my scribbling. 'That I have heard, Dolf,' I said.

'*Meester*,' he persevered, 'thou dost write so much on the Sabbath. Is this to be suffered?' On Sundays he would speak in the language of Scripture.

I continued my writing. Then I looked up and told Dolf that it all depended on what one wrote. This puzzled him. My *bambuse* sang out that lunch in the hunter's three-legged iron pot was ready. It gave me the opportunity to offer Dolf a drop from the cask.

This he considered. A better day providing for a better deed, the hospitality was accepted. The appetizer was also offered to the eldest son.

'May I, father?' he respectfully enquired.

The answer came: 'Son, you may!'

'Dolf,' I said to my friend one day, while we were thus relaxing, 'you should have been present some time ago when King Nambadi received the elders of the laager. He entertained us royally. Don't imagine he offered us *mahongo* to drink. The king may be black, but he offers his guests the good wines of Portugal.'

'It surprises me, *Meester*,' Dolf said, 'but there are many such things in the world today which surprise me. Think of Willem Prinsloo.'

This was one of Old Diederick's sons. The incident which had surprised Dolf Holtzhausen had taken place on the banks of the Cunene. Some boys had spotted what they took to be a martial eagle in a tree on the opposite side. Some older people arrived, and a debate followed: was it an eagle, or was it a baboon?

Willem Prinsloo, impulsive as always, suggested that it be put to the test. Thereupon he took careful aim with a Martini Henry he had recently bought. The object dropped from the tree and lay on the ground. But there was no flapping of wings . . .

'A baboon!' some cried.

Some while later the true answer came in the shape of a band of infuriated Ukuanyamas. Over a distance of some few hundred yards the leader was already informing the Trekker company that Willem Prinsloo had not shot a baboon, but a fellow member of the tribe.

A long argument now followed, with Willem Prinsloo angrily asserting his innocence. It had clearly been an accident, he said.

The accusers shouted him down. Things began to look dangerous, when Old Diederick Prinsloo himself arrived. Perhaps it was the very dignity of the old landdrost in his frock coat and high collar that made the accusers pause.

What was all the trouble about, Old Diederick demanded; why all this noise? And when he was told, he answered: well, an accident was an accident. The Trek would gladly pay compensation. There was nothing more to it. What did Mister Jordan say?

But the Ukuanyama party had started shouting again. Now they were waving spears, fitting arrows to their bows.

I slowly lifted my gun. Old Diederick, however, had taken it all upon himself. He walked back to his wagon, threw his bandolier over a bony shoulder, loaded his gun, and came back. Then, ignoring the spears and arrows pointing at him, never for a moment surrendering his dignity, he bore down upon the leader of the accusers. Training his gun at point-blank range on the man's chest, he then said in a great voice: 'Five oxen! Five oxen thou shalt have—and no more. And let there be no further trouble. Take thou thy five oxen for the life of that man who behaved like a baboon—and get thee away!'

So five oxen it was. And when they had duly been handed over, there was great satisfaction among those who had come so threateningly.

'*Meester*,' Dolf enquired again, 'what then is the object of so much writing?'

'To record all that has taken place, Dolf,' I said. 'To draft the rules by which the new republic will be governed.'

'What will be the name of our republic, *Meester*?'

'Some call it Lydensrust, Dolf,' I said, 'Rest from Suffering. But I think it should be called Upingtonia. Because Sir Thomas

Upington, who is Prime Minister of the Cape Colony, thinks so well of us.'

'*Meester*,' Dolf said, 'I understand thee. But it is the Sabbath.'

I poured him another drop of *aguardente*, for which he thanked me. I looked to the eldest son.

He asked: 'May I, father?'

And Dolf answered: 'Son, you may.' So I poured him a drop.

The sun was setting. It was time for the evening devotions. Old Diederick was already moving towards the great mulemba. Bible and psalter were under his arm, pressed closely to his chest.

'Dolf,' I said before we went to join the others, 'as the carpenter of the Trek, you are a very important man! The hand with the saw, the hammer, the chisel, the plane, is just as necessary as the hand with the pen. Also on the Sabbath.'

'Thou speakest plain words, *Meester*.'

'One day you will see to it that I have a *kist* to lie in when I am dead.'

'That I always have, *Meester*.'

The group under the mulemba had already started to sing, in passionate, ponderous unison. Somehow I wanted to be with them.

2

What had happened to Pieter Maritz-Botha? What had happened to our friendship?

After his marriage to Johanna Meyer the old care-free relationship between us had changed. Piet himself had changed.

He preferred to trek on his own. He had arrived here at Humbe long after the others. There were stories that he had got bogged down badly in the marshy parts west of Humbe.

Johanna, demure, had nevertheless got hold of Piet in her gentle way. Now she held him captive between her dainty fingers. She would eye me with suspicion, as if she knew how amused I was at Piet's eclipse. Then she would seem to say: 'You, Jordan, are the one who has been a bad influence on my husband. All those parties of yours down at Walwich Bay . . . !'

This plump, prim little creature had seemingly taught Pieter Maritz-Botha all her nice, homely little ways. Oh yes, he would still at times depart with the others on hunting expeditions: to the

Shimborro; to the Cunene; to the Sandveld north of the Cunene. But where was the famous hunter of the Debra, the Okavango, the Omuramba Omatako, the White Pan, the Kaoko? What he still liked to do was to tell of those days, as if he had finally done with it all. The big hunters of the present day were Jan Robbertze, Jan Labuschagne, the Venters . . .

I got to the Botha *werf* that night, and was received hospitably enough. Piet offered me a chair.

I had come to hear all about it, I said. Some trek, in all this rain!

Some trek, he affirmed. He had got bogged down. He had had to carry Johanna on his back for miles through all that mud and water.

Johanna, never saying a word, just faintly smiling, served us coffee. Thereupon she extended a warm, soft little hand, wishing me good night.

We sat there in our chairs, drinking coffee, smoking, and in spite of my own light-hearted approach, I discerned the strain of it all. He seemed to resent my very presence. Was it, as I had heard, my growing influence in the community? Why had he elected to join those who were now returning to Damaraland? Why had he not remained at Humpata?

Filling his pipe, he suddenly wished to know: 'Well, what are our plans now? I have no idea yet where we are heading. Nor has anybody, for that matter!'

This was sheer perversity. We were heading for the country purchased by me (or to be finally purchased) from Kambonde Kampingana, King of the Ovambos. And he knew it.

Where was I leading them, he wished to know again. He had been critical of my plans from the start . . .

'There is nothing to hide,' I said after a pause. 'Why should there be?'

This was 1884. Two years earlier, shortly after my return to Humpata from the Cape, Piet and Johanna had visited the Transvaal. During September of 1883 they had returned. This was a few days before the meeting of Trekboers at Humpata concerning their uncertain future. By coincidence I had been off-loading ivory at Moçamedes. The Maritz-Bothas arrived from the Cape. I stood on the mole with great expectations while the dinghy brought them ashore.

Piet was wearing a bowler and was smoking a cigar. Johanna,

half-hidden behind a parasol, was sitting primly erect. They got out of the boat and I went down the steps to meet them.

'Welcome back!' I said, and shook hands. Piet, I thought, was glad to see me again.

We talked about their voyage, the Colonial politics, the situation in the Transvaal. The Transvaal, he said, had consolidated its newly-won freedom. Things were fine there now. A triumvirate had administered the state after the peace had been signed. But now S. P. J. Kruger had been elected as president. He, Botha, had come back, convinced that the people at Humpata should consider returning . . .

I took note of all this, offering only neutral comment. At the time of Majuba I had already wondered how the new developments in the Transvaal would affect my friends of the Trek. Would they return?

Back on the highlands of the Serras a few weeks later, there had been much interest in all that Pieter Maritz-Botha had to tell. Strangely, he could arouse almost no enthusiasm for the idea of repatriation in spite of the general disillusionment. True, I had written letters to Cape newspapers, lauding the excellence of the Humpata highlands. Maybe it was the fever talking. I could never have believed it. Or perhaps I did really believe it at the time.

It had been the meeting fifteen months previously which had finally brought matters to a head. Pieter Maritz-Botha again argued in favour of returning to the Transvaal. But Louw du Plessis, in his quiet, steady way, asked why had he then come back to Humpata? It was quite clear that the Trek community would not easily undertake a return journey over the Thirstland again. I had known from the start that what had moved them was much more than just freedom. Trek! The *idea* of trek, away from the present, away from the known . . .

So, what were my plans? Botha repeated the question. Now I felt myself compelled to answer: 'The idea is to stay just where we are, for the present, at least. Or else we may move on slowly towards Ondangua. And once there, we can discuss the purchase of territory with Kambonde.'

'You well know,' he said, looking sharply at me, 'that the area you wish to occupy is in dispute?'

'By that you presumably mean,' I answered, 'that Robert Lewis claims it on behalf of the Ovaherero?'

He sat there, pulling nervously at his pipe. I knew that he had talked with Lewis when visiting the south. He knew all about the new area I had thought of buying. He had gone down to Otjitambi with Barend Bouwer and myself. With Barend he had signed the contract of sale with Petrus Swartbooi as a witness. Belck had suddenly arrived and had informed us of *Schutzherrschaft* at Rehoboth.

Piet was as taken aback as the rest of us. Why had he joined us on the journey to Otjitambi? I had not invited him. I was pleased when he came to my store one day, saying he would like to go along with us. There had been a lot of palaver the previous weeks on the question of some other area. It would be somewhere in the south, in 'Damaraland'. Botha had agreed: the people of the Trek had to be guided. The war between Namaland and Hereroland had abated. The old idea of Rehoboth could now be revived. Piet agreed. He would come along with us to Otjitambi. Fine, I said. We would like to have him. Did he say something about returning to the Transvaal as being still the best solution? I did not hear it. Why, if he meant it seriously, did he want to accompany us to Otjitambi? Why did he witness the deed of sale? The Germans forestalled us. Piet shared our anger. He, too, said we had entered into a valid contract. The *Reich* was bound to honour it. Well, I said that night around our camp fire, we would have to consider what alternatives there were. There was the fine stretch of country south and south-east of the White Pan. This was still unoccupied.

He agreed with everything. The new area, I said, was perhaps the finest ranching country in all of the Transgariep. It was also good for agriculture.

The new trek had already started when I had heard that Piet was now questioning the whole movement. The remark he had just made now seemed to confirm it. He had seen Robert Lewis; and Lewis had informed him that the area was in dispute. Lewis had always had the idea that his thirty years in the country afforded him a special status above that of everybody else. In the old days, with Palgrave's Union Jack flying at Okahandja, Lewis regarded himself as a power in the land.

Charles Lyon who had touched at Humpata on his way to Moçamedes had told me that Lewis' influence had since by no means weakened. On the contrary, since the departure of the last Resident Magistrate—Musgrave—Lewis had assumed the title of 'High Commissioner'. What exactly had Piet Botha's business been down there? Piet was a Boer. Lewis had never concealed his contempt for his people.

'Robert Lewis,' I now said to Botha, 'had better see to his own business. If he still believes that he can lead people around by the nose, telling tales about the boundaries of Damaraland, he still has much to learn. Kamaherero, as we have heard, has been taking his whole nation on some strange peregrination up and down the borders of Hereroland. No doubt he has been inspired to these exercised by Lewis himself. Listen, I think I know the Nama people better than anybody else here. Jan Jonker has been licked; and even Gamsberg no longer holds the terrors it used to. But Hendrik Witbooi, who says that he has been spoken to by God himself, is a power still to be reckoned with. Lewis pretends that Herero authority includes the area we have in mind. Otavi and the surrounding country belong to the Ovambos, if it belongs to anybody.'

He was cleaning his pipe. His mouth was tense as he blew through the stem. 'I have nothing to do with Lewis,' he muttered. 'I only know that we must know what we are doing, before we do it. Why do you have to decide for us all?'

His question took me by surprise. It was obviously unreasonable. The new trek was the result of a communal decision. True, the majority had gone back on their decision, and had stayed on at Humpata. A large group nevertheless had started the trek southwards. Did Botha really expect me to consult him personally? I was once inclined to ascribe his aloofness to Johanna's influence. But there was more to it.

'You were in favour of the new trek at the meeting,' I said. 'Why? To what end?'

The man was a riddle. True, at the meeting which had taken place in September of the previous year, he had again told of the new order in the Transvaal. But when questioned by Old Diederick, he had not been particularly insistent. The Transvaal was not the only solution. He had listened silently while Old Diederick had said: 'The people are all of one mind to leave Humpata and to trek back. This is because of the unhealthy nature of this land; and also because of its remoteness from the country of our birth, and those who speak our language, believe as we believe.'

Botha's answer to this had been that money was available in the Orange Free State and the Transvaal for those who wished to go back.

And then we had gone down to Otjitambi; and I and others had taken it that it was the last we would hear of Piet's idea. He wished the people to cross the Thirstland. He wished them to go back to the Transvaal. Diederick Prinsloo himself had always been in favour of the 'new proposals of Mr Jordan'.

Now we were here at Humbe on the Cunene, already far advanced on our way to acquire the 'right to settle' which might well, in time, lead to 'legal title'. Why had so many gone back on the decision of the meeting that Angola promised no future? A party of hunters who had been operating successfully in the north had returned with glowing accounts of the fine lands to be had at Qué on the Bié plateau. This had pleased the Albertses, the Van der Merwes, the J. F. Bothas . . . But perhaps it was the news about Rehoboth which finally swayed them.

I could not offer them anything definite now. I could only say: 'I believe that Kambonde Kampingana will sell us that tract of country.'

Finally twenty-five families had started the trek, with others to follow. That would happen, I believed, as soon as the dealings with Kambonde were successfully concluded, and the Trek established; as soon as a *Bestuur* could be formed, and good reports be sent back to Humpata.

'There is no point in hiding my feelings,' I said. 'It has been a great disappointment to me to learn that you do not wish to serve on the *Bestuur*. We need a secretary. David Black? . . . We need someone who has been around a bit, seen something of the world.

'Maybe you feel,' I continued, 'that there is still far too much uncertainty. Agreed. But you will also have to admit that I know Kambonde; that I would not have undertaken this venture had I not known the chances of success.'

'What now if you do not succeed?' He suddenly looked at me.

Something tightened inside of me. 'I shall succeed,' I said.

'You are very sure of yourself. Who is going to pay?'

'I shall pay for it!' I said this with some temper. I got up and walked away from the fire, then looked back at him where he was sitting. He was puffing at his pipe. 'I shall pay for it, I tell you. I was willing and able to pay for Rehoboth. I had already given a bank guarantee for the sum of £1,500. I'll pay Kambonde in full.'

'How will you pay?'

'Cash,' I said. 'If not in cash, then in kind, damn you. Muzzle-loaders, *aguardente*, whatever has value. A horse too, if you like. You might offer me the Arab. I shall present it to Kambonde. He fancies a good horse!'

This was a rather clumsy attempt at levity on my part. The Arab was the one Botha had purchased from Machiel Prinsloo. Machiel had never been too happy about it. He usually fell silent when others teased him, saying that Piet had got the better of the deal. Willem Prinsloo had been very outspoken about it. Botha, he said, thought he had a right to only the best.

'You leave my horse alone.' It was a quick answer, but it afforded me some satisfaction. At least I had ruffled his confidence.

'You would serve the general good in no small way, if you were to clear up your attitude,' I said. 'At the moment everybody is left guessing: you oppose us, and yet you trek after us.'

He threw a log on the fire, then said brusquely: 'My people must get back to where they belong!'

'But you seem to be talking all ways,' I said. 'Now it is the Transvaal, then again some place in Damaraland. Make up your mind, old chap. What if the people have no desire at all for going back? Do you think all these years of trek should end in defeat?'

'There is much confusion,' he said archly. 'My people do not know their own mind. They must be guided. The Trek can go to Damaraland. I shall arrange with Robert Lewis for some place in the Waterberg where the Trek can remain, temporarily. When the people have rested well, they can start trekking back to where they came from.'

'Back through the Thirstland? Have you forgotten all that happened? I was a witness to some of it. We buried more people than we could keep count of.'

'There is no need to cross the Thirstland again.'

'You think the Trek could go by way of Great Namaland, and the northern Cape? The war has not quite come to an end, you know.'

His reference to Robert Lewis had disturbed me.

'Rather watch out for Lewis,' I added, looking straight at him. '*He*'ll take you up the garden path. It is the Trek itself which must decide. Should the *Bestuur* brief me to deal with Kambonde, I'll accept.'

'You wish to give him guns, eh?'

'Guns are no problem, if he wants them. If I pay him in cash, he'll buy guns from the Portuguese here at Humbe. If I can get cap-locks or muzzle-loaders at a special price, why not? My funds are not unlimited. If you want to effect anything here, you must adapt yourself to the land and its ways. Why don't you co-operate for a change, Piet? We need you. We need you on the *Bestuur*.'

I was getting nowhere. He sat there with sulky impassivity, two fingers in the pockets of his waistcoat. What had happened to the man who had once been the life and soul of the company?

'I have my own work to see to,' he said tersely.

It was time for me to get back to my wagon. Why had I come here? I might have known from the start that I was up against it. So, there was nothing else to do but to get on with the dealings with Kambonde. Possibly when he saw the successful outcome of it all, Piet would change his mind. He would then discover that Upingtonia was to be much more than a little republic, lost in the bush.

Apart from the Trekboers there would also be people like the Erikssons, Charles Lyon, Todd, Chapman, Behan . . . Others would come. The Boers would have the first opportunity to choose their farms. But there would be sufficient land for everybody. We would build a strong, civilized community.

'What is the real object of your republic?' he suddenly asked, as if reading my thoughts. 'Why have you gone to so much trouble?'

I knew what he was suggesting: I had ulterior motives. There was someone 'behind' me. Who? He still thought it strange that I, who was altogether different from the Trekboers, should yet go to such trouble for them. But then this would surely have been the case since those first days in the marshes, and at Olifants Pan.

'There is no one paying me for my services,' I said irritably. 'I opened the way for the settlement at Humpata. At first, after coming back from the Cape, I thought it all very fine. But appearances were deceptive. We were all caught that way. I had had qualms before—yes! But only after I had lived at Humpata for some time did I realize that a group of Calvinist Boers, such as you are, would never accept the Portuguese way of life. Besides, *minha terra* is not going to be parcelled out to anybody else, as far as I know the Portuguese. Whatever can be said about forced labour, and the number of black concubines the traders keep in the bush, the Portuguese have been in that country longer than your own people at the Cape. That means close on four centuries.'

There was a blue glint in his eyes.

'What did you expect?' I continued. 'That I should shake off my responsibility? If I erred in imagining that Humpata held a future for us . . .'

'Us?'

He sat there in the firelight, with the red glow on his face, not looking at me. He knew my sensitivity to this: I was an outsider. I was one who had entered the laager as a stranger. What right had I here?

The turmoil of feelings in me was suddenly dispelled with the appearance of Jan Labuschagne. He strode out of the shadows into the firelight, standing there like a tree.

'Mister Jordan!' He greeted me with a wave of his wide-brimmed hat. 'What would you say to it, eh, if I could exchange five good trek-oxen for a reel of cotton and a ramshackle wheel?'

Botha removed his pipe from his mouth, stared at the visitor.

Jan Labuschagne stood there in front of us, cutting himself a chew of tobacco. He was huge and black. 'You, Mister! What do you say to it, eh?'

Something of my good humour of earlier that evening returned. 'I would say you were a clever man,' I answered.

'As clever as I am strong!' His broad shoulders shook with laughter. He chewed away at his cut. 'Now look!' He sat down astride a three-legged stool, suddenly becoming almost intimate. 'I came to the chief here—Nambadi, eh?—and I said to him: "Listen, Chief, I'll give you this old sewing machine, which my good wife has had enough of. Come on, Chief, give me five strong oxen for it! Then you can make yourself clothes such as white men wear." Well, he looked at the little old machine, called in his counsellors. They all said yes; five oxen they would give me for it!'

It was a bargain. And Jan Labuschagne had apparently spent his evening doing the rounds, telling everybody of his cleverness. His exuberance was a sudden relief.

Johanna's plaintive voice now sounded from one of Botha's two wagons, standing some distance away. When, she enquired, was Pieter coming to rest? Rest, I thought, Botha needed little encouragement to do that these days.

'I want to tell you something,' I said while getting up to leave. I was addressing my words to both Piet Botha and Jan Labuschagne. 'Some time before we left Humpata, I wrote a letter to President Kruger of the Transvaal. I asked him for the protection of the Transvaal for the Trek. After many months I received an answer from Dr Leyds, who is the President's secretary. He informed me that we would have to stand on our own feet. I think it necessary that you should know this.'

Johanna called to her husband again. I turned into the darkness. The two others were still sitting at the fire.

'Sleep well, Mister Jordan!' Jan Labuschagne shouted after me, holding his hat aloft.

3

Two days later was another Sabbath, the Day of the Covenant, commemorating the great victory at Blood River in Natal over the massed Zulu impis on 16 December 1838. On that day the vow had been taken: should the battle end in victory for the emigrating Boers, it would ever be honoured as a Sabbath, as a day of thanksgiving.

As a young man Diederick Prinsloo had taken part in the struggle. Most of those in the present trek also had either friends or relations who had participated in the epic events. Blood River had formed the climax of the Great Trek of Boer people from the eastern frontier-districts of the Cape Colony during the thirties.

'We have ordered special services to be held,' Louw du Plessis said. In many respects he had now become the effective leader of the Boers, with Diederick Prinsloo as Principal Reader.

The first service lasted for more than two hours. The people sat around under great trees on stools and benches, the notes of the psalm booming out over the blue Cunene.

On the opposite bank the Ukuanyama Ovambos were watching curiously. Everybody here—men, women, children—was dressed in their Sabbath clothes, taken from their *kists.* At the Prinsloos a Transvaal *Vierkleur* hung from a whip-stick. At Ella Lombard's it hung from the front ribbing of the wagon-hood. Lisa was wearing a brand new polonaise and a pretty, quilted *kappie.* I looked up in surprise, suddenly realizing that she had grown up.

Adriaan Venter, who had helped her to climb into the baobab at Olifants Pan years ago, still followed her around. Adriaan, too, had grown up. He had become a fair-haired young man with gun-blue eyes, slight with a slightness which was deceptive. He was the kind that would follow a lion or elephant spoor for a week, never resting until the chase ended in battle and victory.

Hester Bouwer, who sometimes came to my wagon to consult me about some sick child in the laager, had watched the two walking under the trees one day. With a suggestion of humour she said: 'Adriaan Venter, we hear, is looking out for a wagon-and-team. You have taken enough ivory for him down to Moçamedes, *Meneer.* Well, it seems as if the Portuguese have yet taught us something. Note the manners.' The reference was to Adriaan's bearing, his clothes. He wore a velvet jacket, a wide-brimmed hat, a black ribbon around his shirt collar, and riding-boots. His demeanour was one of almost too much confidence. He had ordered two new Martini-Henrys through Chris Leen who was down at the Bay, but who would join us shortly.

'Yes,' I had answered Hester, 'the wagon-and-team have been ordered. A wedding is as good as a feast!'

'And a feast,' Hester replied, 'is a good way to begin the republic with.'

Adriaan, with his brothers all having remained at Humpata, was now living with the Du Plessis.

'But,' said Hester before going her way, 'only until his own wagon arrives. So, *Meneer*, you will have even more ivory to take down to Moçamedes. Or the Bay.'

'There are more important things to do at present,' I said.

She smiled. 'It is not always the head which matters,' she answered. 'Thank you for the medicine, *Meneer.*'

4

The afternoon of the sixteenth was a time of general visiting. It afforded families the chance to re-tell all the old stories of past heroes. Old Hendrik van Voor sat there on his tamboti chair with its mat of thongs, recounting the adventures of a time when most of his audience were not yet born.

'It was at the time of wanderings among the fever-marshes,' the old man said. 'It was at the Letter Tree.—Got a lion! A great big, black-maned lion that day. Had heart as big as a tsamma-melon!' He needed his arms to indicate the size. 'Was after *Oom* Koos: *old* Koos, father of young Koos Erasmus, who turned back with Kreling, and went to the Transvaal. Kreling himself got there later, so they say.'

He eyed the little ones kneeling in front of him.

'*Oom* Koos was riding up there on the banks of the Kavango one day. His horse's name was Reedbuck. So they rode out one evening, looking for some pot-game. The horse was lively, wild sometimes. *Oom* Koos had a Star Barrel muzzle-loader with him: so, while riding through the mucharra, the horse suddenly noticed the lion, crouching in the thorn-bush. Then the horse gave a *beeg* jump!'

Now the arms and the hands indicated the size of the jump. The children had to duck.

'The horse gave a *beeg* jump, yes!—And the lion gave a *beeger* one!'

The children fell flat with laughter.

'*Beeger*!—But yet not big enough. Where the horse's *hind*legs had been, the lion's *fore*legs landed. So *Oom* Koos got away and came galloping back into the laager. Then we all took our horses and rode out into the mucharra. When we got there, the lion was still about, growling and roaring. I had a dog: his name was Saul—a real little *brak*!*—He nearly fell over his own legs trying to get to the lion. You see, I had shot the lion through the right front shoulder with my first shot. So, little Saul was there, helter-skelter. And suddenly!'

Another quick movement of the hands; and more shrieks.

'Like *that*! And Saul was on *top* of the lion. Sat there biting the lion behind the mane. So!'

A quick pinch on the leg of the small boy sitting nearest to him, made him jump in the air. The others screamed.

'Biting the lion—here in the neck, yes. The lion must have thought it was a bush-tick!—But Saul stuck to the lion's back, until we could fire more shots; until he was dead.'

A round of visits to the different wagons would produce similar scenes. Louw du Plessis would tell of the time he kept the lions at bay with a spade and a bucket. Ella Lombard would recall the incident in the Thirstland; how a wandering 'Galagadi had wanted to sell water to them at a price, until spied upon while sucking water from his own secret well. Old Diederick would as a matter of ritual recount the story of the Prinsloo boy who had got lost and had been murdered by the Bushmen. Piet Botha could add to all this: repeat the account of the mass execution because of

*Cur.

Hendrik van Zyl's summary justice.

The weather was close. High-tiered clouds came drifting down silently from the east, from Nhembaland. We had spent such happy days there. Some of the trek people—including young Venter—had gone into it to hunt elephants. I had told them about it.

Brilliant, humid, and quiet . . . Towards evening, I knew, the clouds would close their ranks. Before long the first lightning would flicker in the gloom. The thunder would roll out over the land. Then the rain would come. Soon it would be a deluge, flooding the land within minutes.

But now all was still serene. People walked sedately about, greeting each other; talking; drinking bowls or cups of coffee; eating pastry or doughnuts.

The children, less sedately, accompanied their elders. And the young people just emerging from their middle-teens were going about self-consciously in their Sunday best. Conspicuous, as always, were the trio Lets Labuschagne, Tina du Plessis and Hannie Venter: newly married, but still the vivacious girls I had always known. A new generation was arising—and my youth had long since receded.

There they were: girls in polonaises, or dresses of print, with high collars and tucks; wearing *kappies* artfully quilted; snow-white where they caught the sun; sometimes resting on the nape of the neck, exposing shiny hair, plaited and fastened with ribbons. Sleeves and collars, often of lace, and shawls were bought in Moçamedes. And also from Moçamedes were the fancy riding boots of the men, going strangely with the short jackets and flap-trousers peculiar to these people. Some of the young men rising to their twenties were already sporting beards, often luxuriant; and formidable pipes. It was the time for such things . . .

And here I sat under my great, cool mulemba, at my X-table, writing, often talking to the passers-by, then absently watching the scene again. Wisps of smoke from *erds* where coffee was brewing hung between the trees. One of the Louwrenses was playing a fiddle, competing with the cicadas. The sky—the dappled blue-white sky stretched over everything. Clouds came drifting by. A fish-eagle called.

The Trekboers, I thought . . . Here they were between the covered wagons, where the God of their Fathers could hear their psalms, their prayers uttered at such length, such solemnity; where the Principal Reader could remind his hearers they were the Lord's people, put here with a Purpose . . . Here these people were themselves.

For them the laager had ever been a rampart, a sanctuary, a refuge in times of stress. And as they had gathered, the world outside receded. Here they were sufficient unto themselves: they and their God . . .

He had always accompanied them on their treks; shown them the sure, the safe, the predestined way. If the Lord Himself were to speak in the midday heat from a burning hookthorn, should a pillar of white cloud lead them by day, a pillar of fire lead them by night, it would be as ordained . . .

The coffee-drinking, doughnut eating, story telling continued as the day ripened. The servants squatted before the *erds*, heads drawn back, eyes half-closed against the smoke. The Portuguese had called these old retainers the *Boers Pretos*: people like Kleinveld Labuschagne, Taliet du Toit, Dina Lombard . . . Black people who had adopted their masters' names as they had adopted their language, their religion and their ways. They sat there tending their fires, serving their mistresses, who were too massive for their stools, too breathless in the heat; manipulating Portuguese fans, talking through the hours, nostalgically remembering the lush highlands of the Serras . . .

Remembering perhaps Gert Alberts, who had married Nellie la Grange, whom he had tended when the crocodile had grabbed her in the waters of the Cunene. Remembering the Van Stadens, who had left the Trek in the old days at Olifants Pan; who had gone off on their own—husband, wife, children, and the husband's brother—into the wild country beyond the Cunene. Remembering how the brother had died and his body had been carried to a *Missao* in the far north; then after years the sudden reunion with these long-lost Trekkers on the High Serras . . .

I, too, remembered Humpata. In my mind's eye I still saw the collection of small farms spread about the cool undulating highland, with lively streams providing abundant water for humans, crops, animals; and fine forest where the trees provided excellent timber for carpentry. So Dolf Holtzhausen had assured me . . .

There was Arthur de Paiva, who was the Portuguese military commander, married to Mina Botha, daughter of the leader of the united Trek. '*Boa Viagem*!' he would shout to me in his exuberant way.

And journeys down from the High Serras to the desert lowlands and Moçamedes . . . The little white-washed port was full of gulls, screeching block-wheel ox-carts, dried fish and cheap wine . . .

Up in the Serras the trees were adorned with bees' nests made out of hollowed-out tree trunks. Majordomo of the community was a wizened little Bushman, rejoicing in the name of Roll-along-the-Path. And roll he did, when the wedding feast had ended. At night one would hear his voice, coming over a distance as he sought his way back to his hut. His song became something in praise of the *escudo, aguardente, 'espera até amanhà'*, and his white masters. Special days too in the community were those on which the hunters returned, laden with the gifts of Africa. The hunters sat around at the various homesteads, drank their coffee, ate their doughnuts, smoked their pipes. But more than anything else they told their stories . . .

By the waters of Babylon, there we sat down and yea, we wept, when we remembered Zion . . .

To them a strange man came from a strange people. He was different to them, but he tried to serve them. In doing so he grew to care for them, as they cared for him . . .

Piet Botha had wished to know why I was going to so much trouble. My true motives were a concern with these people who had become my friends; and a concern with this land, which had been both friend and enemy. My true motive was also a concern with Will Jordan who believed that a man's life should lead somewhere.

Lewies Louwrens's fiddle was still keening. Some were singing:

'Seek, my heart, they long lost friends,
Seek in vain where thou wouldst tarry,
Go then to the wilderness,
Seek them there where they now rest . . .'

An invitation from Ella Lombard to have coffee with them was brought to me by Dina. She had prepared all sorts of fine foods, she said. Lisa and 'that young man Adriaan' would also be there. I went and found it all as promised: good coffee, succulent doughnuts, a festive atmosphere.

A line of spurwing geese came flying up the river. Clouds had by now banked up to the north and lightning was flickering in the gloom. Suddenly a sluice in the sky opened and the rain came pouring down.

5

We sat talking under the wagon-hood, where we had taken shelter. The rain was coming down now like a beaded curtain, the thunder cracking like gun-fire.

Ella Lombard folded her old Transvaal flag—the *Vierkleur*—carefully, lovingly. It would be returned to the wagon *kist,* to be taken out next 16 December.

'Trek? It was always trek,' she said. 'As long as I can remember. For example, Louis Trichardt and his people . . . They were the first to trek from the Old Colony to the far north. And the Van Rensburgs . . . *Oom* Long Hans and his people, who were murdered afterwards on the highveld . . .

'Was still a young girl when we left the Old Colony. In 1838 we were there behind the Drakensberg, on our way to Natal. The mountains in Natal are like the Serras of Humpata. There we were, waiting to cross and go down into the Promised Land. Could see it all, lying there far below us . . .

'Then we had word from Retief and his commission, who had been sent to spy out the land: right down to the kraal of Dingane . . .

'My late father took us some way out of the laager that afternoon, so that we might see the return of Retief and his men. It was all very pretty and the people cheered.

'The commission brought news that Dingane had said that our people might buy the land. But first the Boers had to seek out Siconyella, who had stolen his cattle; then bring these back . . .

'So, there we stood on a hillock, watching the riders come past, cheering. And Retief himself sat up straight on his horse—a chestnut horse, with a white patch on the forehead. Sat there and waved his hat . . .

'My father said: "Well, then we shall do as the King of the Zulu wishes. Go out to look for Siconyella; bring back the cattle . . . When all that has been done, Johanna and Nicholas van Rensburg can get married!"

'Johanna was my eldest sister . . . All were disappointed, because Johanna had long wanted to get married. What did it all mean? What did the Lord intend for us?

'It happened this way: if Johanna and Nicholas had got married as they once had planned, they would have trekked down into Natal, to where the other wagons stood: at Blaauwkrantz and at Murder Spruit. It was there that the Zulu fell upon us that night. All except a few were killed as they lay there in the wagons . . .

'Lost all except Johanna, my sister, who was still up there on the Berg, waiting for Nicholas . . . I lay there on my bed, which was soaked with blood, not daring to move; lay until the sun rose. Then I looked at my body and saw that I was wounded; and yet I lived . . . Lay there not moving, because I could not: twenty other bodies were heaped around me. Then people came and removed the dead. At last I could get up, wounded as I was.'

I remembered the scars I had once seen while she had been kneading dough. So, I thought, she had survived that bloodiest of massacres. Afterwards she had married and had had children; had trekked again, and yet again. She had lost her husband in the Thirstland; she had also lost her sons. All that still remained was Lisa.

'*Meneer*,' she now said, as if she had long nursed the thought, 'now we are really on our way to our land which we have been seeking, and which we shall call Lydensrust . . . We have heard that you, *Meneer*, have arranged with Kambonde to buy this land. It is like it was with Retief!'

'Yes,' I said. 'But, we hope, not too much. The land must still be bought!'

Fine droplets of rain had settled on her face. Some distance away Adriaan and Lisa were sheltering under an awning.

'Much has still to be arranged, *Tante* Lombard,' I answered. 'The Trek will move on slowly. I shall go ahead. Perhaps all will be settled early in the new year.'

'Will Kambonde also ask that cattle of his first be returned, as was the case with Siconyella?'

She was well-informed. I had discussed the matter with a few of the Trek leaders: Louw du Plessis, Barend Bouwer, Diederick Prinsloo. Yes, strange as it seemed, there *was* a Siconyella.

'I shall buy the land around Otavi Spring,' I said. 'Kambonde has, however, asked us to help him bring back some cattle stolen by Bushmen: out there beyond the Omuramba Omatako.'

Her *kappie* dipped. 'Yes,' she said. 'But how long will it still be before all is ready?'

'Six months, nine months!'

'You, *Meneer*, say Upingtonia, but we think of it as Lydensrust. Six months? . . . And then we shall be there!'

That was but a rough estimate. Things had to get moving. This too leisurely progress was good for no one. It gave people like Piet Botha too much time to work up grievances.

The rain suddenly stopped. The after-thunder came booming over the tops of the trees. It was like the spent fury of a lion after a kill. The sun broke through, flooding the world.

Widow Roets, in black, whose wagon stood next to that of Ella Lombard, appeared from her shelter. Her husband had been one of the great hunters of the Trek . . .

'My man,' she said to me, extending a limp hand, 'was choice above all.'

Pity, I said, that he had not been able to undertake the trek to the new republic. I admired her courage, undertaking this trek on her own now.

'As long as the good Lord is with us, *Meneer*,' she said, looking straight, almost vacantly at me, 'there is no hardness for us in trek. My husband always said: the fine land still lies ahead. We must keep on, until we find it.'

6

'How are the guns behaving?' I asked Adriaan Venter later that day.

'They are good, *Meneer*,' he said. He shook his blonde hair out of his eyes. 'They are true, and have great power.'

'Paper cartridge? Pressed bullet?'

'For the elephants, *Meneer*.'

'Please tell him also,' Lisa interrupted, 'every day may be a shooting day, but every day is not a *hunting* day!'

He fixed his gaze on her.

But Lisa was in a playful mood. 'Give *me* a chance with this gun,' she said. 'I'll show him!'

'I fear you'll put us all to shame!' I answered. We laughed. Her new dress and her pretty quilted *kappie* had caught some rain. Her face, turned up towards me, showed all the old alertness. The expression of the mouth was one of sweetness, but also of strength.

Once, I suddenly recalled, I had almost given her up for lost; but she had recovered, and had never looked back. I suddenly felt old and used-up. There was fever in me, I thought.

'Adriaan,' I said, trying to get a hold on myself, 'my brother-in-law down at the Bay, Chris Leen, will be at Ondangua shortly. The wagon-and-team you have ordered will then probably be there for you.'

Lisa blushed. But Mother Ella saved the situation by suddenly reappearing. Had anybody seen the *ginger,* she enquired. Johanna Botha, it appeared, had sent a message, saying that she was suffering from a closeness of the chest. There was a fine remedy made up from ginger, haarlemensis, camphor and alum . . . Did *Meneer* have a remedy?

No, I replied, *Meneer* did not; at least nothing as effective as the remedies of the good women of the Trek. The missing ginger now gave Lisa the opportunity to disappear, taking Adriaan with her. Soon I heard her playful laugh coming from somewhere in the depths of the wagon.

Dina found the ginger in a recess of the wagon *kist.* Slamming the lid down, she muttered some strange threat about seeing to it that Little Miss would not be taken away from them 'before her time'. Whereupon Ella Lombard sighed and reminded her that both of them were not so young as they used to be.

'Remember,' Ella Lombard said, 'you were but a few days old when they picked you up on the battlefield at Mosega.'

That was in the days of the Great Trek, when Boer commandoes had crossed the Vaal to punish Mzilikazi in the Marico country. The Matabeles had attacked the Boer laager at Vegkop and had been driven off. They succeeded, however, in taking with them a great number of cattle. The expedition to Mosega had been a punitive one.

'My dead husband, Hans,' Ella Lombard said, 'found her when the commando was on its way back to the laager with the cattle.' Then turning to Dina again: 'So you lay there in the sun, with the ants crawling over you. And *Baas* Hans stopped and picked you up, put you in his saddle bag: you were so small.'

Dina covered her eyes and wailed aloud, while swaying to and fro. 'Old Miss, Old Miss!'

'You were in the saddle-bag,' Ella Lombard continued, 'and *Baas* Hans brought you back to the laager. I was a young girl at that time. So you see, if you are old, Dina, then I am still older!'

'Oh, oh!' Dina wailed, shaking her little gilded earrings.

'So it all took place. And *Meneer* here must know about it,' Ella Lombard sighed.

Lisa and Adriaan climbed out of the wagon again. Ella Lombard looked critically at her daughter, and said: 'Look how your dress has got wet from the rain.'

Dina looked up, and wiped her eyes. 'My own two hands have ironed that dress!'

'Yes, old Dina,' Lisa answered. 'I know. But we got caught when the rain came down.' She stroked some last droplets off the skirt. 'Only a little wet.'

Dina fixed one coal-black eye on Lisa, while covering the other with a hand. 'It is because there are other things in your head, eh?'

Lisa pouted. 'It is *my* head!'

'*Your* head. But you are your mother's child. You ask Mister here. You must remember me when I am old, eh? You are still a child; and you grew up before me.' The last words were spoken with a quick glance at the young man standing demurely to one side. 'You too were a child, and grew up before me! Old Miss, we have come a long way together, you and I!'

'I tell it to the children every day, Dina.'

'But perhaps Old Miss has also become used to me.'

'Do I become used to my right hand? When we are dead one day, they will bury us together, Dina. And they will put the *Vierkleur* over us.'

Dina wailed again. Deftly she blew her nostrils clean, then shook a finger in Adriaan's face. The Little Master, she said, had a habit of going out into the bush alone. Yes, she knew he went there looking for elephants. But he should also know that there were Bushmen there. How could he think of taking their young Miss along with him among 'those wild things'?

Kleinveld Labuschagne, squatting at the *erd*, looked up and said: '*Oumie*, would you then have Little Miss stay alone?'

Ella Lombard sighed. 'When a child grows up and becomes a man, or becomes a woman, there is no more holding it to one's apron strings.'

'*Confrater*!' Dina addressed Kleinveld in a way she had picked up in Angola. 'You stay and look after Old Miss. I'll go with this child.' With a nod she indicated Lisa. 'I'll go with her. And if anybody is to be married, I must know.'

I laughed, but Adriaan drooped his head. His black, wide-brimmed hat hung limply from his fingers. Dina, gaining confidence, repeated her admonishment: the young couple would have to consult *her,* too, in future.

So there they were before me now: Ella Lombard, sitting on a stool, hands folded; then, removed from us all, the young couple, eager for each other; and Dina Lombard, who had once been picked up as a child on a Matabele battlefield, now folding her shiny black hands under her pure white apron. And Kleinveld Labuschagne, squatting by his fire, poking in the ashes, batting his eyes against thin wisps of smoke . . . he whose father had once been a ring-head Zulu from the kraal of Mpande . . .

'Little Miss,' Kleinveld said, 'if you are out there in the bush one day . . .'

'*Outaaa*!' she protested, meaning Old Father. But it changed almost at once to her merry laugh. Her *kappie* had fallen into the nape of her neck. There was a copper sheen to her hair. She suddenly smiled at me.

7

There was a parasite swimming in my veins . . . Thirteen years before an infected anopheles had pricked a capillary. The only real remedy was to embitter one's blood. One did this with quinine hydrochloride, so that even a parasite would flinch. If one failed to do this, the results might be frightening. Like a great many others, one learnt to drink one's quinine and smile.

Another kind of fever in me was more subtle. It was of the mind. It had developed these past two years and nine months. Now, in the spring of 1885, it had become a disease between two people who had once been friends.

I still liked to think that Pieter Maritz-Botha was not really hostile to our plans. I preferred to see it all as a result of some petty irritation. He would get rid of it in time. Better to stick to the substance of things, I said to myself. In fact, that was what this trek back to Damaraland was all about. Angola had been a mirage, and all of us, including myself, had been led astray. Now it was time to pause.

What were the facts? There was a closer relationship between the Trekboers and myself than ever before. I had been their ambassador to the Portuguese. I had been their trade commissioner; their general agent; their constitutional adviser. I had been their physician . . .

When I finally awoke to the irony of our situation, I thought it possible to revive the Rehoboth scheme. At first it seemed to promise well enough. Piet Botha returned from the Transvaal and supported me. We went down to Otjitambi together, and he signed the deed of sale as a witness with Petrus Swartbooi . . .

Then Belck had turned up and had put an abrupt end to all the Rehoboth dealings. I protested strongly and informed Belck that I would appeal to higher authority, both in Britain and in Germany.

For the time being, however, there was nothing to do but to return. I sought Botha's opinion on all that had happened. He seemed to close up suddenly.

We had been on our way back, and laagered somewhere near the Cunene. At dawn the next morning I shouted to him where he was lying, only half awake: 'Let's get moving!'

He lay there with his head on a propped-up cushion and looked darkly at me. I got up and playfully pulled a blanket off him. Then suddenly he seemed to be irked. What did I think I was doing, he asked. Who was I to give orders? I should know my place . . . By now he was sitting upright.

At the time I dismissed all this; but back at Humpata I became conscious of a growing tension between us. Botha seemed to be resenting my position. He seemed to be questioning the part I was playing in the community. Nevertheless, I still continued to consult him with regard to new developments. He would stand there listening, sucking at his pipe. Then he would finally say: 'Well, we'll see.' This was never said with any warmth. Nor was there any indication that he was willing to help look for an alternative. Maybe the incident on the way back to Humpata, trivial as it was, had wounded me more deeply than I knew.

Some time previously, at Ondangua, Chris Leen had said to me: 'If you and the *Bestuur* wish me to act as secretary to the new state, I am willing. But I don't think Piet Botha would like it. I have heard of things being said. Usually I am indifferent to gossip, but still . . . !'

'Who is Piet Botha to decide who I shall have in the land *I've* paid for?' I interrupted. 'He's been trying to have it all ways for a long time now. What does he want? I hear of his criticism, and then when we move on, he stays put. When we accepted it that he had either stayed at Humpata, or gone off to join Lewis, lo and behold, he turned up again—with the usual ostentation. Well, here we are at Ondangua; and here he is again, playing host to Lewis. Piet is looking for trouble. Should he say anything about your appointment as secretary, ignore him.'

'I've no intention of falling foul of Piet,' Chris said.

'Can you imagine it: here he is, entertaining the arch-enemy of the Boers! Let's get on with the job. We've enough to do.'

So we had talked . . . The pressing work now was the finalizing of the negotiations with Kambonde Kampingana.

What made it bearable in the end was the successful outcome of the sale. The Finnish missionaries had witnessed the contract. I had bought the whole area between the White Pan to Otjovanda Tjongue; to the Omuramba Omatako; to the Waterberg in the south; to Okaukueyo in the north-east. This included all the copper deposits, the waters, the forests. I had bought this land, and it had been carefully described. Kambonde himself had been more than satisfied. I had done all this, and it was the culmination of an ideal. In the daily business there had been little time to think of myself . . .

On the way to Namutoni Hester Bouwer came to me one day while I was sitting at my X-table, writing. 'Piet Botha,' she said, 'is full of loose talk. What does he want us to do?'

'I wish I knew,' I answered. 'He speaks about "Jordan and his place". What do the people understand by it?'

She smiled the gentle smile of a woman whose equanimity I had never seen disturbed. 'He is jealous of you, *Meneer.*'

I looked up in surprise. 'I have never tried to compete with him,' I said. 'I always valued his co-operation.'

'You have done things which he could not do,' she persisted. 'You have bought this land from Kambonde, and paid for it. He is jealous. You are a good man, *Meneer.* You do things for people who are not your own.'

'They are people,' I said after a while.

I saw her thinking deeply. She had strong, well-cut features. 'You are the true leader of our people,' she said, 'although you are different from us.'

'You have your own leaders,' I answered. 'I am merely your adviser. I do not even wish to serve on the *Bestuur.* I shall let every man have a farm for a registration fee of a few shillings.'

'The people have accepted you, *Meneer.* Piet does not like that.'

My feelings were mixed. I felt thankful to hear this from a woman like Hester Bouwer. I was also disturbed by the knowledge that someone who professed to be a Boer through and through and who, presumably, resented a non-Boer leading the Trek, should hobnob with a man like Lewis.

'You must not give up, *Meneer,*' Hester said. 'The people will not fail you.'

Indeed, I thought. Upingtonia had been bought. Rautanen, at the head of the Finnish Mission, and his colleagues, Weikolin and Rocha, had witnessed the deal. They were good friends. They would also be friends of the new state.

'Thank you for your kind words,' I said at last.

When she had left I sat there looking dimly at the writing paper before me. It was a lonely business. A woman like Hester Bouwer would understand it. Perhaps she sensed it in me. There were many things in life beyond my reach . . . I could only keep on, hoping that the fulfilment of one immediate ideal would give one courage. What I really sought was the conviction that I had not lived in vain.

All this was a third kind of fever in me.

8

Chris Leen and I sat in the lee of my wagon under umbrella-shaped acacias near the fine spring of Namutoni.

'So the Trek has completed its own great circle,' I said. 'Six years ago it was here at this very spot, waiting for Gert Alberts and his fellow riders to bring back news of what the country was like to the west. And here they are again—but without *Oom* Gert. Have you any news yet of what the trouble between Botha and Kambonde was about?'

He lit a cigar and stretched his long legs. He was wearing *veldschoens.* 'It was something about a horse,' he said.

'I have it that it was the Arab. I take it that Kambonde wanted it, if I know Kambonde.'

'I asked him about it. He merely shrugged his shoulders. I might even have said that it did not concern me. Perhaps it doesn't!'

'Any possibility of trouble with an Ovambo chief would concern us all,' I said. 'Have you seen Lewis?'

'Just for a few minutes.'

'Why doesn't he move on? Why doesn't he come and see me?'

'He probably thinks that you should go and see him.'

'Damned if I will!'

'I share your sentiments. He asked me about you. He wanted to know whether you were serious about Upingtonia. It's ludicrous, I know. But Lewis is up to mischief, I feel it. He was very outspoken about the contract.'

'The devil take Lewis. Why doesn't he move on? He's a bad influence, always hanging around the laager. Outspoken? About the land not being Ovambo territory? About it belonging to Kamaherero? I have been waiting for him to come and see me. He hasn't got the guts. What does Botha say? I see Jan Labuschagne also going to Lewis's camp. What is *he* up to?'

'When we were at Olukonda there was a lot of talk about the murder in Ukuanyama, with you in the lead.' Chris said this playfully.

'With me in the lead. Maybe you are right. Qualify it by saying that I was a very reluctant principal.'

I had been on my way to Moçamedes with a load of ivory, shortly after the treaty with Kambonde. Observing the custom I had given the King of Ukuanyamaland the usual *passepartout*, a cask of *aguardente.* I had already crossed the river and had passed through Humbe when the trouble started. The king had taken ill. Within a few hours he was dead. This was surely the work of Jordan, some of his counsellors said. He had poisoned the brandy. What nonsense, I rejoined. I poison the king? What for? Surely I would not trek down to Moçamedes, intending to come back. Indeed I *had* to come back. I had bought the land from Kambonde . . .

But the king was dead and the news soon spread. A couple of British traders happened to make some remark, on seeing an Ukuanyama prodding a cow with a spear. This triggered off a mass of pent-up feeling after the death of the king. The two traders took to flight. I, who had been accused of the murder, was already on my way on the far side of Humbe. The only available scapegoats were Fathers Delpech and Rothan. I had often played chess with them. I had also enjoyed their coffee. Then they were killed . . .

On my return from Moçamedes a month later I had heard the news and was shocked. The irony was that the true culprit had meanwhile been exposed by the tribe itself: an ambitious sister of the king who wished to have the throne for her son.

'What did Piet Botha have to say?' I asked Chris.

'Said that what had happened was not so much anger about the king's death, but anger about Kambonde selling Ovambo territory: to you and the Boers.'

'But what does Kambonde have to do with the Ukuanyamas? They and the Ondongas may be related tribes, but they are yet separate.'

'Piet doesn't see it that way. At Olukonda he had an argument with Rautanen about the deed of sale.' Chris looked at me. 'Said there was trouble between Kambonde and his brother Nehale: a direct result of Kambonde's action.'

We sat down to eat. 'Botha,' I said, 'apparently thinks that it has all been a clever bit of fraud on the part of Jordan and Kambonde. What a firm!'

Izak brought us a pot of roasted palla and mashed potatoes. We sipped brandy, and ate.

'I still don't get to the bottom of it all,' I said. 'If Piet thinks that way, what is he doing here?'

'He still wants to take the people back to the Transvaal.'

'Nobody in his right senses will want to cross the Thirstland again. I have an idea that he's merely blowing hot and cold to try us out. He refuses to believe that I am serious about Upingtonia. He must have told Lewis that. Of course, I may give him the proverbial amount of rope to hang himself. It should not be long before he can see how serious we are. Then he may well come to his senses. I would still be glad to have his support.'

'What about Lewis?'

I poured myself some coffee from my little pewter jug. 'That's another mystery,' I said. 'His theatricalities don't bother me. I've got used to that. What I don't like is this strange new *entente* between him and Botha. Even more unnatural is Jan Labuschagne's presence in the company: Jan, who can hardly speak two words of English, while Lewis's Dutch is rudimentary.

How do they talk? In Otjiherero?'

Chris chuckled. 'Jan Labuschagne, by the way, has been spreading the news that our true destination is the Waterberg, according to Barend Bouwer.'

'The Waterberg? To settle there permanently? The Waterberg is part of Damaraland and belongs to Kamaherero.'

'Bouwer mentioned something else some time ago. We have undertaken to help Kambonde get his stolen cattle back from the Bushman Gabriel: out there beyond the omuramba. Well, I have left the matter to develop. If we want to retain Kambonde's friendship, however, we should do it. Botha doesn't like the idea one bit, according to Bouwer. How do you see it?'

'I see it the way you see it.'

'This Gabriel and his crowd are a threat to Upingtonia. We can hardly expect people to go out and live on their distant farms, with these kind of people around. The trek-route through the sandveld to Lake Ngami has to be made safe. Gabriel is a mere bandit. The sooner we get rid of him the better.'

Chris lit a new cigar, blowing out his lucifer with the smoke. We arose and returned to the lee of the wagon.

'There's only one approach which makes sense,' I said. 'That is for every man to do his duty. If he doesn't want it that way? Let him get out and set up on his own. We have no place here for the faint-hearted.'

Chris had been down to the Bay. There he had met hunter-traders like Charles Lyon, Behan, Todd . . . These had indicated that they would like to join us in Upingtonia. What about the Erikssons, I enquired. I had not seen Axel Eriksson for a long time. I missed him. At Ondangua I had written, giving him full details of the new constitution, drawn up with the assistance of the *Bestuur*. I reminded him of his belief that Upingtonia would interest the Erikssons. Omaruru had never got over the shock of the war. The Erikssons were still there, and they were fine people. Their presence in Upingtonia would be of great value to us. Charles Lyon had written to me at Okahandja, saying that he would join us as soon as he could; he still had some affairs to settle. This was encouraging . . .

'Where is Axel at present?' I asked.

'According to Bill Clay, whom I met at Olukonda, as I told you,' Chris answered, 'he was on his way to the Okavango. This was some months ago. He must be up there somewhere; or else on his way back to Omaruru.'

'Let's hope he touches at Otjovanda Tjongue. Let's hope he comes to see us there!'

At three o'clock, while the sun hung as if glued to an azure sky, Chris got up to return to his own wagon. 'By the way,' he said before leaving, 'that wagon-and-team your young friend Venter ordered is on its way! Lewis—believe it or not—brought me some letters from Ondangua. Bill Clay will send it down, as soon as it arrives.'

I was glad about this. 'Fine,' I said, 'then, almost certainly, we shall start the new republic with a wedding. A good omen.'

Chris looked at me, smiling somewhat sadly. The amusement may have been at my expense: me a confirmed bachelor. The sadness was almost certainly because of the thought of his family far away at the Cape.

They would join him, Chris had always said, as soon as everything had been settled. I agreed. His wife, Georgina, was my sister.

9

I made no attempt to see Lewis while we were at Namutoni. His wagon stood between some trees a few hundred yards from my own. There was no obligation on me to look him up. Let him come and talk, I decided, if he so wished.

He came that very afternoon. I was busy making some entries in my journal when he arrived. When I looked up, there he was, approaching on horseback. He dismounted and threw the reins to Kairob in his accustomed way.

'Well, Jordan,' he said, approaching me. 'I would have thought that your sporting instincts would have taken you into the elandveld by this time. We are in for a wet year.' We shook hands.

I poured us some brandy. 'What brings you to these parts?' I asked.

He answered in the old, pedantic way: 'Oh, on the *qui vive*, you know. One never knows what people are up to these days.' He offered me a cigar.

'How's the war going?' I knew quite well enough how the war was going. Hendrik Witbooi had succeeded his father Moses Witbooi as chief of the Witbooi Namas. At Onguheva near

Rehoboth he had forced Kamaherero to accept a 'peace'. This he had managed by intelligent diplomacy, and nothing more than a light military operation. At Gibeon this had nevertheless been celebrated as a great victory.

The news had caused me some satisfaction. If Kamaherero could be brought down a peg or two, it would favour us in the new state. *Schutzherrschaft* which had put paid to the Rehoboth scheme had apparently got bogged down. It had certainly made no impression on either the Namas of the south or the Hereros of the north. The old struggle between the nations was still very much alive. True, Jan Jonker Afrikaander and his tribe had fallen into decadence. Their place had, however, now been taken by the Witboois. Dr Vogelsang, who had been the German *chargé d'affaires* in the Transgariep, had made little impression on Hendrik Witbooi.

Eighteen months earlier Kamaherero had taken his whole nation down to the southern border of Damaraland. They had moved up and down a furrow, drawn by a plough, extending right across Rehoboth. This had been a kind of mass demonstration of national resolve. Thereupon Hendrik Witbooi felt himself compelled to do likewise.

Dr Hans Schinz, a biologist from Zürich, whom I had met at Olukonda when dealing with Kambonde, had told me this. Schinz was on a grand tour of the Transgariep and the surrounding areas, travelling by ox-wagon. In spite of many hardships, he had already absorbed an enormous part of the country.

Here was a man after my own heart. The mass peregrination of the Ovaherero had intrigued him. What intrigued him even more was Hendrik Witbooi's attempt to outdo Kamaherero. By July of the previous year Witbooi and all his people, with all their cattle, carts, horses, wagons, were at Rehoboth, on their way north. To do what? I asked. Schinz, refinedly European, merely smiled. Who knows, he replied. The German authorities like Dr Nels and Dr Goering at Okahandja were worried about it. This seemed like one whole people wanting to fight another.

'So many in this country regard themselves as being called upon by the Most High,' Lewis said. 'This journey of Witbooi's with his entire nation is the latest. People travelling about this country on Heavenly Orders seems to be the fashion these days.'

'From which I deduce,' I said, 'that you object to the Boers on their way to Otjovanda Tjongue. I am taking them there in terms of a valid contract of sale with Kambonde Kampingana.'

His finger with the ring bearing the head of an antelope within a circle seemed to rap the table.

'I am merely giving you formal notice,' he said. 'I do same in my capacity as High Commissioner and Legal Adviser to the Herero nation. Your settlement at Otjovanda Tjongue will be seen in a serious light. It is Damara territory, and Kambonde had no right to sell it.'

I walked away for some yards, trying to control myself. 'Get along, Lewis,' I growled. 'We are going to Upingtonia. Get that into your head, man. The new state, I can assure you, will be constituted in an orderly and correct manner. Which, by the way, may well serve as an example to many others.'

He sat there smoking, seemingly quite at ease.

'I shall not press the matter any further,' he said. 'But be it remembered that we have had this discussion. I might also add that I have made an offer to Labuschagne and others to accommodate them in the Waterberg, should the need arise.'

'Who the hell is Labuschagne?' I was furious now. 'I am the leader here, not Labuschagne!'

'He is a free party,' he answered. 'However, circumstanced as you are, I would meet you this wise: the offer is open to anyone who wishes to avail himself of it. Your good friend, Pieter Maritz-Botha—a fine fellow!—has been so kind as to look things over down there. So you may expect me, should you persist in following the course you have set out upon.' He started walking back towards his horse.

'Never you mind!' I shouted after him. 'We shall be on our way to Otjovanda Tjongue next week! Mark my words!'

I had been determined not to get angry, yet it had happened. I was certainly no diplomat when it came to people like Lewis.

10

'A fine piece of craftmanship,' I said to Adriaan Venter, later that week, while inspecting his recent purchase. It was what in local parlance had come to be known as a 'flower-wagon'. It had been made at Paarl in the Cape and was gaily decorated with paintings of flowers.

'It has come a long way,' I said.

The blond head seemed to glow with pride.

'The wagon is a good one, *Meneer*,' he said. He had taken it down to the spring and had washed it. Now it stood there almost as good as when it had arrived by schooner in the Bay.

'It will have to travel far, *Meneer*. Our banns will be read by *Oom* Diederick this coming Sabbath. But now I have heard that when we get to where the laager is going to stand, we are first to go out on commando. To look for Kambonde's cattle?'

'We have such a commitment,' I said. 'But it should all be over in a few days. This Gabriel fellow should not be too difficult to deal with.'

'In that case, *Meneer*, Lisa and I have decided that we shall not have our wedding until this work has been done.'

I looked at him. He was a man, because he had done difficult, even heroic things, far beyond his years. He was also a boy. The gun-blue eyes, the fair hair, the slight build always reminded me of the youngster I had first met at Olifants Pan. He had recently bought two new Martini Henrys; and the new flower-wagon . . .

'And,' I enquired playfully, 'how far will this wagon trek, when the banns have run, Gabriel has been tamed, and the ceremony performed? You should know that I have decided to offer three hundred farms in Upingtonia at a nominal fee of a few shillings each. Each one will have its own good water. Upingtonia, young man, is the crown of this country. You were there once with Jan Labuschagne, remember?'

'I was there with *Oom* Jan, yes, *Meneer*. But then I was still a milkbeard. And I knew little of the world. I trekked up the 'maramba and came to a fine water at Okasima. There were many elephants there; and many Bushmen too. I would like to go there again.'

'To hunt?'

'To be there for some time, *Meneer*. And then I would like to trek northwards in the 'maramba to the river. From there I would like to go to the Pan where the tree is.'

The 'tree' was the baobab at Olifants Pan on which the names of the hunters in the great elephant slaughter of 1879 had been carved.

'Yes,' I said. 'The tree is still there.'

'I want to carve my own name on that tree.'

His level gaze met mine.

'Good luck to you!' I said. 'But remember, we need you at

Upingtonia. Come back!' I looked at the wagon. 'And may this wagon carry you just as far as mine has carried me. You get to love it afterwards, as much as you could love a wife.'

In the dense reeds around the great spring of Namutoni, the parakeets were chattering excitedly.

11

O, the shining waters of this land . . .

The waters always captured one anew by reason of their preciousness. In great parts of the country rain was an occasion. A year like the present when good rains had fallen early in the season, the Ovaherero, according to their custom, would call Ojomeva, the Year of the Waters.

Names in this country, in their musicality, sang the praises of fountains, lakes, *vleis.* There were Tunobia, Ondangua, Ombonde . . . There were Otjitundua, Kaoko Otavi and Omaruru . . . There were Otjikoto and Guinas: blue bottomless lakes lying in the bush like the eyes of Earth itself . . . Deep down in Great Namaland, where I often came in the early days, there were Hoachanas, Oas, Kubus, Naiams . . . Here was Namutoni where we laagered now. To the west was Okaukueyo. In between was Rietfontein, where Gert Alberts had once buried his wife, after he had returned from the long ride to the west. Ten days' trek to the south-west was Otjovanda Tjongue: the finest water of them all. And nearby was Otavi . . .

At the end of the week Louw du Plessis and I went on a small pilgrimage. We had promised Gert Alberts before our departure from Humpata that we would visit the grave at Rietfontein, when at Namutoni. Rietfontein was a few hours on horseback on the old trek-route to Okaukueyo.

There was open water here in the limestone. The game came down in their thousands from the grasslands to the north and north-west of the White Pan, and from the southern bush. The quelea finches would rise in dense clouds from the reeds, gather into tight, organic balls, go roaring over the plains. The great pan itself shone like the Atlantic at high noon. Sometimes it was like an endless snowfield in the polar wastes.

The kudus would come down quietly, warily, from the mopani. The bulls would lift their great spiral horns; listen, look about them; then come down the white path to the water. The large ears of the cows would remain alert, poised to catch the slightest sound of danger. At the water there were a great many zebras. They would stand there drinking, dreaming. Then suddenly, for no apparent reason, they would start, go thundering away . . .

Louw and I stood there at the little heap of stones between the game paths. We stood there with bared heads, and Louw said a prayer. His hair was thin and wet with perspiration. He spoke in a simple yet moving way. Far to the north-east thunder clouds were building up. The sky was vast and blue.

Louw du Plessis put on his hat again, narrowed his eyes against the glare, as we walked back. 'These are the graves of our people,' he said. 'So we left them on the trek road. One can find them from here to Lake Ngami. And from Ngami to the Crocodile River in the Transvaal. From here to the Cunene; and beyond the Cunene to Humpata. They lie in the sand, in the limestone, in the bush . . . Whether anybody will know about them in ten years' time?' He made a vague gesture. 'Who can tell? The Lord has brought us a long way, Brother Jordan.'

It was getting dark when we eventually reached the laager. Fires were winking between the trees. When we passed Ella Lombard's wagon, Lisa looked up from the *erd* and greeted us.

'*Oom* Louw!' she said. '*Meneer*!'

'Have you seen the new wagon, *Meneer*?' she presently asked.

'It is very fine,' I said. 'I have also seen the young man who ordered it.' She laughed and stirred a three-legged pot.

'He says that he wants to cut his name on a tree; and the wagon will yet take him to that tree: a baobab on which the names of famous hunters have been carved.'

'Goodness!' She deftly stirred her pot, with flicks of the wrist.

'How is your mother?' I asked.

'Ma is better, *Meneer*,' she said. 'This morning she said that she did not feel so well.'

We stood talking for a few minutes; then each one went his way. At my wagon Izak was squatting in front of his own three-legged pot. I suddenly felt lonely, thinking of my own kin whom I had not seen for years. I was thankful when Chris Leen appeared out of the darkness to share my supper. I drew us each an appetizer from the cask. We sat down at my X-table.

'Chris,' I asked when we had eaten well and were relaxing. 'What does a man need from life?'

He looked up, not taking my question seriously.

'Good food,' he said. 'A good wife; and good luck!'

'Here's to good luck,' I answered, raising my glass.

He laughed, as he wished me goodnight.

'You are off to Ondangua tomorrow,' I said. 'If Bill Clay is still up there, please give him some letters of mine to take down to the Bay.'

I wanted to write to my mother. I had not done so for many weeks.

12

At the beginning of October the entire Trek, except a few members who were hunting near the White Pan, was at Otjovanda Tjongue.

Pieter Maritz-Botha had moved down with us from Namutoni. As usual he made up the rear-guard of the long line of wagons slowly making their way through the dense bush south-west of Otjikoto. The remarkable thing was that he had nevertheless remained part of the Trek. It had become a general subject for discussion now: Botha's opposition to the idea of a new republic in the newly purchased territory. On the whole, people were critical of his negative attitude. Jan Labuschagne and a few others were reported to be the only support he had. Robert Lewis, of course, seemed in a strange way still to be an influence.

It was the question of motives which worried me. Was it indeed merely a question of 'jealousy', as Hester Bouwer had suggested? Did Botha indeed envy me my position of influence? Thinking about it as I did, I could only detect a churlishness on the part of Botha which was sad. Who would have thought him capable of this? I sometimes comforted myself; it might all be a passing phase, I reasoned, an attack of bad humour, induced by frustration. Marriage was, no doubt, a fine institution. But it was a curtailment of freedom, all the same.

In spite of the subtle tension, these were good days at Otjovanda Tjongue. The consensus of opinion was that a more beautiful place had never been seen in Damaraland or its neighbouring territories. Water and pasture were abundant here. There was fine soil for produce-gardening and general agriculture. Within the first week some bush had been cleared. Others were building hartebeest-houses: one- or two-roomed structures of daub and poles with roofs of thatch. A few had gone out into the surrounding country to examine the waters. All that was now required to launch the new republic was official acceptance of the constitution at a people's meeting.

The seventeenth of October was provisionally fixed as the date for this. On that day I would formally hand over the necessary deeds to the *Bestuur.* I would also announce on what grounds the new state would be constituted. I would also discuss the allocation of land. So the way would be opened for energetic further development. In time it would become a scheme of things such as this country had never yet seen. Settlers would come from everywhere. We would lay the foundations of a civilized order such as few had thought possible.

The rains remained surprisingly constant. Almost every afternoon there was a sudden, sharp storm. There would be much crashing of thunder with lightning forking over the green bush. Then the rain would come down in torrents. By early evening it would all be over again. The air would be clear; and far to the south the last of the storm clouds, blue-black and massive, would roll away . . .

On the heights of Otjovanda Tjongue itself, the late afternoon sun would lie like a benediction. On grass, shrubs, trees, the raindrops would glisten; and everywhere the cry of francolin, wood-hoopoe and wood-pigeon would ring . . .

I still went about with the suggestion of fever in my blood. It had always been like this. You knew that soon it could get a grip on you. It would start shaking you; and presently it would pull you down on your back. There would be little to be done about it. You would take your quinine, but on the whole just accept it as something to be lived with. You would say to yourself: 'Better not to anticipate it. Live unto the moment. Be thankful for such afternoons, when the world lights up after the rain, and the clouds come drifting by . . .'

13

A sudden shower one afternoon drove the people to their wagons and other shelters. Within minutes it had all passed. Groups soon gathered again, standing or sitting about under the marulas, the sycamores, the anas. There were shrill voices of the children; the boom of hunters' laughter; the plaintive voices of womenfolk, calling their kinsmen to coffee. All this was mixed with the lowing of the cattle, the intricate sound-pattern of the birds, and the tinkling of streams.

I went to Diederick Prinsloo's newly constructed hartebeest-house. There I found the old Principal Reader himself. Louw du Plessis, Barend Bouwer and Pieter Maritz-Botha were also there.

I hesitated for a moment, then thought: 'The sooner we talk to each other as man to man, the better!'

'So you've arrived,' I said to Botha and shook hands.

'We expected you,' Barend Bouwer said. 'Come, here is good coffee, man! Sit down!'

'Well,' Louw du Plessis said, feeling in his pockets for his flint-and-steel. 'It was a sudden downpour, eh? We all got caught.'

'It will be a good year for the veld to grow,' Barend Bouwer said, 'and a good year for the hunt. What are your plans, Mester?'

I lit a cigar. 'What do you mean?' I said. 'For the hunt? I'm not much of a hunter, you know.'

'You are good enough, man. Much better than some who imagine themselves to be something!'

I smiled, and was glad of the opportunity to do so. The atmosphere was strained. Botha, nursing his pipe, was ignoring me.

'Brother Will means,' Louw said, 'that there are things more important than hunting to see to.'

Diederick Prinsloo rapped the ground with his olive-wood stick. 'That thou hast come is as it should be, *Meneer*,' he said. 'It seems that there are many things that are working against us. There are those that are raising a false report about our republic. These are false matters; and it is good that you have come, *Meneer*, to advise us what to do, when we hear such things.'

His words, weighty and solemn as they were, seemed to put me at ease. It was, in a way, a sudden affirmation of my position in the laager. It was a good thing for Botha to witness.

'*Oom* Diederick,' I said, 'there is no other way for us. We are here. This is the land we have bought. It is *our* land.'

'So we believe,' Louw du Plessis said.

Diederick Prinsloo nodded, tapped with his stick, causing me to feel that he was with me. Only Botha sat there, uttering not a sound. His hands were folded. His imperial was cocked at a challenging angle. He was inscrutable.

I suddenly intuited that he had been discussing the future of the new state with these members of the *Bestuur*. That was why Old Diederick had immediately spoken about the raising of 'false reports'. The chances were that neither Old Diederick, nor Du Plessis, nor Bouwer had had time to answer Botha's criticisms before I came.

'*Meneer*,' Old Diederick said. 'We hear now from Piet Botha that there is a murmuring among some of this laager . . . of which we have not yet had advice. Few they must be . . . but it is good that we know what be the cause of their grousing.'

The main cause of all these flying rumours was Botha himself, I thought.

'Such there will always be, *Oom* Diederick,' I said after a while. 'It is not important. We must just get on with the work.'

I was conscious of Botha blowing through his pipe-stem again. This seemed to be the way he expressed his indifference, or maybe his opposition. Since the night at Humbe when I had made an attempt to determine his attitude, I had made little progress. He still seemed to be wanting to have it both ways. That he had in fact been responsible for much of the 'murmuring' Old Diederick had referred to, I had no doubt. I only wished he would express himself in unambiguous terms. This was what the Boers called 'playing at fine weather'. The very fact that the members of the *Bestuur* had spoken in his presence indicated their uncertainty.

Would he find support for his views in the laager? To what extent had he indeed been able to undermine the general morale? Chris Leen had told me that Botha had asked him about the proposed expedition to deal with Gabriel. According to Chris he would rather have us leave Gabriel to carry on his activities, not considering the threat to Upingtonia.

If we were to attack Gabriel, Botha had said, we would invite the wrath of the Bushmen. What! I reacted, was this what our hero had come to? Was he really afraid of a handful of nomadic half-breed Bushmen we were quite capable of dealing with? On the whole it seemed to be the case. What I especially did not like was the way Piet had taken to Lewis: this man who had progressed from elephant hunter to the power behind the Herero throne. Did he realize that Lewis was an admirer of Cecil John Rhodes? There was enough evidence that Rhodes had extensive information regarding the mineral riches of Southern Africa. That was his good right. It was also in order that he should wish to exploit these riches as far as it was in his power. *'Glück zu!'* I would say again, remembering the words of *Missionar* Diehl.

None other than John Caine had assured me, however, that Rhodes had once made enquiries regarding the extensive mineral deposits in the Transgariep. Lewis was not only his personal admirer but also his agent. According to rumours Kamaherero had promised Lewis the Otavi copper for his services.

With regard to Rhodes, if there were to be British intervention in the Transgariep it would not come from the lesser lights. Botha obviously had little idea how chancy his game was . . .

'It's a wet year,' I said, *a propos* of nothing. Old Diederick rapped the ground with his stick.

'Good thing we are here,' Louw du Plessis said.

There was a moment's pause. And then, somewhat to my surprise, Botha looked up and said: 'We can move on to where we need to be. If there are others still to come, they will find it difficult, especially between Namutoni and Otjikoto. It must be like one big *vlei* there now.'

The words seemed to indicate that we still had to 'move on' to somewhere: to some place like the Waterberg, in the south-east. The Waterberg would be a kind of stop-over on the way to the Transvaal.

My throat tightened. A clash here at Old Diederick's would do nobody any good. At the same time I sensed a coming confrontation.

He was cleaning the bowl of his pipe with a pocket-knife now. He snapped it shut. 'Well, I have to be off, *Oom* Died!' he said. 'The wife is not so well. Better you reconsider everything, *Oom*. We shall see each other tomorrow. Meanwhile, I greet you all!'

This he did by a movement of the hand. Then he turned about and walked away, adjusting his hat.

I saw him go, not without some feeling of loss. Maybe the others sensed my discomfort. Bouwer, spreading himself broadly over his chair, said with good humour: 'I dare say, Piet went visiting too long in the Transvaal. He has been bitten by a kind of bush-tick! His head keeps pointing that way! What do you say, Mester?'

I looked up. 'If that's the way his head is,' I said, 'who am I to disagree?'

Old Diederick nodded ponderously.

'What route does he intend taking?' I asked.

'Straight across,' Louw du Plessis said. 'Via Rietfontein!'

'Has he forgotten what the Thirstland is like?'

'That is what we asked him, Mester. Piet is full of idle talk these days. He says if *Oom* Gert Alberts and his people could get through that way, he will too!'

'For what, does he imagine, has everybody been doing what they have been doing all these years? Who does he think he is?'

'Piet has a word for every word,' Louw du Plessis said.

'Gentlemen, I would like nothing better than to have Pieter Maritz-Botha heartily with us in this venture,' I said. 'I admit that would now be difficult. How does *Oom* Diederick see it all?'

The old man looked at me over his high collar. He folded his huge, gnarled hands over the shiny knob of his olive-wood stick and said: 'Thou speakest plain words, *Meneer*—but true! If there are men who will have our state torn to pieces, the Lord will not suffer it.'

'What about Lewis?' I asked. 'Has anybody heard anything about his movements? We have been given to understand that he is coming this way.'

'What to do?' Bouwer asked.

'Who knows,' I said. 'What did he have to say here this afternoon?'

'Not a word about that,' Louw du Plessis answered.

'Piet and Lewis are like *that,*' Barend Bouwer said, and crossed his fingers.

'I find it strange that he can't see through Lewis.'

'All that we have,' Diederick Prinsloo boomed, 'all that we are . . . has been bought for us by the *dead*, *Meneer*. Thou knowest these things; for thou wert a witness of it all, as it happened.'

'So I was, *Oom* Diederick.'

'Whither then this Pieter Botha? What be his intention? What his great talk?'

'As far as I'm concerned,' I said and arose, 'if Botha wants it that way, let him have it. Remember, he was never in the Trek when it came through the Thirstland. He has no idea what it could mean. The main thing we have to stick to is the fact that we have become the owners of a fine country. Here we can yet build something of value. All it needs is work, goodwill and faith. How is it that Pieter Maritz-Botha fails to see it that way?'

'Piet was always stiff-necked, as *Oom* Diederick says,' Louw du Plessis explained. 'He would never accept advice. He always knew better.'

'It would be an excellent thing,' I said, 'if his restiveness could express itself *vis a vis* his present *confrères*. Charity, they say, begins at home!'

'*Meneer,*' said Old Diederick, 'thou knowest this to be no small matter . . . Our enemies are everywhere. But we shall not be put *under*! And not by one who is of us. Sufficient unto the day is the evil thereof . . . We must just keep to the road ahead, deviating neither to the left, nor to the right.'

14

I had become conscious of the first glow of returning fever. It would be disastrous, I said to myself, if I were to be laid up now. As a sick man I would be useless. Neither I nor the laager could afford it. The hard fact was that the *Bestuur* almost completely relied on me. I was still their leader, whether I liked it or not.

The little company around me now seemed to be depressed. Barend Bouwer was slapping his broad chest under his shirt with the flat of his hand in a menacing sort of way. Louw du Plessis was absent-mindedly watching a group of young children playing *hasie.** Old Diederick sat on his stool in motionless silence. I could appreciate their feelings. They had undertaken this trek down to Otjovanda Tjongue with a growing sense of fulfilment. Not that I had even encouraged their thinking of Upingtonia as their long-sought-for 'Land of Rest'. On the contrary, I was at pains to get them to understand the true nature of the venture. The state would be a modern one, I had said. It would, it could not be exclusive. For its very life it was dependent on the goodwill and co-operation of as many people of different backgrounds and capacities as possible. This was no ready-made Eden. We would have to work for it, suffer for it.

'Brother Jordan,' Louw du Plessis said, as if the thought had suddenly struck him. 'You know about the trouble Piet had with Kambonde about the Arab?'

'What happened?'

'Kambonde wanted to buy it,' Du Plessis replied. '*Oom*

*Literally, *the hare.*

Diederick taxed Piet Botha with it this afternoon.'

'So Kambonde helped himself.'

' . . . after he and Piet had had a row.'

'And no payment from Kambonde.'

'Ivory! But not enough to Piet's liking.'

'*Meneer*,' Old Diederick interposed, 'thou knowest the danger of such things. What if the black nation rises against us? We are but a handful.'

To this I might have added that Botha's recklessness contrasted strangely with his solicitude towards Gabriel and his Bushmen.

'If I judge his temper rightly,' I said, 'he'll try to get his horse back somehow. Or will he allow his good sense to dictate for a change? Will he abide?'

'Not Piet Botha,' Bouwer declared.

'So, he will even go back to Ondangua to fetch the Arab? Then he doesn't know Kambonde.'

'Piet likes to be seen on the Arab,' Du Plessis said. 'Dressed up in his fancy waistcoats, hat, Portuguese boots. So, he *wants* his horse!'

'Go for the horse and bring down a war,' I said. 'Kambonde is our friend.'

'War is not to be waged with handfuls of dried peas,' said Old Diederick. 'I *know* war.'

I quietly considered this. Diederick Prinsloo had been trekking with his people for almost half a century. Times of relative quiet had come: of settled existence in a stable society. But these had always been interrupted by the wars against Africa's still tribal peoples; by the spirit of trek itself. These things had often gone together.

'The Ovambos,' I remarked, 'are on the whole a peace-loving nation. But, gentlemen, you will remember what happened at Namutoni when the Trek was in the Kaoko. Three of the Erikssons' men were murdered, merely because they looked like Boers, although they were Swedes. Remember also the murder of Fathers Delpech and Rothan in Ukuanyama. If I sum Piet Botha up correctly, he would be rash enough to attempt some sort of rescue. Set a lucifer to Ondangua, and it may well explode. That would be the end of Upingtonia too.'

It was quite possible, I continued, that Botha could get some further compensation for the Arab from a British court of justice. He might even move the judicial offer to declare the sale null and void. But there were no British courts of justice here; neither were there any German. The 'magistracy' at Okahandja had long since ceased even to be a joke. Botha probably knew this as well as anybody else. Therefore this loose talk of going to Ovamboland to 'fetch' his horse.

'What would he do!' Old Diederick demanded. 'Wage war against Legion and his angels? . . . *Meneer*, how seest thou this thing?'

'Who does he intend taking along with him on this venture?' I replied. 'You, gentlemen?'

There was general dissent. Botha's new domesticity, I thought, might well be so much posturing. Came the hour, the true Pieter Maritz-Botha could suddenly emerge. Under all this partiality towards comfort and homely attentions, there was still the tough romantic I had known in the old days.

'The sooner we get down to the bottom of it all, the better,' I said.

'He shuts himself up, and refuses to say a single word,' Du Plessis reminded us. 'We asked him directly what his plans were. He said we would have to see.'

'See what?' I asked.

'See what we shall see,' Bouwer said. 'What he already sees in his damnfool pig-headedness. I'll say this for Piet, when he has his heart in a thing, there is no stopping him. Remember the time we shot all those elephants in the pan!'

In a way, I thought, Barend Bouwer had now said something which was peculiar to his people as a whole. There was no stopping them—when once they had set their course. This could be turned to positive, worthwhile things. But it could also become disastrous . . .

'Gentlemen,' I said, trying to regulate the hotch-potch of thought and sentiment we had been expressing, 'this matter is serious. As far as I can see, our friend Botha is not here to help us establish and build up the new state. He is here to make things difficult, because he imagines he knows better than the rest of us. Should his madcap scheme to return to Ovamboland and recover his horse ever come to anything, he would no doubt see to it that he is out of the way before trouble starts. Where would he be?'

'In the Thirstland,' Bouwer said. His chair creaked under his weight. 'On his way to the Lake!'

'With the Ovambo nation on his heels!'

'There is talk in the laager that he still wants us all in the Waterberg,' Du Plessis said. 'He's all for the Waterberg.'

'What about Jan Labuschagne?' I asked.

Old Diederick rapped the ground with his stick again.

'Piet talks to Jan, and others too,' Bouwer said. 'But Jan only makes noises with that big mouth of his!'

'This idea of the Waterberg is nothing new,' I said. 'What surprises me, however, is the naivety of our friends who believe—apparently taking Lewis's word for it—that they will be safe there. Don't they know to whom the Waterberg belongs?'

'Kamaherero!' Bouwer said.

'Botha apparently thinks that after his adventure in Ovamboland he can take us all to the Waterberg, and there we shall enjoy the friendly protection of Kamaherero and Lewis.' I looked at the old Landdrost, who was now the President designate of Upingtonia. 'I express myself strongly, and for that my apologies. But perhaps it should be even stronger. If we had taken a firmer attitude from the beginning, we would not have been faced with all this.'

'*Oom* Died!' Barend Bouwer sat up in his chair. 'We all know how Piet can talk. But we must remember: he comes from an old pioneer family. And he will not be easily turned back. I think, Mester, he will stay with Lewis. We must rather be prepared for what may happen.'

I was silent. The fact was that I had been living in something of a fool's paradise these past few weeks. Pieter Maritz-Botha's attitude had never been a secret as far as I was concerned. It was already clear enough at Humbe. In fact, it was clear enough at Humpata. And yet, somehow, I had maintained a rather shallow optimism that things would right themselves. Perhaps I still had some faith in a man who had once been my friend. If anybody had told me in the days we were in the Kaoko, or even afterwards at Humpata, that Piet Botha and Robert Lewis would find common cause, I would have scoffed at it.

I sat looking at the ground. The burden of responsibility suddenly seemed to weigh very heavily on me. There was no longer any avoiding of the true facts. They would have to be faced. With that I would also have to accept in increasing measure the demands made upon me. I had once dreamt of hearty co-operation here between each and every member of the laager. I had hopes of an *ex officio* management by myself and some others who had a wider experience of the modern world than the *Bestuur* itself. The *Bestuur* would function as the government of the new republic. But they would rely on me. I would serve them with advice. They would take it on trust, and I would give it in trust. What I would have welcomed was at least one other—a man like Axel Eriksson—to help me carry the burden. It might even have been Botha. He was the only other one in the laager who had lived and moved in circles beyond the laager and what belonged to the laager. What an exercise in wishful thinking this had been.

And yet, there still remained in me the barely discernible hope that somehow the rupture could be healed. After all, had Piet Botha and I not shared things in the past that were not so easily forgotten? I had talked to him as I had talked to few other men. Five years before we had set out for the Kaoko to look for the Trek. We had been like brothers. We had laughed at, grieved over the same things. When we were up at the river and he had turned up after having been given up for lost, nobody rejoiced more than I.

'I'll have a talk to him,' I said, lost in thought. I looked up. 'One never knows. Reason might yet prevail. I'll do my best, gentlemen. For the rest? You, Louw and you, Barend, try and work on Jan Labuschagne and the others, if there are others.'

'Jan thinks he roars like a lion, but he only brays like a donkey.' Barend Bouwer chuckled.

'How big is the support for the Waterberg?' I asked.

Louw du Plessis turned to me. 'Are they worth taking into account?' he asked.

'They may be but a few,' I answered, 'but one should not underestimate them.'

'Piet Botha is the man we have to work on,' Bouwer declared. 'If he comes to his senses, the others will follow. I'd like to get hold of him.' He tensed his stout, powerful fingers, then suddenly grinned at us.

It was Diederick Prinsloo, however, who wound up the conversation by declaring, with a shade of emotion: '*Meneer*, many wrong things are spoken of us . . . But thou knowest well; it is the underdog which gets the kicks!'

I arose to leave. 'Perhaps the best remedy is to refuse to be the underdog,' I replied. 'Piet Botha and Lewis will yet discover that we are not so easily disposed of. We have not come here to get out again. We have come to stay.'

15

It was clear to me now that I would in any event have to talk to Botha. There was no denying the clash of feelings in the laager. It was bad for morale. What we now needed above all was a respite from tension, so as patiently to work out the details of the new state. There was a task for each one of us.

Within an hour the people would start the evening meal. Then they would gather under the trees for devotions. Presently, the fires would be lit. Here old and young would gather again. Soon someone would be story-telling: the old stories, and the old ritual. Without this the laager would not be the laager. It had been something like this in the early, tribal days of Teutonic man . . .

I looked up at the sky. The air was limpid. Only in the farthest south, as always in the summer, there were dim flashes of lightning. Here and there an old retainer was bent almost double over a smoking *erd*, posterior pointing heavenwards.

Where the slope eased off into level ground again, Kleinveld Labuschagne was cutting wood. The blade of the axe described a circle of light as it moved through the air. When it struck the log, a moment elapsed before the dull thud reached the ears: a single slow drum in the orchestra of bird-song, cattle lowing distantly, the shrill voices of children at play. Then a woman's voice would climb out of these sounds of evening, to disappear again: all remaining wrapped in the warm, sweetly acrid smoke of wood-fires.

I found my servants at the cooking *scherm* behind the wagon, busy smoking their common clay-pipe in turns. The faces—one pitch-black, the other yellow—lighted up on my arrival. Izak, sitting on his haunches, with his arms over his knees and his hands drooping, got up and said: '*Tu go ui!*' meaning: the clouds speak. He narrowed his eyes, examined the sky.

The clouds had spoken, I affirmed, and they had shed tears of anger.

'*Hamtsha?*' he asked. 'Where?'

'Everywhere. There are bad things afoot, old man.'

Izak seemed to get my meaning. '*E!*' both he and Kairob said. Perhaps they had been discussing all this while smoking their pipe.

'*Keia!*' I climbed into the wagon. 'I do not seek what I have not lost! We'll get to where we want to be. What about food?'

'*Sas ku dire ku uha!*' Izak would bring what there was. That he did, some quarter of an hour later, while I sat dispiritedly on the edge of my *katel*, hands on my knees. The fever had got a hold on me again. It was the old story. I had done my best to keep up appearances . . .

Well, for some time it could be done. Then suddenly it would seize you. You would feel yourself disintegrate. And life would drop like a falling barometer . . .

The food was the old indefinable product of the hunters' pot. Into this my servants would put anything from the red-eyed louries they had caught in traps, to termites and fat caterpillars. These they plucked off the mopani trees. On the whole it could be tasty. But I preferred palla steaks, roasted on a grid. This, with pot-bread, honey and butter when available, was food.

I pushed the plate to one side, toppled over into the *katel*.

'All right, *Bambuse*!' I said. 'Never mind!' He stood there looking at me. I leant over, flicked open the lid of a tin box and took out some roll-tobacco.

'*Ikai!* No food?'

'Get along now, old man. Here, take this!' I gave him the tobacco. 'Give Kairob his share.' I embraced the pillow of soft skin and buried my face in it. I heard Izak say thankyou for the tobacco. He still waited at the far end of the wagon. Did he want to tell me something? 'What's the news?' I vaguely asked, lying on my back, eyes closed. 'Where is Lewis?' I felt the blood throbbing in my temples. 'What about this chap, Gabriel? . . . Has stolen Kambonde's cattle. We are going to fetch it! Are there wagons coming?'

I dimly saw him nod. 'Karevapu Katiti!' he then said. His head was drawn in black against the fading light.

'Karevapu!' I said. 'Mr Eriksson!' I pushed myself up with some difficulty. 'Is he coming?'

'He comes!'

'Where is his laager?'

'Otjituuo,' Izak clicked in his own language. I was now wide awake again, feeling around in a box for writing material. 'You take him a letter? Eh?'

What a pleasant surprise, I thought, when Izak had finally left. I sat there on the edge of the *katel* again, pen in hand. Axel Eriksson could not have been in the vicinity more opportunely. I needed him! We all needed him. Charles Lyon would then come up from the Bay. Other people would come. We might even have immigrants from the Cape. Sir Thomas Upington was our friend . . .

I had done the note. The effort had exhausted me. Now I sank back onto the *katel* again. I should be entering up my journal. So much had happened . . . I had not been able to make any entries. But now it was impossible. I did not have the strength . . .

But there was still some resistance. This was not good enough. I lay there on my back, eyes closed. This was taking the line of least resistance. I just could not allow myself to fall ill! There was far too much to do!

A man had to do the right things at the right time. Matters could not just be left to the *Bestuur. Oom* Diederick and Co were fine, but they could hardly stand up to the wiles of Lewis or even those of Botha. Was I being unfair? Hardly. I had given Botha every opportunity to prove himself. But he had gone out of his way to let me know that he had neither faith in my leadership, nor in the new state.

Vaguely I heard Kairob say that there was someone to see me. 'Who is it?' I asked. I was hoping for the moment that it might be Axel. No, Kairob answered, it was only the *oumeid.* This I took to be Dina Lombard.

I raised myself on an elbow again and told Kairob to tell her to look in at the front of the wagon-hood. This she presently did, holding up a dish of veld-fruit for me to see. 'Old Miss Ella said to bring this for Mister!' she declared.

I took the dish from her outstretched hands. 'This is very kind of you,' I said.

'Mupel plums and marula, *Confrater* and I have collected,' she explained.

'Thank you, too, to Kleinveld. And to the Old Miss!'

'Old Miss says please that Mister come to see *oubaas** Diederick after prayers.'

I knew what Old Diederick's trouble was. I had long suspected it. He would die slowly, and with dignity. It was better that way . . .

The coming of Dina and the message she had brought seemed to level things out again. After a while I felt better, and slowly got up.

*Old Master.

16

Now people were drawing nearer for the evening devotions. Between the trees fires were burning. Where the light did not reach, lanterns were suspended from whip-sticks or branches. Oldsters sat in chairs with huge, open Bibles on their laps. Children held candles of wildebeest-fat aloft for them to read by. The night sky was clear with swarms of stars and at times the far-off flicker of lightning.

Hester Bouwer saw me at the edge of the little crowd, and brought me a stool. Old Diederick, Bible and psalter under his arm, climbed onto the wagon. This served as a pulpit. Slowly he looked about him, then closed his eyes, turning his face upwards.

'. . . Lord God!'

Suddenly everything seemed to be in a state of suspense. Everywhere hands were folded, heads bowed.

I heard Old Diederick's voice as if from afar: '. . . . We *children* of Thy covenant . . . Thou hast knowledge of what each and every one has *need* of . . . *Need,* Lord, for we are but miserable sinners . . . Thy arm hath not been shortened; and Thou sufferest *not* thine enemies . . . Lord God, Father of Pity, *shame* not our expectations . . . !'

Slowly, ponderously, it continued. Old Diederick prayed for all to be remembered: those gathered there that night; those whom they had left at Humpata; those in the Transvaal 'beyond the cruel Thirstland'; those 'above us by Thy Holy Will'; those called to lead and give advice; those who were bereaved, lonely, ill . . .

The womenfolk and the old men sat in their chairs, or on their stools. The others stood with bowed heads. The words rumbled over them.

God's purpose, the prayer said, had brought them here to this place: far from where loved ones lay, in the soil of Africa . . .

Peace, the old voice lamented, but there *was* no peace . . . Verses from the Book of Jeremiah were quoted. 'No peace!' it sounded again. But even then God would not forsake the faithful. They were conscious of His commandments; and the Lord was conscious of their needs. *He* would provide. *He* who had brought them here to this land of their being strangers: all the land of Canaan, for an everlasting possession; and *He* would be their God . . .

A long reading from Scripture now followed.

I sat next to Machiel Prinsloo and his brother Jan. They held a large Bible between them. I detected the sweet, musty smell of an old book that had once come from a distant country. Between the binding and its leaves and its brass clasps it had collected the history of the Prinsloos.

Psalm singing, prayers, reading from Scripture . . . At regular intervals a solemn admonishment to the assembled to honour their God . . . This was the old pattern. For more than two centuries now they had borne it with them. They had trekked through Africa. They had shaped their lives to it. Even when critical of it, one respected it. Even when observing it all from the periphery, it held one's attention. This at least had to be admitted: Africa was part of them; and they were part of Africa. Such was God's will for them. Such was His purpose . . .

Strange, I thought, that they who called daily upon their God to see that His will be done, so positively sought their own ends: sought to establish, for all time, their own security, in their own, exclusive land. They had once, in the eighteenth century, come from the settled areas of the Cape to the Eastern Frontier. There they had for the first time clashed with the blacks. In time they had trekked northwards: over the Orange, into vast depopulated lands; over the Drakensberg, into Natal . . .

Not yet the end . . . Deliberately but with deep-seated emotion, they had decided: 'An own free country, where we shall be able to govern ourselves.'

So Gert Alberts had said. So many others had said. To Beulah, Land of Rest; or Lydensrust. But the past was simultaneously part of the Trek. Every 16 December—the day of Blood River, and the triumph over the massed army of King Dingane—the *Vierkleur* would be taken from the *kist,* tied to a whip-stick, fixed to the wagon-head . . .

Once, on such a day, Ella Lombard had looked at the flag and had said to me: 'When I am dead, *Meneer,* please put the *Vierkleur* over me. And if Dina goes before me, I shall put it over her.'

Sitting there next to the Prinsloo brothers, sharing their Bible, I thought: Upingtonia would yet be different. It would have to accommodate itself to the world of our time. It would have to invite all of integrity and character to come and join it.

Problems were everywhere. Were the two Boer republics, the Transvaal and the Orange Free State, without them? The

Transvaal had won the War of Independence at Majuba Mountain. But for imperial Britain this had been but an interlude. Gold had been discovered on the Witwatersrand. There was already much talk of increasing interest in the northern riches. One had only to read the newspapers . . .

Old Diederick, at long last, drew out the final amen. The crowd still stood about under the trees. The servants were carrying away stools and chairs. Some were seeing to the laager fires. Machiel Prinsloo, with his brother Willem jeering, was instructing some youngsters in the art of handling a horse.

'All too soft,' Willem kept saying. 'You must eat more meat. Soft in the legs, soft in the head!'

There was a chorus of protest. 'When I was your age I had a beard down to here!' Jan Labuschagne said. His hand indicated his midriff. The young men laughed; and Jan roared with pleasure.

Hester Bouwer and Jet du Plessis came up to say good evening. Jet pressed her psalter to her bosom and said: 'We wish you all that is good tomorrow, *Meneer.*'

'We are glad that you are here, *Meneer.*'

'I thank you, Hester,' I said, 'and I thank you, Jet. We shall do our best. All will be well!'

'We have heard that Mister Lewis is coming?'

I nodded. 'Maybe.'

They shook hands and said good-night. Barend Bouwer's voice sounded behind me: 'So, we must stick to the spoor, eh!'

'To the spoor, Barend, of course.'

'There are those who will go their own way. Let them go to hell, if they so wish. We stay here. This is our land we have been looking for!'

'Our land,' said Louw du Plessis.

Dimly, I felt the fever rise in me. I pulled myself together, tried to smile.

17

Botha was the centre of the evening's attraction. His sense of theatre had always served him well. Added to this was the way fortune favoured him. When everybody else was down with fever, he was still about. When everybody else was looking for elephants, he found them by the hundreds. When he decided to take ship from Moçamedes to pay a visit to the Transvaal, a schooner was always handy. When he took a wife, he got the most doe-eyed of the lot: to help inflate his ego . . . When he needed a horse in the place of the one he had lost, Machiel Prinsloo sold him the Arab. Only Kambonde Kampingana seemed to have put a stop to his good fortune.

Here he was now, expounding to an audience of young, wide-mouthed listeners. In other days he would have looked up, invited me to join him, while cracking a joke.

Some girls suddenly descended on me, begging me to come and tell of *my* adventures.

'Tell us about the Cape, *Meneer*!' said Lisa Lombard.

'The Cape should be seen,' I reflected.

'The Cape is so *faaar*!' said Lisa.

'You ask *Oom* Piet here. *He* knows the Cape, almost as well as I do. Let him tell you about the governor and his fine house.'

From the corner of my eye I saw the flash of temper move across his face. He remained sitting, not looking at me, annoyed. I was chaffing, but he was in earnest. I was relieved when Ella Lombard intervened: 'Come now, all this cajolery. Get on with you. We must talk to *Meneer.*' She looked at me. 'It is the fever. Better, *Meneer*, that you rest. The laager has great need of you. I shall send you some butter I have made.'

'Dear *Tante*,' I said, 'thank you for your kind thought. But I am well enough. It takes a lot to wear down an old horse.'

'How old then are we who have lived so much longer, and trekked so far?'

'Looking downwards, all still looks fresh and young; and you are old. Upwards? That's the way we keep moving.'

Yes, she agreed. But please, I should take my medicine; and rest; and not walk too much in the sun. The sun, I answered, had burnt us all. We said good-night and I walked back to my wagon.

Dolf Holtzhausen called out from a pipe-smoking group around a small fire. 'Hallo, Dolf,' I said. 'What are *you* doing these days?'

'Making boxes for us to lie in,' said Lewies Louwrens, and the others laughed.

'Thou dost not think that way of me,' Dolf said with careful deliberation.

'No, Dolf,' I said, lighting a cigar with a burning ember. 'But one of these days I'll give you an order.'

'For what, *Meneer*? Hast thou need of it?'

'I have need of a good *katel*,' I said. 'The one I have has been creaking over the land for more than a decade now.'

'Thou art long of limb, *Meneer*. But I shall measure thee.'

'Yes,' I said, 'it is always good to be measured; in time.'

Those standing around us guffawed, letting legs, drooped over knees, swing pendulously. But some were silent: the De Beers, Du Toits, Krugers . . . I had never known them really.

Old Diederick's *vrouw* had just brought him a bowl of shepherd's-tree coffee.

I sat down on a stool next to his bed. He was propped up by some pillows. *Tante* Prinsloo offered me coffee, but I declined it. 'I have just come to see how our President is.' I took his pulse, and examined him as well as I could. Had an attack of 'bile', he said, a burning fullness of the stomach . . . What now?

There was some advancement in his condition, as far as I could judge. Still, there was no reason for alarm. I put a little bottle of laudanum on the *kist* next to his bedside,

'This veld coffee is not so good,' I added. 'One is liable to blow up, like a cow in bad pasture. Rather drink milk, *Oom* Diederick.'

I poured him some drops of the laudanum. He drank it, and it seemed to settle him. Presently he insisted on getting up again, so that he could talk to me.

We sat in front of the hartebeest-house, Old Diederick with a reed-buck karross over his legs. This, *Tante* Prinsloo assured me, had been Old Diederick's father's foot-covering on his *katel* during the Great Trek.

'What now about Lewis?' Old Diederick fixed his eyes on me.

'I can't say. Let him come if he wants to come. We have nothing to hide . . .'

The next day's meeting was intended as a formal handing over of powers to the *Bestuur*. I had bought the land, I was the effective leader, but the *Bestuur* would bear the responsibility and enjoy the legal title.

'All that there is to do for you, *Oom* Diederick,' I said, 'is to preside. Before the proceedings start, however, we shall have a meeting of myself and the *Bestuur*, here at your house.'

His long sinewy fingers closed around the shiny knob of his

olive-wood stick. He nodded.

'We have come from far places, *Meneer* . . . But now there are those that would prevent us having what we have sought for so long . . . *Meneer*, once when I was a young man our people were nearly all murdered by the nations of the lowveld in the Transvaal. They were naked.'

His thoughts now seemed to move swiftly through history. Suddenly he was in the Debra again: the Prinsloo boy had got lost and had been found murdered.

'. . . blood relation,' he assured me. The light of the lantern suspended from a limb of the tree next to the hartebeest-house now fell over him. His face was deeply furrowed and gaunt, with prominent cheek-bones and a noble nose.

'Willem Frederik Prinsloo . . . Aged nineteen years, three months, and seven days.

'. . . In those days, when we lay there at the marshes, stricken by the fever, it all happened. We trekked to the outveld . . . The boy went out early that morning to shoot a palla for the pot. Night came, and he did not return . . . What to do? Nothing . . . Only to hope . . . to pray. And wait until the day broke.

'. . . The moon was not yet properly up that night, when—what did we see? The boy's horse came galloping into the laager: only the horse, no boy. It was a mare, and it dragged its guts as it came galloping . . . From the stab wounds in its stomach.

'The next day we followed the spoor: a long spoor through the dry veld . . . Afterwards we saw vultures wheeling . . . Wheeling, and coming down to sit on the dead trees.

'Spurred the horses! Dust settled . . . And there he lay on the bare sand, at the edge of the pan. Only his cleanly picked bones. Bleached white! It was the work of the Bushmen . . .'

It was the mad time when the Trek had broken up and the various parts were wandering about aimlessly between the marshes and the Debra, with some up at the Okavango.

'Hendrik van Zyl then took his vengeance . . . Caught them who were the murderers. And shot them. We were at Andara at the river at the time, with the Alberts people.'

News had reached the laager that Van Zyl had been killed by one of his own servants, while on a hunting expedition in Damaraland, east of the Waterberg. Was it true, I asked.

'Murdered by his own Bushman he had reared,' Old Diederick answered. 'Was squint-eyed, that old fellow. Couldn't *see* straight. He stabbed himself in his eye when he was at the Okavango. Was cutting up a hippo, when the knife slipped—zipp! Like that; right in his eye. Couldn't *see* straight. But shoot? Better than most. It was his right eye.'

So then, the end of the Great White Hunter of the Debra, I decided. For years Van Zyl had lived there at Ghanzi in his castle-like house, providing accommodation for all he employed. His hunters ranged from the Debra to the marshes, from the marshes up to the river; then westwards to Ovamboland. Great loads of ivory and feathers, skins, hides and trophies had gone down to the Bay. Hendrik van Zyl had considered himself to be Laird of the Ghanzi wilderness.

In the end the ruffianly Paul Visser had got him and had sentenced him to death. But Van Zyl had escaped and seemed set for a series of new and profitable ventures. And now he had been murdered . . . Not by the Orlams, not by the Hereros, but by his own servant; and one he had reared since childhood.

It was a case, I decided, of blood crying out for blood as in the earliest days of the still heroic, still barbarous West. So it was still here in this far-off land, wrapped around Capricorn in its summer heat, in its winter frosts.

18

The conversation turned to Pieter Maritz-Botha. This was inevitable. 'Let him think about his brave efforts, and then try and live with his conscience,' I said. 'Listen, *Oom* Diederick, in this country, too, he who hesitates is lost. Let Piet Botha remember what once happened to Andersson, when on his way to Okahandja, with wife and child. That good-for-nothing Orlam, Piet Wildebeest, came riding up to where Andersson and his company had made camp for the night. Demanded all that they had in the wagon, plus all their money . . . And Andersson said to him: "If you don't get out of my sight within the next minute, I'll inform Jonker Afrikaander. *He'll* deal with you." Thereupon Wildebeest started cursing him. He tried to grab the bridle of Andersson's horse. Luckily he stumbled over some pots and pans at the *erd.* Then he jumped up and struck at Andersson with a horse's bit. Four others came to join Wildebeest, but Andersson stood his ground. Without more ado he shot Wildebeest dead with his pistol. The rest of the gang then fled . . .'

Old Diederick had taken his wife's hand. Her face had puckered at my description of what had once taken place in the veld near Okahandja. Now she was nodding, and clearing away her tears.

'A man who stops because he has lost a spoke of a wheel, is but half a man,' I said. 'You know that too. There is no other way in which we can make this a land fit to live in.'

Old Diederick sat in his armchair with its mat of thongs. His legs were covered by the reedbuck karross. He was a man slowly dying; and whether he knew it or not—I had not told him what I had diagnosed—he bore himself with the old dignity. He was a worthy president.

'Remember to take the laudanum,' I said. 'It will ease you. A few drops in a little water.' There was a smile hidden in his beard.

'*Meneer*, I thank thee,' he said. 'There must ever be *wet en regel.** Otherwise?' He struck the ground with his stick. 'There will be desecration . . . of *all* that we have built up here.'

'We shall have it all settled tomorrow,' I said. 'Let those who still think that we should trek to the Waterberg, or to the Transvaal, then have their say, if they have a case.'

I bade the aged couple good-night. Diederick Prinsloo lifted his right hand. The index finger was pointed upwards. The little finger was bent. It was a large and honest hand: the hand of one who had never faltered on what he believed to be his predetermined way.

At my wagon, Jan and Machiel Prinsloo came to meet me.

'How is Pa?' they enquired.

'He is not so young any more,' I said. 'He has come a long way.'

'Pa says he is all right,' Machiel declared. 'Says it's just a case of too much wind in the stomach. Says he'll fart it all out!'

'What do you say, *Meneer*?' Jan asked when we faced each other. 'You are the doctor. Is it fire inside?'

'Old people can carry on living with this "fire" for a long while. His general condition is good.'

'How long will it take?' asked Machiel.

'I have seen people like him carry on for years. Anyway, the medicine will make him happy. There will be more when supplies

*Law and order.

arrive from the Bay.'

The conversation turned to the next day's meeting.

'Help see to it that all are present,' I said. 'We have work to do.'

Willem Prinsloo suddenly appeared out of the darkness. 'What will happen now?' he enquired, looking at us in turn, with a suggestion of temperament.

'What should happen,' I answered. 'Nothing more, nothing less. Those who think otherwise can fade out of the Upingtonia picture as far as I am concerned. I did not buy this land for the faint-hearted. All this cackle going on behind our backs can then come into the open. We'll see what happens. But Upingtonia is ours; and it will remain ours.'

'What is one's own is one's own,' Jan said.

I liked the way he said it. It was simple and honest, as a man should speak. Willem muttered something about us not knowing all that Piet Botha had said. Piet was no fool, he said.

I looked at him. 'No,' I said coldly. 'Piet is no fool, but he acts like a fool. Good night, gentlemen, we shall see each other in the morning.'

19

He was still there entertaining the young people when I passed the biggest of the laager fires. Some of the older people had also gathered to listen: the Labuschagnes, Oppermans, Du Plessis, Du Toits. Strategically placed in the navel of the audience was young Venter. Lisa Lombard was next to him, leaning with her head against his shoulder.

I hesitated, turned about and stood listening. I should really show my contempt for all this exhibitionism by going my way, I thought. This was Pieter Maritz-Botha trying to impress these people at a critical time. Thinking about Upingtonia and its future as he did, he really did not have any right to be here at all. After all, this was my property. I had bought it. Tomorrow I would hand it over to the *Bestuur*; but at present it was still mine.

The subtle glow of threatening fever had not left me yet. I was getting about on nervous energy. Presently Louw du Plessis came and stood next to me. He winked and offered me his pouch. I filled my pipe, half listening to Botha.

'Jan Robbertze and his team are hunting elephants down in the sandveld,' he said to a question, 'between the Serras and the Cunene; making pots of money; shipping ivory from Moçamedes.'

'We would like to hear about the various hunting methods of *Oom* Hendrik van Zyl!' This was Adriaan Venter, now questioning with a note of authority.

'Well,' the answer came, 'today's methods are different, of course.'

'Did *Oom* and the others concentrate on the waters?'

The questions were being put in the third person; the answers came in the first.

'That we had to do, yes. The Bushmen had to come and tell us how things were at the waters; whether there were spoors. Came the news that there were, we would move on and set up laager, near to it, but note, well away from the game-paths and away from the waters. If not? Well, you could very easily wake up in the middle of the night and discover an elephant astride of you!'

The crowd laughed nervously. But Adriaan, in all seriousness, said: '*Oom,* just that happened to me once.'

'Well, then you know, young man. All right, there you have it: you are in your laager, and some distance away the elephants are drinking. It is midnight, and the jackals and the hyaenas are howling. Somewhere an owl is hooting. The elephants drink their fill, and then set a course, and away they are.—To where? To where they are far enough from the waters. And then they look for a tree to stand—I say *stand*!—and sleep under.—Don't imagine an elephant lies down like a cow. Well, what do you who are still in your laager do? At daybreak you set off for the waters. You examine the spoors and decide. *Oom* Hendrik was the boss—so it was really *his* decision which sent us off. No dilly-dallying either. One would hear the clink of stirrups and the whinneying of the horses: they, too, were eager to get away. You had to jump to it to get everything done: saddlebags packed, guns and ammunition seen to. But no time for coffee, there was not a moment to lose. We would all see to it that everything was ready the night before. We had it all set out, just ready for action: guns, ammunition, bandolier, waterbag, bread, rusks or doughnuts, biltong. Add to this pipe, tobacco, lucifers, saddle, bridle, spurs, sjambok. Every man had his appointed task. And he knew how to go about it. Not like some of you milk-beards these days!'

Much good humoured protest greeted these words.

'So, then we would begin tracking: following the spoors from the waters. But first the horses had to drink their fill for the day. It was usually a hard ride through the sandveld, hardveld, mucharra, hookthorn. Sometimes the fly would pester us, so that we would have to keep away from the *vleis* and the rivers.'

'Who were in the company those days?'

'Usually we were eight hunters. The four Van Zyls—father and three sons; then Brother Barend here: let him tell you more; McDonald too! Later young Llewellyn Andersson joined us: son of the old pioneer. And Ben Orange. *He* was a character! Used to be in the Cape Corps. Was a servant of Sir Harry Smith, governor of the Cape, and took part in the battle of Boomplaats in the Free State. He used to act as interpreter to Dr Livingstone at one time. He had a brown skin, but a white heart. Nobody knew how old he was.'

I suddenly discovered, standing where I was, half in the shadows, with Louw du Plessis at my side, that I was listening intently.

'The *way* we shot? Listen, young man, let's face it: every hunter had only one thing in mind: his own honour. If the spoor became hot, no give, all take! No sense in saying to the man next to you: "This is my first hunt. Let *me* have the first shot at this elephant!" You just had to see to it that your bullet was the first to strike. Ask Barend here. Greenhorns usually went dashing about without *seeing* the elephants. The tendency was always to keep the line of sight too low. Tell you about something I learnt from Barend. Where is he? Ask him if you don't believe me. One hot day we came across the spoor of two great bulls. For some or other reason the two elephants had skipped their nap. They just kept walking: miles and miles through the bush. About midday, however, we caught up with them. Guns?—Usually we had double-barrelled guns.'

'Number 12 cartridges?'

'Cartridges one had to load oneself: 14 to 16 drm—diamond grain gunpowder. The bullet itself was tin-plated, and tapered. These old-fashioned guns had safety stoppers. You put the stopper up when you went out of a morning, and gave the gun to a Bushman bearer. Exactly what I did that day. An old hand like old Barend never told me a thing; probably thought: let this greenhorn learn the hard way. Old *vabond.** . . . The spoor was hotting up, but I never noticed that the other chaps were stealthily taking their guns from their bearers. Suddenly, however, I saw Barend being given his. "What's up?" I asked innocently-like. "You never know," said Barend. "There might be elephants!" And at that I took my own gun and thought: Now for it! One big bull had left a spoor like a coffee tray. I'll get him, I thought. At such time Bushmen had a way of whistling softly through their teeth. Suddenly I heard it, like a snake hissing. I spurred my horse, but the others were already charging past me. Have you ever given your horse—if you have a horse!—its reins through mucharra and hookthorn? You'll never be hunters until you've done that!'

'We have, *Oom*.'

'You, perhaps, young Venter; but one swallow does not make a summer. Listen, the Chimborro of Angola is nothing. The elephants there eat out of your hand! Rather go out into the eastern Sandveld. See what you can bring back, if you do come back. The hookthorn lashes you with fish-hooks. Meanwhile you have to stay put in your saddle. As you know, it is the first strike that counts. Well, that day, I was going flat out, when suddenly I saw the movement in the bush. The horse I had was well-trained: only needed to touch his shoulder, draw in the reins; then he would stop, immediately. Jumping to the ground, raising my gun, I was already congratulating myself: Barend and the rest were still well behind me. Threw the gun to my shoulder; caught the big bull in the sights; pulled the trigger. Not a sound! I had forgotten to loosen the stopper! The next moment, Barend was past me in a whirl of dust, shooting from the saddle. Heard his bullet strike—smack! It was the big bull, a giant with tusks like mulemba branches.'

Listening to all this, I thought: there was never another hunter better than Piet—in his own eyes. But give the devil his due: he could tell a story.

'What did people get for ivory those days, *Oom*?' somebody in the audience asked.

'That bull gave us some sixty pounds of ivory. This was worth forty pounds sterling. The hunters got an eighth of what they brought in. Old Hendrik took the rest.

*Rascal.

'. . . Now that day we had ridden so hard that the laager lay far behind us. By four o'clock that afternoon our water-bags were empty and we were hungry. So we sat down and roasted some elephant meat. What with the sweet taste, when one is thirsty, it is hard to swallow it. Your tongue gets in the way.'

'The nicest part of an elephant is the middle part of the trunk!' Adriaan suddenly declared. 'And then the temple; between the eyes and the ears!'

'Right you are, young fellow. But don't forget the foot!'

'The foot is good, yes!'

'But best still, that finely textured fat one can roast out.'

'The fat, yes, *Oom*. I have said to Lisa here: "Please, when we are married, you will roast me out a barrel full of elephant fat—for me to have, all by myself!" '

Lisa slapped him playfully.

'So, what happened further that day, *Oom*?'

'We had to get back to the laager, but it was dark by now, and the Bushmen had to lead the way. Well, now it was really hellish riding through all that hookthorn, cat-thorn and creeper-rose again. Riding single-file, the one in front had to give the warning when we were approaching a sticky bit. Then he would shout: "Left to the back!" By that he meant that the danger was to the right. So the rider had to keep his head as far left as possible. Should the shout come: "Right to the back!" it would be just the other way around. Of course, you can imagine what language we used when "left" should have been "right", and "right" when it should have been "left". By midnight, God be praised, we reached the laager: still in one piece, but grey with hunger, thirst, and fatigue. So, now you know, it was no easy life, but yet an exciting one.'

Perhaps, I quietly reflected, as at times in the past, I had missed a lot by not taking part in this sort of thing. Temperamentally, I supposed, I was unsuited to the part. I could shoot things for the pot of course. I could also shoot to protect myself or others from danger. What I found no joy in, however, was to shoot for the pride and pleasure of it. I always walked away when someone in the party had brought down an oryx of fine proportions, or a kudu bull of lordly stature. I hated to see animals like these suffocating in their own blood. I was incapable of eating steaks cut of the still warm bodies, or roasting the limp warm livers or parts of the intestines.

And then the sight of the greatest of all land animals, blood-and-dust spurting over his hide, crashing down like a Cape oak in a winter storm . . . It had always depressed me.

'And how did the hunters trek those days, *Oom*?' A young voice broke into my thoughts again.

'Look, we would leave Ghanzi and trek to the first water at Ghams. This was 150 miles. Let us say that you begin on a Monday. By twelve o'clock the trek-oxen would drink for the first time since the previous Saturday. You keep on till about ten o'clock on the Tuesday morning. Then you span the oxen out and send them back to Ghanzi. At about four o'clock you inspan the second team. Now you can keep on till late on Wednesday. Then you do as before: outspan number two team, send them back, and inspan number three. This could take you to Ghams. Of course, one always hoped that Ghams had sufficient water. If not? Well, then there was nothing else to do except look to Providence to get you to the next water.'

'The treks were at night?'

'Yes, we kept on trekking until about nine o'clock in the morning. Then we would rest under trees, if there were any. So we managed to keep in the shade until about five o'clock in the afternoon. Then we would start again. Now you may well imagine that this was a slow business. A thirsty ox stops eating after the third day. So he gets weaker and weaker. Usually by the end of a week's trekking from Ghanzi, we would only be able to manage about one mile an hour. Andrew van Zyl—old Hendrik's eldest son—usually went ahead on horseback. If all went well, we would reach Ghams at seven the next morning.'

'What was Ghams, *Oom*? A well?'

'About twenty or thirty feet deep. One had to lift the water out of it by bucket. The Bushmen were used for this. What they did was to cut forked branches, and place these one atop of the other, down the side of the well. The Bushmen would then stand on this, and the bucket full of water would be handed from one to the other. On reaching the top it would be emptied into a trough of hide. Each ox would then get its turn to come and drink. You can well imagine what it was like when the animals were thirsty, and straining, and bellowing to get to the water. Once we were at Ghams at about eleven on a Saturday morning, but without the wagon. This we had left about two or three miles behind, so as to get the team to the water. Tired and thirsty as we were, that morning we shot eight big elephant bulls near Ghams. This gave us some 500 pounds of choice ivory. A profitable transaction! The Bushmen had to go and hew out the tusks from the carcases. Meanwhile we laagered at Ghams. There was plenty of veld-food that year for the Bushmen. We ourselves had a grand feast to celebrate the end of a difficult trek. We had a menu such as there has never been, before or after. We had elephant foot baked in the ground. We also had boiled elephant heart. This was the food. The decorations were rice, pumpkin, beans!'

'Which came from where?'

'Don't think we were a bunch of barbarians, young fellow. We had it all worked out and neatly planned, man. The things other than the meat we had all brought along with us. Don't laugh. We even had a dessert: a pudding of milk and rice with sugar and cinnamon. Then we finished it all off with groundnuts, a mug of kaffir beer, or tea, coffee, or curds.'

'Heavens, *Oom*, how does one manage such things?'

'Lisa, child, we were men. And we were hunters. After dinner we all looked around for a shady spot, and went to sleep.'

Lisa shrugged her shoulders. Her very innocence was comic. The audience laughed.

I suddenly remembered my own lazy afternoons spent under a shady tree, while trekking through some difficult part. Many of these I had shared with this very man, Pieter Maritz-Botha. We would lie there on our backs, smoking, talking, until the servants brought us coffee. We would discuss Africa, Europe, the ways of man. At times, perhaps, he would fall asleep. Presently his snoring would mingle with the droning of the cicadas. I would lie awake still, watching the sky through the tracery of the camelthorns. The sky would curve infinitely to the horizon. Vultures and marabou storks would show up like points in time and space. With coffee ready, the talk would start again. This was comradeship. Now it had all passed . . .

' . . . That very afternoon we were sleeping off the effects of that great meal, when we heard the Bushmen shouting: "*Kao!*" That means: elephant! In a moment we were all wide awake. In another minute or two we were out looking for the spoor. It was as if an army had passed by the laager. Ahead we could still see the great cloud of dust arising, as the herd moved on. According to the Bushmen there were a few hundred together, a whole generation and a half on the move, heading for the river. To get there, however, they had to go through the fly-belt. But no one likes losing a horse; all our horses were not salted; so we just had to keep out of it. Or where it was unavoidable, have Bushmen walk behind us, waving branches. Far better it was, all the same, to keep to the open veld. The herds had to be headed off before they got to the fly-belt. The fly, of course, was fond of the bush. Many a time we went galloping for all we were worth to keep the elephants in the open. It was like that on the Sabbath, after we had eaten so well. Yes, when you were hunting for Hendrik van Zyl, there was no such thing as a day of rest: had to follow the spoor as you struck it. Maybe weeks or even months could pass before anything like that came your way again. That sort of hunter's life was like waging war. You had ever to be on your guard; act at the shortest notice, even on a Sunday, if the enemy showed up. Enemy? . . . When it was all done with, one sometimes sat down and thought matters over: considered all those great animals we had dispatched; and that for ivory. You needn't look at me that way, young Venter. I have done a lot of hunting in my day; and seen even more.'

I quietly wondered. This was perhaps a new side to Pieter Maritz-Botha, which I had somehow missed.

Adriaan Venter puckered his brow, shifted on his seat: a leadwood-stump. 'That I can well understand,' he said. 'But is it not also true that one's hunter's blood does not easily come to rest, even after one is married?'

Lisa threw her fiancé a sharp glance. Piet Botha looked up from his pipe-stopping, smiling. 'Don't get cold feet,' he said casually.

The crowd was laughing by now. 'Never mind,' Lisa pouted, 'he can *maar* stick to his spoors, if he likes.' She suddenly hung her head, blushing, but also laughing with the rest. The only serious face was that of Adriaan Venter himself.

'Now what about the great battle, *Oom*?' he persisted.

'We were six on horseback that day: McDonald, the three Van Zyls, Barend, myself. After two hours of hard riding we could see the dust again. Before long we caught up with the herd. It was, as the Bushmen had said, the greatest gathering of elephants we had ever seen. Mind you, they didn't appear to be frightened. They were moving steadily; but there was no panic. They were just heading for the river, and within another few hours they would have got there. Well, before long they were bound to discover that they were being followed. The wind changed its direction slightly, and they took our scent. Like that!'

He snapped his fingers.

'One gave the alarm: we could hear the trumpeting like the battle-horn of an Ombalantu. The whole herd suddenly turned about and started stampeding, doubling back on its own spoor. We spurred our horses and kept close to them, not yet shooting: the dust was too thick.'

'Not even a shot?'

'Wild shots, perhaps, into the herd itself. But the real thing still lay ahead. You know how there are pans up in those parts: large pans, little pans, dotted about. The previous year was a good rain year. Everywhere in these pans treacherous mud had collected. Then suddenly there was one which had more than any of the rest. Whether the herd of fleeing elephants misjudged it, I do not know. The next thing we saw was that they were rushing down into the pan like the Gadarene swine. In a few minutes—and now we were shooting for all we were worth!—practically the whole herd had got bogged down in the mud; there they were, struggling like flies in a honey pot. They would push upwards, and forwards, and then just sink down again to their very bellies, trumpeting all the time. The air was thick with powder smoke; torn by the sound of gun-fire, the squealing and trumpeting of the elephants, the death cries of the animals, our own shouts . . .

'Before long all sorts of bush people began collecting; and some from the river: coming in from all sides; licking their chops for the feast ahead. Now I'll tell you what I saw with my own eyes: some of the animals were still alive. Some cows were trying to push their calves ahead of them, out of the stickiness. When it seemed that they would succeed, shots would ring out again—and down they would crash. One hundred and three fell that day: mainly cows and calves.

'By the evening the some three hundred blacks that had gathered were already attacking the carcases. They worked with axes, knives, and whatever could cut, carve, chop. Pools of blood had gathered in the deep hollows in the churned-up mud. It went on for days.

'Meanwhile the sky was black with vultures. Or they would sit like kaffir-beads on the dead leadwoods, stretching their red necks, so heavy from gorging themselves that you could walk past and kick their arses. Talk about the stench? The black meat-cutters, however, kept working through it all. A stink is like that:

afterwards one gets so used to it, fresh air smells abominably. Soon all the trees for miles around were festooned with meat drying in the sun . . .'

A stentorian voice came booming out of the gloom beyond the fire-light. 'This hunting fever, cousin Piet, which gets into the blood, man! It's like the mopani bees, you know! Gets into your nostrils! You swat them and they stink of honey! Others come in swarms—because of the sweet smell. Settle on you, creep into your ears, and your . . . !'

Whatever it was that was crept into, the information got lost in the general banter which accompanied this wisdom, with Labuschagne himself, as usual, hugely enjoying his own jokes.

'Seems to me, Cousin Jan,' Botha said after a moment, looking up leisurely, 'that what your mouth needs is honey!'

The noise continued. Labuschagne, very much the centre of attention now, stood there smiling broadly, towering over those around him. Next to me Louw du Plessis chuckled. 'No end to Jan, eh?' he said.

No end to Jan . . .

20

No end, I added in my thoughts, to the general spirit of these people in a variety of ways. They had come a long way through history: through war-torn Europe of the sixteenth and seventeenth centuries; through Africa itself, with its own enduring conflicts, beyond the knowledge of almost all except those who were closely concerned with it all. They had come a long way and they had survived. Disaster had often threatened. Disaster had often struck. As far as I could judge, they always seemed to carry on with a kind of innocence. On the whole they had survived. They were still surviving. And I, Will Worthington Jordan, was helping them survive . . .

I looked up from my short reverie. Ella Lombard was approaching me. I went out to meet her.

'How are you, *Tante*?' I asked.

'It is you who have not been as well as you should be, *Meneer*,' she said.

'I'm all right,' I replied. 'What about Johanna? Is there still the closeness in the chest?'

'She is better,' she answered. 'But now she is worried about Piet Botha's plans to go to Ovamboland, about the horse. Johanna says Piet moans about it all, like the wind in August. She says he *has* such plans.'

'Indeed,' I said. 'He wants to go to Ovamboland with a commando. He is looking for trouble.'

'*Meneer*, what you are saying disturbs me.'

'I am saying what I am saying, *Tante*.'

'But do you know it?'

'I know the man concerned.'

'But all Johanna said was that Piet was angry about his horse and wished to speak to Kambonde.'

'Guns also speak. But they answer too. Piet has this cock-eyed plan in his head; but please tell Johanna to put him in his right mind again, if she can do it. Otherwise? One wrong step, and it all ends in disaster. There is just no power to exercise authority. If we want to see a quick end to Upingtonia, let Piet carry on with what he is doing.'

I might have spared her this. After all, what could she, Ella Lombard, do about it?

'As you have been talking now, *Meneer*,' her answer presently came, 'it seems that we shall have to do all in our power to keep Piet from doing such things. When one loads a wagon one must see to it that all is well balanced. Otherwise the wagon lists to one side, then turns over at the first steep slope. I am an old woman, *Meneer*, and have no say.'

'In the laager people like you, *Tante*, have as much say as anybody else.'

'We always *maar* trekked along with the others.'

'No trek was ever possible without your consent.'

'You must speak to Piet, *Meneer*. Old Died has said that where there has been strife, peace should be made; the strife put to one side.'

'I'll confess to you, *Tante*, that I am unhappy about all that is taking place here. If you listen to the company here you wouldn't imagine it to be that way. If there are those who have no faith in our cause, let them get out: to where they want to be. But let them not make life difficult for the rest of us.'

For a moment I stood considering this. Was I depressed? A slight shudder seemed to pass through me. Better, I thought, that I get back to my wagon. I looked at Ella Lombard. She smiled at me in a motherly sort of way. I was suddenly touched. Dimly I heard Botha talking: he had taken up his chronicle again.

'. . . after it was all done there at the pan, we cut out our names on the baobab tree: to commemorate the battle. Well, if you young 'uns still have guts enough, you might do likewise. There are still elephants, lots of them, in fact. And there are still trees.'

I looked at the crowd. There was Lisa, sitting on the grass next to Adriaan, directly in front of the presiding figure of Pieter Maritz-Botha, with the firelight on their faces. There was a dreamy expression in Lisa's eyes.

It was Ella Lombard's doing. The next thing I knew, she had brought us to confront each other.

Ella Lombard was there as well, and she was speaking now. She was addressing herself to both of us.

'. . . Do we wish God's judgement to come over us?' she said. 'It is not good that we should stand in each other's dust. Piet? You speak out and say what you have in your heart. *Meneer*, you speak too. We have come to take possession of our land. I leave you, for I am nothing. And you are the leaders; and *Meneer* has bought this land for us.'

With that she left us. For a moment we stood looking at each other.

Then, with an attempt to ease matters, I said: 'There you have it. She has come a long way, and is probably entitled to say what she has said. What's happening? We seem to be walking in circles around each other, like two angry leopards. What for? It's hardly conducive towards stability in the laager. People talk about things, and make wrong judgements. I take it that we both want the best and only the best for our people.'

He had avoided my eyes. But now he looked up sharply at me and asked: 'What is your claim to it, Jordan?'

I was taken by surprise. 'What do you mean?' I asked. 'My claim is surely the claim of one who has engineered the whole project.'

'We all know about what you are supposed to have done. But that's the question!'

'So you think that Will Jordan has gone to all these pains to try and fill his own pocket? You suggested as much at Humbe, when you asked me why I was doing all this. That's so silly that it needs no answer. I have never had much money, and I don't think I shall ever have much.'

'You have mounted a dangerous horse, Jordan. Remember, these are *my* people!'

Two things struck me. There was firstly the fact that he was referring to me as 'Jordan'. We had always used first names when addressing each other. There was secondly the subtle emphasis on the words 'my people'. I was an outsider. I had no right at all to exercise leadership in this company. In my mind, things suddenly began to form a pattern. My true place was where I had been standing here: on the periphery.

His next words affirmed this: 'Every one should know his place. Otherwise there will be trouble!'

There was a start of temper in me. I had heard all this before. So what actually disqualified me here was my descent. I had never taken much notice of all that had reached my ears. Rather I had remembered the trust and good friendship of the majority here. I had even rationalized Botha's own attitude. I had tried to see it as a bit of sheer spitefulness. But his true feelings were surely different . . . We had been the best of friends, and partners. We had sat around the same laager fires, slept in the same trench . . .

'I have no idea what you are getting at,' I said. 'I don't care to know either. That's your indaba. However, since you have referred to my "dangerous horse", you might tell us more about your plans for Ovamboland.'

He looked sharply at me.

'You know what I mean. What happened between you and Kambonde is not my business. But if you have any real feeling for your people, remember, Kambonde is no customer to be trifled with.'

'Is that why you allowed yourself to be taken in by him? That little kaffir is not God himself!'

By now a small crowd had gathered around us, dismayed at the words we were exchanging. 'Consider what you are doing!' I said. 'I warn you.'

'Is this a threat?'

'Only an appeal to your manliness. But there's a lot more you should hear.'

'I have nothing to hide, Jordan. You can say what you like!' He was determined to provoke me.

'All right,' I said. 'If you want it that way: truth is you are making common cause with the enemies of Upingtonia. Remember, as you never tire of saying, they are the enemies of your people, not mine!'

'I know very well what I am doing. I know what they need!'

'Do they need Kamaherero? And Robert Lewis? Lewis is one of Rhodes's men. If you know a better Boer-hater, tell me his name!'

He glared at me.

'Lewis has one passion in life, and that is Lewis. He will lie to you, as he has lied to everyone—including Kamaherero!'

'That's what *you* say!'

'With good reason!'

'You hate him, because he knows what mad thing you are doing. You want to risk the lives of every man, woman and child in this laager. You want to do this simply because Kambonde has talked you into trying to get his cattle back from that Bushman bastard. What about Kamaherero? Have you thought about that? He lays claim to this area. Do you want a murder-feast? Or do you just not care, because you are no Boer, and can never be one?'

Now I was breathing heavily. This was the negation of all reason. People around us were joining in. I was conscious of some taking my side, others supporting Botha. One who had now ranged himself alongside Botha, towering above everybody else, was Jan Labuschagne. I caught a glimpse of Adriaan Venter and Lisa Lombard holding hands, looking with some concern at me.

My resistance suddenly seemed to crumble. I felt a great tiredness come over me. I knew what was happening. It had been threatening for hours. So, I had tried to ignore it. It was no use . . .

'We needn't take this any further,' I said at last. 'Come and say what you have to say at the meeting tomorrow. Let Lewis come, if he so wishes. But for God's sake stay out of Ovamboland!'

'You fool, who said I had a plan to attack Kambonde?'

He was suddenly furious. I saw the blood rush to his face.

'That you can ponder on your own. But I say again, neither I nor the *Bestuur* will suffer any rash adventures in Ondangua.'

'If you think that I would seek your permission to do what I find necessary to do . . . !'

I never heard the rest of the sentence. The tiredness in me had now become a crater. I could feel the fever erupting out of it. I was shaking.

Get back to the wagon, I thought with some confusion, get back!

I turned around with what dignity I could still muster,

mumbling something about this hardly being the place for an argument. Then I walked off, conscious of many eyes being turned on me.

'Where are you off to, Jordan? Come back!'

But I either had to make my wagon, or be carried there.

'Jordan . . . !'

Inwardly I was cursing myself. What had I done? Why had we started this fight? I should have known with whom I was dealing . . .

20

The stage of the dry fever was the worst. You would lie there through the hours, wrestling with a nameless, shapeless monster: lie in semi-consciousness finding no rest, trying to orientate yourself to a strange world . . .

It was like losing your way in the bush. There was no escape from it. All directions had become one.

When after hours you would find yourself returning to your senses, you would be supine on the *katel,* staring at the dirty patch of canvas above you. It glowed softly, and you wondered why; then suddenly knew: it was the moon . . .

All was quiet. You strained your hearing: not a human sound . . . Only the dolorous fiddling of the crickets; and, from very far, the pulsing chorus of the frogs . . .

Who had been here earlier that night? The Bushman . . . I dimly remembered his pursed-up little face, staring at me from out of the darkness. He had said something about water. There was a pail of it, standing on the floor of the wagon, next to the *katel.* Some of it had spilt . . .

He was always worried about his master when he was sick. He would go and perch on the *voorkist.* He would sit there for hours, watching me. I would wake up, see him there at the far end of the wagon in the open, and I would say: 'Come, old fellow, you can go off to sleep now!' I would drop off; and on waking again, he would still be there.

I lay as I had found myself on returning to consciousness. The sheet, tightly twisted between my legs, was warm and limp. The skin cushion under my head was tacky.

You were in an oven. The oven was your own body. You were

being slowly baked alive . . . trying to keep your chin up, look heroic, trying to be brave.

To hell with the fever, you had often said. Let it come . . . But *this* was hell: being baked like bread in a hollowed-out ant-heap . . .

Slowly my fingers crept up to my temples, then rested there. Slowly, deliberately, I pushed my fingers through my hair. My hair was getting thin: because of all this sweating . . . The water? I reached down carefully into the pool of shadow next to the *katel.* My fingers touched the coldness of the metal pail. I gripped it with both hands, lifted it slowly, reached for the water with a quivering mouth. Then the metal hit my teeth and the water splashed. It was wet and cold . . .

I kept on drinking, the water coursing down my chest, reaching to my groin. Presently I heard it tap-tapping under the *katel.* Carefully, exerting myself to the full, I returned the pail to the floorboards, then sank back onto the mattress, relieved.

All this struggling, what was the use . . . ? Only quinine would help . . .

Kairob, I once said to people at the Cape, handled his driving-whip like an artist. No one could outdo Kairob. The Bergdamara made good servants . . .

Mornings Kairob's voice would ring through the freshness. He would wield the longwhip, make it crack like gun-fire.

'England! Kolman!' He loved to make a poem out of the names of the oxen. '*Vaat!*' he would shout, with the crack of the longwhip as accompaniment.

Everywhere wagon spoors went wandering through the sand, the bush, the hardveld . . . In the omurambas they would meet again. The first travellers who had journeyed by ox-wagon through the country had cut these trails. Others had followed and the spoors had deepened. Only when the going could be easier or shorter by cutting a new trail was it done. Spoors lay in the sand for years . . .

Man here was like a broken bottle. Years would pass, the desert sand would blow . . . Wear down its sharpness, its brightness. The way down to the Bay was marked by bottles . . . They lay there in the Namib, reflecting the sun . . .

When you trekked southwards, you soon left the bush. The midveld was savannah, changing gradually to scrub, to desert. The south was a great, golden land, smitten by the light. Hills of gneiss or granite lay like black islands in a burning sea. Those sandflats down at Aus . . . Be on your guard when laagering there. That biologist from Zürich who was travelling through the country—a grand tour of three years by ox-wagon—Hans Schinz . . .

Schinz had said that he had been plagued by sand-lice. He was trekking up from Angra Pequena where his journey had started. That also happened to Andersson. He was out of action for a week. His foot had been poisoned . . .

All these spoors . . . in the bush, in the sand; reaching out to far, to lonely places . . . What sometimes happened was that you got mixed up. This way, that way? Who could tell? It just led you on, and on . . . Like the time you were on your way to Andara and you met the Zulu. How thin he was! You followed his spoor down to the Toahke, down to the marshes. Everywhere in the veld there were these blind trails going this way, that way . . .

The Bushmen were superstitious. They avoided the spoors, jumped over them. They did it because they believed that where men had been . . .

You knew this too. You gave your life to it. You could do it, because it was part of you. You not only became part of your wagon, you became part of the land. It was never a kind land; but it was a land which you loved. It never let you go. It was like a distant proud woman you could not forget. It was like a woman near to you but beyond your reach. It was like Hester Bouwer that day wading through the waters, her dress clinging to her limbs . . . Bold and fine . . .

What thoughts were these? Why did such things come creeping back to mind? Rather concentrate on a single thing, like a Buddhist monk . . .

Of no avail . . . Things worked faster when they were heated. Here I was in this *oven* of the body, and I was being slowly *baked.* So my mind raced . . .

The sun burnt fish-scales on your skin after a summer or two. After years of drought the rain would sweep over the land again, coming down in huge silvery curtains. Everything in the wagon would get wet. It would take days to dry out again. In winter the dryness and the frost and the hooves of the oxen turned the wagon-roads to powder. The dust would rise up from under their feet, settle over the wagon. At nights the Milky Way flowed like a river through the sky: like the Okavango at Andara . . .

Trek! The very word was like the crack of the longwhip. The dust would hang in the air. You would ride your horse to escape it. By late afternoon the sun would be seen as a celestial orange, wanting to be sucked . . .

Sometimes you would stop and rest. You would go to sleep under a camelthorn. You would wake up and scan the firmament for vultures. This was mathematics: those great arches being described in the heavens. Up there it was clean, refined, serene . . . But down here where the birds gorged themselves on carrion . . . All part of the same thing. Heaven and earth were a pair . . .

Days ripened, and faded, and died. Days were always dying. You kept on trekking, just trekking . . . The forenight was rising. The mountains to the east had clean, determined, washing-blue lines. The evening wind caressed the white winter grass. The oxen, sensing the end of their long labour, livened to the shouts of Kairob and the crack of the whip. The wagon jolted over the last of the limestone ridges. Izak, at the head of the team, galloped to keep his lead. Kairob's incantation became a song . . .

Something I always wondered at was the dogs of the Namas: such scrawny creatures. They seemed to be made of paper. What did they eat? When the trek passed the reed huts of the Namas, the whole tribe of Cerberus descended upon you. Kairob would flick his whip over their paper ears—flick, flack! They would howl and scuttle away . . .

One never really knew whither one was heading. I found myself in a Nama hut at Hoachanas once. There were lithographs of Kaiser Wilhelm I, Frederick the Great and Martin Luther against the reed walls. It was said that when Jager Afrikaander brought the Orlams up from the Colony during the early forties, he already had schools for his people. Sir James Alexander, who trekked from Cape Town to the Bay, met him and gave him books. It was a fact that Hendrik Witbooi kept a diary. It was in High Dutch, not Nama. Good for Witbooi. He gave Kamaherero something to think about. I had heard for a fact that when two Hereros met each other these days, they would enquire: '*Otji korta tji ri pi?*' Meaning: 'The little short one, *where* is he?'

Witbooi had once been salved by *Missionar* Ollp. News reaching the laager said that the veld round Okahandja was so full of human skeletons, it looked like a bonemeal-works.

War in this country never came to an end. Blood walked where it did not creep. And blood had run in the Swakop instead of water. Hendrik Witbooi . . . Watch that little Hamite! He was *korta*—short—but he was as tough as a sjambok, shrewd as the gallows . . .

Was I really an ally of the Namas? Kamaherero had said I was, and had damned me for it. What he really believed was what all despots believed: those who were not *for* them were *against* them. I had always refused to believe that one nation in this country was the moral superior of the other. The only real question was: who held the power? That was all that mattered. For years it had been the Namas. Now it was the Ovaherero. Power corrupts. That was the tenor of my letters to the press. Power corrupts; and he who wields the sword will also pay for it.

It was always good to reach the Bay again. The Bay was a tiny centre of civilized life. There were times when you would go and stand on the shore of the open sea, even flash passing ships with a mirror. You hoped that they would pick you up, take you to the Cape . . . It never happened. Then you just wandered back to the little settlement on the edge of the lagoon. The warehouses there held ivory, skins, feathers, brandy, guns, powder, lead . . . They also contained the basic necessities: food and clothes . . . So were the old days. Afterwards things improved with the coming of the British.

Shippard was the consul, and the schooner now arrived . . .

Once we trekked to Nhembaland . . . like children discovering the world. What did we care if the country as a whole was racked by war? We had done our best to stop it . . .

Then the Germans came . . . bringing beer from Bremen, from Hamburg . . . bringing *Ein fester Burg ist Unser Gott* . . . bringing dandy uniforms, and Teutonic efficiency . . . At the Bay the beer bottles collected in a heap behind the warehouse of the Erikssons. Like the Namas, who laid stones one atop of the other in the veld, out of reverence to their God, who was Heitsi-Eibib . . .

Down at the Bay high cirrus would fly over from the Atlantic. At times you would think it was going to rain. But it never rained. The sun burst through again, and the Namib burnt like sodium. In the old days there were only a few schooners from the Cape. The *Isabella Hartley,* the *Swallow,* the *Christina* . . . Later the *Louis Alfred.* Now there were some steamships . . .

The Bay was a long way off. If you were lucky, you would get there in a month. A Bushman runner, carrying a letter in a cleft stick, could make it in a fortnight. You sat here in the bush, you wrote your letters: to people, to the Cape press . . . told about the increasing anarchy in the country, the endless atrocities . . .

Had I taken sides in the struggle? I had taken sides with no one. I had taken sides with what was right. I was an enemy of tyranny. I hated with unrelenting hatred the barbarous disregard for the rights of others. I myself had been the victim of it. My wagons had been 'off-loaded'. I had always been solemnly assured that my goods were merely being 'bought'.

Blast their miserable guts! They never paid. They simply took what they wanted, then cleared off. They drank your brandy, and cursed you to boot. You crept back almost shamefacedly to some little centre, like Otjimbingue, considering yourself fortunate, at least, to be alive . . .

The Namas ate *uintjies, naras,* and puff-adders; distilled *witblitz** with the aid of a gun-barrel . . . They made coffee from ground-up camelthorn seeds and the roots of the shepherd's tree. They smoked elephant dung: there at their waters, playing their reed-flutes . . .

The reed-flute seemed to lament the frailty of man because it was from a reed which once grew in Eden . . . We had got lost in the world . . .

And then there were the tall black people of this country, who had Semitic features, and who sat dreaming around their Holy Fire . . .

Of Kamaherero they said that he wore two pairs of pants, trusting nobody . . . Not even Lewis . . . Lewis was after the copper of Otavi. It was Brincker, I thought, who once said the Boers and the Ovaherero should understand each other. Both were 'God's people' . . . Both believed so utterly in their mission . . .

Jehovah was his name . . . He had chosen them to seek in the wilderness for their Land of Rest. This He had promised them. They were to sing His praises, and honour His Commandments. He in His beneficence would reward them with eternal happiness; here and in the life hereafter . . .

Karunga was His name . . . He was God of the Created World. The omumborombonga was His tree. From its wood the Holy

*Lit. white lightning.

Fire burnt. From its split trunk the first men had emerged, and the first cattle. The Ovaherero were His people; and He was their God. Where His cattle had grazed, there was Hereroland . . .

So they believed; but this land of Upingtonia had never belonged to them. It had belonged to Kambonde Kampingana; and I, Will Jordan, had paid for it.

What would Coates Palgrave have said to all this? Palgrave was the classic example of the ineffectual idealist. Lewis could turn him round his little finger. Lewis claimed almost the whole country for the Ovaherero. But what you did not have, you could not dispose of . . .

Man's understanding had ever been a slave to his emotions. So that, too, had happened to Piet Botha: he had succumbed to the blood . . . Was siding now with the enemies of his people. Thought of me as the 'outsider' . . .

When ill you would pause and ask yourself: what sense in all this? Far better perhaps to clear out, find your own way again. Far better to leave these people to their own salvation . . . And look after yourself . . .

So whom did I see when I looked in a mirror? A stranger with the grey-yellow colour of the fever-stricken . . . And haggard . . .

Your ears had become stopped. Your spleen was like lead. On hands and feet brackish spots had appeared. What you needed with a tremendous, soul-tearing need was some cool and noble spring; in an autumn when a quietness comes over the land, in a year of good rains . . .

Water . . .

Water here had been the cause of the bloodiest battles. You trekked through the bush, the sand, until the oxen showed their bloodshot eyes . . . After many days you eventually got to a place where they could drink their fill . . . You would kneel, look deep down into the shining face of the water . . . You would stop over, piece yourself together again . . . You could bathe, shave, wash your clothes . . . You could bring your journal up to date. You could read a book. Then move on; look for the spoor wandering through the bush; and follow the sun, courage restored . . . You would even sing, and in singing remember the songs of boyhood: blue days at Hout Bay, fishing for Cape lobster out of tin canoes . . .

The loneliness would disappear. The sun and dust would be

forgotten. Thirst and winter frost would be the faintest of memories. It would be good to be alive again . . .

So the day would unwind itself. By evening the black dolomite hill in the bush-plain would have sunk into the horizon. Under stately camelthorns you would set up your laager. The Bushman would prepare palla-liver and mashed potatoes. Rautanen, the Finnish Missionary at Olukonda, had once exchanged potatoes for quinine . . .

You would sleep under the stars. You always slept under the stars when the weather was fine. It was good for the body, good for the soul. At the faintest glimmer of dawn, Kairob would shake himself out of his trench, walk a few steps, stand there piddling with abandon. You would wake to the sound. He would see you and grin with a flash of white. Then he would amble up tell you that the oxen had broken loose in the night, had returned to the last water. You would have to go back; walking, riding, until *erd*-smoke showed up in the dusk. Soon the Great White Pan would shimmer in the evening: lie there like the sea . . . But the cattle would be grazing peacefully among the zebras or the blue-wildebeest. Hunter-traders, coming down from Ovamboland and laagering there, would sing out that you should take things easier. Why all the hurry? Life was short.

A pride of lions would lie at the great spring with its jungle of reeds, indifferent to the men, cattle: they had eaten their fill . . . In the reeds the quelea finches would rise in a great cloud, roar away over the bush. Under the acacias you would eat *omuandis*, take it easy; life indeed was short . . .

Your horse would nudge you. A horse was part of a man. Was that why Botha felt so strongly about the Arab? Did *such* things happen to him as well? I supposed they did.

The thing about a long trek was your growing appreciation for simple things: tea, butter, sugar, bread . . . And a chat with a friend . . . Sometimes a letter . . . Hans Schinz had told me in Ovamboland that after his long journey from Angra Pequena the Irles at Okahandja had given him these things. He was overjoyed.

'Have you seen that the tapered ends of the termite hills all point to the magnetic north?' I had asked him.

'Is that true?' he asked.

'Well, test it!' We did, and he admitted I was right.

'You know,' I had said, 'I was on my way to Moçamedes when it all happened. The two Catholic fathers were living there in perfect amity. Then the king fell ill, and died. At first they tried to blame me, Jordan; but I was already on the far side of Humbe. Then they descended upon the priests. It was like a crucifixion.'

'How does all this affect Ondangua?' Schinz had asked.

'The Ukuanyamas are the most unpredictable of the bunch,' I said, 'Kambonde has given me the assurance that such things could not happen in Ondangua. Anyway, be on your guard. Something else is brewing up there and Kambonde's brother, Nehale, by the way, was violently against the sale of the territory to me.'

'So I have heard from Rautanen,' he said. 'Rautanen, too, is not so happy about Nehale. I'll keep a look out!'

'Fact of the matter,' I said, winding up the conversation, 'is that this is still a barbarous country. One has to calculate one's risk. For the rest? What I am attempting to do at present, *Herr Doktor*, is to establish a centre of civilized government.'

You got nowhere underestimating your abilities. Nothing of any worth at all had come about in this country except by hard work, faith, and courage. The Rhenish missionaries themselves—Diehl, Eich, Irle, and especially Hugo Hahn—would endorse this. When I had expressed myself against the *Missionare*, I had had men like Viehe in mind . . .

Sometimes I would argue with Lewis, even if he were not there.

'Listen, Lewis,' I would say, 'your real trouble is that you have never learnt to know and love this country. It would do you a world of good to forget about your advisership to Kamaherero. There's far more to all this than the question who will be cock o' the roost—war will not make this country, but love will. Give your life to it, man. Sign your name over it in paint, like Thomas Baines, rather than in blood. Did you ever see that painting he made of Charles John Andersson and Fred Green, preparing for the war against Jan Jonker Afrikaander? Three thousand Herero warriors marched past the Holy Fire. Andersson was in front on a white horse, carrying a blue flag with a white cross. Behind him was—who do you think?—Kamaherero wearing the *Missionar*'s night-shirt as battle dress . . .

'Fine, Lewis, if you can laugh about such things. But there's more to grieve about. Do you remember Forsyte? He got to Gobabis and that piece of trash, Freek Vlermuis, complained about the prices of his goods. Poor ingenuous soul, Forsyte . . . He thought he could make a stand of it. They shot him like a sick dog. Then they walked off. They lit their pipes, and sat drinking coffee—Forsyte's coffee . . .

'There's lots more I can tell you, lots more you know yourself. Jan Jonker and Hendrik Ses arrived at Grosz-Barmen one day, and proceeded to baptize the *Missionar*—Brincker it was!—with "blood and fire". Hendrik said: "Shoot this man of God, and see whether the heavens will fall." Well, the heavens *didn't* fall; but afterwards the Hereros caught up with Hendrik Ses. They chopped him into sixty pieces and fed him to the vultures . . .

'God knows, I hold no brief for anyone. I am only telling you this to demonstrate the sorry pattern of things in a country we all love. It has never changed. Blood cries out from the very sand here; from the limestone, from the bush; like the hyaenas under a full moon. The Namas came to avenge the death of Ses. But a few weeks later Kamaherero set off over the Swakop to shoot down every Nama he could find. Round about Omaruru, they say, there was such a stink of rotting flesh, people vomited and fled. The Hereros themselves trekked back the way they had come, but found an empty land. Then ate scorpions to survive . . .

'I know what you wish to tell me, Lewis. You want to say that these things all had their beginnings. I know it. In the forties Jonker Afrikaander led his Orlam bands into the Transgariep from the Old Colony. At Walwich Bay he got rip-roaring drunk and on his way back he demanded the blood of all. Was that the end? No, this very Kamaherero—of whom you are the confidant—emulating Copper Foot, his rickety old father, learnt to kiss the arse of the murderer of his people. In humble subservience, father and son sat at Windhoek, on the *werf* of Jonker. "Please *baas,*" they said, "please allow us to lick your pots clean! Please allow us to play dog on the *werf* of the Hottentot." Shall I remind you of another thing? Kamaherero once killed a lion when the Namas had taken fright and fled. Thereupon your overlord sent the skin to Jonker—Mkuru Oouje, God of the World—as a present. Jonker had a shrewd idea of the man who was doing this to him. He had Kamaherero bound to a wagon-wheel. When after three days they came to loosen him, he prostrated himself before his tormentor, saying: "Thank you, Mkuru, thank you God of the World! Jonker Afrikaander! King of Hereroland! King of Great Namaland!" . . .

'And in 1850 when the final murder-feast began, he fled to the Grosz-Barmen. At Okahandja the Afrikaanders chopped off the hands and feet of the Herero women. And old Copper Foot and his "calf" squatted around the Holy Fire. Jonker went reeling about the battle-field, counting the dead.

'Do you get what I am trying to tell you, Lewis? It amounts to this: the very man who pretends to claim all these lands for the Herero nation once stood by and looked on while the flower of his own people was being murdered. How do you expect anyone to attach much value to the words, to the deeds of such a man?

'I know your answer. You tell me the Namas did the same. That's nothing new. Who would justify it? There are the facts of history. All the letters, all the documents are still in the archives of the Mission. But there's honour among thieves; and loyalty is a virtue. When power corrupts, the first to succumb are the lily-livered. Rather give me old Chief Kahitjene—a true Herero, if ever there was!—who made a pilgrimage to the distant bush to "view" the grave of his son. While he was doing these things, and trying to gather together the remnants of his stricken people, Copper Foot was dying in a bed at Okahandja. Months previously Jonker himself had died in that very place. The two of them sent messages to each other. It was a race to see who could get first to the Styx. Jonker won. Charon said: "Welcome, Mkuru, God of the World! Enter, please enter—into the bottomless pit!" There he was, king at last, in his own country—Tjamuaha, who was called Copper Foot . . .'

'*Morro, Morro!*' The Hereros laughed. They had triumphed at last; but at what a price?

When Tjamuaha expended his last breath, a whirlwind sprang up between the trees. It danced over the plains, pulling up the reed-huts of the Namas. The black nation said: 'See there! It is the spirit of our father! He blows through the *werfs* of the Namas!' And Kamaherero felt his pride arise in him. Ah, the day had come: now he would be God of the World . . .

What does one learn from blood? What does one learn from violence? One thing only: that he who grabs at life and cuts away to get it will be cut down himself.

In 1870 Hugo Hahn had as a last resort compelled the warring parties to make peace. Ten years later—thirty years to the day after Jonker had swept through Hereroland—Kamaherero had every Nama in and around Okahandja caught and slaughtered. The bodies were dragged to a deep hole at the foot of a mountain and thrown into it. Hendrik Witbooi, they said, looked down this hole. He saw the great heap of bones at the bottom. He kept silent. Then he walked away . . .

21

In the grey, hesitant light of dawn I lay there in the wagon, sharply awake. I lay there with a certain resignation, tired but happy; happy in the knowledge that the storm had passed, and I had lived through it all. The little ship of my body had been badly battered. Now it was drifting into calmer waters. I was still sticky with sweat.

God, what a night! Now there just remained the great, blunt impression of an unequal struggle. At times it seemed as if life itself was being eroded. It was like a great rain flooding a landscape, tearing away the soil to bedrock. At other times it was as if I were being slowly trampled by elephants into the soft, squelchy mud of an Okavango marsh. I had talked to people. I had argued, I had racked my brains . . .

Lewis and I had stood next to the white-washed walls of an old Cape house. We had been facing each other. There were leafless oaks about us, and there was a cold snow-wind blowing from the north . . .

Now it had passed. It was good just to lie here, feeling the luminous intensity of perception, the suggestion of light-headedness, the strange empty feeling of the body. It was difficult to lift an arm.

After a while I attempted it, slowly, as if fearful that something might break. I spread my fingers. I lay there looking at their yellow bloodlessness. The tips were puckered like the Bushman's face when he stood next to the *katel* in the night.

I let my arm drop onto the blanket. I lay there flat on my back, dimly wondering what time it was. Was my watch still next to me on the *kist*? It was the gold watch I had inherited from my father. I moved my eyes and saw it lying face upwards. A quarter past six . . .

People in the laager were already astir. The meeting would be at half past ten. I would have to get up. There was a great deal still to be seen to. I would still be shaky, but I could manage. There was much to be arranged. The *Bestuur* had left matters in my hands. Lewis would come: I was certain of that now. I had heard that he was at Nhoosis spring.

The wagons were spread about. Some were in the flats to the north. How many people had Lewis visited? One thing was clear this day, this day, yes, it all would be finalized. Those who had not yet made a personal decision would be called upon to do so. Lewis and Botha and the rest could have their say. The great majority of people would refuse to be intimidated. They would remind their opponents that they were not alone in the world. Their flesh and blood would not abandon them.

I sat on the edge of the *katel*, shoulders bunched, hands gripped tight around the wooden frame. The pail of water stood at my feet. It was nearly empty; and the boards were wet. Voices sounded from outside. I got up and moved unsteadily to the front of the wagon. It was Ella Lombard and Hester Bouwer.

'*Meneer*, we have heard that you have been lying with fever!'

I climbed off the wagon. 'As you say, *Tante*, it is all over and done with: before you are a girl. Good morning to you, *Tante*: good morning, Hester!'

Hester was carrying something in a bowl, covered by a clean white cloth. 'You are pale, *Meneer*,' she said. 'We have brought you some barley soup.'

'Thank you,' I said, feeling a sudden tightness about the throat. Emotions were fluid after a bout of fever.

The bowl was warm in my hands. I looked to Izak, and he got up from his *erd*. He took the bowl and put it down.

'You must eat, *Meneer*,' Ella Lombard said. 'When a man's stomach is troubled, his spirits are too!'

'Will there still be a meeting?' Hester asked.

'Indeed!' I replied. 'At ten thirty. By that time your soup will have made a man of me again.'

Hester smiled. 'There is much talk in the laager about the meeting, *Meneer*.' The sun caught her fine, level teeth.

'I hope the talk is in our favour.'

'The people are mainly *for* Upingtonia. But there are some who see only evil things,' she said.

'Let them be,' I answered. 'No worthwhile thing ever fell into anybody's lap!'

After my visitors had left, I stood there next to the wagon, lost in thought. Izak brought me some of the soup and I slowly ate it all. It was good, but my throat had to be consciously employed. Kairob, squatting next to an iron pot full of curds, grinned at me.

'Old sinner,' I said. The answer was a mixture of clicks and grunts, signifying goodwill. It warmed me, like the soup. I remembered how John Caine once asked me why I didn't get married. I had two excellent old retainers, I said. They looked after me well enough. Caine squinted at me, and I thought: he wanted to tell me there was far more to a woman than just good cooking. Caine was a Lewis man these days . . .

But of course women in Africa had shown their worth as partners, as companions. There was Sarah Jane Andersson—'brave little blue-eyed woman'. When one sat talking to her, telling her of the Transgariep—South West Africa, she preferred to call it—her face would light up. Then she would say: 'A great country, it is!'

And Mary Moffat . . . While Charles John Andersson and his Sarah Jane were here, she married David Livingstone at Kuruman and went to live with him at Kolebeng. Livingstone was busy exploring the Zambesi. Mary died in East Africa and Livingstone stood mourning at her grave.

There were many others who had faced Africa, had struggled with it, loved it . . . like Ella Lombard . . . and Hester Bouwer . . . and Lisa . . . dear Little Lisa . . . she would marry her Adriaan Venter. It would be the first marriage here in Upingtonia . . . bring us good luck perhaps . . .

'Find yourself a good woman,' Charles Lyon had said to me in the Bay. 'It solves a lot of problems.'

'You may be right,' I said. After all, I was human and had human feelings. But things for me were different . . .

Things for me had more or less fallen into a fixed pattern. For example, there was this old wagon. One of a number I had used during my life time. There was this old *katel* which knew me more intimately than even a woman could. It had a coir mattress and a mat of eland thongs. There was a tin box in the *kist*, containing my most personal possessions. There was another *kist* in which I had collected botanical and geological specimens. There was the gun-rack between the hood-ribbings, containing a Wesley Richard, a Winchester Repeater, and two Martini Henrys. There was the ammunition box, the provisions *kist*, containing meal, sugar, coffee, rice, a bag of potatoes . . . Above this was a collection of plates, bowls, cups, cooking pots . . . In the little shelf behind my head as I lay on the *katel*, there was an Authorized Version of the Bible, Andersson's *Lake Ngami* and his *Notes of Travel* . . . There were also some works of Dickens, Shakespeare, a collection of old periodicals . . . On the floor next to me as I lay was the medicine chest, containing Dutch medicines, quinine, ipecac, laudanum, phenol, iodine, purgatives . . . There were my surgical instruments; and a clinical thermometer . . .

I stood looking absently at the soup bowl. This was the way life fell into place. It could so easily become a rut. One could become sentimentally attached to what had been a close witness of suffering. That was precisely what was wrong with some of my friends of the laager. They seemed to relish suffering.

'*Bambuse*,' I said, 'let's get going!'

Izak's face bore a multiple smile. 'Not sick?' he enquired.

'Well enough,' I answered. 'Is there any coffee?'

He stooped over the *erd*. '*Dira ma!*—It is ready.'

'*Garie!*' I clicked. 'Sugar!' I watched the Bushman fill a little jug from the kettle which had been standing on the ash. I tasted the coffee. It was like wine.

'What about the letter? Will *Baas* Eriksson come?'

'Karevapu Katiti.' This was meant to be an affirmative.

'When, *Bambuse*?'

'When the sun is out!'

'Perhaps he will sleep here. You must wash the linen today. Did you come and listen in the night?'

'Mister was dead!' He clicked. '*Atatita!*'

'One doesn't go to bed before one has undressed,' I said.

'*E!*' He agreed.

I relished the sweet intimacy of the coffee. I looked at the little pewter jug from which my bowl had been filled. My mother had given it to me.

UPINGTONIA—LYDENSRUST
(October 1885)

1

When I returned from the spring to my wagon shortly before seven, blue smoke was feathering up between the trees. There was something comforting, home-like about smoke from an *erd.* The very smell was as earthy as that of ripening thatch, a newly spread cow-dung floor, or a thunder-shower on droughty land.

Herdsmen were driving cattle out to pasture. Their cries blended with the lowing of the animals. In clearings between the trees some cows were still being milked. Others were being vigorously pumped by tail-wagging calves. At trestle-tables poke-bonneted women were kneading dough for bread. Two young girls were shaking out bedding and hanging it up. In the grass between the wagons some chickens were chasing insects.

It was a restful scene. But restfulness was not its true content. Of that I was certain, however much I desired the opposite.

Where the water from the spring coursed down the slope, I could see some distance between the trees in a northerly direction. A man on horseback suddenly emerged from the trees. He wore riding breeches, a white jacket, and a topee. It was Robert Lewis.

I stopped in my tracks and watched him dismount. That was Piet Botha's wagon. So, the two had arranged to meet . . .

The next moment my conclusion was confirmed when Botha emerged from behind an awning. He and Lewis shook hands. There was a third party, which I took to be Lewis's 'secretary'. Instinctively I moved behind a tree.

I knelt beside the water, washing my face. Yes, I had expected it; and in a way I had hoped that it would not happen. I had hoped that Botha would come to his senses, however late he had left it. The man was openly ranging himself alongside Lewis! I got up, and started walking back to my wagon, slowly. Botha believed all that Lewis had told him. This was Herero territory: this land of

Upingtonia, for which *I* had paid Kambonde Kampingana.

Adding insult to injury, Lewis thought himself entitled to play the inspector here. He had come to Otjovanda Tjongue—Grootfontein, as some now called it—as 'legal adviser' to the King of Damaraland.

Lewis was barely literate, but could talk so well that he had not only led Kamaherero up the garden path, but also Botha. The whole Herero nation had, in fact, been deceived by Lewis. His own interests were all that mattered.

I was sweating again. Who said I had shaken off the fever? I needed all my bodily strength now to face what was coming.

Axel Eriksson was waiting for me at the wagon.

'Karevapu!' We embraced each other joyfully. Forgetting all that still tended to weigh me down, I looked at him, keeping a hand on his shoulder. 'I'm glad you're here, my friend.' I looked at the sturdy figure with the red beard, dressed in riding boots, corduroy jacket, and bandolier. He looked like a close relation of Barend Bouwer. When he replaced the broad-brimmed hat, he might well have been a Boer.

'So, how is Will Jordan?'

'How is Karevapu? Everywhere I hear where you have just been: the Okavango, Moçamedes, even the Transvaal. We have been crossing and recrossing each other's spoors, and never seeing each other. How's the wife? How are the children?'

'All is well; as well as can be with the human species. Just come to hear how it is here. Wife and kids are at the Cape.'

'I heard that you were in Europe. When did that happen?'

'Middle of '83. To London. To Lissabon. Many places. Yes, even Vänersborg!' He chuckled. 'For all the birds I have collected. Some said: "Stay, stay!" You know what? I just wanted to come back. Was in the Transvaal and looked for farms to buy near Crocodile River.'

'And then back here!'

'No other way, Will.'

'I have seen the ashes of your old fires at quite a few waters. Get my letter? I wrote to Omaruru.'

'Got your letter, yes. So it is well with you here? Good plans for the future, eh? Upingtonia!'

'Remembering what has been happening at Omaruru, I thought you would still be interested.'

'Omaruru is *kaput*. All this war business, Will. When will it all end?'

I looked at him, remembering the days when he was generally acknowledged to be the Trader King of Damaraland. His wagons had gone as far afield as Pretoria, Kimberley, Cape Town. He even had a regular trade with King Kgama, on the far side of the Thirstland.

It was not only the war which had affected the Erikssons. It was also the advent of the Germans. Since *Schutzherrschaft* had crept up from Angra Pequena—now Lüderitz—Otjimbingue had developed as the centre of the German trade. The Erikssons had suffered more than the rest of us.

'Karevapu,' I said, 'one of your lovely bushveld birds must have whispered in that mighty ear of yours that I needed you.' He laughed. 'But who knows,' I added, 'perhaps I catch up with you at the very moment you have decided to shake the dust of this country off your feet.'

'You think there is nothing but defeat for us?'

'Decline is always relative. You needn't worry. You'll always come out on top.'

'Well, we have had bad knocks, you know!'

'You'll keep going, Karevapu.'

We walked to the lee of the wagon. How fine to have found this son of Vänersborg with me again. I looked secretly at him as we found chairs. The sun, the dust, the great impersonal size of Africa, all had left its mark on him. Yet, in a way, there was still something in him of the young man of twenty who had once landed at the Bay, clad in a frock coat and waistcoat; resplendent with watch-chain dangling over the midriff. He had come to work as an ornithologist for Charles John Andersson. In a way he had become his heir. At a price! Fever and dysentery had played its part. There were deep grooves on that fine, broad forehead. The sun, the sun of this land! He had lost some teeth. I myself had drawn one, up at the Okavango . . .

In spite of all, it was still the noble, honest face of my friend whom I trusted. He was like Diederick Prinsloo. The bush and deserts and mountains had not yet been able to extinguish that suggestion of a northern climate.

'You were sick with fever, Will?'

'We get over it quicker, the older we get. Until we get over it no more. What about something to eat? *Bambuse!* Kairob!'

I was taking some things out of the wagon. 'From where have

you come?' I asked. 'Where are you heading?'

'Trek from up there by the river.' His head indicated the direction. 'Now to Omaruru. Very bad weather we have on the way. Rain, rain! Ugh, the wagon is like a ship!'

'Well, you know about all our plans. Today is the day for Upingtonia to be finally constituted. You are here at a propitious moment. So, old *Vite Hövdinger* . . .' This was the name some of his fellow Swedes had given him: White Chief. ' . . . it is up to you to pick your water and your farm. That goes for every man here.'

'Some are still fighting you?'

'Lewis and Co. We need not specify. They can do their worst; we're going through with it. I'm not underestimating our enemies, but I refuse to pay them the compliment of taking them too seriously. Listen, Axel, it's important that the Erikssons become part of the picture here!'

He removed his hat, then polished his shining pate with the palm of his hand.

'My back is strong enough still,' he said. 'Up above a bit thin, eh? I come!'

'I count on that,' I said. 'I am deeply thankful.'

'I have trekked a lot. Now I must first rest a bit. Well, I can come here to Upingtonia; and perhaps there is a farm here.'

'There will be, Karevapu. We meet at ten thirty. Lewis has turned up. What he's going for, I could not say. We'll see. But please be there if you can.'

'I come from outside?'

'I shall decide who is "outside", and who not. This is still my property!'

'I can stay. Our kind does not like to give up.'

'No, of course not. You understand now why Piet Botha's way of doing things is so perverse.'

'This old Piet!'

'Old Piet. Got cold feet, but can still spin yarns about his great deeds of the past. He and Lewis? They're like that.' I crossed my fingers. 'Lewis arrived here all dressed up, and trailing a secretary. And Piet in the offing.'

'But once you were good friends, not so?'

'I have nothing against Piet. I just detest his political counter-jumping. What news have you heard? How is old Witbooi doing?'

'Ugh, Witbooi—the news we hear says he was very heavily defeated at Osona by Kamaherero.'

'What was he doing at Osona? That's just outside Okahandja!'

'Hendrik and his whole Witbooi nation are on the move to the north!'

'We heard all about that. Where exactly were they going?'

'Just to look for land somewhere in the north. You know Witbooi says Almighty God has called him.'

'They started moving up from the south in July, if my information is correct.'

'Correct!'

'So he thought of travelling by way of Damaraland?'

'Came to Osona: and put up a laager there. For his whole "war".'

'His army. How big is that?'

'Six hundred mounted men with good guns. So they come to Osona, and stayed there. No fight yet. They tell me Kamaherero and Witbooi smoked from the same pipe. Only Kamaherero said: "No water for the oxen and the horses, please. Only for coffee".'

'Then they should have given their animals coffee.'

He laughed. 'Perhaps they thought as you say, Will: fill the barrels and make a lot of coffee. But when they rolled the barrels down to the water the Hereros all stood around. And gave orders: "Do this, do that! Throw out this water, it is too much!" Then the Witboois said: "All right, we take the place, and we can shoot it out!" So they *shoot* it out. But Witbooi's "war" was too small; and Kamaherero came with plenty of soldiers. So there was shooting, all round; and women and children were not spared. They say Witbooi lost a son; and another son of his lost an arm. Another *Fest* for the birds!'

'You remember Stephenson?' I asked. 'That fellow who walked through the country with Witbooi, also believing him to be divinely called? John Caine once had an argument with him. Stephenson said whoever doubted Witbooi's divine calling was destined to roast in hell. Meanwhile, it has become Osona. Karevapu, for my part I am beginning to think the sooner *Schutzherrschaft* becomes a reality in Damaraland, the better!'

'You think it will come?'

'Maybe, who knows. The country is full of German officials these days.

'Then Rehoboth is also *kaput*?'

'I protested, wrote all sorts of letters: even to the German Foreign Office. To Shippard at the Bay. And to others. But it needs a greater voice than I have to let the world know. You need muscles too.'

'How strong are the Germans? Goering and Nels and company? Everywhere I come, I hear they have been there. That is like Palgrave.'

'Much sweat and dust from running around; and nothing to show, eh?'

'We hope not. Anyway, this is our territory for which a legal contract exists. We have drawn up a proper constitution. Today will see the formal start of an ordered state. What we still need is *people*! My hope and expectations are that the Erikssons, the Charles Lyons, the Chapmans, Todds, Behans, and many others will yet join us here. Perhaps we shall have others in time; from the Cape, from Europe.'

'When all is ready, we come!'

'That's what I like to hear.'

'What then if *Schutz* is declared?'

'*Schutz* can only come by agreement. We don't need *Schutz*. Would you like to read the constitution?'

I took the documents from my tin box and handed them to him.

'*Wet en regel*, as the Trekboers call it. Well, there it is: law and order. Whatever may be said of the Trekboers, or the Boers in general, they know what an ordered society means.'

He studied the closely written pages for a while. 'And Piet Botha?' he asked. 'He fights you.'

'He fights us. You are coming to the meeting? That's certain. I have to be off just now, to see the *Bestuur*. Meanwhile you make yourself at home.'

We arose. 'Ho, Will,' he said, putting his rock-like arm around me. 'You have a pretty land here. Nice! Everything is nice. Good waters, good land. Plenty of trees, grass!'

'Nothing better in the whole of Capricorn,' I said. If we can get things off to a decent start, this country, this land of Upingtonia is on its way to an excellent future. We carry on as we are. And the future may be left to the future. Agreed?'

'Agreed.'

'Here we have been jabbering, and having nothing to eat. *Bambuse!*'

But the servants had already laid the table. Izak looked over the top of the cooking *scherm*. '*E!*' he said.

2

At nine o'clock that morning the *Bestuur* met at Diederick Prinsloo's.

The president designate sat in front of his hartebeest-house behind a folding table on which lay an open Bible. Splashes of sunlight fell on the pages, on the table, and on Old Diederick himself, highlighting the white hair of his beard. Above and behind him on the ridge of the house sat a brilliantly feathered roller.

He held my hand, and looked me straight in the eye.

'I wish thee good morning, *Meneer*,' he said.

'How are things, *Oom*?'

'I rested well, *Meneer*. The medicine thou gavest me? It was good!'

'It pleases me to hear that, *Oom*.'

The other members of the *Bestuur*—Barend Bouwer, Louw du Plessis, Chris Leen, were now coming up. Each in turn greeted Diederick Prinsloo. Chris Leen, who had just returned from a hunting trip, came up to me.

'I hear you were down with fever?' he asked.

'So I was. But all is right again. By the way, Lewis is here.'

'I was up at your wagon to tell you just that, but you had already left. I wouldn't worry too much about Lewis.'

'I'm not. How was the hunting?'

'Not too good. Our brigand half-breed Bushman, Gabriel, out there near the omuramba, has been shooting.'

Old Diederick's voice, apparently in answer to something Louw du Plessis had said to him, broke in on our conversation '. . . If the Lord finds us pleasing in His eyes, we shall *have* this land!'

With his usual good fellowship, Barend Bouwer came up to me: 'So, Mester!' he boomed. 'The wife says you were sick. But now better! We are glad to hear it.'

'Thank you, Barend. Your wife's powerful broth seemed to work wonders. You know we have visitors? Lewis and an appendage are here.'

'Lewis has been to at least ten wagons this morning, Brother

Jordan.' This was Louw du Plessis. 'Well, I don't think he finds many ears to listen to him.'

'God forbid,' Chris said.

'You know what? I'm heartily sick of all this talk, talk, behind wagons and *scherms*,' I said. 'The sooner things come out into the open, the better.'

'You are right, Brother Jordan.'

Old Diederick lifted his olive-wood stick. '*Meneer*,' he said, 'concerning the things which now be done to us, we stand where we stand!'

David Black, who was field-cornet of the laager now, and a few others, had just arrived. 'Do you perhaps know where Lewis is at present?' I asked.

'He was down at the *werf* of the Krugers,' Black answered. 'They're Botha men.'

'And the De Beers?' I said.

'De Beers,' he confirmed.

I was now remembering the people who had avoided my company the previous night.

The *Bestuur* were all seated around the table.

'It is up to you,' I said. 'If you want to hear what Lewis has to say, we shall have to hang on for some time.' I looked at Chris who was keeping the minutes. 'Meanwhile until His Highness arrives, our chairman may precede us in the usual way.'

We stood with bowed heads while Old Diederick, remaining seated, led the meeting in prayer.

'Thank you, *Oom* Diederick,' I said, when at last the amen had rumbled out.

I now had to give the meeting a general picture of the situation. It was quite simple, I said. In the legal sense I was still the owner of all the lands which had been bought. I passed the contract around for inspection. I had decided, I said, to hand over the whole of the new territory to the *Bestuur*. The *Bestuur*, with my assistance, would then offer the various farms to prospective settlers. I had decided to keep five out of the three hundred farms for myself. I would also retain the mineral rights to the Otavi copper, until such time as it could be developed for the benefit of the whole community. The trouble was its remoteness. A big organization was necessary to undertake the development. The general meeting, I concluded, would just be called upon to witness the formal handing over of the title.

It was half past nine when these matters were finally dealt with. Meanwhile we had decided that Lewis would have to be fetched. We had to know what his business here in the laager was; what he intended doing. Louw du Plessis and David Black offered to go and look for him. Meanwhile some of the womenfolk had brought us refreshment in the form of coffee and milk-tart. *Pièce de résistance* was a pie of fine proportions with a filling of jelly made from the fruit of the omuandi. While being served with this, my hand must have shaken while holding my plate. Jet du Plessis watched me with commiseration.

'*Meneer*,' she said, 'when you lie alone in your wagon, who could know when things are not right? When we are sick, *Meneer* is there to help us all. But when *Meneer* is down? Now we only hear of it all when *Meneer* is up again.'

And Hester Bouwer, serving coffee, remarked that she and *Tante* Ella had been able to provide some strength-giving soup. And pleased she was to hear that I had had it all. But true, she said, why wait until all had passed? The people of the laager were there to help one another.

For no apparent reason I once again felt the faint stirring of emotion. I was, I supposed, still keeping up appearances. This could be dangerous; but it was also necessary. As for Robert Lewis, he could express himself in whatever terms he thought fit. There was one thing, however, he could emulate for his own and the general good: the natural sympathy of these people for the human plight. This was, I suddenly felt, more important than a knowledge of the world.

3

Lewis turned up as expected.

From the very start he assumed the air of a high state official. He was 'inspecting' matters, he said. It was clear that he had taken the titles of Legal Adviser to the Herero Nation and High Commissioner for Damaraland seriously.

Arriving with Louw du Plessis and David Black, he proceeded to greet the other members of the *Bestuur*. From his chair, Diederick Prinsloo eyed him fiercely.

'Mister Lewis!' It was a great rasping voice that suddenly came. Only a troubled movement of the olive-wood stick and a sharp knitting of the bushy eyebrows further indicated Old Diederick's feelings.

When he had completed the rounds of presenting himself to the *Bestuur,* Lewis looked at me in a cursory sort of way.

'Hallo, Jordan,' he then said.

I hesitated for a moment. 'Hallo, Lewis,' I replied.

Somebody offered him a chair, and he sat down. Then he lit a cigar. I looked at Old Diederick and he looked at me. Thereupon he turned towards Lewis and repeated: 'Mister Lewis!'

The silver hair suddenly seemed to stand on end. '. . . I must tell thee, we have had much to *suffer* here from thee!'

Lewis sat up straight and faced Old Diederick. His air of authority had vanished.

'You have some difficulty in understanding the purpose of this visit, Sir,' he said. He spoke English and as far as Old Diederick was concerned, it was a foreign language.

'Listen,' I intervened, 'if you hope to effect anything with these gentlemen, please address them in Dutch.' Only Chris Leen, David Black and myself knew English.

Lewis languished in his chair, legs crossed, thumbs in the pockets of his waistcoat. Switching to the vernacular, I said: 'I have no doubt that we are all eager to hear what our visitor has to say. Perhaps he might find it instructive to hear a few things about our plans for the future.'

He looked up. 'Do you imagine, Jordan,' he said, 'that I am not conversant with the facts?'

'You'll have an opportunity of stating your case, if you have a case,' I said.

'But this is a serious matter, Sir!'

'Of course it is serious. It is serious in the sense that we are here at Otjovanda Tjongue, and in the surrounding country, to stay.'

His eyes were fixed on me. I pointed to the contract and the draft constitution lying on the table. 'In all legality. Examine it, if you please!'

'Pshaw!' It was a studied expression of contempt.

'If you wish to discuss this in a spirit of reasonableness, we would be happy to hear you,' I said. 'If not? We are not going to be misled by your theatricalities.'

'I will have you know, Sir,' he said, 'that I am here in my official capacity. I represent Kamaherero, King of Damaraland!'

'Yes,' I said, 'we know all about that. Representing His

Majesty, then, you might be able to tell us on what grounds do you dispute the legality of this contract?'

'What would you say to it, Sir, if Kambonde Kampingana were to deny all knowledge of ever having signed such a piece of paper?'

He had taken me by surprise. 'Deny it?' I eventually said. 'If you take us for fools, Lewis, then there is no point in continuing this discussion. You obviously wish to imply that the whole business is just a piece of clever chicanery on the part of Will Jordan! Apart from the fact that this document . . .' (I rapped the contract with my knuckles) '. . . has been attested to by Kambonde's own missionaries, do you think that I would lead these people all the way from Humpata to Otjovanda Tjongue, knowing that I, and eventually they, had no rightful title here? Why would I do this? To fill my own pocket? Credit me at least with sufficient sense to know that if I had in fact come here in defiance of rightful ownership, we would not stand a chance. The whole of Ovamboland would have descended upon us. On the contrary, Kambonde Kampingana is well disposed towards us.'

I flicked open the file containing the contract. 'Read and study it, if you can!'

He sat there with a cigar between his fingers, with the smoke creeping up between his whiskers.

'If you refuse to read it, I shall!' I said. I took it up and began reading aloud the terms of the contract.

'I, the undersigned, Kambonde Kampingana, and my mother Namapula, Paramount Chief of the Ondonga tribe of the Ovambos, and hereditary owners of the tract of country embracing the following names and places . . .'

'I have no interest in your silly document, Jordan,' he interrupted. 'You are wasting my time!'

'Were we at the Cape,' I said, 'I would not hesitate to test your claims in a court of law.'

'Is that a threat?'

'. . . The following names are mentioned here: Noolonga, Okahakana, Okakoepa . . .'

'Oh shut up, Jordan! You are making a fool of yourself. Keep your list to yourself, man. Let us get down to business.'

'Business?'

'I also happen to have a little document,' he said, shaking the ash off his cigar. 'It's with my secretary. You are free to examine it: the evidence of the concession granted to me on 9 September, by His Majesty Kamaherero. It is duly sealed with the seal of the Damara nation. This as a reward for my services to these people; being, if it may interest you, the sole right to prospect for minerals and open out mines, especially in this area.'

'Do you imagine that I and these good gentlemen here should be impressed by all this?'

'Well, Sir!' He uncrossed his legs. 'What I do believe is that the sooner you accommodate yourself to the fact of my claims, the better for both you and your *Bestuur*!'

I looked at my friends. They were all tensed up by this time, although only David Black and Chris Leen could have followed the argument.

'If these so-called concessions of 9 September,' I said, 'include the mineral rights to what is included in the purchase of Upingtonia, then Kamaherero has been giving away things which do not belong to him. The contract is perfectly clear. This area has been the property of the Ondonga tribe since time immemorial; that is, until I bought it.'

He was muttering while I was talking.

'Here it all is,' I continued. 'Should you feel that we are playing cock 'o the walk here, it may interest you to know that we have the military support of the Ondonga tribe, as well.'

Picking up the contract again, I quoted: '. . . *and if it should at any time become necessary for Mr W. W. Jordan to hold possession of the above-named country, we pledge ourselves to assist him to do so with the strength of our tribe.'* This document, by the way, was drawn up in both English and Oshindango. As I have said, it has been witnessed by Missionaries Weikolin, Hokala, and Rocha.'

He seemed to be amused at all this. 'Don't act like a fool, Jordan,' he said again. 'Nobody disputes the existence of your so-called contract. The only question is: *how did it all come about?*'

'So you wish to imply that Kambonde Kampingana had pressure brought to bear on him? By me? Trying to push the mighty Ondonga tribe with its three thousand well-armed soldiers into something they don't like?'

Chris Leen, who was noting down as much of the conversation as he could, looked up and caught my eye.

'What you have said, Jordan,' Lewis said, 'is all beside the point. Let's stick to the facts!'

I threw down the contract. 'The central facts lie here. This is not to be dismissed as so much froth, whatever motives you may wish to ascribe to me. This is a legal document and there is no court of law anywhere which could decide against it!'

'Your whole argument, Jordan, rests on the premise that Kambonde Kampingana had the right to sell you this territory!'

'I see,' I said, 'so you, in all seriousness, now wish to maintain the fiction that this country is part of Damaraland!'

'I deal with *facts,* not fiction!'

'Fiction, and of a very poor kind. This area belongs as much to the Ovaherero as does the Cape Flats. For generations it has been the property of the Ondonga tribe; and all people who in fact have lived here have been a few bands of nomadic Bushmen. Where Herero cattle have grazed, there is Hereroland . . .'

'You have said it, Sir!'

'I may have said it, but first hear me out: Herero cattle never grazed here. The nearest they got to it was the cattle stolen by the Bushmen.'

The argument proceeded in circular fashion, presently returning to ground we had already covered. We were not getting anywhere. Maybe Chris was right: we should not take it too seriously.

He brought up the matter of the 'boundaries' of Damaraland again. He repeated the old story he had told Coates Palgrave of Damaraland extending from the mouth of the Cunene to Rietfontein in the east. This shameless piece of presumption was fiction all the way. At what time and how had the Ovaherero exercised authority over all this territory? Regarding Otavi itself, he knew full well how hunter-traders had at various times tried to buy this very area from Kambonde Nampingana, father of the present chief. There was Charles Thomas, for instance; the very Charles who had been killed up at the Okavango and whose death Lewis had helped to avenge. There was Wilmer. There was, in fact, Coates Palgrave himself, who had been interested in the territory as far back as the days of Chief Tjikongo.

Whatever new arguments I tried to raise, they made little impression. Lewis just sat there sucking his cigar, and saying repeatedly: 'I stick to the facts!'

'These are the facts,' I repeated with some heat. 'What you regard as facts, Lewis, have been sucked out of your thumb. You know very well that there is not a civilized government anywhere which would not give judgement for us. All right, I am quite prepared to put it to the test, if you like. I allow you the choice of whatever tribunal you please. Then we can submit the matter for international arbitration.'

'Pshaw, Jordan, what do you take me for?'

I sensed an element of danger. If this was the ruling sentiment, Kamaherero would easily be fired to undertake some adventure up here in the north. After his victory over Hendrik Witbooi at Osona, he was quite capable of it. Not that I wished to admit the truth of anything Piet Botha had said. Botha wished us to clear out before there was even a suggestion of danger. Or rather, he wished to inflate the existing dangers—who would deny them?—to an immediate catastrophe. Of course we would be vigilant here. Only a fool would refuse to recognize the enemy. On the other hand, it would be folly to turn about and run, just because a local potentate had sent a man like Lewis to threaten us.

I looked at the members of the *Bestuur*, sitting tensely in their chairs. Only Chris Leen seemed to be relaxed, maybe because he knew Lewis. For that matter, I knew Lewis as well. There was no true reason for me to take him seriously. He had always been a tongue-wagger. At the same time, I realized something: he could do a lot of damage.

'It is quite apparent that this man has no desire to reach a settlement,' I said at last. '*Ergo*, he does not hesitate to threaten violence.'

Now I had reverted to the vernacular. There was an immediate reaction. Diederick Prinsloo fixed a pair of burning eyes on our visitor.

'There are things we would know of thee!' he rumbled. 'What *plans* art thou hatching? Thou must know, fellow, our hearts are not faint, we tremble not. Neither be we terrified of thee, nor of thy master!'

I could applaud this. For a moment I could also laugh. Old Diederick, who sometimes looked like Wotan, was Moses now.

There was general talk around me: 'Let him do what he will!'—'We shall not give in!'—'Who is this man to talk to us like this?'—'This is the yapping of a *smous**!'—

So it went on, with Lewis ignoring it all. I saw him muttering to himself. No doubt about it: in his own eyes he had the position

*A pedlar.

well in hand.

'I opine, gentlemen,' he said at last, 'that you are worried as to what the future in this country may hold for you. Now come on! Let us understand each other as civilized people. Hard things have been said here today. I would have you know, however, that I am no enemy of your people. There are people in this very laager who would tell you that I have always done my best to meet the Trekboers in a reasonable manner. I would remind you as well that I have on occasion fought with your people for redress of injustice!'

This was a reference to his participation in the expedition across the Okavango, after the death of Charles Thomas.

'*Meneers!* . . .' He had now decided that his English was wasted on Barend Bouwer, Louw du Plessis and Old Diederick. Suddenly he he had switched to his own peculiar version of the Boer dialect.

'We give you the Waterberg to use,' he said. 'It is very pretty there: *mooi tjinene*, as the Mereros say. But please think well how it will be if war were to come. That would not be *tjinene*—pretty. That would be bad. That is not because I wish it, gentlemen. Oh, no! It is because I know the people to whom this place belongs!'

'Don't forget to tell them what your personal interest in the matter is,' I interrupted. 'Especially the copper!'

He looked at me, then pulled at his cigar. 'That I have rightful concessions they may well know,' he said. 'They may also know that one Jordan is much interested in the local trading rights. Not to mention the copper!'

'Listen,' I said, 'this insinuation is so vile that I should not even attempt an answer. You know very well that it would be impossible for me to maintain a local monopoly. What about the Erikssons, the Charles Lyons, the Chapmans? Do you think they would join us, on such terms? Don't be childish, Lewis! They are coming to Upingtonia at my personal invitation.'

He got up as if I had never spoken. Well, he said, he had to leave now. His secretary was waiting. He would see us at the meeting, at ten thirty. He lifted his topee ceremoniously, then walked off.

4

'Lots of bleating, little wool!' David Black said.

'Secretary!' Chris Leen completed his notes, looked up and grinned. Old Diederick's sons, who had been watching the proceedings from the side of the hartebeest-house, now joined us.

'What does he wish of us?' asked Willem, the youngest.

'No matter, let him do what he will!' I replied.

'*Meneer*, you should have chased him away!' Old Diederick tapped with his stick.

'A man like that is rubbish, Pa!' said Willem.

Old Diederick eyed his son. Willem was the most outspoken of the Prinsloos.

'We must have patience,' he said.

'But *this* has not patience, Pa. *Meneer*, do I speak wrongly?'

'The day has only started, Willem.'

'What was all this talk about war?' Jan Prinsloo asked.

Barend Bouwer answered. 'He should think of what he has said. He who shows a fist must know that he himself will feel the blows.'

Others had joined the small crowd. There was much approval of what Bouwer had said. He was the commandant.

'What sort of a fist has he got, Brother Barend?' asked Machiel Prinsloo.

'Man, a fist is not a fist because it *looks* like one. It may be the leg of a baboon!'

This caused merriment. Perhaps this was a good sign. I was still wary of what Lewis would attempt. At the same time I was strengthened in my resolve to go about our business as if he had never arrived.

'Pa must rest now,' Machiel Prinsloo said, and took his father's arm.

Old Diederick replied: 'I am not tired!' He dug the end of the stick into the soft earth. 'We have work to do!'

'The meeting, gentlemen,' I said, taking my leave, 'begins in half an hour.'

5

They sat there under the trees on folding stools, chairs, benches, but mostly on the short veld-grass. An open wagon had been drawn up under a giant sycamore. On this the *Bestuur* assembled, with Old Diederick presiding. To the right of him was Chris Leen and Louw du Plessis; to the left David Black and Barend Bouwer.

I was conscious of the murmur of the audience when I myself mounted the wagon. There was some hand-clapping; and someone called my name. The murmur, I immediately concluded, came from Botha and his supporters. They were there in one of the front rows: the Johannes du Toits, the De Beers, the Krugers . . . The presence of Jan Labuschagne among them would not have surprised me; but I could not see him. The light applause had come mainly from some womenfolk, gathered around Ella Lombard.

Where was Lewis? There was no sign of him. I had no doubt that he would yet show up. His sense of the theatrical would bring him here, probably at what he regarded as the right moment. He was in the vicinity all right; he and his secretary, following him about like a puppy. Well, no doubt the 'High Commissioner for Damaraland' was also in need of the outward symbols of office. Whether any of this showing-off made any impression on the Trekboers was doubtful. Even Piet Botha must have realized how ludicrous it was.

The crowd by now numbered some one hundred and fifty. These would presently constitute themselves as burghers of the state of Upingtonia. From me they would receive the general title to the lands and the waters. This would be the culmination of some twenty months of preparation and negotiation. Or was it twenty years? In a sense, I concluded, one's background, experience, maturity determined one's time 'to gather stones together'.

In January of '84 I had bought Rehoboth. Then Belck had turned up at Otjitambi. That had been the end of it all. The Germans had promised *Schutz*. Maybe they had more in mind. I had made a vain attempt to protect my legitimate interests in Rehoboth by asking for British intervention. The curt refusal from the Cape finally convinced me that if I wanted anything, I had to take matters into my own hands. The Otavi country had been bought in April. Within a few days nearly fifty heads of Trekboer families had co-signed the agreement. Here, at last, was Upingtonia. It was the realization of what had for so many years been but a dream. Could anything finer have come about? Here was water, pasture, soil . . . Here was an earthly paradise.

There had been unpleasantness. There had been threats of violence, and even open enmity. All this was to be expected. *Fide et amore* was the watchword; and it could well become our motto. So we would triumph. Let Robert Lewis and Pieter Maritz-Botha do what they pleased. The cause was a sound one, and would not be defeated. The majority of people in the laager believed in the new state. It was their democratic right to establish the new community, and to be given a reasonable chance to prove themselves.

These were the thoughts moving through my mind while I stood there on the open wagon with the *Bestuur* behind me, facing the assembly.

There were old gaffers with faces like maps, with hands like Cape mid-winter vines, with feet shod in *veldschoens* like flat-bottomed boats. There were the more elderly woman who had come in their usual workaday *kappies* and dresses of print. There were the people between a rising and a passing generation, like Hester Bouwer, Jet du Plessis, the younger Prinsloos, the Louwrens brothers, the upper half of the Holtzhausen clan . . . There were the young people who were having their newly acquired adulthood recognized for the first time.

I caught Lisa Lombard's glance where she was sitting at the feet of Adriaan Venter who was astride a three-legged stool. I saw her greet me with her eyes. I would have liked to have said: 'If you have just a little more patience, Lisa, all will be right. Maybe we shall have to go out this very week to look for Kambonde's cattle. But as soon as that's all over, we shall have a wedding.'

I looked at the President. I nodded as a sign that he could begin. Old Diederick got up, rising to the full six and a half foot of his stature. There he stood next to me on the wagon, clad in his frock coat and high white collar, an open Bible resting on one horny palm. When,.after scanning the assembly and waiting for silence, his voice eventually came, invoking the Almighty's presence:

'Let us pray!' he said.

The prayer itself was the old one: a thanksgiving for grace bestowed; a petition for a blessing on the daily work; a request to newly care for the aged, the infirm, the poor. It was also a reverberating reaffirmation of belief that the Lord God had led the Trek to its true destination: 'Knowing of a surety . . . that Thy seed shall be a stranger in a land . . . which is not theirs.' The

Lord would give them and their seed after them the land wherein they were a stranger, all the land of Canaan—for an everlasting possession. And the Lord would be their God . . .

The final amen was a forceful underscoring of all that had been said. Thereupon Old Diederick gave the number of the psalm. Hendrikus van Voor, in the front row of the audience, sounded the opening note in a voice which was shaky but sonorous. Immediately it was taken up by a keening Ella Lombard. This was the sign for all to join in. Quickly it became a monolith of sound, spreading between the trees, swelling out over their tops. Such was the volume of it all that two bateleurs on an omumborombonga tree nearby took to flight. There they were now, circling, climbing into the sky, with the light catching the black-and-chestnut of their feathers, the deep coral of their legs.

6

With everybody seated again, I began to address the meeting. I used the vernacular, reading from the draft constitution in High Dutch.

This was a meeting called, I said, to constitute formally the state of Upingtonia. The ideal of an own country, owing allegiance to none but God, had been the ideal of the Trek since the early seventies. It had started at the Crocodile River in the Western Transvaal. The hope had once existed that such a community could be established on the Angolan highlands. This had been an error, and there was no point in not admitting it. Neither Humpata, nor Bié to the north, nor any other part of Angola could serve the immigrant people. It had become quite clear that in a Portuguese country there was only a future for them *as Portuguese.*

I sensed that Robert Lewis had arrived. Scanning the audience, I discovered him standing at the back, smoking a cigar, and attended by his secretary in a white suit and carrying a black bag. 'I find it necessary,' I said, 'to put the terms of the draft constitution to the meeting. Should there be any questions or comment, the *Bestuur* and I would be glad to hear it.'

The members of the *Bestuur* would be elected for a period of two years by general franchise, I said. Members who had served their term could be re-elected. Only citizens of the new state could stand for election. Any attempt to influence voting by payment of money would be penalized by loss of the rights of citizenship and a fine of £10. A landdrost and two assessors would also be chosen to hear civil and criminal cases. There would be a right of appeal to the full *Bestuur.* The President and I, W. W. Jordan, would publish the result of such an appeal. A Field-Cornet would be appointed and he would receive his orders from the President himself. The Field-Cornet would be informed about all legal process, and in turn he would have to keep the President informed. No official would be able to relinquish his post without the permission of the *Bestuur.* In cases of neglect of duty or bad conduct on the part of the officials, fines would be imposed according to a fixed scale. All officials, except where otherwise provided, would offer their services to the community for two years without payment. The burghers would show obedience to the officials; and in cases of non-compliance, fines would be imposed. Regarding the division of lands: the area had been bought by me in my personal capacity. Farms would now be allocated, and no payment would be expected. Only persons fully capable of developing their lands would qualify. In the case of the early Trekkers, however (those who had set out from the Transvaal in 1875-1876), exceptions would be made. Farms which had not been occupied within two years of allocation would revert to the *Bestuur.* In this case, too, the early Trekkers would be exempted. Applications for farms would have to be directed to the *Bestuur.* Payment of a registration fee of 2/6d and signing of the allocation by the President would finalize the transaction. The copper-bearing area at Otavi and in the surrounding country, also an area of 6,000 morgen between Ombeka and Etosha, would remain my property. Some 300 farms of 3,000 morgen each would be available. Every enterprising and hard-working family would be entitled to an allocation. Five of these farms would be allocated to me, Jordan, without the obligation to occupy them.

'A word about the motivation for these terms,' I concluded. 'The whole area of Upingtonia was purchased by me in my personal capacity from Kambonde Kampingana. Payment was made in kind; and neither I nor the *Bestuur* expect anything back. The retainment of certain rights and lands, representing a relatively small part of the whole, is regarded by me and the *Bestuur* as a sufficient *quid pro quo.* Regarding the Otavi copper: exploitation by me personally is impracticable. Whatever development may take place here in future, it will need a large amount of capital and organization. If and when this comes about, Upingtonia as a whole will benefit . . .'

'You are dealing with property which doesn't belong to you, Jordan!' Lewis had moved up, and was now standing to the right of the wagon.

I looked at him. 'You'll have your opportunity—without admitting any right on your part—of stating your case, should the meeting so desire,' I said.

'Indeed, Sir, that is what I expect!'

'Meanwhile one may expect from you a measure of decency at a meeting you have forced your presence upon!'

'Tell these good people the truth, Jordan. That is all I ask you!'

Some young bloods were now shouting for Lewis to sit down. He looked around him with an air of innocence.

'Manners', he said, 'should be learnt at an early age!'

Had his English been properly understood, these words might have caused an uproar. Instead, I rejoined, 'You've asked for it, Lewis!'

Another voice now intervened, that of Pieter Maritz-Botha. He got up, looked at the assembly and said: 'Mister Lewis has every right to be here.' Then he turned towards me, and his imperial seemed to quiver. 'Even more than you have, Jordan!'

With protests sounding around me, I stiffened. Old Diederick was rapping the railing of the wagon with his stick. 'Order!' he kept saying.

But Botha was arguing with someone in the crowd. Then he looked at me again and cried: 'This is what you have brought us to, Jordan!'

'You have brought it upon yourself!' I replied.

'You dare say that?'

The crowd was getting restive. Old Diederick again rapped with his stick. 'Mister Jordan has the word!'

'If those who feel that their rights are being affected have any case at all,' I said, 'they will have such opportunity as this meeting is prepared to allow them.' I looked at Lewis. 'Is it too much to ask that you be reasonable?' Botha was still on his legs, looking threateningly at me.

'If these interruptions continue,' I said, 'I shall have no other alternative but to stop the proceedings.'

'Carry on, Jordan!' Lewis shouted.

I picked up my file. 'It is important,' I said, 'for the meeting to realize that the constitution, containing certain legislative regulations, is the basis of our community. It should be fully realized what our aims here are. They may be summed up in two words: colonization and civilization. Is that clear? Is that clear to our visitors who have such experience of statehood in other parts of the country?'

Botha folded his arms over his chest, and Lewis stood looking at me, flicking the ash off his cigar.

'The lands,' I continued, 'will go to those who are able to develop them. It rests therefore with every man to see that he makes the most of what is given him.'

'There is another matter which needs mention here,' I said, 'the relationships with other governments.'

I quoted from the constitution: '*All official parleys or communications with foreign nations or native tribes will be exclusively undertaken by the* Bestuur *and Mr W. W. Jordan.* That means that nobody will be allowed to enter into any negotiations with native chiefs, without prior consent of the *Bestuur*. Those who disregard this will be severely punished. Nobody will be allowed to provide guns and ammunition to any native living within the confines of Upingtonia. Any transgression of this regulation will, likewise, be severely punished. In case of war, the *Bestuur* may appoint a commandant. All male citizens between the ages of eighteen and sixty are liable for military service.'

The most delicate matter for discussion now arose—the promise to Kambonde Kampingana to retake the cattle the Bushman Gabriel had stolen.

'The *Bestuur* has decided,' I said, 'that the cattle should be fetched before the end of next week.'

This, apparently, was what Botha had been waiting for. He got up at once when I said the words and cried: 'Now you are looking for trouble, Jordan!' People were turning their heads. Some had moved from the back to the flanks of the crowd. '. . . You are exposing us to great dangers, Jordan!'

The impersonal form of address was annoying me. He was doing his best to humiliate me. His supporters, among whom I now espied Jan Labuschagne, were encouraging him.

'We have a right to know what your plans are, Jordan!'

'You know my plans,' I answered with rising anger. 'May we

know yours? One day we hear that you intend crossing the Thirstland again. The next we hear that you are considering the offer—what an offer!—by Lewis here to give you the Waterberg, to stop over at. Perhaps you know of something else, like going back to Humpata!'

'Stick to the point! What about Kambonde's cattle?'

'The cattle will be fetched,' I said. 'We don't expect either you or your supporters to participate.'

'Fetch the cattle?' Lewis chimed in. 'At what price?'

'We are quite capable of doing our own arithmetic, Lewis. Should you need some assistance, no doubt someone could be found to help you.' The dig seemed to be lost on him.

'In any case,' I said, 'this matter is not relevant today.'

With trembling fingers I took up my file again, and resumed reading from the constitution:

'*No person shall be allowed to abuse the right to shoot game. Whosoever will be discovered doing the same, will be liable to a fine of £5. No hired person will be allowed to leave his service without due notice . . .*' I looked at Lewis. 'No slavery, please note. I would that the same could be said of all the other nations in this country!'

This sally seemed to stir him.

'What do you wish to imply?' he asked. 'Please speak plainly!'

'What I have said is plain to all but the simple-minded.' I was becoming slightly more at ease now. At the same time I realized that my sallies served little purpose. It was not so difficult to make Lewis look silly. It was more difficult to bring the substance of justice to bear on him.

I quoted again: '*All murderers will be hanged; and any man found guilty of manslaughter will be punished in accordance with the nature of the case . . .*'

Regulations dealing with public moneys, costs of land registration and conveyance, the registration of births, deaths, marriages, followed. Most important was the decision that the system of law in general would be that pertaining in the Cape Colony: the Roman-Dutch.

With that my part in the proceedings was largely disposed of.

'Mr President,' I said, turning towards Old Diederick sitting in the chair just behind me. 'All that remains for me to say is that this constitution is an open book. Anybody, foreigners as well, is free to examine it. Whoever objects to what is contained therein, may express his views. Get this one thing clear, however: we shall suffer no lack of order or discipline. The *Bestuur* will see to that. The President will see to that!'

The crowd applauded and I applauded with them.

The old man sat there like a monument, bolt upright, with his olive-wood stick clasped between his large hands, his head a piece of rough sculpture above a high white collar. The breeze moved in the trees. Little flashes of sunlight fell over Old Diederick's face.

I fell silent for a moment. 'My good friends,' I said, 'I would like to tell you something. In August of '84, with a view to the proposed trek through Damaraland, I wrote to His Honour the President of the South African Republic. I asked him to make it generally known that the people leaving Humpata—that means you—would be travelling under protection of the flag of the Transvaal. I specifically asked the President for his friendly interest in the matter. Some months later I received an answer from the State Secretary, Dr Leyds. He informed me that they who had crossed the frontiers of the Transvaal could no longer be regarded as citizens. The President could therefore not offer us any protection, because then he would be held responsible for what happened outside his dominion. I do not wish to discuss the pros and cons of this decision. In the legal sense Dr Leyds was, no doubt, perfectly correct. I sometimes wonder, however, if President Kruger himself had an inkling for whom I was asking this. What we needed was nothing more than a friendly gesture towards people like Diederick Prinsloo here, your own President.'

The people were cheering now. Louw du Plessis, to my left, sounded the opening notes of the psalm reserved for such occasions:

'*Let, Lord, Thy blessing on him fall . . .*'

The crowd joined in with great power and a certain musicality. Within a few moments the sound was billowing out over the trees and the green, sunlit bush. A line of Namaqua partridges was deploying in a southerly direction. I saw them suddenly change direction and bank up against the pure white of a great thunderhead. I looked at Old Diederick. He had not moved. He still sat there in silence. Then suddenly I saw two great tears, like quartz crystals, break from his eyes and drop into his beard.

7

The Legislative Regulations were approved without any further discussion. The noisy group gathered around Pieter Maritz-Botha had now quietened down. I had hopes that they had learnt their lesson, and that the demonstration of loyalty towards Old Diederick might have moved them to think again. That this was largely a vain hope was borne out by the fact that Robert Lewis had found a seat next to Botha. For a moment I was tempted to refer to this, but I checked myself.

It was time now to hand over the relevant documents. I waited for silence, then faced Old Diederick.

'Mr President,' I said, 'I, Will Worthington Jordan, now hand over to you, Sir, and to the *Bestuur,* representing the burghers of Upingtonia, all the rights and privileges, as described in these documents.'

Old Diederick arose, raising himself to his full height.

'This is the contract, Sir, entered into between Kambonde Kampingana and myself.' I handed it to him. 'And this is the constitution and the accompanying regulations governing the state of Upingtonia!' He took it.

The people were applauding again. Some cheers broke out. Some of the Holtzhausens threw their hats into the air. I heard Dolf shout his approval. The Oppermans, the Louwrenses, the Du Plessis were walking about, congratulating each other. Some of the womenfolk were wiping their eyes. Ella Lombard stood waving to me with a handkerchief. There was Axel Eriksson, too, right at the back, raising his hat to the group on the wagon, grinning. How long had he been there?

When this sudden upsurge of emotion had spent itself, Diederick Prinsloo addressed the crowd. In measured terms and with great solemnity, he spoke.

'*Meneer*, fitting it is that we remember the Word: "And I will make them and the places around my hill . . ." ' (he surveyed the scene around him) ' ". . . a blessing; and I will cause the shower to come down in his season; there shall be showers of blessings . . . And the tree of the field shall yield her fruit . . . And the earth shall yield her increase . . . And they shall be safe in their land . . . And shall know that I am the Lord . . .!" '

He faced the audience again.

'The presentation of Mr W. W. Jordan—be accepted now—for ever!'

Amid cheering he repeated these words: 'For ever! Even should it be required that we of this land take up arms against the nations, to protect it!'

As far as we were concerned, it was over. The state of Upingtonia had been formally established. As far as our enemies were concerned, however, nothing of the sort had taken place.

Pieter Maritz-Botha got up to speak. It was just after Old Diederick had returned to his seat.

'Mr Chairman!'

All eyes turned to look at him. He came forward unhurriedly, hat in hand. Outwardly he appeared to be calm, but I could sense his tension.

'A pity, Sir,' he said, throwing me a glance, 'that you have allowed all this to have taken place here today. This is a great falsehood!' Somebody at the back was vigorously denouncing Botha. One of the Krugers, turning on his stool, shouted an answer.

'If Mr Pieter Maritz-Botha has something to say, he may say it,' I declared. I looked at him uncertainly. 'At the same time, Sir, I warn you not to abuse our patience. Whatever your motives!'

'I have but one motive,' he interjected. 'The well-being of my people. And they are *my* people!'

He knew, I said to myself, where and how to wound. The applause from the Krugers, De Beers, Du Toits and Jan Labuschagne, was proof of this.

'*Meneer!*'

I looked up in surprise when Botha addressed me in this manner. He had never done it before. I thought that he was going to speak to the crowd or the *Bestuur*. Now he was singling me out. I was the enemy.

'We have listened patiently to your many words, *Meneer.* But this meeting cannot adjourn until we have the answer to a number of questions. We *expect* an answer to them!'

'There is no reason whatever,' I said, 'why a civil question should not receive a civil answer!'

Instead of doing what he had just stated he would do, he turned to the crowd again. Ponderously he began repeating all the old things. The situation at Otjovanda Tjongue was fraught with danger, he said. We had exposed ourselves here to attack from all sides. The Trek would seriously have to consider his proposal to return home: to go back to the Transvaal, if not by way of the Thirstland, then by way of Damaraland and Great Namaland.

'You said that you wished to put questions,' I interrupted. 'Well, please do so. We have had all this before!'

He turned upon me with a flash of temper.

'I shall speak as I shall speak!' he said.

'What do you want to know?'

His eyes were boring into mine.

'*Meneer*,' he barked, 'is it still your serious intention of establishing here, in this remote area, an own, free, Boer republic?'

'It is not our intention,' I replied. 'It has already happened.' I looked at the *Bestuur,* and then at the crowd. 'Were you not here when the matter was decided upon?'

'*Meneer*! I wish to hear your own answer!'

'You already know my answer,' I said. 'The Republic of Upingtonia was formally constituted on this seventeenth day of October, 1884. I, Jordan, have transferred all my rights and privileges, except those I have specially reserved. Isn't that clear enough?'

'Do you realize what you are saying?'

'Why should I not realize it? We have been living with all this for months; no, for years. And regarding an own, free state in Africa: your own people, as you say, have certainly not been trekking for nearly a decade just for the outing!'

This was well received. Behind me David Black said: 'Not so that we should now suddenly decide to pack up and go home!'

My interrogator had produced a piece of paper with what were presumably questions on it. Was it true, he first of all wished to know, that I had appealed for assistance to the British Consul at Walwich Bay in April of this year? Had I had dealings with the British?

Yes, I answered promptly, that I certainly had. I had expected the question. There was no reason to hide what I had done. We were but a handful of people here in the new territory, I said, and we would need every friend we could find.

I had hardly finished saying this, when one of the Krugers shouted from the back that it was a pretty poor republic without any friends. To this one of the De Beers added that I was now admitting the danger of our situation. Then it was perfectly right for us to leave this place.

Of course there were enemies, I replied. Nobody had ever denied the existence of enemies. Only a fool would close his eyes to them. This was no reason, however, why we should act like a lot of frightened *dassies.** We would seek our friends and find them wherever they were to be found. This included the British, most certainly. We would also gain the respect of our friends by remaining steadfast. The Boer people had in all their history demonstrated time and again what a group of disciplined and determined men and women could do in the face of danger. Messrs Lewis and Botha would have us shiver in our breeches at the very mention of the name Kamaherero. Perhaps they were acting in this way after the defeat of Hendrik Witbooi at Osona at the hands of the black people. No doubt, Kamaherero regarded himself now as being paramount. There was no reason, however, to be unduly impressed by all this. The fortunes of war in this country had always had a way of changing swiftly. Why, there were many people still living in the country who remembered the time when Kamaherero, as the son of Tjamuaha, had sat at the feet of Jonker Afrikaander—and addressed him as *Baas.*

I was conscious of the fact that my words had gone home. For this I was thankful. At the same time, a persistent chant had set in from Botha's supporters: 'Where—is—the—republic?'

'The republic is here!' I shouted back. 'And the republic will stay. We stand by what we have brought about, and we don't need the assistance of defectors!'

Why the name Upingtonia, Botha demanded. He had narrowed his eyes, as if he had kept this as the decisive question. Why *Upingtonia*? Why not *Lydensrust,* as many people had proposed? What was my *secret purpose*?

'Secret purpose?' I had been taken by surprise. What did he mean? There was no such thing as a 'secret purpose'. Why should there be? What was he driving at? As for the name Upingtonia, I had honestly thought that this had become common knowledge by now.

'Did you never hear of Sir Thomas Upington?' I asked. 'He was Prime Minister of the Cape Colony, and promoted the idea of

*Rock rabbits.

"Africa for the Afrikaner" in the widest possible sense!'

'A lie!' This was Lewis, who had, after holding his tongue for some while, turned on me again. 'Don't make such heavy demands on our goodwill, Jordan!'

'What do you mean?' The blood had rushed to my head. 'Why should it be a lie? It is the simple truth!'

Lewis stepped forward, hands in his pockets, jacket open. He was sporting a gold watch-chain.

'On whose authority do you seek to make such claim?' he asked.

'Never you mind about authority, Lewis. You yourself have never cared much about authority. But if you must have it: the reported speeches of Sir Thomas in every newspaper!'

'Newspapers!'

'Sneer at it if you like, but I attach more value to what I read in the newspapers than what I hear from you!'

'You hear that?' He seemed to be putting the question to Botha and his supporters. They cheered. At the same time others were shouting for Lewis to sit down. The meeting was getting too rowdy. I looked to Diederick Prinsloo to restore the order. This he did by a few sharp raps of his stick. Sternly he demanded silence.

With that it was Botha who seized the opportunity to take the floor again. What right had I, Jordan, he wished to know, to talk about 'being steadfast' in the face of danger? Who would assist us if we were attacked? We were too small to warrant support.

We had no wrong idea about that, I answered. We knew exactly to what extent we could rely on intervention in the case of war. Yes, of course, we were but a few in numbers. But numbers alone had never decided. We had every right to stay where we were. To scuttle away to safety was weakness itself.

'So then,' Botha rejoined, 'to think of the lives of women and children is weakness!'

It suddenly struck me that there was, after all, something of Botha's new domesticity in the charge. At the same time I remembered the talk about Kambonde and the Arab.

'If you are indeed afraid of war,' I asked, 'why do you consider all sorts of hare-brained adventures to attack the Ondonga tribe, to "fetch" a horse? I remind you, the Ovambos are still our allies. We are not as alone as you think!'

The colour rose to his cheeks.

'If you really intend using force,' I persisted, 'I can't think of any surer way to let loose the powers of hell upon us. Do you really want to drive the Ovambos to such things?'

He tried to interrupt, but I gave him no opportunity.

'You have attempted secretly, Botha, to form a Boer commando to take to Ovamboland. You should do your own dirty work.'

This was putting it strongly. He was suddenly furious.

'What proof do you have of such things?' he shouted.

'It is generally known. It was not as secret as you thought.'

'Prove it! Prove what you have now said!'

'Ugh, this is madness!'

I looked up in surprise. It was Axel Eriksson who had stepped forward. He was speaking directly to Botha. He stood there, hat in hand, and repeated his words.

'Madness, I say. The Ovambos will destroy you, man. And then they will come here and destroy us all!'

Botha looked at Eriksson with surprise and contempt.

'What is this old fool doing here?' he demanded.

'You are doing a dumb thing, Botha,' Axel insisted. 'Stay away from Ondangua, man!'

'This chap is an outsider!' cried Botha. 'Tell him to keep his long nose in his own affairs!'

'Outsider?' I asked. 'Presumably your friend and confidant Lewis is an old member of the laager.'

The people laughed. It relieved the tension.

'Jordan,' Botha came forward now. 'I warn you again: you are playing with fire. You are also playing with the lives of women and children. They are *Boer* women, and *Boer* children. Mind out, I tell you, don't drive us too far!' He shook a finger at me.

'If anybody is driving anybody else too far,' I said, 'then it is being done by those who have yet to learn what loyalty means.'

'Loyalty!' he said. 'Who is this man who speaks of loyalty?' He looked at the audience. 'To what nation must *he* now be loyal?'

This was abusive. It also contained an innuendo. For a moment I stood, considering what to say. He, apparently, had sensed the psychological advantage he held. He said, something to his supporters. They all got up and started following him.

We saw them leave: the Van Wyks, De Beers, Du Toits, Krugers. They were people I had never had much contact with.

Rather to my surprise Jan Labuschagne remained seated. Had

he seen the light? He had been largely in the background. Perhaps he was still making up his own mind.

Somebody else was now leaving the meeting. It was the widow Roets. She walked slowly and somewhat sadly. Ella Lombard called after her, but she just kept on walking, looking straight ahead of her.

I felt sorry about this. The other lot could go to blazes for all I cared. They were never much use, anyway. *Tante* Roets was different. She was the widow of one of the outstanding hunters of the Trek. He had died at Humpata. She had once said to me personally that she would 'stand by the laager, come what may'. Now she had decided otherwise.

'Let her go,' I said to Ella Lombard, who was trying in vain to get *Tante* Roets to change her mind. 'Nobody need stay here. We shall build what needs building with those who are prepared to give themselves whole-heartedly to our cause. That is the only criterion.'

'Stop fooling these good people, Jordan!'

Robert Lewis now stood directly in front of me. What had just taken place seemed to fire him to a new exhibition of authority. He had been walking around, talking to people, being closely followed by his white-suited secretary with the black bag.

'I'm fooling nobody, Lewis,' I said. 'It is every man's privilege to decide what he wishes to do. I want to tell you again, however, that this is, strictly speaking, a closed meeting. With what right are you here?'

He ignored my question. Facing the audience from the front of the wagon, he ordered his secretary in a loud voice: 'Take that document out!'

The secretary opened his bag. Then he took out a piece of paper of unusual length.

'Read it aloud!'

The secretary adjusted his eyesight. Then he began to read.

'What's all this supposed to be?' I asked.

'Please continue!'

The secretary cleared his throat. One had to strain one's ears to hear him. It was a 'proclamation', drafted in some kind of legal jargon. It was an official notice of Kamaherero, Paramount Chief of the Herero nation, and of all Damaraland, the territory of which extended from the mouth of the Cunene river in the west, to Rietfontein in the east . . .

Was all this necessary? Did we have to listen to the same dreary old story? It had been disproved so many times. There was not a soul who knew anything about the Transgariep and was even reasonably objective who would support this. It was an empty repetition of the old fraud, presumably in the belief that constant retelling would establish its truth.

'How long is this going to last?' I asked. 'We haven't all day to listen to this drivel, Lewis!'

'Would you like to hand it in?' Chris Leen enquired. 'I'll take it up in the minutes. Few here understand English.'

Lewis motioned impatiently to his secretary to carry on. I listened, fascinated to witness the extent of the man's presumption. The point of it all was reached when we were informed that we had taken possession of Herero territory and that we should remove ourselves 'with all possible speed'. Should we fail to do this, His Royal Highness Kamaherero would be compelled 'to remove same by force of arms . . .'

What struck me now was that all this had been well planned. Lewis's sense of theatre had served him well. He had delayed all this until after Botha and Co had demonstrated their opposition. It might well have been that which he had discussed with Botha.

Was this a declaration of war? If not, it was very near to it. I watched the secretary fold up the proclamation and return it to the black bag. Lewis was looking at me, as if expecting an answer.

'You seem to think that people of the calibre of the Trekboers—except the few who have left this meeting—are going to be stampeded by words!' For the benefit of the Upingtonians, I added in the vernacular: 'This, my friends, has been notice by His Majesty Kamaherero for us to quit. A long document, as you have seen. Lots of words. We are not impressed because we shall not be driven out of a territory which does not belong, and has never belonged, to the Ovaherero.'

The people, having already discovered what it was all about, stood up and cheered.

'That's your true answer, Lewis,' I said, when the clapping had stopped. 'You have a lot to learn about these people. Do you really think they are going to be stampeded by the joint noises you and Kamaherero can produce?'

Members of the *Bestuur* behind me were joining in now.

'Well spoken, Mester Will,' Barend Bouwer grunted.

'Cold pumpkin doesn't scare us!' added Louw du Plessis.

Chris Leen remarked that the very length of the proclamation was proof of its absurdity.

Lewis stood his ground. Then he spoke to me. 'From what you have said, Sir, and from what your *Bestuur* has been saying, I deduce that you intend staying!'

'For once you are right.'

'All to the credit of Will Jordan, eh? All to his benefit!'

'I have least patience with you, Lewis, when you start getting silly.'

'In your view, Sir! But the fact still remains that, if memory serves, you have retained for your exclusive use the Otavi mine, to which you have no right, same having been transferred to me on the ninth day of September; a reward for my years of good service to the Herero people. Mr Jordan claims the plums, which are the mineral resources, for himself and then plays Santa Claus, dispensing "farms"—useless bits of land! Excepting, of course, the pick of the bunch, which, as I understand, you have retained for your own use!'

'What are you trying to do now, Lewis?' I asked. 'Discredit me in the eyes of my friends? You won't succeed! That I promise you. If you could read the legal contract entered into between Kambonde Kampingana and myself—I have already dealt with that!—you will know that I validly bought all there is here—and paid for it. What has been retained—and that, surely, is little enough—will in terms of the Constitution be private property. But only in conjunction with the "special treaty" existing between me and the *Bestuur*.'

'Pshaw!' he said contemptuously. 'Who is there to control your "special treaty"? Has it been committed to paper? Indeed, Sir, you must take us to be fools!'

That was more or less what I was doing at the moment. At the same time prudence warned me not to underestimate Lewis. In fact, I had once given this advice to Goering and Nels, bent on establishing *Schutz* over Damaraland.

These pompous little ways of Lewis, I had said, might easily give a wrong impression. He was no ordinary windbag, lightly to be dismissed. The fact was that he had been in the country since 1858. In his own way he had been a pioneer. His reputation as an elephant hunter was not without substance. There was also the occasion he had joined the Trekboers to avenge the death of Charles Thomas. He himself liked to refer to this as proof of his good intentions towards the 'wanderers'. In any event, no one survived in this country without a fair amount of courage, determination, sagacity. He had never had any scruples about obtaining what he wanted. In the present situation, however, scruples were irrelevant. The only question was whether his threat, contained in the proclamation, had to be taken seriously. I had no doubt now that Lewis and his secretary were the true authors of the document. Kamaherero himself had had little to do with it. It was the language of Lewis, and the writing of his aide.

'I presume we understand each other,' Lewis said. Then he attempted his threadbare Dutch again, directing his words to Old Diederick: '*Mynheer*! War is a bad thing! Nobody wants it. So, we must make to stop it!'

Old Diederick was eyeing him wrathfully.

'Mister Lewis!' he said eventually, pointing the olive-wood stick like a sword at him. 'So we see that we are threatened! Threatened, so that all that we have obtained with great trouble will be taken away from us. What is it now? We see the nations around us and how they live. Live with a great sound of war! What for, Mister Lewis? Because they are still in heathendom. Because they are still naked, and they know not their own nakedness. Our people here are a Christian people, and our strength is in the Lord. So, Mister Lewis, I say to all who have ears to hear: between the nations we *stand*. We *stand* between the nations, and fear not. Who shall go up for us against our enemies? It is the Lord our God, and He will subdue them . . .'

There was a moment of almost complete silence.

'It is apparent,' I said at last, 'that you have no idea of the depth of feeling which has brought these people here. You wish to see all in terms of Jordan's personal greed. But on your own admission, Lewis, your interest here is not that of Prime Minister or Legal Adviser, or High Commissioner, but as the holder of certain "concessions". These, I contend, could hardly bear examination.'

'Stick to the point!'

'It is the point. It is most relevant to the situation. If you wish to become Cecil Rhodes's man here in Damaraland, Lewis, you are on the wrong track. How do you propose developing a mine lying four hundred miles from Walwich Bay, which is the only available harbour? Lying far out in the bush, with no communications worth the name? Sorry, but as I know Rhodes, he has better fish to fry.'

'You have heard the King's proclamation,' he said. 'You must act accordingly, Jordan.'

'And if not?'

'You know what!'

'So this, then, is an ultimatum?'

'A demand, yes, from Kamaherero himself!'

'Threatening women and children?' Chris Leen enquired, looking up from his minute book. He lifted an eyebrow.

'No, Sir! My heart goes out to such. But the facts are the facts, and they must be faced!'

It so happened that a little girl in a red dress, with ribbons in her hair, at that moment came wandering into the open space in front of the wagon. Noticing Lewis, she stopped, put a finger in her mouth and stood rocking on her toes, while looking up at him. This was a child of the Willem Prinsloos, I decided. As such she was a grandchild of Old Diederick.

I saw the old man lean forward and stretch out his hand, as if to protect her. The strange man wearing a topee adorned with a bright red scarf had intrigued the child.

Lewis stood with his thumbs in his waistcoat pockets, a gold watch-chain over his midriff. 'Well, little Missie,' he said, 'and who might *you* now be?' The child laughed up at him. Lewis patted the fair little head. At the same time he turned to the crowd. 'Fie, that the blood of so many like such should rest on the heads of them that should know better!' he said. Signalling his secretary to follow him, he moved off.

Old Diederick, on being told by Chris Leen what Lewis had said, growled after him: 'Thy wickedness, Lewis . . . is far too much. It shall be broken . . . like a tree! For firewood!'

Ella Lombard had arisen from the crowd and now came forward. At the same time Willem Prinsloo's wife came rushing from the back. She swept her child into her arms. Amid wails from the child and laughter from the audience, she bore her off.

'So, our *Bestuur* does accept the offer of Mr W. W. Jordan.' Diederick Prinsloo hesitated for a moment, then raised his voice. 'Of one mind we be!' This was his final word.

Lewis, already on the edge of the crowd, turned round. 'One mind, old fellow, with your best men already leaving!'

'Get along!' I said. 'We've had enough bad manners from you for a day. Clear out now, otherwise we might have to deal with you as a trespasser!'

He wagged his finger at me. 'Then the blood of the innocent will be on *your* head, Jordan!' With that he started walking again.

'Bounce was a good dog,' I threw after him, 'but Hold Fast was a better one!' I watched to see if he would react, but he was moving in among the trees.

'Bring your war, blast you,' I muttered, by now heartily sick of it all. Then to my friends, who were closing around us on the wagon: 'Let them come, if they like, the lot. They'll get a welcome they're not likely to forget. We'll manage until a stronger hand can finally deal with them!'

The vagueness of these words made no difference. It was an emotional moment, and I had surrendered to it. People were shaking my hands, and the hand of every member of the *Bestuur*.

I felt happy, but spent.

8

I found Chris Leen and Axel Eriksson at my wagon. 'Come and have a bite,' I said. 'We need a drink as well.' I poured us some brandy, shouting to Izak to bring us food.

It was good to have this company. 'Karevapu,' I said, 'I'm glad you were there and said what you did. Chris, I'm glad you're secretary.' Chris had taken to the life of this country as if he had been measured for it. In the few years here he had built up an intimate knowledge of large parts of the Transgariep. He was sharp, and a man of integrity. With all my heart I wished that Georgina and the children would join him here. It might yet happen.

'Chris? Karevapu?' I lifted my glass. 'To Upingtonia.'

'Upingtonia!' We drank. 'Well, my friends,' I asked, 'and how do things look to you?'

Eriksson emptied his glass. I poured him another. 'It is well,' he said.

He looked tired, old Karevapu. He was a great pioneer and Botha had spoken to him as if he were dirt. Had he forgotten about the time Eriksson had accompanied him to the Governor of the Cape, Sir Bartle Frere? They had gone to discuss this very matter: territory in Damaraland where the Trekboers could settle. Had Botha forgotten that it was Eriksson who had written to the

Cape newspapers, drawing attention to the disaster of the Trek? This had led to the Cape Relief Committee; to the *Swallow* and the *Christina.*

To refer to Eriksson in public as 'this old fool' was both unfair and dishonest. If less prosperous days had befallen him, then it was because of his preferring service to expediency. I myself had on many an occasion experienced his large-heartedness. In the great drought of '79 he had fed more starving Bergdamaras, Saan, Namas and Hereros than had ever been counted. I had seen him go up to a wreck of a Nama woman one day and press a gold sovereign into her hand. She had been deformed by syphilis.

'Pity that it should all be as it is, friend Will!' Axel's voice broke in on my thoughts. 'But ask me any judgement now. You know what? We shall first have to see *slut*—end, eh?—of it all. How strong is he? Not so very, I think. And now he threatens war!'

'War,' I said, and fell silent, looking at each of my companions in turn. 'He seems to think that the only people in the country are Boers and Hereros. The British are in the Bay, the Germans in the South. Messrs Goering and Nels are well informed, as one hears, and have distinct ideas of their own regarding maintenance of the peace. Not even to mention the Boer peoples of the Transvaal and the Orange Free State. Bloods walks where it cannot creep, they like to say.'

Izak brought the food. It was the nameless stew of his hunter's pot. This time it went reasonably well with salad-beans and sweet pumpkin. As if to honour the occasion, he had also made a plumduff of royal proportions. Doing justice to this, I spoke: 'I'm not worried so much about the talk of war, mind you. I would be less happy if things were more secretive.' I watched as Axel loosened the broad belt he wore. 'Still,' I continued, 'we'll keep a sharp look-out. Even if Lewis lacks the power to attack us, what with Witbooi in the South and Kambonde in the North claiming a large part of Kamaherero's attention, he can still hurt us if he likes.'

'He will try all things,' Axel said, finding a new notch in his belt. 'All to frighten the people here into the bush.'

'Where is Lewis heading?' Chris asked, relishing the plumduff. 'To Okahandja?'

'Maybe Ovamboland,' I said. 'I have an idea that he still believes he can get Kambonde to repudiate the contract.'

'How?' Chris asked.

'My dear Chris, we will just have to face it: our contract is a valid one, but its validity is, for practical purposes, dependent on Kambonde himself. I have given this matter some thought this morning. Whatever our legal rights, our first duty will be to look after Kambonde.'

'You mean, from near enough he is to be trusted!' Eriksson looked at me.

'The uncertain element seems to me still to be Nehale, Kambonde's brother,' I said. 'He might well upset our friend's equilibrium. Of course, this is all on the assumption that Lewis is on his way to Ovamboland by now. Let's get another thing clear: this popular idea that I am an enemy of the Ovaherero. Yes, I have found it necessary, as in my letters to the press some years back, to draw the attention of the public to the senseless cruelties being indulged in here. The Ovaherero were especially named as the culprits. Why? Simply because they held at that time, and still hold, power. And power corrupts. Viehe of Omaruru, however, refused to see it that way. I have often told him that I would have protested as strongly had it been the Orlam Namas going about the country as if they were Lords of Creation. For my trouble, however, Kamaherero had my wagons "off-loaded". I wrote to Manasse Tjisiseta some time ago, saying that I had nothing at all against the Hereros as such. Regarding our aims here, I put it plainly enough: colonization and civilization. We desire nothing more than general peace in this country. We ourselves, I said, want to live in goodwill with everybody else, whatever their race or colour. You, Karevapu, will perhaps be able to tell us how all this was received at Omaruru.'

Axel grimaced. 'Viehe?' he said, dismising him with a gesture of the hand.

'So, I might just as well have been talking to the stones,' I said. 'I wrote to Manasse that I would respect the Damara boundaries. I even offered him an alliance. Granted, he is not at the head of the Herero order; but he is high up, all the same. I wrote to him: "Come along to any place you name, where we can meet and talk." '

Axel finished the last of his plumduff and laid down his fork. He looked at me from underneath a pair of bushy eyebrows.

'Yes, Karevapu? What do you wish to tell me? Am I a miserable optimist?'

He chuckled in his old, warm-hearted manner.

'I don't wish to curry favour with anybody,' I said, 'I merely want justice.'

'No, when a state is a state,' Eriksson said, 'it is necessary, too, that you "curry favour". That is . . . What d'you call it?'

'Diplomacy!' Chris suggested.

'Whatever it may be,' I said, 'I have no quarrel with Manasse. Unfortunately, however, he has been wrongly influenced. What about Viehe's compatriots—Goering and Nels? Axel, what's happening at Omaruru?'

'Omaruru's days are past,' he answered. 'For us, for me. The people, they talk, talk. The Hereros say that they want it all. So!' He shrugged his heavy, rounded shoulders. 'Manasse and the others sit there under the camelthorns and talk. Viehe is not so friendly any more.'

'What will they do to our wagons?' Chris asked. 'Will we be allowed to pass through on our way to the Bay?'

Omaruru was almost impossible to bypass on the journey to the coast. To the south-east was Okahandja, where Kamaherero was at the height of his power. To the west lay the Namib. No trek could make it to the Bay by a wide outflanking movement through the desert.

'As things stand at present, our wagons will probably be stopped,' I answered. 'However, we have no present need to send wagons to the coast. Meanwhile, it may yet happen that Manasse comes to his senses. But Viehe at Omaruru is like Lewis at Okahandja: the personal adviser to the chief. Not that the two have much in common, mind you. Viehe is obsessed by his "calling" in life. As usual few other people share these convictions of divine approval. Result? The true interests of the flock are neglected in favour of political considerations. I'll give Manasse some more time to answer my letter. If he doesn't do that, I'll go and see him. What do you say to that, Karevapu?'

'Are we thieves, eh? Are we robbers?'

He had said 'we'. It warmed my heart to hear it. This I interpreted as an affirmation of the expressed intention of the Erikssons to settle in the new republic. The imprint of the Erikssons was manifest everywhere in the Transgariep. If Omaruru had passed, Upingtonia offered a new future.

'We come before the frost!' Eriksson spread himself broadly in his chair. 'Wife, kids, eh! They too. But you must look out for what Piet Botha has in his head to do!'

'The first frost usually comes in May, or early June,' I said. 'Before that time we'll either have sent Piet Botha packing, or else have come to terms with him. By the way, that reference of his to "outsiders" . . . If anybody belongs here, it is the Erikssons. Who the hell is Lewis to talk?'

'I have trekked far on life's road,' Eriksson said after a moment. 'I do not worry much about Piet's mumbling. Now, perhaps, there are the others who followed him.'

'For my part they can all go hang themselves,' I said.

'Where are they intending to go?' Chris asked. 'With Botha in the lead?'

'Botha's talk was back to the Transvaal via Rietfontein and the Thirstland,' I said. 'But there's still this matter of the horse. If I know him, he's still considering an adventure in Ovamboland. *Then* there will be war; and we might as well clear out.'

Axel thumped his knees. 'For what now? How many in his commando? Twenty, thirty, eh? No chance. Three thousand Ovambos will come!'

'*And* the rest,' I said, 'He thinks because they shoot with caplock-muskets they cannot do any damage. He'll go ahead with that cock-eyed idea, and bring disaster upon us all.'

My anger was still mixed with other feelings. Axel sensed what I was thinking. 'We were together at the Cape,' he said. 'Good friends!'

'Now you're the "outsider",' I reminded him. 'And so am I.'

'Perhaps he is just jealous of you, Will.'

'Jealous of what?' I asked. 'He has every opportunity to take a lead here. But he refuses to do it. Am *I* on the *Bestuur*? Whatever his intentions, they seem conducive to no good. One thing I can promise you: I will not allow him to carry on as if we have nothing to say in the matter.'

Chris looked at me. 'Do you want to go to Ovamboland?'

'If need be, yes!'

'On your own? *Samt* nobody?' Eriksson asked.

'You seem to think that I am taking a risk. Don't worry, old chap, I've learnt to keep my eyes open. I've been in this business long enough. Hans Schinz is still up there. I'd like to see him again.'

'Kambonde?' Eriksson persisted.

'You don't trust him,' I said.

Eriksson folded his hands over his stomach. 'The 'Vambos can do bad things,' he said, 'when they get mad.'

I thought about it for a moment. 'One thing we have to face,' I continued, 'and that is that we cannot stay here where we are without accepting at least some risk as being normal.' An odd thought struck me. It was Robert Lewis himself who had once expressed a similar sentiment. In this country, he had said, one had to accept danger as part-payment for the privilege of being here. For once I could agree.

The afternoon light was a white blaze. Trees stood silently, unmoving, in deep pools of shadow. The cicadas were in a frenzied mood. At odd intervals a red-eyed lourie would cock a head at us from some nearby branch. 'Go away!' it would caw, as if it had eavesdropped, and was now deriding our efforts.

'Go away,' I said back to it, forming the words with my mouth.

I looked at my empty plate. My *bambuse* suddenly appeared and took it away. He had put the little pewter jug on the table in front of us. I thought of my mother. I had not seen her for more than four years . . .

'*Mooi tjinene!*' Axel said, and shook some tobacco out of his pouch into Izak's cupped hands. 'Give to Blackface too.' Blackface was Kairob.

'Karevapu Katiti,' Izak's face creased into smiles.

We drank our coffee. Then we stretched ourselves out on a patch of grass next to the wagon. We lay there smoking, sipping brandy as a liqueur, talking.

'What we always have to remember,' I said, 'is what we have here. Show me a better piece of Africa, if you can. Chris and I have discussed the possibility of building a railway from the Bay, Karevapu. Then the copper deposits can be mined.'

'Railway?'

'Why not? The Portuguese have been talking of a railway from Benguela to the east for a long time now. Remember, the inner parts of Southern Africa are still largely *terra incognita.* To develop it properly you will need communications. It will come, you watch!'

'Can the Portuguese do all that?'

'If not, they'll get somebody else to do it,' I said.

'Some international organization can undertake the building of the railway as a concession. That is what they are all waiting for. Everybody is falling head over heels to claim the best parts of

Africa. Well, if the Portuguese can sell concessions, so can we. Cecil Rhodes has even been talking about a railway from the Cape to Cairo.'

'The Cape was full of such talk a year ago,' Chris said. 'The idea is to build the railway over the interior of the Colony to Kimberley; and from there through the Republics to the north.'

'There's another being considered,' I said. 'It is to run from Durban in Natal to the Transvaal Highveld. Then there's a proposal for a line to Delagoa Bay, also to the Transvaal: Pretoria in fact. Well, Karevapu, you know Southern Africa as well as anybody else; if not better. Why should we not do something similar here? A line from the Bay, through Upingtonia, north-eastwards to the lands north of the Limpopo; or even north of the Zambezi? Then you watch Upingtonia.'

'This is a good land, Will,' Eriksson said. 'I have not seen many as good; for ranching, eh? *Omkring* Otjovanda Tjongue good farms can be established. Look at the cattle. They are in good condition. No bad sicknesses either. This is a pretty place.'

'Three hundred farms,' I said. 'Each with its own water. What we now need is the old spirit of survival, and plenty of it. Of course, we'll have some "outsiders": like the Erikssons, the Charles Lyons, the Chapmans! And whoever believes in his fellow man. Will they come?'

'They'll come,' Eriksson replied, smiling in his red beard. Then he suddenly rubbed his shining pate with the palm of his hand. 'What we say in Swedish, Will, my *sötebrödsdager* are past now. I want a restful life: a little bit of hunting, and plenty of looking for the birds, eh? My son, so big!' He indicated the height with his hand. 'He paints them. Paints fine! My trust is in God, Will.'

I suddenly felt a great sympathy for my friend. He was my senior by but a few years. But life here had told upon him. Was I really the younger? At times I too felt spent, used-up.

'Saw Charles Lyon at the Bay some time back,' Eriksson said. 'Said to me he will come in the new year, to see all there is here. So, friend Will, you will have the "outsiders"; perhaps too many, eh? What do you say, Chris?'

'I have been wondering,' Chris said, 'whether we are not playing into the hands of our enemies by even discussing this. Those people that left the meeting all say this is not going to be a Boer republic.'

True, in the laager the dominant thought was still that of the

Land of Rest. But this was to be expected. My friends had been wandering through Africa now for more than a decade, pursuing their ideal. Still, I had put this to the *Bestuur* on a number of occasions: one had to face realities.

Fewer people had undertaken the trek from Humpata than I had hoped. Our numbers here were but a handful. Of the three hundred farms available here about one third would be taken by the Trekboers. That would leave much empty land awaiting settlers. The land should be occupied.

'Immigration!' I said, expressing my thoughts. 'That's what we need!' I was resting on an elbow. 'No arguments about that. Whatever the doubts of some may be. We must get more people: from Humpata; from the Cape; even from the Transvaal, if possible.'

'Foreigners?' Chris asked. 'People from the Continent? Germans?'

'The Germans are excellent pioneers,' I said. 'Like the Swedes.'

'Plenty Germans here already,' Eriksson said.

Perhaps too many, I thought. The Erikssons' trade at Omaruru had suffered when the Germans had set up shop at Otjimbingue.

'Osona!' Eriksson remembered. 'They say that Goering, Nels, Diehl, cut a barrel full of lead out of the black flesh. The Ovaherero were mighty pleased.'

'What are you trying to say, Karevapu? Is *Schutz* coming?'

'Well, *Schutz* is down there in Namaland and in Rehoboth. So why not at Okahandja?'

'You are right,' I said. 'It may well happen after Osona. What about Lewis?'

'He won't just accept *Schutz.* He has too many vested interests here. Don't forget, there is still the memory of *Protection.* But Dr Goering and *Kanzler* Nels are duty-conscious Fatherlanders. I accept it that what they intend doing will be done thoroughly.'

9

Chris went off to his own wagon, Axel filled his glass with brandy again. There he sat against a wagon wheel, looking dimly at me. 'Will,' he suddenly asked, 'I ask you if you can remember when last we were like this together?'

'It was our trip to Nhembaland,' I said. 'Those were great days, my friend!'

'I think much, Will, of the time we were there . . .'

Nostalgia puckered the skin around his eyes. 'Remember old King Ekari of Ombandja, eh? Yes, yes, we also ate of your plumduff that day! And His Majesty came all shiny and black to have dinner with us. Ho! We gave pudding, and he said: "Nice *otjecera*—porridge"!' His shoulders shook with laughter. 'Then I gave a horse for a present. A *horse,* man!'

'I suppose we could afford it,' I said. 'We had fifty-eight!'

'Remember the time our hunters were caught in the veld, and their guns were taken from them? Ugh! Robbery! But we did not worry so much, eh? It was a good trek, Will. King Xahanga at Humbe was so scared, remember? Thought it was Piet Botha and the Boers come to punish them for the affair at the river. And in Nhemba the King came to look at my book with the birds. Wanted to know: now how is it that the birds come so *flat*? And another chief wondered at our saw which could divide wood, so that the sides remained smooth.'

So we sat there chatting, laughing, our words swimming in the heat which had grown imperceptibly around us. Present problems had receded. The fair days of enjoyment of the land had come alive again.

In Nhembaland we had reached places where the people had never yet seen a white man. Yelling, they had taken shelter in the bush. King Nambinga of the Evare tribe visited us in state, with a retinue of hundreds. Axel's book on ornithology, containing illustrations, also of the brilliant birds of Southern Africa, caused great excitement. With our Martini Henrys we aimed rapid fire at the trunk of a baobab. I watched through a pair of binoculars. In turn the king watched me with a pair of golden eyes. When the shooting stopped, he sent some of his men to examine the tree. These soon returned with the news that it was full of holes. Thereupon King Nambinga stood up, raised his hands, and praised us all as mighty men . . .

Now I was here, more than four years later, with the very man who had led that trek with so much good judgement, such human feeling . . .

'Listen,' I said, 'when all is settled here, when we have finally got everything properly launched, we'll make another trek.

There's lots more of Africa I want to know about. We may even go back to Nhembaland. We only saw a part of it those days.'

I looked at Axel. He sat there against the wagon wheel, his glass of brandy in his hand, smiling.

'So we remember all, Will,' he said. 'All the long roads we have trekked, eh? You know, when we came back that time, I was bad with dysentery. On the trek I was ill sometimes, but not so very much. Afterwards? For nine months, man.'

He patted his belly. 'Other troubles too. You know, I went down to Moçamedes that time and was robbed. How much? Four hundred thousand kroner. Well, I got tired of it all, and went to the Cape, Transvaal. But you know how it all keeps on biting you? You want to come back here! I don't know why, I was sometimes nearly *opu*, as the Hereròs say.'

He had aged, and I knew what he meant by *opu*. His big hands had folded around the glass, and his head drooped. His hair—what still remained of it—was thick and grizzly at the neck.

'Don't talk like that, my friend,' I said. 'We must just find time to get some rest. Then watch us. Disease, losses, disappointments? We've all had our fair share of them. Some less, some more. But the land here is good, Karevapu.'

He sat there, deep in thought, with his hat on his lap, a splash of dappled sunlight on the shiny top of his head. With an impulsive movement he rolled up his trouser leg, kicking off the riding boot.

'Look!' he said. I saw the purple scar running the length of the calf. A wounded leopard had got him there, shortly after Llewellyn Lloyd, father of Charles John Andersson, had sent him from Vänersborg to Damaraland.

He pushed his leg out to its full length. 'Nearly dead,' he said. 'But my dogs saved me. Came and got hold of the leopard, and dragged him away from me. But he bit two of them *kaputu*.'

Other memories had awoken in him. He rolled his trousers down again, pushing the ends into his riding boots. 'You know, Will,' he said, 'we were together at the Cape that time, and *Chef* Andersson was there too, lying in bed, also with a leg!'

'That was after he had been wounded in the fight against Jan Jonker,' I said.

'They brought him to the Cape. Some said: "Now all is *slut*. You will never go back to Damaraland." Not so. A great longing came over him and he said to me: "Axel, man, we must go north again!" His wife, Sarah Jane, she said no, he was too sick to go. He would not rest. Said he wanted to go back so that he could write a book about the birds. Eriksson would help. So what to do? They let him go in the end; and I went with him. Came up to the Bay in the *Isabella*. And no waiting: as soon as we got there the trek started. He was still a sick man.'

'That was in '67,' I said dreamily. 'It was a wet year . . . Like this one.'

'. . . Like this one. People everywhere sick with fever. And plenty of dysentery. You know what? The people at Otjimbingue and at Okahandja did not like it that Andersson was in the country again. You see, his money was *opu*, and he had to do some trade to keep going. So the others did not like it. Said he was a scientist, no trader!'

'What drivel!'

'How was he to live, eh? I was in his service, but got little money. No matter. It was grand to work for such a man. I was angry when people said bad things about him. All untrue. I knew him like I knew my own father. He *was* my father. You know what? Hugo Hahn's wife refused to have him. Then that piece of rubbish, Samuel, and his people, came and stole all his things. Nobody helped him; not even the Hereros he fought with against Jan Jonker. So he said to me: "Axel, man, we go up to the Cunene. I once tried to get there, and turned back at Okonjenje." He tried another time . . .!'

'And got to the Okavango!'

' "*Chef*," I said, "you are tired and a sick man. You must rest. We can't go look for the Cunene now!" He said to me: "Axel, I must go, man. I must see the country again, and find all my old spoors! I must see the river!" He was in a hurry. Like a man who knows this is *avsked*. Nights we sit in our laager and talk. He tells me about all the things he has seen on his travels. Remember the time he was in such danger up at the Okavango. The nations wanted to attack him. He sent a message to Fred Green in Matabeleland. And Green trekked from so far to get to him. They met at Omatako. *Chef* said it was like two brothers who found each other again after many years.'

I marvelled at all this. Andersson and Green had fought together in the war against Jan Jonker. Matabeleland was many weeks' trek to the east.

'*Chef* told me things. Listened to it all, because I was still fresh from Sweden; in a wild country. Every day we trekked a bit further to the north, looking for the river. Getting weak now. The sickness was eating him up, but he still kept going. When he saw a good tree which might have birds' nests, he said: "Come on, Axel, boy; let's go and have a look!" His eating was poor, but he kept on, kept on. The fever got hold of me too, but if the *Chef* would not lie down, how could I?

'In April of that year we were at Ondangua. Good friends with the 'Vambos! But now he was just all bones: like the Hereros in a year of bad drought. Still, he said we must push on, and on. No rest, till we got to the river. Well, after a long time we got to the river, just below Humbe. Ho, he was glad to see it! He had tears in his eyes that day. Then we started trekking back. I knew what was going to happen, and for me these were days of great sadness. Not so far from the river, and he said: "Axel, now it is *slut*—finish!" I stood there by him, and said, no, he should not speak like that. You know what? Now he asked me whether I had ever seen a man die. I said, no. Well, he said, *now* I would see it. So he lies there in the tent; and when his voice is already weak, he asks me to read. I do so, and he listens, there on his little folding-bed. Afterwards he just says: "How beautiful are the Swedish psalms. Now I am ready to die. I trust in God's mercy!" But three more days he lies there. And I just sit; and sometimes do not even know whether he is still alive or dead. On Friday, 9 July, at last, I see that he is cold. That great heart beats no more.'

I rested with my head on a cushion formed by my folded hands. Eriksson was still sitting with his back to the wagon wheel. The brandy glass, empty now, had dropped from his fingers, and lay in the grass. I thought about what he had told me. We had all heard of Andersson's death at Ukuambi, near the Cunene. Eriksson himself had often referred to it in conversation. Now, however, I had heard the full story for the first time.

'What then?' he said. 'I was only twenty, as I told you. Stood there in the wild veld with only the Hereros, Tjirongo and Tjimanda, who came with us on the trek. Only them, and the body of my dead friend, *Chef* Andersson. Now all the *omsorger*—care for all, eh?—came on my shoulders . . .'

'Good broad shoulders!'

'Not those days, Will. Small still! So I decided I must trek. It was already sunset when *Chef* sighed for the last time. Darkness was coming, but I must trek. To Naumi's kraal, so that I can bury my friend. We trekked—a funeral procession! We trekked through the veld. The moonlight was so white, and the jackals and hyaenas were howling in the bush. I was frightened of it all. I was still a boy, Will. Noon next day at Naumi's kraal. He says no, not to bury *Chef* in his veld. So we had to trek. To where? I do not know. Afterwards we came to a big antheap, and I say we must halt. There I dig a grave with an axe and a tin plate. Tjirongo and Tjimanda watch to see that all is safe. I dig the grave, and when it is finished, we lay *Chef* in it, and put hookthorn over, for the animals. So we buried him, Will, in a very humble grave, far out in the wild veld. What then? We trekked back to Omaruru; and I became a man. Ugh, perhaps it is the sun which does it: makes you a man when you are still a boy.'

He showed me his hands. They were rough and blotched.

'My eyes are not so good any more, Will.'

He rolled up a shirt-sleeve. Where the skin had been protected from the elements, it was white and tender. Where it had been exposed, it was brown and leathery.

'The sun blinds us, Will! From too much walking about, and too much looking up. It is there, like God's own eye!'

I repeated the words to myself. 'Yes, Karevapu,' I said. 'You are right. Like God's own eye . . . Are you still at Otjituuo?'

'Half a day's ride from here. My horse is grazing down on the flats. Left it with my servant. One wagon already on its way to the Bay: to Omavare, I think.'

'Are you in a hurry? Do you need to be at Omaruru? We haven't finished talking yet!'

'I come again!' The red beard had spread over his chest as his head sank lower. The hair around his ears was sweaty.

'Here is a lot of work for us to do, Karevapu. We need you, man. In a few days' time the commando must go out to look for Kambonde's cattle. To the omuramba, and beyond. Is the Bushman Gabriel still down there?'

'I hear talk about him!'

'This is a thing we have to do. I gave my word to Kambonde. Botha is strongly against it. To hell and back with him. You stay a few days, and you can give us good advice. You can have the *katel* in the wagon. I have a folding bed as well. I take it you brought a servant to look after your horse?'

I could discern the slightest of smiles. His eyes seemed to be closing. His eyes, he had told me, were troubling him.

'Your people won't expect you back so soon, Karevapu,' I said. 'A week won't make any difference. Will you stay?'

He had not heard me. I watched his chest rise and fall.

'Karevapu . . .' I said, a little helplessly.

But he was beyond my reach. I sat up and looked at him. All the tension had left his body as he lay against the wagon wheel, sleeping.

I had a lost, lonely feeling as I watched. Should I shift him to a more comfortable position? He had collapsed against the wheel, and he presented an ungainly picture: arms hanging limply at his sides, his head dropping to his chest, with the red beard spread out, his legs apart. There was a wet patch on his trousers where some brandy had spilt.

Sleep on, old fellow, I said to myself. I got up, pulled my hat over my eyes, and walked out into the sun.

10

Days of growing tension followed. The sharp blade of war had been shown, and the effect was apparent. The words Old Diederick, Louw du Plessis and I had used after the meeting were meant to ease matters, but a feeling of uncertainty prevailed.

Everywhere little groups were talking. There was a lasting impression of pipes being filled, lit, smoked, emptied. One saw gestures being made, indicating resistance, grievance, chagrin, but also vagueness. The older people sat around under the trees on stools and chairs, consulting each other, offering advice, then falling silent again.

The attempt on my part to feign normality might well have succeeded, had I not found it difficult to escape the question: whither now? Would we have sufficient time to show what we were capable of? Would we be allowed to develop a community which could serve as a model for the country?

I countered a threatening pessimism by reminding myself that emerging societies all had their growing pains. Of course there would be problems. But nothing worthwhile had ever come about in any other way.

One unmoving fact, however, remained: our numbers were small. We needed people. These we would have to bring here: neither by force nor by persuasion, simply by virtue of the land itself.

When the Trek had been at Humbe, I had written to the Erikssons, the Charles Lyons, the Todds, Chapmans, and others in the Bay. They knew the country. They knew what a fine stretch of land this was. They knew the great possibilities it held. Come over and help us, I had said.

The *Bestuur*, too, had known about this. They, too, had approved of it. Still, I was conscious of the danger it held for me personally. Unscrupulous people might easily exploit it. The people of the laager were deeply conservative. This had to be faced. Most here thought of Upingtonia as a 'Boer Republic'. The possibility that it might be something more had never occurred to them. A few, like Louw du Plessis and David Black, realized how things might develop. One never heard them commenting on this.

Why hadn't I spoken to them, openly and courageously? Perhaps I knew, but would not admit it to myself. This was not something I could force. A group, embedded in rigid isolation, could not be coerced. The members themselves would have to discover the truth. The republic could never be a lost little enclave up here in the northern bush. Facts were slow but irresistible forces.

Keeping up a semblance of normality, I went about my business in a way which suggested a permanence of tenure. We were not just sojourners here. We had come to stay; to build; to love. There were daily discussions with the various families about the lands, the waters they had examined and preferred. I talked to the Prinsloos, the Van Voors, the Oppermans, Holtzhausens, Louwrenses, Du Plessis. Many had already chosen names for their new farms: *Zoetdoring, Ondira, Rietfontein, Klipgebou, Om Eerste te Zijn, Vergenoeg* . . . My own farms I called *Olive Grove, Namutonia, Nhoosis* . . . Chris Leen put his beacons up, claimed his water, called his land *Retreat* . . .

Adriaan Venter still dreamt of Okasima, far down the omuramba, his 'water' where the elephants roamed, and he could no longer see the smoke from another's *erd*. He also dreamt of following the 'maramba right up to Olifants Pan, where the baobab was with the names of great hunters cut into its bark.

'Well,' I enquired from Barend Bouwer one day, 'have you made up your mind where you wish to settle?'

Hester, his wife, was expecting a child, and I knew that he would like to be among the first to fix his boundaries and set up house. Barend Bouwer smiled enigmatically. 'Mester!' he boomed. 'The water I have found, yes! But not yet the name!'

Sitting in front of his hartebeest-house, whisking away flies with an ox-tail, Diederick Prinsloo nodded thoughtfully. There he sat, hands clasped around his olive-wood stick, surveying the scene around him.

'Now, what is it?' he said as I regarded him. 'When nought comes to aught . . .' He was referring to Lewis. '*Meneer*, this man is not thy equal. He speaks such high words! . . . We must wait, and see . . . See what comes, *Meneer* . . . And what he will do. To us . . . We who now seek our waters . . . I hear he is still here in the bush.'

'For my part,' I replied, 'he can stay in the bush. I've heard that he has trekked in the direction of Otavi.'

'What to do?' Old Diederick asked.

'It may be that he is already on his way to Ovamboland,' I said. 'I, too, will have to go soon.'

'To pull the wires!' Barend Bouwer said. 'That is what Lewis will do!'

'Let him try,' I answered. 'He may discover that wire-pulling can well be hazardous: become a trip-wire. We have a contract, *Oom* Diederick. And even although there is no central authority here to help enforce it, it is not the worthless document some make it out to be. Kambonde's own missionaries were parties to it, and they are not without influence. In any event, Lewis is Kamaherero's man. Kambonde has no particular love for the King of Damaraland. The crux of the matter still is: to whom did this territory belong before I, Jordan, bought it? Kambonde had no doubt about the answer. Since time immemorial it has been Ovambo property.'

'So, *Meneer*, then thou goest? . . . To Ovamboland.'

'It seems like it. The *Bestuur* will discuss it. There's no point in us just hanging about here, waiting for things to happen. Lewis will use every advantage he can get. He'll also do his best to ruffle Kambonde, as I know him. May even threaten him. Kambonde is still a young man, and Lewis is full of tricks. What about the Finns? Lewis can prove to be too clever for even the likes of Rautanen or Weikolin. I'll simply have to travel to Ondangua and see what's brewing.'

Later that day Chris Leen, Axel Eriksson and I discussed all this. Eriksson had had reservations about my going to

Ovamboland. The Ovambos, he reminded me, were still a barbarous nation, and there was no telling when their peaceable natures would explode. I had had personal experience of this, of course, when Fathers Delpech and Rothan had been murdered. John Caine, who still seemed to think that he owed me fatherly advice, had also written, warning me against my 'black allies in the north'. Caine, in fact, played on my more tender feelings by reminding me once again of his old friendship with my father.

I had read his letter with some annoyance. Confound him, I thought, who was Caine to come and lecture me on the Ovambos? I could tell him far more than he had ever known. He had brought up the murder of Skoglund and Bjorklund as an example of what the Ovambos were capable of. Well, I could cap all that: worse things had since happened. Still, it didn't really affect the issue . . .

Truth was, I had nevertheless decided that John Caine was treating me in a rather patronizing way, and I had now had enough of it. Violence? I had witnessed more violence, also in Ovamboland, than most. In any event, I was by no means too trustful. I knew just how artful the Ovambos could get. Kambonde himself, of course, was a consummate scrounger. If articles in one's wagon caught his fancy, he would start throwing broad hints that he would like such or such a thing. With this stratagem failing to work, he would demand what he wanted outright. Then there was no alternative but to give him what he wanted: powder, lead, a bag of flour, a razor . . . Even soap and other household articles had at other times to be laid at his feet. All this, I wryly decided, was tax.

At nights I now often lay awake. The key to everything was still Kambonde. On the whole, I supposed, one had to be thankful for small mercies. On the whole, Kambonde was still the best of the bunch. After all, he had been able to resist the machinations of his brother Nehale. And he sometimes sent me gifts in return. More important: he governed his people efficiently. In spite of all the begging, the unpredictable upsurge of primitive emotion, and the lack of any effective sanction to enforce the contract between us, I still kept faith. Lewis, I believed, would find Kambonde a tougher customer than he had imagined.

Keeping faith . . .

Was I really doing that? Or was I still constantly being assailed by deep-lying doubts? By the eroding feeling that Lewis had perfected his methods to an alarming degree? At times I would say to myself: 'He'll have to climb over my dead body to do what he would do!' Almost immediately, I would then think: 'Don't tempt the gods. You know Lewis. You'll have to beat him at his own game. He'll stop at nothing. Alive you are worth far more to your friends than dead. Do what must be done. But keep him guessing!'

All a strange criss-cross of speculations . . .

What really made things easier was the pleasant company. Axel Eriksson had decided to stay for a few more days. He had made himself at home on my *werf*, and I could almost believe that he had always been part of it. The *katel* he eschewed, preferring a stretcher set up under an awning. Here he seemed to be comfortable enough. Soon his peaceful snoring became part of my domestic scene.

For hours we would sit talking. Sometimes we would go out on horseback and examine the waters, the pastures, the forests. Constantly Axel would assure me that there was no finer bit of country anywhere in the territory. In all Southern Africa he had not seen much to compare with it. As far as the Erikssons were concerned, they could happily settle down here. And should the wanderlust take hold of him, Axel, again, well, then he would be off! . . . But he would always return, as he had always returned to Omaruru . . . Omaruru was now a thing of the past. They were pulling up their tentpegs there . . .

The days were warm and sultry. Great clouds would come drifting over the north-eastern horizon. By the later afternoon they would close their ranks, and the heavens would shake. Blue-white lightning would dance in the piled-up cumulus, and the thunder would applaud. Soon the rain would come, moving in finely woven drapes over the green tops of the trees; swishing in like a Spanish dancer. White egrets would V-fly against a darkening firmament. Presently the gentle onset of the rain would become a steady downpour. But after an hour it would all have passed. Then the sky would unfold again, smiling at the caprice of it all. In the bush the wood-hoopoes would chatter . . .

11

A regular visitor these days was Ella Lombard.

'Where then is God's work? she asked one day. 'Why do such sinners go about?' Presumably, this was Lewis.

'The ways of the Lord, *Tante*,' I said sagely, 'are not our ways . . .'

'True, *Meneer*,' she said, thinking deeply, 'we should not murmur. But these things come to one at nights. Then you think: can *one* man do such evil? What then is the state of the world? We must just stand fast, *Meneer*. Stand fast and stay where we are, here on these heights. To see all, and for all to see. And they who would hinder us, we must stop. Stop them and make them turn back to where they came from. We have been seeking this land for a long, long, time now. We have trekked for many a year, and for many, many miles. My child, everything has its day, and passes. Troubles too. All that I have seen and lived through, I'll tell you about one day! The heat of the day, the frost by night . . . And sleep was not in our eyes . . . With all the things of these days I wish I were younger and angrier; to speak hard words to them who do us evil.'

Dina brought me a cup of coffee on a tray.

'Old Miss Ella? Old Miss is tired and must go to sleep!' she said.

'No, Dina,' the answer came, 'I am not tired. I am only inquisitive to know all that will take place. And what there is, I take to heart; for it is my people who are here; and we have come a long way.'

Dina clicked. 'Now, how does Old Miss talk? You think we are going to die, eh?'

'That is the way of everyone who lives, *Oumie*,' Kleinveld said. He was tending the *erd*. 'You must ask Mister, who is a clever man, and has seen things.'

'Mister knows what we shall do,' Dina said. 'Because he is over all our people. But Saturday, Little Miss will marry!'

Lisa, who had been listening to all this in a dreamy sort of way, looked up sharply, then smiled her quick, gleaming smile.

'*Ai* Dina,' she said, 'it is you who have kept me here for so long. But Saturday, Dina?' Lisa turned, poised like a bird about to fly. 'Away!'

'To where now, Little Miss?'

'Don't ask, Dina; and you will hear no lies!'

This caused Dina to shake a crooked black finger. The children—Adriaan Venter and Lisa—could not do such things, she warned. They had to remember who had raised Little Miss, and her brothers. Also Old Master, whose grave was far away, on the edge of the marshes. They should think about this, and not do as they pleased. She, Dina, would not allow it. They had to be careful of the Bushmen, who were like wild animals, stalking one in the bush, shooting poisoned arrows . . .

'So, Lisa,' I later said to her, 'then we are doing as we decided: bringing luck to Upingtonia. What do you think of Mister Lewis?'

'Pooh!' she replied. This was eloquent speech.

'I have heard that the commando will go out this coming week, *Meneer*?' Adriaan asked. 'That is as it should be. We cannot allow everything to remain as it is. We must go out and do what we can do.'

'Even before one gets married?'

'Even before that, *Meneer*. For it is our duty.'

'Do the other young men of the laager feel that way too?'

'All that I know of, *Meneer*.'

'What does Lisa say?'

'That if there is a gun and no one to use it, call me, *Meneer*. I want to go with you!'

We laughed at this. But I noticed a suggestion of emotion in Lisa's smile. It was as if a sudden apprehension had taken hold of her. For the moment I was sensitive to her lonely fear. Then she seemed to read my thoughts, and her merriment returned.

'Yes!' she said, and held her head proudly. 'I can ride too!'

'Very well, Lisa,' I answered, 'if we need you, we shall let you know.'

'*Meneer* won't need me!' She pulled Adriaan's hat over his eyes.

Dear Lisa, I thought, you are so tenderly young. I stand with reverence before your dreams. Here we all are in a far country, in the bush of Southern Africa. We are a little island of humanity in a sea of dangers. What hope have we to survive a storm? And yet, we will survive. We have no alternative. There is no turning back. What was suffered in the Thirstland was only a hardening for the true struggle . . .

Such were my thoughts. What pleased me was that I had used the word 'us'. This was the true indication that I had accepted the laager as my home. I had joined them in the enduring fight against Africa. I had accpeted them with all their limitations, giving myself to their cause, even when doubting it. Here they were in their Land of Rest, or so they thought. Why break their illusions? They were happy in it. This was their final horizon. So far they had trekked, and here they wished to stay. This was the *eindbestemming*—their true destiny. I could be with them and yet be on my own. I could give myself to them and gradually they would give themselves to me and to the cause of a greater concept than Rest from Suffering. Upingtonia would become that. Here would be the heartland of real progress. We would set standards, and we would bring peace to a torn country.

Was it all the dream again of one lying under a tree on a lazy afternoon, listening to the call of the spotted turtle, being mesmerized by the incessant droning of the cicadas? Or of one standing beside the Atlantic, watching the day sink beneath the horizon? Or of one resting against a tree, sitting in its blue shadow, seeing the bush stretching to infinity, like another sea, like the sky itself?

No! I would force myself back to the facts. To dream about the future was to court disaster. It was precisely this that I had always been critical of. Of far greater importance were the things of the present. There was no other way.

12

I proposed to the *Bestuur* that the commando set out on its task early in the new week: on the Tuesday, if possible. Reports had reached the laager that Gabriel and his band were lying low. They had probably got wind of our plans.

'Gentlemen,' I said, 'we may be away for two or three days. Gabriel and his lot, as we have heard, are out there, east of the omuramba. How far? Nobody seems to be able to tell us. Anyway, the stolen cattle have been grazing in the omurambas, according to the Bushmen. We hope that the expedition will be able to do its work without recourse to violence. None of us likes a shooting party. Should we meet resistance, however, there may be no alternative. From what I know of Gabriel, he'll clear out before we catch up with him. With Lewis around here, anything can happen. Driving a large herd of cattle, however, is another matter. For my part Gabriel can get away to the other side of the Thirstland, as long as we can recover Kambonde's property.'

I looked to Barend Bouwer, who was the commandant.

'Mester is right,' he said presently. 'We must go out, and get the job done!'

'How many will we be?' I asked.

He spread open his powerful fingers, as if he were counting them. 'Thirty, or so!' he then decided.

'It all depends,' David Black remarked.

'On those that are still in two minds,' Louw du Plessis added.

'Thirty, with all who are to be spared here,' Barend said. 'We'll see what Piet Botha has in his head to do.'

I sat thinking. There was no point in discussing Botha again. Chris Leen had remarked that this would also be a good opportunity to see who were loyal to the cause. I agreed with him. Old Diederick, too, approved of this by tapping with his stick, then remarking that the disloyal would have to 'splinter away' as fast as their legs could carry them. We here in the laager would carry on, not for one moment deviating from the 'measured out' road.

Those at the meeting who had supported Botha and had followed him in the end when he left had not given any indication yet of what they intended doing. Even Botha himself showed no particular haste to shake the dust of Upingtonia off his well-shod feet. Yes, indeed, there were many stories doing the rounds of what he had said here or there. It was difficult to pin it down.

Some of Botha's followers like the De Beers and the Krugers had shifted their *werfs* to outlying waters. The Van Wyks and Du Toits, however, stayed where they were; so, too, the widow Roets.

Once or twice I passed her wagon. She greeted me in the old manner. I hesitated and thought: should I talk to her again? No, I decided, I would not. It was the old reserve which held me fast. It had plagued me all my life. I had always baulked at the thought of forcing my presence on anybody. Perhaps it was pride; perhaps it was my determination to avoid any impression that I was looking for support. Or was I just feeling myself to be the outsider again? What was the truth? I did not know.

Jan Labuschagne was still an enigma. I had no qualms about approaching him, making no bones about it. He was the kind one could do it to. But Jan was an old hand, parrying my thrusts with a certain cunning. He explained to me at length the attractions of the Waterberg. Often he had hunted in the vicinity, he said. There was 'nowhere better'. To this I drily remarked that we had undertaken the founding of a new state and were not looking for a hunter's paradise. Nothing daunted, he roared back that it would nevertheless be a good thing to stay on the 'right side' of Mister Lewis, 'because one never knows'. We 'should look things through', and decide where it was best for us.

Here, I roughly answered, just *here*, and nowhere else. This had been said often enough. Those who still had other thoughts were welcome to have them, but should go.

What about the commando, I asked. Would he join it? Could we count on him? Or had he been moved to see Gabriel as an angel, and not as a brigand?

This was lost on Jan. Nevertheless he assured me with much waving of arms that he was 'quite willing to help shake out that old *schelm*'.*

But dominant in my thoughts was always Pieter Maritz-Botha . . .

I spent hours thinking about all that had happened. So doing, I relived the old emotions. But now they seemed to be concentrated. I felt vexation, impatience, bitterness at the thought of the man's unjust treatment of me. I was newly irritated by his studied disregard of the truth; revolted by his apparent smugness. But then, suddenly, it would all change: I would feel sorrow at the knowledge that something of one piece, our good friendship, had fallen apart. In between it all there were little darts of hope that all was not lost. Somehow we would find each other. Somehow we would sit down and talk again, as men . . .

Things in the daily rote constantly took my mind back to what had been. There had been the early morning fire after a frosty night. There had been the morning salute when we met over freshly-made coffee; the lively talk of the road we had come; and the road ahead . . .

Nights we would sit next to the glowing leadwood fires, cooking doughnuts, discussing Southern Africa and the world 'outside'. I would like to pull his leg; I would say: 'Let's go to Europe together one day! But long before that you'll have a matrimonial noose around your neck!' He had always wagered me he would not . . .

In the early hours of the morning I lifted a corner of the wagon-tent. I could see down the gentle slope of the heights of Otjovanda Tjongue: Grootfontein—Great Fountain—as it now was called. There it lay in the moonlight. Between the dark forms of the trees

*Rascal.

low fires still burnt like sleepy eyes. I could count the white tents of the wagons . . .

Here, near me, under the awning, Karevapu lay like an old lion, sawing benignly through the hours. Good old Karevapu . . .

And here, where the heap of leadwood coals still glowed, were my servants in their trenches.

The moon was so bright that the stars had faded. There was Crux, balancing above a treetop . . . There were the Pleiades, in the branches of an ana . . .

I gripped the tent-ribbing, dimly wishing that I could pray. But my words were slight, my thoughts confused . . . Better just to lie back on the pillow and think . . . There was only one thing for us to do . . . To go forward to wherever it would lead us . . .

Personal feelings had suddenly receded. Upingtonia was far more important.

Pieter Maritz-Botha and most of his supporters left the laager the next day. I stood there on the heights watching the convoy of wagons moving off in the western bush. At times they would disappear, then become visible once more. There was little dust as the veld was lush.

'Where are they heading?' I asked Chris.

'Nobody knows for sure,' he replied. 'There's still talk about Ovamboland.'

'To fetch the horse?'

'Maybe!'

'What then? If he survives it!'

'The Old Transvaal,' Chris looked at me.

'Surely he does not intend taking Johanna and her baby along with him?'

'I have an idea they'll laager somewhere near here at one of the waters. He is still very outspoken about the commando going out.'

'I'm afraid I have yet to discover what his outspokenness amounts to, unless it's all personal.'

'That's more than likely,' Chris said.

I turned around and walked back to the laager. I had a feeling that I had still not seen the last of this man, who had once been my friend.

13

The day we set out against Gabriel dawned with a brittle clarity. I had got up at four o'clock to see to ammunition, provisions and horses.

Izak, preparing breakfast, looked at me with some apprehension. 'The 'maramba Bushman is wild like a veld animal,' he said.

'Yes, *Bambuse*,' I said. 'We know that only too well.'

'Now why do you go so far after him? He will see you coming.'

'Well, then they must see us coming. But we'll go out, all the same.'

'Gabriel lies in the bush. He knows our plans.'

'We'll catch up with him, never mind.'

The Bushman grinned, as if he didn't believe me.

'If the cattle have left the 'maramba, where will they be?' I asked.

'Far . . .!'

'I can't say that you're an encouragement. Never mind, old man, we have done this sort of thing before. The likes of Gabriel are not as clever as all that. You should have come along with us. But now you stay here and look after everything.'

'When will Mister come?'

'We'll see. Maybe on Friday. You see to it that all goes well here.'

'*E!*'

'I'll tell you what: if things work out as they should, we'll go down to the Bay in a week or two. We need things.'

His face brightened.

'*E!* Karevapu Katiti?'

'He is leaving for his own laager.'

'*Hamtsja!* Will he come?'

'He will come, in time. As soon as he gets all his things settled at Omaruru. We'll clean up the land around here, and the people will go out to their farms. Many people will come to Upingtonia, *Bambuse*.'

His eyes crinkled. To myself I said: all great things had small beginnings. At the same time I reminded myself that small beginnings were no assurance of growth. It was wholly a matter of individual disposition. I was quietly determined that lack of success would rather be my fate than my fault.

Axel Eriksson and I had a farewell breakfast together. I had hoped that he would still be here on our return. No, he said, he had to get to Omaruru. His brothers had expected him more than a week before. And now he had been holidaying so pleasantly here at Otjovanda Tjongue . . .

'Well, old warrior,' I remarked with some sadness, 'when do we see each other again?'

He was cutting choice bits off his cutlet with a penknife.

'Ho, Will,' he grinned, 'maybe very soon. Who knows, eh?'

He finished the cutlet, and started nibbling at some marula nuts Izak had gathered.

'I have bought land at Crocodile River too. Did I tell you?'

'You mentioned something,' I said. 'The name of the farm is Marseille. Listen, that may be fine, my friend. But we need you here. You shall have two like Marseille—for the price of registration, which will be five shillings.'

He enjoyed this.

'Marseille is a good farm,' he stated. 'Plenty of game, Will. Good for hunting, man.'

'Oh, to hell with your hunting!' I replied. 'You want a real farm where you can raise cattle, and work the land. You saw the waters here. Which one will be yours?'

'Now!'

Axel thought for a moment, then looked at me from underneath his bushy eyebrows, as if confiding.

'Aukas, eh? As the Bushmen call it.'

'Then Aukas it will be. And a fine choice!'

'If not Aukas, then Okaukueyo!'

'You can have them both, as far as I am concerned. What about your brother Albert?'

'Remember the place where so many quelea finches were, eh?'

'Palmietfontein we called it. Fine, then that is set aside for brother Albert. When can we expect you?'

'Plenty of things we have to do still.'

'I realize that. But come as soon as you can!'

'You make *slut* with all your work; and by that time we are here.'

'Yes,' I said, 'unless someone makes *slut* with me.'

'Ugh, Will, man, what do you say!'

I had shocked him.

'I'm only joking, Karevapu,' I said. 'I'll see to it that your beacons are erected at those places. We'll have a feast the day you arrive. Tell the wife and kids we'll have a band out to welcome them. Violin by the Brothers Louwrens, harmonica by Jan Labuschagne, jew's harp by Jordan.'

He roared with laughter.

'By the way,' I said, 'you can put in a good word for us at Omaruru, in spite of the efforts of the Reverend Viehe. Try and get Manasse to see reason. I have no desire to argue with him. I'll write to him again. But use your good influence. We have nothing but peaceable intentions as far as all the native peoples of this country are concerned. Anybody ready to enter into a treaty will find us only too willing. By the way, I have written to *Kanzler* Nels, and asked him to please come and have a look at Viehe's doings. Viehe still believes, like Botha, that the whole affair here is all to the material benefit of Jordan. How? My dear Karevapu, I don't mind telling you, from a business point of view, Upingtonia is a dead loss. It has cost me a lot of money, and there is little prospect of getting it back. In fact, I don't *want* it back!'

'We know all about that. All these stories are because they themselves have interests, eh? Not to think of it, Will!'

'I won't, if I can help it. But it's not always so easy to avoid, though. Here's Kairob with the horses!'

Axel Eriksson gathered his things together. When he was ready to depart, he pressed half a sovereign in each of the servants' hands.

'For all the food that had tasted so good,' he said to Izak, who was beaming like the rising sun.

'For looking after the horse and good driving!' he said to Kairob.

His smile was a splash of white in the pitchy darkness of his face. Thereupon Eriksson turned to me.

'So, Will,' he said, 'then it is *avsked* again!'

Our hands clasped.

'Let's hear from you,' I said. 'We are out in the bush here. We want to know what is happening in the world. Maybe we'll trek down to the Bay before the month is out. It all depends.'

'Keep good courage. Not be frightened.'

'That's not likely.'

'Only joking. I know the stuff you're made of.'

'Pretty moth-eaten stuff sometimes, what with fever and the rest. But we'll manage. Goodbye, old chap. Look after yourself.

And think of us, when you can!'

'Like a brother, Will, who knows all about our cries, troubles, dangers to life. Nice that I would have been here, Will. I say then—*Wiederschauen*!'

'*Wiederschauen* Karevapu!'

He mounted his gelding which had been having a quiet conversation with the mare. He rested easily in the saddle: a stocky figure with a red beard and a bald pate. He held his hat aloft by way of farewell. For the last time I felt his warm, comforting humanness.

'Karevapu Katiti!' This was from my servants, paying their farewell homage.

The horse, arching his neck, moved through the long grass. I watched them disappear between the trees. The last I saw of Axel Eriksson was his broad-rimmed hat, waving us a final goodbye.

I had an empty feeling as I walked back to the wagon. He had said that he would return. He would come to Aukas, or to Okaukueyo. He would seek a new life in Upingtonia. Omaruru was the past, and the past was done with . . .

'Farewell, old blazer of trails!' I said with savage affection.

So it was, and there was nothing more to it. We had to 'keep good courage, not be frightened.' Of course. And yet, I had the deeper feeling that I had now reached the end of something fine in my life. Was it lack of confidence? Heaven forbid. I preferred to see it as the usual 'little death' of every parting.

Or perhaps, I thought, it was all part of what this country was: this south-western land of Capricorn. It took hold of you, like no loved one could. It went with you wherever you went. It fed on your life. Gradually it devoured you . . .

The mare whinnied from where she was fastened under a tree.

I looked up. My servants were tidying the *werf.* They grinned at me, as if they had divined my thoughts.

'I must be off,' I said. 'Are the saddlebags packed? Bring the horse!'

In the east the sun was rising between the branches of a camelthorn.

STRYFONTEIN
(October 1885)

1

By eight o'clock that October morning the commando assembled at a water a few miles from the laager. This happened to be the place Barend Bouwer had chosen for himself, even long before the Trek had arrived. Dabe, the Bushmen called it: *vlei.* The water from a fine spring gathered here in a clay pan bordered by luxuriant reeds. This had always been a favourite watering place for the game. With the laager at Otjovanda Tjongue, however, and much cattle grazing in the vicinity, the game had gone elsewhere.

'How many are we?' I enquired on arrival. 'Thirty-two, Mester,' Barend Bouwer replied, 'and four still to come!'

'Who?'

'The Labuschagnes, and Adriaan Venter.'

'We have had word of their coming,' Louw du Plessis said. 'Piet Botha is also nearby.'

I offered no comment. I had expected Botha to stick around until he saw exactly what we were doing. Apparently he had appointed himself custodian *in absentia.* Well, we would see. He certainly was no easy one to shake off. I had once seen him follow the spoor of a wounded lion for more than twenty miles.

'Does anybody know what Botha intends doing?' I asked. 'Is he coming this way?'

Louw du Plessis looked at me in surprise. 'I'm simply enquiring,' I said. 'Let Botha come if he wants to. It will make no difference!'

We were on our horses under the trees, ready to go off as soon as the commando was fully constituted. There were the Louwrenses, Oppermans, Du Plessis, the Grobbelaars . . . Some like Jan Prinsloo and Koos Opperman had dismounted and were seeing to their guns or bandoliers. Lewies Louwrens was filling a water bottle at the fountain. Machiel Prinsloo was fixing a stirrup.

The day unfolded. It was sultry and there was the promise of thundery weather in the afternoon. I mopped brow, temples, neck. My hands were sweaty too, and I wiped them on my trousers. It would have been even better had we passed through the omuramba before the sun was out. A sense of urgency in our mission was, however, hardly to be expected. My friends were temperamentally unsuited to all this, as yet. That was why we had to sit here waiting for some to turn up. Would the Labuschagnes arrive? Adriaan Venter was with them, and I could not imagine him staying away.

I took out my watch and looked at it. A quarter past seven . . . Few here in the laager measured time by an instrument. They watched the sun.

'Before sundown of the first day we have to know how the land lies,' I had said. 'Before sundown of the second day we have to have the stolen cattle together. By sundown of the third day we have to be back at the laager with the cattle. What then? We'll let Kambonde know to come and fetch them.'

'We must just finish the job!' Barend Bouwer said thoughtfully. 'We have better work to do.'

'Perhaps the bird has already flown,' said Louw du Plessis.

'As long as we get the cattle,' I said, 'Gabriel can fly to where he will.'

'We'll find him!' Barend Bouwer said.

'When we've completed our task, will you go to Ovamboland, Brother Jordan?' Louw du Plessis's beard was thrust pointedly against the blue-white of the sky.

'There are many things to be seen to at the laager,' I replied. 'What's the news about Lewis? Is he trekking north?'

'He is near Otavi spring,' David Black said.

'My bet is he is on his way to Ovamboland.' Chris Leen got off his horse to adjust the saddle-cloth.

'In that case,' I answered, 'I'll go.'

'Alone?' asked Du Plessis.

'It will be better to go alone. *You* look after the laager.'

'And Piet Botha?' Bouwer asked.

'We'll see about Botha,' I said.

'He's very angry about this commando,' Bouwer said.

'Why?' I asked. 'Can anybody tell me, precisely *why*?'

'We should have inspanned him from the start,' Bouwer said. 'Then we wouldn't have had the chance to get about with people like Lewis.'

'Brother Barend, you speak now as if you do not know your own people.' Louw du Plessis eyed him steadily. 'Always it was like that: when a man had decided on a course, he just pressed on, come what may. When he saw that what he was aiming to reach was a mirage—did he turn back? No, never. He still pressed on, until the bitter end.'

I knew what he was referring to. It was that feud between him and Kreling in the days of the Second Trek, west of the Crocodile River. Kreling had lost his leadership when the people had demanded a vote. He had refused to accept this defeat.

'Good!' Kreling had shouted on that occasion for all to hear. 'We shall trek into the Thirst. Every man shall stand on the soles of his own feet!'

So, the trek had fallen into two parts. Kreling and his people had gone ahead obstinately with no idea at all where the waters lay and how they could be reached. The result had been disastrous.

All these things were still fresh in the minds of the people. Fresh in my mind, too, was the story of the reconciliation, after all the bitterness of the trek, on the shores of Lake Ngami.

'When we sat there near the waters,' Louw du Plessis had once told me, 'after all the sufferings of the Thirstland, we shook hands. We sat there in the cold night, around a little fire. Sat there and thought about all the people we had lost . . . We didn't say much. There was still too much sadness about all that had happened. Would it henceforth go better? Well, we hoped that it would. But so it was not to be. Jan Kreling wished to be near the waters, trekking up the west bank of the river. That is what he and his people did, and they got fever, and a great many died. You were there, Brother Jordan; and you saw what had happened.'

I had seen what had happened. It was like a scar inside my mind. There was that wagon with the dead people lying inside, on the *katel*. The man had had a Bible clutched between his fingers. There were vultures on the draught-pole . . .

Such was Jan Kreling. Later, at Leeu Pan, he had turned back and had looked for the spoor to the Transvaal. He never admitted that he had been wrong. He simply left the laager at Olifants Pan, stating that he and his people were going out to hunt. He never came back.

And now Piet Botha was acting in a similar way. He still regarded me as an intruder in the laager. I had to know what my 'place' was, he was still fond of saying. This angered me when I had first heard about it. Botha had hated the idea that I had bought Upingtonia; that I had largely worked out the constitution and was allocating the lands. I was no Boer, he had said. What right had I to interfere in their affairs?

Still very strange, I now reflected. He had said all this and had yet found common cause with Robert Lewis. Lewis had been the enemy of Botha's people from the very start. How far could a man go when reason left him? Now he would save the laager from the wrath of the Bushmen; but at the same time he was willing to lead a crackpot expedition against Kambonde Kampingana, all for the sake of a horse. He would do that, and war would come. Was he indeed prepared to risk all this for the sake of getting even with me? I had done him no wrong . . .

Pieter Maritz-Botha was from old pioneer stock and also would not easily be turned. His grandfather was Gert Maritz, who had led the Great Trek of '36, and who had died in Natal. The arguments between him and Potgieter in the days before Umzilikazi had been defeated were generally known. The Cape was still full of stories of the deep differences which sometimes existed between other leaders of that first mass emigration. Retief and Uys, and Uys and Potgieter, had clashed. Retief and his men had been murdered at the kraal of Dingane. Uys had also been murdered . . .

What did one learn of experience? Not much. What had I, Will Jordan, learnt of experience? I had dreams of a strong, well-ordered state up here in the north-west. I saw it as an entirely new order. It would put this land we loved on a healthy, sound foundation . . .

Did I have the right to think this way? Botha and his followers thought not. But the others in the laager—the majority—accepted me. I did not serve on the *Bestuur*; but it had been my own choice not to do so. I wished to be free to advise and to act as the occasion demanded. It was generally agreed that, at least for the present, I would have to be the effective leader. This was simply because I could not shake off responsibility as a dog shakes off water. Upingtonia had been my idea and I had to see to its implementation.

Did I care for the special 'regard' in which I was held? Was I, unknown to myself, concerned about it? It was quite true that I would not like to see all the management suddenly taken out of my hands. We had to do with enemies who had learnt their political tricks in a tough school. This country had had more than its share of deceit, intrigue, and lust for power. The long isolation of the Trekboers had left them ill-equipped to deal with such things. It would have been far more pleasant, surely, to have picked a farm and to have retired peacefully. This was what Axel Eriksson was doing. I envied him. Nothing would be finer than to leave all this tension behind and set out on some long trek to some new part of Africa . . .

2

I looked up. The sun struck me and I was momentarily blinded. When my sight had adjusted itself, I saw the group of riders coming towards us through the bush. The mare pricked her ears and whinnied.

'The Labuschagnes?' I asked.

'The Labuschagnes too,' David Black replied.

I did not ask who the others were. I shaded the sun from my eyes. It was the Labuschagnes, yes; and Adriaan Venter. Six of them were together. There was Jan and his two brothers, Daniel and Cornelis. Adriaan Venter was the fourth. Who were the other two? Intuitively I suddenly knew. It was Louw du Plessis who confirmed this. 'Piet Botha,' he said. 'And Jan Kruger.'

A variety of comment came from those around us. 'So, the hind-ox also gets to the kraal!' Barend Bouwer shouted.

Jan Prinsloo wanted to know whether such an ox could still do that in lion country. Not at all, his brother Willem replied. And Machiel, the third of Old Diederick's sons, laconically remarked that this ox was so noisy that no lion would risk it near him . . .

In fact, Jan Labuschagne was approaching with an arm raised and a voice to quicken the dead. What! he enquired, had we been waiting?

I turned my horse about. Waiting? I repeated. Indeed, we had been waiting. Come along, we had to get a move on. I was partly conscious of Adriaan Venter riding up to me and apologizing for the delay. *Oom* Piet had held them up, he explained; *Oom* Piet had spoken to them . . .

I cut him short and shouted back to the riders still behind me: 'Gentlemen, please now, we must move on. It is getting late!'

He sat there on his horse, some fifty yards from where I had stopped. He was under a tamboti tree. My impression was that he had said something to my fellow riders which had caused them to hesitate. What was happening?

I controlled myself and came back slowly till only a few yards separated us. He sat there on his horse, dressed in riding breeches and a straw hat. He carried a sjambok in his hand and was casually flicking it against his right gaiter.

What was all this about? Why had Botha come? Obviously he was up to no good. Had he not had enough? I had hoped that he had gone off for ever. But here he was again. It seemed that he wished to prevent the commando from setting off. It was clear that he had already tried to get the Labuschagnes and Adriaan Venter not to participate. He had timed it to perfection. Here at Dabe he stood a better chance of upsetting our plans. He knew that Old Diederick would not suffer his presence in the laager. He had a certain respect for Old Diederick . . .

My heart was hammering, slowly, heavily. I pulled the mare in and stopped in the game path leading from the spring. I should not get angry. It would do no good. It would give him the exact advantage he was looking for . . .

I caught a glimpse of Barend Bouwer's face, red with annoyance. Louw du Plessis snapped a pocket knife shut. Adriaan Venter had removed his hat and was wiping his forehead. Suddenly it was very quiet. Then I heard a francolin calling from the bush. I also heard Jan Prinsloo say: 'I think it is better that you turn about, Cousin Piet, and go back!'

He had no such plans. He looked askance at me. 'I hoped that you would come to your senses, Jordan,' he said. 'But now I see that you still intend carrying on with all this madness. You are playing with fire. I tell you that. You are also playing with the lives of women and children. You can do that because these people are not your own!'

'Why don't you clear off, Botha?' I said.

I found it difficult to conceal my emotions. Feelings were pushing up in me that even the meeting had not provoked. The mare turned sideways to the game path so that I had to look at him over my shoulder. He had not moved.

'You know very well what we intend doing here,' I said. 'It has nothing more to do with you. You've made your choice and you have gone off with your own supporters. Fine, let that be as it may. But, for God's sake, leave us alone. Don't meddle in our affairs!'

'Meddle?' He said something to Kruger I could not hear.

I swung the mare around and confronted him. 'You're as meddlesome as an old woman!' I said.

I saw him flush with anger.

'One meddles when one sticks one's nose into affairs which one has no right to!' he shouted.

I got the innuendo. I didn't belong there. I was an outsider. When I had first heard of such talk, I had been angry but had soon shrugged it off. Now it was different. Botha was in deadly earnest. This was his final, desperate attempt to humiliate me in the eyes of his fellow Boers.

'If you are going to get personal . . .' I said, 'I warn you.' My voice was shaky.

'I must speak the truth, and the truth hurts! Do you think I came here to shake hands?'

'Get along, man! You've left the laager. Now get back to your friends at Okahandja!'

'. . . When I have done my duty. These are my people, and I must look after their interests!'

'Did any of them ask you to do that? Not even the lot who seem to support you. You're childish, Botha. Get on your way, man, and take your *claque* with you. These are men here. They know whom they can trust.'

'You've told our people enough lies, Jordan,' he rejoined. 'It all fits nicely into your schemes, eh?'

'Like what?' Chris moved up to me.

'You've kept a lot of farms—the best!—for yourself!' Botha said this with a note of triumph as if he had been brooding on it.

'Farms! The best? You mean I've retained less than one per cent of what I paid for?'

'A Boer Republic! And this Jordan, our learned friend, sees to it that he gets the best of the deal!' He turned to the others who had gathered around us on foot and on horseback. 'I tell you as I told you at the meeting, he'll sell you up without your even knowing it! He wants to bring in all sorts of people here. The Erikssons . . . the Chapmans . . . and Lyon, and Todd; and the rest of that crowd! All from the Bay. All they know about is drinking, playing cards, and trading. A whole bunch of Englishmen. He wants them here, yes—to further his own ends. What will be left of the *republic* you have striven for so long? Just a few months and you'll have the English here. Then you'll have to salute the Union Jack. Come on now, Jordan, be a man, and admit that you have always had a secret purpose with this scheme!'

By now I was breathing heavily. 'You've said enough!' I snapped back. I spurred the mare closer, till only a yard or two separated us. I saw him raise the sjambok as if to defend himself.

'You threaten me?'

'No, I would not threaten you, Botha. But I despise the things you do and say, especially what you insinuate. Farms kept for my own use? The best of them all? Ask yourself why I didn't keep the lot? Or charge for those allocated to the burghers?'

'You won't fool me, Jordan. All your tricks! It's sheer hypocrisy.'

'You know very well there is not a single one among those who would settle here who is not a good friend of the Trekboers. This applies especially to the Erikssons. Every man we have approached will be an asset here. It is also necessary to win the good friendship of great powers like Britain and Germany. Sell you up? Hypocrisy? But not for a moment do you hesitate to sell up your own kind to that arch-hater of your people, Robert Lewis!'

'You leave out Lewis. If you had done half of what Lewis has done for this country . . . !'

I looked around me at the men listening to all this. 'There you have it,' I said. 'Lewis has now become the great benefactor of the Boer people. If that's the case, gentlemen, there is, surely, little more to say!'

But he persisted: 'Oh no, there's a lot more to say, Jordan. And these people here should hear it all!'

I turned on him. 'Shout it from the house-tops, man!' I said. 'God knows, I couldn't care a tinker's cuss what the hell you do! I've had enough of all your sickly moaning, Botha! Go lick your liege-lord's backside: Kamaherero wants to set you up in the Waterberg! You rat! What do you think you are going to get out of all this?'

I was well aware that I was saying things I would later regret. But the words were breaking out beyond my control.

'For the past few months,' I continued, 'you have been nothing but an embarrassment to your own people. Worse, you have been traitorous. But do what you will, Botha, you won't scare us into submission. We are not so bloody useless. There is not a single man here today who does not despise your so-called manliness. Get out of here: you have become a positive danger to the community. To hell with you, Botha!'

I could keep the mare reasonably quiet up to this point. But now, as if sensing what was taking place, she became restless. I pulled her in roughly, then finally threw at him: 'You fool! You fool!'

The others were listening to all this in amazement. At the same time a small voice was warning me: 'Better to keep calm and tell him what he should hear, carefully, but unanswerably. Better to quit this company, and get back to the laager; or else summon the commando to follow you, and set off against Gabriel!'

Reason, however, had momentarily deserted me. The struggle between Botha and myself had now deteriorated into this clumsy hitting out at each other.

There he sat on his horse, looking at me. In a sense he had now gained the upper hand. He had provoked me to these harsh words; and this was exactly what he wanted. The opportunity had now arrived for him to do something; say something he had probably been keeping in reserve for a long while. There had always been the insinuations, the preparedness to wound, but not to strike.

Suddenly I saw him undo his shirt-sleeve and begin to roll it up. Watching as if something had warned me what was coming, I saw him expose the inside of his arm to above the elbow. The arm, to some distance above the wrist, was as brown as my own. On the soft underside, however, where the sun had never reached, it was soft and white.

'All your ranting, Jordan,' he said, 'passes me by. Say whatever you like. I won't take any notice of it.' He now lifted the exposed part of his arm for all to see. 'Do you see, Jordan?' He was waving the arm as if it were a banner. 'Dare you talk as you have talked? Here you see the colour of an *opregte witte man*!'*

*A genuine white man.

I suddenly seemed to have been struck by something from behind. I sat on my horse, momentarily too shocked to speak. Perhaps I did react: did say something. I might have used words like: *What do you mean?—Why do you say such things?—This is insulting* . . . Whatever I could have said, however, would have been ineffectual.

In the inner confusion which came over me, I was yet conscious of my pain. Yes, indeed, he had used those words. He had said: *Here you see the colour of an opregte witte man.*

Automatically I turned the mare. Botha was still adding to what he had said; but I did not hear his words. As if from a distance I heard someone call my name. It might have been Louw du Plessis. But I had to get away now, to somewhere in the bush . . . The mare shuddered under me, as if she shared my pain. Her walk became a canter, her canter a gallop. She was following the game path. Somebody behind me was still calling me. Now it could have been Chris . . .

The mare's hooves clattered over a rocky section of the path. A francolin went scampering through the grass and the trees seemed to close around me. I felt relieved, but I was still breathing heavily.

3

Half an hour later I was sitting against the bole of an omumborombonga, locked within myself. Slowly perspectives were adjusting themselves. I had found a cigar which Axel Eriksson had given me in a shirt pocket. Absently I watched the blue smoke drift slowly through my fingers, until it finally dispersed. My hand was unsteady.

Well, I quietly decided, so that was how matters stood. What Pieter Maritz-Botha had been wanting to say for a long time, he had finally said. He had struck me in my most vulnerable part. I had to face it.

The question remained: what now? It was clear enough that my position might have to be reviewed. Would those who had stood by me so loyally still do so in the light of what had taken place? Yes, I decided at once, they would. I could not imagine men like Louw du Plessis, Barend Bouwer, David Black, Old Diederick himself, and many others, suddenly shunning me because the matter of what race I belonged to had been brought up in this rough and unmannerly way. I had never hidden anything about my personal life.

Yet, it would have been rash to have drawn conclusions. I should not have worried too much about the effects of Botha's words. Neither could I stay out here where I now was, keeping everybody in a state of suspense. Botha had done his best to stop the commando from setting out, and to a certain extent he had succeeded. He had delayed the expedition; and some members would in all probability now withdraw. Nevertheless, we would go on. To stop now would be an acknowledgement of defeat, an admission that my enemies had always been right.

One simply had to dig one's heels in and refuse. You got nowhere by turning tail and getting out. Was this what I had thought of doing? Heaven forbid. The shock of it all had momentarily confused me. Botha had dealt me a hard blow in a most vital part . . .

I had let the mare find her own way. Only after about ten minutes had I begun to take notice of where I was. I had dismounted here and had sat down against the tree. Perhaps I had done the best thing in the circumstances. If I had stayed on, the clash between Botha and myself might have produced something worse. What had taken place was bad enough.

The thing was now to get back and carry on as if nothing had happened. Should Botha still be there, one simply had to ignore him, then proceed as planned. Meanwhile, what conclusions had my friends come to? How would they interpret my flight? Botha might well have remarked: 'You see? There he goes. When he heard the truth he couldn't face it!'

What then was this 'truth'? That I was of mixed parentage? I had always regarded myself as an Englishman by birth and education. This I had said often enough. In such terms, too, I had written to Nachtigall of the German Foreign Office. I had done so because I wished to present the case for Upingtonia in the clearest possible light. Indeed, I was of mixed parentage; but what of it? There were thousands like me at the Cape. There were millions like me in the world. And a great many of them had helped to make history. I was of mixed parentage because my mother—all honour to her name—was a Cape woman. Why had Botha waited until today to point this out in that scornful, melodramatic way? What he wished to imply was that I had no right to a point of view of my own. I was no *opregte witte man.* Therefore, everything I did was discounted.

It had profoundly shocked me. I had never made a secret of my parentage. He, Botha, had often been to the Cape. There had been many opportunities for him to visit my parental home in Wynberg; to investigate, if he so wished, my background. 'Go and look up my folks,' I had often said to him. 'They will welcome you like a son.'

Never had he given any indication that he held my lineage against me. What had happened to him now? Was all this also the doings of Robert Lewis? It might well have been the case. On the other hand this, at least, had to be said of Lewis: he had no racial prejudices. The only conclusion one could therefore come to was that Botha's attitude was deep-seated; or of his own recent making.

He seemed to have been nursing it for a long while, waiting for the right moment to announce it. When at last it had all been made known the effect was devastating. For the moment, at least, it had shattered my confidence. In its place had come self-consciousness of a painful, blinding clarity. It was like suddenly, inadvertently, looking at the sun.

Perspectives were slowly rebuilding themselves, but the pain remained. The simple fact was that I had been attacked not on merit, but because of my race. This was the ultimate argument *ad hominem.* What Botha had said affected not only me, but also Chris. He was married to my sister. Would he attack Chris as well? Chris had gained the respect of people like Barend Bouwer, Louw du Plessis, Diederick Prinsloo. Chris was doing the secretarial work. He was doing it well . . .

I had to return. I could not sit here much longer. I had to get back to Dabe and see what was happening. The commando might have returned to Otjovanda Tjongue, for all I knew. Or maybe they were still at Dabe awaiting my return.

But could matters ever be the same again? I was no *opregte witte man . . . This* had been said by a man who had been like a brother to me. And many had heard it.

Maybe I had identified myself too closely with the laager. In a way it was true: I was no Boer. I would never be a Boer. This was also because I had never desired to be one. What was true, however, was that among these people I had found some of the finest friends I had ever known. But how far in fact had I got to know and understand them? Had I not simply carried on with something I had sought to express myself in personally? Had I done what I had done because of my genuine feeling for these people?

Now I had to remind myself that we differed in almost every respect. From the start I had been attracted and repelled by the simplicity, but also the hardness of their reformed faith. It was a confession so stern, so unsympathetic, so spare. These Thirstlanders were a people without nuances. They knew only believers or unbelievers, black or white; those within the laager, those without. They were so limited, so caught up in their own inadequate knowledge of the world. And yet, within these narrow confines they were capable of greatness.

Their convictions were rarely the product of reason; nearly always they were instinctive. They rode westwards, following the sun: westwards, not because they had any knowledge of the geography of Africa, simply because a 'moving spirit' had set them on their course . . .

And then, one afternoon, when the sea did appear beyond the last dunes, no one was unduly surprised. So it was, and so it had to be. So it had been ordained from the start. There was no other way. God was the Great Team-leader. God was also the Great Wagon-driver. Those that found a place on the Wagon could only be thankful. The Wagon was the Laager-on-Wheels. Somewhere beyond the Last Horizon lay the Land of Rest. What room was there left for disillusionment, inner conflict, the search for the Unknown God? There was no God of the lonely questing individual. There was only the God of the *volk,* the people on trek . . .

The awe, the loneliness had become too much for them. They had sought refuge in the laager. But this was the greater loneliness. The laager was all: cradle, school, parental home. Ultimately it was God's acre. More than anything else, however, the laager was the Fortress-on-Wheels. From behind these ramparts the world could be kept at bay and the future shaped. How then could there be room for loners with questions on the mind and deep doubt in the heart? How could it accommodate loose wanderers who had nothing left but their own tattered selves, burdened down by their own individual problems? How could such compare their beliefs with the unbending, unquestioning simplicity of this puritan faith? Yet, an answer had to be found. The Old Covenant was not enough.

Here I sat on this humid, peaceful morning, delving into my own inner depths. It was only when I suddenly became conscious of the anxious *oc-oc-oc* of guinea fowl that I removed my fingers from my eyes and looked up. There they were, scurrying through the long grass, in under the low-hanging branches of the trees. I watched them and suspected the cause of it all. Looking upwards through the branches of the trees, I saw the martial eagle sweep into view.

There it was, sailing through the heavens like the Holy Cross in flight. The sun caught the white breast as the bird tilted against the sky. I thought I could see the golden eyes taking in every detail of the land below: the scampering guinea fowl; the kudus moving warily between the trees; the blue wildebeest where the trees were less dense; the palla; the zebra; the mare grazing unconcernedly here near me in the sweet-grass; the man against the tree, with knees drawn up, hat over his eyes, hands hanging loosely in front of him . . .

Something glowed inside of me. I recalled a time at the Okavango when Axel Eriksson had shot a martial eagle for his collection. The bird had had a wingspan of seventy-two inches. Axel had been sad in this moment of triumph . . .

How I wished my friend were here now. He would have viewed the flight of the *polemaetus* with joy. 'Well, now,' he would have breathed, while fixing his gaze on the bird in flight, 'how fine that is!'

This, I suddenly thought, was Africa. Here it was, drifting through the bright air of summer. This was Africa, which seized one so lovingly, so cruelly. This was what had brought back people like Charles John Andersson, Axel Eriksson, and even Will Jordan. On a certain level, I supposed, we had a common denominator. It was the land itself which held us. Wryly I decided that even I and Robert Lewis might, on this score at least, find a common interest.

4

Slowly I rode back through the bush. I said to myself: 'If they have left Dabe, I'll go back to the laager. If they are still there, I'll behave as if nothing has happened.'

When I came to myself, I saw the wisp of smoke rising among the trees. Hearing a horse whinny, I hesitated, and drew the mare in. Then I gently touched her with the spurs again, and she moved forward.

They were gathered under a giant sycamore when I arrived. A coffee kettle was boiling over a small fire. Someone seemed to be addressing the company. It sounded like Labuschagne. It *was* Labuschagne. I heard him say something about a load of ivory going down to the Bay. I saw his arms stop halfway through a gesture. Then he looked sharply at me.

It was a critical moment. All eyes seemed to turn towards me. Comment was coming from various quarters, and it did not sound unfriendly. Dismounting, I said: 'I think it is time for us to get moving now, gentlemen: those who wish to come along. Should anybody have changed his mind by now, it is his good right to withdraw from the commando. The rest of us will then carry on with what we have to do. Barend Bouwer, I take it, will still lead us.'

Bouwer seemed to have been waiting for this. I saw him jam his hat onto his head and get up. 'We must go, yes,' he said brusquely. Quickly he walked to his horse, tethered to one side, flipped open a saddle bag, and threw the remains of a piece of biltong* into it. 'Yes,' Louw du Plessis said, rising from a root of the sycamore. 'The day is already far shorter than it should be.' He spoke in the old dispassionate but encouraging manner.

The others, some still slightly hesitant, seemed to be following the lead. From the corner of my eye I saw Adriaan Venter sling his gun over his shoulder. David Black was untethering his horse. Chris Leen, who had been relieving himself in the bush, came back with long, rangy steps and said: 'My God, I'm glad you're here! Things were truly upset!'

'Never mind,' I said, 'it's past now.' Dolf Holtzhausen shook me by the hand. 'Dolf,' I asked, 'are you coming along?'

'Yes, *Meester*,' he replied, 'I am coming. And so are the sons. Thou hast given us much to talk about, *Meester*; and much to think about.'

I suddenly found it difficult to find any words for him. What

*Sun-dried meat.

levelled me off again was Botha. I had not noticed him. He had been sitting behind a tree. Now he suddenly appeared and spoke: 'This is on your head, Jordan. Don't say I didn't warn you!'

'Then it is on my head,' I answered.

'Well then, just remember what I said!'

'You have been saying far too much of late, Botha. Isn't it time you shut up for a change?'

I had other things on my mind to say to him; but prudence checked me. There was no point in restarting the mutual slander. I pulled over the mare's reins and she swung around sharply. The game-path I had taken earlier that morning once again stretched before me. Bouwer, Du Plessis and the Holtzhausens were already waiting.

'You're in the lead, Barend,' I said. 'Let's head for the 'maramba.'

Within a few moments the commando was moving through the bush at a steady pace. I was thankful. It could have been infinitely worse. I was not even counting how many had stayed behind at Dabe with Botha. We were a strong enough force; and we would complete our task.

I was quietly determined now. If Piet Botha had thought to upset an ideal by such means, he had better think again. This was a matter of human lives. If it was my own life, it was also the lives of my charges. What we now needed was action.

The morning was already far advanced, and heat-waves were trembling against a sky like steel. The hornbills were wailing, while flapping listlessly from tree to tree. Thunder clouds were building up to the north-east.

5

All the tension of that day led to somewhat of an anti-climax. By four o'clock in the afternoon it began to rain.

The rain had suddenly changed its quality. It was not the sudden deluge after violent thunder-and-lightning as had become the rule during the past few weeks. Usually this had been all over and done with within an hour or two.

Now the rain came over a broad front, and the clouds were a level field of smudgy white at high altitude. The start was more or less as usual: flickering bolts, and crashing thunder rolling distantly away. The quick climax, however, was missing. Instead the clouds seemed to spread out evenly over the land, becoming a tide of mist and fine rain, reminiscent of the Cape.

There was no opportunity to take shelter. We just kept on riding, heads low against the rain. Barend Bouwer and I kept to the fore, finding the way, which was not easy, there being a dearth of landmarks and visibility being limited. Makalani palms would loom up through the mist like ships' masts. Old trees which had been upset by the elephants would lie there like wrecks.

It was getting dark by the time we reached the omuramba. There it lay, wet and desolate before us. The only sign of life was a solitary bull-giraffe standing like a toy in the middle of the broad, sandy watercourse. Suddenly it turned and moved off with a pendulum-like action.

We followed the omuramba. The first indication that we had reached Otjituuo was the fresh ash in old *erds*. These had been left by treks moving between the Bay and the Okavango. This was where Axel Eriksson had been only a few days previously. Much game had also visited the waters here. A variety of spoors excited the interest of the hunters among us. Fresh elephant dungballs were collapsing. Every now and then a group of riders, usually with Jan Labuschagne or with one of his brothers in the lead, would go galloping off into the surrounding bush. After a time they would reappear with the news that all the game had fled, 'fed up with the wetness'. This was accompanied by a flick of a sjambok against the left buttock of Adriaan Venter's horse. The animal leapt forward and the young man had to balance precariously in the stirrups.

With much laughter resounding around us, I thought: 'As long as there is fun, I am comforted. When things begin to get quiet, it is time to worry.'

They still called me *Meneer*; or Mester; or Mister; or *Meester*. At times it would be 'Brother Will'. On rare occasions it was just 'Will'. This seemed to light something inside of me. It was because I was still sensitive about what had taken place at Dabe. Inevitably I had become defensive, extremely alert to changes in the atmosphere.

Plodding along through the wetness, I discussed the advisability of sending down wagons to the Bay with Barend Bouwer, Louw du Plessis, the Prinsloo brothers. To Machiel Prinsloo I said that should he come across some good horse for sale, he should let me know. Well, he replied in good spirit, there was always the possibility of buying back Piet Botha's Arab—'*My* Arab', he said—from Kambonde Kampingana. We laughed at this, and I felt relieved.

Night fell and we stopped under giant anas where we managed to keep relatively dry. We even got a fire going, and sat huddled around it, drinking coffee: eating hard Boer rusks, whittling away at biltong, smoking our pipes. There was a pungent smell of wet clothes, strong tobacco and strong coffee. It was like old times.

The talk was now about hunting, the weather, and again hunting. For a long while the main topic was whether Upingtonia could send hunters north-westwards to the river, or westwards to Ngami, 'like the time when we were in the Kaoko'. Ah, yes, the Kaoko! It seemed to raise nostalgic memories.

Jan Robbertze, David Black said, was hunting so many elephants in the Kaoko from Humpata these days, he was becoming a rich man.

This seemed to challenge Jan Labuschagne who broadly announced that he himself had considered going to the Kaoko. For that reason it would be a good thing to consider the Waterberg as a 'stopping-over place'; it was so much nearer to the Kaoko. It was also nearer to the Bay, and also nearer to Humpata.

I heard this in silence, thinking: the Waterberg was Robert Lewis's idea. So, we had to give up Otjovanda Tjongue and settle there, relying on the goodwill of Kamaherero.

I sat there, immobilized in the fug which had built up between the fire and the men huddled around it: steaming, sweating, breathing smoke from the fire and from their pipes. I sat there, holding my tongue. There would be time enough to get all this cleared up when we returned to the laager.

6

Long before dawn we were on our way again. The rain had temporarily stopped. A cloud-ceiling of sooty grey stretched from horizon to horizon. The horses splashed through miles of *vlei*. Shallow courses feeding the omuramba had already collected a fair amount of water. We kept due east. The surface was sandy, and the vegetation became sparser. If we were to continue in this way, we could reach the marshes of the Okavango and Lake Ngami within a week.

Dreamily I thought: I would have liked to have seen the places where I met the Trekkers some six years before. I would have liked to have found the place where I discovered the laager with its stricken people . . . I would have liked to have seen the river again . . . To have walked along on its banks, watching its shining waters quietly flowing past . . .

I rode for some distance lost in these thoughts. Then I pulled in the mare and surveyed the country. Cattle had been here. In this area it had not rained so much. The veld was full of dung and spoors. At times we would find a deserted *scherm*, but there was no sign of the humans who had lived there. Even game was scarce.

By early afternoon we reached a stretch of open water in a depression. A collection of deserted huts under the trees showed up. *Erds* were everywhere. At one place a great heap of bones, hides and horns had collected. Wagon spoors criss-crossed those of animals. Two tracks were relatively fresh and disappeared in a south-easterly direction. The spoors of a great many sheep and cattle and humans accompanied them. Bushmen had been the herdsmen.

This had been Gabriel's nest; but the bird had flown as Louw had predicted. Now he was deep down in the sandveld somewhere. Would he return? In a way it was a satisfying thought that he had cleared off rather than give fight. On the other hand, it would have given me particular pleasure to have dealt with Gabriel.

Patrols were hastily sent out in various directions. One under Machiel Prinsloo followed the large trekspoor southwards. The tracks kept going for a few hours. There was no sign of an outspan.

Adriaan Venter, returning with this patrol, declared that this had proved what he had always said: people like Gabriel, any Bushman for that matter, would give way to determined action. One brave man was enough to frighten them off.

I remembered Adriaan's enthusiasm for the 'good water' of Okasima down in the omuramba. There, he had often said, he would go when he and Lisa had got their things settled. There he would 'stand', and from there he would eventually set out for 'the tree'.

Well, I said, we would have to discuss that some later day. Okasima was a fine water but it was remote. Anyway, we would see. In my heart I knew that I would never contain this young man. He had always followed his own head. It was a strong head.

The patrols came back one by one. The desolate *werf* began to liven up again. The rain which had held off for a few hours now came sweeping back. With heads held down we rode back in single file towards the omuramba. We were pretty wet and miserable by this time, having little to say to each other. There was just the steady splashing of the horses through the water, relieved at times by the lusty cursing of somebody who had got his legs entangled in the hookthorn.

By evening the rain was coming down with such force that it was almost impossible to see more than ten yards ahead. We pressed on, trying to keep on our course. Afterwards we were compelled to take what shelter we could find under stately anas, on what seemed to be the east bank of the omuramba. There was no hope of getting a fire going. Everything around us was swimming. Hour after hour we stood there, as close to the boles of the trees as we could manage. The rain came down incessantly, falling out of a pitchy sky. Only the white smudge of a man's face, the soft glow where somebody had managed to light a pipe, the glint in a horse's eye, relieved the blackness. The night seemed to be without end.

I sat there on my horse, half asleep. The images of the past, the dreams of the future, seemed to surface again. It was like a new bout of fever.

I fell asleep, and awoke with a start when I nearly fell off my horse. Louw du Plessis, next to me, caught my arm and said: 'Brother Will!'

I laughed. I tried to see the time, but I couldn't make it out. After another hour, I heard Du Plessis say: 'Dawn is breaking. There's enough light to see the trees. Shall we go?'

'Yes,' I agreed. 'Let's go. What does Barend Bouwer say?'

He grunted. 'Mester Will? If we can swim . . . So, let's *maar* swim then!'

He forged ahead, and we followed him.

The white gleam behind the clouds in the east showed that the sun had risen. Soon we were crossing the omuramba, which had become a broad shallow river, fed from all sides by strongly running *spruits*. It was still raining and the water was stirrup-high. At times a horse and his rider would sink away into some depression, and would then have to swim.

After what seemed to be a long while, we reached firmer ground again. I shared a flask of brandy with some others.

'Is it good, Dolf?' I asked Holtzhausen when he had swallowed his tot. His eyes were alight.

'It is good, *Meester*,' he said. 'Thy hand is always ready to help a poor sinner!'

'If the poor sinner could but help himself,' I said. There was a drop left in the flask. I offered it to Dolf's eldest son.

'May I, father?' he enquired respectfully.

'You may, son,' his father replied.

The others had meanwhile been collecting veld-fruits. We ate some, and then continued our journey.

7

The afternoon was already half spent when we discerned the slight rise in the west. Half an hour later I could see the white of wagon-tents.

When, at long last, we galloped up to the still streaming heights of Otjovanda Tjongue people waved to us from their wagons, hartebeest-houses, and *scherms*. I saw Old Diederick standing in his doorway, holding his stick aloft.

We shook hands. 'Good-day, *Oom* Diederick. We got to where Gabriel had made his nest, *Oom*, but the bird had flown.'

'They knew we were coming, *Oom*,' Louw du Plessis added, 'so they trekked off, taking all the cattle!'

Oom Diederick nodded slowly. 'Then no strike.'

'No strike, *Oom*,' Du Plessis confirmed. 'But we shall keep an eye on that part. Gabriel won't come back so easily.'

Tante Prinsloo offered us some coffee, but I was in a hurry to get to my own wagon. When I arrived there, I found my servants sitting around a fire under a *scherm*.

'*Ara!*' they cried when they saw me.

The Bushman took the reins of my horse, and examined me curiously. 'Mister is wet!' A series of clicks further expressed his feelings.

'West, *Bambuse*,' I sat down on the provisions *kist* under the *scherm* and extended a leg. 'Take'm off, old fellow!'

He knelt before me and started undoing my boot. At the same time I stripped the wet clothes from the upper part of my body.

Kairob picked up my clothes, then started puffing at the fire.

Well now, what had happened to me, my servants wished to know. It had rained so much here at Otjovanda Tjongue, everything got so wet; there was no more firewood for the laager. The cattle were standing knee-deep in water on the flats where they were grazing. What had happened to the *schelm*? Did we hang him from a tree?

No, I replied, in all seriousness, we did not hang him from a tree. He had got wind of our coming and had skedaddled. Ho, my servants assured me, that was a bad thing! Gabriel was as clever as a jackal. He would come back some time.

I sat there in front of the fire, which was now burning pleasantly, with only a pair of trousers on. Soon the aroma of freshly made coffee gathered under the *scherm*. A palla steak was sizzling in the pan. Izak brought me some hot water to wash and shave in, also some dry clothes to put on.

It was home-like. My own mother could not have cared for me more lovingly.

Half an hour later I lay down on the *katel* in the wagon. Hardly had I done so, when sleep removed me from this world.

When I awoke it was late afternoon. There I lay watching splashes of dappled sunlight falling on the wagon-hood. It was the colour of ripe Cape apricots. Birds were chattering in the trees. Somewhere children at play were calling to each other.

I swung my feet over the edge of the *katel* and lifted a part of the canvas. A flood of light had fallen over the world. Everything seemed to be brilliantly green, blue, golden. The rain had passed and the whole northern sky had cleared. Surprising . . . At one time I had thought never to see the sun again. Coming through the omuramba it had seemed to be a general rain. So it sometimes happened. Then the whole country would come to a standstill.

Extremes were inherently part of things here. Great droughts were so devastating that the Hereros walked through the dry bush like living skeletons. Then the rains would return and Ovamboland would become a land of a thousand lakes, a thousand palm-fringed islands. The Hereros named the years after the most important event, or the main characteristic. 1848 was *Ojomeva Omanene*, the Year of the Great Waters; 1875 was *Ojejuva*, the Year of the Sun. In 1881 Kamaherero had driven back the Namas to the far south. This was *Ojohara*, the Year of the Great Army. In 1883 I had marvelled from the High Serras of

South Angola at the Great Comet: the most brilliant since that of Brooks in the late fifties. This then became *Ojonjose*, the Year of the Comet . . .

What would this one be called? I played with the thought. There was certainly no dearth of important events. According to all reports reaching the laager, Osona had been a massacre. Hendrik Witbooi, who had terrorized Damaraland for a number of years, had been heavily defeated, and his forces scattered. The year 1885 might well become the Year of Kamaherero, Chief of Chiefs . . .

Had it indeed been his final triumph? Osona! There was still the possibility that the power behind Kamaherero might claim the year for himself: Robert Lewis. Why not the Year of Pieter Maritz-Botha?—Or the Year of Kambonde Kampingana?—Or of Will Worthington Jordan?

I was being facetious at my own expense. Better to call it the Year of Otjovanda Tjongue: The Ridge where the Leopard had done its Evil . . .

I stood up. Was there any reason for staying here on my own *werf?* Why did I not go down to the spring as usual? Well, I supposed, I had not yet got over the shock of what had happened at Dabe. Worst of all was my self-consciousness, my painful memory of what had happened . . .

He had rolled up his shirt-sleeve . . . He had shown all who were there the white, inner part of his upper arm . . . The sun had never burnt him there . . . He had shown this to the whole commando . . . Then in a calculated way he had said: 'Here you see the colour of an *opregte witte man* . . .'

That, he added, was more than I, Jordan, could claim. True enough, were I to roll up my shirt-sleeve, the inside part of my upper arm would not be as pale as his. It was tawny, like an old calabash. There was also little difference between the colour of my upper arm on the inside, and that of my face and hands. But it had never worried me. After a hot summer we were all pretty much the same hue, including Piet Botha, unless one wore a *kappie* . . .

The queston nevertheless remained: how had the Dabe incident affected my position in the laager? Well, I quickly decided, I could soon put it to the test . . .

8

At the Lombard *werf* a task force of stout *tantes* had gathered here to assist old Ella and Dina in the wedding preparations. I liked the happy way everything had gone on as usual.

Ella Lombard informed me, almost in confidence: 'We were mindful of the young people's plans. When we got word of the commando's return and saw, too, that the rain was passing, we said: "As the Lord wills it, Saturday we'll have a wedding." When nature burns so strongly, *Meneer*, 'tis better that one hangs one's kettle over one's own *erd*.'

Lisa herself, radiantly busy, looked up from the table where she was rolling out strips of dough.

'*Meneer*,' she said, 'we have heard from the old people that marriage is no horse-buy. Well, it isn't, *Meneer*: you see, a horse must drink in the end from the waters you ride it to. But *Meneer*, we have now chosen our own water. And we'll drink from it! Ma, *Oom* Died need but say the word, and give us his blessing; and off we go, far away!'

'In the new flower wagon?'

'In the flower wagon.'

Dina served me with strong black coffee. I sat there viewing the proceedings. This sausage, pastry and sweetmeat making was reminiscent of the great hippo-fat days up at the Cunene. The stout *tantes* in their print dresses, poke-bonnets and *velaschoens* went bustling about: working, laughing, making sly digs at Lisa who was more than equal to it.

'You see, *Meneer*,' Lisa said, holding her pretty head proudly, 'it is as I told you. There is much ado, and much talk, and we would have been off in a jiffy. But Ma wouldn't have it.'

'For all who may come to wish us good luck, my child, there must be readiness.' There was a choir of support for Ella Lombard from her helpers. What, then, was the consensus of opinion, if days of christening, marriages, funerals went by like any other? Did Lisa not remember how finely things were done when they were up on the Serras?

Lisa threw back her head. That was a long, long time ago, she said. And the world, so she had heard from *Meneer*, turned on its own axis. Things went ahead.

'We must always honour the old days, Lisa, child,' her mother said. 'And the Lord will give us his blessing.'

There was a merry glint in Lisa's eye as she looked at me. I was watching her move lithely and gracefully between the well-fleshed *tantes*, playing each of them in turn like an angler playing his fish. There was a fine self-confidence about her. Was it possible, I thought, to have so much youth, so much faith in life?

Those years we spent up on the Serras . . . They were happy days, for me as well . . . Maybe I had just taken a holiday from myself. Maybe I had just entered willingly into the strange, lost little life of this tight little community in search of Utopia, forgetting what moved deeper, more strongly in me.

Now I began talking, telling about the feast-days of the Serras, in a sudden, piquant mood. Yes, I said, it had been quite a time. I remembered the way a team of choice oxen had been inspanned in front of a Cape cart, adorned with flowers, flags. As many as could got onto the cart with the bridal pair. There was much firing of crackers, rockets, music-making. The marriage would first have to be solemnized before the Portuguese authorities. In most cases Diederick Prinsloo had been the marriage officer. But in 1881 the Reverend Cachet had arrived from the Cape, a sharp-witted cleric with a sense of humour . . .

To me he had said: 'My people here thought they had an eagle; it turned out to be a sparrow. They trust you, Mr Jordan; take them back to where they belong . . .'

Ai Dina and her *confrater* were now engaged in a lively dialogue concerning the merits of the famous cuisinier of Humpata: a strange combination of Bushman legend and *maître d'hôtel*, the inimitable Paadjierol.

This was enough to raise the ire of old Dina, who scolded *Confrater* for being a better-knowing ingrate. He was eating and getting fat on the good food she and Old Miss provided him with having said such things. Kleinveld, whose spare frame hardly bore out the accusation of living too well, withdrew into himself, batting his eyelids against the *erd* smoke.

I nevertheless comforted him by saying that old Roll-Along-the-Path was an artist, no doubt. He could cook and he could sing. I myself had on more than one occasion encountered him on a pathway, loaded with some of the goodies he had had a hand in. He had walked along with a sack over his shoulder, singhing his drunken songs, leaving a zig-zag spoor in the dust.

To all this Jet du Plessis, preparing pastry dough, added that Paadjierol could cut up and 'work' a hippo carcase all on his own. Did *Meneer* remember the time up at the Cunene?

Five years had elapsed. Much had happened. Were we all up there at the Cunene once? . . . Pieter Maritz-Botha had had a narrow escape, trying to get away from the Ombalantu Ovambos . . . And when he had turned up, there had been much rejoicing . . . I, too, had laughed and cracked jokes with him . . . I, too, had thought: 'This is a man after my own heart: free, adventurous, daring . . . We could *do* things together . . .'

'*Meneer* had fever then,' I heard *Tante* Louwrens say.

'I had fever then,' I said, returning to myself.

And Hester Bouwer, newly arriving, set off a lively discussion about the incident with the crocodile. Hester had only managed to do what she did, Jet declared, because she was so strongly limbed. That went for Nellie too, who had the crocodile still hanging on to her leg. Hester, whose baby was due any day now, just smiled and remarked that it was all simply nonsense. Why, Lisa with her 'waspish' figure would certainly have done likewise. Lisa, in her proud little way, said yes, she would have done likewise; perhaps even better. Why, if Nellie had been out in the middle of the river, she would have taken off her clothes and *swum* after her. This shocked the *tantes*, until Lisa's merry laughter eased them again, and they all joined in. However it may be, Jet du Plessis declared firmly, she believed in being well covered. These modern girls seemed to be made of air. Never mind, once they were married, they would soon discover what kept a man happy.

A word of wisdom in this debate was provided by Ella Lombard herself. Now, if one *did* become so stout, she said, that the children had to be asked to tie your shoe-*riempies*,* there was a good remedy: cream of tartar from the baobab tree, with honey. All of this, Dina added, in a bottle of boiling water.

Not every baobab, Kleinveld sagely remarked. It had to be *ripe* fruit from an *old* tree. This, he said, was also good for rheumatism, indigestion, and spots before the eyes . . .

Ah, yes, we were happy here . . . But here, now, I was happy again because of something which could not have been apparent to my company. I was glad and relieved because it seemed as if my new self-consciousness had, after all, been unnecessary. We were

*Laces of hide

sharing memories . . .

'We will just have to keep a sharp look-out,' I said looking up. 'This is our land; and this is our republic. We will love it and look after it. Those that will not share the future with us are better away.'

A thought struck me. 'What has the Widow Roets decided to do?' I asked.

'To wait,' Hester Bouwer replied, 'for a word from Piet Botha; to trek!'

'To where?' Ella Lombard asked.

'Some say the Waterberg,' I replied. 'Some say the Transvaal.'

'And Piet did not go with the commando?' *Tante* Louwrens asked.

'No,' I answered, 'we left him at Dabe.'

All these good women here must surely have heard about Dabe, I decided. Yet, we seemed to be on the same footing as always. Or had they not properly understood what Botha, in fact, had said to me? Would it ultimately yet become apparent, as time went on? Would the issue yet arise crisply as Botha himself repeated his accusations, if they were accusations?

Somebody had brought up Botha's own story of their trek from Humpata in wet weather.

'Johanna said the river was full at Humbe,' Hester Bouwer said. 'So the oxen had to swim.'

'She came through in a *maghor*,'* Ella Lombard said. '*Meneer* will know, Mister Eriksson left a cable up at Humbe with which the wagons could be pulled through the river. Not by the cable; by the oxen, *guided* by the cable.'

'Piet Botha,' *Tante* Louwrens said, 'put his wagon on two of the *maghors,* with a rope around the cable. Johanna was in another *maghor* and the river was flowing strongly. *She* was pulled, against all that angry water. And they say she just sat there in the *maghor*, hands tightly clasped over her eyes. They all pulled and she never stopped praying. When at last she reached the river bank, she said: "Thank you, Lord!"'

Lisa giggled, but I sat wondering.

'Well,' Jet du Plessis remarked, 'Johanna *stood* by Piet; and even when he is wrong, it is good for a woman to *stand* by her man.'

*Dug out canoe.

I caught Lisa's eye and she smiled. Yes, she seemed to say, it is good for a woman to *stand* by her man.

'. . . Like the time,' Ella Lombard said, 'in the days of the Great Trek from the Old Colony. Barend de Lange and his wife . . . They called him Hippo-eye. When the Trek started, she said no, she would not go; she would stay where she was: Barend's wife, whose name was Jacoba. She said her own family was not going to trek, so why should she? Old Barend did not say a word. The day came, and he packed up and inspanned and started greeting all who stayed behind. At last he came to his own wife, Jacoba, and smack!—he kissed her goodbye. Then he climbed on to the *voorkist* and was just about to leave the *werf*, when Jacoba shouted: "Hippo-eye, wait! I'll get onto your wagon!" And she gathered up her dresses and got onto the wagon. And so they trekked away.'

Kappies were nodding gravely. Yes, they seemed to say, a woman should *stand* by her man . . .

I looked at Hester Bouwer. 'I hear that *Meneer* wishes to go to Ovamboland,' she said.

'Maybe I'll have to go,' I said thoughtfully. 'Lewis is probably on his way there by now. What is the news about the Waterberg? Do those who intend leaving still think they can settle there? What does Jan Labuschagne have to say?'

'Jan has many tricks,' *Tante* Louwrens said.

'Many tricks and much wind,' Jet du Plessis added with some force.

'My child,' Ella Lombard sighed, 'there are many kinds of people in this world. It is best to suffer them all: to hear them, and *maar* do as you please.'

This, I reflected, was sound advice. It was quite possible that Ella Lombard was now trying to say something to me: more than what appeared on the surface. If that were the case, well, I was thankful.

In a way I was thankful, too, that the conversation around the trestle tables had switched back to the immediate business of preparing for the wedding. All the arts acquired during a generation of trekking and living off the land had already been employed to a remarkable degree. Veld-fruits like num-num, yellow-apples, toop-toopies, wild grapes, medlars, mupels from the red milkwood, jackal-berries, omuandi: all had been turned into sweetmeats. There was a promise of fine baking and good cooking.

This was Eden, I mused. But wryly I was reminded, once again, of that other Eden we had once shared, up on the Mountains of the Sky at Humpata . . .

'There,' someone had once remarked, 'sweet potatoes came out of the soil as fat as *dassies*.' The hills were full of woodbush, yellow-wood and waterberry. Mare's-teat trees grew to a hundred feet or more. The trees everywhere were fitted with bees' nests made from hollowed out logs. At the time the baobabs bore their great lamp-like flowers; the honey was as white as lard . . .

That was the other Eden. That was the first one; and we had abandoned it . . .

I had abandoned it. I had said farewell to it, because in time I knew the sweet deception of it all. Sooner or later in life one was faced, and in turn had to face, the uncomplicated, immovable fact of things . . .

I had taken the final, momentous, all-risking step of buying, of establishing this land of Upingtonia . . .

Lydensrust some called it . . .

If they preferred it so, I was happy to let them have their way.

9

Sitting there with the *Bestuur* in front of Old Diederick's house, later that afternoon, we somehow seemed to avoid the pressing problems of the moment. The talk was rather about the old things that had always intrigued the laager: the weather, the hunt, births and deaths and states of health. It was as if what had taken place at Dabe had never happened.

'That time I was with Old Hendrik van Zyl,' I heard Barend Bouwer say, 'it was a wonderful thing to get a letter from somewhere. You had no thought *where* such a letter came from. Well now, I remember a day when we were hunting in the Mbukushu area, below Andara. A Bushman arrived carrying a letter in a cleft stick. We were far out in the bush, and sat there arguing about who could have sent the letter, and what was it all about. It was still the time before we met, or even properly knew about, the Trek. When the Bushman was still about a thousand paces off, we could definitely see that he was carrying a letter; so we charged off to meet him. Old Hendrik just sat there in his chair, looking at us with his one good eye, waiting for us to bring him the letter to read. You can well imagine how eager we all were to learn all about it. There we stood laughing and cracking jokes and urging the old chap to open the letter and tell us what it said. Well, as you know, Old Hendrik was not the kind of person to be ordered about. There he just sat, took out his hunting knife—no hurry at all!—and carefully, very carefully, slit open the letter. Then he unfolded it just as carefully, and spread it on his knees. There it lay, while he squinted at it; and carefully, very carefully, he put his hunting knife back into its sheath. He was still adjusting his eye to see better. There we still were to one side, laughing and cracking jokes and telling the old chap that now we *had* to know. Then suddenly—whirr! Can you think what it was?'

I looked up. 'A thermal,' I said, 'a whirlwind.'

'Right you are. A whirlwind. The sort, you know, that picks up the vultures and carries them up, up; so high that they just become specks in the sky. Sometimes even the speck disappears. Well now, what do you think? This time it was not a vulture or a leaf or a tuft of grass which the wind had snatched up and carried into the sky. It was the *letter*!'

Bouwer, his chair creaking under his weight, chuckled.

'The letter, yes. What we did? I tell you, we just stood there open-mouthed, and looked at the piece of paper going up, and up. Old man Hendrik just sat there in his chair, sat and looked up with a tilt of the head, and never said a word. The piece of paper was going up, up. Afterwards it looked like one of the gulls you see at Moçamedes. At length I said: "Well, now it is too high; surely it must come down again!" Now don't you believe it. You know how it is: you look and look at something in the sky. Then suddenly, in an eyewink, it is gone!

'That was the last we saw of it. But *who* wrote that letter? Mester Will, we never found out. The Bushman said it came from a white man whose name was Campbell. His laager was towards sundown, some way below the river.'

'I remember him,' I mused. 'He and his son turned up at the Bay one day. Went hunting in Damaraland, if memory serves. So you never saw them?'

'Never. You will know how disappointed we were. For days we spoke about nothing else but the bad luck which we had had!'

We were there under the trees in front of Old Diederick's house.

The sons—Machiel, Jan Willem—were whitewashing the walls of the little building. For this they used a mixture of silver-white leadwood ash and buttermilk . . .

Old Diederick was lying on his bed in the pleasant dusk of the little room, propped up against some pillows, but fully dressed. Even the olive-wood stick lay alongside him.

Well, I enquired, and how was the President? I poured him a few drops of laudanum in a glass of water. He drank it slowly.

I examined him and found his general condition to be unchanged. The old man was tough: like the long, lean biltong one cut from the carcase of a full grown oryx or kudu. The 'fire' inside would cause him some discomfort; but he would yet keep going . . .

'Take it when the need arises, *Oom*,' I said, putting the bottle down beside him. I sat there talking to him for some while, drinking the coffee *Tante* Prinsloo had brought, telling him of our expedition across the omuramba. Even if we were not as successful as we had hoped, I said, we had, at least, given notice to the world that we were here to stay.

He nodded solemnly. 'Let it be known,' he said at length, that we *are* of one mind—to stay; to *stay*; and *build* our state; and be steadfast. As the Lord wills it.'

As the Lord wills it . . .

I suddenly attached an own private meaning to these words. Perhaps, who could say, I had been affected by my living here in a way I had not yet been able to recognize. I had always viewed things from the periphery of the laager. This reliance on Providence . . . My own experience of the numinous had been fluid, presenting itself at odd unexpected intervals, usually leaving me for a while in a state of quiet elation, trembling, wonder . . . Like that afternoon near the Bay when all existence seemed to sink into an ocean like infinity itself . . . Usually such feelings were soon dispersed in the strenuous activity of the day's trek, the day's work.

Now, after all that had happened, I seemed to be looking at my friends in another light. Strangely, I was now conscious of a certain change in perspective. They were a people who had wandered far through Africa, pursuing their own earthly happiness. Men like Robert Lewis, Caine, and many others regarded them as wanderers, nomads, who had no clear idea who they were, what they wanted, where they were going. A lost tribe chasing a dream . . .

But I, Will Worthington Jordan, had been drawn to them, had taken up their cause as my own. Why exactly had I done this? Was there, in spite of everything, some deep rapport between us? Were they really so different to so many others in history cast in the puritan mould who had attempted to construct for themsleves a Holy Commonwealth, which they, collaborating with Providence, would set up for time and eternity?

Memory stirred deeply, formlessly in me. I knew that my own Anglo-Saxon antecedents had in centuries past been moved in a similar way: to establish as an earthly kingdom the visible evidence of their election, of God's special grace. This, surely, had once taken place in both Old and New England . . . and perhaps proceeded from there in ways beyond our immediate comprehension.

Some day, I decided quietly, sitting here at the bedside of a dying man—that of Old Diederick—President-designate of the Republic of Upingtonia—some day I would explore it all in greater detail, seek to understand it all more fully.

Meanwhile I could but be thankful, could find a certain comfort in the knowledge: my friends were just not the kind to be stampeded into new attitudes by the bad manners of Pieter Maritz-Botha. All the way back to Otjovanda Tjongue the thought had plagued me: would there be a change after what had happened at Dabe? Would my position as leader here be affected? I had struggled on my own with this. Eventually I had found the courage to put it to the test. I had gone out into the laager as if nothing had happened. I had been accepted, so it seemed, as if nobody had ever heard of Dabe. I had feared something different. My fears had been groundless. Secretly I was deeply thankful. And my thankfulness was accompanied by a sense of inadequacy. I lacked so much.

I got up, and wished Old Diederick goodnight. We would see each other in the morning, I said. He raised his hand, smiled slowly, and said, 'Thou doest much for us, *Meneer*.'

For a moment I was silent. Then I nodded abruptly and said: 'Not enough yet, *Oom*. But things will improve. We'll keep the faith. We'll see each other tomorrow!'

Outside, in the gathering dusk, I found Machiel Prinsloo. He had just put the finishing touches to his whitewashing. 'So,' he said, regarding his work, 'if we do such things, then we mean to *stay*, not so?'

I offered him a cigar. 'We mean to stay,' I replied.

'Will Lewis declare war against us?' Jan Prinsloo put the question as if he had been pondering the matter.

'If he does, it makes no difference,' Machiel said. 'We are prepared for what he can bring.'

I looked at Machiel. I remembered how this man and his horse had once been cornered by an angry lioness, with Machiel's gun out of reach. The animal had walked in circles around him for more than an hour. He had stood his ground, and had never allowed his eyes to move off his adversary. The lioness kept up her walk, going round and round. Then at last she had turned and made off into the bush. Asked later why he had not ridden away, Machiel had answered: 'Then my *horse* would have suffered. The lioness would have got *him*.'

'If Lewis wishes to bring an army here, let him bring it,' Willem Prinsloo said. 'We can shoot straight!'

'You realize, of course,' I reflected, 'that it may all take place sooner than we imagine. I have to go to Ovamboland, gentlemen. I don't know whether Lewis is there already. It is reasonable to expect that Piet Botha will also make the journey.'

'Piet has already left,' Louw du Plessis said. 'Piet has gone off to do what we said he should not do.'

This news disturbed me afresh. 'If it's only a matter of the horse,' I said, 'one could ignore it. Piet on his own without a commando? But *is* he on his own?'

'Nobody else trekked with him,' Du Plessis said. 'They are all still here in the vicinity.'

'He's a greater optimist than I have credited him with being,' I said, looking up. 'Let's be thankful for that, at least.'

Chris Leen had joined the company and had sensed the tenor of the discussion.

'When do you want to leave?' he pointedly asked me.

'Monday,' I replied. 'Tomorrow we are to have the wedding. On Sunday we rest. We leave Monday morning early.'

'Who?' Chris asked.

'I'm going on my own,' I suddenly decided. 'Everybody else will be needed here in the laager. Don't think because we never dealt with Gabriel, he does not know what is happening here.'

'How long away then, Mester Will?' Barend Bouwer asked.

'If I can make it, I'll be back within a month,' I answered.

'Meanwhile you burghers can carry on with the fixing of beacons and boundaries for the lands.'

'Brother Barend here has a new name for his farm,' Du Plessis said. I saw a twinkle in his eye. But his beard was pointing towards me.

'It is no longer Dabe. It is—what do you think, Brother Will?'

'Stryfontein!' William Prinsloo announced from the side.

'Stryfontein?' I queried.

'Because that is the place, Mester Will,' Bouwer said, 'where the big *argument* took place.'

I was intrigued. '*Stryfontein*,' I mused. 'The Fountain of the Argument . . .'

I was touched, and smiled. Not because of the renaming of the place, but because I had been told of it in this light-hearted way. This was, in fact, a motion of confidence, such as I had never expected.

'I thank you, my friends,' I said quietly. I looked up and saw them smiling at me. 'Well, it was a big *stry*, of course! However, it is something of the past now. And our work here will continue. I don't wish to conceal anything from you. There is no advantage in illusion. If Upingtonia is to be Fools' paradise, then we had better get out while we still can. Better to know exactly where we stand. Our position remains a precarious one, until we can add to our numbers with the right type of colonist. Meanwhile, we are a small speck of civilization in a huge, still barbarous land. I must endorse what *Oom* Diederick said to me a few minutes ago: "Let it be known to all the world what our manly behaviour is." This should not be difficult for people who have done so much in Africa; and done it with such courage.'

'One can only do one's best,' Du Plessis said.

'If that is the case,' I answered, 'then there is nothing to worry about. We will survive.'

I looked at my company. 'I have some letters to write,' I said. 'By the way, Barend, we'll be needing post, and some provisions. Some wagons will have to go down to the Bay shortly. Would you consider undertaking the journey? As a matter of state? There is the possibility, of course, of having some trouble with Manasse Tjisiseta at Omaruru.' I paused. 'But I'm writing to him. There is no reason why we should not come to terms.'

'We'll trek as we trek,' Barend Bouwer said. 'When must we go?'

'When I come back from Ovamboland,' I thought.

'Never mind, we'll get through,' said Louw du Plessis.

But Willem Prinsloo was of another mind.

'We should stay out of the Bay,' he said again.

Some of the others immediately challenged him on this. I let it pass. Willem Prinsloo had always been unpredictable.

Walking back to my wagon, I thought: No doubt you have a lot to learn still—about everybody here.

10

The early morning sounds of the laager seemed to indicate the festive nature of things. Women were calling to each other from *werf* to *werf*. The children had been sent out to play at an early hour. Even the cattle being taken down to the grazing lands were lowing with particular resonance. There was no lying abed for anybody. Each one seemed to have his set task.

This, I said to myself, was not only the wedding-day of my young friends. It was also, in a way, the celebration of the establishment of the world's youngest and maybe most unusual, republic.

Diederick Prinsloo, ignoring my suggestion that he should rather take things quietly, was the marriage officer. With the bridal pair before him, and reading from Scripture at a special chancel made for the occasion by Dolf Holtzhausen, his voice resounded through the morning freshness.

'And Cush begat Nimrod . . . he began to be a mighty one in the earth . . . He was a *mighty hunter* before the Lord . . . Whether it is said, even as Nimrod the *mighty hunter* before the Lord . . .!'

The crowd solemnly participating in the rites nevertheless smiled. Behind the stern features of Old Diederick one could discern an element of play.

Adriaan, slight but manly, was taking it all in with great seriousness. Next to him stood Lisa, as pretty as I had ever seen her.

The wedding guests, too, had entered into the spirit of it all. When the President announced the psalm to be sung, it was the occasion for extraordinary abandon. The notes pealed through the trees. Even the peculiar nasal keening of the women sounded like the treble notes of organ accompaniment: a contrapuntal pattern between the heavier tones of the men. The very birds seemed to join in, lauding the day in acacias, sycamores, marulas, as I had seldom heard. Men, women and children were dressed for the occasion in the best their *kists* contained. Diederick Prinsloo in a frock coat with cravat, as head of state, was presiding over all as if he had been specially trained for it. The beard, following the contour of the high cheekbones, spread broadly downwards under deeply sunken eyes and a patrician nose.

'. . . And I will give unto thee, and to thy seed *after* thee . . . the *land* wherein thou art a stranger: *all* the land of Canaan, for an everlasting possession; *and I will be their God . . .!'*

I looked at Lisa, so attractive in her simple white dress, topped by a veil of mosquito netting. A sudden proud reserve seemed to have come over the playful girl of yesterday. The bridegroom, alert, ready, dapper, wore a coat of black velvet, a black bow, a black wide-brimmed Portuguese hat balanced neatly on his right arm. I looked at the fair hair, the gun-blue eyes, the tightly closed mouth . . . Adriaan Venter seemed to be saying: 'This is the real start of all the great things I still want to do!'

The marriage rites at last expended themselves. Old Diederick finally announced the young couple to be man and wife. Something seemed to open up in Lisa: a womanliness, I thought, which had always been kept in abeyance. She was smiling, accepting the good wishes of all who were now coming up to them.

Ella Lombard embraced her daughter, kissed her new son-in-law, and wiped away a tear. Then she admonished them both before the others to remember their God, always to do their duty. The young couple stood before her in elation, but also in reverence.

All the others now took the opportunity to wish them well. Lisa's old friends, dressed in their own fineries, embraced her, one by one. Lets Labuschagne pinned a miniature bouquet of the flowers of the tearbush to Adriaan's coat. This caused Jan Labuschagne, her uncle, to shout a warning: 'Mind you don't kiss him, Niece!' At the same time he laid an outsize pumpkin at the feed of the bridal couple: a wedding gift. It was meant to start the farming with: to feed all the children the marriage would produce.

The young people laughed, sprinkled a few kernels of rice over the bridal couple, then made way for the older ones to begin their congratulations. Some did it by handshakes, others by kisses, others by embraces. A few took the opportunity to add their own words of admonishment.

Many more gifts were added to the Labuschagne offering: a finely embroidered cushion; bits of well executed crochet work; a collection of fine feathers; some choice syrups, confitures, veld-fruit chutneys . . . There was also a new bandolier; a coffee pot; a riding whip; a sjambok—to keep the bride in the boat, as Jan Labuschagne described it. There was also a bag of sugar, a box of cutlery, a leather-bound psalter . . .

The Holtzhausens, with Dolf at the head, brought a chair made of Dolfswood. Dina and Kleinveld, emerging from the group of black retainers who were viewing the proceedings, contributed a *lappie*—a piece of embroidered linen. Dina, respendent in a newly starched apron and a matching bonnet, announced that it was meant to cover a tray. The tray, she assured with a wagging finger, would be carried by her, Dina Lombard.

Into all this show of interest and affection, Louw du Plessis then introduced the customary note:

'Let, Lord, Thy blessing
On them fall . . .'

The psalm having been struck up by the single leader-voice grew swiftly in volume. The louries, cocking their tufted heads, listened curiously from the trees, cawing at intervals.

When the singing had finally ceased, I approached my young friends. Adriaan's hand was rough and hard in mine; Lisa's was delicate, but had a firmness of its own. 'Remember,' I said, 'you are the first bridal pair of Upingtonia. Bring our land some of the luck we wish you; and all of your happiness.'

'That we shall do, *Meneer*,' Adriaan promised.

'*Oom* . . .?' This was the first time since she had been a child that Lisa had addressed me thus. I saw her throat tighten.

'Now look!' she said, and folded her bottom lip over the top one.

'Well,' I said light-heartedly, 'it seems as if Lisa is having second thoughts?—Adriaan?'

'Yes,' she blurted out playfully, but also with incipient tears, 'I want to run away from him!'

The tears, which had been held back, came with the laughter. With an endearing movement Lisa took her husband's arm again.

Adriaan, slightly taken aback by these quick changes of mood, held himself erect, looking squarely at me.

'Go carefully,' I cautioned. 'Watch the land. Adriaan, I have put a carton of cartridges in your wagon for you. And for you, Lisa . . .' She looked up at me. 'There is a box with some medicine.'

'*Meneer*,' Adriaan said, 'we are thankful for all you do for us. When it is possible you must come and visit us, *Meneer*, at our water; or wherever we may be.'

The company, comprising almost everybody in the laager except one or two of the old and infirm, retired to Ella Lombard's *werf*. Trestle tables under the trees here had been loaded with goodies. The bustling *tantes* of the previous day were ready for the feast. Soon coffee was being served, with sweetmeats, cakes and pastry to go with it. Dina was offering num-num rolls: delicate twists of goodness, decorated with leaves and flowers. In no time she had to shrug her crooked little shoulders, muttering to herself, displaying an empty wooden bowl to those who had discovered her sweetmeats too late.

The sad violin of Lewies Louwrens struck up from somewhere. The young people sang:

'Seek, my heart, thy long lost friends,
Seek in vain where thou wouldst tarry,
Go then to the wilderness,
Seek them there where they now rest.'

Ella Lombard repeated the old advice: 'And remember, a wagon which is badly loaded will overturn at the first big bump!'

'This is a flower-wagon,' Jet du Plessis reminded us. 'It *may* not bump!'

'If it bumps, *Tante*,' Lisa said, 'then I'll jump off in time!'

There was song, laughter, and much pleasant, carefree talk.

'Now,' Hester Bouwer said, 'you must speak to the *ooms*, Adriaan; that when they come there, they first shoot to let you know that they are on their way.'

'Never mind,' Lisa assured her, 'we'll see them from afar!'

'Especially when it is *Oom* Jan,' Adriaan said. 'For he is taller than any grass can be.' Jan Labuschagne, flattered by this, bayed like a dog.

The wagon, carefully loaded, was already awaiting its owners. Adriaan and Lisa mounted the *voorkist*. The team leader sprang to attention. The driver cracked his longwhip. Kairob, who had been helping to get things ready, waved his hat, calling out the names of oxen.

The wagon moved forward. Soon it was clattering down the stony incline at a fair pace, accompanied by children and dogs.

Swarms of birds were rising out of the trees. A line of Namaqua partridges flew swiftly away to the north-east. This was the route the wagon would take: the flower-wagon, which had come all the way from the Cape, and was now serving its purpose as never before.

Ella Lombard stood watching the departure, not saying a word. After a while, when the joyous tumult around her had subsided somewhat, she looked up and said: 'So we are left with not a child . . .'

The crowd was still throwing veld flowers at the disappearing wagon. The dogs were barking only desultorily.

Ella Lombard blew away her tears into a handkerchief.

'Old Miss,' said Dina, 'this is the way the world is. Don't cry, eh!'

Kleinveld remarked crossly that it was the good right of Old Miss to cry as she wished.

The day had been undappled. Now clouds came drifting down from the north once more. They were like dreamed-up galleons on a sea of sky. Over the laager which had known such light-heartedness these past few days, shadows crept once more.

The frivolity had exhausted man of the oldsters. Most of the people had retired to their respective *werfs*. But the young people were still laughing, playing, singing somewhere. Lewies Louwrens, sadly sawing away at his violin, smiled quickly, obliquely.

I stood surveying the scene. It was still difficult at times to believe that I was part of it all . . .

THE YEAR OF LIES
(November 1885–December 1885)

1

Ten days later I was creeping over the Oshana plain, a day and a half's trek south-east of Olukonda in Ovamboland. The veld was brilliantly green with hip-high grass. The horizon was broken only by the feathery tops of distant makalanis.

By the late afternoon the serried clouds had finally packed together. Darts of lightning were flickering in them. There was water everywhere. Where the makalanis grew next to the lakelets, the landscape had a south-sea air. The year was a propitious one. But I had been in Africa long enough to know that it was at its most unpredictable when it was at its most beautiful.

I was certainly not here to admire the view. I had come to finally put an end to tension, threats, uncertainty. For the proper establishment of Upingtonia it needed at least some measure of security.

So I reminded myself. And yet, the land in its early summer abundance was giving me particular joy. How many times had I followed this road to Ovamboland? It had not always been so pleasant. There had been years of drought, when the blue wildebeest had stood here unmoving, heads drooping, dust-covered. There had been times of flood when the whole of Ovamboland had become an inland sea.

Sometimes I had come up from the Bay via Otavi, Namutoni, Ondangua, then on to Humbe, Lubango, and Moçamedes. Sometimes I had come from Andara on the Okavango; at times from the south again via Otjikondo, Okaukueyo, Okomdeka . . . My oxen could almost do without a driver.

On the 8th November I at last discerned the steep roofs of the mission buildings at Olukonda in the distance. The oxen, too, had sensed the end of the journey. After half a day's trek on the Oshana plain I had discovered a fresh wagon spoor ahead of mine. Was this Lewis? I enquired. Yes, my *bambuse* assured me, it was Lewis.

It was not unexpected. After all, I had undertaken this very journey because I had feared that Lewis would come to see Kambonde. He would do his best to upset the agreement between us. Legally he could not do it. A contract was a contract, even here. But he was still a threat . . .

Another spoor ran alongside that of Lewis. We had found sections of it since we had passed Otavi. This, my servants assured me, was *Baas* Botha. So, Botha, too, had preceded us by three or four days. Coming up on the north-eastern edge of the White Pan, however, we found an *erd* in which the ash was still warm. Botha had left here the previous day. He would arrive at Olukonda a day ahead of us.

The sky was already darkening when we arrived at the mission house. Rautanen, the head of the Finnish Mission in Ovamboland, appeared in the front door with a lamp in his hand and his face spoke a welcome. He gripped my hand and pulled me inside.

'Mister Jordan!' he cried, 'we have been expecting you!'

From inside the house Rautanen's colleagues, Rocha and Weikolin, too, came forward to greet me. We shook hands and clapped each other on the shoulders. Ondonga Ovambos had brought the news that I was on my way, they said. Rautanen looked at me approvingly. 'All sorts of other messages have been arriving here,' he said. 'We heard that you were having some trouble down there at Grootfontein. Is that the name now?'

'That is the name,' I assured him. We spoke English and German, alternating it as it suited us. 'Regarding our troubles . . . They're not so serious, really. Growing pains. Anyway, I am glad to be here.'

We sat in the living room of the mission-house, made comfortable and furnished with a variety of articles brought all the way from Finland. Soon Mrs Rautanen appeared with a tray of coffee. There was another happy renewal of acquaintance.

Ovamboland was having a fine year, I said. I had never seen it looking so kindly. I hoped that the landscape was a reflection of conditions generally.

Things were reasonably quiet, my friends assured me. There was this enmity between Kambonde and his brother. Nehale was doing his best to exploit the sale of the Otavi country to bring

Kambonde into disrepute. But Kambonde was standing up to these onslaughts well enough . . .

What had happened at Osona, I was asked. The news of Hendrik Witbooi's heavy defeat had penetrated to Ovamboland 'How many people did Witbooi lose?'

'We heard that the whole way to Gibeon was marked with dead bodies,' I said. 'Those who had not died of their wounds died of hunger and thirst.'

In turn I was informed that the Hereros had been so impressed by the good services of Dr Goering, Pastor Buettner and others, that the matter of *Schutz* had now become practical politics. I looked up in some surprise. What was the source of this information? Pieter Maritz-Botha, I was immediately told.

This was interesting. Where had he obtained the news? It seemed to point to Robert Lewis. If that were the case, how would he react? *Schutz* would put paid to all his schemes . . .

'Who told Botha this?'

'Viehe of Omaruru,' Rautanen replied. 'Botha saw a letter he had written.'

Stirring my coffee, I reflected: Viehe of Omaruru . . . Should I tell my friends of my true mission; and of all the events which had taken place in the laager? They had a right to know about it. This I then proceeded to do.

'The whole matter rests with Kambonde himself,' I concluded.

'You, Mr Weikolin, you, Mr Rocha, were witnesses to the contract. Lewis wants to ignore this. According to him, the whole business is but a swindle on the part of Will Jordan, and at the expense of Kambonde Kampingana. If you had been at Grootfontein these past few weeks, you would no doubt understand why I feel this way.

'Lewis has threatened war if we do not clear out. If German occupation does in fact come about, we may, presumably, forget about Lewis. But we may have other worries then. How will the Germans establish *Schutz*? Are they going to ship troops to South West Africa?

'. . . Of one thing you can be certain: we have not settled in Upingtonia with the idea of moving on as soon as things begin to get difficult. We are there to stay. I see great possibilities in Upingtonia: not only for our own state, but for the country as a whole. What this country needs more than anything else is an ordered, civilized community, which can serve as a starting point.'

My words made some impression on my friends. Indeed, I reminded myself, there was no reason why all these empty, undeveloped lands could not, in time, support a large and industrious population.

'Come down and pay us a visit some day,' I said. 'The country will appeal to you. There's an abundance of good soil, and good waters! One fountain some way up the omuramba—Okasima, it's called—runs so strongly, you can follow the stream by horseback for more than an hour. When you write back home,' I continued, 'tell the folks we would welcome them as settlers in Upingtonia.'

My Finnish hosts laughed at this, not taking me seriously. 'Thank you for the kind thought,' Rautanen said, 'but will your friends like that? All these strange people coming to their country?'

'The first consideration remains that of a civilized community,' I replied.

Rautanen folded his hands. 'Yes,' he nodded, 'of course. But now it all depends on the Boers themselves, not so?'

'To a certain extent,' I conceded. 'But they are by no means as intractable as people make them out to be.'

'They have trekked far,' Weikolin added. 'And they have suffered much. For their sakes, we wish them every success.'

'All that we ask,' I said, 'is to be left alone; to work out our own salvation. What we also ask, of course, is that solemn agreements be honoured. We have our troubles inside the laager, as I have mentioned. But men like Diederick Prinsloo, Louw du Plessis, Barend Bouwer and others, are steadfast. They are the real leaders of the community.

'If *Schutz* comes,' I continued, 'supported by troops from Germany or not, I cannot see how it will affect our position. We are prepared to enter into any agreement with the German authorities they deem necessary, and we find congenial.'

'By the way,' Rautanen asked, 'is it true about the way the Osona battle started? We heard that Witbooi was sent coffee and sugar by Kamaherero when he arrived at the Swakop with all his people. *That*—but no water!'

'So he and his men went down to the river to fetch the water themselves,' I confirmed. 'It became a shooting match. The moral of the story, of course, is: don't drink coffee!'

We were in a light-hearted mood now. For the next few minutes we were regaling each other with the latest stories about Hendrik

Witbooi. He was no ordinary, freebooting Nama, I explained. He had a Divine Mission—to conquer the land for the Nama people. His Heavenly Orders he wrote down in High Dutch. And then wrote letters to everybody, explaining this.

'How is Hans Schinz?' I enquired.

'. . . has had strange adventures,' said Weikolin.

'You remember when you met him for the first time?' Rocha asked.

'On my way back from Moçamedes. In August.'

'Mister Jordan brought us the first full news of the murder in Ukuanyama of Fathers Delpech and Rothan,' Rautanen reminded his colleagues.

'For a time,' I explained, 'I was regarded with suspicion, even here. I hope it's all over. Neither Delpech, nor Rothan, nor Jordan murdered the king with poisoned *aguardente.* It was the king's own sister, as we all know. Has this knowledge become general in Ovamboland?'

'The important thing about that incident,' Rautanen said, 'is the nature of the Ovambo people themselves. You realize that the whole matter was kept secret from us, until you arrived?'

I considered this for a moment. 'So anything can still happen,' I concluded.

'I told you that Hans Schinz has been having strange adventures,' Weikolin repeated. 'Some time after you left, at the end of September to be exact, a band of Swartbooi-Hottentots carried out a raid here in Ondangua. There was a lot of shooting around the mission station, and we had to lie on the floor most of the time to keep out of the firing line. Well, fortunately the Ondonga proved more than equal for the Swartboois. They fled, leaving two wagons behind.'

'Why the raid?' I queried. 'Or was it just robbery?'

'It concerned the intrigue of one Jifa,' Rautanen explained. 'One of the royal princesses of the house of Ondonga. She had had an argument with Kambonde about the succession of her son to the throne.'

'It seems to be a bad habit up here,' I interjected, 'ambitious mothers wanting thrones for their minor sons!'

'It is not a laughing matter,' Rocha said. 'Jifa was in league with the Swartboois, so it would seem. They came in closed formation. Near Ondangua they were met by Ondonga defectors. They were no match for the Ondongas, however.'

'What about Schinz?'

'Schinz was up somewhere near Ukuambi at the time,' Weikolin said. 'Kambonde sent him a message advising him to return to Ondangua at once. There was no telling what the Swartboois might do.'

'So he arrived here in time?'

'Only just,' said Weikolin. 'There was shooting all round here, as we have told you. The Swartboois were driven back, and Kambonde seized all Jifa's cattle, for her part in the affair.'

'When it was all over,' Rautanen continued, 'the veld here lay full of dead bodies.' He grinned. 'Now, this Hans Schinz is a man such as his slight build would not cause one to suspect. He found a well preserved body of an Ondonga not far from here. He needed this, said he, with a view to his scientific investigation. Rather not, I said, it might cause trouble. No, he would do it and take all responsibility, he said. So, hup! He put the dead Ondonga into a box and brought him here. By this time *we* were part of the plot, I'm afraid . . .'

My three friends looked slightly guilty.

'What Schinz wanted was the skeleton,' Rautanen continued. 'So we worked at it: helped him rub the skeleton with arsenious soap. Then we placed the skeleton—in the box again—on top of Schinz's wagon to dry in the sun. Alas, a thermal sprang up one day, came waltzing over the plain. The wind struck the wagon and—boom! Down came the box, skeleton and all. It so happened that some Ondongas were standing nearby. When they saw all those white bones lying in the grass, they fled, screaming. We did our best to try and explain what had really happened; but I'm afraid it was too late.'

'So the Professor has now become a sorcerer in the eyes of our black friends,' Weikolin added.

'Which might well have its advantages,' I remarked. 'Where is Schinz at the moment?'

'Botanizing in the upper Ondonga area,' Rocha replied. 'But he may be here tomorrow.'

Rautanen refilled our coffee cups.

'His idea was to trek to the Okavango,' he said, 'then to follow its course down to Lake Ngami. Now, however, he has had all sorts of difficulties with his servants. There is only the Herero, Michiel, assisting him at present. He has therefore decided to spend the rest of the rainy season here in Ovamboland, and to record as much as he can: botanically, geologically, anthropologically speaking. We built a room for him down there near the big fountain. He is usually up very early in the morning, and goes out to look for his specimens. After that he arrives here at the Mission house for *Frühstück*. Then I teach him the Oshindongo language for an hour or two. At the same time I see whether I can analyse some more of the grammar.'

Hans Schinz, I reflected, was the sort of man I could happily spend a holiday with alone, somewhere in virgin bushveld. Andersson had been a Swede, like Axel Eriksson. Alexander Green, Galton and the Chapmans had been Englishmen. Hugo Hahn, Rath, Diehl, Brincker and others like them were Germans. Hans Schinz was a Swizz from Zürich . . . The strange thing, I decided, was that the best pioneers were invariably men with a European background, in love with this country . . . I had only met Schinz for a few hours after my return from Moçamedes in August. It was enough, however, to make me decide that we had many common interests. What appealed to me in Schinz was what appealed to me in Charles John Andersson and Axel Eriksson: he was uncompromising, in the best sense of the word. He was also human.

Here was a man who had already distinguished himself in the fields of enthnography, philology, botany. A wild thought struck me: what if *he* could join us in Upingtonia? Was it really so unimaginable?

Hans Schinz had already been in South West Africa for more than two years. He had travelled the country. Obviously it had appealed to him. If a man of the stature of Charles John Andersson had found this a field for his most creative talents, it was not impossible that Hans Schinz could do likewise. As an adviser he could be of inestimable value.

I had to see Schinz again. Whatever his future plans might be, I needed his views on Kambonde Kampingana. It was reasonable to assume that he had by this time formed a shrewd idea of what was really taking place here in Ovamboland. Kambonde was, whichever way one looked at it, still a relatively young man, with limited experience. It had also to be faced that he suffered from the same illusions as any other tribal chief in a position of power. When approached from the right angle, Kambonde was tractable and positive; but I also knew his fickleness.

'Kambonde was angry with Schinz,' Rocha said, 'because he

refused to give him everything he asked for. Afterwards Kambonde ordered him to quit the country. The Professor could not trek, however, because his servants had absconded. Neither did he have any draught-oxen left. Then, one day, he was visited by a number of black warriors who told him to leave at once. Schinz refused. Somehow his courage impressed the Ovambos. Well, he is *still* around!'

'What happened,' Rautanen explained, 'was that Kambonde demanded a great amount of lead and powder for a hunting expedition. Schinz refused to give it. The hunting was not so successful and Kambonde put the blame on Schinz. Then the soldiers came to Schinz's place!'

'Right into his room,' Weikolin added. 'I take my hat off to Schinz. You know what he did? He said: "Let the eldest among you take what he wants, according to the custom of the land." At the same time he held his gun at the ready. Well, the eldest just never came!'

The mood in which all this was being told to me was still reasonably light-hearted. At the same time I experienced a new touch of anxiety. The contract between Kambonde and myself had been witnessed by these very people. If Kambonde had been prepared to intimidate a man like Hans Schinz on the property of the mission . . .

I checked myself. Kambonde and I had always been friends, I decided. I would know how to deal with him. One had to make allowances for him. He was young and impulsive; but he would mature . . .

'Well,' Rautanen said, 'finally we made our peace with Kambonde. Now, I am happy to relate, Schinz is no longer plagued by all this begging.' This put my mind at rest again.

Mrs Rautanen, a fine woman, Swedish in looks, appeared once more and requested me to examine her youngest child. It was possibly fever, she said. The difficulty was to get a child to swallow quinine, she said.

We walked to the bedroom where the young patient lay. He had fever, yes. What could we do? It was a real problem. I had been faced with this difficulty in the old days when the Trek was at Olifants Pan. To disguise quinine with sugar or mik was no easy matter.

The direct approach, I decided, was still the best. We administered the quinine through the corner of the mouth, almost as one would do to a sick puppy. Somewhat to my own surprise, the child swallowed the medicine, spluttering slightly. After having had some hot milk, he was soon asleep.

'Please come and stay with us,' Mrs Rautanen said graciously when I took my leave. 'Our home is open to you.'

We were standing at the garden gate of the mission house, when the dogs started barking. Dimly we could discern the crack of a whip and the shouts of a driver. Rautanen walked to a group of makalanis and peered into the moonlit distance.

'The Professor!' he stated, after a minute had passed. It could also be Lewis, I thought.

What uncertainty there was, however, was resolved as the shape of the wagon-and-team materialized out of the darkness. It was Schinz all right. Confirmation came a moment later in the form of his voice over some distance announcing his arrival. Soon we were greeting each other like old friends. Then it was back to the mission house again, where more coffee was waiting, now accompanied by fresh bread and butter, and a bowl of umuandi plums. Our Swiss friend was eager to hear about all that was taking place. The news of my coming was everywhere, he said. But he had also heard that Robert Lewis had sent a message to Kambonde Kampingana that he would visit him at Ondangua the next day.

I considered this. Should this be the case, I eventually replied, then I would have to arrange my own meeting with Kambonde, possibly also for the next day. Lewis would certainly not have it all his own way. I had the right to be present at any discussions Lewis might want about the contract.

Correct, Schinz affirmed. And if there was any way in which he could be of assistance to us, he would be only too pleased to help.

'When do you propose going?' Rautanen asked.

'I want to get this thing cleared up, once and for all,' I stated. 'At the same time, I certainly don't intend racing Lewis to get to the king's kraal first. I can wait until Monday.'

Kambonde, my friends assured me, was astute enough not to be rushed into any quick decisions to suit Lewis. And he was still a friend of Upingtonia.

This heartened me and 'By the way,' I said, 'it may be a good idea to have you with us, Dr Schinz, if you can attend our palaver. Of course, Mr Rautanen here will accompany us. I take it he will keep the minutes.'

'What about Lewis?' Rautanen asked.

'Lewis can get there as he likes,' I said. 'We can expect him to turn up, whatever his plans. We have nothing to hide. Better we all go together. That leaves less room for arguments later on as to what happened, or did not happen.'

'Kambonde is shrewd enough,' Schniz said again. 'Lewis will have to watch out, or he may get caught.'

It rained again that night. I lay awake, listening to the great drops splashing down on the canvas. Too many things were still nervously active in me. Afterwards I sat up with a lamp at my elbow, writing up my journal:

I reached Olukonda at sunset. Mr Pieter Maritz-Botha had arrived the previous day and is laagering somewhere nearby. The news has come that Mr Robert Lewis intends having an interview with King Kambonde Kampingana tomorrow. It seems as if the dispute regarding the ownership of the Otavi country will now finally be settled. I am satisfied that I can rely on the king. Men of integrity signed the contract of sale between myself and the king, entered into on the 21st day of April, 1884. They were Messrs Weikolin, Hakala and Rocha. These gentlemen will all be able to testify to the legality of the agreement. It is to be hoped that the next few days will finalize matters for the state of Upingtonia.

I am eager to return to the laager at Grootfontein (Otjovanda Tjongue) as soon as possible. The various lands have not as yet been fully surveyed. Many allocations have still to be made. What Upingtonia needs is people of the right kind. We hope that settlers of British, German and Colonial stock will come to Upingtonia within the next few years. With the Trekboers as a nucleus, and good relationships with the various peoples of the country, growth may be assured. With reasonable support by those European Powers with interests here, we might well see the realization of a long existing ideal: a truly civilized community in a land too long neglected . . .

I laid down my pen while a thought occurred to me: why not see Kambonde before even Lewis could get there? The idea excited me for a minute. This would be bad diplomacy, I decided. It was wise not to give a tribal chief the impression that you were eager for his favours.

Swinging my legs off the *katel*, I pulled on my boots and clambered out of the wagon. What was now indicated was coffee, I decided. My servant had already interpreted my movements, however, and was crawling out of his trench by the fire-side. Soon the flames were, once again, licking the sides of the little black kettle.

'Almost daybreak, *Bambuse*,' I noticed. He clicked in agreement, and looked towards the east, where the morning star was suspended like a dew-drop. The Bergdamara, Kairob, had also by this time shaken off his sleep and came squatting next to the fire, bare as at the moment of his birth.

'*Mo-le*!'* he grunted with his open hands turned towards the flames.

2

I did not know about Botha. The thought that he was in the vicinity worried me. I could see his laager a mile and a half to the south-east, on the level grass plain. Thinking of using my binoculars to see what was going on down there, I decided against it: I could see well enough what he was doing. He was spending most of the time in his wagon. But sometimes I saw him walk over to the mission house at Olukonda.

'I know all about him,' I thought wryly, 'and he knows all about me. Yet we probably won't meet. We are worlds apart.'

By ten o'clock that Saturday morning, Izak came to tell me that Lewis had arrived. I walked around my wagon to see whether he had joined Botha in his laager. I could see no one, however, and returned to my folding-chair. There I sat, smoking, thinking, acutely aware of the delicate balance of things.

My hand seemed to be shaking. Had I lost self-confidence? It could well have been another bout of fever. I had been conscious of the aura of it during the past few days. It could well have been the weather. I had never reacted well to humidity. The days were sticky, and one was in a continual sweat.

Or were these all attempts to rationalize my own secret fears? Surely there was no need for it. I had a cause to serve. It was an honourable cause, because it was not confined to me personally, but affected others. This did not mean the Trekboers only. This meant all who believed that this was a worthwhile country; that they could find a future here.

*Morning!

Lewis left his laager after about an hour and took the road to Ondangua. I was again left in some doubt. Perhaps I should have been there at Kambonde's kraal by now. It was quite possible that Lewis could spin him a yarn about the cattle stolen by Gabriel and the failure of our commando to bring any back. On the other hand, what certainty was there that Kambonde would receive Lewis? After all, it was common knowledge that Lewis was Kamaherero's confidant, his 'High Commissioner'.

The day passed all too slowly. What made it bearable was a visit to the mission house again. Our friend from Zürich had built up a remarkable collection of botanical, geological and other specimens: Schinziana, I dubbed them.

One could listen to Schinz. He already knew more about the country than the great majority of the 'authorities'. Of the Ovaherero he said: 'They have burnt their land in the Holy Fire.' It was true. For some square miles around each Herero *werf*, every single omumborombonga had been cut down. The Fire had to burn for ever. Should the Fire die, the nation, too, would die. But the price of the Eternal Fire was also the life of the nation . . .

I pondered this. For our own situation it seemed to hold some meaning, the content of which still escaped me.

'Well now, *Herr* Jordan,' Schinz inquired, 'what about *Schutz*? Do you favour it?'

'If *Schutz* can put an end to the general free-for-all in this country,' I replied, 'then, by all means, let it come. I dare say we of Upingtonia could come to some agreement with the Germans. Whether they are really serious about it all remains to be seen. And whether a *Pax Germanica* would be acceptable to Lewis and Co is another matter. Neither should the *Reich* underestimate his—Lewis's—capabilities.'

It was a fact, I added, that Kamaherero had given hs 'Prime Minister' the complete mineral rights of all Damaraland for a period of twenty years. He had even stipulated that Lewis had the right to protect these interests with 'white troops'.

'But where would these come from?' I asked. 'Anyway, Lewis has every intention of hanging on to whatever he's got; or thinks he's got. His mineral rights, of course, according to him, include those of the Otavi mine and whatever else is to be found in the Upingtonia territory.'

'Kamaherero is then giving mineral rights to Mr Lewis and at the same time thinking about *Schutz*?'

I shrugged my shoulders. 'Such is the country,' I said. 'And such is the justification for Upingtonia, if you like.'

He considered this, then nodded approval. 'And good luck to you, *Herr* Jordan. *Wer immer strebend sich bemüht/den können wir erlösen** . . . *Nicht?*' That was one way of putting it.

That same afternoon I ran into Pieter Maritz-Botha, unexpectedly. We met each other at the entrance gate just as I was leaving the mission house. For a moment or two there was a comic attempt to avoid a collision. Then we stood looking at each other.

'What's the news about the horse?' I asked. I was surprised at my own question. I had put it hastily, for lack of anything better.

'You ought to know!'

His face was in deep shadow because the light was bad and he wore a hat. I could note the tension in his voice.

'What do you mean?' I asked, suddenly more at ease. 'How should I know?'

'You have done enough damage, Jordan. Let it be!'

I was puzzled.

' . . . You knew well how to put obstacles in my way. I could have expected it from one like you.'

'What do you mean, Botha?' I asked. 'What are you referring to, specifically?'

'You know very well that you went and told Kambonde that I had a plan to invade his country!'

It was suddenly laughable. 'For heaven's sake,' I exclaimed. 'Where did you get this information? I have no idea what you are talking about.'

'And if Kambonde had been able to carry out his murder-plan, the blood of innocent people would have been on *your* head!'

This was something new on the part of Pieter Maritz-Botha, I thought: this air of injured innocence.

'Do you really wish to imply that *I* . . .' (I pointed to myself) ' . . . have been instigating Kambonde to murder *you*? My God, you must be mad! I don't know who told you this, but to believe such bloody tripe needs more than just imagination!'

'You told Kambonde I had such a plan!'

'Who told you this bit of fiction? Lewis, probably! So, that is the story he brought back to you from Kambonde Kampingana!'

'Kambonde won't see me. Why not?'

*Goethe: *Faust* I.

'That's a question *you* have to answer yourself, old chap. Don't expect me to do it for you. As far as I know, you discussed that scheme of yours to bring a commando here to Ovamboland quite freely with a number of people. If the news has got about, don't blame me.'

'This is treachery!'

I stared at him. Was this man in his right senses? Treachery! The effrontery had almost taken my breath away.

'Listen,' I said, 'in the first place: I have seen nobody here in Ovamboland since my arrival but my friends of the mission, and Dr Schinz. Get this clear: I have lost all interest in your personal matters. How do you think I could have got to see Kambonde since my arrival? You just don't go over and chat to him. At least, I don't. Do you imagine I have some sort of secret service informing Kambonde of the latest developments? Apart from anything else, with what right do you use the word "treachery"? You do not acknowledge me as belonging to your *witte bloed*—white blood—so presumably there is no reason to be particularly loyal to you. That idea of yours was completely daft; but in any event, I decided that it was your own funeral, and you were free to arrange it.'

'You're abusive!'

'Maybe I am. But you need some abuse, Piet. You need to hear the truth. Whether I convince you or not, what I have said is on record. Leave it at that. I repeat: *I have not yet seen Kambonde Kampingana, and I have sent him no messages.*'

'Even the headmen refuse to greet me. But one of Kambonde's advisers told Lewis that he, Kambonde, had a plan to murder me, so I had better get out of Ovamboland. All right, so now I'm leaving. I'm going back to the Transvaal; and others are coming with me. Everybody there at Grootfontein will yet do the same.'

I was having some difficulty in interpreting his attitude. There was just the suggestion that he was moved by something. Was it the loss of the horse? Was it an injury to his pride? Could it possibly be that he, too, was grieved by what had happened?

'So you think you can explain to Kambonde,' he said, 'why he did not get his cattle back?'

He was switching from one point to another, trying to provoke me.

'I have no intention of explaining anything,' I said. 'Why don't you stick to the true issue? I have been accused by you of treachery, of instigating murder, of doing all sorts of evil! How and when did I do these things? Come along, let's go inside and talk to men like Rautanen and Schinz. If there is any doubt about their answers, you win!'

For a moment this seemed to make an impression on him. He stood looking at me. Then his mouth shut. He adjusted his hat, turned about and walked away. I stood watching him in despair. For a while I still heard the dull thud of his footsteps.

I supposed I could have made an appeal to him once more. I could have said something like: 'Is there any sense in all this bickering? I still think we can work together for the good of Upingtonia, for the good of this country as a whole.' I might even have said: 'You have decided to return to the Transvaal via the Thirstland. We are sorry about this, but we wish you a good journey. Perhaps we shall see things in a better perspective, in time . . !'

I did not say this. I stood there at the gate where we had met, listening to the crickets and a dog barking.

Once more, faintly, where the pathway passed some makalanis, I could see the shape of the man who had once been to me like a brother: the brother I had never had.

Then he disappeared. I never saw him again.

3

Shortly after sunrise the next morning I went on horseback to the royal kraal at Ondangua.

I found Rautanen, Schinz, and their servants, already there, resting under a giant diospyros. The arrangement was that Rautanen would take the minutes. Lewis could also be present if he so wished, I had said. It was necessary, in fact, that he be present so that things could be put beyond all doubt. All this loose chatter about what had happened between Kambonde Kampingana and Will Jordan would now be resolved. I was sick of it all.

It afforded me some satisfaction that Lewis had vainly tried to see Kambonde Kampingana the previous Saturday. According to Rautanen, Kambonde had informed Lewis that he could only see him with his own missionary in attendance. Lewis had tried to argue about this, but the king was adamant. This at least was something to be thankful for.

'What does Lewis intend doing?' I asked, dismounting. 'Where is he?'

'Right behind you,' replied Rautanen.

So it was. He, too, had just arrived. He went around, greeting each of us by hand, lifting his topee with the red scarf ceremoniously.

'So you have arrived,' he said to me. We shook hands.

For some time we stood there, making small talk. Rautanen and Schinz kept up a lively commentary on the state of the weather, the difficulties of travelling, the complete absence of stones in Ovamboland.

'I understand you are accompanying us to King Kambonde?' I asked.

'Not if I am intruding, Sir!'

'Don't be silly. Mr Rautanen here has obliged to keep the minutes. He will also interpret. Dr Schinz will assist generally.'

Two royal counsellors approached and there was an exchange of greetings. The king was now ready to receive us, we were informed. Mr Rautanen was required to be present, please. Yes, we were ready, I replied. Mr Rautanen would accompany us.

Behind me I heard Lewis mumbling something about Rautanen having been available during the week-end. I took this to indicate that he was by no means happy about matters. Probably he had thought that he would be able to see Kambonde on his own.

Half an hour later we entered the kraal, the usual strangely palisaded labyrinth of all royal Ovambo kraals, with the counsellors leading the way. We marched in single file behind them through a series of narrow passageways, formed by long stakes driven in to the sand. Gradually we penetrated deeper and deeper into the complex until eventually the *sanctus sanctorum* was reached.

I knew the ritual; I had already been here on a number of occasions. Sitting on a variety of stools, we had to wait patiently for the appearance of the king. Usually he was in no hurry. This, I conceded, was his good right. After all, in his own country, and especially in his own sanctuary, he was supreme. Besides, patience paid good dividends. Tribal potentates were quite tractable, as long as one realized that they were human. They loved their own egos.

When the king ultimately arrived, he was accompanied by still more counsellors, and a servant bearing a pot of *mahongo*. The king, not noticing our presence, took his seat on a heavy tamboti chair. The counsellors and the servant wore tribal dress, but Kambonde himself was sporting a linen jacket of European origin, decorated with the gaudiest of kerchiefs.

I looked at the king, confirming my own earlier conclusions: he was about twenty-five, athletically built, with a face showing a certain refinement, but with restless eyes.

At last he 'saw' us, and the customary greetings took place. Rautanen, taking the lead, enquired after His Majesty's health. The king in turn asked what gifts had been brought. The gifts, I replied, were powder, lead, and a new coat. Lewis, not to be outdone, announced similar offers.

A servant had brought all these articles in and they were placed at the king's feet. Looking at them somewhat critically, he asked to be handed the coat. This—a Norfolk jacket—seemed to please him. Thereupon he indicated that we could go ahead.

The purpose of this visit, Rautanen explained in Oshindongo, was to discuss the contract of sale between the king and Mr Jordan. Meanwhile the servant had poured the *mahongo* into wooden bowls and served us with the drink. It was thin and refreshing.

Rautanen rounded off his introduction, and looked at me to add something. It was Lewis, however, who seized the opportunity. 'Please ask the king,' he said, 'whether I may address him.' Rautanen in turn waited for my reaction. I gestured somewhat impatiently that Lewis could go ahead. Schinz smiled broadly. In his usual pompous way Lewis proceeded: 'No doubt,' he said 'your Majesty already has an idea what the purpose of this discussion may be.'

Rautanen, whose knowledge of English was very limited, was nevertheless managing well enough with the translation, with me offering assistance at times, all to Lewis's obvious annoyance.

He had been specially delegated, Lewis weightily explained, by His Majesty Kamaherero, King of Damaraland, to come and have these talks with His Majesty Kambonde Kampingana, King of Ovamboland, concerning the alleged sale of the district of Otavi, where the copper mines were situated. Had this territory in fact been sold to Jordan?

The answer, through Rautanen, came at once. Indeed, yes, the area in question *had* been sold to Mr Jordan. The people of the mission—Messrs Hakala, Rocha and Weikolin—who were not present at this meeting had witnessed the deed.

At this stage I felt myself compelled to produce the relevant document. This I handed to Rautanen, who, in turn, presented it to the king. Kambonde scrutinized it with a deep frown, then handed it to his counsellors, who likewise studied it carefully, palpably not being able to read it. Thereupon they handed it back to Rautanen who gave it to Lewis. 'Tell the king,' Lewis interposed, 'that I am not here to dispute the fact that this document was indeed drawn up and signed by the parties concerned. The district of Otavi, however, has always belonged to the Ovaherero. Granted, your Majesty and counsellors have in all probability been under the *bona fide* impression that this area was part of Ondangua. I would be failing in my duty, however, if I did not remind your Majesty that the old adage is still the proper guide: where Herero cattle have grazed, *there* is Hereroland.'

I was finding it difficult to conceal my chagrin. It was the old story, I breathed to myself. All the evidence pointed to Kambonde Kampingana's ownership. I watched the king closely: Lewis was still enlarging on his claim, with Rautanen interpreting as best he could. At regular intervals Kambonde would thump his thighs in disagreement, at the same time shake his head vigorously. No, no, no, he then forcefully interrupted Lewis, not true! The Ondonga tribe through their rightful king were the true owners of the territory. Impatiently he signalled that Lewis had said enough. Thereupon he started a voluble palaver with his counsellors. The Bushmen, I gathered from this excited discussion in Oshindongo, were *his*, Kambonde Kampingana's subjects. The *Bushmen* had dug the copper and had regularly carried this as tribute to his kraal. This they had done for generations . . .

We sat there listening, at times sipping *mahongo*—mainly, I supposed, as a gesture of politeness—then again consulting each other in low voices. After about twenty minutes of too-fluent discussion with his counsellors, the king indicated that Rautanen could continue. Rautanen, however, looked to me: did *I* now wish to say anything?

I took the opportunity. It was quite clear, I said, that the whole matter turned on the ancient ownership of the Otavi territory. By the way, I interrupted myself, I wished to apologize to the king and the people of Ondangua that the Upingtonia commando had been unable to bring back the cattle stolen by Gabriel. The copious rains, however, had made matters very difficult. There had also been some delay in setting out: some members of the laager were in disagreement regarding the procedure. Nevertheless, the king could rest assured, we would yet catch up with the robbers . . .

I returned to the claims as stated by Lewis. Kamaherero, I said, was claiming the Otavi territory on the grounds that the Ovaherero had grazed cattle there and had also mined the copper ore. But had there really been this occupation? After all, one had only to remember that the Herero, who had been living in the south for the past century and a half, had never had an own word for *copper*. They simply provided the English word with an Otjiherero prefix, making it *otjikoporo* or *ongoporo*. In the Ovambo dialects, however, the ore of Otavi had always been known as *uueyendye* . . .

Deep noises from the king and his counsellors indicated that they were in full agreement with this philological deduction. I was heartened.

In any event, I continued, the Bushmen had been digging ore at the Otavi site since time immemorial. In fact, the families of headmen had traditionally used this copper to make foot-rings for their wives. The Bushman copper-miners had always lived in the vicinity of Okambuti. As such, they acknowledged only one chief: Kambonde Kampingana . . .

'And the Ovaherero lived at Otjovanda Tjongue,' Lewis, with a note of triumph in his voice, interjected. 'What answer do you have to that, Sir? After all, it is an Otjiherero name!'

'That might well be so,' I replied, 'but it proves nothing. If Herero cattle have grazed in the country surrounding the Otavi fountain, including Otjovanda Tjongue, it happened a long time ago, and has long since been proscribed. Ovambo hunters, in fact, have been operating there for generations.' This Lewis dismissed with an impatient gesture of the hand.

The early explorers, I nevertheless continued, like Sir Francis Galton and Charles John Andersson, could bear me out. By 1851 Galton and Andersson had penetrated as far north as Ondangua, but had found no Herero cattle north of Okambati. Their records testified to this. Galton had stated specifically that what cattle he found in the disputed area had belonged to one Tjapupa, who was a subject of king Naugolo of Ondangua.

Oh yes, Kambonde interposed, after quickly consulting

Rautanen, he knew all about the visit by this man Galton. Why, as a child he had been present when Galton had once visited the royal kraal . . .

It was also shortly after that visit, the counsellor Aramaomo confirmed, that the Ovaherero had withdrawn to the south again. His father had told him all about that. And since that day no Ovaherero had ever come further north than the sandstone wall of Otjozondjupa in the Waterberg. This was common knowledge, surely? The counsellor looked to the king for agreement; and the king nodded assent. So it had happened, he then added to the counsellor's observation; further referring, somewhat out of context, I thought, to claims by his brother Nehale to the throne, something which was equally spurious . . .

A moment of quiet fell over the company. I looked at Lewis, who was still smiling to himself, implying that he accepted nothing of what had been said by any of us.

'Whatever the claims of the Ovaherero to Otjovanda Tjongue may be,' I repeated, 'whatever they once might have been, they have no basis in law any longer.'

But there was something else, I continued. It concerned the arrival of the Ovaherero in South West Africa during the seventeenth century, according to tradition. Originally they had settled in the Kaoko and had then clashed with the Ogandjera of Ovamboland. In the Kaoko, however, the Ovaherero had had just as much trouble with the Bergdamaras: so much so, in fact, that they had moved to the south in the twenties of the present century. It was then that the subjection of the Nama peoples had started. In 1851, however, the Namas, led by the formidable Jonker Afrikaander, had turned the tables and had subjected the Ovaherero. So indisputably was this the case that when Jonker had visited Ovamboland in 1852, he had brought a herdsman who was a son of Chief Tjamuaha with him. Today he was widely known as the Paramount Chief of Damaraland, Kamaherero . . .

From the corner of my eye I watched Rautanen's reaction to all this. He was smiling slightly, thereby signifying his agreement largely with what I had said. Lewis, however, was drawing at his cigar and eyeing me with some contempt.

So it was, I confirmed: the young herdsman in the employ of Jonker Afrikaander later became the present king of the Ovaherero. Tradition had it that Jonker required him to approach him on all fours, never allowing him to turn his back on his master.

'This is scandalous,' Lewis suddenly blurted out. 'What do you pretend to establish, Sir?'

'I am not relating this to score easy points off Kamaherero,' I rejoined. 'I only wish to remind all of us here that the Ovaherero were, until fairly recently, a subservient people. It was only in 1863 that they were at last able to throw off the Nama yoke. This they did with the assistance of Charles John Andersson and Fred Green. It nevertheless took a further seven years to become completely free. The question now is: what substance can there be in Kamaherero's claim that he and his people had always held sovereignty in the Otavi district? Remember that when Dr Palgrave as Special Commissioner from the Cape Colony was here in 1876 he asked Kamaherero to describe the boundaries of his country to him. This he was unable to do. Mister Lewis here, however, has had no difficulties in defining them: according to him the boundaries of Damaraland ran from the mouth of the Cunene river to Rietfontein in the east.'

Lewis was busy sorting all this out for himself. 'You shall have your answer, Jordan,' he said, without looking at me. 'All in good time.'

'It is King Kambonde who is entitled to an answer,' I replied.

'Oh, he shall have it as well!'

'Were there any real substance in these claims of Kamaherero and his agent,' I said to our Ovambo hosts, 'it would mean that tribes like the Ondonga and the Oruandunili would become subservient to the Ovaherero. Why, even the Ogandjera and the Onguambi would lose a substantial part of their ancestral lands: that to a nation which has only enjoyed its own sovereignty for the past fifteen years or so.'

Lewis was still largely unaffected by what I had said. 'We shall see, we shall see . . .' he kept muttering. Turning to Rautanen he asked: 'Would His Majesty be able to tell me exactly where the boundaries of the tract of land sold to Jordan and Co run?'

'If you consult the deed of sale,' I answered for Rautanen, 'you will find a complete list of the names of places within our territory.'

'Why don't you let the king himself answer, Jordan?' he immediately came back.

'All right,' I said, 'let the king himself inform you—if you can't read properly for yourself.'

This was a dig, of course, at his relative illiteracy. I had not been able to withstand the temptation.

It was unbearably close now, here in this inner sanctuary of the kraal. Between the high-palisaded walls the air hardly moved. The king, shiny with sweat, kept mopping his face. The atmosphere was thick with humidity, sticky with the strong body odour of bare torsos.

I longed for the cool evening wind which moved over the plains of Ovamboland in a year like the present. I longed to stand in it, to take off my shirt and feel the wetness fold around me with tenderness. Fever was always in my blood . . .

I had nothing more to add to what I had said. Lewis, too, had had his say. But the discussion still continued between Rautanen and Kambonde, between Kambonde and his counsellors. They listened to the king, and approved. Then Kambonde signed to Rautanen to interpret.

'I, Paramount Chief of the Ondonga tribe of the Ovambo nation,' he stated, make it known to all here today: for generations we have been the owners of the land I sold to Mr Jordan on the twenty-first of April. I also make known that the Bushmen at present living there are my subjects. Since time immemorial they have been paying tribute to us in the form of ivory, feathers and copper ore. I also wish to say that all the firearms still in possession of the Bushmen came from me. They are still my property.'

Rautanen put a question, and Kambonde replied:

'It has been asked what are the boundaries of the area. Our answer is: the names of the places as they appear in the contract of sale in possession of Mr Jordan. We can do with those places what we wish to do. All the waters south of these places belong to the Ovaherero.'

Kambonde having addressed Rautanen, now turned to Lewis. 'Tell Kamaherero that he knows very well what my rights are,' he said. 'That land has always belonged to us. What has not been sold still belongs to us.'

It seemed as if this had apparently got through to Lewis. He arose, shook his head, and turned to Rautanen.

'I don't see the point in pursuing this matter here any further,' he said. 'However, this does not dispose of it either. I shall have to consult my principal. Then, you may rest assured, you will be hearing from us again.'

The man was a stickler, I thought. One had to grant him this. I despised his methods, but he was tough and shrewd. We would be hearing more from him . . . Indeed, I believed he would be as good as his word. But after all, was there any point in all this argument here? Lewis was irrelevant now. The matter was between Kambonde and Upingtonia.

The thickness of the air, the subtle glow of fever, the sheer pressure of human beings in an area far too confined for their numbers, suddenly became too much. I wanted to return to my laager. Kambonde had ratified the agreement of 21 April. That was all that really mattered; and Lewis knew it.

Raising my arm to the king, I said to Rautanen: 'Please tell His Majesty that we are thankful that matters have been cleared up. The state of Upingtonia seeks to live in friendship with the Ondonga tribe and with Ovamboland. We greet you.' Kambonde and his counsellor returned my salute.

We departed. It was a great relief to escape out of the intricate maze of passageways. The brilliance of the noon sky was overpowering. I had to shade my eyes.

The servants had made coffee for us under the giant diospyros. I swallowed it black, and relished it. The *mahongo* we had drunk still seemed to stick to my palate.

Lewis was uncommunicative. He accepted our hospitality but avoided any comment on what had transpired at the kraal. He still seemed to have all sorts of tricks up his sleeve. Obviously he wished to keep us guessing.

'We'll have another chat, Jordan,' he said darkly, finishing his coffee. 'I'll be moving along now. Good day to you all!'

4

I swallowed some quinine and relaxed on the *katel* in my wagon. I felt exhausted. To fall ill here in Ovamboland might well prove disastrous. I had to return to Otjovanda Tjongue. There was much to be done.

Barend Bouwer had to attempt the journey to the Bay with a convoy of wagons. The way to Moçamedes in a wet year like the present was impossible. If it kept on raining as it had during the past few weeks, one would have to cross Ovamboland by boat.

I lay in a state of incipient sleep, staring through the hood at a piled-up formation of snow-white cumulus. The clouds were drifting lazily through a sky which had now become the purest azure . . .

Once more a dream seemed to carry me off. I was standing on the banks of a great river . . . It flowed so serenely, with such limpidity . . . A great, strongly flowing stream . . . Suddenly I found myself between dunes and marshes and dark, silent pools . . . Clouds of mosquitoes seemed to rise from them and blot out the sun . . . Was there an abandoned wagon somewhere here? Was there a vulture with fiery eyes perched on a draught-pole?

I awoke with a start. Then I heard the distant staccato prelude of the thunder, and lifted the canvas. It had become overcast. Somewhere someone was talking to my servants. It was Hans Schinz.

'Hallo!' I shouted, pleased to see him. The evening air was suddenly cool over my body. I pulled on my boots and clambered out of the wagon.

'So!' he greeted me. 'Are you resting?'

I grimaced. 'We could call it that,' I said.

'You have a touch of fever?' he enquired, peering closely at me. 'Yes, I think so!'

'Who hasn't,' I answered, 'in a year as wet as this!'

'Have you enough medicine, *Herr* Jordan?'

'Enough. But enough is never sufficient, is it? If it really gets bad. *Ach du lieber Gott, was für ein Land ist das!*'

'*Ein wundervolles Land!*' He smiled.

I could agree with Hans Schinz: a wonderful land . . . To this I could add: also a cruel land . . . Schinz had been here long enough to get the feel of it; to feel its hold on you. I noticed the sallow tinge of his skin. He himself had suffered illness. He had been 'off-loaded' by robbers, was ever exposed to danger, had been threatened with his life on many occasions. But he was still here, still planning to continue his grand tour through a wild and unknown country. He was planning to travel to the Okavango from here; and from there to Ngami . . .

'What were your impressions of Kambonde?' I asked.

He pursed his lips. 'I wish I knew what was going through his mind while you were speaking,' he said.

'You don't quite trust him,' I said.

'I would not put it that way,' he answered.

'This business with Nehale is the real difficulty, I think.'

'Did you know that they have decided to *divide* the kingdom?'

'No!' I said.

'Nehale does not like the idea of any white people being in Ovamboland. He does not even like the missionaries. Remember? Kambonde referred to him.'

'I have heard as much,' I said. 'But has Nehale any real power? I don't think so. He wants the throne of the whole of Ovamboland, of course. But he seems to me to be pretty shifty: the kind who never stops making threats, you know; and never effects anything. I'm more afraid of the quiet sort, who work in the dark. By the way, *Herr Doktor*, when you go to the Okavango, you will pass through Nehale's territory. Mind you, I would not be too apprehensive about it, for the very reasons I have just stated. As far as Kambonde is concerned, I still trust him. I may be wrong, but I have sufficient reason to be right. The very fact that a man like Rautanen still has a great deal of influence over him says a lot. Do you agree?'

He did agree. What about the murder in Ukuanyama, he wanted to know. How did I view that? Was this typical of Ovamboland? According to all the reports, I had dealt with it all in a competent manner. He had long since decided that one had to be a *schlauer Fuchs* to survive in this country. Those who were not strong had, at least, to be clever. He was only joking, he said. But still, it was quite true that one had to employ as much guile as one could . . .

'Well, Kambonde seemed to be tractable enough,' I replied. 'That at least is something to be thankful for.'

'Would this be the influence of the Mission?' he asked.

'It may well be the case,' I replied. 'At times I have expressed myself strongly regarding certain aspects of the missionaries' work here in this country. It has not always accorded with the true spirit of the Christian faith. Nevertheless, I would be the first to acknowledge the work of many fine men in this field. Our friends here at Olukonda are among them. By the way, I understand you had a lot of trouble with all the begging.'

'If I had not put a stop to it by absolutely refusing to give away anything more, I would have been reduced to abject poverty,' he affirmed. 'Some even looked at the trousers I was wearing, and asked me to please let them have it!'

We laughed at this.

'There is no point in trying to win favours by giving things away,' I said. 'Gifts are bad envoys. "Gifts" is hardly the correct word. Bribes, if you like. Better to say: "This is where I stand, I can do no other. So help me, Lord." '

'Do you know who is the real culprit behind much of the intrigue here?' he suddenly asked.

I gazed at him.

'Namapula. Kambonde's mother.'

'What about the old father—Kampingana?'

'Just as bad,' he said. '*Gleich und gleich gesellt sich gern.* Well, all honour to Kambonde, perhaps: that the son seems to be somewhat more of a statesman than the father.'

I remembered the story of the skeleton.

'Meanwhile,' I said, 'Hans Schinz has been building up quite a reputation as a sorcerer, I understand.'

He grinned. 'You see, Schinz went around with a big book, placing plants between the covers. Those that saw him came and told the king he was stealing the land.' He chuckled.

'You have referred to Queen Mother Namapula,' I reminded him. 'She also put her mark to the contract of sale, you know. Where is she? Why was she not at the palaver this morning?'

'I heard that she was with Nehale,' he said. 'But she is about somewhere. I have seen her a few times.'

'What does she say about Jordan? What is she telling Nehale?'

'I would like to know the answer to that,' he answered. 'So we all have our little problems, *nicht*? But if we do our duty, all will come right, *Herr* Jordan.'

'Yes,' I agreed, 'perhaps you are right. One should ever be thankful for grace bestowed. Can we expect you at Grootfontein one of these days? You wouid like to meet the Thirstlanders, I'm sure!'

'I would like to do that, yes. If I go to the Okavango, I'll come down to Grootfontein, and from there I may trek to Ngami. Is there a direct route?'

'Through the Omaheke—the Sandveld,' I said. 'Where that arch-brigand Gabriel kept house until some time ago. In a good rain-year you can take that road. How long are you still going to be here?'

'That you will have to ask the Kampinganas,' he replied. 'When will you be leaving?'

'Tomorrow morning,' I said. '*Deo volente.*'

We chatted for some time about the wealth of trees on the great

Ovambo plain. I thought absently how wonderful it would be just to trek along with a man like Hans Schinz: botanizing, examining the trees of the country, writing about them . . .

5

I was busy making an entry into my journal that afternoon when Izak came to inform me that Mister Lewis had arrived. I looked up in surprise, to see him approaching. This was an old way of his: sudden visits, with no indication beforehand that he was coming.

I had been caught unawares. I pointed vaguely to a chair: the very one on which Hans Schinz had been sitting half an hour before.

'Hope I'm not intruding,' he said cheerily.

Uncertainly I looked around. 'Some brandy?' I took the flask from under the table, and poured us a tot each.

'What can I do for you?' I then asked.

He sat there with his glass in his hand. 'Just a friendly chat, Jordan,' he replied, crossing his legs.

'Carry on. What have you on your mind? It's always a good thing, Lewis, for a man to know when he is beaten.'

'Agreed,' he said.

Maybe he wasn't taking me seriously. Or perhaps he was saying to himself: 'Jordan knows very well that the final round has yet to come. Upingtonia is a lost little community far out in the virgin bush. Jordan knows this very well. He knows they haven't got a chance there. He thinks he has the support of Kambonde Kampingana. But since when do the Boers seek alliances with the blacks of Africa?'

I was eager to know what he had to say. It was a morbid interest. There was also the strange little hope in me that Lewis had perhaps seen the light. Maybe he had seen Hans Schinz come to my laager. Schinz was a man of considerable international standing in Europe, with a great deal of influence in European academic circles. Lewis might have realized this. He might have realized that the very fact that Schinz had travelled safely through the country reflected the high regard in which he was generally held. Or was I just thinking wishfully . . .

'What is it you wish to know, Lewis?' I asked.

'Never really had the opportunity to speak to you, Jordan. As man to man, that is.'

'You think I don't know my own mind?'

He pulled thoughtfully at his cigar. 'Not always, to be quite honest.'

'But Robert Lewis presumably knows his. In fact, he knew it so well that he came up to Ovamboland expecting Kambonde Kampingana to repudiate a contract everybody can attest to.'

Now he was looking at me from underneath the brim of his topee.

'I have my duty, Jordan,' he said. 'Granted, you might have yours, as you see it. More's the pity, I often think, that you should waste your undoubted talents on such.'

He was keeping me guessing; this was a rare mixture of flattery and damnation.

'You are referring to the Trekboers,' I said. 'I thought we had been through all that to the point of exhaustion.'

'Not to my knowledge.'

'Then you have a stronger stomach than I have. We talked about this as far back as 1880, in the Bay, remember. I have a better knowledge of "such" than you could ever hope to have. I have lived with these people for years now.'

'That is your difficulty. I have been here a long time, Jordan. More than twice as long as you have. I don't think you always see the wood for the trees, my friend.'

'What trees? What wood? Don't demonstrate your ignorance, Lewis.'

'You have rather a poor view of my intelligence, I think.'

'I think it wise for any man to know what his limitations are.'

'Agreed. But the important thing still is to keep your wits about you, my boy. Don't ever get forwandered in the stars.'

'Damn it, Lewis, who are you to tell me this?'

'Don't get angry. You speak about limitations. Well, let's look at things squarely. Your association with the Boers, for example. You like playing Father Christmas to them, it seems. Or the Rich Uncle. You imagine *you* give the lead; but in fact you go after them. Forwandering!'

A drop of rain fell on my nose. Another hit me on the right cheek. The temper I still felt was quickly flushed out by rain falling over us like a huge, beaded curtain. I grabbed my hat from my X-table where we had been sitting, and jumped onto the wagon.

The servants had already taken shelter underneath. My *bambuse* was grinning at me from behind the spokes of a wheel.

Lewis had followed me. Here we were underneath the hood now. 'Anon you may want to know . . . !' The rest of his words were shattered by a sudden crash of thunder.

I sat on a *kist* wiping the rain from my eyes. Lewis was sitting astride of a provision-box. His cigar had been extinguished by the rain, but he still chewed at it.

'What I want to tell you, Jordan,' he began again, 'is not something . . . !'

'Oh, dry up, Lewis!' I retorted. 'I'm not really interested in what you think of me, man.'

'I think well enough of you, Sir, when you behave according to your endowments!'

Now I felt like laughing.

'It is your talents that you should use to better purpose,' he added.

'Talents? Blast you. Let me get on with whatever you may think I have; call it talents, call it what you will.'

'What goes on inside these Boers?' he chirped, trying to relight his cigar. 'I hope you don't mind my questions. As you say, you have been living in close proximity to them for some years now. *You* should know.'

'Even if I did know, what would it benefit you to know? You obviously don't share their beliefs.'

'I'm merely interested. This was intended as a friendly sort of chat.'

'Friendly? I have other ideas of good company.'

'Well, take it or leave it, as you like. But you would still like to hear what I think.'

'It would not affect me either way.'

It was raining so hard now that the hood had sagged where water had collected. The canvas was dripping in places.

'You're right,' he suddenly conceded. 'We *did* talk about these things in the Bay once or twice. That was a long time ago. If memory serves, I asked you where the immigrants were heading. Got no answer as far as I can recall. Still rather a mystery to me.'

'Why the hell should it worry you so much, man? If you don't fathom it, what about it? How does it concern you?'

'I told you I was just interested.'

'You mean you are an interested party. That's more like it.'

'I must remind you that I am High Commissioner to the Herero nation.'

'With an unduly large share in the spoils of office. By manipulation you acquire every single worthwhile mineral concession in Damaraland. It all looks very pretty, until Will Jordan and his "forwandered" Boers turn up to spoil the view.' Something struck me. 'By the way, you might discover that there are others who may do more than just occupy the landscape.'

'Germany, eh?'

'So you know of the coming *Schutz*!'

'I think I know the Ovaherero better than Messrs Goering, Nels and Co. King Kamaherero will send them packing.'

'You may be in for a shock.'

'I know my own business,' he said.

The rain pelted down with fresh violence. From underneath the floor of the wagon, I could hear the chatter of my servants. It had become so dark that I could hardly see Lewis's face.

'Maybe that is what you would like, Jordan!' he shouted above the noise of the elements. 'German *Schutz* for Upingtonia!'

'That's *our* affair!' I yelled back. 'Damn you!'

'Or British protection? I heard that you asked for this earlier this year. Shippard down at the Bay knows all about it. I understand you even want Germans to come and settle at Otjovanda Tjongue! Wrote to Bieber, eh?'

'What about it? I can write to whom I like!'

'Nothing wrong with it, except that the Boers won't have either *Schutz* or Protection, as far as I can see!'

'How do you know what they will have and what they won't have?'

'You're a romantic, my friend. Come on, admit it!'

'You're presumably Master of the True Facts. What rubbish!'

'Take a good look at your friends, and you'll have to admit that they, at least, are romantics. That means that you share their romantic ideas, unless you are prepared to repudiate them. What do they do? A group of reasonably well-off people, from what I gather, decide one day to abandon their good farms in the western Transvaal. They do this with no apparent rhyme or reason. God only knows why they do it. But what God? The Old Man of the Skies comes down to travel along with them on the *disselboom*.* So they wander away into the Thirstland, because

*Draught-pole of wagon.

they believe the Old Man has specially called them to do His bidding. As a reward they are to find a nice little Promised Land, tucked away somewhere in Africa: all white and all Boer; except for the servants.'

'You would not have lasted a day with them, Lewis.'

'Maybe not. But so much more the mystery. People die. The trek-route is marked by graves, as they are fond of telling. And yet they go on, and on. Bent on a quest . . . For what? They get bogged down in the marshes—after having got over the Thirstland. But more die. Of fever this time. And while they die, Will Jordan meets up with them. Does he ask: *why? To what purpose?* No. He writes to the Cape papers, giving them a harrowing account of the adventures of the Trekboers. Now, please do not imagine I am decrying your human feelings, my friend. But the question still remains: *why did they do it?* Why carry on obstinately when people are dying around you like flies? Why carry on when all the good, sound reasons point the other way? I hear they have always been searching for "freedom". A fine sentiment. But how do they set about it all? They dream about freedom and being on their own: together on their own. What happens? In the end Will Jordan takes them to *oorkant*—with the Old Man still on the *disselboom*. Flint-hard Calvinists these; and where do you take them to? And where do they ultimately settle? *Amongst the Catholic Portuguese!*'

'They are not in Angola any more.'

'Some are, some are not. However it may be, and wherever they are—and that also goes for those Boers living in the Transvaal and the Orange Free State—as far as I can see, they sit tightly in their little laagers, dreaming about Kingdom Come. They have no idea what time it is.'

'Oh, shut up, man. You talk as if you had a fine idea of the modern world. I know these people. Limitations and all, I prefer them vastly to your ilk!'

'Do you imagine they will welcome people from outside in your "civilized state"? People like Charlie Lyon, Behan, Todd, the rest of that moth-eaten crowd? These are all British *smouse*—pedlars—in the eyes of the Boers. In fact, I have an idea that you and your friends were at cross purposes from the start.'

I suddenly had no inclination to answer him. Weariness had overtaken me again. Perhaps it was the brandy which I had been drinking, coupled with my incipient fever. I looked at Lewis, sitting there on a packing case with a dead cigar clenched between his teeth. Why did I not throw him out? Why had I even listened to the man? Strangely I had maintained a certain objectivity while doing so. I was saying to myself: 'Here you are, sitting under a wagon-hood with your arch-enemy, Robert Lewis. Is this possible? Why do you listen to what he is saying? It might well be that this man has said things which have surprised you. Has he *thought* all this out on his own? Who has given him these ideas? He is barely literate. Even his natural sagacity cannot explain the way he had been talking . . . I have never had any illusions about my friends of the laager. They are human beings and they suffer from the same anxieties, the same confusion of vision as the rest of us. I have never found it necessary to explore all this to the last detail. Why should I? They are my friends and we understand each other. In spite of what people like Pieter Maritz-Botha and others have said about me, we belong together. I have increasingly felt that their coming has been something more than mere contingency. It has given meaning to my life. It has brought me face to face with things, as I have never dreamed possible . . .'

'They won't have you in the end, Jordan,' Lewis interrupted my thoughts. 'The sooner you realize that, the better. Stick to your own kind, old fellow. That is the way of the world! I'll tell you something else. Piet Botha is the only one among them with any real sense. He knows a blind trail when he sees one. So he has decided to go back to the Transvaal; and for my part I wish him the best of luck.'

'The pity of it all is that he should gang up with the likes of you against his own people,' I said with some bitterness. 'If Botha had but a fraction of the moral strength of men like Diederick Prinsloo, Louw du Plessis, and many more like them, he could be proud of himself. Instead he goes about helping you to pull wires.'

The old paralysing lassitude had got hold of me properly by now. I slipped off the *kist,* and lay down on the *katel.* When I felt like this, I lost all interest in what was happening around me. This was the case now with Lewis.

'Do your worst,' I said. 'We'll carry on with what we have to do.'

The rain had ceased. Under the floor of the wagon my servants clicked away in conversation. Lewis was preparing to leave.

'Well,' he said with a foot on the *voorkist,* 'You have heard what I had to say. Think it over. Come over for a drink some time, and we can talk some more.'

'Bugger off!' I breathed into the pillow.

I heard him say something to my servants in Otjiherero. They chuckled.

For a long time I lay there in the dark. I heard Izak going about his business, preparing the evening meal.

The stars were out, and from a thousand places the brilliant ringing of the frogs came. The air was cool and fresh. To the far south lightning still played on the horizon.

6

The next day I took leave of my friends at Olukonda. I followed my own wagon spoor of the previous week. It had become faint in places due to the rains, but I could still see it.

Long lines of people followed our trek, hoping apparently to pick up something we had abandoned or decided to give away. The air was so quiet that the smoke of kraal-fires hung like morning mist over the great plain.

In the late afternoon, however, a cool west wind began blowing. We reached the end of the Oohama flats. I was elated. It was not so much because we were leaving Ovamboland. It was mainly because the fever seemed to have left me. I felt like singing. I had a feeling that I was going home.

We trekked with difficulty through flat grass country which had become marshland. A few times we got bogged down badly and had to dig ourselves out again. Nevertheless, a fortnight later we reached Otjovanda Tjongue. It was the last week of November.

Nearly all the men were out hunting. I was quite relieved to find Diederick Prinsloo and his son, Jan, in front of their hartebeest-house. Old Diederick arose when he saw me coming. He took my hand, obviously moved.

'*Meneer*,' he said, looking me straight in the eye, 'glad we are that thou hast returned safely. We have had great anxiety.'

'How are you, *Oom* Diederick? How are you, Jan?'

They were well, they told me. But they were eager to know from me what had happened in Ovamboland. For days nobody in the laager could talk of anything else. Was it true, they wanted to know, that Piet Botha and Robert Lewis were both in Ondangua?

Yes, I replied, it was perfectly true. They were there.

'Many rumours, *Meneer,*' Old Diederick said. 'What to believe? To believe only what we would hear from thine own mouth.'

'Piet's supporters received a message from him to come and join his trek,' said Jan. 'They said he was on his way back to the Transvaal. Is this true?'

'It seems to be so,' I answered. 'He left Olukonda with the declared intention of doing just that. Have Kruger, Du Toit and the others left yet?'

'There is talk that they will meet at the Waterberg,' replied Jan.

'What then?'

'The Thirstland,' Old Diederick said.

I was silent. At length I spoke: 'I wish them a good journey.' I meant it.

'What about Widow Roets?'

'She has left,' Jan said. 'Through the south; Great Namaland; and up along the Orange, to the Free State.'

I thought of all the violence that had also torn Great Namaland these past years. Hendrik Witbooi had been defeated at Osona, but that was by no means the end of the struggle. As I knew the Namas, Witbooi would return.

The Germans had extended *Schutzherrschaft* from Angra Pequena to Rehoboth. Now there was this talk of it going to Okahandja. What would it all mean in practical terms? At the most, as things were at present, a handful of *Schutztruppen,* who would be quite ineffective in the event of real trouble. *Schutz* would mean nothing until it could grow its own teeth. Lewis probably realized this. That was the reason why he had not taken much notice of the rumours.

Widow Roets was a brave woman, I thought. We could have used her here. There was no dearth of courage in the laager. Even Pieter Maritz-Botha was brave in his own way . . . He was prepared to cross the Thirstland again. This was no easy task. The risks were enormous.

I wished them well. Together we had shared many things, however much we had differed in our views . . .

' . . . *Meneer,* we have decided now to sign a declaration.' I looked up at Old Diederick.

' . . . It is to be by those of us who stand fast, *Meneer.* Thou knowest how each man must *decide* what he must do according to his *own* conscience. But what stands fast, stands fast . . . And there is no giving way to the forces which bear on us so strongly. The whole land must *know* what our will is. Be it otherwise, all will come to a standstill.'

Old Diederick looked more gaunt than ever. Now I could even discern the angularity of his great shoulders beneath the frock-coat. His cheeks were hollowed out. Yet, he had lost nothing of his dignity.

'To stand by your own people,' he continued, 'to be strong as iron, *Meneer*. The nations always have a clamour of war.'

He looked searchingly at me. '*Meneer,* how now with our lands?'

'The farms will now be allocated as the demand is there, *Oom*,' I replied. 'As soon as everybody is back here in the laager, we must set to work. What's the news about the Bushmen?'

'Not a word about Gabriel,' Jan said. 'Louw du Plessis and his party were out hunting down that way about a week ago. He sent a letter. He said that the *werf* we found on the other side of the 'maramba was still deserted.'

'Adriaan and Lisa Venter?' I enquired.

'They were here,' replied Jan. 'Like two spring lambs they were!' He chuckled. 'Then Adriaan was out for a time with the Labuschagnes, hunting. Now the two have gone off again, this time to their water. And the elephants.'

'Chris Leen has gone down to Otjimbingue,' I said. 'Did he say anything about when we could expect him?'

'Said he would send a letter,' Jan answered, as *Tante* Prinsloo brought us coffee.

'We are glad that *Meneer* has come,' she said warmly. 'We had so much illness here in the laager. Many people lay with fever. Cousin Ella, too.'

This was to be expected, in a wet summer. I had left a fair stock of quinine here, but it had run low. Now it was becoming a matter of urgency to obtain new supplies from the Bay. There would be outbreaks of dysentery as well. Some wagons should have reached the Bay by this time. My journey to Ovamboland could well prove to have been expensive.

'While I have been away, you have laid out some fine gardens,' I said, cheering myself up.

'This is good land, *Meneer*,' *Tante* Prinsloo said.

'Good and fruitful!' Old Diederick added. 'Nowhere soil which gives such crops.'

'Pumpkins!' *Tante* Prinsloo opened her arms enthusiastically. 'That size! We have sent you some, *Meneer.*'

'I thank you, *Tante.*'

'Mealies! Beans!' Old Diederick said. 'With what the hunt brings in, *Meneer*, we are well provided for. Truly, this is Eden.'

I recalled what Lewis had said at Olukonda.

' . . . As far as I can see,' he had said, 'they sit tightly in their little laagers, dreaming about Kingdom Come.'

He was judging things from the outside. It might well be true that my friends' idea of the state of Upingtonia did not quite agree with my own. What I also believed, however, was that the practical demands of the situation would ultimately decide. Upingtonia could become the heartland of a civilized order in this country. The Trekboers were not unreasonable: they would not deny the true facts of their situation when ultimately faced with it.

The very fact that they accepted me as they did, indicated this. I would not press them into sudden new attitudes. Things would come in their own good time.

7

'So, *Tante* Ella,' I said, 'you have also been laid low?'

She was lying on a *katel* under a *scherm* of grass and poles, which Kleinveld had erected for her. It was cool and pleasant here under the leadwoods, better than lying in the wagon.

Her pleasure at seeing me again made me happy. She had been enquiring about our return, and had sent me a message bidding me welcome.

I told her about the journey, the outcome of the palaver at Ondangua, and the days spent at Olukonda.

'The main thing,' I said, 'is that we had the contract ratified. It has been confirmed beyond all dispute that we are the legal owners of this tract of country. Well, now we have work to do. What about the newly-weds? I hear they have gone down the 'maramba to their water!'

She smiled. Yes, she confirmed, they had left. They were so happy to go. Adriaan had just returned from hunting with the Labuschagnes. They were here to say goodbye.

She looked drawn. Her skin had the pallor of fever. I placed a bottle of quinine on the trestle-table next to the *katel.*

'This will make you feel better,' I assured her. 'We all have to take it.'

'*Meneer* is good to us,' she said. 'We always just asked: "When will *Meneer* come back?" '

'When did the young folk leave?' I asked.

'*Meneer* had been away about a week when they came back to the laager: full of stories, and laughing; you know how it is with the children when they get married. Then Adriaan went off with the Labuschagnes for about fourteen days. Then he came back and they stayed here for a few more days. Then they trekked off to Okasima.'

She lifted a tired arm and pointed towards strings of dried meat hanging from the trees.

'Biltong,' she explained. 'Enough for the whole year. But how to make biltong when the weather is so rainy? Feathers he brought, too. Enough to sell, when *Meneer* goes down to the Bay again.

'I said to the children: "Stay until *Meneer* is back. Then we can see whether the country around here has been cleared. Then you can go to your water." You know how it is with young folk? They only have time and eyes for each other. *Meneer*, is there danger for them being so far away and alone? They are but children still.'

I thought about this.

'Gabriel and his lot have not showed up again, from what I hear,' I said. 'I do not think they will risk it either, with all the men at various places in the hunting veld. When Adriaan was with the Labuschagnes, did Bushmen help in the hunting?'

'One day they were there; the next day they were gone. You know how it happens. They used them for tracking and for cutting up the meat and bringing in what had been shot. Did I tell you, *Meneer*, that Kleinveld went to Okasima to see how it was with the children?'

'So he went! What news did he bring back?'

'They are at the water. Adriaan is hunting and Lisa goes out with him to where he wants to be. They have also made a garden. Old Dina here fussed a lot, of course: wanted to go down to be with the children. No, I said, it was not to happen. She had to stay here and look after her Old Miss. The children she could visit later, when everything was more settled.'

'So, how did Kleinveld travel?'

'On horseback. Took the old nag we have, and went along. Stayed there for a day, and took three days back. A week in all. Well now, when I am strong again, I'll see if I can go down to visit the children. Perhaps *Meneer* will also go?'

'Why not?' I said.

She lay there on the *katel,* musing. 'Our numbers have grown small here in the laager, not so?' she continued. 'With all the menfolk away on the hunt, it is just us few who are old, and some who are ill . . . But we must never grumble. The Lord is good to us. He has kept us as his own for many years and over many, many miles . . . But a handful, but strong in our resolve.'

'Within a few months our numbers may well be doubled. It is not impossible.'

'No, it is not impossible . . . Do you know what I said to Sannie Roets, just before she left? God would not have brought us all this way just to leave us here to fend for ourselves. God had His own purpose for us. We should just be trustful and do our duty as we find it. But Sannie said, no, she had wandered far enough. Now she was only desirous of one thing: to get back home again, after all these years. "But Sister," I said, "have you no fear of the nations, trekking alone as you wish to?" And she replied: 'Cousin Ella, is it not true that you too have trekked along and stood alone, when all had fallen away from you?" Yes, I said, that was so. You must know we were together in all the treks since we were young girls with long plaits of hair trailing behind our backs. And here we had come, at last, to Lydensrust . . . where we would be happy and contented . . . as the Lord intended it to be.'

Listening to all this with distant thoughts of my own, I knew there was only one thing to do: carry on with what we were engaged in; to continue building the state of Upingtonia, *fide et amore* . . . Ella Lombard was right, one had to keep faith in what one was doing, believe that this was the realization of a long sought for ideal. What we still lacked in terms of the modern world would come in God's own time. This might well be soon . . .

Dina approached me. 'Mister?' she asked, looking at me with a hand over one eye, 'is this *Mister* that has come?'

'This is Mister,' I replied. 'How are you, Dina?'

'I am well, Mister; and hoping to hear the same from Mister. If not, the Lord will tell us why . . . *Illness* here, Mister, as you see;

Old Miss is on her back, but already better now. Eh, Old Miss?'

'Better, yes, Old Dina. And we are thankful.'

'And Mister must know that I too must go and see what Little Miss is doing; and where she is going.'

She held up her hands for me to see.

'Look, Mister, crooked! Cos' the joints are stiff. But these hands raised all the children of Old Miss. Eh, Old Miss? *Raised* them all, yes: they who are now dead and gone; and the one little ewe-lamb she still had, she has now also lost.'

'Not lost, Old Dina; why do you say "lost"?' Ella Lombard turned her eyes towards her.

'Lost, because lost is *mos* lost. And when a man comes, he has his own plans. And a woman can *maar* only say: *Yes, my lord, so I will do, my lord*. But before I die, I will go down to that water; and see all for myself.'

'You won't die, *Oumie*,' Kleinveld said philosophically.

'Not die? We *all* die, man.'

'You are still good for a long time, *Oumie*. To *tell* us things.'

'Things you must know, eh?'

'What is the country like towards Okasima, Kleinveld?' I asked.

'*Mooi tjinene*, Mister. Grass that high.' He indicated with his hand. 'A man on a horse disappears in it. Pans and pans of water; everywhere.'

'Are there elephants? What has Little Master been shooting?'

'Well, when he was with the Labuschagne people, Mister,' Kleinveld replied, 'they shot birds and camels . . .'

'Giraffes, you mean.'

'Camels, yes; and plenty of buck. Eland and kudu. But elephants? Uh-uh. There are only spoors down in the 'maramba. Perhaps the elephants don't like it when it is so wet down there. Then they rather go out to the drier parts. But Little Master *did* shoot two: a cow and a young bull. He says there is a big bull there that he is after. And he will yet follow him right up to the river.'

'What have they planted in the garden?'

'Everything that can grow. Pumpkins; and sweet potatoes; and mealies; and beans. It is even prettier than it is here.'

But Dina admonished: 'You must not make up stories, Kleinveld.'

'Perhaps it is just because it is new,' Ella Lombard said. 'But it is beautiful here. And other people must come to see what a fine land we have. And there is work for everybody.'

'Yes, there is always work,' Dina said. 'Even when these hands are crooked, and the joints are stiff, like mine. We just do our best.'

'Yes, *Oumie*,' Kleinveld agreed. 'We do our best.'

8

The letter from Chris arrived a few days later. A runner who said that he had come from Otjimbingue brought it.

'I have an idea that Kamaherero himself is not so much against our presence here, as the traders at Otjimbingue, with Robert Lewis in the van.'

So Chris had spoken before I had left for Ovamboland. He had said that he wanted to determine once and for all who were our friends, and who our enemies.

'Richard Stevens, James Lewis, Charles Rule and J. L. B. Caine are definitely not on our side,' he now wrote. 'Clay, on the other hand, is still a good friend of Upingtonia and the Trekboers, and will give us as much assistance as is compatible with his own safety. The others are not all as outspoken and uncompromising as John Caine. It is difficult to believe that this man once professed to be your friend. As far as I can see, he spends most of his time drafting letters to the Cape press wherein he attacks you and the whole idea of Upingtonia. The attitudes of the others vary from scepticism on the part of a man like Rule to the downright enmity of a man like Stevens. By the way, Stevens, J. Lewis and Rule signed as witnesses to the concession of 9 September, in which Kamaherero granted Robert Lewis "the sole right to prospect for minerals and other precious stones in perpetuity on payment of a royalty of 2/6d per ton on all minerals save coal".

'What Ka-Robbie thus claimed to have had seems to be a fact. The question remains, of course, whether Kamaherero had any right to make such awards. The concession further grants the beneficiary the 'sole rights to explore, prospect and dig for minerals throughout the whole country". This for a period of twenty years, mark you. You may now well understand why our schemes for the development of Upingtonia caused such passion on the part of Robert Lewis!

'Now, of course, fate itself has intervened. Lewis left for Ovamboland to get to Kambonde Kampingana first and, to quote John Caine, "to have a face to face discussion with the young upstart". Until yesterday I had no idea what had taken place at Ondangua. The previous evening, however, Lewis had arrived back from Ovamboland. His arrival had been so noisy that I at once got the impression that things had not gone too well for him. The next day (yesterday) my impressions were confirmed. John Caine got hold of me and told me with some bitterness that you had succeeded in "misleading" Kambonde. He had come to ask me to please intervene, in the name of reason and good sense. Can you believe it? I was to please use my influence on you, Caine said. You should voluntarily quit the area and leave Upingtonia to its rightful owners.

'Well, this angered me, although I did not show much of it. Anyway, I refused to be a party to this. "I hope you don't mind my telling you to do your own dirty work," I said to Caine. He lost his temper, but I did not react. When at last he concluded his rant, I added that he obviously did not know the Trekboers; nor did he know Will Jordan. They would not be intimidated.

'Meanwhile something else has happened of which you may already have received some word. Goering and Co were at Okahandja when Witbooi arrived with his "war" . . .'

The letter then gave an account of the battle of Osona, with details which I had not yet heard. There was also some information about the *Schutzherrschaft* which had been proclaimed over Damaraland during Lewis's absence in Ovamboland.

'You may well understand the flutter the news caused here at Otjimbingue,' Chris's letter went on. 'Caine, Stevens, Rule and others refused to believe it at first. *Missionar* Brickner arrived to confirm it, however, and the result? There is much confusion here among the British hunter-traders. How was it possible, the question is being asked, for Kamaherero to grant Robert Lewis all the mineral rights of Damaraland on 9 September, and to accept official German protection six weeks later?

'What had Robert Lewis to say to all this? To put it mildly, he was livid. The failure of his mission to Ovamboland had, of course, left him in a bad mood. Stevens was soon upon the scene, informing Ka-Robbie of what had taken place. The next day he was here, there and everywhere. The reports were all the same: Lewis refused to accept the *Schutzvertrag*. He told all and sundry that he would protest to Prince von Bismarck himself. This, he stated, was a scandalous negation of existing rights. He exhibited the document of 9 September. This bore the royal seal of Damaraland: the one showing a circle, enclosing the head of an antelope.

'I stayed out of his way, but this was not easy. Otjimbingue is as big as you know it is: a few houses and one or two "streets" However, we ran into each other at *Hälbichs*. There was a lively exchange of words between us. It amounted to this: that he, Lewis, had decided that war would be declared against Upingtonia. Does this frighten you? I should think not. Especially in view of the fact that Lewis has now acquired the Germans as enemies as well. The Germans, he stated in no uncertain terms, were power-seekers, who had misled Kamaherero. He, Lewis, would leave for Okahandja that same afternoon and see that matters be put right. I understand he left.

'Regarding the Boers, Lewis's theme remained one of "the dream world of these people being shattered". They were an "evil influence" in the country, he maintained. I don't suppose it is necessary to go into all the abuse he poured on the heads of W. W. Jordan and Chris Leen. There is one thing, however, I feel it my duty to tell you, however unpleasant it may be. Nevertheless, I hesitate to do so. I know what a shock it may be. Still, I am so convinced of the utter maliciousness of the charge, that I am prepared to tell you about it. The origin of the story? It may well be our friend Piet Botha. I would rather not think so, but in repeating the story, Lewis seemed to indicate that he had all this on "the highest authority, from a man who knows the laager better than anybody else I know of". Who else could this be but Pieter Maritz-Botha?'

Something seemed to warn me what was coming. I turned over the page slowly. With a tightening heart I read what stood there.

'It concerns Hester Bouwer, a woman I have always held in the greatest esteem. I know that this applies to you as well. I have admired her as a woman of great courage and strength of character. You remember how often you spoke about what she did that time up at the Cunene when you went hippo-hunting? Perhaps I was to blame for Lewis's outburst. If I was, I beg your forgiveness. When he realized I was getting the better of the argument, he resorted to abuse. I said to him: "Will Jordan is a man of great talent and integrity. One always knows exactly where one stands with him." To this he replied: "Do the God-fearing members of the laager know, for example, that he is the father of Hester Bouwer's youngest child?" I was speechless. Then he repeated the story, and affirmed that he had it on "the highest authority". I was angered and challenged him to name the source of his information. This he refused to do, saying that he would not name the person and so allow you to victimize him.

'All this is grossly slanderous, of course. It may just be possible that the story has reached your ears, and that you have treated it with the right amount of contempt. On the other hand, it may be that you are completely innocent as yet of the methods being used to defeat you, and so to defeat us all . . .'

I sat there with the letter in my hands. The handwriting seemed to fade. What I had read had shocked me. Deeper than the shock, however, was a sense of intense hurt. Was this really the sort of thing my enemies had stooped to, and would stoop to again? The terrible thing about it was that they did not care a rap how it would affect the life of someone entirely outside the whole issue.

I got up and walked about, muttering to myself: 'Is this necessary? Is this the price one has to pay for high ideals and fine intentions? Does it all ultimately resolve to a sordid *ad hominem* of this kind? I don't care a damn for myself. But I do care for Hester Bouwer and what she may suffer, were any of this to reach her ears. How does one face her again? What does one say?'

This continued for some time. I realized at last that my servants were looking at me. I stopped in my tracks. Then I walked back to my chair. I was probably a peculiar figure in the eyes of Izak, the Bushman, and Kairob, the Bergdamara. They were grinning at me; not that I could blame them. It must have seemed funny to them to watch their master striding up and down between the trees without going anywhere. They must have wondered at his talking to himself, being so preoccupied that he probably did not even hear their question whether anything was wrong!

Things then had come to this pass . . .

What was there to do? It was like the incident at Dabe. I just had to get over it. I just had to carry on as if it had never happened. This I had to do because of Hester herself; and also because of Barend. How would Barend react if he heard this story? Would he discount it, recognizing it to be just a piece of malicious libel?

Slowly, with some difficulty, I commenced reading once more.

'It may afford you some comfort to know,' Chris wrote, 'that Lewis excepted no one in his attacks. The Germans, he declared, were power-seekers of the worst kind. Kamaherero had obviously been deceived. He would leave for Okahandja that same afternoon to "get things straightened out again". As far as the Boers were concerned, they were heading for disaster. Their little "Kingdom Come" would soon be shattered. The sooner the country was rid of them, the better. Will Jordan and Chris Leen, apart from anything else, were traitors to the "British cause". How Lewis can see his nefarious dealings as "British" is beyond me. In any case, there you have it, as fully as I am capable of putting it down on paper.

'One more thing. I do not think we should view Lewis's declaration of war too lightly. I doubt whether you would do this, but I must point it out. The mineral concessions of which Lewis is the "owner" are of considerable value. True, the Otavi mine would be difficult to exploit, because of its remoteness. Yet in time it will have to be developed . . . Lewis knows this and one can expect any sort of thing from him if he sees that his interests are threatened. What his true position in the Herero hierarchy now is, in view of the establishment of *Schutz*, is a mystery. If I know Lewis at all, I am willing to bet that he will prove more than a handful for the Germans, too. After all, does *Schutz* mean anything more than *Protection* did? There are no *Truppen* in the country to give it any strength.

'I hope that your journey to Ovamboland was as successful as Lewis has indicated. I am burning to hear all about it . . .'

My feelings were now a strange mixture of personal hurt, anger, determination not to allow Lewis to have his way. I realized how exposed we were to danger here, what with most of the menfolk away in the hunting veld. Should they not turn up within a day or two, I would have to send out messages. At Olukonda I had been ill and not fully capable of standing up to Lewis. I listened to him, and even allowed him some truth in what he had been saying. Now I was no longer prepared to give him any quarter. He had become the sworn enemy of Upingtonia, and of Will Jordan. There was no other way to deal with him but the hard way. This was the only language he understood. He should also be made to know that whatever adventure he considered undertaking against the laager, it would be resisted to the full.

9

Another letter arrived. It was from Axel Eriksson.

Missionar Viehe of Omaruru, Axel wrote, was still violently opposed to the establishment of an independant Boer State in the Otavi area. It had become generally known that Manasse Tjisiseta had rejected my offer of a meeting to discuss matters. I had pointed out to him that the new state wished to have cordial relations with all its neighbours. Our struggle was not against the Ovaherero, but against certain individuals based at Okahandja who were instigating strife. Viehe, according to Axel, was making no secret of it that he was influencing Manasse.

Regarding Upingtonia, Axel wrote, the Eriksson brothers had discussed matters and were agreed that the cause should be supported. Without a strong civilized community which could develop into a central authority, there was no future in this country. Brother Albert had already indicated that he would apply to the *Bestuur* for an allocation. Possibly the Erikssons would come in the new year to have a look around. Who could say, Axel concluded, what adventures lay ahead for us? It was a grand idea that we who had given what we possessed to this land would now at last be able to see something of real value. What about another trek to virgin hunting country? Now that trade had slackened, his interest seemed to be turning to ornithology in increasing measure. He would like to complete his collection for the museum at Vänersborg . . .

The letter left me with a longing to see my friend again. I sat with the pages in my hand, hearing his voice: 'So it is, friend Will. You know of all the hard things which have happened to you in this country. You think you must pack up and go away, perhaps back to Sweden, perhaps to the Cape. Ugh, man, you just think these things. Like *Chef* Andersson, you always come again. But sometimes I am tired . . .'

'That is the way it is, Karevapu,' I said to myself. His company now would have given me the moral support I needed. What Chris had written to me about Hester Bouwer had badly shaken me. What could I do? I had already decided that I could only continue, never indicating that I had any knowledge of the wild, libellous talk Lewis and others were indulging in. Had Piet Botha put this idea into Lewis's head? I had every reason to feel bitter about it. It was a useless passion, and I preferred to forget Botha altogether. No, I could hardly believe that a man who had been my friend would have stooped so low. More likely the story was Lewis's own fabrication, arising out of some loose remarks made by someone in his presence. It was best to concentrate on immediate matters.

We had to open the portals of Upingtonia. We had to bring in as many sound, pioneering people as we could. The world should get to know about us. We would have to see to it that this small beginning could yet lead to great things. The whole of south-western Africa would yet come to play a great part in the affairs of the continent. Did my friends also think of it in this way? Lewis had said that Will Jordan and the laager were at cross purposes . . .

I cursed myself. Why did my thoughts keep reverting to what Lewis had said? I had been determined to put him out of my mind. I was finding it difficult. Was it perhaps because, in spite of everything, I was forced to admit at least an element of truth in Lewis's charges? Hardly. Were there anything in the accusation of a sick isolation as far as the Boers were concerned, then time would cure it. These people had been at grips with Africa for generations now. What was more natural than a certain wariness on their part? A thousand hazards had taught them to be on their guard. But now they were settled; and with an increase in security, they would soon adapt themselves to a larger life, to a wider community.

The High Serras which had promised so much had turned out to be unworkable. I might have known it from the start. Firstly, it was a matter of religion. The Portuguese were Catholics. Within their Catholic system, they did not know the taboos concerning mixture of the races. At Humbe, and beyond Humbe, there were many *mesticos*—the descendants of Portuguese traders and black concubines. At the same time it was a fact that slavery had by no means been abolished. It would hardly be known by that name, but the recruitment of '*indigenas* with facilities' by the government was, in fact, a system of forced labour.

The Boers were different. It was part of their particular *ethos* that their whiteness be jealously preserved. On the other hand, it was also true that black people like Dina Lombard, Kleinveld Labuschagne, Paadjierol van der Merwe and many others like them were for all practical purposes part of the tightly closed community of the laager. Yes, most certainly, Lewis and others like Lewis would say that this was because the black retainers of the laagers were also slaves. The test was whether they were free to come and go. Indeed they were free. Should someone like *Ai* Dina decide one day that she had had enough of her Boer liege-folk, there was nothing to prevent her from leaving. That she preferred to remain, was because this was her home. She belonged here.

It had to be faced: I, Will Worthington Jordan, was the effective leader of these people. Pieter Maritz-Botha had told me that day at Dabe that I did not have the colour of an *opregte witte man.* I had never claimed that I did. Why should I? Botha's words had shocked me intensely. For one moment I had been knocked off balance. I had struggled to my feet and had decided that it was best to get away. But I had returned. I had led my friends on the expedition against Gabriel. Once more I had taken part in the pleasant business of the laager. Nobody had made me feel that I was not welcome any more. Surely the news of Dabe had been spread around . . .

Now there was this other business about Hester Bouwer. If the people of the laager also knew about this, why did I have to hear about it through Chris Leen, writing from Otjimbingue? This seemed to confirm what I believed: the practical task of building a new state was of primary import. This was our common passion. Without some sort of task to believe in, life was empty. At times my friends exasperated me by their lack of knowledge of the modern world; by their excessive psalm-singing and scripture-reading; by their stubborn resistance to facts, and their strange emotionalism.

But one thing was certain: in the general picture of confusion in this country, they were the one stable element. Their courage, their love of order, their fierce adherence to values which had their roots in the heroic Beggars' League of the Netherlands and the equally heroic Huguenots of France, made them outstanding pioneers. If Rome had not been built in a day, neither would Upingtonia be. This meant that the people of the laager would find their feet as time went by. Patience was the watchword. Patience and prudence . . .

There I was sitting, bent forward, hat low over the eyes, Axel's letter in my hand. A spotted turtle called. I looked up. It was a quiet, luminous afternoon, mild and pleasant. Everything was so peaceful. The *werfs* were all at rest. Only here and there an old retainer was poking an *erd.* On the shady side of the two hartebeest-houses some old people were drinking coffee and chatting.

On the whole, I decided, I would have preferred a scene of greater activity. Things had to get going. The temptation would always be there just to sit back and enjoy the life. This, after all, had been the ideal so many in the laager had striven for, in all sincerity. It was a hopeless ideal. If there were still too many who thought of matters in that way, they would have to be helped, as gently as practicable, to a new perspective.

I stood up. The pages of the two letters I had received lay scattered over the X-table. For many miles they had been carried in a cleft stick through the bush. As humans we had need of each other, I mused. We fought each other bitterly; but neither could we do without each other.

Two days later, on 28 November, it arrived: the official declaration of war against Upingtonia. It was addressed to the *Bestuur.*

If something of this nature had been expected, it nevertheless came as a shock. It was Izak who brought the runner with the letter to me. Diederick Prinsloo was resting and the other members of the *Bestuur* had not yet returned from their hunting.

I tore the letter open. There it was, in an ostentatious handwriting which I recognized as that of Lewis's amanuensis.

'Be it made known to all concerned that after due warning being given to vacate the said territory, which falling within the legal confines of Damaraland, and as such being under the dominion of Kamaherero, Paramount Chief, the Bestuur *and burghers of the so-called state of Upingtonia ignoring same, and disregarding all reasonable demands to acknowledge the rightful ownership . . .'*

My primary impulse was to tear the document to pieces. I hesitated, only crumpling a corner of the single sheet. At the same time I cursed Lewis.

I walked to my wagon, climbed in and sat down on the *katel.* Again I studied the letter. It was sickening.

War!

I flung the letter to one side. My God, so it had really come to this! I knew well that there was little sense in dismissing it all as just another empty gesture on the part of Lewis. It had to be faced: Lewis was determined to hold to his guns. Much was at stake, and he would stop at nothing. Not even the Germans at Okahandja would deter him from following his course.

He was tough. That I had to admit. One would have thought that after the failure of his diplomacy in Ovamboland, he would think again. The establishment of *Schutzherrschaft* should have deterred him. Obviously he had nothing but contempt for it. He still thought of himself as the true power behind the throne. He also refused to accept Kambonde's own answers to the questions he had put to him.

What now?

I got up so quickly that I knocked my head on one of the hard-wood ribbings and saw stars. I scrambled out of the wagon. I had to see Diederick Prinsloo. One never knew what might happen. The laager was particularly vulnerable at present. I would have to send out messages at once, asking everybody to return to Otjovanda Tjongue. I still believed that Lewis had drafted this declaration on his own, without even consulting Kamaherero. The latter probably still had his hands too full with Hendrik Witbooi. Witbooi had been defeated at Osona, but as I knew the Namas, and especially as I knew Witbooi, this was not the end of the matter.

This did not mean that Lewis was bluffing. It was still quite possible that he could persuade some part of the Herero nation to take action. What then? Outside help had already been considered. How soon could troops, say from the Cape, arrive at the Bay? Months . . . From the Bay to Upingtonia would need weeks. Perhaps I had been living in the happy illusion that the people at the Cape were well conversant with conditions here. I had written to the newspapers . . . Nevertheless, it took time for something like that to establish itself in the public mind.

We had written and used various addresses. We had given it as Ovamboland; Okahandja; Otjimbingue; Otavi; Walwich Bay . . . Usually, when the letter appeared after some three months in *The Cape Times* it bore the legend *Upingtonia*. How many people cared to read this? And when reading it, how many had any inkling where it was situated? Or who the Trekboers were? Or who Will Jordan was? Who cared?

So, in the main, we had only ourselves: here on the limestone heights of Otjovanda Tjongue, this rise in the level expanse of bush from where one could see far to the north to where the river was; to the east where the bush swept down to the Omuramba Omatako and where, beyond the omuramba, slender makalanis grew, as they did in Ovamboland.

I found old Diederick in front of his humble little dwelling busy whittling at a roll of tobacco.

'There we have it, *Oom*,' I said without more ado. I threw the letter I had received down on the table in front of him.

'Lewis wants to shoot it out!'

He looked up in surprise, then knotted his huge eyebrows. 'Shoot?' he asked.

'Yes, *Oom*, shoot!'

Old Diederick could not read the English. I picked up the sheet of paper and translated the words on it.

'There you have it,' I said. 'As plain as a *disselboom*. If we don't get out, he'll start a war. This letter arrived about an hour ago.'

Old Diederick was silent. Perhaps I was giving him a wrong impression now and I hastened to add: 'Not that there is anything in this that we haven't heard before.'

'So, *Meneer*, Lewis wants war!'

'It looks like it,' I said.

Jan Prinsloo arrived, and he heard these words.

'What now?' he asked, looking first at me, then at his father.

'We are where we are,' I said. 'At the same time, it would be foolish to take risks. The menfolk are all out in the veld. We'll have to get them together. The laager at full strength will not easily be attacked, I can assure you. After all, the Boers have fought against great odds on many other occasions in their history. Am I right?'

Old Diederick folded his large hands together. 'Vegkop!' His eyes were blazing. 'Sod Laager in Natal! . . . Blood River! . . . Thou art right, *Meneer*.'

'Majuba,' Jan Prinsloo added.

'We have to get the *Bestuur* together,' I said. 'It must be done this week, and no later.' I looked at Jan. 'Is there anybody here we can send out with the letters?'

'Two of our old servants,' Jan said.

'I'll draft the letters,' I said. 'Let the two who are to go come and fetch them at my wagon in half an hour's time. The main group of hunters is still up at the White Pan.'

The news of what had happened seemed to spread through the laager. Soon women were appearing, meeting each other, talking in low voices. Diffidently they approached us where we stood. One of the first to arrive was Hester Bouwer.

'What has happened?' she asked quietly. 'Is it true what we hear? Will there be war?'

'Not necessarily,' I said.

'Then why does Lewis threaten us?'

'Because he is Lewis.'

'Will our wagons be safe?' she asked again.

'As safe as they have always been.'

'We must do what we must do,' she said, looking at me steadily. She was thinking of Barend.

'Yes,' I said. 'There is no other way. We'll win through.'

Ella Lombard said, 'All must help.'

'What all you good ladies can do,' I said, 'is just to see that nothing be lacking when the menfolk arrive.'

A little crowd had now gathered in front of the hartebeest house.

'To bark is one thing,' I said. 'To bite is another.'

Old Diederick lifted his olive-wood stick. 'Dogs that do easily bark, seldom bite!'

I left them there discussing it, and returned to my wagon.

10

It was like the days when I had to write my matriculation. All was tensed up and pointed. There was too much adrenalin in my blood.

I sat down and started writing a letter to Manasse Tjisiseta. He hadn't answered my friendly letter to him, dispatched at the beginning of October. There was no doubt in my mind that Viehe had influenced him not to answer it. The difficulty was that Manasse had no real conception of who and what Robert Lewis was. Perhaps he would yet see the light. It had become a matter of great urgency to have our wagons move down to the Bay without interference. As soon as Barend Bouwer was back in the laager, the wagons would have to leave.

'My purpose in this country,' I again wrote to Manasse, 'is

colonization and civilization. We wish to live in peace and amity with all peoples here, irrespective of race or colour. I would, however, be failing in my duty if I did not warn you against a man like Robert Lewis. He is a barely literate, corrupt specimen of humanity. A man like that could never be of any real use to you as a nation.'

This was hardly subtle. I had reached the stage, however, when I was no longer prepared to mince words. Manasse himself was hardly subtle.

'It has come,' I wrote to Axel Eriksson as well. 'Lewis was obviously driven to desperate action by the success of my dealings with Kambonde. Chris Leen has written to tell me that when Lewis got back to Otjimbingue and heard about *Schutz* at Okahandja, he was furious. He left immediately to see Kamaherero, but what he effected there nobody knows. The fact is that he sent us a "declaration of war" the very next day. If the worst comes to the worst, I am quite sure that we shall be able to give a good account of ourselves.

'We would like to have you here again, Karevapu. Aukas, the farm you had in mind, will be set aside for you. Your brother Albert may have Palmietfontein. Meanwhile, it seems as if some other Omaruru hunter-traders are becoming interested. I hear that Carlson has been making enquiries. The news from the Bay is that Thomas and Sichel are to join Chapman, Lyon, Todd, and the others. I expect them all here during the next month or two to talk about allocations. Chris is still down at Otjimbingue, and I have an idea that he might come to some agreement with Bill Clay regarding trade in Ovamboland. There is much work to do here, but meanwhile we and our dependants have to live. Chris and Bill will probably proceed to Mocamedes when they go to Ovamboland. It would afford many of the people in the laager the opportunity to send personal messages and letters to their kinsfolk on the Serras. We still have hopes of getting more of them to settle in Upingtonia. If the letters are encouraging they will most certainly come.

'A heavy responsibility now rests on the *Bestuur*. Chris is doing his job most efficiently; but if Lyon arrives he can assist him. Many of the official documents still have to be copied. By the way, what about an own flag for Upingtonia? When I was in Cape Town in 1881, Sarah Jane Andersson showed me a drawing in the scrapbook of her late husband. It was of the flag the Herero army bore, led by Andersson and Green, against Jan Jonker Afrikaander in 1864. If I remember rightly, it had a dark blue background with a white star on it. The vertical and horizontal points of the star had been elongated to form a white cross. A red cross was superimposed on it. What made an impression on me at the time was the note in Andersson's own handwriting underneath the drawing: *Damara flag riddled with ball in the memorable fight of 22 June 1864—CJA*. Well, more is the pity that the Ovaherero do not have such an honourable banner to fight under today.'

I called my *bambuse*. 'You'll have to go to Omaruru with these letters,' I said. 'Take a horse; and see that you keep riding.'

Izak screwed up his eyes.

'Never mind, *Bambuse*,' I said. 'They are not after your blood. Just keep going. Travel by night, if you prefer it that way. But see to it that Mister Eriksson gets these letters. Come back at once with an answer, if possible.'

'Will *Baas* Eriksson come?'

'He will come, yes. And the others will also come. 'Take the canvas bag for your food, *Bambuse*. You must be off before nightfall.'

He left in the late afternoon. Kairob brought me some coffee, and I sat down to write the letters for the men in the hunting veld. By five o'clock they were ready. I handed them over to Jan Prinsloo.

'The messages will be there in three days,' Jan assured me.

Fortune favoured us. The messengers had only been travelling for a day when they met some of the hunters returning to the laager, their wagons loaded to the hood-ribbings with meat, feathers and a reasonable amount of ivory. The wet weather had made things difficult; but on the whole the hunting had been successful.

The laager which had been so quiet suddenly seemed to live again. News of Lewis's threat of war had reached the hunters even before my letters had arrived. It was the details of Lewis's declaration which the returning hunters now wished to know. I translated the document for them and they studied it silently.

To my surprise Chris Leen arrived from Omaruru the next day. I embraced him as a brother, eagerly hearing what news he had. 'The whole of Damaraland is agog with the story of Lewis's letter to you,' he said. 'I was expecting it, as I wrote to you; but I honestly did not think it would come so soon. On the other hand, the very fact that it has come in this way seems to indicate its impulsive nature. Rule and Stevens confirmed it all for me at Otjimbingue. So I decided to come home at once.'

To come home . . . Otjovanda Tjongue—Grootfontein—had come to be our home. No, it was Upingtonia itself: this land of royal trees and fine waters. Disease, poverty, threats of violence, the loneliness of the laager, the pressing uncertainty of the future, nothing could prevent us striking root here.

'Louw, Blackie, Barend!' I greeted each in turn. It was good to see them all again.

From their side it was: 'Brother Will!'—'Mister Jordan!' —'Mester Will!'

In Barend's attitude I could detect no change. Either the story Chris had told of in his letter had not reached his ears; or else he had recognized it as being preposterous.

To Chris, drinking coffee at my wagon, I said: 'I've been taken for many things in my life, but never for an adulterer.' Chris suddenly laughed out aloud. I could only smile. I poured us some brandy to go with the coffee.

'Here's to a good marriage,' Chris said, eyeing me carefully. 'You need a wife, Will. Man was not meant to sleep alone.'

To this I had no answer. Others had told me that before.

11

We found each other at Diederick Prinsloo's in the late afternoon.

I told the company all about the journey to Ovamboland. Chris told about his time spent at Otjimbingue. The hunters told of their many adventures in and around the White Pan.

'As far as we could see,' Louw du Plessis said, 'we were hunting strictly within the limits of Upingtonia.' He said this in mock seriousness.

'We hope so,' I said.

'You see, Mester,' Barend Bouwer said, 'we can *maar* go by the names of the places as they stand in the contract!'

'Where is Willem?'

We all fell silent. I looked at Old Diederick, who had put the question.

'. . . What is up with Willem?' The old man turned his eyes on us.

Willem Prinsloo had not arrived with the others. Soon Old Diederick was enquiring after him. His son, Machiel, answered: 'Pa, I have told Pa that Willem will come within the week.'

'Where is he? Why does he not come?'

Old Diederick was sitting in his chair, swishing the flies away with a wildebeest-tail. His eyes were blazing.

'He does not come, Pa, because he has gone out after a leopard with Jan Labuschagne.'

'To do what, son?'

'To go after the leopard. They got tired of all the wetness, Pa, and said that it was drier in the Omaheke sandveld. So they went. There's a leopard there that Jan has been after for many a day.'

'A leopard is the devil himself.' Old Diederick pointed his swish at Machiel. 'He changes his spots!'

This was a new way of looking at it. I laughed with the others. At the same time, I would probably have been happier if Willem Prinsloo had been here. I didn't care too much for his hobnobbing with Labuschagne.

The womenfolk were serving coffee now. The scene was becoming festive. The old trio, who had once been Lisa Lombard's closest friends, and whom I had known as Hannie Venter, Lets Labuschagne, and Tina du Plessis—all married now—were carrying trays about. I missed Lisa herself.

'What is the news from Okasima?' I asked.

It was Louw du Plessis who answered: 'I sent a message to Adriaan Venter that he is wanted to join our company. He should come. We have heard that there are elephants in the 'maramba.'

'All that are away must return,' Old Diederick said. 'Thou sayest so, too, *Meneer*.'

'We need everybody.' I looked at Louw du Plessis. 'Do you expect the Venters?'

'It is very likely that they will come, Brother Will.'

'Each must come to his rightful place, which is here,' Old Diederick emphasized. 'What is this we hear of the Waterberg?'

I looked at the old man. There had always been those in the laager who had favoured the Waterberg as the centre of a settlement in South West Africa. Otjozondjupa was an abandoned mission station, lying at the foot of the mountain. Jan Labuschagne had lauded its properties and had roundly declared that this was where 'the laager should have been.'

Was Willem Prinsloo perhaps a new convert to this point of

view? Was this the reason for Old Diederick's close questioning of Machiel? Families inside the laager were closely knit. It would be a matter of great concern to Old Diederick if one of the Prinsloos were to desert the cause and defect to the Waterberg. Who else was there likely to accompany Jan Labuschagne if he should decide to leave? The Labuschagnes were as much a clan as the Du Plessis, the Holtzhausens, or the Prinsloos . . .

There had always been the story that Lewis had personally made Jan Labuschagne the offer of Otjozondjupa. There he (Labuschagne), and whoever wished to accompany him, would live happily as the subject of Kamaherero. Jan was clever in his way. His broadness of humour was very much a diversion. What had happened to the runner who had brought Lewis's declaration of war? Perhaps he had gone eastwards to the omuramba, looking for Jan.

'Well, then it is time for us to close our ranks!'

This was Barend Bouwer speaking in answer to something David Black had said.

'Yes,' I said, 'it is about time.'

The *Bestuur* met after the evening devotions.

'It is quite clear, gentlemen,' I said, 'that we need not regard the matter of Lewis's threat to us too solemnly. At the same time, we should not disregard it altogether. The man is obviously going all out to get what he wants; or to hold what he has; or thinks he has. Whether Kamaherero himself knows anything about this declaration is difficult to say.'

Chris thought about the matter. 'You don't easily get to know what Kamaherero has on his mind,' he said. 'Most of the day he just sits there at Okahandja under the camelthorns, wearing a seaman's jacket, and a woollen cap on his head. Even his own missionaries can't make up their minds about him.'

I was listening intently. Kamaherero had had my wagons 'offloaded' on a number of occasions. He had informed me, more or less officially, that this was only 'part payment' for the 'disservice' I had done the Herero nation. The fact that I had done nothing else than try and draw the attention of the outside world to the general anarchy persisting in the country did not seem to make any impression on him. Yet, on the personal level, I bore him no ill will.

A thought struck me. '*Oom* Diederick,' I said, 'We might well consider the possibility of your writing to Kamaherero personally.

No later than tonight. The letter should be on its way to Okahandja tomorrow. Kamaherero should have it before the week is out.'

It was quiet around the table, as the members of the *Bestuur* waited for me to continue.

'It is quite possible,' I said, 'that Kamaherero is not fighting the Boers as much as he is fighting Will Jordan. If that is the case, the sooner the record is put straight the better. This is not my private venture here. It never was, and could never be. It is just possible that our enemies might take another view of things if we make a personal approach.'

Old Diederick considered it carefully. We waited patiently for him to answer.

'If the *Bestuur* thinks thou has judged rightly, *Meneer*,' he said at last, 'we shall do it.'

'Then that has been decided,' I said.

Other matters now demanded our attention. There were the wagons to be sent down to the Bay. There were the final arrangements regarding the allocation of lands. Settlers would have to establish their beacons before the end of December. For the rest, we had to see to it that business here at Otjovanda Tjongue—Grootfontein—went on as usual, and new settlers were encouraged.

The old urge to isolation had by no means been changed. Still, facts had to be met. The Erikssons were definitely coming, I said. Then there was Carlson of Omaruru, and almost certainly Charles Lyon, also the Chapmans, and Todd . . . I named a number of others who had been well-known to the Boers as hunters, or hunter-traders.

It was only Chris who signified his agreement. This was a matter we would have to face courageously, I said. There was no hope of our meeting the challenge before us if our numbers remained as meagre as they were at present. We would have to go forward together, accepting all the support we could get from people of strong character from outside.

I left it there for the while, and returned to the question of which wagons would go to the coast; and when they would leave. What we needed, I said, was medicines, ammunition, guns, material for clothing, cotton for sewing, coffee beans. Pity, I said, that there were no more Segals about. Segal was a *smous**

*Pedlar.

who had kept on overcharging the Trekboers for necessary things, until his wagon broke down one day and only the wheelwrights of the Trek could assist him—at a price. The reference caused laughter around the table. The tension which had build up subtly during the discussion on immigration was dispersed.

'Old Segal, yes!' Louw du Plessis chuckled. Barend hooked his thumbs underneath his braces and rocked his chair, smiling broadly. Even Old Diederick smiled.

'I have written to Manasse, gentlemen,' I said. 'Told him what sort of man Lewis is, said that he would yet discover it for himself. Furthermore, we have no feeling of enmity towards the Ovaherero. On the contrary.'

It was almost midnight when we eventually broke up. There was no chance of getting much sleep. I was called out about three o'clock to come and see a sick child. It was past four when I had done what I could. The child, who had got violently ill after eating some poisonous veld-fruit, was over the worst, and sleeping again.

It was a comforting thought that I was still regarded as the physician of the laager.

12

Early in the new week I heard the news that Jan Labuschagne was back. I went to look for him, wishing to know what his plans were. I found him recounting his adventures in the leopard-hunt. Seeing me, he raised his right arm by way of salute. 'Mister Will!' he said.

'Was just telling,' he continued, 'how the leopard came and crept in under my blanket, with me there too!' He laughed with his head thrown back, displaying his epiglottis. 'Come on, take a seat, man!' He showed me a tree-stump, but I remained standing. The rest of the company, sitting around, some lying on the grass, were obviously amused.

'. . . As I have been saying, it was the Bushmen who came and told us up there that the eland were salt-licking in the pans. Got there, and soon shot a string of eland. Others came along with the wagons and loaded the meat. Had to cut biltong for three days, Mister Will. In summer you pickle them first in the hide itself.

Otherwise you'll never get a proper biltong with all this rain. Then off again. This time taking Brother Daniel along with me. And old Piet du Prés, who joined us some time ago. We pickled all that biltong first. Had to use a wagon-hood, because the skins were not big enough. Trekked away, man, and fixed up a laager for the night. You know how it is when time presses. We just cut grass as we found it in the bush. Made up a big bed for us all. So we went to sleep; Brother Daniel in the middle, Piet du Prés on his right, I on his left.'

Much comment was now coming from the audience: Why did *he* not sleep in the middle? Were his feet too big? Were they looking after Brother Daniel? Was the right side nearest to the fire?

'. . . Well, there I lay. Next to me was my hat, pipe, tobacco pouch. There was my dog, old Spoor, also lying on the grass. I say, *kerels*,* have you seen how dark darkness can be, eh? When it comes to a slow drizzle in the bush, and the sky is thick with clouds, and the moon is dark? You can't even see your own toes.

'Well now, there was a kind of bump near to us: must have been an old termite nest. What happened then? Was just dozing off when—woop!—something jumped right at me from the top of the bump: right onto old Spoor, snoring just next to me.'

From all sides there was now much laughing and cajoling: 'Come on Jan, tell us another!'—'Now can this be true?'—'What a story to think up when one is sober!'

'. . . Before you could say knife, we all jumped out of the grass bed, and shouted: "Lion!" . . . Searched for my lucifers. Could not find them! Dark, dark, as I have been telling you. There we were charging about, bumping into each other, all the time, shouting. You couldn't make out what was dog and what was leopard. There I stood, trying to get in a shot. Could just see old Spoor standing his ground while the leopard had hold of his throat. And everywhere, by this time, there was blood. Piet du Prés got in a shot. The next thing we saw was the leopard passing us like a yellow flash. Piet was knocked down; but he still fired another shot into the darkness of the bush.'

I looked at the laughing men, sitting about on stumps of wood, lying on the grass, reclining against the boles of trees. They were smoking pipes, chewing tobacco, wiping sweat off their faces, whittling at lean strips of biltong. This was something of the old,

*Chaps.

carefree life on the High Serras: before thoughts of the future had returned to plague them. This was also the life many had thought finally to establish here in Upingtonia.

Here now, in the clear light of afternoon, I was deeply conscious of the fine balance of things. Here in the enormous incandescence of the day we were reduced to nothing. We were tiny spots in the green ocean of the bush.

'. . . So then some Bushmen arrived with some fire, Mister,' Jan Labuschagne continued. 'Brother Daniel also got a light burning. There we saw old Spoor had got messed up properly. Well, we washed him with what do you think? *Aguardente!* Washed him, and sewed up his pieces of skin hanging from him like rags. Next morning we followed the blood-spoor—with Spoor leading all the way. Some three miles, and there, suddenly, we saw the leopard's mug through the grass. I threw my gun to my shoulder—and—bang!—there he lay, with a bullet between the eyes. Come to my wagon, Mister, I'll show you the skin!'

It was only towards the late afternoon that I could corner him.

'What's all this I hear about your plans for the Waterberg, Jan?' I asked. He looked at me askance. 'Don't cause any dissension here, please. Your people have come a long way. We can make Upingtonia something which the world will know about. If each one tries his own luck in some scatter-brained sort of way, where do you think we'll land? You know what bitter things strife and discord have caused in the history of your people. What are your plans? Or are they secret?'

His face had become tight with anger.

'What our plans are?' he said. 'We do only what is best for us!'

All the *bonhomie* had now disappeared. Suddenly he had become full of bluster and loud talk again.

'Our plan is our plan!' he said.

'In the laager there are also women and children,' I said. 'There are also old people.'

He narrowed his eyes and peered at me. 'We have always been saying that we should go to the Waterberg,' he rasped. 'Then we would not have had all this trouble.'

Words leapt to my tongue, but I did not speak them. There was no point in a verbal fight with this man. 'I don't know what you had on your mind when we first came here,' I eventually said. 'I only know that you came, and you settled here. All I ask of you is that you consider your own flesh and blood.' I looked up at him. I was six feet tall, but he towered over me.

'What do you mean?' he said. 'Surely it is right for our people to find their *own* place!'

'But this *is* their own place.'

'Not for the Boers only, Mister!'

I looked for words. It was the old trouble. My God, had there been no progress? How did his attitude accord with his acceptance of Lewis's offer? It didn't make sense.

'Whom do you object to?' I asked. 'Your own people had the first opportunity to select lands and waters. Why don't you follow the example of your leaders?'

'They might be our leaders, but Mister Jordan says what is to happen!'

'Where? How? When?' I was losing control over myself. 'You must be daft, man.'

He looked at me, then suddenly walked off with great swinging strides. Then he turned about again and shouted in a loud voice: 'You have a plan, Mister, to bring people here who are not *our* people! They don't believe in *our* God, and they don't belong to *our* Church! They speak English, or they speak some other strange language. Where now is the Republic we have striven for?'

For the moment I seemed to be hearing Pieter Maritz-Botha again. Something was beating in my throat. A sweat-bead crept over my left cheek. It would have been easy to have told this man that one did not preserve one's own by running to an area where a black potentate held sway. Neither did one do it by making common cause with, by accepting favours from, a man like Robert Lewis.

'You are very foolish,' I said. 'Don't you know Robert Lewis? Here he has declared war against the laager; and you still think that you can co-operate with him, or appease him?'

'We must do our best for our people!' he shouted. And Willem Prinsloo, appearing from nowhere, added with the old impulsiveness: 'What we must see to is that war doesn't come.' He had probably heard what I and Jan Labuschagne had been saying and could not contain himself any longer. 'We are not strong here, but we can prevent things happening!'

I looked at him in surprise. In a sense this was nothing new. Piet Botha had always insinuated that even 'those close to *Oom* Diederick' did not support us. He had said this in public on 20 October, at the people's meeting. Had Willem Prinsloo, and the others who were leaving for the Waterberg, felt that way at that time? If so, why hadn't they spoken up?

'Do you really believe you are going to effect anything at all with Lewis?' I asked.

'Lewis is not king!' said Labuschagne.

Some others who had gathered around us were now gaping at us in surprise. I was suddenly sickened by it all. Was what was happening inevitable? Did I have to waste time and patience and energy in trying to convince people who seemed to be inherently short-sighted?

'We must go to find a place where we can stay without being threatened,' Willem Prinsloo said. Had he spoken in this way to his father, Old Diederick? Had he said this to his brothers, Machiel and Jan?

I looked sharply at him. 'You'll come off badly in any deal you are trying to make with Lewis,' I said. 'Mark my words!'

'We have our own plans,' Willem said. 'We are grown-up people, not children!'

I turned about and started walking away. Behind me some voices were still being raised. What it was all about, I could not say. Neither did I care. It suddenly seemed to me as if I was now destined to clash with all sorts of people. This had never been my disposition. Thirty-plus of my thirty-seven years I had spent in relative calm. I had known difficult years, yes. No year in the Transgariep was ever easy. The land itself made its own rigorous demands. But I had never known the soul-destroying tension of these latter days. It had only become part of me since I had thrown in my lot with my friends of the Trek; and especially those who had come down to settle in Upingtonia.

I had given myself to their cause. Or had they given themselves to mine? My cause, I had often said and written, was one of 'colonization and civilization'. It still was. With the Trekboers as the hard core, my dreams could become reality. I had thought about all this until my mind spun. It was still my ideal. In spite of all that had happened, there was no turning back. I had set my course, I had to follow it.

The sun was coming down in waves of light and heat on my bare head. I put my hat on. A lourie fluttered past. I saw its black shadow moving over the grass. 'Go away!' it presently cawed at me from the limb of an acacia. I looked up and saw Chris Leen approaching.

'Hallo, Chris,' I said vaguely. 'What about a drink?' He said something I could not hear, and we walked together to my wagon.

If I still had any hopes that the 'Waterbergers' would see the folly of their ways, they were soon dispelled. Many a time I heard Jan Labuschagne's voice booming over the laager, telling his audience of his fine plans and what benefits they would reap if they joined him.

The laager itself was quiet. One could nevertheless discern signs of uneasiness. In a family like the Prinsloos there was unhappiness about Willem's decision.

'Willem must follow his own head,' Old Diederick said to me somewhat sadly. 'And let him *bump* it!—Bump it hard. *Meneer*, thou knowest how such things do come.'

Having spoken in this way Old Diederick would relapse into silence, sitting motionless for long spells, his large, bony hands clasped around the head of his olive-wood stick.

The Prinsloo brothers themselves would have long talks. Usually it ended with Willem pulling his hat over his eyes and stalking off. Jan and Machiel would watch him go, shake their heads, and stand around talking.

I was also vaguely conscious now that some in the laager were becoming critical of my dominant position. If this were the case, I said to myself, if indeed I was having too much to say, how was it to be avoided? I was the only one who could see and deal with things in their entirety. It would certainly have been far more pleasant to have abandoned my responsibilities, to have said: 'Then you carry on from here. I have brought the matter so far. Now I wish to return to my hunting and trading. Regarding the expense I have had in buying this tract of country, well, let's regard it as my contribution to stability in South West Africa. Let's part company here, as good friends, each going his own way. In the material sense, I can no longer afford the luxury of leadership. I have had no opportunity to take a single load of ivory or feathers or anything else down to the Bay for months. My agents in Cape Town must be wondering what has happened to me. Before the idea of Upingtonia came up, I was doing well enough. Every now and again I could send my mother and sisters a generous sum of money through Krynauw and Co.'

Chris had heard from Georgina. She had said that they were very worried about me. Why did they not hear from me, she asked? I had my folks constantly on my mind. It was worrying me deeply. I did not have a steady income any longer. I had neglected my primary duties in favour of the greater idea. But charity still started at home. What if I were suddenly to die? What would be left for distribution? I did not even have a proper will. There were my wagons, some cattle, the few personal possessions, a little bit of cash. There was also the land of Upingtonia. What this all amounted to was problematical. Very likely in case of death my possessions would have to be collected by some good friend. What then?—He would send them down to the Bay. There was little hope that cattle would get there. The property of a dead man was fair game in this country. However vigilant my still anonymous good friend might be, the cattle would almost certainly just disappear on the trek to the Bay. If even some did get there, who would buy them? What about my lands? Would Kambonde still honour the contract? Would my heirs be compensated for what I had paid for? The copper deposits were certainly worth something. But all was dependant on the goodwill of Kambonde.

These were morbid thoughts. One attracted things to one by dwelling on them in this negative way. Keep going, be alive, that was the only way to set things here on an even keel again. The ship had to be saved . . . Saved? There I went again. I shouldn't think of it all like this. Conditions were not really so bad. I was being unnecessarily defensive. Why? Was it Upingtonia or the concept of Upingtonia I was trying to defend, to justify? Or was it just Will Jordan who had increasingly found himself to be identified with the success of everything?

'Don't be side-tracked,' I would breathe to myself. 'Carry on as if nothing has ever happened to make things difficult. Don't be side-tracked . . .'

Within days I opened the register for the occupation of lands. For a small fee the allocations could be officially noted. What was necessary now was for every settler to survey his own lands and erect the beacons. The traditional pattern would be honoured: an hour's ride on horseback in a fixed direction, a beacon . . . Then another hour's ride, at right angles to the first leg, another beacon . . . The farm became more or less a square. Where squares overlapped, the *Bestuur* would decide. It was easier said than done, most of the time.

Where trees and grass were high, where hills, omurambas, depressions and water courses made the going difficult, the square was out of alignment. The wonder was that farms still seemed to find their shape. The heart of every new settlement was its water. From the water, development would spread. Many in the laager were referring to their farms as if they were already living there . . .

I was surprised one day to receive a request from three of the Waterbergers for allocations. Yes, they said, they were on their way to Otjozondjupa, but they would like the land in Upingtonia as well. I was speechless. Well, I eventually found my voice, how nice. We who were remaining here at Otjovanda Tjongue to keep things going, to get things on a firm basis, should do so for the benefit of those who were playing safe elsewhere.

'That is not as we intend it, Mister Jordan,' Jan Labuschagne said.

'Yes,' I answered quickly, 'I think it is. You are quite prepared to share in all the benefits here, as long as you are not called upon to help look after them.'

I was angry. Yet I also knew that it would serve no purpose in trying to prevent the Waterbergers from having any land at all in Upingtonia. There were enough harsh things being said against me at present. I certainly did not want to have the reputation that I was preventing Trekkers from living in their own republic, even if they had become defectors. It was already held against me that I was bringing people to Upingtonia who spoke English, or 'in other languages' . . .

No doubt Jan Labuschagne and his lot would find out in due course that even the Waterberg was not Kingdom Come. I smiled wryly. Here I was thinking like Robert Lewis. In the end I compromised. The lands would be kept for a reasonable time, I informed Labuschagne. Should there be no attempt to settle them, then other arrangements would be made.

'Well, just as Mister Jordan thinks good!' he said generously.

Like Pieter Maritz-Botha, the man was an enigma.

13

The Waterbergers were to leave in the coming week. They attended the Sabbath devotions for the last time. Old Diederick read them the strange history of King Jehoiachim, stressing certain words.

'. . . So the king sent Jehudi to fetch the roll; and he took it out of Elishima the scribe's chamber . . . And Jehudi read it in the ears of the king . . . And in the ears of all the princes that stood *beside* the king . . . Now the king sat in the winter house in the ninth month . . . and there was a fire on the hearth *burning* before him . . . And it came to pass that when Jehudi had read three or four leaves, he cut it with the *penknife*, and cast it into the fire that was on the hearth . . . And all the roll was *consumed* in the fire that was on the *hearth* . . .'

I knew that Old Diederick had Robert Lewis's war-letter in mind. In my mind's eye I could see him cutting the letter to shreds with his sheath-knife, burning the pieces in the laager fire, until 'all the roll was *consumed* in the fire that was on the *hearth*.'

The psalm-singing, the long prayer and scripture-reading sounded tired that day. The new development weighed heavily upon the laager. Everywhere there was evidence of heart-searching. But, I decided, there was no turning about for us who still believed in our cause.

The Waterbergers came to say good-bye on the Monday: the Labuschagnes, the Piet du Prés, Rudolph du Toits, Willem Prinsloos . . . There were eleven families. From Jan Labuschagne I heard a cheery announcement that they had selected their farms here. These were the lands lying around the waters at Omambonde, Ou Tefans and Rietfontein.—For the moment, after having been told this, I was not quite sure where all these places lay. I knew the traditional names of waters, but not those which had been given to places by the Trekboers.

'Next month we'll be here to pack our beacons, Mister Jordan!' Jan Labuschagne said. I managed a bit of a wry smile.

I said good-bye to the Waterbergers, shaking hands with each one in turn. At least, I reflected, it was something to be thankful for that we were parting without undue enmity.

'Chris,' I said, as we stood watching the convoy leave the heights of Otjovanda Tjongue, 'I suppose I am just a damned idiot dreaming my own dreams.' I stood looking at the distant southern sky. It was summer at the Cape now. The southeaster was blowing the skies to limpidity. The sea water, too, was clear and cold. At Hout Bay the Cape lobster would abound in the rock-pools. 'You know what, Chris? I also have a dream of lying on a Cape beach again some day. I'd like to lie there in the nude, with the sun and the wind and the sea spray on my body. What's happening to me, Chris?'

Barend Bouwer left on 14 December with the wagons for Omaruru. He would try to get through to the Bay, he said. I knew full well that he would run into difficulties with Manasse Tjisiseta: if not with his own wagons, then certainly with mine.

'We'll just do our best,' Barend said. 'Now, should it happen that Manasse wants to know *whose* wagon is *whose* wagon?'

'Then you tell him the facts.'

'And should he seize the wagon?'

'I doubt whether he will go as far.' Secretly I was hoping that the Erikssons had been able to use their influence by now. The uncertain element, however, was still Viehe. If he had been meddling again in matters which did not concern him, other measures would have to be taken. I had, for instance, considered approaching *Kanzler* Nels at Okahandja himself. Nels was very much German *chargé d'affaires* here.

'Just do your best, Barend,' I said in conclusion.

He considered it for a moment. Then he pulled his hat over his eyes, and grunted. 'Sometimes a man's best is not good enough.' Had I detected something in his attitude which was new? It was difficult to say.

Shortly before Barend's departure the next day, an answer arrived from Kamaherero to Diederick Prinsloo's letter. Old Diederick was seated on his chair in front of the house, with the open letter on his knees. It had been drafted in German. Possibly Brincker or Diehl had been the writer. It could also have been Nels. What pleased me at once was the realization that Lewis, at least, did not seem to have had a hand in it.

The letter was dated 10 December. I took it up and scanned it.

Yes, Kamaherero wrote, he was quite prepared to discuss peace. War had to be avoided. The Boers should come to Okahandja to talk things over . . .

I translated this freely to those who had come with me to Old Diederick's. Louw du Plessis looked pensive.

'So it seems, Brother Jordan,' he said, 'that the Waterbergers may still serve some good purpose? I mean, let them go and talk to Kamaherero first. Then we here will better be able to know what to do.'

David Black shared this view. He and Louw du Plessis had always been the steadiest elements in the laager. Well now, how did this accord with the popular idea that the Boers were stodgy, unemotional, blunt? The opposite was more like it. They were deep-feeling, sensitive, even to the point of sentimentality. In a way this was the explanation for the belief that the *rapprochement* with Kamaherero would yet lead to positive results. I could not share this belief. I knew too well the fickle natures of tribal potentates. The half century of bloody warfare in this country had demonstrated this. Kamaherero's sudden reasonableness might have been dictated by the knowledge that his victory over Hendrik Witbooi at Osona had by no means put an end to the Nama threat.

The letter from Kamaherero seemed to have an enlivening effect on Barend Bouwer. Manasse regarded himself very much as a power on his own. On the other hand, he could ill afford to break with Kamaherero. He was still very much dependent on Okahandja for his influence.

14

On 16 December the laager once again remembered the Boer victory at Blood River, fifty years before.

There was a special religious service, conducted by Louw du Plessis, as Diederick Prinsloo was ill. I looked up Old Diederick where he lay on the *katel* in his little house. A faded Transvaal *Vierkleur* hung above the doorway. The old man bade me welcome by lifting his hand.

'Sorry to find you in bed today, *Oom*,' I said.

He turned his eyes on me. I could see that his thoughts were far away. After all, he, like Ella Lombard, had been part of the Great Trek from the Old Colony to Natal.

Many thousands of miles through Africa lay mapped on the long, deeply hewn face of Old Diederick. He had participated in nearly all the great battles of the mass immigration of the thirties. He had fought at Mosega where the Ndebele might had been broken after the disaster of Vegkop. He had fought at the Sod Laager. Ultimately he had also fought at Blood River . . .

The past had always been carried along with him, in wagon after wagon. Here I was sitting now in a little room in the northern bush of South West Africa, listening to the tales of a heroic time.

'Was October . . .' I heard the deep, rasping voice of Old Diederick say. 'Was October of 1838. Our Commandant General,

Gert Maritz . . . he died of sickness . . . Was the grandfather of Pieter Maritz-Botha.'

He said these words with sudden spiritedness, and looked slowly at me, as if expecting comment. I remained silent.

'So he died,' Old Diederick continued, 'Gert Maritz . . . Beginning of December we of the Trek were all together at Danskraal . . . Pretorius—Andries Pretorius—was now our leader, chosen by us all . . . A whole fleet of wagons to welcome him . . . for he had come from the Old Colony after the death of Maritz, and also the death of Uys . . . Cilliers had gone to fetch Pretorius down at Graaff-Reinet; *Koloniesplaats* . . . So we were there together at Danskraal. And Pretorius said: "If God give us the victory over the Zulu nation, whenever we should clash with them, then we will remember the day for ever as a Sabbath." That he said to Cilliers: and Cilliers said it to the *volk* . . . Whoever was *against* it should stand to one side.'

A thin shaft of sunlight had penetrated through the wooden shutter of the room. It fell over Old Diederick's face, emphasizing its gauntness.

'How many were there to *one* side?—Only *two.*—What did they say?—They said they did not know how we could keep such a vow . . . Then Cilliers spoke. And Pretorius spoke *too* . . . Cilliers said: "The Lord has never deserted us. *And I will give unto thee, and to thy seed after thee, the land wherein thou art a stranger* . . . *Two* against it. But all others *for* it." So we made the vow—there at Danskraal . . . December 7 of '38. Next day the commando of four hundred trekked out to Blood River to await the enemy. Only the men . . . Evenings when we had devotions we spoke the vow again: every day until the Saturday, when we drew a laager next to a river, which we later called *Blood River*: next to a mountain, and alongside a deep sluit . . . The laager was right up against the sluit; and also against the river . . . Patrols went out. They came back and said: "Beware, the enemy is at hand!" So what did we do? . . . Fastened lanterns to whipsticks and tied them to the wagons. There was much rainy weather, like this year here; and great mists lay over the land. At night we heard the clamour of war from the enemy. But they did not come . . . Came not that night but *did* come the next morning: it was the Sabbath . . . Many thousands came . . . Came from everywhere, like the waves of the sea. But we stood our ground, shooting from behind the wagons.

Everybody was brave in the struggle, because Pretorius was always ahead, and leading us . . . There was a cannon too. Fought until the enemy lay dead as high as the roof here . . . Then the men went out on the horses and chased the enemy, shooting all who were still fighting us. We counted the dead bodies . . . until we counted three thousand. There were more too. And we? . . . Only one or two wounded; and that was Pretorius himself; and some other . . .'

I had heard this story on previous occasions. Every year on 16 December Old Diederick would recount it. So I had always been reminded of the way in which my friends of the Trek had carried their strange, heroic past along with them in all their wanderings.

What had happened at Blood River had been one of the decisive battles in the history of Western man. The popular idea was that the Boers had trekked out of the Cape Colony because of the emancipation of the slaves. There was far more to it. The prime motive had been the universal urge to freedom . . .

In Natal they had negotiated with Dingane, King of the Amazulu. They had bought from him a tract of country in which the Republic of Natalia was to be established. While having a parley with Dingane, Pieter Retief and seventy men had been murdered. The laagers lying below the Drakensberg had been attacked, and a great many people killed. Nevertheless, the Trekboers had not despaired. Blood River had finally brought them victory . . .

As a boy I had heard these stories: all the terrible details of the massacres of Weenen and Blaauwkrantz. Ella Lombard had been at Blaauwkrantz: one of the few who had survived to tell the tale . . .

I found her towards evening sitting in a chair under a *scherm*. There was a *Vierkleur* fastened to the hood-ribbing of her wagon. She was pleased to see me, but seemed depressed.

'It is because she thinks this day of Little Miss far out there in the bush, Mister,' Dina explained.

To this Kleinveld added: 'Old Miss has thought: perhaps Little Miss would be here today, see. Now she has not come.'

Dina brought us some coffee, and I asked: 'Well, what did Lisa say? When can we expect her?'

'A child says many things,' Ella Lombard said. 'And does not always think of the heart of a mother.'

'Probably she is just waiting for the new year,' I said. 'Then she'll be here, and will stay for a long while.'

The Day of the Vow, I thought, was firstly a day for the oldsters of the laager. That was why Ella Lombard was feeling the way she did. She needed her loved ones on a day like this.

'So you see, *Meneer*,' she said pensively, 'this happens to an old woman.'

'Old Miss isn't old,' Dina said with some heat. 'And we are here, so Old Miss is not alone.'

'Yes, Dina. I know I am not alone. The Lord is with me; and you are here too.'

Dina grunted approval. 'She sits here thinking too many things,' she said. 'Not good for the heart.'

'We have come a long way, Dina,' Old Miss herself answered. 'It is time to think about all that has happened.'

'We have come far; but we are not tired. We can go yet farther.'

'Who all were left on the trek road, Dina? They who lie in the bush, in the sand, whose graves we ne'er shall find.'

I let her talk. The following day the *Vierkleur* would be taken down again and put away in the *voorkist.* Should Adriaan and Lisa Venter not turn up early in the new year, I would send them a message to come.

Ella Lombard unbuttoned the sleeve of her dress: slowly, deliberately, as if it were part of the ritual of the day.

'They thought I was dead,' she said, displaying the scars which ran the length of the forearm. 'But it was not yet my time.

'*Meneer*, perhaps you have thought sometimes: what happened to me after they had murdered all who were with me, and I alone remained? Well, I think I have told you about Sister Hannie and brother-in-law Nicholas van Rensburg. They had got married, and only came down from the Berg after all had taken place.—They found me there at Sod Laager, where I was. Then they cared for me until I was well again. Those were hard days for us all because we had to struggle against the nations of Natal, which were the Amazulu. Pieter Retief and all his men were murdered by Dingane, who was their king. *Meneer*, can you see now that we had reason to think that all was lost? The land which we had been seeking, and which Retief had bought and paid for. Just as you, *Meneer*, bought and paid for what is now our Lydensrust. Then came Blood River, and the enemy was given into our hand.'

Natalia, I thought, another dream that had faded and

disappeared . . . The trek turned back over the mountains and went to the Trans-Orange and the Transvaal.

'So there we were, *Meneer*; and General Pretorius went to catch Dingane, who was not dead after Blood River. Chased him over the Pongola River . . . And only afterwards we heard from Carel Trichardt that Dingane was dead. How that happened? The laagers were everywhere, still: we had not yet left Natalia. I, with Sister Hannie and brother-in-law Nicholas van Rensburg, was in the laager of Landman: Willem Landman, who was a brother of Commandant Carel Landman, as you may know. The laager stood at a river, not far from the sea. One day the women saw a band of knobnosed *volk*—black *volk*!—approaching with pack-oxen. Some of us were frightened and started running to the wagons. But Sister Hannie and others suddenly saw that there was a white man among them. Well, we had already had tidings about the Trichardt people, and how they had all died of fever when they trekked down from the lowveld to Delagoa Bay. Well, we thought they were all dead. And there suddenly was *Oom* Carel: thin as a plank, and dried out by fever. But so glad to see us all again. He jumped off his horse, and many ran up to him, embracing him, and crying for joy . . .

'An own free destiny, *Meneer*, that is what our people have always sought. Louis Trichardt was the first of the Voortrekkers, because he went ahead of us all. Afterwards he came to the Zoutpansberg, in the northern Transvaal; and from there he trekked down to Delagoa Bay; and they all died there, except Carel, and a few others. What Carel then did was to go and see what land he could find even further north. He went by ship, *Meneer*, all the way to Egypt.'

I knew the story. It had been a big discussion point in the old days at the Cape: whether Carel Trichardt had indeed got as far as Egypt. According to his reports it rather seemed that he had penetrated to the upper reaches of the Nile, crossing a part of Abyssinia on the way. He had not found his Land of Promise, and had come back to look for his people in Natal.

'*Oom* Carel then brought us the news that Dingane had been killed, *Meneer*. It was up there on the banks of the Pongola River, so they said. Sopoza, who was king of the Swazi nation, caught Dingane and defeated his armies and killed him. That is what *Oom* Carel said. He also said that the nations were very strong all around Natal, and it would be better if we were looking for our land on the sunset-side. That is what we did. We left Natalia. We stayed there until the English came; but the English were too strong for us. We were but few in numbers. When the people in the highveld heard that the English were there, they came down over the mountains to help us. That was Jan Mocke and his commando. But the English were still too strong for us. Some of our people stayed on in Utrecht. But others kept on saying: Back! We must go back: over the Berg to the highveld again. There we would be free!—*Meneer*, I was seventeen when I married Hans Lombard. We had four sons—all dead now. I had four sons; and when I had already thought that my time was past, another one came. That was Lisa. Hans and I were married in Pietermaritzburg. It was at the very time when Jan Mocke and his commando came down over the Berg. You know what? They just kicked up a lot of dust, and then they went back to Winburg, which is in the Free State. Well, when we saw that our people were leaving Natal and going back over the Berg, we also packed up and trekked. Three months, and we settled at Mooidorp in the Transvaal; which was later called Potchefstroom . . . Had two children there. Hans then wanted to go to Schoemansdal, because there was much ivory to be had here; and ivory had a price. Then we came back to Potchefstroom; and then went to Rustenburg, in the western Transvaal. Stayed there. Hans and the sons were hunting together. The names of my sons were Tobias, Little Hans, Petrus, Willem.'

She went on. She told of the death of each son. Tobias had been killed while lion-hunting near Ohrigstad in the lowveld. Little Hans had fallen in the campaign against Makapan in the Zoutpansberg, Petrus had died while on an expedition across the Limpopo to Barotseland. Willem, the youngest, had also been killed by a lion: at Lake Ngami, when the Trek was crossing the Thirstland. Hans Lombard himself had died of fever in the marshes. Many thousands of miles separated these graves.

'I first wanted to go back, because Lisa was still a small child. But what could a woman do alone on the trek-road? Machiel Roets also died. As you know, *Meneer*, he was a great hunter. Sannie was his widow. Well, we found each other and then decided no, we would stay with the Trek. We remembered how the first Voortrekkers had already gone into the wilderness to seek a new land; to freedom, and perhaps the sea. Think of all the graves everywhere, *Meneer*. There must be a great many by this time.

Now who could there be who could find them all again?—*Oom* Carel Trichardt went as far as Egypt and came back to where we found him. And later, when we saw that we had not yet found what we were seeking, Hans Lombard, my husband, said to me: "Then we must trek, woman! The *volk* want to go through the Thirstland. It will be difficult to trek where there is no water and the sand is thick and the sun beats down. But this is what the Lord has called us to do. So we must *maar* trek, come what may On the other side of the Thirstland is the land we are seeking; the good land where we shall live in peace and happiness forever."

'Why? Do you ask *why* we trekked, *Meneer*? There was no other reason but that we had the *feeling,* the spirit of trek, as the Lord had given it. It was always our ideal, *Meneer.* It was our fine land, our Land of Rest.—What we have lost?—We have lost nothing, *Meneer*, because the Lord is always with us: Emmanuel. And here is our Lydensrust after all these years. You must keep faith in your God, and He will lead you to where the land is that He has given you.'

I arose. My thoughts and feelings were in a state of flux. It was, however, neither the time nor the place to give expression to them. I simply said, 'You are right. This is the end of your journey. We have got here; and here you should remain, believing in what has been attained, and what is still to be attained. To this purpose, we must have faith in each other.'

She was drying her tears. Her face had suddenly become deeply lined. There was also the sallow dullness of fever about the skin. 'Dina,' I said. 'You must let Old Miss rest now. She is tired. Fever eats one up. I'll tell you what, if Little Miss is not back here by the end of next week, Kleinveld must go and look for her.'

Kleinveld turned up his eyes at me where he was squatting in front of the *erd.* 'I'll go, Mister,' he said.

'Mister,' Dina intervened, 'that is what he should have done a long time ago. They must come home, those two. I'm telling Old Miss, and telling you too, Mister. It is a wrong thing that they are away. Look at Old Miss now! She is without a child.'

'Old Dina,' Ella Lombard said. 'We mustn't grumble, Dina. It is not good when we grumble, *oumeid.*'

'That is what I know, Old Miss. But I must talk of what is in my heart. Not so?'

'We must be patient, Dina. We can rest here and wait. The children will come back when they have had enough.'

Four days later, to my joy, I heard the lively barking of dogs and heard a trek approaching through the bush. A few minutes later, the flower-wagon of the Venters rumbled up the limestone slope of Otjovanda Tjongue.

The sombre atmosphere which had prevailed in the laager seemed to vanish with the arrival of Adriaan and Lisa Venter. Even the aged Hendrikus van Voor, who was now spending his days in an ever diminishing world, seemed to look up and take notice. From all sides the young people came to see what was happening. Lisa's old friends—Lets Labuschagne, Tina du Plessis, Hannie Venter, as they once were—ran up to embrace her.

At Ella Lombard's a moving little scene took place. Mother and daughter held and kissed each other. Kleinveld was performing a veritable dance which rattled the bones of his spare frame. Dina was wailing aloud, just for the pleasure of it.

When my chance came at last, I said: 'Hallo, Lisa!' I looked down at her shining little face. 'So you have come,' I said. 'We were just about to set out to look for you!'

'I am glad to be here, *Meneer*. Is it well with *Meneer* too?'

'Well enough, Lisa, thank you. Good day, Adriaan.' We shook hands. 'Well, what news do you bring?'

I saw his head lift proudly. The ostrich feather in his hat bent towards the wagon, which was well loaded. I guessed what it was all about. 'Ivory,' I said.

'Ivory, *Meneer*. We went down the 'maramba, *Meneer*. There are big herds coming in from the Sandveld.'

'I didn't know there were any big herds still left,' I said. 'After all the great shooting of some years ago.'

'*Meneer*, there are more elephants in the world than we can ever shoot. They just disappear for a time. But then they always come back. They come in from the Sandveld on the other side of Korakobis. I think they cross there on their way to the White Pan. But because the year is so wet, they come back again to the 'maramba. It is not always so easy to find them, because there is no need for them to return to the waterholes. Water is everywhere. So we have to trek after the elephants and try to catch up with them. The Bushmen come and tell us where they are. Then we stay in hiding and wait for them to pass. Got five big bulls, *Meneer*, with good tusks, as *Meneer* can see. There are still many others. We'll get them all, *Meneer*!'

'What does Lisa do while you are out on the hunt?' I asked.

'Heavens, *Meneer*, I am always with him.'

'My apologies to you, Lisa, of course. But don't you long to be back here sometimes?'

'That is what I have asked Little Miss,' Dina mumbled.

'Yes, we long to be here sometimes,' Lisa said, smiling out of the corner of her mouth, while her eyes said: 'Ah, if you only knew what fun we have out there where we are! Life is such an adventure!'

Africa had got a hold on these two. There was even the smell of the veld about them. I had always been sensitive to it. The Cape mountains left it on you when you went climbing. The bushveld left it on you when you spent days, weeks, months walking, trekking, riding through it. When sleeping you were nearest to it. You lay close to the earth and listened to the great heart beating underneath you. When I was a boy, hunters, traders, and hunter-traders leaned over the counter at Krynauw and Co, in Cape Town. They had arrived in the schooner, which had docked that morning. They leaned over the counter and told their stirring tales. Their hats, their jackets, their guns were impregnated with the aroma of Africa. This was a holy contagion; and I had caught it. We had all caught it.

'So there are Bushmen aplenty,' I said.

'Many, *Meneer*,' Lisa said. 'They just come out of the bush. They are always there when there is meat to be had.'

'Are you sure they are not Gabriel's lot?'

'They are dog-tame, *Meneer*,' Adriaan said. 'Gabriel is *kaputu*, they say. I asked them about him. They say Gabriel got such a fright when he heard about us coming that he fled right across the Thirstland, *Meneer*.'

I looked at him. He had grown tougher these few months. He was a man now and had the bearing of a man. Even his beard which had always been relatively slight had become fuller. There was no sense in trying to keep him inside the laager. His spirit was too restless.

'Well, this is a nice collection of ivory you have,' I said, inspecting it.

'Will *Meneer* be able to take it down to the Bay?'

'Either the Bay or Moçamedes,' I said. 'All in good time, Adriaan. Things are still rather upset at present. But in a month or two, no doubt, normal communications will be restored.

Meanwhile I could advance you some money on this. What about feathers?'

'Birds are scarce, *Meneer*,' he answered. 'I have only the one feather, as *Meneer* can see.'

Lisa struck at it playfully where it waved on her husband's hat. I looked at her. She too had matured these last few months. She was probably expecting, if I judged rightly. I noted the roughness of her hands, and knew that she had not spared herself.

'So, how long are we to have you here?' I asked. 'Or are you back for keeps?'

Others voiced the same question. In conclusion, Ella Lombard said: 'We women do what our men do. It is as it always was. Oh, my child, if your man is not with you anymore! Then you know what a good man is; and you have deep thoughts while you lie alone.'

'We do as we must do, Ma,' Lisa said.

'And as the Lord wills it, my child. But, oh, I am so glad that you have come for the new year. And I am so thankful to the Lord that it is going well with you at your water.'

Tina du Plessis fingered Lisa's dress. 'It is a pretty dress,' she said. Hannie Venter also came up to admire it. And Lets Labuschagne said: 'Such nice stuff, where did you get it? From a *smous*?'

'Adriaan bought it in Moçamedes,' Lisa said.

'It's for the man,' *Ai* Dina said.

Lisa smiled.

15

Things happened fast those last days of December.

Izak returned unexpectedly from Omaruru with some letters. He also brought the news that Barend Bouwer's convoy had been stopped by Manasse Tjisiseta. Ultimately Barend had been allowed to proceed with his own wagons, but not with mine.

'*Baas* Bouwer was very angry,' Izak said. 'But he went off to the Bay.'

I wasn't quite clear who the object of Barend's anger was.

I turned round and walked away. What had happened was disturbing. I was apprehensive now of opening the letter my *bambuse* had brought from Axel Eriksson. When at last I plucked up enough courage to do so, I sat in the lee of my wagon and started reading, my hat drawn over my eyes.

The letter was again in Axel's strange mixture of English, Swedish and German.

My faithful servant, Izak, had probably told me what had happened, Axel wrote. Barend Bouwer had already been stopped by Manasse's people long before he had reached Omaruru. Barend refused to be intimidated and continued his trek. At Omaruru, however, Manasse seized two wagons, identifying them as belonging to 'Mister Jordan'. Barend resisted this and said that it had been Jordan's own decision to send the wagons down to the Bay. Manasse wouldn't listen to anything, but said that he would allow Barend to proceed, but only with his own wagons. Those belonging to Jordan would have to remain at Omaruru. It was quite easy to see the hand of Gustav Viehe in everything. He had great influence over Manasse. Without any doubt, Viehe could have moved Manasse to let the wagons pass.

Axel and his brother Albert had gone to Viehe, and had pointed out that it was not a matter of Jordan's private interests being at stake. There were women and children in the laager at Otjovanda Tjongue badly in need of medicines, food and clothing. Viehe then said that he would put it to Manasse, but he did not think it would make any difference. Manasse was adamant. In any event, Barend then left with his own wagons and had probably reached the Bay by that time. My two wagons were still at Omaruru. They, the Erikssons, would do their best to get them back for me. I would have to exercise patience, however. There were so many rumours about . . .

I sat there against a wagon wheel. The leaves of Axel's letter lay on the ground in front of me. It was all very disheartening. I took up a leaf of the letter again and looked at the closely written words. There was something I had not yet read. It dealt with the Waterbergers.

It seemed, Axel wrote, as if Jan Labuschagne must have had some secret agreement with Robert Lewis. It was general talk at Omaruru that Lewis had told Labuschagne that he was offering them the Waterberg in the name of Kamaherero. Then they could live in peace at Otjozondjupa and other waters. They could also depend on Kamaherero to protect them from anybody who tried to molest them. This news had been brought to Omaruru by traders from Otjimbingue. Viehe himself had confirmed it from reports reaching him from Okahandja. At almost the same time, however, another rumour began to do the rounds. It was to the effect that Lewis had told Kamaherero that the Boers had decided to claim the Waterberg for themselves. They were, in fact, committing a new aggression against the Herero nation.

As long as he could remember there had never been a time in the Transgariep when so many base rumours were flying about, Axel said. If he had still been sceptical about Lewis's machinations at Okahandja regarding the true intentions of the settlers in the Waterberg, he now knew the truth. Manasse himself had come to tell the Erikssons that he had been in contact with Robert Lewis. Lewis had told him of the 'secret plans' of the Boers there.

It was all as complicated as a melodrama. Still, the facts were the facts. My source was a man in whom I had implicit trust. What was interesting, Axel wrote, was that Lewis's manoeuvres soon became known at Otjozondjupa. Jan Labuschagne and Co had hardly got there when they heard of the things Lewis had told at Okahandja and other places. Luckily for them, Axel concluded, Kamaherero himself had not been far from the Waterberg at the time. The Waterbergers at once sent a commission to Otjikango to meet the king. They found him at Kanjoli. The news was that after some difficulty they succeeded in convincing Kamaherero of their peaceable intentions. Now there was talk—it was hard to believe!—that Kamaherero had offered Windhoek to the Waterbergers. Here was the old headquarters of Jan Jonker Afrikaander. He was not so much against the Boers as against Will Jordan.

I walked over to Chris Leen. There I also found David Black and Louw du Plessis. I showed them Axel's letter, and gave them a short summary of its contents. They each read the letter in turn, looking up blankly when they had done with it.

'What's the next step?' Chris asked.

I saw the muscles in David's face working tensely. 'What can one say?' he asked.

'When you mix yourself with the bran, the pigs will devour you,' Louw growled. He said it with a touch of emotion, which was rare in him.

'Are we just going to see matters deteriorate?' Chris asked.

'Hardly,' I said. 'We have to get on with what we have to do. There is no time to waste.'

My companions agreed.

'Louw is right,' I said. 'Mix yourself with the bran, and the pigs get you. Then you can start thinking of home again. The Bible tells us as much. Our Waterberg friends can forget about Windhoek.'

I wasn't expressing myself very clearly. But nothing around us was clear. It was enormously involved. What caused me to wonder suddenly was that in such a sparsely populated country so many human motives could intertwine. The fact was, I supposed, that things were no different here than they had been anywhere else, at any other time. The human race everywhere was cut out of the same cloth.

'Brother Jordan has spoken well,' Louw du Plessis said. 'We should just go on as usual. We are here to stay. And we are here to work.'

'Yes,' David Black said. 'That is so. We mustn't falter!'

This was good to hear. The *Bestuur* had once publicly declared that the rightful settlers of Otjovanda Tjongue, who were now the burghers of Upingtonia, would not leave their lawfully acquired territory. The terse, meaningful words of my friends newly confirmed this.

Axel had added a postscript to his letter.

There was talk, he said, that the Ovaherero had called 1885 Ojovitenda—The Iron Year. There was, however, another name: The Year of Lies. This was because of all the lies Hendrik Witbooi had told at Osona and at other places. But there was much support for the theory that Kamaherero himself had decided on this name after having discovered the guile of Robert Lewis. Once the enemy start fighting each other, we could go our way.

Good old Karevapu. Yes, he was right, there were encouraging signs, in spite of the disappointments. Our main source of strength was still the conviction that we were fighting for a worthwhile cause. It was no small matter to establish a civilized community here in the bush of Africa. Only a settled, stable community, basing its conduct on the tried values of the Western community of nations, could put an end to the anarchy which had ever plagued this country. We could play a meaningful part in the opening of Africa to the world, and the opening of the world to Africa.

It mattered little that only I still thought like this.

LOST EDEN
(January 1886 - July 1886)

1

The new year brought much activity, in spite of the continuing wet weather. Or, who could say, perhaps it was because of it. These were close, humid days. But generally the rains kept the temperatures down. I had experienced summers in this country when it was so dry and hot that you were continually moving from one bit of shade to the other. Now the rains were coming down with monotonous regularity. By the late afternoon there would be a thunderous announcement. Soon it would be followed by heavy rain and a sharp drop in temperature. The lightning would play and often cause even the hardiest to duck and cover their eyes.

Often it would rain through the night. Then it would be pleasant to ride through the bush the next morning to the various farms where the new settlers had already erected their beacons; to the waters where they intended establishing their homes. This would take place as soon as everything was on a sound footing. Fever in the laager was on the increase again.

Barend Bouwer eventually returned from the Bay. It was a relief to see him. He brought medicines, ammunition, post, and the general necessities of life. It would have been even better had my own two wagons not been held at Omaruru. I was consequently unable to implement my stocks.

On the surface Barend was his old self: broad in speech, broad in body, yet extremely active. He was always on the move. He went out to inspect beacons, waters, lands. He spent some time at each separate *werf*, telling of what he had seen and heard at the Bay. To the *Bestuur* he reported fully on what had taken place at Omaruru; and on the situation generally, as he had noted it. It was a vain hope, he said, to believe that Kamaherero had abandoned his warlike intentions. It was perfectly true that the Waterbergers had had discussions with him. Jan Labuschagne and Co were being led by the nose. On the other hand there was no doubt that the Germans at Okahandja were a restraining influence. Of one thing we could be perfectly sure: the enemies of Upingtonia were as many as we could cope with. If we really wanted to go ahead, we had better look around for some friends. Lewis was full of tricks again. He would not rest before he had frightened us off. The Bay was humming with rumours. Even 'the lot' who had previously promised support for Upingtonia—Lyon, Todd, Chapman, and others—had begun to have doubts. They continually asked him, Barend, what the prospects were. Could we stand against our enemies?

I was silent. I didn't quite like Barend's tone of voice. He kept looking at me. He seemed to be challenging me, wanting to know what I had to say about it all?

He was difficult to fathom. He had stressed the necessity of looking for friends. Did he mean the Germans? Had he spoken to any of them? Had he perhaps spoken to Viehe himself? On the other hand there was nothing to indicate that Barend had seen the value of 'foreign' settlers in Upingtonia. He suggested as much by the way in which he referred to 'the lot' down at the Bay, those now having doubts.

There was another thing. It was quite possible that what Chris had written about was now asserting itself. After all, the evil little bit of gossip had been hatched at Otjimbingue. It was probably being told at the Bay as a joke. Will Jordan, the father of Hester Bouwer's child . . . Could one believe it? So he was human, after all . . .!

I shook it off. This was no good. If I allowed such thoughts to take possession of me, it was the surest way to collapse. It was the easiest thing in the world to succumb to morbid introspection. Action counted. There was no time to sit and mope.

'Listen,' I said one day, 'as far as German aid is concerned, we can stop fooling ourselves. The German *Gewalt* in this country isn't even the equal of British power here at its most elementary.'

How could it be, if it was unable to prevent the sort of wanton robbery a man like Manasse had been indulging in? I had protested to Nels as German *chargé d'affaires* at Okahandja against the dubious part played by Gustave Viehe at Omaruru. Neither Nels nor Goering took much notice of what I was saying. They probably regarded it as all just part of a private feud between myself and Viehe. Now Barend Bouwer had, in effect, said that we should try for German support.

I had enough wits about me to realize that I should not press my point of view. However, I was obviously still required to take the lead. The *Bestuur*, though, would have to make the final decision. I would rather not take the responsibility. In fact, this is what had already taken place, in a sense. It was very much Barend Bouwer who was calling the tune. The others—Diederick Prinsloo, David Black, Louw du Plessis—heard his arguments in silence. And their silence was approval.

What was being privately discussed between them was difficult to say. Louw du Plessis informed me that Barend Bouwer had been delegated to go and talk to the Germans. Barend himself confirmed this. I did not enquire about the details. Fine, I said, if the burghers of Upingtonia could enjoy some of the benefits of *Schutz*, by all means let them. I personally had little doubt that they would soon discover what a futile gesture *Schutz* still was.

In a way the new trend of thought was a blessing in disguise. There was not so much talk any more about 'outsiders' coming to Upingtonia. In fact, I sensed that many people were now becoming conscious of our utter loneliness. We needed friends, and ever more friends.

The Erikssons could be expected soon. Charles Lyon as well. It was quite possible that with the newcomers we could do without *Schutz*. Others would follow. Within six months we might well double our numbers.

Having said this, the *Bestuur* looked at me in silence.

'Gentlemen,' I said, 'there are no two ways about it now. If we want to keep on existing as a state, we have to face the facts.'

It was Barend Bouwer who eventually answered. 'Mester Will,' he said, 'you mustn't think we Boers are the sort to cry halt before we have got to the end of the trek! If we must get to a place, we'll get there, I say!'

'I have no doubt, Barend,' I said. 'If it had been otherwise, I certainly would not have been where I am'.

There was still a faint suggestion of tension between us. It was almost impossible to determine. Well, I decided, that was something else that would just have to work itself out. It would indeed have been remarkable had we been in full agreement on all issues.

I wrote further pieces for the Cape press. Some hunters were trekking down the omuramba on their way to the Bay and could take them along. They would be there in about six weeks' time. It might last another few weeks before a schooner could take the letters to the Cape. It was quite possible, of course, that they would never reach their destination. Yet, it was part of the unwritten code existing between hunter-traders that letters were sacrosanct. Even warring peoples honoured the rule. The remarkable thing was that so many letters got to their destinations. The hazards were many. Letters might well get lost somewhere between this northern bush and the distant Peninsula.

I wrote to my mother, too. I said: 'I am sorry that I can't get away here to come and see how you all are. It will be a good thing for Upingtonia as well if I could get to the Cape. I would dearly like to discuss the future of our state with men like Hofmeyr (of the Afrikaner Bond), Sprigg, Scanlen, and especially Sir Thomas Upington, whose name our republic bears. I would like to have their active support in the general cause of civilization here. When this could take place, I do not know. We have much to do.

'There is, for example, the matter of allocating the various lands in an equitable way. Then there is the more arduous task of developing the farms. You will understand that an area which has always been the hunting ground of wild Bushmen could hardly change overnight. But change it must. At the same time we have to see to the establishment and preservation of good relationships with the indigenous peoples . . .'

My mother had always been worried about my health and my safety here. I reminded her of conditions here in the days when Galton, Andersson and Green opened new trek-routes in an unchartered country. I reminded her of a man like David Livingstone. 'Who will deny that things are easier these days,' I wrote. 'Communications have improved, and there have been technical advances in medicine which have benefited us greatly. Quinine is a boon, and fever is no longer the scourge it used to be. Regarding the "dangers" which threaten: it is better to view the matter philosophically. The chances of my losing my life in the streets of Cape Town by being run over are as good as those of being murdered in Ovamboland. I long to see you all and I certainly will be home at the first opportunity. Meanwhile, remember me as your ever loving son . . .'

In my journal I noted down: 'It can reasonably be expected that the distribution of lands in the district of Upingtonia will be completed by the end of March. This is a difficult task.

Fortunately the writer can rely on a number of people who have grown up in a tradition of self-help. Judging from the gardens which have been developed here in the immediate vicinity of Otjovanda Tjongue, we have indeed been fortunate in procuring the finest agricultural land in the territory. With the difficulties we are experiencing in establishing a line of supply with Walwich Bay, the crops raised locally have satisfied the wants of the community. It has been a good year. With continuing good rains it will not be necessary to irrigate lands and crops.'

Deep in January the laager once again took leave of Adriaan and Lisa Venter. They were returning to their water at Okasima, far down the Omuramba. Adriaan had been fired to resume his hunting. I had managed to sell his ivory to Bill Clay and Chris Leen. Now, he said, the time had come to go right down the omuramba to the Tree.

Chris Leen's new partnership with Clay was working well. They were undertaking all sorts of journeys: to Ovamboland, to the Okavango, and back to the Bay. Passing through Omaruru they were left unmolested, although it was common knowledge by this time that Chris was my brother-in-law.

Barend Bouwer, the Oppermans, Louw du Plessis, the Louwrens brothers and David Black were also undertaking new hunting expeditions. They worked in the vicinity of the White Pan. I once suggested to Adriaan that he join this company. He merely smiled, saying in effect: 'I have my own plans, they have theirs . . .'

I saw his eyes and knew he was thinking of the baobab at Olifants Pan. It bore the names of great hunters on its bronze bark. I looked at Adriaan and suddenly remembered a time when similar things had stirred in me. Was I getting old? I was thirty-seven . . . But somehow I felt that I had lived longer than my days. Would I have time enough to relax? Just to sit back and enjoy the calm, the peace, the richness of life? Or was this all an idle wandering with a loss of memory in the way of the Thirstlanders? Indeed, it would be ironic if it was. Whatever the case, there were times when I thought that nothing could be finer than just to trek out into the blue once again: just to go on in a leisurely sort of way, enjoying the land; looking up in surprise when crossing an old trek spoor; recognizing it as your own, then laagering somewhere under great trees by some quiet water . . .

I sometimes saw my servants squatting around the *erd.* There they sat enjoying life in their own way, demanding nothing from it, satisfied with the little that came their way. God, I supposed, had given them a certain wisdom which we of more delicate fibre somehow lacked.

2

At the end of February, when the great rains had eased somewhat, many of the 'outside people' arrived at Otjovanda Tjongue. They had come to inspect their prospective farms. Among them were those we had always relied on as supporters of Upingtonia: Lyon, Thomas, Todd, Chapman.

They stayed a while. They visited the various waters and erected their beacons. They had talks with the people of the laager and did some trading, giving special terms to their future compatriots. Then they departed to various regions: Todd and Chapman to the Okavango, Thomas down to the south. They left behind them new farms with new names: *Okambutafontein, Steenbokrug,* and *Lowland* . . . These were the waters they had carefully selected. Charles Lyon was at Ombeka, at the south-western extremity of the White Pan. Here he had opened up the waters and cleared a great deal of bush. After some weeks he returned to Otjovanda Tjongue. In the absence of Chris Leen, he became acting secretary. After some few weeks of intelligent labour on behalf of the new republic, he returned to the Bay with the promise of coming back to the settlement as soon as he had wound up his affairs. Meanwhile, he would do his best to counteract the influence of men like Rule, Caine, and Robert Lewis. It was an encouraging sign that Upingtonia was receiving a growing amount of support from people like Charles Lyon: men of integrity and talent. Was it clear by this time that they would be welcomed by the members of the laager? I had not completely shed my uncertainties. But common sense would prevail.

This would also have to determine our attitude to the Germans. And the Waterbergers? I had to confess that even this could be approached soberly. On what other basis could a lasting relationship be found? There had been far too much vagueness in everything.

The Erikssons arrived at the beginning of March: Axel and his brother Albert. The waters at Aukas and Palmietfontein were re-examined. Albert thereupon left for the Okavango. Axel went off to inspect the water at Okaukueyo at the eastern tip of the White Pan. He had been discussing this for a long time. There were great concentrations of game around the spring there, he said.

Axel was his old, genial self. We sat for hours talking, reminiscing. One day I said: 'Karevapu, when one thinks so much of what has been, it may be a sign that one is done for.'

He rubbed his shining pate, bearing against the broad belt he wore. 'And now all is so fine here. As much as one could wish for, eh? This is like Eden!'

I looked at him. He had put on some weight since I had last seen him. Perhaps this was because life had become easier for him. He was looking forward to settling at Aukas.

'After all the bad things that were, Will, the good will come again. It's here already, look!' He indicated the scintillating landscape.

'This is a worthwhile country,' I said, 'and we have to do worthwhile things. Yet you haven't answered my question.'

'*Opu*, eh? As the Hereros say. You are just a little tired, like we all are sometimes. So I was too, some time back. You come down to the Bay, my friend. Get some fresh sea-air again. Then you will be up and lively, as always!'

'I'm lively enough,' I said. 'Except when my blood thickens. How are the wife and children? They tell me you have a son who paints well.'

'Axel, yes! Paints, draws. My birds, eh!'

'Why not? Take him along with you on your treks, Karevapu. Show him the land. Tom Baines was here and said that one would need a life-time to catch all the moods of this country.'

'All the moods, yes. And all the reasons why it catches you around the heart.' He grimaced, as if he were experiencing a pain which was also a pleasure. 'So it is.'

Yes, I thought, so it was. The land got hold of you, even when you were tired.

At nights you lay awake and images lived in you.

The Martini Henry was suspended from a nail in the hood-ribbing. The bandolier with ammunition also hung there. There were times when you would come wandering into the laager with a steenbuck or a duiker over your shoulders dangling from its hind legs, the one threaded through the other. Great rains would come and for days the heavens would weep. Nowhere was there a piece of firm ground to use as an outspan. For hours the oxen would just have to stand in their yokes with sad faces and ghostly eyes.

These were the years of the Great Waters. But there were also the Years of the Sun: Ojorukata, the Hereros said, the Year of the Great Drying Up. Then there would hardly be sufficient water for the morning porridge. Your very appetite seemed to have dried up too. In the veld the hyaenas lay gnawing at the bleaching bones of long-dead animals. You walked past them and they hardly noticed you.

There was the wounded kudu-bull lying under the wreck of a camelthorn. Your dog went for him and grabbed him by the throat. Kairob sat there on his haunches with a piece of half-raw meat between his teeth. He pulled it out and sawed it off with a knife. He sat there chewing, blinking his eyes. The mare walked sadly between leafless trees, looking for grass, pawing the ground. From the trees, a line of palla biltong hung drying, shrivelled by the heat. On a termite nest the vultures sat with drooping wings, too heavy from gorging themselves to fly away. Only the martial eagle still sailed serenely through the heavens . . .

'Karevapu?' I said one day. 'Can it be that Robert Lewis has spent himself? He has threatened us with war, but nothing has yet come of it. He has been found out by Kamaherero, too. That is why the Ovaherero have called it the Year of Lies.'

You talked this way when you had had a tot of brandy and your inhibitions left you.

I poured us some coffee from the pewter jug my mother had given me. That was a long time ago. One so easily forgot things here . . .

3

If we had thought that the great rains had finally receded, we had been too optimistic. During March the wet weather returned. The laager was forced to take shelter most days of the week. Luckily, by this time, many of the people had built themselves snug hartebeest-houses. Those that had gone out to the hunting veld returned fed-up. There they sat smoking the fierce tobacco they themselves had grown. At times they would spit mightily, drink bowls of coffee, clean their guns, tell about their adventures. The womenfolk prepared doughnuts and always replenished the coffee jugs. They talked about food, the trek, the graves of their children. They also talked about births, deaths, marriages, illnesses, funerals. Often they would remind each other of the balmy days on the Serras, before things began to change. Sometimes I would join a group around a fire eating from an iron pot full of roasted meat. Most times, however, while it rained, I would just stay in my wagon, attend to my correspondence, bring my journal up to date.

At the Cape there was still a deplorable vagueness regarding Upingtonia. At the end of November I had written:

'The District of Upingtonia,
Ovamboland, 25 November 1885.

To the Editor of the Cape Times
Sir—You will no doubt search the map of South Africa through and through in order to find the above named district, and fail to do so. Allow me then to give you particulars as to its situation and origin . . .'

I proceeded to give an account of my journey to Ovamboland; of the parley between Kambonde Kampingana, Robert Lewis and myself. I once again pleaded the cause of the immigrant Boers, and disputed the right of Robert Lewis to claim the territory on behalf of the Herero nation.

'Your moral support is what I ask for at present. In a short time I hope our little colony will be augmented by a number of respectable Cape farmers. Let there be an established European colony here and the massacres of Bushmen, Bergdamaras etc will soon be a thing of the past . . .'

I had put it that way. It still had to be put that way. I knew that Robert Lewis had used the press for his own purposes. John Caine, who had once been my friend, was now writing his letters for him . . .

I considered a journey to Moçamedes. This was in view of the fact that the Bay was, practically speaking, closed to me. The loss of my wagons at Omaruru had been a hard blow. Still, I would manage. I would get along with the one remaining wagon, and perhaps another I could rent. I would take the old trek-road through Ovamboland. I would cross the Cunene at Humbe, and then go via Humpata and the Serras down to the coastal desert. The distance was some five hundred miles.

Possibly I might even get to see Kambonde again. I would like to hear him affirm the agreement. He had done this already, but it was best to keep him alive.

What had happened to Hans Schinz? He had spoken about trekking to the Okavango. The northern flatlands were now a chain of lakes. I would have enjoyed having Hans Schinz at Otjovanda Tjongue. There was so much to talk about. At Humpata I might look up all the old friends again. They were living on their remote highland and seemed to have lost contact with the outside world. What future could they as die-hard Calvinists possibly have in a Catholic country? Yes, there had been a time when I had been enthusiastic about Angola. I soon came to realize the faultiness of my judgement.

On the afternoon of 12 March my *bambuse* appeared with two fellow Bushmen bearing a skin bag with a letter in it. I tore it open. It was from Schinz. His trek had got bogged down between Namutoni and Lake Otjikoto. Would I please come to his assistance?

I sat down at my X-table and re-read the letter. *Strapazen* with Kambonde, and especially with his difficult old father, had caused Schinz to flee from Ondangua. His life had been in danger. The root of the evil? Probably still the skeleton of the Omandonga. There was another immediate cause, however, and it concerned the so-called Stone of the Land. He had been accused of dishonouring it. He would tell me all the involved details when we met again. Meanwhile, I probably knew enough about Ovamboland to know that the people there took their stones seriously.

I smiled. Of course they did. Ovamboland was stoneless; and whatever stones there were had been imported. Schinz must have helped himself to one of these and brought the wrath of the tribe down on his intelligent head.

The situation became difficult, the letter said. So the flight began at the dead of night. A day's trek from Olukonda, however, they begán to find the going heavy, due to the incessant rain. *Missionar* Rautanen had sent trek-oxen, however, and they could resume the journey. A hunter-trader who had also found Ondangua too turbulent to be safe joined forces with him. *Schade*, a trek-stage from Oshando his wagon had got bogged down to the axles. It contained all the collected specimens of three years of travelling. The combined wagon-teams of Schinz and his hunter-trader—whoever he was—could not move the wagon. The latter was forced to move on, and there he, Schinz, was now stuck in the mud . . .

I put down the letter. I would send oxen at once. This, I reflected, was at least one tradition which civilization had brought to this country; people helped each other when they were in trouble.

The days were brightening. Thin mare's-tail clouds at great heights stretched over a sky washed to purity-blue by the rains. I spent days looking for trek-oxen in the veld. It was no easy matter. In the flatland around Otjovanda Tjongue *vleis* had also become a chain of lakelets. Springs were gushing. We found the oxen in due course, however, and by 15 March Izak and Kairob had set off with the team to Oshando.

At the beginning of April, when I was already wondering whether my two servants had ever got to their destination, I set out in a north-westerly direction. It may have been the result of a premonition. After a few hours of riding, I faintly discerned the crack of a driver's whip. Half an hour later I saw the trek approaching. Hans Schinz was standing on his *voorkist*, balancing precariously, waving his hat.

4

'So what is the story about the Stone of the Land?' We were sitting around a laager fire. My friend from Zürich was as lively as ever.

'Well, as I have told you,' he said, 'we had always had the intention of going to the northern parts of the Ondangua area. Apart from my general interest, we had often heard about the Stone. Close questioning had elicited the information that the Stone was so deeply buried in the earth that it could not be moved. My geological senses being stirred, I was determined to get to the bottom of the Stone, if not of the riddle. You see, I *had* already found some fairly youthful limestones at places in Amboland, but nothing like a large boulder deeply imbedded in the earth. Rautanen and his colleagues knew nothing about it, and we concluded that the Stone must be a meteorite. In fact it was general talk amongst the Ondongas that it had been sent from heaven by Kalunga—God.'

'So you set off!'

'So we set off. Between Olukonda and Omipa there is the Oshiheke formation which we also wished to investigate. After a day or two we got to Nembungu's kraal. What about the Stone, we asked? Who could tell us something? No answer. Nembungu himself was closed up like an oyster. Well, you know, *Herr* Jordan, how tobacco can set tongues moving again. I offered Nembungu a piece long enough to last him a month. Straight away I was taken to the *sanctus sanctorum* of the kraal and shown—what do you think? A piece of white quartzite, as big as a man's hand!'

What followed had been comical, but also very nearly tragic. The true Stone, so Nembungu had told my friends, lay some two hours further on, in open veld. After assurances had been given that the religious feelings of the tribe would be honoured, the trek moved on.

'*Ach, du lieber Gott!*' Schinz laughed. 'There we were all set to find a great meteorite. What an anti-climax!—It turned out to be just an ordinary piece of quartzite—one quarter of a metre long, and one eighth of a metre wide. This was then the great stone which could not be moved.'

The Stone lay in the sand, and had a polished surface. In order to examine it more carefully and at his leisure, Schinz had broken a corner off. The expedition had then moved on. Schinz had seen some remarkable *scelerocaya* trees, and wished to take pictures of them. With that done, the return journey to Olukonda was undertaken.

'What a consternation,' Schinz said. 'The very next morning two messengers from Kambonde turned up. They wished to know whether the rumours were true. Had I brought the Stone of the Land with me? The Place of the Stone, I was so solemnly informed, was holy. Omandongas had to keep away from it. Should the stone be damaged or removed, evil would befall the tribe. I offered no comment on this, nor would I admit any sacrilege. So we moved on. By the Thursday of that week Rautanen and I—the two guilty ones!—reached the *werf* of Nampingana. Rautanen did the talking and explained—very finely, I thought!—that no harm had been intended. In any event we were humbly sorry if we had offended the tribe. We had all been ignorant of the true meaning of the Stone.

'Nampingana wouldn't relent. He remained aloof and declared outright that Kalunga could only be appeased by an offer of blood. Meanwhile we could go. The elders of the tribe would decide our fate. We would be informed.

'So, onwards again. You may well understand that we were filled with uncertainties. Now, our hope was centred on Kambonde himself. He had known white people from his earliest days. Surely he could intervene and move his father to take up a more reasonable attitude. At the same time we were constantly remembering what had happened to the Catholic fathers, Delpech and Rothan. They had, after all, been murdered precisely because they had "threatened" the existence of the tribe.

'We eventually got back to Olukonda. We sat there in Rautanen's *Stube*, discussing the prospects of survival. Then suddenly, one day, a large force belonging to Nampingana arrived and demanded lead, powder, lucifers—and also the Piece of the True Stone which we still had in our possession.' Schinz chuckled. 'I wasn't going to give up so easily. So I gave them another piece of quartzite I had brought from Damaraland. The next morning brought some relief when we were informed that Rautanen, because of his good services in the past, would be forgiven his misdeed. Hans Schinz, however, would have to pay the penalty . . .

'*Abscheulicher!* What was my life worth? Not very much, as you can see, *Herr* Jordan. The only glimmer of hope was that Kambonde was still arguing our case before the tribe. His father, Nampingana, was adamant, however. The tribe would only escape the most horrible fate if the blood of Schinz appeased Kalunga. No, Kambonde said, that was not necessary. All that should be done was to seize my property. Kalunga would be satisfied with that. The magic objects which I had collected had especially to be removed from my possession. These, as you probably have decided, *Herr* Jordan, included the famous skeleton, and also my botanical and other specimens. After seizure of my property, Kambonde said, I had to be banned from the country. Rautanen—*gottlob!*—would be forgiven.

'The following morning brought little change. Rumours were everywhere. Now I would hear that Kambonde had successfully pleaded for my life. Then I would hear again that the whole matter was still being considered. Hours of rare tension! At the command of Nampingana some servants left me. Some one hundred sheep and goats I had collected were lost in this way. For days a band of Kambonde's warriors lay near my little sod-house, keeping me guessing. Apparently they were just waiting for the royal command to grab my property. It became pretty awful afterwards, I can assure you. I do not ordinarily suffer from nerves, but by the end of the week, I was beginning to feel the strain. Did I tell you that trader Leen was in Ondangua too?'

I looked up in surprise. 'Chris Leen is my brother-in-law,' I said. 'He is in partnership with Bill Clay at present. So, Chris is the mysterious figure who fled Ovamboland with you? I knew that he was up in the north, of course, but I had no idea he was at Ondangua. What happened to him?'

'Well, after we parted company and he suggested I send a letter to you asking for assistance, he set off for the Okavango, saying that we would probably meet again at Otjovanda Tjongue. But I am leaping ahead. Let me get back to where I was. Things were coming to a pass, so Leen and I put our heads together. We had to get out as soon as possible. It was quite clear that Kambonde was not standing up to his father, Nampingana, as we had expected. So, at the dead of night we packed our things and Leen tore down the store he had put up temporarily. You might well wish to know how we managed to do this while we were being so closely watched. The answer is that the dispute between father and son concerning our fate had now reached such proportions that attention was diverted. There were certain complications in the matter, too. Kambonde's brother Nehale had joined in, seeing an opportunity to assert himself. You see . . .' He chuckled again. '. . . Kambonde and Nehale had already divided the kingdom between them. They now sought to divide Schinz's estate as well. One was greedier than the other. And while they were arguing about who would get what, father Nampingana lost patience with his sons and went off in a huff. Now Kambonde was determined to show Nehale who was boss in Amboland. In this way we managed to get out. The rest of the story you know . . .'

I lay that night thinking about everything Schinz had told me. I was immensely glad for his part that things had turned out well for him. At the same time there were aspects of his story which were disturbing. The truth was that what had happened at Ondangua not only affected Hans Schinz, Chris Leen, and the Ovambos. It also affected Upingtonia.

There was firstly the fact that Chris had been drawn into it all and had been forced to flee. There was the further complication that Nehale and Kambonde had found a new bone of contention. I had always got on well enough with Kambonde Kampingana. Whether he would hold it against me and Upingtonia that Chris Leen had got out of the country in fear of his life would still have to be seen. As far as Nehale was concerned, I was uneasy. I did not know him, but from many reports I gathered that he was an ambitious type. He would seize the least opportunity to further his own interests. It might well be that he would exploit the situation. The matter was complicated and exhausting.

I tossed in my bed. My God, I thought, was there never an end to the involvements of existence? One thing had now become clear. I myself had to get back to Ovamboland. It would be difficult to get away from Otjovanda Tjongue, but I had to go. With some luck I might make the journey in ten days. Schinz had taken six weeks, but the weather had improved. I had to get to Ondangua and set things right again. Kambonde was not the sort of man to be left to himself. He needed encouragement.

I had to get to Ovamboland. At the same time, my attention was needed here in the laager. So much was in a state of precarious balance. The *Bestuur* alone would find it difficult to cope. Perhaps if Charles Lyon or Axel Eriksson would turn up, I could ask them to assist . . .

5

Amidst much which weighed me down, these days at Otjovanda Tjongue were full of interest. Hans Schinz was fine company. He sat for hours talking about the modern world, the future of Africa. We would get interested in the magnificent collection of specimens collected in the course of three years trekking through the Transgariep.

Schinz liked to visit the people of the laager in their hartebeest-houses. There he would sit talking to them about the Trek across the Thirstland, making notes. I gave him my journal to read, and he pored over it, putting many questions to me about the days when I had first met the immigrants in the marshes.

What about his future plans? He had intended to reach Lake Ngami through the eastern Sandveld, he said. Would it be safe? He had heard of Gabriel and his robber-band. But he had also heard that we had chased them off. Well, I answered, that was what we believed. There had been no sign of Gabriel for months now. Still, one had to remember that characters like Gabriel had a habit of showing up when least expected. That was the history of the country. Schinz nodded and I saw his eyes sparkle behind his spectacles. Yes, he said, he would be on his guard, but he would still like to reach Ngami by the direct route. I knew that he would continue his journey as planned, undaunted.

'We must never stop believing in our own special little guardian angel, *Herr* Jordan,' he said. 'Look what happens. I have been surrounded for weeks by clouds of mosquitoes, and yet I did not fall ill. What now? This morning my teeth are chattering. But I am here among friends; and I know a good physician when I meet him.'

There was a pleasing lightness about those days, whatever the threats from afar. We rode into the veld, spending days botanizing, examining the rocks, noting the flow of the waters. When the opportunities arose for me to contribute something to my friend's great wealth of knowledge, I felt myself privileged.

Schinz's weak Ovambo oxen could hardly have got him to Lake Ngami through the eastern Sandveld. I bought them from him, giving him in the place thereof twenty strong *Hererorinder,* as he called them. On 27 April he finally took leave of us: Hans Schinz of Zürich. He had done much during these weeks to relieve our tensions. He had reminded us and reminded me personally that the richness of life never lessens. It was there for us to discover, and to make our own.

I saw his wagon disappearing through the trees. In the foliage the tints of autumn were showing. He stood with one foot on his *voorkist*, holding onto a hood-ribbing. He was waving his hat to us by way of a last farewell. I saw the early sun catch the lenses of his glasses and reflect from it. There was a deep sense of loss in me when the wagon finally disappeared. Something seemed to have gone forever.

A few days later the first frost of winter lay upon the ground. It had suddenly turned cold. The servants sat huddled around their little fires. The night-sky was brilliantly clear. The stars were like bees.

In the laager the days were becoming quieter too. It was as if a general expectancy of coming things had got hold of us. One day I returned to my wagon and found Dina Lombard there.

'Mister must please come,' she said. 'It is Old Miss.'

'What about Old Miss?'

'Is sick, Mister.'

'What's wrong?' I gave my horse's reins to Kairob. 'How long has Old Miss been sick?'

'Two days, Mister. Wanted to come and call Mister; but Old Miss said no, Mister was too busy. Not fever now, Mister.'

I walked over to the Lombard *werf* a few minutes later. Outside the sod-house Adriaan Venter had built for Ella Lombard when he had been here in January, I found a little group of women. Jet du Plessis and Hester Bouwer came to meet me.

'I hear *Tante* Ella is not well?' I said to Hester.

'She is resting now,' Hester answered.

'*Tante* is very tired, *Meneer*,' Jet answered.

I heard a sharp, rasping little cough from inside the one-roomed house. I looked to Hester, then to Jet. 'May I go inside?' I asked.

'We have been waiting for *Meneer*,' Jet said.

I pushed open the door of grass and poles and entered the room. I had to bend. In the room there was only space enough for the *katel*, a *kist* and one or two small benches. It was close, and sunlight filtered through the single window covered with a piece of white linen.

She lay there on the *katel* under a sheet and two karrosses. Her breathing was laboured and fast. The features of her face seemed sharper, as if the skin was sagging. In her cheeks deep lines had been etched. Her colour was high. I took her hand from under the sheet and felt her pulse.

The *katel* had been set up in one corner of the room. The late afternoon sunlight poured through one side of the linen curtain, spilling over a wall of the room. There was a picture there hanging from a wooden peg. It was one of Ella Lombard and her dead husband and her dead sons. She was already a middle-aged woman there. There was a child in her arms. That was Lisa.

I stood next to the *katel* for some while, watching to see if Ella Lombard would react. But there were only her set features, her heavy breathing, and the feeling that this was someone who had grown tired of wandering. Years of fever, dysentery, the rigours of the trek, had finally been too much for the frail vessel of the body. She was sixty. In a way she had lasted the pace better than most. The sudden change in the weather during the past few weeks had affected people of stronger constitution.

There was a Bible and psalter on the *kist* next to the *katel* . . . There was also an earthenware bowl with some water in it, and a wash-rag. There was a calabash containing drinking water, a cup and saucer with gilt rims. On the wall above the katel a wall-board bore the inscription: *I am the Lord thy God which hath brought thee out of the Land of Egypt, out of the house of bondage.*

I opened the door as wide as I could. The group of women were still outside. Behind them Dina and Kleinveld were standing. They looked up questioningly when I appeared. Dina was frowning and shaking her head.

'Did she complain of any discomfort?' I asked Jet du Plessis.

'She said she had a pain here, *Meneer*,' Jet answered. She indicated the chest.

I stepped outside and the fresh air spilled over me.

'*Tante* Ella is not one to complain,' Hester Bouwer said.

'Did it come on suddenly?' I asked Dina.

'In the night, Mister. I heard Old Miss groaning. Then I went to see. She said it was a pain she had. And she had a great thirst.'

'When did the coughing start?'

The women looked at each other, then at Dina.

'We just heard it at times, *Meneer*,' *Tante* Louwrens said.

It was inflammation and congestion of the lungs, I decided. Everything pointed to this. Final confirmation of what I had diagnosed, came the very next moment. Another hard, brittle little cough came from the room.

I went inside again. There was some rusty coloured sputum round Ella Lombard's mouth. Somebody behind me whispered:

'It is the blood cough!'

I wiped her mouth with the wash-rag, and she opened her eyes. 'How do you feel, *Tante*?' I asked. She smiled weakly, and the deeply etched lines on her face became even more severe.

'Keep yourself well covered, *Tante*,' I said. 'Don't move about too much.' She lay there quietly looking at me. Her lips moved.

'*Meneer* is good to me,' I heard her whisper at last.

I stood there next to the *katel*, sharply conscious of my inadequacy. We might relieve her discomfort by applying cold compresses to the head, warm fomentations to the chest. We might give her a little alcohol to increase perspiration. A steaming kettle on a pan of live coals next to the bed might help relieve the cough. All these things the good women standing in the doorway and outside might do. There had never been a remedy for pneumonia, even in local folk-lore.

A variety of 'medicines', ranging from the crushed liver of a tortoise or the oil of wild-hemp for cancer, to hyaena dung and acacia bark for croup, was always at hand. For the 'blood cough' there had never been an answer. A vomitive perhaps, a little sweet-oil to ease the cough, a little haarlemensis . . .

Jet du Plessis stood next to me at the bedside. '*Tante*, are you close in the chest?' she asked aloud.

The patient reacted slowly. She nodded slightly, and indicated the calabash with a movement of the fingers. I poured some water in the cup and gave it to her. She drank it with great difficulty.

We left the room, and stood outside. Dina was wailing like a dog, Kleinveld was becoming irritable with *Oumie*. Frowning deeply he wished to know from me what was going to happen to Old Miss. Would she die? When I gave him no straight answer, he enquired about Little Miss. Would she have to be fetched?

Yes, I said, after a while, Little Miss would have to be fetched. How, precisely, I did not know. The chances were that the Venters were deep in the veld somewhere, with Adriaan chasing the elephants. He might even have trekked up to Olifants Pan to see the Tree. I stood thinking.

Perhaps I should have prevented their going. Ella Lombard had been in indifferent health for some time now. In any event, it was definitely risky for two young people to be out there alone. Yes, of course, a man like Hans Schinz was also alone. I myself had been alone for many thousands of miles, trekking through this country. And yet it was different. Or was it different? I did not know. One thing I did know: it was perfectly useless to try and contain one of these far-ranging Boers when once he had been bitten by the huntsman's bug. No, not even that. When once their own peculiar type of *wanderlust*, a complication of the general trek-fever, had taken hold of them, they were beyond reason. There was Van Staden who had left Olifants Pan in the bitter days of the Trek. He had crossed the Okavango with his wife, child, and brother in only one wagon. He had just trekked off into the unknown, and after many months the family, minus the brother, had reappeared somewhere in north-eastern Angola. If you tried to tell Adriaan Venter that he should not go after the elephants on his own, he would look up in surprise and want to know: 'Well, *Meneer*, now why not?' Perhaps he would be right. This was the tradition in which he had grown up to manhood.

The immediate question now was to find the young couple. A spell of dry weather had afforded the hunters in the laager the opportunity to go out biltong-shooting. The previous expeditions in wet conditions had been less successful.

6

Hester Bouwer, who was watching at Ella Lombard's bedside, sent Kleinveld to me at three o'clock in the morning. Would I please come? Miss Hester thought Old Miss's time had come. I got up at once. I pulled on my boots, for I had been lying on my *katel* fully clothed. I walked between the great trees to the Lombard *werf.* The laager was asleep, but at the foot of the northern slope of the rise a fire winked. As I came nearer I heard someone howling like a spanked child. It was Dina.

So, it had come, I thought. A few minutes later I saw Jet du Plessis and Hester Bouwer in front of the little sod-house. Jet's large, strong face was wet and flushed. She wiped her eyes and said: '*Tante* is dead, *Meneer.*' Hester Bouwer looked at me, smiling sadly. I stooped and walked into the dim little room. A single mopani wax-candle was burning on the *kist* next to the bed. In its gentle light I saw her lying under a sheet which had been pulled up to cover her face. I lifted it.

There she lay now, in the serenity of death. I took her hand and felt it. It was cold, like an egg removed from a bird's nest. On the inside of the arm I saw the scars the assegais had left half a century before. It was livid, and the skin was puckered.

Hester Bouwer was standing behind me. I was glad she was there. 'Did it come suddenly?' I asked.

'She spoke to me,' Hester answered quietly. 'She just said that the night was so long. I got up to give some water; and then suddenly she just seemed to sigh, and give up the ghost.'

'The heart can take a lot,' I said. 'It's a tough little muscle. It keeps on working, working. And then, someday, it just goes snap, from bearing too much.'

It was very quiet in the room. I pulled the sheet over the dead woman's face.

'It is as *Meneer* says,' Hester Bouwer whispered.

Something seemed to grip me. I stood there shaking. Opposite me on the wall was the family picture hanging from the wooden peg. It was a stern little group. There was great courage and determination in those set faces. The only relieving feature was the smiling mouth and eyes of Lisa, who was still a baby then. Outside Dina was still wailing against the wall of the house. Kleinveld stood in the doorway with his hat pressed to his chest.

'*Tante* Ella,' I just said. She had sometimes addressed me as 'My child'. It had warmed me, and I remembered the occasions.

She had come a long way, this Boer woman, who in many respects had been like a mother to me. She had come a long way, searching for her Land of Rest. Those who had been with her had fallen by the trek-routes. She had always gone on, and on, believing that in the end her Lydensrust would make it all worth while. As a young girl she had left the Old Colony. She had survived the massacre of Blaauwkrantz. After many years she had got to the High Serras of southern Angola. Then she had come to Upingtonia, with us . . .

At last she had been gathered to those whom she had loved. But what had she found eventually?

It was hard to say.

'Thank you for what you have done,' I said.

'It is nothing,' Hester Bouwer answered.

We left the room together.

We buried her the next day in a *kist* of kiaat Dolf Holtzhausen had made. We hung the faded *Vierkleur* over it, as Ella Lombard had always said should be done. I had been told that all her children had been born under this flag, literally. This was not only the flag of the Transvaal which had been her country. It had also ever remained for her the symbol of freedom.

7

I returned to my wagon and wrote a letter to Adriaan and Lisa Venter. I drafted it as factually and soberly as the custom of the Boers required.

The messengers were provided with a wagon, team, a gun, and sufficient food to last them a week or two. They were to go straight to Okasima. If the Venters had left the water and were down the omuramba somewhere, they were to be found. Izak was as good a tracker as his people had ever produced. He would locate Little Master and Little Miss.

'No,' Dina emphatically declared, 'not the Bushman, but *I* will find them. Is *my* people!'

'Then you must find them, Dina,' I said. 'And if you are not back within the week, I'll come and look for you.'

The days passed slowly. I kept myself occupied with much of the clerical work which had accumulated, but it was difficult to concentrate. My thoughts were constantly turning to Adriaan and Lisa Venter. Perhaps I should have set off to find them myself. The chances were that Adriaan Venter had got to the Tree. The three servants would take a long time to catch up with him. I should have gone on horse-back. I could have completed my mission in four days.

There was a growing uneasiness in me as the days passed. Towards the end of the week I rode out in a north-easterly direction. I kept going until the bush began to thin and the feathery tops of distant makalanis started showing up against the horizon. I sat in the fork of a camelthorn, peering through binoculars over the veld, trying to discern some sign of an approaching trek. The grass was hip-high and already white from the recent frost. In the distance I could see herds of palla, hartebeest, blue wildebeest, and a line of eland. There was no indication of a wagon; and there were no humans. Here the spoor of the servants' wagon lay. They had passed here some five days before. They were heading straight for Okasima and the omuramba. Some vultures were wheeling to the north at a great height. Would that I could be up there to spy out the land.

I rode back to the laager, slowly, deep in thought. It could be, of course, that the Venters themselves had run into trouble somewhere. Or perhaps Adriaan had gone right down the omuramba, intending to get to Olifants Pan. I was blaming myself now. I should have told them to stay at Otjovanda Tjongue until there was greater certainty about Ella Lombard's condition. She was old. Her body had been racked by fever for many years. I should have said to Adriaan: 'Listen, let Lisa stay here for a while. Go off hunting if you like. But be within easy fetching-distance from the laager . . .'

'There is no other way,' I said on my return. 'I'll have to go and find out what has happened.'

Louw du Plessis saw that I was deeply worried. 'Brother Jordan,' he said, 'I would like to come with you.'

'What about the laager?' I said. 'They need you here. There are too many people away. Besides, there are rumours that the Waterbergers are coming back. If they do arrive, a member of the *Bestuur* should be here. I don't think *Oom* Diederick will walk again.'

It was difficult to get to the origin of the story. But people were discussing it openly. The Waterbergers had been sadly disillusioned, they said. They had discovered how much substance there had been in Robert Lewis's promises. They had also discovered that Kamaherero's talk about their settling at Windhoek had been meaningless. What now? There was even a rumour that Jan Labuschagne was preparing to trek back to the Serras. He was already in Ovamboland.

We sat next to my laager fire. I poured some coffee and asked Louw about this. Was this likely? If some of the Waterbergers had indeed been forced to face reality, would they seriously consider returning to Angola? I found it hard to believe. Surely they knew by this time that they had no real future among the Portuguese as Boers. I put it to him pointedly: were there people here in the laager too who had lost faith in Upingtonia? Were there more who had decided that this wasn't the 'free Boer state' they had so long sought? That Will Jordan had, in fact, led them to something they had never desired?

I watched him as he sat there filling his pipe. The firelight played on his features. He wore a skin jacket with its collar turned up. The night-air was chilly. His beard had become splotched with grey these last few months. His face was leaner. After more than two centuries his Gallic origin was still clearly visible. He filled his pipe, and deftly took a live ember from the fire, playing it in the palm of his hand until it rested on the bowl of the pipe.

'Let us suppose,' I said, 'that our enemies succeed in their objective and destroy Upingtonia. I may just as well tell you, Louw, that as far as I am concerned, I shall defend it to the end, with my life if it must be. I have given all I have to this cause. What would you do, Louw?

'What would the Du Plessis, Prinsloos, Louwrenses, Holtzhausens, Oppermans and others do? Would they want to remain in Damaraland—if it is Damaraland—hoping for German *Schutz*? This is what Barend Bouwer seems to want. If the people no longer have the strength or belief to remain here, where do they wish to go to? Back to Humpata? Or back to the Transvaal?'

He sat looking at the fire. 'Brother Jordan,' he said at last, 'these are not easy questions to answer. We would just have to see where our ideals can best be served. North or south, it makes no difference. It is the *ideal* which is important.'

His words were cryptic. I did not react to them in words of my own. I knew intuitively that even Louw had been seriously thinking of returning to the Serras. I was momentarily depressed, but was determined to show no sign of it. The fact of the matter was, I decided, that only one thing could make these people true burghers of the state of Upingtonia: the concrete proof of success.

'Looking back on the long way you have come, Louw,' I said, 'and thinking of all that has happened, would you cross the Thirstland again, if given a second chance? Has there been any sense in it at all?'

The question was not merely hypothetical. News had arrived at the laager these last few months that other groups in the Transvaal were considering the journey.

'A people must find its own true destiny.' I caught his glance. 'We are very thankful towards you, Brother Jordan', he looked up, 'for all that you have done for our *volk*.'

I was suddenly irritated. I never intended 'doing things' for these people. I had merely done what I believed to be meaningful for this country which I loved. I had served an ideal in the best way I could.

I got up and walked to my wagon. Louw remained sitting at the fire. I stood there in the dark, until my feelings had subsided. Then I drew some brandy from the little cask, and walked back to the fire. I poured us each a tot, but my hand was shaking. We drank our brandy in silence. Then he got up, saying that it was time to get to bed. When would I be leaving?

'Tomorrow morning very early,' I said.

'And how long do you think you will be away, Brother Jordan?'

'I don't know,' I said. 'It may be a day. It may be a week. Or even longer. I leave everything to you here, Louw.'

'I'll do my best, Brother Jordan,' he said. 'Sleep well!'

8

When the sun, a blood-red disc, had broken free of the horizon, I was already two hours' distance from the laager. I was following the wagon spoor of Kleinveld and Co. It wandered crazily towards the omuramba.

The last time I had come this way, I thought, was when we had set out after Gabriel. We were some thirty men in the commando and the rain descended upon us as in a Cape winter. It was a barren task looking for Gabriel in this northern bush. It was also a time of barrenness within. Piet Botha had told me at Dabe that I did not have the colour of an *opregte witte man* . . .

Strange, I was yet remembering that expedition with a certain nostalgia. The men were in good spirits, in spite of what had happened. Jan Labuschagne and Barend Bouwer would laugh so loudly that herds of palla would be set running. We found shelter where we could, and the young men went out looking for veld-fruits. We even succeeded in boiling a kettle at times, and roasting a few steaks. Wet and weary, we arrived at the laager again after some five days. I was filled with tension about the reäction of people in the laager to what had taken place at Dabe. I had visited Ella Lombard and had sat there talking, drinking coffee, and eating sweetmeats, while preparations were being made for Lisa's wedding. I had listened to all the women-wise talk, and had decided that nothing had changed . . .

The sun was now in a sky the colour of iron. The brightness of the day lay over everything. Details in the landscape were visible over many miles where the bush allowed it. Herds of game were everywhere. In the trees the winter had already set in. Yet each still carried in its own subtle way the poetry of Africa. Three spurwing geese came flying low against the sky where it curved steeply to the horizon. In other times and in other circumstances I would have paused to take all this in, listening to the music of the land. But now there was no time for it. Still, when I reached a stretch of open country where the oryx had been ploughing up the earth in their search for wild cucumbers and the eland-bean, I did stop for a moment. There was the smell of freshly turned damp soil. My spirits lifted, and I pressed on. The wagon spoor still ran on ahead of me. I myself had learned to read the record of a trek. Here they had stopped to prepare food. Here they had changed the oxen. Here a lion had followed them for a few miles . . . I even saw where somebody—presumably my *bambuse*—had climbed into a red milkwood to spy out the land.

By eleven o'clock I reached the first outspan. I examined the *erd* and could see what they had been preparing for supper. With luck, I decided, I might be able to catch up with the trek by the evening or the next morning.

I rode in the elongated shadow of great anas and sycamores. This was Okasima. Beyond the trees, near the powerful fountain which lay between dense reeds, the bush had been cleared and a garden established.

There was deep, fruitful soil here. One could live here pleasantly, and profitably. Quelea finches were whirring up in dense clouds from the reeds. They closed into a tight ball like a swarm of bees. Then they went droning away in the direction of the omuramba. Kudu, eland, zebra, blue wildebeest visited the water regularly. The lions had been here too. There were many bones lying about. A line of Namaqua partridges flew up from the pool where the water gathered and streaked away into the setting sun. Their shrill cries sounded lonely, as if they were trying to express inexpressible things.

There had once been a stout hedge of thorn branches around the garden. There had also been a kraal for the cattle and sheep. Both had been burnt down. Only ash and charred branches still indicated what had been. A one-roomed house of reed and poles had also been destroyed. The garden had been trampled flat. The remains of a patch of mealies and the dry tendrils of outsize pumpkin plants were all that was left of what had obviously been singularly lush. There were spoors everywhere; the spoors of animals—game and cattle—and the spoors of humans. Who had they been? Some were familiar, but others puzzled me. I judged the majority of the spoors to be those of wild Bushmen. What had they been doing here? Had they burnt down the kraal, the garden hedge, and the reed-house? It was easy to draw conclusions which would be deeply disturbing. I avoided doing this. It was quite possible, I argued, that all this was just the debris of a normal break-up. Adriaan Venter might have decided that Okasima, in spite of its good water and fine soil, was confining him too much. He might have done the burning himself. The Bushmen could have been in his employ as trackers. It was impossible to go after the elephants alone. The Bushmen were necessary for hewing out tusks and for tracking. Yes, of course, this was more likely what had happened. The Venters were probably down the omuramba. The servants had also been here. A fresh *erd* showed where they had laagered.

I walked around for some time, examining everything as carefully as I could, weighing the possibilities, trying to settle my own anxieties, not succeeding wholly in doing so. How long ago had the Venters left this place? It was difficult to say.

I spent the night at Okasima. It had been a long day, but I could not sleep. I lay there wide awake, staring up at the heavens. Just after midnight a herd of elephant came crashing through the bush from the direction of the omuramba. They splashed about in the pool until I was forced to fire a few shots. Trumpeting hysterically they thundered off into the night.

I lay down again. There was no moon and Arcturus was a jewelled brightness to the north. Directly above was Scorpio; and Crux was low in the south-west . . .

I drew the blanket over my head, but sleep would not yet come. Everything in me was strangely alerted. Old hunters like Barend Bouwer and Jan Labuschagne had always said that the elephants had left the omuramba and the Debra permanently after the great slaughter at Olifants Pan. Adriaan Venter did not believe them. I myself had already had proof that there were still many elephants in this area. Okasima had probably been a fine base for Adriaan Venter to operate from. No doubt he had gone north after some big herd. These were young people, I said to myself, with a zest for life and a taste for adventure. Still, if he had gone off to the pan, Adriaan should have sent a message to the laager. He knew that Ella Lombard wasn't so well any more . . .

There was no point in furthering this argument with myself. I got up, threw some logs on the fire, and put the kettle on to boil. There were still three hours to daybreak. The mare whinnied softly behind me. It was as if she were trying to remind me that I was not alone.

9

Two sets of wagon spoors intertwined for many miles between the trees of the omuramba. Sometimes they had been obliterated by the spoors of game moving in great herds across the broad, sandy watercourse. Fresh elephant dung and shallow excavations in the sand caused me to hope that those whom I was seeking were not too far off. There was also the possibility, of course, that the servants had caught up with them and that they had taken a short-cut through the bush to Otjovanda Tjongue. Was it a short-cut? Hardly. The omuramba was open, easy going for a wagon, even if its sinuosities made the distance longer. The bush itself was difficult.

I kept the mare going at a steady pace. At midday we rested for some time under giant anas. Then we resumed the search, following the double track down the omuramba. Giraffes were staring at us over the umbrella tops of young camelthorns. To the north vultures were wheeling.

By five o'clock in the afternoon, when I had already left Okasima some thirty miles to the south-west, in the vicinity of Korakobis water, I came across an outspan which had recently been used. There was a spring here; and close by were the remains of three great elephant bulls. The tusks had been removed and from the spoors it was apparent that a great many Bushmen had been here to do the hewing. The other wagon—the one the servants were using—had also stopped here. My spirits rose. These spoors were only a few days old. If I pressed on, I could possibly overtake the wagons within the next twenty four hours.

Somehow I seemed prepared for what was coming. Some two hours from where the dead elephants lay, the double track came to an end. One wagon had stood there under a marula. The other had come to within a few hundred yards of it. Here it had turned about and had left the omuramba, travelling in a south-westerly direction. It was puzzling, but I knew at once that something untoward had happened.

I followed the spoor to the south-west on foot for half a mile. Between two trees, so close to each other that a wagon could not pass between them, there were the spoors of humans again. The broad, flat one—I had known it for years—belonged to my *bambuse*. The small one had been made by a light *veldschoen*. I knew that as well. It belonged to Lisa Venter. It was quite apparent that Izak had been tracking her.

I stood here with my hat in my hand, feeling the sweat trickling over my cheeks. Why had Lisa been walking here alone? Where had she been going to? Where was her husband?

I walked back slowly, apprehensively, to where the mare was tied to a tree. The light had deteriorated and the trees in the omuramba were already starkly black.

I mounted my horse and rode back to where the two wagons had diverged. Had I missed something? I already knew what it was. I dismounted again and stood looking about me. There it was, the mound of earth with hookthorn piled over it. I had seen it the first time but had taken it to be the wreck of an acacia which had collapsed.

A single vulture was perched on a tree a short distance away. I looked up slowly. The bird suddenly launched itself into the lifeless air and sailed away. I absently followed its flight, trying to order my feelings.

This was the grave of Adriaan Venter, I kept saying to myself. I knew it. This was his grave . . .

The feelings of many months seemed to be compressed into a tight little ball, sticking in my throat.

He was dead; the blonde boy who had too suddenly become a man, and yet had never shed his boyhood.

10

I overtook them near Buchuvlei in the Omuramba Omatako during the early afternoon of the next day.

She was very tired. She lay in the wagon on a bed the servants had made for her. The child rested in her arms, and as far as I could judge, he was in reasonable shape.

I listened to her as she slowly told me her story.

'My child was born in the veld, *Meneer*,' she said. 'I first thought that he was dead. I also thought that I too would die. But the Lord was with us, *Meneer. Ai* Dina came, when I thought that there would be nobody who would even know how I had died. *Ai* Dina found me where I lay in the veld. *Ai* Dina helped me, and my child was born. He wasn't dead, as you can see, *Meneer*.'

There were signs of what she had passed through on her face. She was thin and her skin had been affected by sun and wind. There were fine lines about her eyes. Lacerations on her arms and hands showed where the hookthorn had caught her. In spite of everything, I could still discern the old Lisa.

'How long had you been walking?' I asked. 'How long were

you alone in the veld after you had fled?'

'It was two days and two nights, *Meneer.*'

'Did you have any water?'

'Only some in a calabash, *Meneer.*'

'When did you first discover that there was danger nearby?'

'We were in the 'maramba. And there was the great herd of elephants, as I have already told you, *Meneer.* They had come down from the top. Then my husband shot three, as you found them at the water. The Bushmen came out of the veld, and we hired them, and they started chopping out the tusks. We loaded the ivory and my husband said we must trek further down the 'maramba, because there was surely much more ivory to be had. Then the Bushmen just disappeared. We didn't know where they had gone to. So we just kept on trekking. By evening the Bushmen appeared again and told my husband that there was a big herd of elephants on the sunrise side of the 'maramba. He must come and look. I became frightened and said to Adriaan: "No, you mustn't go. Why do they come and tell you this in this way? Why did they disappear and suddenly come again?" He said: "You mustn't worry. These people have done good work for us. I'll go with them, just to see if there are any spoors."—Well, he went with them and he was just a little way from the place where the wagon stood, when I heard a shot. It was an old cap-lock gun, *Meneer.* And they shot my husband with it. I heard the shot ring out, and then I jumped out of the wagon and ran towards them. When I got there, he was already dead. I lay there next to him, and I said they must shoot me too, because I didn't want to live any more.'

Tears broke from her eyes. For a moment or two she sobbed. Then with a quick, irritable movement, she controlled herself again.

'They took the wagon, *Meneer.* The flower-wagon. They took all our things. Our own servants also went with them. They left me there, because they thought perhaps I would die. I thought of Ma here in the laager; and I thought of my child which was coming. Ma?' Her voice broke again, and I saw her mouth tighten. 'I did not know about Ma. I wanted to come back to the laager and our people. And where *Ai* Dina was. And all of you, *Meneer.* Then Ma also died. And I knew nothing of it.'

'Where did you sleep in the veld, Lisa?'

'The first night I sat in a tree, *Meneer.* I heard lions roaring.

The next day I was very tired. So I crept under a hookthorn-bush. I just lay there, and slept for some while. I did not mind whether I died or not. And yet again I thought of my child. I wanted to bring my child into this world, because he was also Adriaan's child.' She glanced down at the baby in her arms. 'Will he live, *Meneer*?'

'Was he before his time?'

'Only a little while, *Meneer*. We wanted to come back to the laager for his birth.'

'A child is much tougher than you think, Lisa. It needs a lot of killing.'

She smiled faintly. I hadn't intended this as humour. Still, she seemed to be encouraged by my words.

'Besides,' I added, 'there's a good reason for him to live.'

'Yes, *Meneer*,' she said quietly. 'There is a good reason.'

Many good reasons, I repeated silently to myself. In a way, I supposed, this was also the personal plea—of Will Jordan.

Dina appeared with a plate containing cooked maize-meal with gravy over it. Lisa shook her head. 'I am not hungry, *Aia*,' she said.

'Little Miss must eat. Else, who will feed the child, eh?'

Lisa smiled to herself.

'She will eat, Dina,' I said. 'When she feels like it. But not now.' Dina mumbled something and climbed out of the wagon.

'When can we go to Grootfontein?' Lisa asked.

'If we leave tomorrow morning very early,' I said, 'we can be in the laager by nightfall. I am sending Izak on ahead to tell the people what has happened.'

Dina was moving outside somewhere. I heard her say, 'The devil was there in the bush!'

She had allowed Kleinveld and Izak hardly any time to rest. When eventually they had got to Lisa where she was lying under the hookthorn, it was not a moment too soon. Dina had chased the other two away, and had done what had to be done.

'When I came to my senses again,' Lisa said, 'my child was born. *Ai* Dina stood there holding him up for me to see. And then they put me in the wagon. And then after a long while *Meneer* came.'

I still wondered at it all.

11

Lisa lay there in the bed the servants had made for her. A faint little life beat against her own. She seemed resigned to everything now. At the same time there was a clear determination to cling to whatever was left to her. This was not courage born of despair, but of belief.

I clambered out of the wagon. The old tiredness had taken hold of me again. In a way I was also emotionally exhausted. I hadn't realized the extent of my own involvement with all that had taken place.

Kleinveld Labuschagne, grey-black and as thin as a Herero in a dry year, told me about the grave I had found in the omuramba.

'Little Miss made it, Mister,' he said. 'She made it with her own hands. And she buried Little Master. She first rolled him in a skin and then dug the hole, and put him into it. She dug with an axe, and a broken spade, and her hands. She chopped the branches of the hookthorn to put over the grave, because the hyaenas had already been digging there.'

Izak told me how he had followed Lisa's spoor all through the veld until he had found her under the bush. She had walked a long distance. Lions' spoors had followed hers at times. With the ancient hand-signs of his race he showed how it had all happened. With Izak doing the tracking, and Kleinveld driving, *oumie*—Dina Lombard—had been compelled to lead the oxen. She had refused at first to do 'the Bushman's work'. She had grumbled, but had nevertheless taken the *trekriem* and had led the team.

'How many days and nights had Little Miss been walking?' I asked Kleinveld.

'Two nights and two days, Mister,' he said.

This, I calculated, was about thirty miles through thick sand and difficult bush, with no open water. There had constantly been the danger of wild animals. The servants had eventually caught up with her when she struck the omuramba again, due east of Otjovando Tjongue.

I had said to Lisa: a child needs a lot of killing. It was even true of one prematurely born. It was true of the human species generally. As long as the will to live was there, men would survive, somehow.

Lisa herself had shown this. The night temperature in June dropped to below zero. By day the winter sun could be subtly fierce. If you didn't know where to look for water, you would have great difficulty in finding it in the bush. Lisa had emptied her calabash by the end of the first day. Her feet were badly blistered and her clothes had been torn to shreds by the hookthorn and mucharra. She had not only carried herself but also her unborn child. When her time came, she lay down under a bush and gave birth. Dina had been there to assist, but it had been Lisa herself who had risen to the occasion. In a sense, it was life itself returning with the one hand what it had taken with the other.

Breaking into this probing of my thoughts there suddenly came a sound which was raw, sharp, but also magnificent to hear. It came from the wagon which had been drawn up under a camelthorn. It was the vociferous affirmation of all that I had been thinking. The child was bawling mightily, and for my part it could go on doing so right through the night. The child was in effect shouting and telling the world: 'I am here to stay. I, too, have claimed the world!'

Dina stuck her head out of the wagon-hood and told Kleinveld to bring her some warm water. He did it readily, carrying it in a black three-legged pot. Kleinveld was grinning.

The mare stood under a tree where I had fastened her. I put my arm around her neck, I pressed my cheek to hers. I wished I had a handful of sugar for her.

Guinea fowl were calling from the omuramba: *oc, oc, oc!* . . . In the fading light I saw a lordly kudu bull watching me, head erect, horns spiralling nobly upwards. He was there at a hundred paces between the mopani. The night was rising in a purple wave behind the trees. The grass was the colour of ripe corn in the summer grainlands of the Cape . . .

Who was it that once said: 'When a horse has horse-sickness, it must be ridden until it is well again?' This, I was assured, was an old Boer remedy. Sometimes it worked, and sometimes not. The important thing was that it offered a certain hope. Or was it illusion? Maybe this was the same thing. I did not know. Maybe this little bit of veterinary wisdom was part of the general pattern. Ride him, my friends said. Carry on, and to hell with the consequences. Keep going through the bush, the desert, the dry river beds, to where you wished to be. No matter what it cost in heaving lungs, in quivering, sweat-covered muscles, you just kept on in faith, they said. One morning you would find your horse sound as a bell again.

Sometimes it worked, and sometimes it didn't.

Look at Barend Bouwer. There was no stopping him these days. He had gone off on his own to talk to the Germans about *Schutz*. He was at Omaruru now. Axel Eriksson had written that they had talked for hours about Upingtonia, and Barend had also met Nels, the German *chargé d'affaires*. Barend had rattled on, and Nels seemed to be impressed. Yes, *Herr* Bouwer, he had said, in High Dutch, if Upingtonia is all it was claimed to be, then the *Reich* would most certainly consider extending its imperial protection to the territory. He would discuss it all with *Reichskommissar* Goering. Nels might possibly yet turn up at Grootfontein, Axel said. So we were to be on the alert. It would be best to accept his good faith. It seemed as if Kamaherero, since the advent of the *Reich* officials, had been a little more subdued. He wasn't making such grandiose claims anymore. A silly story was doing the rounds that Kamaherero was, in fact, not the Paramount Chief of Damaraland and that there had never been a proper struggle for freedom against the Nama nation. It had all just been the personal caprice of a petty potentate. Kamaherero was no different to his father Copper Foot (Tjamuaha), who had lived in comfortable subservience at the court of the Nama tyrant, Jonker Afrikaander. This, Axel said, was the typical loose talk that one heard in Damaraland these days. The previous year had been called the Year of Lies. It was still the Year of Lies.

The Waterbergers were a fine example of the general confusion. What did they want?—As far as he, Axel, could ascertain, they were trekking about more or less aimlessly. They were staying at various waters. They were raising crops—enough to keep themselves going. They were also sending out letters and making enquiries about *Schutz*.

Jan Labuschagne had been telling everybody that he was fed up with everything down there in the south. One thing was certain, there would have to be a far greater sense of reality if these people hoped to develop, or help develop, a meaningful, settled community.

12

I was having little rest these days. I couldn't help it. There was a growing feeling inside of me that the whole movement was losing its momentum. I was doing my utmost to keep things going.

Charles Lyon arrived from the Bay, and we spent some reasonably fruitful days drafting letters, seeing to minutes and deeds of title. In the absence of Chris Leen, who was still up at the Okavango, he made a number of copies of the constitution. I had earnestly hoped that Charles would come and settle. One morning, however, without warning, he came and told me that he would have to leave for the Bay again. It was a disappointment, but I took it with the necessary grace. I wished him a good journey.

In the laager the people had quietly gathered. Since the beginning of December forty-three farms had been allocated. Some people had even gone out to settle at their waters. Then they had come back again to Grootfontein. There were only about ten families now who could be regarded as stable members of our little society. This was far too meagre. There had been much talk, many promises, many fine intentions but almost nothing had yet materialized. Perhaps I was in too much of a hurry. The Erikssons would most certainly come at the first opportunity. As far as I could judge, however, this could not take place before the last quarter of the year. Other people—in Angola, at the Cape, in the Transvaal—would have to be approached.

So then, Jan Labuschagne was definitely on his way to Humpata. I had reluctantly concluded that Louw du Plessis himself was considering it. It would be completely nonsensical. There was nothing to be gained in returning to an even greater isolation. That is exactly what Humpata and the Serras would mean. There was no hope for the Boers to establish an own free state in Angola. I knew the Portuguese. They jealously guarded what was theirs. Angola belonged to them. It had belonged to them for some four centuries. There was far more meaning in building up contacts with related peoples like the Germans, the British, the Cape Colonials.

I myself would go to Humpata. I just wanted to get things a little more settled here. Then I would leave. There had been some talk of going after the murderers of Adriaan Venter. By this time, however, they would be deep in the Omaheke. There was very little chance of catching up with them. We would have to bide our time, wait for information from friendly Bushmen, then try and surprise the guilty ones. Personally I had no doubt that the Bushmen who had attacked Adriaan Venter belonged to Gabriel's band. So Gabriel had triumphed after all; for the meanwhile, at least.

I remembered now what Diederick Prinsloo had read from the Old Testament the day the Waterbergers had left. He had read from the Book of Jeremiah: the strange history of King Jehoiachim. '. . . *And it came to pass that when Jehudi had read three or four leaves he cut it with the penknife, and cast it into the fire that was on the hearth . . .*'

The trouble was, I wryly decided, that the King of Babylon arrived all the same. Old Diederick had not completed his reading. Yes, the enemy arrived and the land was laid waste.

I couldn't prevent thoughts such as these from arising within me. It served little purpose. Of course, one had to avoid being deluded. At the same time there was no advantage to be gained by meeting trouble half-way. To see the local Nebuchadnezzar in a format he did not possess was illusion of another sort. He had to be taken for what he was, nothing more, nothing less. The main thing was just to keep your wits about you; to be fully alive to the situation, in all its nuances.

But was I, Will Jordan, still capable of doing this? At least, I could do my best.

The land lay about us in its winter resignation. The grass had been bleached to whiteness by recurrent frost. Was this the same landscape of a few months before? Then everything grew mightily. Now it had all quietly run down. The early sun hung between the acacias like a ball of fire. The sky was a gentle blue. There was not a single cloud in it.

It was no longer a question whether I would go to Humpata. It was only a question of fixing the date. I would take the opportunity of transporting a load of feathers and ivory down to Moçamedes. In spite of everything I had managed to do a little trading here. I needed the money. Funds were running low. I had spent an inordinate amount on Upingtonia. I had never expected to get it back.

State finances, I supposed, went by way of international loan, when local revenue was not enough. But who would lend us money? Perhaps it was not so impossible as I imagined. If I could only get to the Cape, I could do a lot to set things right, financially too. The earliest this could take place, however, was the end of the year. The Erikssons and perhaps some other 'outsiders' would be here by then. Then I could go off. Possibly some form of reason would have been restored by then, and the road to the Bay would be open again . . .

So, *Referendar* Nels was coming to Grootfontein. I had not yet had the opportunity of discussing this with the *Bestuur.* Diederick Prinsloo was still confined to his bed, and would probably stay there. Barend Bouwer had returned from Omaruru but had almost immediately left on a hunting trip. He was uncommunicative, except for hinting darkly that the Germans would 'put things right'.

I listened to this, but did not discuss it. Nels would have to come and look around, if he wished to do so. I would use the opportunity to tell Nels that *Schutzherrschaft* in Damaraland had done precious little to prevent people like Manasse Tjisiseta, aided and abetted by Gustav Viehe, from behaving in a high-handed manner. Was it right for the *Reich* to allow robbery such as I had suffered to go unpunished? I had no idea when Nels would arrive. He was welcome here, as long as he came in the proper spirit. He would have to realize that the Trekboers would not easily relinquish the ideal of an own, free state, in spite of what Barend Bouwer might have said to him. He would have to understand that nobody was really enthusiastic about German protection. This was not to be reconciled with the ideal of true autonomy. It was clear from the newspapers that the German imperium in Africa was beginning to discover its strength. A free Upingtonia could hardly exist as part of the *Reich*. What we would accept gladly was an agreement of mutual friendship and assistance by the stronger for the weaker. The heart of the matter was still my agreement with Kambonde Kampingana. Here the contract lay in my tin box. Here were also the minutes taken by Rautanen of Olukonda. Everything had been confirmed.

Where was Robert Lewis these days? One heard little of him. Axel Eriksson had written that he was about. What was he doing? What was he doing at Okahandja? What, with the Germans now established at the court of Kamaherero, had happened to his many concessions?

I had the uncomfortable feeling that Lewis would yet come up with something new. The Germans would discover that he was no easy customer. If I were Nels, I wouldn't be so sure about Kamaherero either. After all, there was something like a tradition of changeability at Okahandja. Not only at Okahandja.

The *Vierkleur* was still over the grave of Ella Lombard. Kleinveld had laid branches over it to keep the dogs and wild animals away. Lisa sometimes went and stood at the graveside. I saw her there with her head bowed and her fingers intertwined. She stood there for some time. At last Dina would come down to fetch her and they would walk back together.

In spite of everything it was going well with Lisa. Her son was the pride of the laager.

'Will he live, *Meneer*?' she had asked that day in the wagon at the omuramba.

One had only to walk past the Lombard *werf*. The lively little fellow would give his own answer.

13

The second week in July brought a surprise, but also a shock. Chris Leen arrived, not from the Okavango as I had expected, but from Otjimbingue. He and Bill Clay had trekked down the omuramba to fetch stores, and had sent me a letter telling me of their intentions. The runner had never got to Grootfontein, for reasons nobody knew.

I was immensely glad to see Chris. I was shocked, however, by what he gave me to read. 'This is a copy of a letter which arrived at Okahandja for Kamaherero,' he said. 'The whole of Damaraland is talking about it. John Caine has had various copies made and has sent some to the Cape newspapers for publication. Lewis has been very active these last few months. He is certainly not taking *Schutz* very seriously.'

I picked up the piece of paper, and read the words.

'My dear eldest brother Kamaherero,

Your letter I have received and I must inform you that I have not sold the Otavi Mine and the ground in question to Mr Jordan, and I have no idea whatever about the same being sold; all that I know is that I have sold Mr Jordan a piece of ground near my station for guns and ammunition. So, as you are my eldest brother and adviser, please write and let me know what I must do with these things, whether I shall return them or not. I am only a child, and I do not know the tradition of my forefathers; or even how far my country extends. So, please, my eldest brother, kindly inform me how far my boundary extends . . .'

I sat there with the document in my hands. I looked up slowly as if something had lost its flexibility in me and said: 'Then Lewis was there, of course. These are his words, not Kambonde's.'

'He's been about a lot,' Chris said, 'according to reports. You can take it that he has been in touch with Kambonde somewhere. Apparently he has also written to Prince Von Bismarck and protested against *Schutz*. He has stated that all the mineral rights of Damaraland belong to him.'

I got up. I felt horrible. I took hold of a spoke of the wagon-wheel to steady myself. This wasn't true, I said. There was a mistake, a misunderstanding, somewhere. Here in my tin box was the agreement. How could Kambonde come along and deny its terms? This was irrefutable proof of what had happened between us. It was witnessed by Kambonde's own missionaries. Everybody there at Olukonda would testify to this. Hans Schinz would testify to it.

My revolt, my feelings of bitter protest gradually subsided. I knew full well that whatever my evidence, it would not affect the matter at all.

I turned round. I drew some brandy from the cask in the wagon and sat down at my X-table. 'Sorry, Chris,' I said, pouring the brandy in two glasses, 'the Year of Lies has indeed not passed. Axel was right. Or else it has repeated itself. What more is there to say?'

We drank in silence. Chris lit a cigar. He offered me one, but I refused it. 'Has this letter already been sent off to the Cape?' I asked.

'It seems like it,' Chris answered. 'There are wagons passing through Otjimbingue almost every day now.'

'What is behind all this?' I asked. 'We know about Lewis. But is there more to it? What about Nehale, who has been fighting Kambonde for possession of the Kingdom of Ovamboland? Is Kambonde trying to counter Nehale's scheming? I knew that one of the arguments he was using was that Kambonde has "given away" the land belonging to the Ovambo nation.'

Chris thought about it for a while. Then he shrugged his shoulders.

My mind was working under pressure. I was seeing a thousand

possibilities. I tried to put my feelings into words, but it was no good. 'Hans Schinz was here,' I said at last. 'He had to get out of Ovamboland in a hurry because of what happened to both of you. You know all about it. It all turns on the same thing, Chris, as far as I can see: the argument about who is going to rule Ovamboland. Lewis has sized it all up and has decided that the position can be exploited. Kambonde has been told that he can outbid Nehale by repudiating Jordan. Nehale is no fool, apparently. He will take advantage of the situation as much as Lewis is doing. One thing must be clear: this was Ovambo territory until I bought it. The tribe itself never lived here and there was no reason for not wanting to sell it. Do you see it that way?'

'Yes,' Chris said, 'I do.'

'But you would like to add: this doesn't alter the situation materially. No, it doesn't. What has really astonished me, however, is that Kambonde should suddenly turn to his "dear eldest brother" Kamaherero. There has never been any love lost between them. Can it be that Caine is bluffing? That Lewis has put him up to all this?'

'Caine says that he examined the original and can find no fault with it,' Chris said.

'Caine was once my friend,' I recalled with some bitterness. 'He was also my father's friend. Then he became my enemy, because I was doing what I sincerely believed to be right for this country.'

Chris lay on the dry grass, his long, lean body stretched out to its full length, his head resting on his folded hands.

'What now, Chris? You are my brother-in-law. You are more like my brother. Please tell me what to do. Do we just pack up and pull out? It is unthinkable.'

'I don't know what I should tell you, Will,' he said, bearing up on an elbow.

Was Chris also losing faith in our cause? He had undertaken his new treks with Bill Clay because he had to make a living. That was not to be avoided. Still, I had always counted on Chris to give his full support to the end. I now had the feeling that Upingtonia was not so important any more.

I resisted this line of thought and feeling. It would get me nowhere. Chris was human like we all were, and we were all depressed by what had happened.

'I'll have to go to Ovamboland again,' I said after some while.

'To do what?'

'To hear from Kambonde exactly what he means by writing in this vein to Kamaherero. To make an appeal to his better nature. To see whether the missionaries can't assist me.'

'You realize the risk,' Chris said.

'Risk or no risk,' I said, 'It will have to be done. After twenty odd years of risky living, another few weeks of it will do me no harm.'

Chris was silent. 'I'm not so worried about Kambonde himself,' he said.

'About whom then?'

'Nehale!'

'Why?'

'For the very reason you have stated. His eagerness to oust Brother Kambonde.'

I looked at Chris. 'You don't have much hope for me,' I said.

Chris took it lightly.

'Well, be careful how you go about things,' he said. 'Don't tempt fate.'

'Fate,' I said and left it at that.

'You mean a lot for us in this country, Will,' he added. 'And I don't just mean Upingtonia.'

I offered no comment. I knew one thing deep inside me: I would go to Ovamboland, fate or no fate. There was no other way for me. I would set out before the week had run its course. I would follow the old trek-route I had followed so many times before: Otavi Spring, Lake Otjikoto, Namutoni; then the eastern boundary of the White Pan; on to Olukonda . . .

In a strange way I was looking forward to it.

The difficult task of informing the *Bestuur* of the newest developments and my immediate plans now lay on me. I told them all about it as soberly as I could.

David Black, Louw du Plessis and Diederick Prinsloo himself were amazed. Barend Bouwer who had returned from his hunting expedition reacted strongly. He swore mightily, as I had never heard him do before. 'Mester Will,' he said, and his face was red with chagrin, 'this is a thundering, damned shame. You see, it is because I had the feeling all along something like this was happening that I went down to Okahandja to talk to the Germans. Well now, Nels must come and see for himself what we are doing here. And he must *verdomp* well come quickly, or else I'll go and fetch him!'

Barend's outspokenness was in a way a healing of the breach which had opened between us. At least, I was thankful for that.

'There is a possibility, of course,' I said, 'that Nels and Goering will get out of Okahandja. Lewis has still got a legal document signed by Kamaherero giving him all the mineral rights in Damaraland. Lewis has written to the German Foreign Office. All right, let Nels come, if it will give comfort to some. I'm afraid I can't be here when he arrives. I'm leaving this afternoon for the north. You will have to deal with Nels. I may be away for some time. From Ovamboland, I'll go on to Humpata; and from there to Moçamedes.'

They stood listening to me in silence. Even Barend Bouwer seemed to be subdued.

'Maybe there are some others at Humpata who would like to join us here,' I said. 'I still believe we are going to win through. Things are not so bad, after all. If Kambonde has addressed himself to his dear "elder brother" in these respectful terms, then there is surely no reason why "dear elder brother" should attack the laager.'

They laughed.

'In any event,' I said, 'as long as Messrs Goering and Nels keep shop there in Okahandja, it is very unlikely that Kamaherero will undertake any adventures. Kambonde is a young man and given to impulsiveness. It is highly probable that he has been tricked into writing this letter by our enemies. I am confident that I can bring him back to reason.'

Perhaps this was whistling in the dark. Were it so, it was all I could do. And in fact I was not altogether without hope. Everything was not yet lost.

'We'll let things find their own course for a while,' I said presently. 'I'll do my best with Kambonde. Should he refuse to honour his contract? Well, we are still the legal owners. And we still have strength enough to defend ourselves.'

14

I stood in the hartebeest-house at the bedside of Diederick Prinsloo. He was lying on the *katel,* and his skin drooped from his huge, bony frame like the sails of a ship becalmed. Old Diederick's condition had deteriorated considerably since the onset of the winter. I gave him a few bottles of laudanum. This was all I could do for him.

I told him what had happened, and he listened with burning attention. 'I have to leave for Ovamboland today,' I said. 'I'll get to the bottom of the whole business, *Oom.* There is still the possibility that the whole thing is a fraud; that Kambonde never wrote such a letter. Anyway, it is only Kambonde who can confirm or deny it. I have every hope that things will turn out well for us.'

Maybe I was trying to soften the hardness of things for a dying man.

'All these sorrowful happenings . . .' He turned his eyes upon me and they shone like great coals of leadwood beneath his banked-up eyebrows. '*Meneer* . . .'

'We must keep faith, *Oom*,' I said.

'Until all is restored as it was . . .' He sighed deeply.

'We'll shake it out, and get on with the work,' I said.

Somebody had once used similar words, I thought. Who had it been? I couldn't remember.

'. . . Of substance we must be,' Old Diederick said ponderously, as if he had long been considering the words. 'God's mills grind! . . . Slowly!'

We talked for a few more minutes. Then I saw his eyelids droop. Soon he was asleep. Then he suddenly awoke again. 'We are not . . .' He seemed to have difficulty in finding the words now. 'We are . . . not a handful of flies!'

I took his hand. It was huge and cold and bony. Yet I discerned the goodwill in it. 'All that is best for you, *Oom* Diederick,' I said. I stood for a moment in the doorway. He lifted his hand slightly and nodded, as if by way of saying: 'Godspeed to thee.'

Outside the Prinsloo sons were waiting for me. 'The cancer is eating Pa up now,' Jan said curtly.

'We have thought that Pa would perhaps want to lie in the Transvaal,' Machiel said. 'At Wildebeestfontein, where he grew up. That is our birthplace.'

I stood wondering how things would be if I were to return from my journey and find the Prinsloos gone, crossing the Thirstland, on their way back to the Transvaal.

'Willem has sent a message,' Machiel said. 'That he is coming back. It was as we said it would be at the Waterberg. He knows about Pa.'

We shook hands.

'A good trek, *Meneer*!' Jan said.

'And do not stay away so long,' Machiel added. 'We need *Meneer* here.'

His words affected me. For some moments I stood there lost in thought, staring at the distant tops of trees. Then a lourie called and I returned to myself.

I ran into another old friend while walking back to my wagon. It was Dolf Holtzhausen: he who had spent his years making useful things for other people. He had made them with love.

'Hallo, Dolf,' I said.

He took hold of my hand with a quick, impulsive movement. He seemed unable to speak. 'Dolf,' I teased him. 'You haven't got so far as to make what I once ordered, have you?'

'*Meester* . . .?' He looked up. 'What would that be?'

'One of your excellent *kists,* made to measure.'

He shook his head firmly. A tear dropped from his eyes. I couldn't help it, I laughed.

'Never mind, Dolf,' I said. 'I'm only pulling your leg. Long after all of us have been forgotten, people will still talk of your fine teak of these northern parts: *Dolfswood*!'

'*Meester,*' he said, displaying a heartfelt seriousness. 'Every man must *maar* do what he can for others, *Meester*.'

'Yes, Dolf,' I said. 'There is wisdom in what you say. And it so easily escapes us. You have given much, and you have never talked about it. That is important.'

'Yes, *Meester*. But I don't know. Is *Meester* going far?'

'Not too far.'

'We shall wait here, *Meester*. I and all the sons. And the wife too.'

'Thank you, Dolf,' I said. 'It means a lot to me to know that. Come over to the wagon, when I am back. We'll have a glass together. And chat!'

'I'll come, *Meester*!'

15

'So, Lisa,' I said 'You are looking very well.'

She had a new *kappie* on, and she was carrying her son in her arms.

'The Lord has been good to me, *Meneer*,' she said. 'And good to my child.'

Indeed, her pristine freshness seemed to have returned. She would go out to meet whatever life demanded from her. She would not suffer herself to be defeated.

'What are your plans, Lisa?'

'Goodness, *Meneer*!' She seemed eager to tell me about them. 'I would like my child to go to Adriaan's people in the Transvaal. Here nobody belonging to me is left; only the two old blacks. They will go with me, *Meneer*.'

I nodded, and had mixed feelings. Was everybody leaving? Still, for Lisa it was right, perhaps. She would take the long road back. Dina and Kleinveld would be with her. How she would manage it exactly, I did not know. But I knew she would, somehow.

'I am staying with the Du Plessis now,' she said. 'With *Oom* Louw and his people. They are very good to us.' She looked up straight at me. 'And I hear that *Meneer* is also about to trek?'

'Yes,' I said. I had a heavy heart.

'Then we will have to take leave, *Meneer*.'

'Perhaps!'

It was Dina Lombard who saved me from some embarrassment. My feelings were getting too fluid.

'Mister,' she said, 'so we are old—*opu*, eh? But we think of Little Miss, and the child. Such a pretty child.' She clicked her tongue.

For a long time after we had parted company I still carried the image of Lisa and her child. The boy had smiled at me.

16

A week later, at Namutoni, a giant of a man came striding through the bush to meet me. A voice bellowed through the quiet winter air: 'Mister Will!' It was Jan Labuschagne.

Strangely enough, in spite of less pleasant associations, I was glad to see this man. Here in the loneliness of the White Pan he seemed to take me back to those I had left behind. We talked and he explained at length that he did not think there was any future 'for us Boer people in Damaraland'. He had now decided to return to Angola. Word had come that the people at Humpata were helping the Portuguese 'clean up' the country. When they had disposed of all the warlike blacks, the Portuguese would give the Boers their own country as a reward. They would then receive full title to the land, and everything would be fine.

The old idea of a benign isolation had not yet died. As I now knew my friends, I doubted whether it would ever die. It was odd, I thought, that this should still be the driving motive in a man who had sought the favour of Robert Lewis.

I was tired and did not feel like arguing the point.

'And now, Mister Will, you are trekking again, eh?' He stood there in front of me, arms akimbo: 'Now where to this time?'

Before I could answer, he said: 'Well, here I am standing as well, before I trek on through Ovamboland. Two arrived from Ondangua, Mister Will, and brought news. They were two of our own people.'

'What news?'

'Well, they say they had to flee because there are all sorts of war-shoutings up there!'

'Was any harm done to them?'

'No, not harm. But they just got away in time. Got a big fright, Mister Will!'

'That does one good sometimes.'

He guffawed at this.

'So what are your plans?' I asked.

'I'll stay here, Mister Will, and see how the hunting is. The birds are few, and the elephants haven't come through from the Sandveld yet. If news comes that it is all right with the 'Vambos, I'll *maar* trek on. Lewis is up there.'

I did not enquire what he meant by 'up there'. Presumably it was Ondangua. If Lewis was up there, fine. We would meet each other. I would tell him exactly what I thought about the matter. I would ask the missionaries at Olukonda to accompany me to Kambonde's kraal again. I would get Lewis there too. I would challenge Kambonde to deny the terms of the contract before people like Rautanen, Weikolin, Roche. The missionaries wouldn't suffer his blatant lying. Kambonde knew that if he harmed the missionaries he was in for trouble.

To start off with, he would lose face with the other tribes of the country. To have your own missionaries was a sign of status.

'We hear that young Venter was murdered by the Bushmen, Mister,' Jan Labuschagne said. 'Just as I said would happen.

They shouldn't have gone off so far from the laager alone. It is a pity that it happened in this way. But he tried to do too much when he was still too young . . . Now where is she?'

'Presumably you mean Lisa? We fetched her.'

'And it goes well with her now? What is her plan? Where is she going to now?'

'She will probably go back to the Transvaal, when the opportunity arrives to travel safely.'

'Well, that is what I thought would happen. Mister Will, you must come and stay over with us there at the reed-fountain. But if you are staying here, then you may send someone for a haunch of palla.'

On this charitable note the conversation was closed.

By nine o'clock I was already lying in my *katel*. I hadn't sent for the palla meat. I didn't need it.

An hour before sunrise the next morning we were already astir. When we passed the Labuschagne laager near the spring there was no sign of movement. A naked servant lay curled up around a smouldering little fire.

The old trekspoor wandered on ahead of us. The great White Pan, which had been a lake the previous summer, was almost dry again. It lay there like a snowfield in the polar wastes; or like the sea, as Gert Alberts had once said . . .

We trekked for three days without incident. The land was peaceful. The smoke from kraal fires hung in the windless air. Makalanis with feathery tops cut the distant horizon.

At the end of the third day we were but one trek-stage from Olukonda. Perhaps if we had forced the pace we might already have reached the mission house. I was looking forward to a re-union with Rautanen and his colleagues. There was so much to talk about. After all, the issues were far greater than the private dreams of Will Jordan. Or was there, in spite of everything, also this desperate need for self-expression? Did each man carry inside of him the Little Laager, which had to be defended at all costs?

17

I lie awake again. Izak brought me some coffee an hour or two ago. I have lain here and my thoughts and memories have ranged over many years and over many miles. How far have I come to reach this point in time? The image of all that was, all that I have tried to be, has been in my mind's eye. I have looked upon all the roads, all the people, all the strivings, all the secret pain of these past years. I have experienced again the anger, the protest, but also the tenderness of feeling, which I have known. I have remembered those who were near to me, but never knew it.

How enormous is the task of the human being who tries to make life come to something. What then is to be done when in the end there is just the recognition of failure? When hope has burnt to a silver-white ash, like the leadwood logs of this northern forest? It is like the river. It is like the Okavango which collects its clear waters in a distant highland, gathers it to make a strong, clear-running stream; which gradually loses its momentum, then its life, in the sand and reedlands of the Thirstland . . .

I was down there in the marsh that day. I had gone to find the people I had heard of. I reached that part of the river where it was no longer a stream but only a series of stagnant fever-pools.

I lift the canvas of the wagon hood and look outside. All is so quiet here in the moonlight. The oxen are still tied to their yokes and the moon is in their eyes. In the trenches by the fire my two servants lie . . .

Arcturus is brilliant to the north. Directly above is Scorpio. And Crux is low in the south-west. All is immensely quiet. One might almost hear the frost descending . . .

Why do we always creep back to safety? To the Great Laager, and to the Little Laager? Why do we carry it along with us, like a tortoise its carapace?

We wander in some forgotten Thirstland, not knowing where we have come from, or where we are going to. How shall we find faith again, and love? Where is Eden . . . ?

All this thinking tires me, this remembering. When all my work is done here, I want to go back home. I want to see my mother again, in the little house under the oaks of Table Mountain, in the city in which I was born. She is my mother, and I honour her memory. In the end, one always has to go back home again . . .

Perhaps that is what Lisa is doing. There are stronger things in life than armies, laagers, the call of Eden, man's endless designs for living, his impossible ideals. Life itself is stronger . . .

The moonlight is now like a flood after great summer rains. It fills the landscape. There is no end to it. But the oxen are peaceful there, tied to their yokes.

Next to the little mound of glowing embers lie the others who have walked with me through this land. I love them too. I love all here who have been part of what I have been part of: these people, these animals . . .

One has arisen now and is throwing logs on the fire. A stream of sparks is mingling with the stars.

POSTSCRIPT

Early next morning Jordan heard the voices of strange people who had come to his wagon. He also heard his servants talking to them. No, his servants said, the baas *was still asleep. If they wanted to talk to him about an ox they wished to barter, they would have to wait until he was up.*

When the visitors insisted on seeing Jordan, Kairob angrily asked them whether they had no manners. Who came to talk business so early in the morning? The sun was not yet up. The baas *had not even had his early morning coffee. They should go and return later.*

The visitors would not hear of this. It was an urgent matter, they insisted. They had to see Jordan. He should be aroused.

By this time Jordan was already up. He had heard the raised voices outside and had lifted the canvas to see who it was. This was Nehale, he decided. This was the brother of Kambonde Kampingana. His kraal was nearby and if he had really come to talk about an ox, he could have come the previous evening . . . This was Nehale.

Nevertheless he got up and started dressing. He called his bambuse, *and asked him to bring him some hot shaving-water and a cup of coffee. Nehale would have to wait.*

Izak returned with the water and Jordan set it down on his X-table next to a wheel of his wagon. Izak was bringing the coffee on a tray, when the visitors—there were four of them—suddenly reappeared around the back of the wagon. Nehale was leading them and he had a gun in his hands. Jordan had only time to look up in surprise when a shot rang through the morning. There was another, and Jordan fell to the sand.

With a terrible cry Kairob now came running up, trying to grab a gun which had been lying on the voorkist *of the wagon. Before he could get there, he too was shot down.*

Izak, the Bushman, shaking in every limb, was now ordered to take Jordan's clothes off. Thereupon the fore-ox of the wagon team was also shot. Some other people from the nearby kraal of

Nehale had now arrived. They could cut meat from the dead ox, Nehale said, and eat. But first they had to make a deep hole, and bury Jordan and his servants and the remains of the ox. Izak, the Bushman, was forced to assist.

When it was eventually all done, Nehale took Jordan's wagon to his kraal and claimed its contents.

On the great plain, there was now almost no sign of the violent happenings of the morning. Only a heap of loose sand showed where a grave had been made.

At nightfall Izak emerged from the bush where he had crept away while the others had been busy feasting on the slaughtered ox. Here he had sat all day long with his head in his hands, stricken with grief.

When the moon rose, he warily came out into the open again. The long white road wandered away to the south-west. He set off and followed it for many days.

1 Ghanzi, where Van Zyl built his castle and organized massive elephant hunts
2 Rietfontein, resting place for Trek
3 Andara
4 Olifants Pan, resting place
5 Leeu Pan, resting place
6 Namutoni, great spring; resting place
7 Olukonda; in this area Jordan was murdered
8 Ondangua
9 Okaukueyo
10 Ombeka
11 Otjitambi
12 Otjitundua; the Trek stayed here for sixteen months
13 Rocky Point (Felsenfort) on the Skeleton Coast, where riders arrived from Namutoni
14 Kaoko Otavi, great spring of the Kaokoveld; the Trek stayed here for sixteen months
15 Tjimahaka, ford over Cunene River; here the great hippo hunt took place
16 Humbe (Angola)
17 Okuambi (Angola)
18 Humpata, on the Serra da Chela, where the Trekkers thought they had found their Land of Rest
19 Mocamedes
20 Grootfontein (Otjovanda Tjongue), heart of the embryonic republic of Upingtonia
21 Okasima; Adriaan and Lisa Venter's great water
22 Otjituuo
23 The Waterberg
24 Otavi, heart of the copper area
25 Otjozandjupa
26 Omaruru
27 Okahandja
28 Osona
29 Otjimbingue
30 Walwich (or Walfish) Bay
31 Gurumanas
32 Windhoek
33 Rehoboth, heart of the Baster territory, once purchased by Jordan
34 Hoachanas
35 Gibeon
36 Keetmanshoop
37 Lüderitz (Angra Pequena)

——— Trek route from the Crocodile River, Transvaal, to Humpata

\- - - - Trek route from Humpata to Otjovanda Tjongue